D0966634

EUDORA WELTY

EUDORA WELTY

STORIES, ESSAYS, & MEMOIR

A Curtain of Green, and Other Stories
The Wide Net, and Other Stories
The Golden Apples
The Bride of the Innisfallen, and Other Stories
Other Stories
Selected Essays
One Writer's Beginnings

THE LIBRARY OF AMERICA

The paper used in this publication meets the minimum requirements of the American National Standard for Information Sciences—Permanence of Paper for Printed Library Materials, ANSI Z39.48—1984.

Distributed to the trade
in the United States by Penguin Group (USA) Inc.
and in Canada by Penguin Books Canada Ltd.

Library of Congress Catalog Number: 97—46691
For cataloging information, see end of Notes.
ISBN 1–883011–55–8
ISBN 978–1–883011–55–0

Fourth Printing
The Library of America—102

Manufactured in the United States of America

Richard Ford and Michael Kreyling
selected the contents and wrote the notes
for this volume

Eudora Welty: Stories, Essays & Memoir
is kept in print in honor of

THE EUDORA WELTY FOUNDATION

by a gift from

Evelyn & Michael Jefcoat

to the Guardians of American Letters Fund,
established by The Library of America
to ensure that every volume in the series
will be permanently available.

Contents

A CURTAIN OF GREEN

and Other Stories

To

Diarmuid Russell

Contents

Lily Daw and the Three Ladies

MRS WATTS and Mrs Carson were both in the post office in Victory when the letter came from the Ellisville Institute for the Feeble Minded of Mississippi. Aimee Slocum, with her hand still full of mail, ran out in front and handed it straight to Mrs Watts, and they all three read it together. Mrs Watts held it taut between her pink hands, and Mrs Carson underscored each line slowly with her thimbled finger. Everybody else in the post office wondered what was up now.

"What will Lily say," beamed Mrs Carson at last, "when we tell her we're sending her to Ellisville!"

"She'll be tickled to death," said Mrs Watts, and added in a guttural voice to a deaf lady, "Lily Daw's getting in at Ellisville!"

"Don't you all dare go off and tell Lily without me!" called Aimee Slocum, trotting back to finish putting up the mail.

"Do you suppose they'll look after her down there?" Mrs Carson began to carry on a conversation with a group of Baptist ladies waiting in the post office. She was the Baptist preacher's wife.

"I've always heard it was lovely down there, but crowded," said one.

"Lily lets people walk over her so," said another.

"Last night at the tent show——" said another, and then popped her hand over her mouth.

"Don't mind me, I know there are such things in the world," said Mrs Carson, looking down and fingering the tape measure which hung over her bosom.

"Oh, Mrs Carson. Well, anyway, last night at the tent show, why, the man was just before making Lily buy a ticket to get in."

"A ticket!"

"Till my husband went up and explained she wasn't bright, and so did everybody else."

The ladies all clucked their tongues.

"Oh, it was a very nice show," said the lady who had gone.

"And Lily acted so nice. She was a perfect lady—just set in her seat and stared."

"Oh, she can be a lady—she can be," said Mrs Carson, shaking her head and turning her eyes up. "That's just what breaks your heart."

"Yes'm, she kept her eyes on—what's that thing makes all the commotion?—the xylophone," said the lady. "Didn't turn her head to the right or to the left the whole time. Set in front of me."

"The point is, what did she do after the show?" asked Mrs Watts practically. "Lily has gotten so she is very mature for her age."

"Oh, Etta!" protested Mrs Carson, looking at her wildly for a moment.

"And that's how come we are sending her to Ellisville," finished Mrs Watts.

"I'm ready, you all," said Aimee Slocum, running out with white powder all over her face. "Mail's up. I don't know how good it's up."

"Well, of course, I do hope it's for the best," said several of the other ladies. They did not go at once to take their mail out of their boxes; they felt a little left out.

The three women stood at the foot of the water tank.

"To find Lily is a different thing," said Aimee Slocum.

"Where in the wide world do you suppose she'd be?" It was Mrs Watts who was carrying the letter.

"I don't see a sign of her either on this side of the street or on the other side," Mrs Carson declared as they walked along.

Ed Newton was stringing Redbird school tablets on the wire across the store.

"If you're after Lily, she come in here while ago and tole me she was fixin' to git married," he said.

"Ed Newton!" cried the ladies all together, clutching one another. Mrs Watts began to fan herself at once with the letter from Ellisville. She wore widow's black, and the least thing made her hot.

"Why she is not. She's going to Ellisville, Ed," said Mrs Carson gently. "Mrs Watts and I and Aimee Slocum are paying her way out of our own pockets. Besides, the boys of Victory are on their honor. Lily's not going to get married, that's just an idea she's got in her head."

"More power to you, ladies," said Ed Newton, spanking himself with a tablet.

When they came to the bridge over the railroad tracks, there was Estelle Mabers, sitting on a rail. She was slowly drinking an orange Ne-Hi.

"Have you seen Lily?" they asked her.

"I'm supposed to be out here watching for her now," said the Mabers girl, as though she weren't there yet. "But for Jewel—Jewel says Lily come in the store while ago and picked out a two-ninety-eight hat and wore it off. Jewel wants to swap her something else for it."

"Oh, Estelle, Lily says she's going to get married!" cried Aimee Slocum.

"Well I declare," said Estelle; she never understood anything.

Loralee Adkins came riding by in her Willys-Knight, tooting the horn to find out what they were talking about.

Aimee threw up her hands and ran out into the street. "Loralee, Loralee, you got to ride us up to Lily Daws'. She's up yonder fixing to get married!"

"Hop in, my land!"

"Well, that just goes to show you right now," said Mrs Watts, groaning as she was helped into the back seat. "What we've got to do is persuade Lily it will be nicer to go to Ellisville."

"Just to think!"

While they rode around the corner Mrs Carson was going on in her sad voice, sad as the soft noises in the hen house at twilight. "We buried Lily's poor defenseless mother. We gave Lily all her food and kindling and every stitch she had on. Sent her to Sunday school to learn the Lord's teachings, had her baptized a Baptist. And when her old father commenced beating her and tried to cut her head off with the butcher knife, why, we went and took her away from him and gave her a place to stay."

The paintless frame house with all the weather vanes was

three stories high in places and had yellow and violet stained-glass windows in front and gingerbread around the porch. It leaned steeply to one side, toward the railroad, and the front steps were gone. The car full of ladies drew up under the cedar tree.

"Now Lily's almost grown up," Mrs Carson continued. "In fact, she's grown," she concluded, getting out.

"Talking about getting married," said Mrs Watts disgustedly. "Thanks, Loralee, you run on home."

They climbed over the dusty zinnias onto the porch and walked through the open door without knocking.

"There certainly is always a funny smell in this house. I say it every time I come," said Aimee Slocum.

Lily was there, in the dark of the hall, kneeling on the floor by a small open trunk.

When she saw them she put a zinnia in her mouth, and held still.

"Hello, Lily," said Mrs Carson reproachfully.

"Hello," said Lily. In a minute she gave a suck on the zinnia stem that sounded exactly like a jay bird. There she sat, wearing a petticoat for a dress, one of the things Mrs Carson kept after her about. Her milky-yellow hair streamed freely down from under a new hat. You could see the wavy scar on her throat if you knew it was there.

Mrs Carson and Mrs Watts, the two fattest, sat in the double rocker. Aimee Slocum sat on the wire chair donated from the drugstore that burned.

"Well, what are you doing, Lily?" asked Mrs Watts, who led the rocking.

Lily smiled.

The trunk was old and lined with yellow and brown paper, with an asterisk pattern showing in darker circles and rings. Mutely the ladies indicated to each other that they did not know where in the world it had come from. It was empty except for two bars of soap and a green washcloth, which Lily was now trying to arrange in the bottom.

"Go on and tell us what you're doing, Lily," said Aimee Slocum.

"Packing, silly," said Lily.

"Where are you going?"

"Going to get married, and I bet you wish you was me now," said Lily. But shyness overcame her suddenly, and she popped the zinnia back into her mouth.

"Talk to me, dear," said Mrs Carson. "Tell old Mrs Carson why you want to get married."

"No," said Lily, after a moment's hesitation.

"Well, we've thought of something that will be so much nicer," said Mrs Carson. "Why don't you go to Ellisville!"

"Won't that be lovely?" said Mrs Watts. "Goodness, yes."

"It's a lovely place," said Aimee Slocum uncertainly.

"You've got bumps on your face," said Lily.

"Aimee, dear, you stay out of this, if you don't mind," said Mrs Carson anxiously. "I don't know what it is comes over Lily when you come around her."

Lily stared at Aimee Slocum meditatively.

"There! Wouldn't you like to go to Ellisville now?" asked Mrs Carson.

"No'm," said Lily.

"Why not?" All the ladies leaned down toward her in impressive astonishment.

" 'Cause I'm goin' to get married," said Lily.

"Well, and who are you going to marry, dear?" asked Mrs Watts. She knew how to pin people down and make them deny what they'd already said.

Lily bit her lip and began to smile. She reached into the trunk and held up both cakes of soap and wagged them.

"Tell us," challenged Mrs Watts. "Who you're going to marry, now."

"A man last night."

There was a gasp from each lady. The possible reality of a lover descended suddenly like a summer hail over their heads. Mrs Watts stood up and balanced herself.

"One of those show fellows! A musician!" she cried.

Lily looked up in admiration.

"Did he—did he do anything to you?" In the long run, it was still only Mrs Watts who could take charge.

"Oh, yes'm," said Lily. She patted the cakes of soap fastidiously with the tips of her small fingers and tucked them in with the washcloth.

"What?" demanded Aimee Slocum, rising up and tottering before her scream. "What?" she called out in the hall.

"Don't ask her what," said Mrs Carson, coming up behind. "Tell me, Lily—just yes or no—are you the same as you were?"

"He had a red coat," said Lily graciously. "He took little sticks and went *ping-pong! ding-dong!*"

"Oh, I think I'm going to faint," said Aimee Slocum, but they said, "No, you're not."

"The xylophone!" cried Mrs Watts. "The xylophone player! Why, the coward, he ought to be run out of town on a rail!"

"Out of town? He is out of town, by now," cried Aimee. "Can't you read?—the sign in the café—Victory on the ninth, Como on the tenth? He's in Como. Como!"

"All right! We'll bring him back!" cried Mrs Watts. "He can't get away from me!"

"Hush," said Mrs Carson. "I don't think it's any use following that line of reasoning at all. It's better in the long run for him to be gone out of our lives for good and all. That kind of a man. He was after Lily's body alone and he wouldn't ever in this world make the poor little thing happy, even if we went out and forced him to marry her like he ought—at the point of a gun."

"Still——" began Aimee, her eyes widening.

"Shut up," said Mrs Watts. "Mrs Carson, you're right, I expect."

"This is my hope chest—see?" said Lily politely in the pause that followed. "You haven't even looked at it. I've already got soap and a washrag. And I have my hat—on. What are you all going to give me?"

"Lily," said Mrs Watts, starting over, "we'll give you lots of gorgeous things if you'll only go to Ellisville instead of getting married."

"What will you give me?" asked Lily.

"I'll give you a pair of hemstitched pillowcases," said Mrs Carson.

"I'll give you a big caramel cake," said Mrs Watts.

"I'll give you a souvenir from Jackson—a little toy bank," said Aimee Slocum. "Now will you go?"

"No," said Lily.

"I'll give you a pretty little Bible with your name on it in real gold," said Mrs Carson.

"What if I was to give you a pink crêpe de chine brassière with adjustable shoulder straps?" asked Mrs Watts grimly.

"Oh, Etta."

"Well, she needs it," said Mrs Watts. "What would they think if she ran all over Ellisville in a petticoat looking like a Fiji?"

"I wish *I* could go to Ellisville," said Aimee Slocum luringly.

"What will they have for me down there?" asked Lily softly.

"Oh! lots of things. You'll have baskets to weave, I expect. . . ." Mrs Carson looked vaguely at the others.

"Oh, yes indeed, they will let you make all sorts of baskets," said Mrs Watts; then her voice too trailed off.

"No'm, I'd rather get married," said Lily.

"Lily Daw! Now that's just plain stubbornness!" cried Mrs Watts. "You almost said you'd go and then you took it back!"

"We've all asked God, Lily," said Mrs Carson finally, "and God seemed to tell us—Mr Carson, too—that the place where you ought to be, so as to be happy, was Ellisville."

Lily looked reverent, but still stubborn.

"We've really just got to get her there—now!" screamed Aimee Slocum all at once. "Suppose——! She can't stay here!"

"Oh no, no, no," said Mrs Carson hurriedly. "We mustn't think that."

They sat sunken in despair.

"Could I take my hope chest—to go to Ellisville?" asked Lily shyly, looking at them sidewise.

"Why, yes," said Mrs Carson blankly.

Silently they rose once more to their feet.

"Oh, if I could just take my hope chest!"

"All the time it was just her hope chest," Aimee whispered.

Mrs Watts struck her palms together. "It's settled!"

"Praise the fathers," murmured Mrs Carson.

Lily looked up at them, and her eyes gleamed. She cocked her head and spoke out in a proud imitation of someone—someone utterly unknown.

"O.K.—Toots!"

The ladies had been nodding and smiling and backing away toward the door.

"I think I'd better stay," said Mrs Carson, stopping in her tracks. "Where—where could she have learned that terrible expression?"

"Pack up," said Mrs Watts. "Lily Daw is leaving for Ellisville on Number One."

In the station the train was puffing. Nearly everyone in Victory was hanging around waiting for it to leave. The Victory Civic Band had assembled without any orders and was scattered through the crowd. Ed Newton gave false signals to start on his bass horn. A crate full of baby chickens got loose on the platform. Everybody wanted to see Lily all dressed up, but Mrs Carson and Mrs Watts had sneaked her into the train from the other side of the tracks.

The two ladies were going to travel as far as Jackson to help Lily change trains and be sure she went in the right direction.

Lily sat between them on the plush seat with her hair combed and pinned up into a knot under a small blue hat which was Jewel's exchange for the pretty one. She wore a traveling dress made out of part of Mrs Watts's last summer's mourning. Pink straps glowed through. She had a purse and a Bible and a warm cake in a box, all in her lap.

Aimee Slocum had been getting the outgoing mail stamped and bundled. She stood in the aisle of the coach now, tears shaking from her eyes.

"Good-by, Lily," she said. She was the one who felt things.

"Good-by, silly," said Lily.

"Oh, dear, I hope they get our telegram to meet her in Ellisville!" Aimee cried sorrowfully, as she thought how far away it was. "And it was so hard to get it all in ten words, too."

"Get off, Aimee, before the train starts and you break your neck," said Mrs Watts, all settled and waving her dressy fan gaily. "I declare, it's so hot, as soon as we get a few miles out of town I'm going to slip my corset down."

"Oh, Lily, don't cry down there. Just be good, and do what they tell you—it's all because they love you." Aimee drew her mouth down. She was backing away, down the aisle.

Lily laughed. She pointed across Mrs Carson's bosom out the window toward a man. He had stepped off the train and just stood there, by himself. He was a stranger and wore a cap.

"Look," she said, laughing softly through her fingers.

"Don't—look," said Mrs Carson very distinctly, as if, out of all she had ever spoken, she would impress these two solemn words upon Lily's soft little brain. She added, "Don't look at anything till you get to Ellisville."

Outside, Aimee Slocum was crying so hard she almost ran into the stranger. He wore a cap and was short and seemed to have on perfume, if such a thing could be.

"Could you tell me, madam," he said, "where a little lady lives in this burg name of Miss Lily Daw?" He lifted his cap—and he had red hair.

"What do you want to know for?" Aimee asked before she knew it.

"Talk louder," said the stranger. He almost whispered, himself.

"She's gone away—she's gone to Ellisville!"

"Gone?"

"Gone to Ellisville!"

"Well, I like that!" The man stuck out his bottom lip and puffed till his hair jumped.

"What business did you have with Lily?" cried Aimee suddenly.

"We was only going to get married, that's all," said the man.

Aimee Slocum started to scream in front of all those people. She almost pointed to the long black box she saw lying on the ground at the man's feet. Then she jumped back in fright.

"The xylophone! The xylophone!" she cried, looking back and forth from the man to the hissing train. Which was more terrible? The bell began to ring hollowly, and the man was talking.

"Did you say Ellisville? That in the state of Mississippi?" Like lightning he had pulled out a red notebook entitled, "Permanent Facts & Data." He wrote down something. "I don't hear well."

Aimee nodded her head up and down, and circled around him.

Under "Ellis-Ville Miss" he was drawing a line; now he was flicking it with two little marks. "Maybe she didn't say she would. Maybe she said she wouldn't." He suddenly laughed very loudly, after the way he had whispered. Aimee jumped back. "Women!—Well, if we play anywheres near Ellisville, Miss., in the future I may look her up and I may not," he said.

The bass horn sounded the true signal for the band to begin. White steam rushed out of the engine. Usually the train stopped for only a minute in Victory, but the engineer knew Lily from waving at her, and he knew this was her big day.

"Wait!" Aimee Slocum did scream. "Wait, mister! I can get her for you. Wait, Mister Engineer! Don't go!"

Then there she was back on the train, screaming in Mrs Carson's and Mrs Watts's faces.

"The xylophone player! The xylophone player to marry her! Yonder he is!"

"Nonsense," murmured Mrs Watts, peering over the others to look where Aimee pointed. "If he's there I don't see him. Where is he? You're looking at One-Eye Beasley."

"The little man with the cap—no, with the red hair! Hurry!"

"Is that really him?" Mrs Carson asked Mrs Watts in wonder. "Mercy! He's small, isn't he?"

"Never saw him before in my life!" cried Mrs Watts. But suddenly she shut up her fan.

"Come on! This is a train we're on!" cried Aimee Slocum. Her nerves were all unstrung.

"All right, don't have a conniption fit, girl," said Mrs Watts. "Come on," she said thickly to Mrs Carson.

"Where are we going now?" asked Lily as they struggled down the aisle.

"We're taking you to get married," said Mrs. Watts. "Mrs Carson, you'd better phone up your husband right there in the station."

"But I don't want to git married," said Lily, beginning to whimper. "I'm going to Ellisville."

"Hush, and we'll all have some ice-cream cones later," whispered Mrs Carson.

Just as they climbed down the steps at the back end of the train, the band went into "Independence March."

The xylophone player was still there, patting his foot. He came up and said, "Hello, Toots. What's up—tricks?" and kissed Lily with a smack, after which she hung her head.

"So you're the young man we've heard so much about," said Mrs Watts. Her smile was brilliant. "Here's your little Lily."

"What say?" asked the xylophone player.

"My husband happens to be the Baptist preacher of Victory," said Mrs Carson in a loud, clear voice. "Isn't that lucky? I can get him here in five minutes: I know exactly where he is."

They were in a circle around the xylophone player, all going into the white waiting room.

"Oh, I feel just like crying, at a time like this," said Aimee Slocum. She looked back and saw the train moving slowly away, going under the bridge at Main Street. Then it disappeared around the curve.

"Oh, the hope chest!" Aimee cried in a stricken voice.

"And whom have we the pleasure of addressing?" Mrs Watts was shouting, while Mrs Carson was ringing up the telephone.

The band went on playing. Some of the people thought Lily was on the train, and some swore she wasn't. Everybody cheered, though, and a straw hat was thrown into the telephone wires.

A Piece of News

SHE HAD BEEN out in the rain. She stood in front of the cabin fireplace, her legs wide apart, bending over, shaking her wet yellow head crossly, like a cat reproaching itself for not knowing better. She was talking to herself—only a small fluttering sound, hard to lay hold of in the sparsity of the room.

"The pouring-down rain, the pouring-down rain"—was that what she was saying over and over, like a song? She stood turning in little quarter turns to dry herself, her head bent forward and the yellow hair hanging out streaming and tangled. She was holding her skirt primly out to draw the warmth in.

Then, quite rosy, she walked over to the table and picked up a little bundle. It was a sack of coffee, marked "Sample" in red letters, which she unwrapped from a wet newspaper. But she handled it tenderly.

"Why, how come he wrapped it in a newspaper!" she said, catching her breath, looking from one hand to the other. She must have been lonesome and slow all her life, the way things would take her by surprise.

She set the coffee on the table, just in the center. Then she dragged the newspaper by one corner in a dreamy walk across the floor, spread it all out, and lay down full length on top of it in front of the fire. Her little song about the rain, her cries of surprise, had been only a preliminary, only playful pouting with which she amused herself when she was alone. She was pleased with herself now. As she sprawled close to the fire, her hair began to slide out of its damp tangles and hung all displayed down her back like a piece of bargain silk. She closed her eyes. Her mouth fell into a deepness, into a look of unconscious cunning. Yet in her very stillness and pleasure she seemed to be hiding there, all alone. And at moments when the fire stirred and tumbled in the grate, she would tremble, and her hand would start out as if in impatience or despair.

Presently she stirred and reached under her back for the newspaper. Then she squatted there, touching the printed page as if it were fragile. She did not merely look at it—she watched it, as if it were unpredictable, like a young girl watching a baby. The paper was still wet in places where her body had lain. Crouching tensely and patting the creases away with small cracked red fingers, she frowned now and then at the blotched drawing of something and big letters that spelled a word underneath. Her lips trembled, as if looking and spelling so slowly had stirred her heart.

All at once she laughed.

She looked up.

"Ruby Fisher!" she whispered.

An expression of utter timidity came over her flat blue eyes and her soft mouth. Then a look of fright. She stared about. . . . What eye in the world did she feel looking in on her? She pulled her dress down tightly and began to spell through a dozen words in the newspaper.

The little item said:

"Mrs Ruby Fisher had the misfortune to be shot in the leg by her husband this week."

As she passed from one word to the next she only whispered; she left the long word, "misfortune," until the last, and came back to it, then she said it all over out loud, like conversation.

"That's me," she said softly, with deference, very formally.

The fire slipped and suddenly roared in the house already deafening with the rain which beat upon the roof and hung full of lightning and thunder outside.

"You Clyde!" screamed Ruby Fisher at last, jumping to her feet. "Where are you, Clyde Fisher?"

She ran straight to the door and pulled it open. A shudder of cold brushed over her in the heat, and she seemed striped with anger and bewilderment. There was a flash of lightning, and she stood waiting, as if she half thought that would bring him in, a gun leveled in his hands.

She said nothing more and, backing against the door, pushed it closed with her hip. Her anger passed like a remote flare of elation. Neatly avoiding the table where the bag of coffee stood, she began to walk nervously about the room, as if a teasing indecision, an untouched mystery, led her by the hand. There was one window, and she paused now and then, waiting, looking out at the rain. When she was still, there was a passivity about her, or a deception of passivity, that was not really passive at all. There was something in her that never stopped.

At last she flung herself onto the floor, back across the newspaper, and looked at length into the fire. It might have been a mirror in the cabin, into which she could look deeper and deeper as she pulled her fingers through her hair, trying to see herself and Clyde coming up behind her.

"Clyde?"

But of course her husband, Clyde, was still in the woods. He kept a thick brushwood roof over his whisky still, and he was mortally afraid of lightning like this, and would never go out in it for anything.

And then, almost in amazement, she began to comprehend her predicament: it was unlike Clyde to take up a gun and shoot her.

She bowed her head toward the heat, onto her rosy arms, and began to talk and talk to herself. She grew voluble. Even if he heard about the coffee man, with a Pontiac car, she did not think he would shoot her. When Clyde would make her blue, she would go out onto the road, some car would slow down, and if it had a Tennessee license, the lucky kind, the chances were that she would spend the afternoon in the shed of the empty gin. (Here she rolled her head about on her arms and stretched her legs tiredly behind her, like a cat.) And if Clyde got word, he would slap her. But the account in the paper was wrong. Clyde had never shot her, even once. There had been a mistake made.

A spark flew out and nearly caught the paper on fire. Almost in fright she beat it out with her fingers. Then she murmured and lay back more firmly upon the pages.

There she stretched, growing warmer and warmer, sleepier and sleepier. She began to wonder out loud how it would be if Clyde shot her in the leg. . . . If he were truly angry, might he shoot her through the heart?

At once she was imagining herself dying. She would have a nightgown to lie in, and a bullet in her heart. Anyone could tell, to see her lying there with that deep expression about her mouth, how strange and terrible that would be. Underneath a brand-new nightgown her heart would be hurting with every beat, many times more than her toughened skin when Clyde slapped at her. Ruby began to cry softly, the way she would be crying from the extremity of pain; tears would run down in a little stream over the quilt. Clyde would be standing there above her, as he once looked, with his wild black hair hanging to his shoulders. He used to be very handsome and strong!

He would say, "Ruby, I done this to you."

She would say—only a whisper—"That is the truth, Clyde—you done this to me."

Then she would die; her life would stop right there.

She lay silently for a moment, composing her face into a look which would be beautiful, desirable, and dead.

Clyde would have to buy her a dress to bury her in. He would have to dig a deep hole behind the house, under the cedar, a grave. He would have to nail her up a pine coffin and lay her inside. Then he would have to carry her to the grave, lay her down and cover her up. All the time he would be wild, shouting, and all distracted, to think he could never touch her one more time.

She moved slightly, and her eyes turned toward the window. The white rain splashed down. She could hardly breathe, for thinking that this was the way it was to fall on her grave, where Clyde would come and stand, looking down in the tears of some repentance.

A whole tree of lightning stood in the sky. She kept looking out the window, suffused with the warmth from the fire and with the pity and beauty and power of her death. The thunder rolled.

Then Clyde was standing there, with dark streams flowing over the floor where he had walked. He poked at Ruby with the butt of his gun, as if she were asleep.

"What's keepin' supper?" he growled.

She jumped up and darted away from him. Then, quicker than lightning, she put away the paper. The room was dark, except for the firelight. From the long shadow of his steamy presence she spoke to him glibly and lighted the lamp.

He stood there with a stunned, yet rather good-humored

look of delay and patience in his face, and kept on standing there. He stamped his mud-red boots, and his enormous hands seemed weighted with the rain that fell from him and dripped down the barrel of the gun. Presently he sat down with dignity in the chair at the table, making a little tumult of his rightful wetness and hunger. Small streams began to flow from him everywhere.

Ruby was going through the preparations for the meal gently. She stood almost on tiptoe in her bare, warm feet. Once as she knelt at the safe, getting out the biscuits, she saw Clyde looking at her and she smiled and bent her head tenderly. There was some way she began to move her arms that was mysteriously sweet and yet abrupt and tentative, a delicate and vulnerable manner, as though her breasts gave her pain. She made many unnecessary trips back and forth across the floor, circling Clyde where he sat in his steamy silence, a knife and fork in his fists.

"Well, where you been, anyway?" he grumbled at last, as she set the first dish on the table.

"Nowheres special."

"Don't you talk back to me. You been hitchhikin' again, ain't you?" He almost chuckled.

She gave him a quick look straight into his eyes. She had not even heard him. She was filled with happiness. Her hand trembled when she poured the coffee. Some of it splashed on his wrist.

At that he let his hand drop heavily down upon the table and made the plates jump.

"Some day I'm goin' to smack the livin' devil outa you," he said.

Ruby dodged mechanically. She let him eat. Then, when he had crossed his knife and fork over his plate, she brought him the newspaper. Again she looked at him in delight. It excited her even to touch the paper with her hand, to hear its quiet secret noise when she carried it, the rustle of surprise.

"A newspaper!" Clyde snatched it roughly and with a grabbing disparagement. "Where 'd you git that? Hussy."

"Look at this-here," said Ruby in her small singsong voice. She opened the paper while he held it and pointed gravely to the paragraph.

Reluctantly, Clyde began to read it. She watched his damp bald head slowly bend and turn.

Then he made a sound in his throat and said, "It's a lie."

"That's what's in the newspaper about me," said Ruby, standing up straight. She took up his plate and gave him that look of joy.

He put his big crooked finger on the paragraph and poked at it.

"Well, I'd just like to see the place I shot you!" he cried explosively. He looked up, his face blank and bold.

But she drew herself in, still holding the empty plate, faced him straightened and hard, and they looked at each other. The moment filled full with their helplessness. Slowly they both flushed, as though with a double shame and a double pleasure. It was as though Clyde might really have killed Ruby, and as though Ruby might really have been dead at his hand. Rare and wavering, some possibility stood timidly like a stranger between them and made them hang their heads.

Then Clyde walked over in his water-soaked boots and laid the paper on the dying fire. It floated there a moment and then burst into flame. They stood still and watched it burn. The whole room was bright.

"Look," said Clyde suddenly. "It's a Tennessee paper. See 'Tennessee'? That wasn't none of you it wrote about." He laughed, to show that he had been right all the time.

"It was Ruby Fisher!" cried Ruby. "My name is Ruby Fisher!" she declared passionately to Clyde.

"Oho, it was another Ruby Fisher—in Tennessee," cried her husband. "Fool me, huh? Where 'd you get that paper?" He spanked her good-humoredly across her backside.

Ruby folded her still trembling hands into her skirt. She stood stooping by the window until everything, outside and in, was quieted before she went to her supper.

It was dark and vague outside. The storm had rolled away to faintness like a wagon crossing a bridge.

Petrified Man

"Reach in my purse and git me a cigarette without no powder in it if you kin, Mrs Fletcher, honey," said Leota to her ten o'clock shampoo-and-set customer. "I don't like no perfumed cigarettes."

Mrs Fletcher gladly reached over to the lavender shelf under the lavender-framed mirror, shook a hair net loose from the clasp of the patent-leather bag, and slapped her hand down quickly on a powder puff which burst out when the purse was opened.

"Why, look at the peanuts, Leota!" said Mrs Fletcher in her marveling voice.

"Honey, them goobers has been in my purse a week if they's been in it a day. Mrs Pike bought them peanuts."

"Who's Mrs Pike?" asked Mrs Fletcher, settling back. Hidden in this den of curling fluid and henna packs, separated by a lavender swing door from the other customers, who were being gratified in other booths, she could give her curiosity its freedom. She looked expectantly at the black part in Leota's yellow curls as she bent to light the cigarette.

"Mrs Pike is this lady from New Orleans," said Leota, puffing, and pressing into Mrs Fletcher's scalp with strong red-nailed fingers. "A friend, not a customer. You see, like maybe I told you last time, me and Fred and Sal and Joe all had us a fuss, so Sal and Joe up and moved out, so we didn't do a thing but rent out their room. So we rented it to Mrs Pike. And Mr Pike." She flicked an ash into the basket of dirty towels. "Mrs Pike is a very decided blonde. *She* bought me the peanuts."

"She must be cute," said Mrs Fletcher.

"Honey, 'cute' ain't the word for what she is. I'm tellin' you, Mrs Pike is attractive. She has her a good time. She's got a sharp eye out, Mrs Pike has."

She dashed the comb through the air, and paused dramatically as a cloud of Mrs Fletcher's hennaed hair floated out of the lavender teeth like a small storm cloud.

"Hair fallin'."

"Aw, Leota."

"Uh-huh, commencin' to fall out," said Leota, combing again, and letting fall another cloud.

"Is it any dandruff in it?" Mrs Fletcher was frowning, her hair-line eyebrows diving down toward her nose, and her wrinkled, beady-lashed eyelids batting with concentration.

"Nope." She combed again. "Just fallin' out."

"Bet it was that last perm'nent you gave me that did it," Mrs Fletcher said cruelly. "Remember you cooked me fourteen minutes."

"You had fourteen minutes comin' to you," said Leota with finality.

"Bound to be somethin'," persisted Mrs Fletcher. "Dandruff, dandruff. I couldn't of caught a thing like that from Mr Fletcher, could I?"

"Well," Leota answered at last, "you know what I heard in here yestiddy, one of Thelma's ladies was settin' over yonder in Thelma's booth gittin' a machineless, and I don't mean to insist or insinuate or anything, Mrs Fletcher, but Thelma's lady just happ'med to throw out—I forgotten what she was talkin' about at the time—that you was p-r-e-g., and lots of times that 'll make your hair do awful funny, fall out and God knows what all. It just ain't our fault, is the way I look at it."

There was a pause. The women stared at each other in the mirror.

"Who was it?" demanded Mrs Fletcher.

"Honey, I really couldn't say," said Leota. "Not that you look it."

"Where's Thelma? I'll get it out of her," said Mrs Fletcher.

"Now, honey, I wouldn't go and git mad over a little thing like that," Leota said, combing hastily, as though to hold Mrs Fletcher down by the hair. "I'm sure it was somebody didn't mean no harm in the world. How far gone are you?"

"Just wait," said Mrs Fletcher, and shrieked for Thelma, who came in and took a drag from Leota's cigarette.

"Thelma, honey, throw your mind back to yestiddy if you kin," said Leota, drenching Mrs Fletcher's hair with a thick fluid and catching the overflow in a cold wet towel at her neck.

"Well, I got my lady half wound for a spiral," said Thelma doubtfully.

"This won't take but a minute," said Leota. "Who is it you got in there, old Horse Face? Just cast your mind back and try to remember who your lady was yestiddy who happ'm to mention that my customer was pregnant, that's all. She's dead to know."

Thelma drooped her blood-red lips and looked over Mrs Fletcher's head into the mirror. "Why, honey, I ain't got the faintest," she breathed. "I really don't recollect the faintest. But I'm sure she meant no harm. I declare, I forgot my hair finally got combed and thought it was a stranger behind me."

"Was it that Mrs Hutchinson?" Mrs Fletcher was tensely polite.

"Mrs Hutchinson? Oh, Mrs Hutchinson." Thelma batted her eyes. "Naw, precious, she come on Thursday and didn't ev'm mention your name. I doubt if she ev'm knows you're on the way."

"Thelma!" cried Leota staunchly.

"All I know is, whoever it is 'll be sorry some day. Why, I just barely knew it myself!" cried Mrs Fletcher. "Just let her wait!"

"Why? What 're you gonna do to her?"

It was a child's voice, and the women looked down. A little boy was making tents with aluminum wave pinchers on the floor under the sink.

"Billy Boy, hon, mustn't bother nice ladies," Leota smiled. She slapped him brightly and behind her back waved Thelma out of the booth. "Ain't Billy Boy a sight? Only three years old and already just nuts about the beauty-parlor business."

"I never saw him here before," said Mrs Fletcher, still unmollified.

"He ain't been here before, that's how come," said Leota. "He belongs to Mrs Pike. She got her a job but it was Fay's Millinery. He oughtn't to try on those ladies' hats, they come down over his eyes like I don't know what. They just git to look ridiculous, that's what, an' of course he's gonna put 'em on: hats. They tole Mrs Pike they didn't appreciate him hangin' around there. Here, he couldn't hurt a thing."

"Well! I don't like children that much," said Mrs Fletcher.

"Well!" said Leota moodily.

"Well! I'm almost tempted not to have this one," said Mrs Fletcher. "That Mrs Hutchinson! Just looks straight through you when she sees you on the street and then spits at you behind your back."

"Mr Fletcher would beat you on the head if you didn't have it now," said Leota reasonably. "After going this far."

Mrs Fletcher sat up straight. "Mr Fletcher can't do a thing with me."

"He can't!" Leota winked at herself in the mirror.

"No siree, he can't. If he so much as raises his voice against me, he knows good and well I'll have one of my sick headaches, and then I'm just not fit to live with. And if I really look that pregnant already——"

"Well, now, honey, I just want you to know—I habm't told any of my ladies and I ain't goin' to tell 'em—even that you're losin' your hair. You just get you one of those Stork-a-Lure dresses and stop worryin'. What people don't know don't hurt nobody, as Mrs Pike says."

"Did you tell Mrs Pike?" asked Mrs Fletcher sulkily.

"Well, Mrs Fletcher, look, you ain't ever goin' to lay eyes on Mrs Pike or her lay eyes on you, so what diffunce does it make in the long run?"

"I knew it!" Mrs Fletcher deliberately nodded her head so as to destroy a ringlet Leota was working on behind her ear. "Mrs Pike!"

Leota sighed. "I reckon I might as well tell you. It wasn't any more Thelma's lady tole me you was pregnant than a bat."

"Not Mrs Hutchinson?"

"Naw, Lord! It was Mrs Pike."

"Mrs Pike!" Mrs Fletcher could only sputter and let curling fluid roll into her ear. "How could Mrs Pike possibly know I was pregnant or otherwise, when she doesn't even know me? The nerve of some people!"

"Well, here's how it was. Remember Sunday?"

"Yes," said Mrs Fletcher.

"Sunday, Mrs Pike an' me was all by ourself. Mr Pike and

Fred had gone over to Eagle Lake, sayin' they was goin' to catch 'em some fish, but they didn't, a course. So we was settin' in Mrs Pike's car, is a 1939 Dodge——"

"1939, eh," said Mrs Fletcher.

"—An' we was gettin' us a Jax beer apiece—that's the beer that Mrs Pike says is made right in N.O., so she won't drink no other kind. So I seen you drive up to the drugstore an' run in for just a secont, leavin' I reckon Mr Fletcher in the car, an' come runnin' out with looked like a perscription. So I says to Mrs Pike, just to be makin' talk, 'Right yonder's Mrs Fletcher, and I reckon that's Mr Fletcher—she's one of my regular customers,' I says."

"I had on a figured print," said Mrs Fletcher tentatively.

"You sure did," agreed Leota. "So Mrs Pike, she give you a good look—she's very observant, a good judge of character, cute as a minute, you know—and she says, 'I bet you another Jax that lady's three months on the way.' "

"What gall!" said Mrs Fletcher. "Mrs Pike!"

"Mrs Pike ain't goin' to bite you," said Leota. "Mrs Pike is a lovely girl, you'd be crazy about her, Mrs Fletcher. But she can't sit still a minute. We went to the travelin' freak show yestiddy after work. I got through early—nine o'clock. In the vacant store next door? What, you ain't been?"

"No, I despise freaks," declared Mrs Fletcher.

"Aw. Well, honey, talkin' about bein' pregnant an' all, you ought to see those twins in a bottle, you really owe it to yourself."

"What twins?" asked Mrs Fletcher out of the side of her mouth.

"Well, honey, they got these two twins in a bottle, see? Born joined plumb together—dead a course." Leota dropped her voice into a soft lyrical hum. "They was about this long—pardon—must of been full time, all right, wouldn't you say?—an' they had these two heads an' two faces an' four arms an' four legs, all kind of joined *here*. See, this face looked this-a-way, and the other face looked that-a-way, over their shoulder, see. Kinda pathetic."

"Glah!" said Mrs Fletcher disapprovingly.

"Well, ugly? Honey, I mean to tell you—their parents was first cousins and all like that. Billy Boy, git me a fresh towel from off Teeny's stack—this 'n's wringin' wet—an' quit tick-lin' my ankles with that curler. I declare! He don't miss nothin'."

"Me and Mr Fletcher aren't one speck of kin, or he could never of had me," said Mrs Fletcher placidly.

"Of course not!" protested Leota. "Neither is me an' Fred, not that we know of. Well, honey, what Mrs Pike liked was the pygmies. They've got these pygmies down there, too, an' Mrs Pike was just wild about 'em. You know, the tee-niniest men in the universe? Well honey, they can just rest back on their little bohunkus an' roll around an' you can't hardly tell if they're sittin' or standin'. That 'll give you some idea. They're about forty-two years old. Just suppose it was your husband!"

"Well, Mr Fletcher is five foot nine and one half," said Mrs Fletcher quickly.

"Fred's five foot ten," said Leota, "but I tell him he's still a shrimp, account of I'm so tall." She made a deep wave over Mrs Fletcher's other temple with the comb. "Well, these pyg-mies are a kind of a dark brown, Mrs Fletcher. Not bad lookin' for what they are, you know."

"I wouldn't care for them," said Mrs Fletcher. "What does that Mrs Pike see in them?"

"Aw, I don't know," said Leota. "She's just cute, that's all. But they got this man, this petrified man, that ever'thing ever since he was nine years old, when it goes through his diges-tion, see, somehow Mrs Pike says it goes to his joints and has been turning to stone."

"How awful!" said Mrs Fletcher.

"He's forty-two too. That looks like a bad age."

"Who said so, that Mrs Pike? I bet she's forty-two," said Mrs Fletcher.

"Naw," said Leota, "Mrs Pike's thirty-three, born in Jan-uary, an Aquarian. He could move his head—like this. A course his head and mind ain't a joint, so to speak, and I guess his stomach ain't, either—not yet anyways. But see—his food, he eats it, and it goes down, see, and then he digests it"—Leota rose on her toes for an instant—"and it goes out to his joints and before you can say 'Jack Robinson,' it's stone—pure stone. He's turning to stone. How'd you like to be married to a guy like that? All he can do, he can move his head just a quarter of an inch. A course he *looks* just *terrible*."

"I should think he would," said Mrs Fletcher frostily. "Mr Fletcher takes bending exercises every night of the world. I make him."

"All Fred does is lay around the house like a rug. I wouldn't be surprised if he woke up some day and couldn't move. The petrified man just sat there moving his quarter of an inch though," said Leota reminiscently.

"Did Mrs Pike like the petrified man?" asked Mrs Fletcher.

"Not as much as she did the others," said Leota deprecatingly. "And then she likes a man to be a good dresser, and all that."

"Is Mr Pike a good dresser?" asked Mrs Fletcher skeptically.

"Oh, well, yeah," said Leota, "but he's twelve- fourteen years older 'n her. She ast Lady Evangeline about him."

"Who's Lady Evangeline?" asked Mrs Fletcher.

"Well, it's this mind reader they got in the freak show," said Leota. "Was real good. Lady Evangeline is her name, and if I had another dollar I wouldn't do a thing but have my other palm read. She had what Mrs Pike said was the 'sixth mind' but she had the worst manicure I ever saw on a living person."

"What did she tell Mrs Pike?" asked Mrs Fletcher.

"She told her Mr Pike was as true to her as he could be and besides, would come into some money."

"Humph!" said Mrs Fletcher. "What does he do?"

"I can't tell," said Leota, "because he don't work. Lady Evangeline didn't tell me near enough about my nature or anything. And I would like to go back and find out some more about this boy. Used to go with this boy got married to this girl. Oh, shoot, that was about three and a half years ago, when you was still goin' to the Robert E. Lee Beauty Shop in Jackson. He married her for her money. Another fortune teller tole me that at the time. So I'm not in love with him any more, anyway, besides being married to Fred, but Mrs Pike thought, just for the hell of it, see, to ask Lady Evangeline was he happy."

"Does Mrs Pike know everything about you already?" asked Mrs Fletcher unbelievingly. "Mercy!"

"Oh yeah, I tole her ever'thing about ever'thing, from now on back to I don't know when—to when I first started goin' out," said Leota. "So I ast Lady Evangeline for one of my questions, was he happily married, and she says, just like she was glad I ask her, 'Honey,' she says, 'naw, he idn't. You write down this day, March 8, 1941,' she says, 'and mock it down: three years from today him and her won't be occupyin' the same bed.' There it is, up on the wall with them other dates—see, Mrs Fletcher? And she says, 'Child, you ought to be glad you didn't git him, because he's so mercenary.' So I'm glad I married Fred. He sure ain't mercenary, money don't mean a thing to him. But I sure would like to go back and have my other palm read."

"Did Mrs Pike believe in what the fortune teller said?" asked Mrs Fletcher in a superior tone of voice.

"Lord, yes, she's from New Orleans. Ever'body in New Orleans believes ever'thing spooky. One of 'em in New Orleans before it was raided says to Mrs Pike one summer she was goin' to go from state to state and meet some gray-headed men, and, sure enough, she says she went on a beautician convention up to Chicago. . . ."

"Oh!" said Mrs Fletcher. "Oh, is Mrs Pike a beautician too?"

"Sure she is," protested Leota. "She's a beautician. I'm goin' to git her in here if I can. Before she married. But it don't leave you. She says sure enough, there was three men who was a very large part of making her trip what it was, and they all three had gray in their hair and they went in six states. Got Christmas cards from 'em. Billy Boy, go see if Thelma's got any dry cotton. Look how Mrs Fletcher's a-drippin'."

"Where did Mrs Pike meet Mr Pike?" asked Mrs Fletcher primly.

"On another train," said Leota.

"I met Mr Fletcher, or rather he met me, in a rental library," said Mrs Fletcher with dignity, as she watched the net come down over her head.

"Honey, me an' Fred, we met in a rumble seat eight months ago and we was practically on what you might call the way to the altar inside of a half an hour," said Leota in a guttural voice, and bit a bobby pin open. "Course it don't last. Mrs Pike says nothin' like that ever lasts."

"Mr Fletcher and myself are as much in love as the day we married," said Mrs Fletcher belligerently as Leota stuffed cotton into her ears.

"Mrs Pike says it don't last," repeated Leota in a louder voice. "Now go git under the dryer. You can turn yourself on, can't you? I'll be back to comb you out. Durin' lunch I promised to give Mrs Pike a facial. You know—free. Her bein' in the business, so to speak."

"I bet she needs one," said Mrs Fletcher, letting the swing door fly back against Leota. "Oh, pardon me."

A week later, on time for her appointment, Mrs Fletcher sank heavily into Leota's chair after first removing a drugstore rental book, called *Life Is Like That*, from the seat. She stared in a discouraged way into the mirror.

"You can tell it when I'm sitting down, all right," she said.

Leota seemed preoccupied and stood shaking out a lavender cloth. She began to pin it around Mrs Fletcher's neck in silence.

"I said you sure can tell it when I'm sitting straight on and coming at you this way," Mrs Fletcher said.

"Why, honey, naw you can't," said Leota gloomily. "Why, I'd never know. If somebody was to come up to me on the street and say, 'Mrs Fletcher is pregnant!' I'd say, 'Heck, she don't look it to me.' "

"If a certain party hadn't found it out and spread it around, it wouldn't be too late even now," said Mrs Fletcher frostily, but Leota was almost choking her with the cloth, pinning it so tight, and she couldn't speak clearly. She paddled her hands in the air until Leota wearily loosened her.

"Listen, honey, you're just a virgin compared to Mrs Montjoy," Leota was going on, still absent-minded. She bent Mrs Fletcher back in the chair and, sighing, tossed liquid from a teacup onto her head and dug both hands into her scalp. "You know Mrs Montjoy—her husband's that premature-gray-headed fella?"

"She's in the Trojan Garden Club, is all I know," said Mrs Fletcher.

"Well, honey," said Leota, but in a weary voice, "she come in here not the week before and not the day before she had her baby—she come in here the very selfsame day, I mean to tell you. Child, we was all plumb scared to death. There she was! Come for her shampoo an' set. Why, Mrs Fletcher, in a hour an' twenty minutes she was layin' up there in the Babtist Hospital with a seb'm-pound son. It was that close a shave. I declare, if I hadn't been so tired I would of drank up a bottle of gin that night."

"What gall," said Mrs Fletcher. "I never knew her at all well."

"See, her husband was waitin' outside in the car, and her bags was all packed an' in the back seat, an' she was all ready, 'cept she wanted her shampoo an' set. An' havin' one pain right after another. Her husband kep' comin' in here, scared-like, but couldn't do nothin' with her a course. She yelled bloody murder, too, but she always yelled her head off when I give her perm'nent."

"She must of been crazy," said Mrs Fletcher. "How did she look?"

"Shoot!" said Leota.

"Well, I can guess," said Mrs Fletcher. "Awful."

"Just wanted to look pretty while she was havin' her baby, is all," said Leota airily. "Course, we was glad to give the lady what she was after—that's our motto—but I bet a hour later she wasn't payin' no mind to them little end curls. I bet she wasn't thinkin' about she ought to have on a net. It wouldn't of done her no good if she had."

"No, I don't suppose it would," said Mrs Fletcher.

"Yeah man! She was a-yellin'. Just like when I give her her perm'nent."

"Her husband ought to could make her behave. Don't it seem that way to you?" asked Mrs Fletcher. "He ought to put his foot down."

"Ha," said Leota. "A lot he could do. Maybe some women is soft."

"Oh, you mistake me, I don't mean for her to get soft—far from it! Women have to stand up for themselves, or there's just no telling. But now you take me—I ask Mr Fletcher's advice now and then, and he appreciates it, especially on something important, like is it time for a permanent—not that I've told him about the baby. He says, 'Why dear, go ahead!' Just ask their *advice*."

"Huh! If I ever ast Fred's advice we'd be floatin' down the Yazoo River on a houseboat or somethin' by this time," said Leota. "I'm sick of Fred. I tole him to go over to Vicksburg."

"Is he going?" demanded Mrs Fletcher.

"Sure. See, the fortune teller—I went back and had my other palm read, since we've got to rent the room agin—said my lover was goin' to work in Vicksburg, so I don't know who she could mean, unless she meant Fred. And Fred ain't workin' here—that much is so."

"Is he going to work in Vicksburg?" asked Mrs Fletcher. "And——"

"Sure, Lady Evangeline said so. Said the future is going to be brighter than the present. He don't want to go, but I ain't gonna put up with nothin' like that. Lays around the house an' bulls—did bull—with that good-for-nothin' Mr Pike. He says if he goes who'll cook, but I says I never get to eat anyway—not meals. Billy Boy, take Mrs Grover that *Screen Secrets* and leg it."

Mrs Fletcher heard stamping feet go out the door.

"Is that that Mrs Pike's little boy here again?" she asked, sitting up gingerly.

"Yeah, that's still him." Leota stuck out her tongue.

Mrs Fletcher could hardly believe her eyes. "Well! How's Mrs Pike, your attractive new friend with the sharp eyes who spreads it around town that perfect strangers are pregnant?" she asked in a sweetened tone.

"Oh, Mizziz Pike." Leota combed Mrs Fletcher's hair with heavy strokes.

"You act like you're tired," said Mrs Fletcher.

"Tired? Feel like it's four o'clock in the afternoon already," said Leota. "I ain't told you the awful luck we had, me and Fred? It's the worst thing you ever heard of. Maybe *you* think Mrs Pike's got sharp eyes. Shoot, there's a limit! Well, you know, we rented out our room to this Mr and Mrs Pike from New Orleans when Sal an' Joe Fentress got mad at us 'cause they drank up some home-brew we had in the closet—Sal an' Joe did. So, a week ago Sat'day Mr and Mrs Pike moved in.

Well, I kinda fixed up the room, you know—put a sofa pillow on the couch and picked some ragged robbins and put in a vase, but they never did say they appreciated it. Anyway, then I put some old magazines on the table."

"I think that was lovely," said Mrs Fletcher.

"Wait. So, come night 'fore last, Fred and this Mr Pike, who Fred just took up with, was back from they said they was fishin', bein' as neither one of 'em has got a job to his name, and we was all settin' around in their room. So Mrs Pike was settin' there, readin' a old *Startling G-Man Tales* that was mine, mind you, I'd bought it myself, and all of a sudden she jumps!—into the air—you'd 'a' thought she'd set on a spider—an' says, 'Canfield'—ain't that silly, that's Mr Pike—'Canfield, my God A'mighty,' she says, 'honey,' she says, 'we're rich, and you won't have to work.' Not that he turned one hand anyway. Well, me and Fred rushes over to her, and Mr Pike, too, and there she sets, pointin' her finger at a photo in my copy of *Startling G-Man*. 'See that man?' yells Mrs Pike. 'Remember him, Canfield?' 'Never forget a face,' says Mr Pike. 'It's Mr Petrie, that we stayed with him in the apartment next to ours in Toulouse Street in N.O. for six weeks. Mr Petrie.' 'Well,' says Mrs Pike, like she can't hold out one secont longer, 'Mr Petrie is wanted for five hunderd dollars cash, for rapin' four women in California, and I know where he is.' "

"Mercy!" said Mrs Fletcher. "Where was he?"

At some time Leota had washed her hair and now she yanked her up by the back locks and sat her up.

"Know where he was?"

"I certainly don't," Mrs Fletcher said. Her scalp hurt all over.

Leota flung a towel around the top of her customer's head. "Nowhere else but in that freak show! I saw him just as plain as Mrs Pike. *He* was the petrified man!"

"Who would ever have thought that!" cried Mrs Fletcher sympathetically.

"So Mr Pike says, 'Well whatta you know about that,' an' he looks real hard at the photo and whistles. And she starts dancin' and singin' about their good luck. She meant our bad luck! I made a point of tellin' that fortune teller the next time

I saw her. I said, 'Listen, that magazine was layin' around the house for a month, and there was five hunderd dollars in it for somebody. An' there was the freak show runnin' night an' day, not two steps away from my own beauty parlor, with Mr Petrie just settin' there waitin'. An' it had to be Mr and Mrs Pike, almost perfect strangers.' "

"What gall," said Mrs Fletcher. She was only sitting there, wrapped in a turban, but she did not mind.

"Fortune tellers don't care. And Mrs Pike, she goes around actin' like she thinks she was Mrs God," said Leota. "So they're goin' to leave tomorrow, Mr and Mrs Pike. And in the meantime I got to keep that mean, bad little ole kid here, gettin' under my feet ever' minute of the day an' talkin' back too."

"Have they gotten the five hundred dollars' reward already?" asked Mrs Fletcher.

"Well," said Leota, "at first Mr Pike didn't want to do anything about it. Can you feature that? Said he kinda liked that ole bird and said he was real nice to 'em, lent 'em money or somethin'. But Mrs Pike simply tole him he could just go to hell, and I can see her point. She says, 'You ain't worked a lick in six months, and here I make five hunderd dollars in two seconts, and what thanks do I get for it? You go to hell, Canfield,' she says. So," Leota went on in a despondent voice, "they called up the cops and they caught the ole bird, all right, right there in the freak show where I saw him with my own eyes, thinkin' he was petrified. He's the one. Did it under his real name—Mr Petrie. Four women in California, all in the month of August. So Mrs Pike gits five hunderd dollars. And my magazine, and right next door to my beauty parlor. I cried all night, but Fred said it wasn't a bit of use and to go to sleep, because the whole thing was just a sort of coincidence—you know: can't do nothin' about it. He says it put him clean out of the notion of goin' to Vicksburg for a few days till we rent out the room agin—no tellin' who we'll git this time."

"But can you imagine anybody knowing this old man, that's raped four women?" persisted Mrs Fletcher, and she shuddered audibly. "Did Mrs Pike *speak* to him when she met him in the freak show?"

Leota had begun to comb Mrs Fletcher's hair. "I says to her, I says, 'I didn't notice you fallin' on his neck when he was the petrified man—don't tell me you didn't recognize your fine friend?' And she says, 'I didn't recognize him with that white powder all over his face. He just looked familiar,' Mrs Pike says, 'and lots of people look familiar.' But she says that ole petrified man did put her in mind of somebody. She wondered who it was! Kep' her awake, which man she'd ever knew it reminded her of. So when she seen the photo, it all come to her. Like a flash. Mr Petrie. The way he'd turn his head and look at her when she took him in his breakfast."

"Took him in his breakfast!" shrieked Mrs Fletcher. "Listen—don't tell me. I'd 'a' felt something."

"Four women. I guess those women didn't have the faintest notion at the time they'd be worth a hunderd an' twenty-five bucks apiece someday to Mrs Pike. We ast her how old the fella was then, an' she says he musta had one foot in the grave, at least. Can you beat it?"

"Not really petrified at all, of course," said Mrs Fletcher meditatively. She drew herself up. "I'd 'a' felt something," she said proudly.

"Shoot! I did feel somethin'," said Leota. "I tole Fred when I got home I felt so funny. I said, 'Fred, that ole petrified man sure did leave me with a funny feelin'.' He says, 'Funny-haha or funny-peculiar?' and I says, 'Funny-peculiar.' " She pointed her comb into the air emphatically.

"I'll bet you did," said Mrs Fletcher.

They both heard a crackling noise.

Leota screamed, "Billy Boy! What you doin' in my purse?"

"Aw, I'm just eatin' these ole stale peanuts up," said Billy Boy.

"You come here to me!" screamed Leota, recklessly flinging down the comb, which scattered a whole ash tray full of bobby pins and knocked down a row of Coca-Cola bottles. "This is the last straw!"

"I caught him! I caught him!" giggled Mrs Fletcher. "I'll hold him on my lap. You bad, bad boy, you! I guess I better learn how to spank little old bad boys," she said.

Leota's eleven o'clock customer pushed open the swing door upon Leota paddling him heartily with the brush, while he gave angry but belittling screams which penetrated beyond the booth and filled the whole curious beauty parlor. From everywhere ladies began to gather round to watch the paddling. Billy Boy kicked both Leota and Mrs Fletcher as hard as he could, Mrs Fletcher with her new fixed smile.

"There, my little man!" gasped Leota. "You won't be able to set down for a week if I knew what I was doin'."

Billy Boy stomped through the group of wild-haired ladies and went out the door, but flung back the words, "If you're so smart, why ain't you rich?"

The Key

IT WAS QUIET in the waiting room of the remote little station, except for the night sounds of insects. You could hear their embroidering movements in the weeds outside, which somehow gave the effect of some tenuous voice in the night, telling a story. Or you could listen to the fat thudding of the light bugs and the hoarse rushing of their big wings against the wooden ceiling. Some of the bugs were clinging heavily to the yellow globe, like idiot bees to a senseless smell.

Under this prickly light two rows of people sat in silence, their faces stung, their bodies twisted and quietly uncomfortable, expectantly so, in ones and twos, not quite asleep. No one seemed impatient, although the train was late. A little girl lay flung back in her mother's lap as though sleep had struck her with a blow.

Ellie and Albert Morgan were sitting on a bench like the others waiting for the train and had nothing to say to each other. Their names were ever so neatly and rather largely printed on a big reddish-tan suitcase strapped crookedly shut, because of a missing buckle, so that it hung apart finally like a stupid pair of lips. "Albert Morgan, Ellie Morgan, Yellow Leaf, Mississippi." They must have been driven into town in a wagon, for they and the suitcase were all touched here and there with a fine yellow dust, like finger marks.

Ellie Morgan was a large woman with a face as pink and crowded as an old-fashioned rose. She must have been about forty years old. One of those black satchel purses hung over her straight, strong wrist. It must have been her savings which were making possible this trip. And to what place? you wondered, for she sat there as tense and solid as a cube, as if to endure some nameless apprehension rising and overflowing within her at the thought of travel. Her face worked and broke into strained, hardening lines, as if there had been a death—that too-explicit evidence of agony in the desire to communicate.

Albert made a slower and softer impression. He sat motionless beside Ellie, holding his hat in his lap with both hands—a hat you were sure he had never worn. He looked home-made, as though his wife had self-consciously knitted or somehow contrived a husband when she sat alone at night. He had a shock of very fine sunburned yellow hair. He was too shy for this world, you could see. His hands were like cardboard, he held his hat so still; and yet how softly his eyes fell upon its crown, moving dreamily and yet with dread over its brown surface! He was smaller than his wife. His suit was brown, too, and he wore it neatly and carefully, as though he were murmuring, "Don't look—no need to look—I am effaced." But you have seen that expression too in silent children, who will tell you what they dreamed the night before in sudden, almost hilarious, bursts of confidence.

Every now and then, as though he perceived some minute thing, a sudden alert, tantalized look would creep over the little man's face, and he would gaze slowly around him, quite slyly. Then he would bow his head again; the expression would vanish; some inner refreshment had been denied him. Behind his head was a wall poster, dirty with time, showing an old-fashioned locomotive about to crash into an open touring car filled with women in veils. No one in the station was frightened by the familiar poster, any more than they were aroused by the little man whose rising and drooping head it framed. Yet for a moment he might seem to you to be sitting there quite filled with hope.

Among the others in the station was a strong-looking young man, alone, hatless, red haired, who was standing by the wall while the rest sat on benches. He had a small key in his hand and was turning it over and over in his fingers, nervously passing it from one hand to the other, tossing it gently into the air and catching it again.

He stood and stared in distraction at the other people; so intent and so wide was his gaze that anyone who glanced after him seemed rocked like a small boat in the wake of a large one. There was an excess of energy about him that separated him from everyone else, but in the motion of his hands there was, instead of the craving for communication, something of reticence, even of secrecy, as the key rose and fell. You guessed that he was a stranger in town; he might have been a criminal or a gambler, but his eyes were widened with gentleness. His look, which traveled without stopping for long anywhere, was a hurried focusing of a very tender and explicit regard.

The color of his hair seemed to jump and move, like the flicker of a match struck in a wind. The ceiling lights were not steady but seemed to pulsate like a living and transient force, and made the young man in his preoccupation appear to tremble in the midst of his size and strength, and to fail to impress his exact outline upon the yellow walls. He was like a salamander in the fire. "Take care," you wanted to say to him, and yet also, "Come here." Nervously, and quite apart in his distraction, he continued to stand tossing the key back and forth from one hand to the other. Suddenly it became a gesture of abandonment: one hand stayed passive in the air, then seized too late; the key fell to the floor.

Everyone, except Albert and Ellie Morgan, looked up for a moment. On the floor the key had made a fierce metallic sound like a challenge, a sound of seriousness. It almost made people jump. It was regarded as an insult, a very personal question, in the quiet peaceful room where the insects were tapping at the ceiling and each person was allowed to sit among his possessions and wait for an unquestioned departure. Little walls of reproach went up about them all.

A flicker of amusement touched the young man's face as he observed the startled but controlled and obstinately blank faces which turned toward him for a moment and then away. He walked over to pick up his key.

But it had glanced and slid across the floor, and now it lay in the dust at Albert Morgan's feet.

Albert Morgan was indeed picking up the key. Across from him, the young man saw him examine it, quite slowly, with wonder written all over his face and hands, as if it had fallen from the sky. Had he failed to hear the clatter? There was something wrong with Albert. . . .

As if by decision, the young man did not terminate this wonder by claiming his key. He stood back, a peculiar flash of interest or of something more inscrutable, like resignation, in his lowered eyes.

The little man had probably been staring at the floor, thinking. And suddenly in the dark surface the small sliding key had appeared. You could see memory seize his face, twist it and hold it. What innocent, strange thing might it have brought back to life—a fish he had once spied just below the top of the water in a sunny lake in the country when he was a child? This was just as unexpected, shocking, and somehow meaningful to him. Albert sat there holding the key in his wide-open hand. How intensified, magnified, really vain all attempt at expression becomes in the afflicted! It was with an almost incandescent delight that he felt the unguessed temperature and weight of the key. Then he turned to his wife. His lips were actually trembling.

And still the young man waited, as if the strange joy of the little man took precedence with him over whatever need he had for the key. With sudden electrification he saw Ellie slip the handle of her satchel purse from her wrist and with her fingers begin to talk to her husband.

The others in the station had seen Ellie too; shallow pity washed over the waiting room like a dirty wave foaming and creeping over a public beach. In quick mumblings from bench to bench people said to each other, "Deaf and dumb!" How ignorant they were of all that the young man was seeing! Although he had no way of knowing the words Ellie said, he seemed troubled enough at the mistake the little man must have made, at his misplaced wonder and joy.

Albert was replying to his wife. On his hands he said to her, "I found it. Now it belongs to me. It is something important! Important! It means something. From now on we will get along better, have more understanding. . . . . Maybe when we reach Niagara Falls we will even fall in love, the way other people have done. Maybe our marriage was really for love, after all, not for the other reason—both of us being afflicted in the same way, unable to speak, lonely because of that. Now you can stop being ashamed of me, for being so cautious and slow all my life, for taking my own time. . . . . You can take hope. Because it was I who found the key. Remember that—I found it." He laughed all at once, quite silently.

Everyone stared at his impassioned little speech as it came from his fingers. They were embarrassed, vaguely aware of some crisis and vaguely affronted, but unable to interfere; it was as though they were the deaf-mutes and he the speaker.

When he laughed, a few people laughed unconsciously with him, in relief, and turned away. But the young man remained still and intent, waiting at his little distance.

"This key came here very mysteriously—it is bound to mean something," the husband went on to say. He held the key up just before her eyes. "You are always praying; you believe in miracles; well, now, here is the answer. It came to me."

His wife looked self-consciously around the room and replied on her fingers, "You are always talking nonsense. Be quiet."

But she was secretly pleased, and when she saw him slowly look down in his old manner, she reached over, as if to retract what she had said, and laid her hand on his, touching the key for herself, softness making her worn hand limp. From then on they never looked around them, never saw anything except each other. They were so intent, so very solemn, wanting to have their symbols perfectly understood!

"You must see it is a symbol," he began again, his fingers clumsy and blurring in his excitement. "It is a symbol of something—something that we deserve, and that is happiness. We will find happiness in Niagara Falls."

And then, as if he were all at once shy even of her, he turned slightly away from her and slid the key into his pocket. They sat staring down at the suitcase, their hands fallen in their laps.

The young man slowly turned away from them and wandered back to the wall, where he took out a cigarette and lighted it.

Outside, the night pressed around the station like a pure stone, in which the little room might be transfixed and, for the preservation of this moment of hope, its future killed, an insect in amber. The short little train drew in, stopped, and rolled away, almost noiselessly.

Then inside, people were gone or turned in sleep or walking about, all changed from the way they had been. But the deaf-mutes and the loitering young man were still in their places.

The man was still smoking. He was dressed like a young doctor or some such person in the town, and yet he did not seem of the town. He looked very strong and active; but there was a startling quality, a willingness to be forever distracted, even disturbed, in the very reassurance of his body, some alertness which made his strength fluid and dissipated instead of withheld and greedily beautiful. His youth by now did not seem an important thing about him; it was a medium for his activity, no doubt, but as he stood there frowning and smoking you felt some apprehension that he would never express whatever might be the desire of his life in being young and strong, in standing apart in compassion, in making any intuitive present or sacrifice, or in any way of action at all—not because there was too much in the world demanding his strength, but because he was too deeply aware.

You felt a shock in glancing up at him, and when you looked away from the whole yellow room and closed your eyes, his intensity, as well as that of the room, seemed to have impressed the imagination with a shadow of itself, a blackness together with the light, the negative beside the positive. You felt as though some exact, skillful contact had been made between the surfaces of your hearts to make you aware, in some pattern, of his joy and his despair. You could feel the fullness and the emptiness of this stranger's life.

The railroad man came in swinging a lantern which he stopped suddenly in its arc. Looking uncomfortable, and then rather angry, he approached the deaf-mutes and shot his arm out in a series of violent gestures and shrugs.

Albert and Ellie Morgan were dreadfully shocked. The woman looked resigned for a moment to hopelessness. But the little man—you were startled by a look of bravado on his face.

In the station the red haired man was speaking aloud—but to himself. "They missed their train!"

As if in quick apology, the trainman set his lantern down beside Albert's foot, and hurried away.

And as if completing a circle, the red haired man walked over too and stood silently near the deaf-mutes. With a reproachful look at him the woman reached up and took off her hat.

They began again, talking rapidly back and forth, almost as one person. The old routine of their feeling was upon them once more. Perhaps, you thought, staring at their similarity—her hair was yellow, too—they were children together—

cousins even, afflicted in the same way, sent off from home to the state institute. . . .

It was the feeling of conspiracy. They were in counter-plot against the plot of those things that pressed down upon them from outside their knowledge and their ways of making themselves understood. It was obvious that it gave the wife her greatest pleasure. But you wondered, seeing Albert, whom talking seemed rather to dishevel, whether it had not continued to be a rough and violent game which Ellie, as the older and stronger, had taught him to play with her.

"What do you think he wants?" she asked Albert, nodding at the red haired man, who smiled faintly. And how her eyes shone! Who would ever know how deep her suspicion of the whole outside world lay in her heart, how far it had pushed her!

"What does he want?" Albert was replying quickly. "The key!"

Of course! And how fine it had been to sit there with the key hidden from the strangers and also from his wife, who had not seen where he had put it. He stole up with his hand and secretly felt the key, which must have lain in some pocket nearly against his heart. He nodded gently. The key had come there, under his eyes on the floor in the station, all of a sudden, but yet not quite unexpected. That is the way things happen to you always. But Ellie did not comprehend this.

Now she sat there as quiet as could be. It was not only hopelessness about the trip. She, too, undoubtedly felt something privately about that key, apart from what she had said or what he had told her. He had almost shared it with her—you realized that. He frowned and smiled almost at the same time. There was something—something he could almost remember but not quite—which would let him keep the key always to himself. He knew that, and he would remember it later, when he was alone.

"Never fear, Ellie," he said, a still little smile lifting his lip. "I've got it safe in a pocket. No one can find it, and there's no hole for it to fall through."

She nodded, but she was always doubting, always anxious. You could look at her troubled hands. How terrible it was, how strange, that Albert loved the key more than he loved

Ellie! He did not mind missing the train. It showed in every line, every motion of his body. The key was closer—closer. The whole story began to illuminate them now, as if the lantern flame had been turned up. Ellie's anxious, hovering body could wrap him softly as a cradle, but the secret meaning, that powerful sign, that reassurance he so hopefully sought, so assuredly deserved—that had never come. There was something lacking in Ellie.

Had Ellie, with her suspicions of everything, come to know even things like this, in her way? How empty and nervous her red scrubbed hands were, how desperate to speak! Yes, she must regard it as unhappiness lying between them, as more than emptiness. She must worry about it, talk about it. You could imagine her stopping her churning to come out to his chair on the porch, to tell him that she did love him and would take care of him always, talking with the spotted sour milk dripping from her fingers. Just try to tell her that talking is useless, that care is not needed . . . And sooner or later he would always reply, say something, agree, and she would go away again. . . .

And Albert, with his face so capable of amazement, made you suspect the funny thing about talking to Ellie. Until you do, declared his round brown eyes, you can be peaceful and content that everything takes care of itself. As long as you let it alone everything goes peacefully, like an uneventful day on the farm—chores attended to, woman working in the house, you in the field, crop growing as well as can be expected, the cow giving, and the sky like a coverlet over it all—so that you're as full of yourself as a colt, in need of nothing, and nothing needing you. But when you pick up your hands and start to talk, if you don't watch carefully, this security will run away and leave you. You say something, make an observation, just to answer your wife's worryings, and everything is jolted, disturbed, laid open like the ground behind a plow, with you running along after it.

But happiness, Albert knew, is something that appears to you suddenly, that is meant for you, a thing which you reach for and pick up and hide at your breast, a shiny thing that reminds you of something alive and leaping.

Ellie sat there quiet as a mouse. She had unclasped her purse and taken out a little card with a picture of Niagara Falls on it.

"Hide it from the man," she said. She did suspect him! The red haired man had drawn closer. He bent and saw that it was a picture of Niagara Falls.

"Do you see the little rail?" Albert began in tenderness. And Ellie loved to watch him tell her about it; she clasped her hands and began to smile and show her crooked tooth; she looked young: it was the way she had looked as a child.

"That is what the teacher pointed to with her wand on the magic-lantern slide—the little rail. You stand right here. You lean up hard against the rail. Then you can hear Niagara Falls."

"How do you hear it?" begged Ellie, nodding.

"You hear it with your whole self. You listen with your arms and your legs and your whole body. You'll never forget what hearing is, after that."

He must have told her hundreds of times in his obedience, yet she smiled with gratitude, and stared deep, deep into the tinted picture of the waterfall.

Presently she said, "By now, we'd have been there, if we hadn't missed the train."

She did not even have any idea that it was miles and days away.

She looked at the red haired man then, her eyes all puckered up, and he looked away at last. He had seen the dust on her throat and a needle stuck in her collar where she'd forgotten it, with a thread running through the eye—the final details. Her hands were tight and wrinkled with pressure. She swung her foot a little below her skirt, in the new Mary Jane slipper with the hard toe.

Albert turned away too. It was then, you thought, that he became quite frightened to think that if they hadn't missed the train they would be hearing, at that very moment, Niagara Falls. Perhaps they would be standing there together, pressed against the little rail, pressed against each other, with their lives being poured through them, changing. . . . And how did he know what that would be like? He bent his head and tried not to look at his wife. He could say nothing. He glanced up once at the stranger, with almost a pleading look, as if to say, "Won't you come with us?"

"To work so many years, and then to miss the train," Ellie said.

You saw by her face that she was undauntedly wondering, unsatisfied, waiting for the future.

And you knew how she would sit and brood over this as over their conversations together, about every misunderstanding, every discussion, sometimes even about some agreement between them that had been all settled—even about the secret and proper separation that lies between a man and a woman, the thing that makes them what they are in themselves, their secret life, their memory of the past, their childhood, their dreams. This to Ellie was unhappiness.

They had told her when she was a little girl how people who have just been married have the custom of going to Niagara Falls on a wedding trip, to start their happiness; and that came to be where she put her hope, all of it. So she saved money. She worked harder than he did, you could observe, comparing their hands, good and bad years, more than was good for a woman. Year after year she had put her hope ahead of her.

And he—somehow he had never thought that this time would come, that they might really go on the journey. He was never looking so far and so deep as Ellie—into the future, into the changing and mixing of their lives together when they should arrive at last at Niagara Falls. To him it was always something postponed, like the paying off of the mortgage.

But sitting here in the station, with the suitcase all packed and at his feet, he had begun to realize that this journey might, for a fact, take place. The key had materialized to show him the enormity of this venture. And after his first shock and pride he had simply reserved the key; he had hidden it in his pocket.

She looked unblinking into the light of the lantern on the floor. Her face looked strong and terrifying, all lighted and very near to his. But there was no joy there. You knew that she was very brave.

Albert seemed to shrink, to retreat. . . . His trembling

hand went once more beneath his coat and touched the pocket where the key was lying, waiting. Would he ever remember that elusive thing about it or be sure what it might really be a symbol of? . . . His eyes, in their quick manner of filming over, grew dreamy. Perhaps he had even decided that it was a symbol not of happiness with Ellie, but of something else—something which he could have alone, for only himself, in peace, something strange and unlooked for which would come to him. . . .

The red haired man took a second key from his pocket, and in one direct motion placed it in Ellie's red palm. It was a key with a large triangular pasteboard tag on which was clearly printed, "Star Hotel, Room 2."

He did not wait to see any more, but went out abruptly into the night. He stood still for a moment and reached for a cigarette. As he held the match close he gazed straight ahead, and in his eyes, all at once wild and searching, there was certainly, besides the simple compassion in his regard, a look both restless and weary, very much used to the comic. You could see that he despised and saw the uselessness of the thing he had done.

Keela, the Outcast Indian Maiden

ONE MORNING in summertime, when all his sons and daughters were off picking plums and Little Lee Roy was all alone, sitting on the porch and only listening to the screech owls away down in the woods, he had a surprise.

First he heard white men talking. He heard two white men coming up the path from the highway. Little Lee Roy ducked his head and held his breath; then he patted all around back of him for his crutches. The chickens all came out from under the house and waited attentively on the steps.

The men came closer. It was the young man who was doing all of the talking. But when they got through the fence, Max, the older man, interrupted him. He tapped him on the arm and pointed his thumb toward Little Lee Roy.

He said, "Bud? Yonder he is."

But the younger man kept straight on talking, in an explanatory voice.

"Bud?" said Max again. "Look, Bud, yonder's the only little clubfooted nigger man was ever around Cane Springs. Is he the party?"

They came nearer and nearer to Little Lee Roy and then stopped and stood there in the middle of the yard. But the young man was so excited he did not seem to realize that they had arrived anywhere. He was only about twenty years old, very sunburned. He talked constantly, making only one gesture—raising his hand stiffly and then moving it a little to one side.

"They dressed it in a red dress, and it ate chickens alive," he said. "I sold tickets and I thought it was worth a dime, honest. They gimme a piece of paper with the thing wrote off I had to say. That was easy. 'Keela, the Outcast Indian Maiden!' I call it out through a pasteboard megaphone. Then ever' time it was fixin' to eat a live chicken, I blowed the sireen out front."

"Just tell me, Bud," said Max, resting back on the heels of his perforated tan-and-white sport shoes. "Is this nigger the one? Is that him sittin' there?"

Little Lee Roy sat huddled and blinking, a smile on his face. . . . But the young man did not look his way.

"Just took the job that time. I didn't mean to—I mean, I meant to go to Port Arthur because my brother was on a boat," he said. "My name is Steve, mister. But I worked with this show selling tickets for three months, and I never would of knowed it was like that if it hadn't been for that man." He arrested his gesture.

"Yeah, what man?" said Max in a hopeless voice.

Little Lee Roy was looking from one white man to the other, excited almost beyond respectful silence. He trembled all over, and a look of amazement and sudden life came into his eyes.

"Two years ago," Steve was saying impatiently. "And we was travelin' through Texas in those ole trucks.—See, the reason nobody ever come clost to it before was they give it a iron bar this long. And tole it if anybody come near, to shake the bar good at 'em, like this. But it couldn't say nothin'. Turned out they'd tole it it couldn't say nothin' to anybody ever, so it just kind of mumbled and growled, like a animal."

"Hee! hee!" This from Little Lee Roy, softly.

"Tell me again," said Max, and just from his look you could tell that everybody knew old Max. "Somehow I can't get it straight in my mind. Is this the boy? Is this little nigger boy the same as this Keela, the Outcast Indian Maiden?"

Up on the porch, above them, Little Lee Roy gave Max a glance full of hilarity, and then bent the other way to catch Steve's next words.

"Why, if anybody was to even come near it or even bresh their shoulder against the rope it'd growl and take on and shake its iron rod. When it would eat the live chickens it'd growl somethin' awful—you ought to heard it."

"Hee! hee!" It was a soft, almost incredulous laugh that began to escape from Little Lee Roy's tight lips, a little mew of delight.

"They'd throw it this chicken, and it would reach out an' grab it. Would sort of rub over the chicken's neck with its thumb an' press on it good, an' then it would bite its head off."

"O.K.," said Max.

"It skint back the feathers and stuff from the neck and sucked the blood. But ever'body said it was still alive." Steve drew closer to Max and fastened his light-colored, troubled eyes on his face.

"O.K."

"Then it would pull the feathers out easy and neat-like, awful fast, an' growl the whole time, kind of moan, an' then it would commence to eat all the white meat. I'd go in an' look at it. I reckon I seen it a thousand times."

"That was you, boy?" Max demanded of Little Lee Roy unexpectedly.

But Little Lee Roy could only say, "Hee! hee!" The little man at the head of the steps where the chickens sat, one on each step, and the two men facing each other below made a pyramid.

Steve stuck his hand out for silence. "They said—I mean, I said it, out front through the megaphone, I said it myself, that it wouldn't eat nothin' but only live meat. It was supposed to be a Indian woman, see, in this red dress an' stockin's. It didn't have on no shoes, so when it drug its foot ever'body could see. . . . When it come to the chicken's heart, it would eat that too, real fast, and the heart would still be jumpin'."

"Wait a second, Bud," said Max briefly. "Say, boy, is this white man here crazy?"

Little Lee Roy burst into hysterical, deprecatory giggles. He said, "Naw suh, don't think so." He tried to catch Steve's eye, seeking appreciation, crying, "Naw suh, don't think he crazy, mista."

Steve gripped Max's arm. "Wait! Wait!" he cried anxiously. "You ain't listenin'. I want to tell you about it. You didn't catch my name—Steve. You never did hear about that little nigger—all that happened to him? Lived in Cane Springs, Miss'ippi?"

"Bud," said Max, disengaging himself, "I don't hear anything. I got a juke box, see, so I don't have to listen."

"Look—I was really the one," said Steve more patiently, but nervously, as if he had been slowly breaking bad news. He walked up and down the bare-swept ground in front of Little Lee Roy's porch, along the row of princess feathers and snow-on-the-mountain. Little Lee Roy's turning head followed him. "I was the one—that's what I'm tellin' you."

"Suppose I was to listen to what every dope comes in Max's Place got to say, *I'd* be nuts," said Max.

"It's all me, see," said Steve. "I know that. I was the one was the cause for it goin' on an' on an' not bein' found out—such an awful thing. It was me, what I said out front through the megaphone."

He stopped still and stared at Max in despair.

"Look," said Max. He sat on the steps, and the chickens hopped off. "I know I ain't nobody but Max. I got Max's Place. I only run a place, understand, fifty yards down the highway. Liquor buried twenty feet from the premises, and no trouble yet. I ain't ever been up here before. I don't claim to been anywhere. People come to my place. Now. You're the hitchhiker. You're tellin' me, see. You claim a lot of information. If I don't get it I don't get it and I ain't complainin' about it, see. But I think you're nuts, and did from the first. I only come up here with you because I figured you's crazy."

"Maybe you don't believe I remember every word of it even now," Steve was saying gently. "I think about it at night—that an' drums on the midway. You ever hear drums on the midway?" He paused and stared politely at Max and Little Lee Roy.

"Yeh," said Max.

"Don't it make you feel sad. I remember how the drums was goin' and I was yellin', 'Ladies and gents! Do not try to touch Keela, the Outcast Indian Maiden—she will only beat your brains out with her iron rod, and eat them alive!' " Steve waved his arm gently in the air, and Little Lee Roy drew back and squealed. " 'Do not go near her, ladies and gents! I'm warnin' you!' So nobody ever did. Nobody ever come near her. Until that man."

"Sure," said Max. "That fella." He shut his eyes.

"Afterwards when he come up so bold, I remembered seein' him walk up an' buy the ticket an' go in the tent. I'll never forget that man as long as I live. To me he's a sort of—well——"

"Hero," said Max.

"I wish I could remember what he looked like. Seem like

he was a tallish man with a sort of white face. Seem like he had bad teeth, but I may be wrong. I remember he frowned a lot. Kept frownin'. Whenever he'd buy a ticket, why, he'd frown."

"Ever seen him since?" asked Max cautiously, still with his eyes closed. "Ever hunt him up?"

"No, never did," said Steve. Then he went on. "He'd frown an' buy a ticket ever' day we was in these two little smelly towns in Texas, sometimes three-four times a day, whether it was fixin' to eat a chicken or not."

"O.K., so he gets in the tent," said Max.

"Well, what the man finally done was, he walked right up to the little stand where it was tied up and laid his hand out open on the planks in the platform. He just laid his hand out open there and said, 'Come here,' real low and quick, that-a-way."

Steve laid his open hand on Little Lee Roy's porch and held it there, frowning in concentration.

"I get it," said Max. "He'd caught on it was a fake."

Steve straightened up. "So ever'body yelled to git away, git away," he continued, his voice rising, "because it was growlin' an' carryin' on an' shakin' its iron bar like they tole it. When I heard all that commotion—boy! I was scared."

"You didn't know it was a fake."

Steve was silent for a moment, and Little Lee Roy held his breath, for fear everything was all over.

"Look," said Steve finally, his voice trembling. "I guess I was supposed to feel bad like this, and you wasn't. I wasn't supposed to ship out on that boat from Port Arthur and all like that. This other had to happen to me—not you all. Feelin' responsible. You'll be O.K., mister, but I won't. I feel awful about it. That poor little old thing."

"Look, you got him right here," said Max quickly. "See him? Use your eyes. He's O.K., ain't he? Looks O.K. to me. It's just you. You're nuts, is all."

"You know—when that man laid out his open hand on the boards, why, it just let go the iron bar," continued Steve, "let it fall down like that—bang—and act like it didn't know what to do. Then it drug itself over to where the fella was standin' an' leaned down an' grabbed holt onto that white man's hand as tight as it could an' cried like a baby. It didn't want to hit him!"

"Hee! hee! hee!"

"No sir, it didn't want to hit him. You know what it wanted?"

Max shook his head.

"It wanted him to help it. So the man said, 'Do you wanta get out of this place, whoever you are?' An' it never answered—none of us knowed it could talk—but it just wouldn't let that man's hand a-loose. It hung on, cryin' like a baby. So the man says, 'Well, wait here till I come back.' "

"Uh-huh?" said Max.

"Went off an' come back with the sheriff. Took us all to jail. But just the man owned the show and his son got took to the pen. They said I could go free. I kep' tellin' 'em I didn't know it wouldn't hit me with the iron bar an' kep' tellin' 'em I didn't know it could tell what you was sayin' to it."

"Yeh, guess you told 'em," said Max.

"By that time I felt bad. Been feelin' bad ever since. Can't hold onto a job or stay in one place for nothin' in the world. They made it stay in jail to see if it could talk or not, and the first night it wouldn't say nothin'. Some time it cried. And they undressed it an' found out it wasn't no outcast Indian woman a-tall. It was a little clubfooted nigger man."

"Hee! hee!"

"You mean it was this boy here—yeh. It was him."

"Washed its face, and it was paint all over it made it look red. It all come off. And it could talk—as good as me or you. But they'd tole it not to, so it never did. They'd tole it if anybody was to come near it they was comin' to git it—and for it to hit 'em quick with that iron bar an' growl. So nobody ever come near it—until that man. I was yellin' outside, tellin' 'em to keep away, keep away. You could see where they'd whup it. They had to whup it some to make it eat all the chickens. It was awful dirty. They let it go back home free, to where they got it in the first place. They made them pay its ticket from Little Oil, Texas, to Cane Springs, Miss'ippi."

"You got a good memory," said Max.

"The way it *started* was," said Steve, in a wondering voice, "the show was just travelin' along in ole trucks through the country, and just seen this little deformed nigger man, sittin' on a fence, and just took it. It couldn't help it."

Little Lee Roy tossed his head back in a frenzy of amusement.

"I found it all out later. I was up on the Ferris wheel with one of the boys—got to talkin' up yonder in the peace an' quiet—an' said they just kind of happened up on it. Like a cyclone happens: it wasn't nothin' it could do. It was just took up." Steve suddenly paled through his sunburn. "An' they found out that back in Miss'ippi it had it a little bitty pair of crutches an' could just go runnin' on 'em!"

"And there they are," said Max.

Little Lee Roy held up a crutch and turned it about, and then snatched it back like a monkey.

"But if it hadn't been for that man, I wouldn't of knowed it till yet. If it wasn't for him bein' so bold. If he hadn't knowed what he was doin'."

"You remember that man this fella's talkin' about, boy?" asked Max, eying Little Lee Roy.

Little Lee Roy, in reluctance and shyness, shook his head gently.

"Naw suh, I cain't say as I remembas that ve'y man, suh," he said softly, looking down where just then a sparrow alighted on his child's shoe. He added happily, as if on inspiration, "Now I remembas *this* man."

Steve did not look up, but when Max shook with silent laughter, alarm seemed to seize him like a spasm in his side. He walked painfully over and stood in the shade for a few minutes, leaning his head on a sycamore tree.

"Seemed like that man just studied it out an' knowed it was somethin' wrong," he said presently, his voice coming more remotely than ever. "But I didn't know. I can't look at nothin' an' be sure what it is. Then afterwards I know. Then I see how it was."

"Yeh, but you're nuts," said Max affably.

"You wouldn't of knowed it either!" cried Steve in sudden boyish, defensive anger. Then he came out from under the tree and stood again almost pleadingly in the sun, facing Max where he was sitting below Little Lee Roy on the steps.

"You'd of let it go on an' on when they made it do those things—just like I did."

"Bet I could tell a man from a woman and an Indian from a nigger though," said Max.

Steve scuffed the dust into little puffs with his worn shoe. The chickens scattered, alarmed at last.

Little Lee Roy looked from one man to the other radiantly, his hands pressed over his grinning gums.

Then Steve sighed, and as if he did not know what else he could do, he reached out and without any warning hit Max in the jaw with his fist. Max fell off the steps.

Little Lee Roy suddenly sat as still and dark as a statue, looking on.

"Say! Say!" cried Steve. He pulled shyly at Max where he lay on the ground, with his lips pursed up like a whistler, and then stepped back. He looked horrified. "How you feel?"

"Lousy," said Max thoughtfully. "Let me alone." He raised up on one elbow and lay there looking all around, at the cabin, at Little Lee Roy sitting cross-legged on the porch, and at Steve with his hand out. Finally he got up.

"I can't figure out how I could of ever knocked down an athaletic guy like you. I had to do it," said Steve. "But I guess you don't understand. I had to hit you. First you didn't believe me, and then it didn't bother you."

"That's all O.K., only hush," said Max, and added, "Some dope is always giving me the low-down on something, but this is the first time one of 'em ever got away with a thing like this. I got to watch out."

"I hope it don't stay black long," said Steve.

"I got to be going," said Max. But he waited. "What you want to transact with Keela? You come a long way to see him." He stared at Steve with his eyes wide open now, and interested.

"Well, I was goin' to give him some money or somethin', I guess, if I ever found him, only now I ain't got any," said Steve defiantly.

"O.K.," said Max. "Here's some change for you, boy. Just take it. Go on back in the house. Go on."

Little Lee Roy took the money speechlessly, and then fell

upon his yellow crutches and hopped with miraculous rapidity away through the door. Max stared after him for a moment.

"As for you"—he brushed himself off, turned to Steve and then said, "When did you eat last?"

"Well, I'll tell you," said Steve.

"Not here," said Max. "I didn't go to ask you a question. Just follow me. We serve eats at Max's Place, and I want to play the juke box. You eat, and I'll listen to the juke box."

"Well . . ." said Steve. "But when it cools off I got to catch a ride some place."

"Today while all you all was gone, and not a soul in de house," said Little Lee Roy at the supper table that night, "two white mens come heah to de house. Wouldn't come in. But talks to me about de ole times when I use to be wid de circus——"

"Hush up, Pappy," said the children.

Why I Live at the P.O.

I WAS getting along fine with Mama, Papa-Daddy and Uncle Rondo until my sister Stella-Rondo just separated from her husband and came back home again. Mr Whitaker! Of course I went with Mr Whitaker first, when he first appeared here in China Grove, taking "Pose Yourself" photos, and Stella-Rondo broke us up. Told him I was one sided. Bigger on one side than the other, which is a deliberate, calculated falsehood: I'm the same. Stella-Rondo is exactly twelve months to the day younger than I am and for that reason she's spoiled.

She's always had anything in the world she wanted and then she'd throw it away. Papa-Daddy gave her this gorgeous Add-a-Pearl necklace when she was eight years old and she threw it away playing baseball when she was nine, with only two pearls.

So as soon as she got married and moved away from home the first thing she did was separate! From Mr Whitaker! This photographer with the popeyes she said she trusted. Came home from one of those towns up in Illinois and to our complete surprise brought this child of two.

Mama said she like to made her drop dead for a second. "Here you had this marvelous blonde child and never so much as wrote your mother a word about it," says Mama. "I'm thoroughly ashamed of you." But of course she wasn't.

Stella-Rondo just calmly takes off this *hat*, I wish you could see it. She says, "Why, Mama, Shirley-T.'s adopted, I can prove it."

"How?" says Mama, but all I says was, "H'm!" There I was over the hot stove, trying to stretch two chickens over five people and a completely unexpected child into the bargain, without one moment's notice.

"What do you mean—'H'm!'?" says Stella-Rondo, and Mama says, "I heard that, Sister."

I said that oh, I didn't mean a thing, only that whoever Shirley-T. was, she was the spit-image of Papa-Daddy if he'd cut off his beard, which of course he'd never do in the world. Papa-Daddy's Mama's papa and sulks.

Stella-Rondo got furious! She said, "Sister, I don't need to tell you you got a lot of nerve and always did have and I'll thank you to make no future reference to my adopted child whatsoever."

"Very well," I said. "Very well, very well. Of course I noticed at once she looks like Mr Whitaker's side too. That frown. She looks like a cross between Mr Whitaker and Papa-Daddy."

"Well, all I can say is she isn't."

"She looks exactly like Shirley Temple to me," says Mama, but Shirley-T. just ran away from her.

So the first thing Stella-Rondo did at the table was turn Papa-Daddy against me.

"Papa-Daddy," she says. He was trying to cut up his meat. "Papa-Daddy!" I was taken completely by surprise. Papa-Daddy is about a million years old and's got this long-long beard. "Papa-Daddy, Sister says she fails to understand why you don't cut off your beard."

So Papa-Daddy l-a-y-s down his knife and fork! He's real rich. Mama says he is, he says he isn't. So he says, "Have I heard correctly? You don't understand why I don't cut off my beard?"

"Why," I says, "Papa-Daddy, of course I understand, I did not say any such of a thing, the idea!"

He says, "Hussy!"

I says, "Papa-Daddy, you know I wouldn't any more want you to cut off your beard than the man in the moon. It was the farthest thing from my mind! Stella-Rondo sat there and made that up while she was eating breast of chicken."

But he says, "So the postmistress fails to understand why I don't cut off my beard. Which job I got you through my influence with the government. 'Bird's nest'—is that what you call it?"

Not that it isn't the next to smallest P.O. in the entire state of Mississippi.

I says, "Oh, Papa-Daddy," I says, "I didn't say any such of a thing, I never dreamed it was a bird's nest, I have always been grateful though this is the next to smallest P.O. in the state of Mississippi, and I do not enjoy being referred to as a hussy by my own grandfather."

But Stella-Rondo says, "Yes, you did say it too. Anybody in the world could of heard you, that had ears."

"Stop right there," says Mama, looking at *me.*

So I pulled my napkin straight back through the napkin ring and left the table.

As soon as I was out of the room Mama says, "Call her back, or she'll starve to death," but Papa-Daddy says, "This is the beard I started growing on the Coast when I was fifteen years old." He would of gone on till nightfall if Shirley-T. hadn't lost the Milky Way she ate in Cairo.

So Papa-Daddy says, "I am going out and lie in the hammock, and you can all sit here and remember my words: I'll never cut off my beard as long as I live, even one inch, and I don't appreciate it in you at all." Passed right by me in the hall and went straight out and got in the hammock.

It would be a holiday. It wasn't five minutes before Uncle Rondo suddenly appeared in the hall in one of Stella-Rondo's flesh-colored kimonos, all cut on the bias, like something Mr Whitaker probably thought was gorgeous.

"Uncle Rondo!" I says. "I didn't know who that was! Where are you going?"

"Sister," he says, "get out of my way, I'm poisoned."

"If you're poisoned stay away from Papa-Daddy," I says. "Keep out of the hammock. Papa-Daddy will certainly beat you on the head if you come within forty miles of him. He thinks I deliberately said he ought to cut off his beard after he got me the P.O., and I've told him and told him and told him, and he acts like he just don't hear me. Papa-Daddy must of gone stone deaf."

"He picked a fine day to do it then," says Uncle Rondo, and before you could say "Jack Robinson" flew out in the yard.

What he'd really done, he'd drunk another bottle of that prescription. He does it every single Fourth of July as sure as shooting, and it's horribly expensive. Then he falls over in the hammock and snores. So he insisted on zigzagging right on out to the hammock, looking like a half-wit.

Papa-Daddy woke up with this horrible yell and right there

without moving an inch he tried to turn Uncle Rondo against me. I heard every word he said. Oh, he told Uncle Rondo I didn't learn to read till I was eight years old and he didn't see how in the world I ever got the mail put up at the P.O., much less read it all, and he said if Uncle Rondo could only fathom the lengths he had gone to to get me that job! And he said on the other hand he thought Stella-Rondo had a brilliant mind and deserved credit for getting out of town. All the time he was just lying there swinging as pretty as you please and looping out his beard, and poor Uncle Rondo was *pleading* with him to slow down the hammock, it was making him as dizzy as a witch to watch it. But that's what Papa-Daddy likes about a hammock. So Uncle Rondo was too dizzy to get turned against me for the time being. He's Mama's only brother and is a good case of a one-track mind. Ask anybody. A certified pharmacist.

Just then I heard Stella-Rondo raising the upstairs window. While she was married she got this peculiar idea that it's cooler with the windows shut and locked. So she has to raise the window before she can make a soul hear her outdoors.

So she raises the window and says, *"Oh!"* You would have thought she was mortally wounded.

Uncle Rondo and Papa-Daddy didn't even look up, but kept right on with what they were doing. I had to laugh.

I flew up the stairs and threw the door open! I says, "What in the wide world's the matter, Stella-Rondo? You mortally wounded?"

"No," she says, "I am not mortally wounded but I wish you would do me the favor of looking out that window there and telling me what you see."

So I shade my eyes and look out the window.

"I see the front yard," I says.

"Don't you see any human beings?" she says.

"I see Uncle Rondo trying to run Papa-Daddy out of the hammock," I says. "Nothing more. Naturally, it's so suffocating-hot in the house, with all the windows shut and locked, everybody who cares to stay in their right mind will have to go out and get in the hammock before the Fourth of July is over."

"Don't you notice anything different about Uncle Rondo?" asks Stella-Rondo.

"Why, no, except he's got on some terrible-looking flesh-colored contraption I wouldn't be found dead in, is all I can see," I says.

"Never mind, you won't be found dead in it, because it happens to be part of my trousseau, and Mr Whitaker took several dozen photographs of me in it," says Stella-Rondo. "What on earth could Uncle Rondo *mean* by wearing part of my trousseau out in the broad open daylight without saying so much as 'Kiss my foot,' *knowing* I only got home this morning after my separation and hung my negligee up on the bathroom door, just as nervous as I could be?"

"I'm sure I don't know, and what do you expect me to do about it?" I says. "Jump out the window?"

"No, I expect nothing of the kind. I simply declare that Uncle Rondo looks like a fool in it, that's all," she says. "It makes me sick to my stomach."

"Well, he looks as good as he can," I says. "As good as anybody in reason could." I stood up for Uncle Rondo, please remember. And I said to Stella-Rondo, "I think I would do well not to criticize so freely if I were you and came home with a two-year-old child I had never said a word about, and no explanation whatever about my separation."

"I asked you the instant I entered this house not to refer one more time to my adopted child, and you gave me your word of honor you would not," was all Stella-Rondo would say, and started pulling out every one of her eyebrows with some cheap Kress tweezers.

So I merely slammed the door behind me and went down and made some green-tomato pickle. Somebody had to do it. Of course Mama had turned both the niggers loose; she always said no earthly power could hold one anyway on the Fourth of July, so she wouldn't even try. It turned out that Jaypan fell in the lake and came within a very narrow limit of drowning.

So Mama trots in. Lifts up the lid and says, "H'm! Not very good for your Uncle Rondo in his precarious condition, I must say. Or poor little adopted Shirley-T. Shame on you!"

That made me tired. I says, "Well, Stella-Rondo had better thank her lucky stars it was her instead of me came trotting in with that very peculiar-looking child. Now if it had been me that trotted in from Illinois and brought a peculiar-looking child of two, I shudder to think of the reception I'd of got, much less controlled the diet of an entire family."

"But you must remember, Sister, that you were never married to Mr Whitaker in the first place and didn't go up to Illinois to live," says Mama, shaking a spoon in my face. "If you had I would of been just as overjoyed to see you and your little adopted girl as I was to see Stella-Rondo, when you wound up with your separation and came on back home."

"You would not," I says.

"Don't contradict me, I would," says Mama.

But I said she couldn't convince me though she talked till she was blue in the face. Then I said, "Besides, you know as well as I do that that child is not adopted."

"She most certainly is adopted," says Mama, stiff as a poker.

I says, "Why, Mama, Stella-Rondo had her just as sure as anything in this world, and just too stuck up to admit it."

"Why, Sister," said Mama. "Here I thought we were going to have a pleasant Fourth of July, and you start right out not believing a word your own baby sister tells you!"

"Just like Cousin Annie Flo. Went to her grave denying the facts of life," I remind Mama.

"I told you if you ever mentioned Annie Flo's name I'd slap your face," says Mama, and slaps my face.

"All right, you wait and see," I says.

"I," says Mama, "*I* prefer to take my children's word for anything when it's humanly possible." You ought to see Mama, she weighs two hundred pounds and has real tiny feet.

Just then something perfectly horrible occurred to me.

"Mama," I says, "can that child talk?" I simply had to whisper! "Mama, I wonder if that child can be—you know—in any way? Do you realize," I says, "that she hasn't spoken one single, solitary word to a human being up to this minute? This is the way she looks," I says, and I looked like this.

Well, Mama and I just stood there and stared at each other. It was horrible!

"I remember well that Joe Whitaker frequently drank like

a fish," says Mama. "I believed to my soul he drank *chemicals.*" And without another word she marches to the foot of the stairs and calls Stella-Rondo.

"Stella-Rondo? O-o-o-o-o! Stella-Rondo!"

"What?" says Stella-Rondo from upstairs. Not even the grace to get up off the bed.

"Can that child of yours talk?" asks Mama.

Stella-Rondo says, "Can she what?"

"Talk! Talk!" says Mama. "Burdyburdyburdyburdy!"

So Stella-Rondo yells back, "Who says she can't talk?"

"Sister says so," says Mama.

"You didn't have to tell me, I know whose word of honor don't mean a thing in this house," says Stella-Rondo.

And in a minute the loudest Yankee voice I ever heard in my life yells out, "OE'm Pop-OE the Sailor-r-r-r Ma-a-an!" and then somebody jumps up and down in the upstairs hall. In another second the house would of fallen down.

"Not only talks, she can tap-dance!" calls Stella-Rondo. "Which is more than some people I won't name can do."

"Why, the little precious darling thing!" Mama says, so surprised. "Just as smart as she can be!" Starts talking baby talk right there. Then she turns on me. "Sister, you ought to be thoroughly ashamed! Run upstairs this instant and apologize to Stella-Rondo and Shirley-T."

"Apologize for what?" I says. "I merely wondered if the child was normal, that's all. Now that she's proved she is, why, I have nothing further to say."

But Mama just turned on her heel and flew out, furious. She ran right upstairs and hugged the baby. She believed it was adopted. Stella-Rondo hadn't done a thing but turn her against me from upstairs while I stood there helpless over the hot stove. So that made Mama, Papa-Daddy and the baby all on Stella-Rondo's side.

Next, Uncle Rondo.

I must say that Uncle Rondo has been marvelous to me at various times in the past and I was completely unprepared to be made to jump out of my skin, the way it turned out. Once Stella-Rondo did something perfectly horrible to him—broke a chain letter from Flanders Field—and he took the radio back he had given her and gave it to me. Stella-Rondo was furious!

For six months we all had to call her Stella instead of Stella-Rondo, or she wouldn't answer. I always thought Uncle Rondo had all the brains of the entire family. Another time he sent me to Mammoth Cave, with all expenses paid.

But this would be the day he was drinking that prescription, the Fourth of July.

So at supper Stella-Rondo speaks up and says she thinks Uncle Rondo ought to try to eat a little something. So finally Uncle Rondo said he would try a little cold biscuits and ketchup, but that was all. So *she* brought it to him.

"Do you think it wise to disport with ketchup in Stella-Rondo's flesh-colored kimono?" I says. Trying to be considerate! If Stella-Rondo couldn't watch out for her trousseau, somebody had to.

"Any objections?" asks Uncle Rondo, just about to pour out all the ketchup.

"Don't mind what she says, Uncle Rondo," says Stella-Rondo. "Sister has been devoting this solid afternoon to sneering out my bedroom window at the way you look."

"What's that?" says Uncle Rondo. Uncle Rondo has got the most terrible temper in the world. Anything is liable to make him tear the house down if it comes at the wrong time.

So Stella-Rondo says, "Sister says, 'Uncle Rondo certainly does look like a fool in that pink kimono!' "

Do you remember who it was really said that?

Uncle Rondo spills out all the ketchup and jumps out of his chair and tears off the kimono and throws it down on the dirty floor and puts his foot on it. It had to be sent all the way to Jackson to the cleaners and re-pleated.

"So that's your opinion of your Uncle Rondo, is it?" he says. "I look like a fool, do I? Well, that's the last straw. A whole day in this house with nothing to do, and then to hear you come out with a remark like that behind my back!"

"I didn't say any such of a thing, Uncle Rondo," I says, "and I'm not saying who did, either. Why, I think you look all right. Just try to take care of yourself and not talk and eat at the same time," I says. "I think you better go lie down."

"Lie down my foot," says Uncle Rondo. I ought to of known by that he was fixing to do something perfectly horrible.

So he didn't do anything that night in the precarious state he was in—just played Casino with Mama and Stella-Rondo and Shirley-T. and gave Shirley-T. a nickel with a head on both sides. It tickled her nearly to death, and she called him "Papa." But at 6:30 A.M. the next morning, he threw a whole five-cent package of some unsold one-inch firecrackers from the store as hard as he could into my bedroom and they every one went off. Not one bad one in the string. Anybody else, there 'd be one that wouldn't go off.

Well, I'm just terribly susceptible to noise of any kind, the doctor has always told me I was the most sensitive person he had ever seen in his whole life, and I was simply prostrated. I couldn't eat! People tell me they heard it as far as the cemetery, and old Aunt Jep Patterson, that had been holding her own so good, thought it was Judgment Day and she was going to meet her whole family. It's usually so quiet here.

And I'll tell you it didn't take me any longer than a minute to make up my mind what to do. There I was with the whole entire house on Stella-Rondo's side and turned against me. If I have anything at all I have pride.

So I just decided I'd go straight down to the P.O. There's plenty of room there in the back, I says to myself.

Well! I made no bones about letting the family catch on to what I was up to. I didn't try to conceal it.

The first thing they knew, I marched in where they were all playing Old Maid and pulled the electric oscillating fan out by the plug, and everything got real hot. Next I snatched the pillow I'd done the needlepoint on right off the davenport from behind Papa-Daddy. He went "Ugh!" I beat Stella-Rondo up the stairs and finally found my charm bracelet in her bureau drawer under a picture of Nelson Eddy.

"So that's the way the land lies," says Uncle Rondo. There he was, piecing on the ham. "Well, Sister, I'll be glad to donate my army cot if you got any place to set it up, providing you'll leave right this minute and let me get some peace." Uncle Rondo was in France.

"Thank you kindly for the cot and 'peace' is hardly the word I would select if I had to resort to firecrackers at 6:30 A.M. in a young girl's bedroom," I says back to him. "And as to where I intend to go, you seem to forget my position as postmistress of China Grove, Mississippi," I says. "I've always got the P.O."

Well, that made them all sit up and take notice.

I went out front and started digging up some four-o'clocks to plant around the P.O.

"Ah-ah-ah!" says Mama, raising the window. "Those happen to be my four-o'clocks. Everything planted in that star is mine. I've never known you to make anything grow in your life."

"Very well," I says. "But I take the fern. Even you, Mama, can't stand there and deny that I'm the one watered that fern. And I happen to know where I can send in a box top and get a packet of one thousand mixed seeds, no two the same kind, free."

"Oh, where?" Mama wants to know.

But I says, "Too late. You 'tend to your house, and I'll 'tend to mine. You hear things like that all the time if you know how to listen to the radio. Perfectly marvelous offers. Get anything you want free."

So I hope to tell you I marched in and got that radio, and they could of all bit a nail in two, especially Stella-Rondo, that it used to belong to, and she well knew she couldn't get it back, I'd sue for it like a shot. And I very politely took the sewing-machine motor I helped pay the most on to give Mama for Christmas back in 1929, and a good big calendar, with the first-aid remedies on it. The thermometer and the Hawaiian ukulele certainly were rightfully mine, and I stood on the step-ladder and got all my watermelon-rind preserves and every fruit and vegetable I'd put up, every jar. Then I began to pull the tacks out of the bluebird wall vases on the archway to the dining room.

"Who told you you could have those, Miss Priss?" says Mama, fanning as hard as she could.

"I bought 'em and I'll keep track of 'em," I says. "I'll tack 'em up one on each side the post-office window, and you can see 'em when you come to ask me for your mail, if you're so dead to see 'em."

"Not I! I'll never darken the door to that post office again if I live to be a hundred," Mama says. "Ungrateful child! After all the money we spent on you at the Normal."

"Me either," says Stella-Rondo. "You can just let my mail lie there and *rot*, for all I care. I'll never come and relieve you of a single, solitary piece."

"I should worry," I says. "And who you think's going to sit down and write you all those big fat letters and postcards, by the way? Mr Whitaker? Just because he was the only man ever dropped down in China Grove and you got him—unfairly—is he going to sit down and write you a lengthy correspondence after you come home giving no rhyme nor reason whatsoever for your separation and no explanation for the presence of that child? I may not have your brilliant mind, but I fail to see it."

So Mama says, "Sister, I've told you a thousand times that Stella-Rondo simply got homesick, and this child is far too big to be hers," and she says, "Now, why don't you all just sit down and play Casino?"

Then Shirley-T. sticks out her tongue at me in this perfectly horrible way. She has no more manners than the man in the moon. I told her she was going to cross her eyes like that some day and they'd stick.

"It's too late to stop me now," I says. "You should have tried that yesterday. I'm going to the P.O. and the only way you can possibly see me is to visit me there."

So Papa-Daddy says, "You'll never catch me setting foot in that post office, even if I should take a notion into my head to write a letter some place." He says, "I won't have you reachin' out of that little old window with a pair of shears and cuttin' off any beard of mine. I'm too smart for you!"

"We all are," says Stella-Rondo.

But I said, "If you're so smart, where's Mr Whitaker?"

So then Uncle Rondo says, "I'll thank you from now on to stop reading all the orders I get on postcards and telling everybody in China Grove what you think is the matter with them," but I says, "I draw my own conclusions and will continue in the future to draw them." I says, "If people want to write their inmost secrets on penny postcards, there's nothing in the wide world you can do about it, Uncle Rondo."

"And if you think we'll ever *write* another postcard you're sadly mistaken," says Mama.

"Cutting off your nose to spite your face then," I says.

"But if you're all determined to have no more to do with the U.S. mail, think of this: What will Stella-Rondo do now, if she wants to tell Mr Whitaker to come after her?"

"Wah!" says Stella-Rondo. I knew she'd cry. She had a conniption fit right there in the kitchen.

"It will be interesting to see how long she holds out," I says. "And now—I am leaving."

"Good-by," says Uncle Rondo.

"Oh, I declare," says Mama, "to think that a family of mine should quarrel on the Fourth of July, or the day after, over Stella-Rondo leaving old Mr Whitaker and having the sweetest little adopted child! It looks like we'd all be glad!"

"Wah!" says Stella-Rondo, and has a fresh conniption fit.

"*He* left *her*—you mark my words," I says. "That's Mr Whitaker. I know Mr Whitaker. After all, I knew him first. I said from the beginning he'd up and leave her. I foretold every single thing that's happened."

"Where did he go?" asks Mama.

"Probably to the North Pole, if he knows what's good for him," I says.

But Stella-Rondo just bawled and wouldn't say another word. She flew to her room and slammed the door.

"Now look what you've gone and done, Sister," says Mama. "You go apologize."

"I haven't got time, I'm leaving," I says.

"Well, what are you waiting around for?" asks Uncle Rondo.

So I just picked up the kitchen clock and marched off, without saying "Kiss my foot" or anything, and never did tell Stella-Rondo good-by.

There was a nigger girl going along on a little wagon right in front.

"Nigger girl," I says, "come help me haul these things down the hill, I'm going to live in the post office."

Took her nine trips in her express wagon. Uncle Rondo came out on the porch and threw her a nickel.

And that's the last I've laid eyes on any of my family or my family laid eyes on me for five solid days and nights. Stella-Rondo may be telling the most horrible tales in the world about Mr Whitaker, but I haven't heard them. As I tell everybody, I draw my own conclusions.

But oh, I like it here. It's ideal, as I've been saying. You see, I've got everything cater-cornered, the way I like it. Hear the radio? All the war news. Radio, sewing machine, book ends, ironing board and that great big piano lamp—peace, that's what I like. Butter-bean vines planted all along the front where the strings are.

Of course, there's not much mail. My family are naturally the main people in China Grove, and if they prefer to vanish from the face of the earth, for all the mail they get or the mail they write, why, I'm not going to open my mouth. Some of the folks here in town are taking up for me and some turned against me. I know which is which. There are always people who will quit buying stamps just to get on the right side of Papa-Daddy.

But here I am, and here I'll stay. I want the world to know I'm happy.

And if Stella-Rondo should come to me this minute, on bended knees, and *attempt* to explain the incidents of her life with Mr Whitaker, I'd simply put my fingers in both my ears and refuse to listen.

The Whistle

NIGHT FELL. The darkness was thin, like some sleazy dress that has been worn and worn for many winters and always lets the cold through to the bones. Then the moon rose. A farm lay quite visible, like a white stone in water, among the stretches of deep woods in their colorless dead leaf. By a closer and more searching eye than the moon's, everything belonging to the Mortons might have been seen—even to the tiny tomato plants in their neat rows closest to the house, gray and featherlike, appalling in their exposed fragility. The moonlight covered everything, and lay upon the darkest shape of all, the farmhouse where the lamp had just been blown out.

Inside, Jason and Sara Morton were lying between the quilts of a pallet which had been made up close to the fireplace. A fire still fluttered in the grate, making a drowsy sound now and then, and its exhausted light beat up and down the wall, across the rafters, and over the dark pallet where the old people lay, like a bird trying to find its way out of the room.

The long-spaced, tired breathing of Jason was the only noise besides the flutter of the fire. He lay under the quilt in a long shape like a bean, turned on his side to face the door. His lips opened in the dark, and in and out he breathed, in and out, slowly and with a rise and fall, over and over, like a conversation or a tale—a question and a sigh.

Sara lay on her back with her mouth agape, silent, but not asleep. She was staring at the dark and indistinguishable places among the rafters. Her eyes seemed opened too wide, the lids strained and limp, like openings which have been stretched shapeless and made of no more use. Once a hissing yellow flame stood erect in the old log, and her small face and pale hair, and one hand holding to the edge of the cover, were illuminated for a moment, with shadows bright blue. Then she pulled the quilt clear over her head.

Every night they lay trembling with cold, but no more communicative in their misery than a pair of window shutters beaten by a storm. Sometimes many days, weeks went by without words. They were not really old—they were only fifty;

still, their lives were filled with tiredness, with a great lack of necessity to speak, with poverty which may have bound them like a disaster too great for any discussion but left them still separate and undesirous of sympathy. Perhaps, years ago, the long habit of silence may have been started in anger or passion. Who could tell now?

As the fire grew lower and lower, Jason's breathing grew heavy and solemn, and he was even beyond dreams. Completely hidden, Sara's body was as weightless as a strip of cane, there was hardly a shape to the quilt under which she was lying. Sometimes it seemed to Sara herself that it was her lack of weight which kept her from ever getting warm.

She was so tired of the cold! That was all it could do any more—make her tired. Year after year, she felt sure that she would die before the cold was over. Now, according to the Almanac, it was spring. . . . But year after year it was always the same. The plants would be set out in their frames, transplanted always too soon, and there was a freeze. . . . When was the last time they had grown tall and full, that the cold had held off and there was a crop?

Like a vain dream, Sara began to have thoughts of the spring and summer. At first she thought only simply, of the colors of green and red, the smell of the sun on the ground, the touch of leaves and of warm ripening tomatoes. Then, all hidden as she was under the quilt, she began to imagine and remember the town of Dexter in the shipping season. There in her mind, dusty little Dexter became a theater for almost legendary festivity, a place of pleasure. On every road leading in, smiling farmers were bringing in wagonloads of the most beautiful tomatoes. The packing sheds at Dexter Station were all decorated—no, it was simply that the May sun was shining. Mr Perkins, the tall, gesturing figure, stood in the very center of everything, buying, directing, waving yellow papers that must be telegrams, shouting with grand impatience. And it was he, after all, that owned their farm now. Train after train of empty freight cars stretched away, waiting and then being filled. Was it possible to have saved out of the threat of the cold so many tomatoes in the world? Of course, for here marched in a perfect parade of Florida packers, all the way from Florida, tanned, stockingless, some of them tattooed.

The music box was playing in the café across the way, and the crippled man that walked like a duck was back taking poses for a dime of the young people with their heads together. With shouts of triumph the men were getting drunk, and now and then a pistol went off somewhere. In the shade the children celebrated in tomato fights. A strong, heady, sweet smell hung over everything. Such excitement! Let the packers rest, if only for a moment, thought Sara. Stretch them out, stained with sweat, under the shade tree, and one can play the guitar. The girl wrappers listen while they work. What small brown hands, red with juice! Their faces are forever sleepy and flushed; when the men speak to them they laugh. . . . And Jason and Sara themselves are standing there, standing under the burning sun near the first shed, giving over their own load, watching their own tomatoes shoved into the process, swallowed away—sorted, wrapped, loaded, dispatched in a freight car—all so fast. . . . Mr Perkins holds out his hard, quick hand. Shake it fast! How quickly it is all over!

Sara, weightless under the quilt, could think of the celebrations of Dexter and see the vision of ripe tomatoes only in brief snatches, like the flare-up of the little fire. The rest of the time she thought only of cold, of cold going on before and after. She could not help but feel the chill of the here and now, which was not to think at all, but was for her only a trembling in the dark.

She coughed patiently and turned her head to one side. She peered over the quilt just a little and saw that the fire had at last gone out. There was left only a hulk of red log, a still, red, bent shape, like one of Jason's socks thrown down to be darned somehow. With only this to comfort her, Sara closed her eyes and fell asleep.

The husband and wife now lay perfectly still in the dark room, with Jason's hoarse, slow breathing, like the commotion of some clumsy nodding old bear trying to climb a tree, heard by nobody at all.

Every hour it was getting colder and colder. The moon, intense and white as the snow that does not fall here, drew higher in the sky, in the long night, and more distant from the earth. The farm looked as tiny and still as a seashell, with the little knob of a house surrounded by its curved furrows of tomato plants. Cold like a white pressing hand reached down and lay over the shell.

In Dexter there is a great whistle which is blown when a freeze threatens. It is known everywhere as Mr Perkins' whistle. Now it sounded out in the clear night, blast after blast. Over the countryside lights appeared in the windows of the farms. Men and women ran out into the fields and covered up their plants with whatever they had, while Mr Perkins' whistle blew and blew.

Jason Morton was not waked up by the great whistle. On he slept, his cavernous breathing like roars coming from a hollow tree. His right hand had been thrown out, from some deepness he must have dreamed, and lay stretched on the cold floor in the very center of a patch of moonlight which had moved across the room.

Sara felt herself waking. She knew that Mr Perkins' whistle was blowing, what it meant—and that it now remained for her to get Jason and go out to the field. A soft laxity, an illusion of warmth, flowed stubbornly down her body, and for a few moments she continued to lie still.

Then she was sitting up and seizing her husband by the shoulders, without saying a word, rocking him back and forth. It took all her strength to wake him. He coughed, his roaring was over, and he sat up. He said nothing either, and they both sat with bent heads and listened for the whistle. After a silence it blew again, a long, rising blast.

Promptly Sara and Jason got out of bed. They were both fully dressed, because of the cold, and only needed to put on their shoes. Jason lighted the lantern, and Sara gathered the bedclothes over her arm and followed him out.

Everything was white, and everything looked vast and extensive to them as they walked over the frozen field. White in a shadowed pit, abandoned from summer to summer, the old sorghum mill stood like the machine of a dream, with its long prostrate pole, its blunted axis.

Stooping over the little plants, Jason and Sara touched them and touched the earth. For their own knowledge, by their hands, they found everything to be true—the cold, the rightness of the warning, the need to act. Over the sticks set in among the plants they laid the quilts one by one, spreading them with a slow ingenuity. Jason took off his coat and laid it over the small tender plants by the side of the house. Then he glanced at Sara, and she reached down and pulled her dress off over her head. Her hair fell down out of its pins, and she began at once to tremble violently. The skirt was luckily long and full, and all the rest of the plants were covered by it.

Then Sara and Jason stood for a moment and stared almost idly at the field and up at the sky.

There was no wind. There was only the intense whiteness of moonlight. Why did this calm cold sink into them like the teeth of a trap? They bent their shoulders and walked silently back into the house.

The room was not much warmer. They had forgotten to shut the door behind them when the whistle was blowing so hard. They sat down to wait for morning.

Then Jason did a rare, strange thing. There long before morning he poured kerosene over some kindling and struck a light to it. Squatting, they got near it, quite gradually they drew together, and sat motionless until it all burned down. Still Sara did not move. Then Jason, in his underwear and long blue trousers, went out and brought in another load, and the big cherry log which of course was meant to be saved for the very last of winter.

The extravagant warmth of the room had sent some kind of agitation over Sara, like her memories of Dexter in the shipping season. She sat huddled in a long brown cotton petticoat, holding onto the string which went around the waist. Her mouse-colored hair, paler at the temples, was hanging loose down to her shoulders, like a child's unbound for a party. She held her knees against her numb, pendulant breasts and stared into the fire, her eyes widening.

On his side of the hearth Jason watched the fire burn too. His breath came gently, quickly, noiselessly, as though for a little time he would conceal or defend his tiredness. He lifted his arms and held out his misshapen hands to the fire.

At last every bit of the wood was gone. Now the cherry log was burned to ashes.

And all of a sudden Jason was on his feet again. Of all things, he was bringing the split-bottomed chair over to the hearth. He knocked it to pieces. . . . It burned well and brightly. Sara never said a word. She did not move. . . .

Then the kitchen table. To think that a solid, steady four-legged table like that, that had stood thirty years in one place, should be consumed in such a little while! Sara stared almost greedily at the waving flames.

Then when that was over, Jason and Sara sat in darkness where their bed had been, and it was colder than ever. The fire the kitchen table had made seemed wonderful to them—as if what they had never said, and what could not be, had its life, too, after all.

But Sara trembled, again pressing her hard knees against her breast. In the return of winter, of the night's cold, something strange, like fright, or dependency, a sensation of complete helplessness, took possession of her. All at once, without turning her head, she spoke.

"Jason . . ."

A silence. But only for a moment.

"Listen," said her husband's uncertain voice.

They held very still, as before, with bent heads.

Outside, as though it would exact something further from their lives, the whistle continued to blow.

The Hitch-Hikers

TOM HARRIS, a thirty-year-old salesman traveling in office supplies, got out of Victory a little after noon and saw people in Midnight and Louise, but went on toward Memphis. It was a base, and he was thinking he would like to do something that night.

Toward evening, somewhere in the middle of the Delta, he slowed down to pick up two hitch-hikers. One of them stood still by the side of the pavement, with his foot stuck out like an old root, but the other was playing a yellow guitar which caught the late sun as it came in a long straight bar across the fields.

Harris would get sleepy driving. On the road he did some things rather out of a dream. And the recurring sight of hitch-hikers waiting against the sky gave him the flash of a sensation he had known as a child: standing still, with nothing to touch him, feeling tall and having the world come all at once into its round shape underfoot and rush and turn through space and make his stand very precarious and lonely. He opened the car door.

"How you do?"

"How you do?"

Harris spoke to hitch-hikers almost formally. Now resuming his speed, he moved over a little in the seat. There was no room in the back for anybody. The man with the guitar was riding with it between his legs. Harris reached over and flicked on the radio.

"Well, music!" said the man with the guitar. Presently he began to smile. "Well, we been there a whole day in that one spot," he said softly. "Seen the sun go clear over. Course, part of the time we laid down under that one tree and taken our ease."

They rode without talking while the sun went down in red clouds and the radio program changed a few times. Harris switched on his lights. Once the man with the guitar started to sing "The One Rose That's Left in My Heart," which came over the air, played by the Aloha Boys. Then in shyness he stopped, but made a streak on the radio dial with his blackly calloused finger tip.

"I 'preciate them big 'lectric gittars some have," he said.

"Where are you going?"

"Looks like north."

"It's north," said Harris. "Smoke?"

The other man held out his hand.

"Well . . . rarely," said the man with the guitar.

At the use of the unexpected word, Harris's cheek twitched, and he handed over his pack of cigarettes. All three lighted up. The silent man held his cigarette in front of him like a piece of money, between his thumb and forefinger. Harris realized that he wasn't smoking it, but was watching it burn.

"My! gittin' night agin," said the man with the guitar in a voice that could assume any social surprise.

"Anything to eat?" asked Harris.

The man gave a pluck to a low string and glanced at him.

"Dewberries," said the other man. It was his only remark, and it was delivered in a slow and pondering voice.

"Some nice little rabbit come skinnin' by," said the man with the guitar, nudging Harris with a slight punch in his side, "but it run off the way it come."

The other man was so bogged in inarticulate anger that Harris could imagine him running down a cotton row after the rabbit. He smiled but did not look around.

"Now to look out for a place to sleep—is that it?" he remarked doggedly.

A pluck of the strings again, and the man yawned.

There was a little town coming up; the lights showed for twenty miles in the flat land.

"Is that Dulcie?" Harris yawned too.

"I bet you ain't got no idea where all I've slep'," the man said, turning around in his seat and speaking directly to Harris, with laughter in his face that in the light of a road sign appeared strangely teasing.

"I could eat a hamburger," said Harris, swinging out of the road under the sign in some automatic gesture of evasion. He looked out of the window, and a girl in red pants leaped onto the running board.

"Three and three beers?" she asked, smiling, with her head poked in. "Hi," she said to Harris.

"How are you," said Harris. "That's right."

"My," said the man with the guitar. "Red sailor-boy britches." Harris listened for the guitar note, but it did not come. "But not purty," he said.

The screen door of the joint whined, and a man's voice called, "Come on in, boys, we got girls."

Harris cut off the radio, and they listened to the nickelodeon which was playing inside the joint and turning the window blue, red and green in turn.

"Hi," said the car-hop again as she came out with the tray. "Looks like rain."

They ate the hamburgers rapidly, without talking. A girl came and looked out of the window of the joint, leaning on her hand. The same couple kept dancing by behind her. There was something brassy playing, a swing record of "Love, Oh Love, Oh Careless Love."

"Same songs ever'where," said the man with the guitar softly: "I come down from the hills. . . . We had us owls for chickens and fox for yard dogs but we sung true."

Nearly every time the man spoke Harris's cheek twitched. He was easily amused. Also, he recognized at once any sort of attempt to confide, and then its certain and hasty retreat. And the more anyone said, the further he was drawn into a willingness to listen. I'll hear him play his guitar yet, he thought. It had got to be a pattern in his days and nights, it was almost automatic, his listening, like the way his hand went to his pocket for money.

"That 'n's most the same as a ballat," said the man, licking mustard off his finger. "My ma, she was the one for ballats. Little in the waist as a dirt-dauber, but her voice carried. Had her a whole lot of tunes. Long ago dead an' gone. Pa 'd come home from the courthouse drunk as a wheelbarrow, and she'd just pick up an' go sit on the front step facin' the hill an' sing. Ever'thing she knowed, she'd sing. Dead an' gone, an' the house burned down." He gulped at his beer. His foot was patting.

"This," said Harris, touching one of the keys on the guitar.

"Couldn't you stop somewhere along here and make money playing this?"

Of course it was by the guitar that he had known at once that they were not mere hitch-hikers. They were tramps. They were full blown, abandoned to this. Both of them were. But when he touched it he knew obscurely that it was the yellow guitar, that bold and gay burden in the tramp's arms, that had caused him to stop and pick them up.

The man hit it flat with the palm of his hand.

"This box? Just play it for myself."

Harris laughed delightedly, but somehow he had a desire to tease him, to make him swear to his freedom.

"You wouldn't stop and play somewhere like this? For them to dance? When you know all the songs?"

Now the fellow laughed out loud. He turned and spoke completely as if the other man could not hear him. "Well, but right now I got *him*."

"Him?" Harris stared ahead.

"He'd gripe. He don't like foolin' around. He wants to git on. You always git a partner got notions."

The other tramp belched. Harris laid his hand on the horn.

"Hurry back," said the car-hop, opening a heart-shaped pocket over her heart and dropping the tip courteously within.

"Aw river!" sang out the man with the guitar.

As they pulled out into the road again, the other man began to lift a beer bottle, and stared beseechingly, with his mouth full, at the man with the guitar.

"Drive back, mister. Sobby forgot to give her back her bottle. Drive back."

"Too late," said Harris rather firmly, speeding on into Dulcie, thinking, I was about to take directions from him.

Harris stopped the car in front of the Dulcie Hotel on the square.

" 'Preciated it," said the man, taking up his guitar.

"Wait here."

They stood on the walk, one lighted by the street light, the other in the shadow of the statue of the Confederate soldier, both caved in and giving out an odor of dust, both sighing with obedience.

Harris went across the yard and up the one step into the hotel.

Mr Gene, the proprietor, a white-haired man with little dark freckles all over his face and hands, looked up and shoved out his arm at the same time.

"If he ain't back." He grinned. "Been about a month to the day—I was just remarking."

"Mr Gene, I ought to go on, but I got two fellows out front. O.K., but they've just got nowhere to sleep tonight, and you know that little back porch."

"Why, it's a beautiful night out!" bellowed Mr Gene, and he laughed silently.

"They'd get fleas in your bed," said Harris, showing the back of his hand. "But you know that old porch. It's not so bad. I slept out there once, I forget how."

The proprietor let his laugh out like a flood. Then he sobered abruptly.

"Sure. O.K.," he said. "Wait a minute—Mike's sick. Come here, Mike, it's just old Harris passin' through."

Mike was an ancient collie dog. He rose from a quilt near the door and moved over the square brown rug, stiffly, like a table walking, and shoved himself between the men, swinging his long head from Mr Gene's hand to Harris's and bearing down motionless with his jaw in Harris's palm.

"You sick, Mike?" asked Harris.

"Dyin' of old age, that's what he's doin'!" blurted the proprietor as if in anger.

Harris began to stroke the dog, but the familiarity in his hands changed to slowness and hesitancy. Mike looked up out of his eyes.

"His spirit's gone. You see?" said Mr Gene pleadingly.

"Say, look," said a voice at the front door.

"Come in, Cato, and see poor old Mike," said Mr Gene.

"I knew that was your car, Mr Harris," said the boy. He was nervously trying to tuck a Bing Crosby cretonne shirt into his pants like a real shirt. Then he looked up and said, "They was tryin' to take your car, and down the street one of 'em like to bust the other one's head wide op'm with a bottle.

Looks like you would 'a' heard the commotion. Everybody's out there. I said, 'That's Mr Tom Harris's car, look at the out-of-town license and look at all the stuff he all time carries around with him, all bloody.' "

"He's not dead though," said Harris, kneeling on the seat of his car.

It was the man with the guitar. The little ceiling light had been turned on. With blood streaming from his broken head, he was slumped down upon the guitar, his legs bowed around it, his arms at either side, his whole body limp in the posture of a bareback rider. Harris was aware of the other face not a yard away: the man the guitar player had called Sobby was standing on the curb, with two men unnecessarily holding him. He looked more like a bystander than any of the rest, except that he still held the beer bottle in his right hand.

"Looks like if he was fixin' to hit him, *he* would of hit *him* with that gittar," said a voice. "That'd be a real good thing to hit somebody with. Whang!"

"The way I figure this thing out is," said a penetrating voice, as if a woman were explaining it all to her husband, "the men was left to 'emselves. So—that 'n' yonder wanted to make off with the car—he's the bad one. So the good one says, 'Naw, that ain't right.' "

Or was it the other way around? thought Harris dreamily.

"So the other one says bam! bam! He whacked him over the head. And so dumb—right where the movie was letting out."

"Who's got my car keys!" Harris kept shouting. He had, without realizing it, kicked away the prop, the guitar; and he had stopped the blood with something.

Nobody had to tell him where the ramshackle little hospital was—he had been there once before, on a Delta trip. With the constable scuttling along after and then riding on the running board, glasses held tenderly in one fist, the handcuffed Sobby dragged alongside by the other, with a long line of little boys in flowered shirts accompanying him on bicycles, riding in and out of the headlight beam, with the rain falling in front of him and with Mr Gene shouting in a sort of plea from the hotel behind and Mike beginning to echo the barking of the rest of the dogs, Harris drove in all carefulness down the long tree-dark street, with his wet hand pressed on the horn.

The old doctor came down the walk and, joining them in the car, slowly took the guitar player by the shoulders.

"I 'spec' he gonna die though," said a colored child's voice mournfully. "Wonder who goin' to git his box?"

In a room on the second floor of the two-story hotel Harris put on clean clothes, while Mr Gene lay on the bed with Mike across his stomach.

"Ruined that Christmas tie you came in." The proprietor was talking in short breaths. "It took it out of Mike, I'm tellin' you." He sighed. "First time he's barked since Bud Milton shot up that Chinese." He lifted his head and took a long swallow of the hotel whisky, and tears appeared in his warm brown eyes. "Suppose they'd done it on the porch."

The phone rang.

"See, everybody knows you're here," said Mr Gene.

"Ruth?" he said, lifting the receiver, his voice almost contrite.

But it was for the proprietor.

When he had hung up he said, "That little peanut—he ain't ever goin' to learn which end is up. The constable. Got a nigger already in the jail, so he's runnin' round to find a place to put this fella of yours with the bottle, and damned if all he can think of ain't the hotel!"

"Hell, is he going to spend the night with me?"

"Well, the same thing. Across the hall. The other fella may die. Only place in town with a key but the bank, he says."

"What time is it?" asked Harris all at once.

"Oh, it ain't *late*," said Mr Gene.

He opened the door for Mike, and the two men followed the dog slowly down the stairs. The light was out on the landing. Harris looked out of the old half-open stained-glass window.

"Is that rain?"

"It's been rainin' since dark, but you don't ever know a thing like that—it's proverbial." At the desk he held up a brown package. "Here. I sent Cato after some Memphis whisky for you. He had to do something."

"Thanks."

"I'll see you. I don't guess you're goin' to get away very shortly in the mornin'. I'm real sorry they did it in your car if they were goin' to do it."

"That's all right," said Harris. "You'd better have a little of this."

"That? It'd kill me," said Mr Gene.

In a drugstore Harris phoned Ruth, a woman he knew in town, and found her at home having a party.

"Tom Harris! Sent by heaven!" she cried. "I was wondering what I'd do about Carol—this *baby*!"

"What's the matter with her?"

"No date."

Some other people wanted to say hello from the party. He listened awhile and said he'd be out.

This had postponed the call to the hospital. He put in another nickel. . . . There was nothing new about the guitar player.

"Like I told you," the doctor said, "we don't have the facilities for giving transfusions, and he's been moved plenty without you taking him to Memphis."

Walking over to the party, so as not to use his car, making the only sounds in the dark wet street, and only partly aware of the indeterminate shapes of houses with their soft-shining fanlights marking them off, there with the rain falling mist-like through the trees, he almost forgot what town he was in and which house he was bound for.

Ruth, in a long dark dress, leaned against an open door, laughing. From inside came the sounds of at least two people playing a duet on the piano.

"He would come like this and get all wet!" she cried over her shoulder into the room. She was leaning back on her hands. "What's the matter with your little blue car? I hope you brought us a present."

He went in with her and began shaking hands, and set the bottle wrapped in the paper sack on a table.

"He never forgets!" cried Ruth.

"Drinkin' whisky!" Everybody was noisy again.

"So this is the famous 'he' that everybody talks about all

the time," pouted a girl in a white dress. "Is he one of your cousins, Ruth?"

"No kin of mine, he's nothing but a vagabond," said Ruth, and led Harris off to the kitchen by the hand.

I wish they'd call me "you" when I've got here, he thought tiredly.

"More has gone on than a little bit," she said, and told him the news while he poured fresh drinks into the glasses. When she accused him of nothing, of no carelessness or disregard of her feelings, he was fairly sure she had not heard about the assault in his car.

She was looking at him closely. "Where did you get that sunburn?"

"Well, I had to go to the Coast last week," he said.

"What did you do?"

"Same old thing." He laughed; he had started to tell her about something funny in Bay St Louis, where an eloping couple had flagged him down in the residential section and threatened to break up if he would not carry them to the next town. Then he remembered how Ruth looked when he mentioned other places where he stopped on trips.

Somewhere in the house the phone rang and rang, and he caught himself jumping. Nobody was answering it.

"I thought you'd quit drinking," she said, picking up the bottle.

"I start and quit," he said, taking it from her and pouring his drink. "Where's my date?"

"Oh, she's in Leland," said Ruth.

They all drove over in two cars to get her.

She was a slight little thing, with her nightgown in some sort of little bag. She came out when they blew the horn, before he could go in after her. . .

"Let's go holler off the bridge," said somebody in the car ahead.

They drove over a little gravel road, miles through the misty fields, and came to the bridge out in the middle of nowhere.

"Let's dance," said one of the boys. He grabbed Carol around the waist, and they began to tango over the boards.

"Did you miss me?" asked Ruth. She stayed by him, standing in the road.

"Woo-hoo!" they cried.

"I wish I knew what makes it holler back," said one girl. "There's nothing anywhere. Some of my kinfolks can't even hear it."

"Yes, it's funny," said Harris, with a cigarette in his mouth.

"Some people say it's an old steamboat got lost once."

"Might be."

They drove around and waited to see if it would stop raining.

Back in the lighted rooms at Ruth's he saw Carol, his date, give him a strange little glance. At the moment he was serving her with a drink from the tray.

"Are you the one everybody's 'miratin' and gyratin' over?" she said, before she would put her hand out.

"Yes," he said, "I come from afar." He placed the strongest drink from the tray in her hand, with a little flourish.

"Hurry back!" called Ruth.

In the pantry Ruth came over and stood by him while he set more glasses on the tray and then followed him out to the kitchen. Was she at all curious about him? he wondered. For a moment, when they were simply close together, her lips parted, and she stared off at nothing; her jealousy seemed to let her go free. The rainy wind from the back porch stirred her hair.

As if under some illusion, he set the tray down and told her about the two hitch-hikers.

Her eyes flashed.

"What a—stupid thing!" Furiously she seized the tray when he reached for it.

The phone was ringing again. Ruth glared at him.

It was as though he had made a previous engagement with the hitch-hikers.

Everybody was meeting them at the kitchen door.

"Aha!" cried one of the men, Jackson. "He tries to put one over on you, girls. Somebody just called up, Ruth, about the murder in Tom's car."

"Did he die?" asked Harris, without moving.

"I knew all about it!" cried Ruth, her cheeks flaming. "He told me all about it. It practically ruined his car. Didn't it!"

"Wouldn't he get into something crazy like that?"

"It's because he's an angel," said the girl named Carol, his date, speaking in a hollow voice from her highball glass.

"Who phoned?" asked Harris.

"Old Mrs Daggett, that old lady about a million years old that's always calling up. She was right there."

Harris phoned the doctor's home and woke the doctor's wife. The guitar player was still the same.

"This is so exciting, tell us all," said a fat boy. Harris knew he lived fifty miles up the river and had driven down under the impression that there would be a bridge game.

"It was just a fight."

"Oh, he wouldn't tell you, he never talks. I'll tell you," said Ruth. "Get your drinks, for goodness' sake."

So the incident became a story. Harris grew very tired of it.

"It's marvelous the way he always gets in with somebody and then something happens," said Ruth, her eyes completely black.

"Oh, he's my hero," said Carol, and she went out and stood on the back porch.

"Maybe you'll still be here tomorrow," Ruth said to Harris, taking his arm. "Will you be detained, maybe?"

"If he dies," said Harris.

He told them all good-by.

"Let's all go to Greenville and get a Coke," said Ruth.

"No," he said. "Good night."

" 'Aw river,' " said the girl in the white dress. "Isn't that what the little man said?"

"Yes," said Harris, the rain falling on him, and he refused to spend the night or to be taken in a car back to the hotel.

In the antlered lobby, Mr Gene bent over asleep under a lamp by the desk phone. His freckles seemed to come out darker when he was asleep.

Harris woke him. "Go to bed," he said. "What was the idea? Anything happened?"

"I just wanted to tell you that little buzzard's up in 202. Locked and double-locked, handcuffed to the bed, but I wanted to tell you."

"Oh. Much obliged."

"All a gentleman could do," said Mr Gene. He was drunk. "Warn you what's sleepin' under your roof."

"Thanks," said Harris. "It's almost morning. Look."

"Poor Mike can't sleep," said Mr Gene. "He scrapes somethin' when he breathes. Did the other fella poop out?"

"Still unconscious. No change," said Harris. He took the bunch of keys which the proprietor was handing him.

"You keep 'em," said Mr Gene.

In the next moment Harris saw his hand tremble and he took hold of it.

"A murderer!" whispered Mr Gene. All his freckles stood out. "Here he came . . . with not a word to say . . ."

"Not a murderer yet," said Harris, starting to grin.

When he passed 202 and heard no sound, he remembered what old Sobby had said, standing handcuffed in front of the hospital, with nobody listening to him. "I was jist tired of him always uppin' an' makin' a noise about ever'thing."

In his room, Harris lay down on the bed without undressing or turning out the light. He was too tired to sleep. Half blinded by the unshaded bulb he stared at the bare plaster walls and the equally white surface of the mirror above the empty dresser. Presently he got up and turned on the ceiling fan, to create some motion and sound in the room. It was a defective fan which clicked with each revolution, on and on. He lay perfectly still beneath it, with his clothes on, unconsciously breathing in a rhythm related to the beat of the fan.

He shut his eyes suddenly. When they were closed, in the red darkness he felt all patience leave him. It was like the beginning of desire. He remembered the girl dropping money into her heart-shaped pocket, and remembered a disturbing possessiveness, which meant nothing, Ruth leaning on her hands. He knew he would not be held by any of it. It was for relief, almost, that his thoughts turned to pity, to wonder about the two tramps, their conflict, the sudden brutality when his back was turned. How would it turn out? It was in this suspense that it was more acceptable to him to feel the helplessness of his life.

He could forgive nothing in this evening. But it was too

like other evenings, this town was too like other towns, for him to move out of this lying still clothed on the bed, even into comfort or despair. Even the rain—there was often rain, there was often a party, and there had been other violence not of his doing—other fights, not quite so pointless, but fights in his car; fights, unheralded confessions, sudden love-making—none of any of this his, not his to keep, but belonging to the people of these towns he passed through, coming out of their rooted pasts and their mock rambles, coming out of their time. He himself had no time. He was free; helpless. He wished he knew how the guitar player was, if he was still unconscious, if he felt pain.

He sat up on the bed and then got up and walked to the window.

"Tom!" said a voice outside in the dark.

Automatically he answered and listened. It was a girl. He could not see her, but she must have been standing on the little plot of grass that ran around the side of the hotel. Wet feet, pneumonia, he thought. And he was so tired he thought of a girl from the wrong town.

He went down and unlocked the door. She ran in as far as the middle of the lobby as though from impetus. It was Carol, from the party.

"You're wet," he said. He touched her.

"Always raining." She looked up at him, stepping back. "How are you?"

"O.K., fine," he said.

"I was wondering," she said nervously. "I knew the light would be you. I hope I didn't wake up anybody."

Was old Sobby asleep? he wondered.

"Would you like a drink. Or do you want to go to the All-Nite and get a Coca-Cola," he said.

"It's open," she said, making a gesture with her hand. "The All-Nite's open—I just passsed it."

They went out into the mist, and she put his coat on with silent protest, in the dark street not drunken but womanly.

"You didn't remember me at the party," she said, and did not look up when he made his exclamation. "They say you never forget anybody, so I found out they were wrong about that anyway."

"They're often wrong," he said, and then hurriedly, "Who are you?"

"We used to stay at the Manning Hotel on the Coast every summer—I wasn't grown. Carol Thames. Just dances and all, but you had just started to travel then, it was on your trips, and you—you talked at intermission."

He laughed shortly, but she added:

"You talked about yourself."

They walked past the tall wet church, and their steps echoed.

"Oh, it wasn't so long ago—five years," she said. Under a magnolia tree she put her hand out and stopped him, looking up at him with her child's face. "But when I saw you again tonight I wanted to know how you were getting along."

He said nothing, and she went on.

"You used to play the piano."

They passed under a street light, and she glanced up as if to look for the little tic in his cheek.

"Out on the big porch where they danced," she said, walking on. "Paper lanterns . . ."

"I'd forgotten that, is one thing sure," he said. "Maybe you've got the wrong man. I've got cousins galore who all play the piano."

"You'd put your hands down on the keyboard like you'd say, 'Now this is how it really is!' " she cried, and turned her head away. "I guess I was crazy about you, though."

"Crazy about me then?" He struck a match and held a cigarette between his teeth.

"No—yes, and now too!" she cried sharply, as if driven to deny him.

They came to the little depot where a restless switch engine was hissing, and crossed the black street. The past and present joined like this, he thought, it never happened often to me, and it probably won't happen again. He took her arm and led her through the dirty screen door of the All-Nite.

He waited at the counter while she sat down by the wall table and wiped her face all over with her handkerchief. He carried the black coffees over to the table himself, smiling at her from a little distance. They sat under a calendar with some picture of giant trees being cut down.

They said little. A fly bothered her. When the coffee was all gone he put her into the old Cadillac taxi that always stood in front of the depot.

Before he shut the taxi door he said, frowning, "I appreciate it. . . . You're sweet."

Now she had torn her handkerchief. She held it up and began to cry. "What's sweet about me?" It was the look of bewilderment in her face that he would remember.

"To come out, like this—in the rain—to be here. . . ." He shut the door, partly from weariness.

She was holding her breath. "I hope your friend doesn't die," she said. "All I hope is your friend gets well."

But when he woke up the next morning and phoned the hospital, the guitar player was dead. He had been dying while Harris was sitting in the All-Nite.

"It *was* a murderer," said Mr Gene, pulling Mike's ears. "That was just plain murder. No way anybody could call that an affair of honor."

The man called Sobby did not oppose an invitation to confess. He stood erect and turning his head about a little, and almost smiled at all the men who had come to see him. After one look at him Mr Gene, who had come with Harris, went out and slammed the door behind him.

All the same, Sobby had found little in the night, asleep or awake, to say about it. "I done it, sure," he said. "Didn't ever'body see me, or was they blind?"

They asked him about the man he had killed.

"Name Sanford," he said, standing still, with his foot out, as if he were trying to recall something particular and minute. "But he didn't have nothing and he didn't have no folks. No more 'n me. Him and me, we took up together two weeks back." He looked up at their faces as if for support. "He was uppity, though. He bragged. He carried a gittar around." He whimpered. "It was his notion to run off with the car."

Harris, fresh from the barbershop, was standing in the filling station where his car was being polished.

A ring of little boys in bright shirt-tails surrounded him and the car, with some colored boys waiting behind them.

"Could they git all the blood off the seat and the steerin' wheel, Mr Harris?"

He nodded. They ran away.

"Mr Harris," said a little colored boy who stayed. "Does you want the box?"

"The what?"

He pointed, to where it lay in the back seat with the sample cases. "The po' kilt man's gittar. Even the policemans didn't want it."

"No," said Harris, and handed it over.

A Memory

ONE SUMMER MORNING when I was a child I lay on the sand after swimming in the small lake in the park. The sun beat down—it was almost noon. The water shone like steel, motionless except for the feathery curl behind a distant swimmer. From my position I was looking at a rectangle brightly lit, actually glaring at me, with sun, sand, water, a little pavilion, a few solitary people in fixed attitudes, and around it all a border of dark rounded oak trees, like the engraved thunderclouds surrounding illustrations in the Bible. Ever since I had begun taking painting lessons, I had made small frames with my fingers, to look out at everything.

Since this was a weekday morning, the only persons who were at liberty to be in the park were either children, who had nothing to occupy them, or those older people whose lives are obscure, irregular, and consciously of no worth to any thing: this I put down as my observation at that time. I was at an age when I formed a judgment upon every person and every event which came under my eye, although I was easily frightened. When a person, or a happening, seemed to me not in keeping with my opinion, or even my hope or expectation, I was terrified by a vision of abandonment and wildness which tore my heart with a kind of sorrow. My father and mother, who believed that I saw nothing in the world which was not strictly coaxed into place like a vine on our garden trellis to be presented to my eyes, would have been badly concerned if they had guessed how frequently the weak and inferior and strangely turned examples of what was to come showed themselves to me.

I do not know even now what it was that I was waiting to see; but in those days I was convinced that I almost saw it at every turn. To watch everything about me I regarded grimly and possessively as a *need*. All through this summer I had lain on the sand beside the small lake, with my hands squared over my eyes, finger tips touching, looking out by this device to see everything: which appeared as a kind of projection. It did not matter to me what I looked at; from any observation I would conclude that a secret of life had been nearly revealed to me—for I was obsessed with notions about concealment, and from the smallest gesture of a stranger I would wrest what was to me a communication or a presentiment.

This state of exaltation was heightened, or even brought about, by the fact that I was in love then for the first time: I had identified love at once. The truth is that never since has any passion I have felt remained so hopelessly unexpressed within me or appeared so grotesquely altered in the outward world. It is strange that sometimes, even now, I remember unadulteratedly a certain morning when I touched my friend's wrist (as if by accident, and he pretended not to notice) as we passed on the stairs in school. I must add, and this is not so strange, that the child was not actually my friend. We had never exchanged a word or even a nod of recognition; but it was possible during that entire year for me to think endlessly on this minute and brief encounter which we endured on the stairs, until it would swell with a sudden and overwhelming beauty, like a rose forced into premature bloom for a great occasion.

My love had somehow made me doubly austere in my observations of what went on about me. Through some intensity I had come almost into a dual life, as observer and dreamer. I felt a necessity for absolute conformity to my ideas in any happening I witnessed. As a result, all day long in school I sat perpetually alert, fearing for the untoward to happen. The dreariness and regularity of the school day were a protection for me, but I remember with exact clarity the day in Latin class when the boy I loved (whom I watched constantly) bent suddenly over and brought his handkerchief to his face. I saw red—vermilion—blood flow over the handkerchief and his square-shaped hand; his nose had begun to bleed. I remember the very moment: several of the older girls laughed at the confusion and distraction; the boy rushed from the room; the teacher spoke sharply in warning. But this small happening which had closed in upon my friend was a tremendous shock to me; it was unforeseen, but at the same time dreaded; I recognized it, and suddenly I leaned heavily on my arm and fainted. Does this explain why, ever since that day, I have been unable to bear the sight of blood?

I never knew where this boy lived, or who his parents were. This occasioned during the year of my love a constant uneasiness in me. It was unbearable to think that his house might be slovenly and unpainted, hidden by tall trees, that his mother and father might be shabby—dishonest—crippled—dead. I speculated endlessly on the dangers of his home. Sometimes I imagined that his house might catch on fire in the night and that he might die. When he would walk into the schoolroom the next morning, a look of unconcern and even stupidity on his face would dissipate my dream; but my fears were increased through his unconsciousness of them, for I felt a mystery deeper than danger which hung about him. I watched everything he did, trying to learn and translate and verify. I could reproduce for you now the clumsy weave, the exact shade of faded blue in his sweater. I remember how he used to swing his foot as he sat at his desk—softly, barely not touching the floor. Even now it does not seem trivial.

As I lay on the beach that sunny morning, I was thinking of my friend and remembering in a retarded, dilated, timeless fashion the incident of my hand brushing his wrist. It made a very long story. But like a needle going in and out among my thoughts were the children running on the sand, the upthrust oak trees growing over the clean pointed roof of the white pavilion, and the slowly changing attitudes of the grown-up people who had avoided the city and were lying prone and laughing on the water's edge. I still would not care to say which was more real—the dream I could make blossom at will, or the sight of the bathers. I am presenting them, you see, only as simultaneous.

I did not notice how the bathers got there, so close to me. Perhaps I actually fell asleep, and they came out then. Sprawled close to where I was lying, at any rate, appeared a group of loud, squirming, ill-assorted people who seemed thrown together only by the most confused accident, and who seemed driven by foolish intent to insult each other, all of which they enjoyed with a hilarity which astonished my heart. There were a man, two women, two young boys. They were brown and roughened, but not foreigners; when I was a child such people were called "common." They wore old and faded bathing suits which did not hide either the energy or the fatigue of their bodies, but showed it exactly.

The boys must have been brothers, because they both had very white straight hair, which shone like thistles in the red sunlight. The older boy was greatly overgrown—he protruded from his costume at every turn. His cheeks were ballooned outward and hid his eyes, but it was easy for me to follow his darting, sly glances as he ran clumsily around the others, inflicting pinches, kicks, and idiotic sounds upon them. The smaller boy was thin and defiant; his white bangs were plastered down where he had thrown himself time after time headfirst into the lake when the older child chased him to persecute him.

Lying in leglike confusion together were the rest of the group, the man and the two women. The man seemed completely given over to the heat and glare of the sun; his relaxed eyes sometimes squinted with faint amusement over the brilliant water and the hot sand. His arms were flabby and at rest. He lay turned on his side, now and then scooping sand in a loose pile about the legs of the older woman.

She herself stared fixedly at his slow, undeliberate movements, and held her body perfectly still. She was unnaturally white and fatly aware, in a bathing suit which had no relation to the shape of her body. Fat hung upon her upper arms like an arrested earthslide on a hill. With the first motion she might make, I was afraid that she would slide down upon herself into a terrifying heap. Her breasts hung heavy and widening like pears into her bathing suit. Her legs lay prone one on the other like shadowed bulwarks, uneven and deserted, upon which, from the man's hand, the sand piled higher like the teasing threat of oblivion. A slow, repetitious sound I had been hearing for a long time unconsciously, I identified as a continuous laugh which came through the motionless open pouched mouth of the woman.

The younger girl, who was lying at the man's feet, was curled tensely upon herself. She wore a bright green bathing suit like a bottle from which she might, I felt, burst in a rage of churning smoke. I could feel the genie-like rage in her narrowed figure as she seemed both to crawl and to lie still, watching the man heap the sand in his careless way about the larger legs of the older woman. The two little boys were running in wobbly ellipses about the others, pinching them indiscriminately and pitching sand into the man's roughened hair as though they were not afraid of him. The woman continued to laugh, almost as she would hum an annoying song. I saw that they were all resigned to each other's daring and ugliness.

There had been no words spoken among these people, but I began to comprehend a progression, a circle of answers, which they were flinging toward one another in their own way, in the confusion of vulgarity and hatred which twined among them all like a wreath of steam rising from the wet sand. I saw the man lift his hand filled with crumbling sand, shaking it as the woman laughed, and pour it down inside her bathing suit between her bulbous descending breasts. There it hung, brown and shapeless, making them all laugh. Even the angry girl laughed, with an insistent hilarity which flung her to her feet and tossed her about the beach, her stiff, cramped legs jumping and tottering. The little boys pointed and howled. The man smiled, the way panting dogs seem to be smiling, and gazed about carelessly at them all and out over the water. He even looked at me, and included me. Looking back, stunned, I wished that they all were dead.

But at that moment the girl in the green bathing suit suddenly whirled all the way around. She reached rigid arms toward the screaming children and joined them in a senseless chase. The small boy dashed headfirst into the water, and the larger boy churned his overgrown body through the blue air onto a little bench, which I had not even known was there! Jeeringly he called to the others, who laughed as he jumped, heavy and ridiculous, over the back of the bench and tumbled exaggeratedly in the sand below. The fat woman leaned over the man to smirk, and the child pointed at her, screaming. The girl in green then came running toward the bench as though she would destroy it, and with a fierceness which took my breath away, she dragged herself through the air and jumped over the bench. But no one seemed to notice, except the smaller boy, who flew out of the water to dig his fingers into her side, in mixed congratulation and derision; she pushed him angrily down into the sand.

I closed my eyes upon them and their struggles but I could see them still, large and almost metallic, with painted smiles, in the sun. I lay there with my eyes pressed shut, listening to their moans and their frantic squeals. It seemed to me that I could hear also the thud and the fat impact of all their ugly bodies upon one another. I tried to withdraw to my most inner dream, that of touching the wrist of the boy I loved on the stair; I felt the shudder of my wish shaking the darkness like leaves where I had closed my eyes; I felt the heavy weight of sweetness which always accompanied this memory; but the memory itself did not come to me.

I lay there, opening and closing my eyes. The brilliance and then the blackness were like some alternate experiences of night and day. The sweetness of my love seemed to bring the dark and to swing me gently in its suspended wind; I sank into familiarity; but the story of my love, the long narrative of the incident on the stairs, had vanished. I did not know, any longer, the meaning of my happiness; it held me unexplained.

Once when I looked up, the fat woman was standing opposite the smiling man. She bent over and in a condescending way pulled down the front of her bathing suit, turning it outward, so that the lumps of mashed and folded sand came emptying out. I felt a peak of horror, as though her breasts themselves had turned to sand, as though they were of no importance at all and she did not care.

When finally I emerged again from the protection of my dream, the undefined austerity of my love, I opened my eyes onto the blur of an empty beach. The group of strangers had gone. Still I lay there, feeling victimized by the sight of the unfinished bulwark where they had piled and shaped the wet sand around their bodies, which changed the appearance of the beach like the ravages of a storm. I looked away, and for the object which met my eye, the small worn white pavilion, I felt pity suddenly overtake me, and I burst into tears.

That was my last morning on the beach. I remember continuing to lie there, squaring my vision with my hands, trying to think ahead to the time of my return to school in winter.

I could imagine the boy I loved walking into a classroom, where I would watch him with this hour on the beach accompanying my recovered dream and added to my love. I could even foresee the way he would stare back, speechless and innocent, a medium-sized boy with blond hair, his unconscious eyes looking beyond me and out the window, solitary and unprotected.

Clytie

IT WAS late afternoon, with heavy silver clouds which looked bigger and wider than cotton fields, and presently it began to rain. Big round drops fell, still in the sunlight, on the hot tin sheds, and stained the white false fronts of the row of stores in the little town of Farr's Gin. A hen and her string of yellow chickens ran in great alarm across the road, the dust turned river-brown, and the birds flew down into it immediately, sitting out little pockets in which to take baths. The bird dogs got up from the doorways of the stores, shook themselves down to the tail, and went to lie inside. The few people standing with long shadows on the level road moved over into the post office. A little boy kicked his bare heels into the sides of his mule, which proceeded slowly through the town toward the country.

After everyone else had gone under cover, Miss Clytie Farr stood still in the road, peering ahead in her nearsighted way, and as wet as the little birds.

She usually came out of the old big house about this time in the afternoon, and hurried through the town. It used to be that she ran about on some pretext or other, and for a while she made soft-voiced explanations that nobody could hear, and after that she began to charge up bills, which the postmistress declared would never be paid any more than anyone else's, even if the Farrs were too good to associate with other people. But now Clytie came for nothing. She came every day, and no one spoke to her any more: she would be in such a hurry, and couldn't see who it was. And every Saturday they expected her to be run over, the way she darted out into the road with all the horses and trucks.

It might be simply that Miss Clytie's wits were all leaving her, said the ladies standing in the door to feel the cool, the way her sister's had left her; and she would just wait there to be told to go home. She would have to wring out everything she had on—the waist and the jumper skirt, and the long black stockings. On her head was one of the straw hats from the furnishing store, with an old black satin ribbon pinned to it to make it a better hat, and tied under the chin. Now, under the force of the rain, while the ladies watched, the hat slowly began to sag down on each side until it looked even more absurd and done for, like an old bonnet on a horse. And indeed it was with the patience almost of a beast that Miss Clytie stood there in the rain and stuck her long empty arms out a little from her sides, as if she were waiting for something to come along the road and drive her to shelter.

In a little while there was a clap of thunder.

"Miss Clytie! Go in out of the rain, Miss Clytie!" someone called.

The old maid did not look around, but clenched her hands and drew them up under her armpits, and sticking out her elbows like hen wings, she ran out of the street, her poor hat creaking and beating about her ears.

"Well, there goes Miss Clytie," the ladies said, and one of them had a premonition about her.

Through the rushing water in the sunken path under the four wet black cedars, which smelled bitter as smoke, she ran to the house.

"Where the devil have you been?" called the older sister, Octavia, from an upper window.

Clytie looked up in time to see the curtain fall back.

She went inside, into the hall, and waited, shivering. It was very dark and bare. The only light was falling on the white sheet which covered the solitary piece of furniture, an organ. The red curtains over the parlor door, held back by ivory hands, were still as tree trunks in the airless house. Every window was closed, and every shade was down, though behind them the rain could still be heard.

Clytie took a match and advanced to the stair post, where the bronze cast of Hermes was holding up a gas fixture; and at once above this, lighted up, but quite still, like one of the unmovable relics of the house, Octavia stood waiting on the stairs.

She stood solidly before the violet-and-lemon-colored glass of the window on the landing, and her wrinkled, unresting fingers took hold of the diamond cornucopia she always wore in the bosom of her long black dress. It was an unwithered grand gesture of hers, fondling the cornucopia.

"It is not enough that we are waiting here—hungry," Octavia was saying, while Clytie waited below. "But you must sneak away and not answer when I call you. Go off and wander about the streets. Common—common——!"

"Never mind, Sister," Clytie managed to say.

"But you always return."

"Of course. . . ."

"Gerald is awake now, and so is Papa," said Octavia, in the same vindictive voice—a loud voice, for she was usually calling.

Clytie went to the kitchen and lighted the kindling in the wood stove. As if she were freezing cold in June, she stood before its open door, and soon a look of interest and pleasure lighted her face, which had in the last years grown weather-beaten in spite of the straw hat. Now some dream was resumed. In the street she had been thinking about the face of a child she had just seen. The child, playing with another of the same age, chasing it with a toy pistol, had looked at her with such an open, serene, trusting expression as she passed by! With this small, peaceful face still in her mind, rosy like these flames, like an inspiration which drives all other thoughts away, Clytie had forgotten herself and had been obliged to stand where she was in the middle of the road. But the rain had come down, and someone had shouted at her, and she had not been able to reach the end of her meditations.

It had been a long time now, since Clytie had first begun to watch faces, and to think about them.

Anyone could have told you that there were not more than 150 people in Farr's Gin, counting Negroes. Yet the number of faces seemed to Clytie almost infinite. She knew now to look slowly and carefully at a face; she was convinced that it was impossible to see it all at once. The first thing she discovered about a face was always that she had never seen it before. When she began to look at people's actual countenances there was no more familiarity in the world for her. The most profound, the most moving sight in the whole world must be a face. Was it possible to comprehend the eyes and the mouths of other people, which concealed she knew not what, and secretly asked for still another unknown thing? The mysterious smile of the old man who sold peanuts by the church gate returned to her; his face seemed for a moment to rest upon the iron door of the stove, set into the lion's mane. Other people said Mr Tom Bate's Boy, as he called himself, stared away with a face as clean-blank as a watermelon seed, but to Clytie, who observed grains of sand in his eyes and in his old yellow lashes, he might have come out of a desert, like an Egyptian.

But while she was thinking of Mr Tom Bate's Boy, there was a terrible gust of wind which struck her back, and she turned around. The long green window shade billowed and plunged. The kitchen window was wide open—she had done it herself. She closed it gently. Octavia, who never came all the way downstairs for any reason, would never have forgiven her for an open window, if she knew. Rain and sun signified ruin, in Octavia's mind. Going over the whole house, Clytie made sure that everything was safe. It was not that ruin in itself could distress Octavia. Ruin or encroachment, even upon priceless treasures and even in poverty, held no terror for her; it was simply some form of prying from without, and this she would not forgive. All of that was to be seen in her face.

Clytie cooked the three meals on the stove, for they all ate different things, and set the three trays. She had to carry them in proper order up the stairs. She frowned in concentration, for it was hard to keep all the dishes straight, to make them come out right in the end, as Old Lethy could have done. They had had to give up the cook long ago when their father suffered the first stroke. Their father had been fond of Old Lethy, she had been his nurse in childhood, and she had come back out of the country to see him when she heard he was dying. Old Lethy had come and knocked at the back door. And as usual, at the first disturbance, front or back, Octavia had peered down from behind the curtain and cried, "Go away! Go away! What the devil have you come *here* for?" And although Old Lethy and their father had both pleaded that they might be allowed to see each other, Octavia had shouted as she always did, and sent the intruder away. Clytie had stood as usual, speechless in the kitchen, until finally she had repeated after her sister, "Lethy, go away." But their father had not died. He was, instead, paralyzed, blind, and able only to call out in unintelligible sounds and to swallow liquids. Lethy still would come to the back door now and then, but they never let her in, and the old man no longer heard or knew enough to beg to see her. There was only one caller admitted to his room. Once a week the barber came by appointment to shave him. On this occasion not a word was spoken by anyone.

Clytie went up to her father's room first and set the tray down on a little marble table they kept by his bed.

"I want to feed Papa," said Octavia, taking the bowl from her hands.

"You fed him last time," said Clytie.

Relinquishing the bowl, she looked down at the pointed face on the pillow. Tomorrow was the barber's day, and the sharp black points, at their longest, stuck out like needles all over the wasted cheeks. The old man's eyes were half closed. It was impossible to know what he felt. He looked as though he were really far away, neglected, free. . . . Octavia began to feed him.

Without taking her eyes from her father's face, Clytie suddenly began to speak in rapid, bitter words to her sister, the wildest words that came to her head. But soon she began to cry and gasp, like a small child who has been pushed by the big boys into the water.

"That is enough," said Octavia.

But Clytie could not take her eyes from her father's unshaven face and his still-open mouth.

"And I'll feed him tomorrow if I want to," said Octavia. She stood up. The thick hair, growing back after an illness and dyed almost purple, fell over her forehead. Beginning at her throat, the long accordion pleats which fell the length of her gown opened and closed over her breasts as she breathed. "Have you forgotten Gerald?" she said. "And I am hungry too."

Clytie went back to the kitchen and brought her sister's supper.

Then she brought her brother's.

•

Gerald's room was dark, and she had to push through the usual barricade. The smell of whisky was everywhere; it even flew up in the striking of the match when she lighted the jet.

"It's night," said Clytie presently.

Gerald lay on his bed looking at her. In the bad light he resembled his father.

"There's some more coffee down in the kitchen," said Clytie.

"Would you bring it to me?" Gerald asked. He stared at her in an exhausted, serious way.

She stooped and held him up. He drank the coffee while she bent over him with her eyes closed, resting.

Presently he pushed her away and fell back on the bed, and began to describe how nice it was when he had a little house of his own down the street, all new, with all conveniences, gas stove, electric lights, when he was married to Rosemary. Rosemary—she had given up a job in the next town, just to marry him. How had it happened that she had left him so soon? It meant nothing that he had threatened time and again to shoot her, it was nothing at all that he had pointed the gun against her breast. She had not understood. It was only that he had relished his contentment. He had only wanted to play with her. In a way he had wanted to show her that he loved her above life and death.

"Above life and death," he repeated, closing his eyes.

Clytie did not make an answer, as Octavia always did during these scenes, which were bound to end in Gerald's tears.

Outside the closed window a mockingbird began to sing. Clytie held back the curtain and pressed her ear against the glass. The rain had stopped. The bird's song sounded in liquid drops down through the pitch-black trees and the night.

"Go to hell," Gerald said. His head was under the pillow.

She took up the tray, and left Gerald with his face hidden. It was not necessary for her to look at any of their faces. It was their faces which came between.

Hurrying, she went down to the kitchen and began to eat her own supper.

Their faces came between her face and another. It was their faces which had come pushing in between, long ago, to hide some face that had looked back at her. And now it was hard to remember the way it looked, or the time when she had seen it first. It must have been when she was young. Yes, in a sort of arbor, hadn't she laughed, leaned forward . . . and that vision of a face—which was a little like all the other faces, the trusting child's, the innocent old traveler's, even the greedy barber's and Lethy's and the wandering peddlers' who one by one knocked and went unanswered at the door—and yet different, yet far more—this face had been very close to hers, almost familiar, almost accessible. And then the face of Octavia was thrust between, and at other times the apoplectic face of her father, the face of her brother Gerald and the face of her brother Henry with the bullet hole through the forehead. . . . It was purely for a resemblance to a vision that she examined the secret, mysterious, unrepeated faces she met in the street of Farr's Gin.

But there was always an interruption. If anyone spoke to her, she fled. If she saw she was going to meet someone on the street, she had been known to dart behind a bush and hold a small branch in front of her face until the person had gone by. When anyone called her by name, she turned first red, then white, and looked somehow, as one of the ladies in the store remarked, *disappointed.*

She was becoming more frightened all the time, too. People could tell because she never dressed up any more. For years, every once in a while, she would come out in what was called an "outfit," all in hunter's green, a hat that came down around her face like a bucket, a green silk dress, even green shoes with pointed toes. She would wear the outfit all one day, if it was a pretty day, and then next morning she would be back in the faded jumper with her old hat tied under the chin, as if the outfit had been a dream. It had been a long time now since Clytie had dressed up so that you could see her coming.

Once in a while when a neighbor, trying to be kind or only being curious, would ask her opinion about anything—such as a pattern of crochet—she would not run away; but, giving a thin trapped smile, she would say in a childish voice, "It's nice." But, the ladies always added, nothing that came anywhere close to the Farrs' house was nice for long.

"It's nice," said Clytie when the old lady next door showed her the new rosebush she had planted, all in bloom.

But before an hour was gone, she came running out of her house screaming, "My sister Octavia says you take that rosebush up! My sister Octavia says you take that rosebush up and move it away from our fence! If you don't I'll kill you! You take it away."

And on the other side of the Farrs lived a family with a little boy who was always playing in his yard. Octavia's cat would go under the fence, and he would take it and hold it in his arms. He had a song he sang to the Farrs' cat. Clytie would come running straight out of the house, flaming with her message from Octavia. "Don't you do that! Don't you do that!" she would cry in anguish. "If you do that again, I'll have to kill you!"

And she would run back to the vegetable patch and begin to curse.

The cursing was new, and she cursed softly, like a singer going over a song for the first time. But it was something she could not stop. Words which at first horrified Clytie poured in a full, light stream from her throat, which soon, nevertheless, felt strangely relaxed and rested. She cursed all alone in the peace of the vegetable garden. Everybody said, in something like deprecation, that she was only imitating her older sister, who used to go out to that same garden and curse in that same way, years ago, but in a remarkably loud, commanding voice that could be heard in the post office.

Sometimes in the middle of her words Clytie glanced up to where Octavia, at her window, looked down at her. When she let the curtain drop at last, Clytie would be left there speechless.

Finally, in a gentleness compounded of fright and exhaustion and love, an overwhelming love, she would wander through the gate and out through the town, gradually beginning to move faster, until her long legs gathered a ridiculous, rushing speed. No one in town could have kept up with Miss Clytie, they said, giving them an even start.

She always ate rapidly, too, all alone in the kitchen, as she was eating now. She bit the meat savagely from the heavy silver fork and gnawed the little chicken bone until it was naked and clean.

Halfway upstairs, she remembered Gerald's second pot of coffee, and went back for it. After she had carried the other trays down again and washed the dishes, she did not forget to try all the doors and windows to make sure that everything was locked up absolutely tight.

The next morning, Clytie bit into smiling lips as she cooked breakfast. Far out past the secretly opened window a freight train was crossing the bridge in the sunlight. Some Negroes filed down the road going fishing, and Mr Tom Bate's Boy, who was going along, turned and looked at her through the window.

Gerald had appeared dressed and wearing his spectacles, and announced that he was going to the store today. The old Farr furnishing store did little business now, and people hardly missed Gerald when he did not come; in fact, they could hardly tell when he did because of the big boots strung on a wire, which almost hid the cagelike office. A little high-school girl could wait on anybody who came in.

Now Gerald entered the dining room.

"How are you this morning, Clytie?" he asked.

"Just fine, Gerald, how are you?"

"I'm going to the store," he said.

He sat down stiffly, and she laid a place on the table before him.

From above, Octavia screamed, "Where in the devil is my thimble, you stole my thimble, Clytie Farr, you carried it away, my little silver thimble!"

"It's started," said Gerald intensely. Clytie saw his fine, thin, almost black lips spread in a crooked line. "How can a man live in the house with women? How can he?"

He jumped up, and tore his napkin exactly in two. He walked out of the dining room without eating the first bite of his breakfast. She heard him going back upstairs into his room.

"My thimble!" screamed Octavia.

She waited one moment. Crouching eagerly, rather like a

little squirrel, Clytie ate part of her breakfast over the stove before going up the stairs.

At nine Mr Bobo, the barber, knocked at the front door.

Without waiting, for they never answered the knock, he let himself in and advanced like a small general down the hall. There was the old organ that was never uncovered or played except for funerals, and then nobody was invited. He went ahead, under the arm of the tiptoed male statue and up the dark stairway. There they were, lined up at the head of the stairs, and they all looked at him with repulsion. Mr Bobo was convinced that they were every one mad. Gerald, even, had already been drinking, at nine o'clock in the morning.

Mr Bobo was short and had never been anything but proud of it, until he had started coming to this house once a week. But he did not enjoy looking up from below at the soft, long throats, the cold, repelled, high-reliefed faces of those Farrs. He could only imagine what one of those sisters would do to him if he made one move. (As if he would!) As soon as he arrived upstairs, they all went off and left him. He pushed out his chin and stood with his round legs wide apart, just looking around. The upstairs hall was absolutely bare. There was not even a chair to sit down in.

"Either they sell away their furniture in the dead of night," said Mr Bobo to the people of Farr's Gin, "or else they're just too plumb mean to use it."

Mr Bobo stood and waited to be summoned, and wished he had never started coming to this house to shave old Mr Farr. But he had been so surprised to get a letter in the mail. The letter was on such old, yellowed paper that at first he thought it must have been written a thousand years ago and never delivered. It was signed "Octavia Farr," and began without even calling him "Dear Mr Bobo." What it said was: "Come to this residence at nine o'clock each Friday morning until further notice, where you will shave Mr James Farr."

He thought he would go one time. And each time after that, he thought he would never go back—especially when he never knew when they would pay him anything. Of course, it was something to be the only person in Farr's Gin allowed inside the house (except for the undertaker, who had gone there when young Henry shot himself, but had never to that day spoken of it). It was not easy to shave a man as bad off as Mr Farr, either—not anything like as easy as to shave a corpse or even a fighting-drunk field hand. Suppose you were like this, Mr Bobo would say: you couldn't move your face; you couldn't hold up your chin, or tighten your jaw, or even bat your eyes when the razor came close. The trouble with Mr Farr was his face made no resistance to the razor. His face didn't hold.

"I'll never go back," Mr Bobo always ended to his customers. "Not even if they paid me. I've seen enough."

Yet here he was again, waiting before the sickroom door.

"This is the last time," he said. "By God!"

And he wondered why the old man did not die.

Just then Miss Clytie came out of the room. There she came in her funny, sideways walk, and the closer she got to him the more slowly she moved.

"Now?" asked Mr Bobo nervously.

Clytie looked at his small, doubtful face. What fear raced through his little green eyes! His pitiful, greedy, small face—how very mournful it was, like a stray kitten's. What was it that this greedy little thing was so desperately needing?

Clytie came up to the barber and stopped. Instead of telling him that he might go in and shave her father, she put out her hand and with breath-taking gentleness touched the side of his face.

For an instant afterward, she stood looking at him inquiringly, and he stood like a statue, like the statue of Hermes.

Then both of them uttered a despairing cry. Mr Bobo turned and fled, waving his razor around in a circle, down the stairs and out the front door; and Clytie, pale as a ghost, stumbled against the railing. The terrible scent of bay rum, of hair tonic, the horrible moist scratch of an invisible beard, the dense, popping green eyes—what had she got hold of with her hand! She could hardly bear it—the thought of that face.

From the closed door to the sickroom came Octavia's shouting voice.

"Clytie! Clytie! You haven't brought Papa the rain water! Where in the devil is the rain water to shave Papa?"

Clytie moved obediently down the stairs.

Her brother Gerald threw open the door of his room and called after her, "What now? This is a madhouse! Somebody was running past my room, I heard it. Where do you keep your men? Do you have to bring them home?" He slammed the door again, and she heard the barricade going up.

Clytie went through the lower hall and out the back door. She stood beside the old rain barrel and suddenly felt that this object, now, was her friend, just in time, and her arms almost circled it with impatient gratitude. The rain barrel was full. It bore a dark, heavy, penetrating fragrance, like ice and flowers and the dew of night.

Clytie swayed a little and looked into the slightly moving water. She thought she saw a face there.

Of course. It was the face she had been looking for, and from which she had been separated. As if to give a sign, the index finger of a hand lifted to touch the dark cheek.

Clytie leaned closer, as she had leaned down to touch the face of the barber.

It was a wavering, inscrutable face. The brows were drawn together as if in pain. The eyes were large, intent, almost avid, the nose ugly and discolored as if from weeping, the mouth old and closed from any speech. On either side of the head dark hair hung down in a disreputable and wild fashion. Everything about the face frightened and shocked her with its signs of waiting, of suffering.

For the second time that morning, Clytie recoiled, and as she did so, the other recoiled in the same way.

Too late, she recognized the face. She stood there completely sick at heart, as though the poor, half-remembered vision had finally betrayed her.

"Clytie! Clytie! The water! The water!" came Octavia's monumental voice.

Clytie did the only thing she could think of to do. She bent her angular body further, and thrust her head into the barrel, under the water, through its glittering surface into the kind, featureless depth, and held it there.

When Old Lethy found her, she had fallen forward into the barrel, with her poor ladylike black-stockinged legs up-ended and hung apart like a pair of tongs.

Old Mr Marblehall

OLD MR MARBLEHALL never did anything, never got married until he was sixty. You can see him out taking a walk. Watch and you'll see how preciously old people come to think they are made—the way they walk, like conspirators, bent over a little, filled with protection. They stand long on the corners but more impatiently than anyone, as if they expect traffic to take notice of them, rear up the horses and throw on the brakes, so they can go where they want to go. That's Mr Marblehall. He has short white bangs, and a bit of snapdragon in his lapel. He walks with a big polished stick, a present. That's what people think of him. Everybody says to his face, "So well preserved!" Behind his back they say cheerfully, "One foot in the grave." He has on his thick, beautiful, glowing coat—tweed, but he looks as gratified as an animal in its own tingling fur. You see, even in summer he wears it, because he is cold all the time. He looks quaintly secretive and prepared for anything, out walking very luxuriously on Catherine Street.

His wife, back at home in the parlor standing up to think, is a large, elongated old woman with electric-looking hair and curly lips. She has spent her life trying to escape from the parlor-like jaws of self-consciousness. Her late marriage has set in upon her nerves like a retriever nosing and puffing through old dead leaves out in the woods. When she walks around the room she looks remote and nebulous, out on the fringe of habitation, and rather as if she must have been cruelly trained—otherwise she couldn't do actual, immediate things, like answering the telephone or putting on a hat. But she has gone further than you'd think: into club work. Surrounded by other more suitably exclaiming women, she belongs to the Daughters of the American Revolution and the United Daughters of the Confederacy, attending teas. Her long, disquieted figure towering in the candlelight of other women's houses looks like something accidental. Any occasion, and she dresses her hair like a unicorn horn. She even sings, and is requested to sing. She even writes some of the songs she sings

("O Trees in the Evening"). She has a voice that dizzies other ladies like an organ note, and amuses men like a halloo down the well. It's full of a hollow wind and echo, winding out through the wavery hope of her mouth. Do people know of her perpetual amazement? Back in safety she wonders, her untidy head trembles in the domestic dark. She remembers how everyone in Natchez will suddenly grow quiet around her. Old Mrs Marblehall, Mr Marblehall's wife: she even goes out in the rain, which Southern women despise above everything, in big neat biscuit-colored galoshes, for which she "ordered off." She is only looking around—servile, undelighted, sleepy, expensive, tortured Mrs Marblehall, pinning her mind with a pin to her husband's diet. She wants to tempt him, she tells him. What would he like best, that he can have?

There is Mr Marblehall's ancestral home. It's not so wonderfully large—it has only four columns—but you always look toward it, the way you always glance into tunnels and see nothing. The river is after it now, and the little back garden has assuredly crumbled away, but the box maze is there on the edge like a trap, to confound the Mississippi River. Deep in the red wall waits the front door—it weighs such a lot, it is perfectly solid, all one piece, black mahogany. . . . And you see—one of *them* is always going in it. There is a knocker shaped like a gasping fish on the door. You have every reason in the world to imagine the inside is dark, with old things about. There's many a big, deathly-looking tapestry, wrinkling and thin, many a sofa shaped like an S. Brocades as tall as the wicked queens in Italian tales stand gathered before the windows. Everything is draped and hooded and shaded, of course, unaffectionate but close. Such rosy lamps! The only sound would be a breath against the prisms, a stirring of the chandelier. It's like old eyelids, the house with one of its shutters, in careful working order, slowly opening outward. Then the little son softly comes and stares out like a kitten, with button nose and pointed ears and little fuzz of silky hair running along the top of his head.

The son is the worst of all. Mr and Mrs Marblehall had a child! When both of them were terribly old, they had this little, amazing, fascinating son. You can see how people are taken aback, how they jerk and throw up their hands every time they so much as think about it. At least, Mr Marblehall sees them. He thinks Natchez people do nothing themselves, and really, most of them have done or could do the same thing. This son is six years old now. Close up, he has a monkey look, a very penetrating look. He has very sparse Japanese hair, tiny little pearly teeth, long little wilted fingers. Every day he is slowly and expensively dressed and taken to the Catholic school. He looks quietly and maliciously absurd, out walking with old Mr Marblehall or old Mrs Marblehall, placing his small booted foot on a little green worm, while they stop and wait on him. Everybody passing by thinks that he looks quite as if he thinks his parents had him just to show they could. You see, it becomes complicated, full of vindictiveness.

But now, as Mr Marblehall walks as briskly as possible toward the river where there is sun, you have to merge him back into his proper blur, into the little party-giving town he lives in. Why look twice at him? There has been an old Mr Marblehall in Natchez ever since the first one arrived back in 1818—with a theatrical presentation of Otway's *Venice*, ending with *A Laughable Combat between Two Blind Fiddlers*—an actor! Mr Marblehall isn't so important. His name is on the list, he is forgiven, but nobody gives a hoot about any old Mr Marblehall. He could die, for all they care; some people even say, "Oh, is he still alive?" Mr Marblehall walks and walks, and now and then he is driven in his ancient fringed carriage with the candle burners like empty eyes in front. And yes, he is supposed to travel for his health. But why consider his absence? There isn't any other place besides Natchez, and even if there were, it would hardly be likely to change Mr Marblehall if it were brought up against him. Big fingers could pick him up off the Esplanade and take him through the air, his old legs still measuredly walking in a dangle, and set him down where he could continue that same old Natchez stroll of his in the East or the West or Kingdom Come. What difference could anything make now about old Mr Marblehall—so late? A week or two would go by in Natchez and then there would be Mr Marblehall, walking down Catherine Street again, still exactly in the same degree alive and old.

People naturally get bored. They say, "Well, he waited till

he was sixty years old to marry, and what did he want to marry for?" as though what he did were the excuse for their boredom and their lack of concern. Even the thought of his having a stroke right in front of one of the Pilgrimage houses during Pilgrimage Week makes them only sigh, as if to say it's nobody's fault but his own if he wants to be so insultingly and precariously well-preserved. He ought to have a little black boy to follow around after him. Oh, his precious old health, which never had reason to be so inspiring! Mr Marblehall has a formal, reproachful look as he stands on the corners arranging himself to go out into the traffic to cross the streets. It's as if he's thinking of shaking his stick and saying, "Well, look! I've done it, don't you see?" But really, nobody pays much attention to his look. He is just like other people to them. He could have easily danced with a troupe of angels in Paradise every night, and they wouldn't have guessed. Nobody is likely to find out that he is leading a double life.

The funny thing is he just recently began to lead this double life. He waited until he was sixty years old. Isn't he crazy? Before that, he'd never done anything. He didn't know what to do. Everything was for all the world like his first party. He stood about, and looked in his father's books, and long ago he went to France, but he didn't like it.

Drive out any of these streets in and under the hills and you find yourself lost. You see those scores of little galleried houses nearly alike. See the yellowing China trees at the eaves, the round flower beds in the front yards, like bites in the grass, listen to the screen doors whining, the ice wagons dragging by, the twittering noises of children. Nobody ever looks to see who is living in a house like that. These people come out themselves and sprinkle the hose over the street at this time of day to settle the dust, and after they sit on the porch, they go back into the house, and you hear the radio for the next two hours. It seems to mourn and cry for them. They go to bed early.

Well, old Mr Marblehall can easily be seen standing beside a row of zinnias growing down the walk in front of that little house, bending over, easy, easy, so as not to strain anything, to stare at the flowers. Of course he planted them! They are covered with brown—each petal is a little heart-shaped pocket of dust. They don't have any smell, you know. It's twilight, all amplified with locusts screaming; nobody could see anything. Just what Mr Marblehall is bending over the zinnias for is a mystery, any way you look at it. But there he is, quite visible, alive and old, leading his double life.

There's his other wife, standing on the night-stained porch by a potted fern, screaming things to a neighbor. This wife is really worse than the other one. She is more solid, fatter, shorter, and while not so ugly, funnier looking. She looks like funny furniture—an unornamented stair post in one of these little houses, with her small monotonous round stupid head—or sometimes like a woodcut of a Bavarian witch, forefinger pointing, with scratches in the air all around her. But she's so static she scarcely moves, from her thick shoulders down past her cylindered brown dress to her short, stubby house slippers. She stands still and screams to the neighbors.

This wife thinks Mr Marblehall's name is Mr Bird. She says, "I declare I told Mr Bird to go to bed, and look at him! I don't understand him!" All her devotion is combustible and goes up in despair. This wife tells everything she knows. Later, after she tells the neighbors, she will tell Mr Marblehall. Cymbal-breasted, she fills the house with wifely complaints. She calls, "After I get Mr Bird to bed, what does he do then? He lies there stretched out with his clothes on and don't have one word to say. Know what he does?"

And she goes on, while her husband bends over the zinnias, to tell what Mr Marblehall (or Mr Bird) does in bed. She does tell the truth. He reads *Terror Tales* and *Astonishing Stories.* She can't see anything to them: they scare her to death. These stories are about horrible and fantastic things happening to nude women and scientists. In one of them, when the characters open bureau drawers, they find a woman's leg with a stocking and garter on. Mrs Bird had to shut the magazine. "The glutinous shadows," these stories say, "the red-eyed, muttering old crone," "the moonlight on her thigh," "an ancient cult of sun worshipers," "an altar suspiciously stained . . ." Mr Marblehall doesn't feel as terrified as all that, but he reads on and on. He is killing time. It is richness without taste, like some holiday food. The clock gets a fruity bursting tick, to get through midnight—then leisurely, leisurely on.

When time is passing it's like a bug in his ear. And then Mr Bird—he doesn't even want a shade on the light, this wife moans respectably. He reads under a bulb. She can tell you how he goes straight through a stack of magazines. "He might just as well not have a family," she always ends, unjustly, and rolls back into the house as if she had been on a little wheel all this time.

But the worst of them all is the other little boy. Another little boy just like the first one. He wanders around the bungalow full of tiny little schemes and jokes. He has lost his front tooth, and in this way he looks slightly different from Mr Marblehall's other little boy—more shocking. Otherwise, you couldn't tell them apart if you wanted to. They both have that look of cunning little jugglers, violently small under some spotlight beam, preoccupied and silent, amusing themselves. Both of the children will go into sudden fits and tantrums that frighten their mothers and Mr Marblehall to death. Then they can get anything they want. But this little boy, the one who's lost the tooth, is the smarter. For a long time he supposed that his mother was totally solid, down to her thick separated ankles. But when she stands there on the porch screaming to the neighbors, she reminds him of those flares that charm him so, that they leave burning in the street at night—the dark solid ball, then, tongue-like, the wicked, yellow, continuous, enslaving blaze on the stem. He knows what his father thinks.

Perhaps one day, while Mr Marblehall is standing there gently bent over the zinnias, this little boy is going to write on a fence, "Papa leads a double life." He finds out things you wouldn't find out. He is a monkey.

You see, one night he is going to follow Mr Marblehall (or Mr Bird) out of the house. Mr Marblehall has said as usual that he is leaving for one of his health trips. He is one of those correct old gentlemen who are still going to the wells and drinking the waters—exactly like his father, the late old Mr Marblehall. But why does he leave on foot? This will occur to the little boy.

So he will follow his father. He will follow him all the way across town. He will see the shining river come winding around. He will see the house where Mr Marblehall turns in at the wrought-iron gate. He will see a big speechless woman come out and lead him in by the heavy door. He will not miss those rosy lamps beyond the many-folded draperies at the windows. He will run around the fountains and around the Japonica trees, past the stone figure of the pigtailed courtier mounted on the goat, down to the back of the house. From there he can look far up at the strange upstairs rooms. In one window the other wife will be standing like a giant, in a long-sleeved gathered nightgown, combing her electric hair and breaking it off each time in the comb. From the next window the other little boy will look out secretly into the night, and see him—or not see him. That would be an interesting thing, a moment of strange telepathies. (Mr Marblehall can imagine it.) Then in the corner room there will suddenly be turned on the bright, naked light. Aha! Father!

Mr Marblehall's little boy will easily climb a tree there and peep through the window. There, under a stark shadeless bulb, on a great four-poster with carved griffins, will be Mr Marblehall, reading *Terror Tales*, stretched out and motionless.

Then everything will come out.

At first, nobody will believe it.

Or maybe the policeman will say, "Stop! How dare you!"

Maybe, better than that, Mr Marblehall himself will confess his duplicity—how he has led two totally different lives, with completely different families, two sons instead of one. What an astonishing, unbelievable, electrifying confession that would be, and how his two wives would topple over, how his sons would cringe! To say nothing of most men aged sixty-six. So thinks self-consoling Mr Marblehall.

You will think, what if nothing ever happens? What if there is no climax, even to this amazing life? Suppose old Mr Marblehall simply remains alive, getting older by the minute, shuttling, still secretly, back and forth?

Nobody cares. Not an inhabitant of Natchez, Mississippi, cares if he is deceived by old Mr Marblehall. Neither does anyone care that Mr Marblehall has finally caught on, he thinks, to what people are supposed to do. This is it: they endure something inwardly—for a time secretly; they establish a past, a memory; thus they store up life. He has done this;

most remarkably, he has even multiplied his life by deception; and plunging deeper and deeper he speculates upon some glorious finish, a great explosion of revelations . . . the future.

But he still has to kill time, and get through the clocking nights. Otherwise he dreams that he is a great blazing butterfly stitching up a net; which doesn't make sense.

Old Mr Marblehall! He may have years ahead yet in which to wake up bolt upright in the bed under the naked bulb, his heart thumping, his old eyes watering and wild, imagining that if people knew about his double life, they'd die.

Flowers for Marjorie

HE WAS one of the modest, the shy, the sandy haired—one of those who would always have preferred waiting to one side. . . . A row of feet rested beside his own where he looked down. Beyond was the inscribed base of the drinking fountain which stemmed with a troubled sound up into the glare of the day. The feet were in Vs, all still. Then down at the end of the bench, one softly began to pat. It made an innuendo at a dainty pink chewing-gum wrapper blowing by.

He would not look up. When the chewing-gum wrapper blew over and tilted at his foot, he spat at some sensing of invitation and kicked it away. He held a toothpick in his mouth.

Someone spoke. "You goin' to join the demonstration at two 'clock?"

Howard lifted his gaze no further than the baggy corduroy knees in front of his own.

"Demonstration . . . ?" The tasteless toothpick stuck to his lip; what he said was indistinct.

But he snapped the toothpick finally with his teeth and puffed it out of his mouth. It landed in the grass like a little tent. He was surprised at the sight of it, and at his neatness and proficiency in blowing it out. And that little thing started up all the pigeons. His eyes ached when they whirled all at once, as though a big spoon stirred them in the sunshine. He closed his eyes upon their flying opal-changing wings.

And then, with his eyes shut, he had to think about Marjorie. Always now like something he had put off, the thought of her was like a wave that hit him when he was tired, rising impossibly out of stagnancy and deprecation while he sat in the park, towering over his head, pounding, falling, going back and leaving nothing behind it.

He stood up, looked at the position of the sun, and slowly started back to her.

He was panting from the climb of four flights, and his hand groped for the knob in the hall shadows. As soon as he opened the door he shrugged and threw his hat on the bed, so Marjorie would not ask him how he came out looking about the job at Columbus Circle; for today, he had not gone back to inquire.

Nothing was said, and he sat for a while on the couch, his hands spread on his knees. Then, before he would meet her eye, he looked at the chair in the room, which neither one would use, and there lay Marjorie's coat with a flower stuck in the buttonhole. He gave a silent despairing laugh that turned into a cough.

Marjorie said, "I walked around the block—and look what I found." She too was looking only at the pansy, full of pride.

It was bright yellow. She only found it, Howard thought, but he winced inwardly, as though she had displayed some power of the spirit. He simply had to sit and stare at her, his hands drawn back into his pockets, feeling a match.

Marjorie sat on the little trunk by the window, her round arm on the sill, her soft cut hair now and then blowing and streaming like ribbon-ends over her curling hand where she held her head up. It was hard to remember, in this city of dark, nervous, loud-spoken women, that in Victory, Mississippi, all girls were like Marjorie—and that Marjorie was in turn like his home. . . . Or was she? There were times when Howard would feel lost in the one little room. Marjorie often seemed remote now, or it might have been the excess of life in her rounding body that made her never notice any more the single and lonely life around her, the very pressing life around her. He could only look at her. . . . Her breath whistled a little between her parted lips as she stirred in some momentary discomfort.

Howard lowered his eyes and once again he saw the pansy. There it shone, a wide-open yellow flower with dark red veins and edges. Against the sky-blue of Marjorie's old coat it began in Howard's anxious sight to lose its identity of flower-size and assume the gradual and large curves of a mountain on the horizon of a desert, the veins becoming crevasses, the delicate edges the giant worn lips of a sleeping crater. His heart jumped to his mouth. . . .

He snatched the pansy from Marjorie's coat and tore its

petals off and scattered them on the floor and jumped on them!

Marjorie watched him in silence, and slowly he realized that he had not acted at all, that he had only had a terrible vision. The pansy still blazed on the coat, just as the pigeons had still flown in the park when he was hungry. He sank back onto the couch, trembling with the desire and the pity that had overwhelmed him, and said harshly, "How long before your time comes?"

"Oh, Howard."

"Oh, Howard,"—that was Marjorie. The softness, the reproach—how was he to stop it, ever?

"What did you say?" he asked her.

"Oh, Howard, can't you keep track of the time? Always asking me . . ." She took a breath and said, "In three more months—the end of August."

"This is May," he told her. . . . He almost warned her. "This is May."

"May, June, July, August." She rattled the time off.

"You know for sure—you're certain, it will happen when you say?" He gazed at her.

"Why, of course, Howard, those things always happen when they're supposed to. Nothing can stop me from having the baby, that's sure." Tears came slowly into her eyes.

"Don't cry, Marjorie!" he shouted at her. "Don't cry, don't cry!"

"Even if you don't want it," she said.

He beat his fist down on the old dark red cloth that covered the couch. He felt emotion climbing hand over hand up his body, with its strange and perfect agility. Helplessly he shut his eyes.

"I expect you can find work before then, Howard," she said.

He stood up in wonder: let it be the way she says. He looked searchingly around the room, pressed by tenderness, and softly pulled the pansy from the coat.

Holding it out he crossed to her and dropped soberly onto the floor beside her. His eyes were large. He gave her the flower.

She whispered to him. "We haven't been together in so long." She laid her calm warm hand on his head, covering over the part in his hair, holding him to her side, while he drew deep breaths of the cloverlike smell of her tightening skin and her swollen thighs.

Why, this is not possible! he was thinking. The ticks of the cheap alarm clock grew louder and louder as he buried his face against her, feeling new desperation every moment in the time-marked softness and the pulse of her sheltering body.

But she was talking.

"If they would only give you some paving work for the three months, we could scrape something out of that to pay a nurse, maybe, for a little while afterwards, after the baby comes——"

He jumped to his feet, his muscles as shocked by her words as if they had hurled a pick at the pavement in Columbus Circle at that moment. His sharp words overlaid her murmuring voice.

"Work?" he said sternly, backing away from her, speaking loudly from the middle of the room, almost as if he copied his pose and his voice somehow from the agitators in the park. "When did I ever work? A year ago . . . six months . . . back in Mississippi . . . I've forgotten! Time isn't as easy to count up as you think! I wouldn't know what to do now if they did give me work. I've forgotten! It's all past now. . . . And I don't believe it any more—they won't give me work now—they never will——"

He stopped, and for a moment a look shone in his face, as if he had caught sight of a mirage. Perhaps he could imagine ahead of him some regular and steady division of the day and night, with breakfast appearing in the morning. Then he laughed gently, and moved even further back until he stood against the wall, as far as possible away from Marjorie, as though she were faithless and strange, allied to the other forces.

"Why, Howard, you don't even hope you'll find work any more," she whispered.

"Just because you're going to have a baby, just because that's a thing that's bound to happen, just because you can't go around forever with a baby inside your belly, and it will really happen that the baby is born—that doesn't mean everything else is going to happen and change!" He shouted across at her desperately, leaning against the wall. "That doesn't mean that I will find work! It doesn't mean we aren't starving to death." In some gesture of his despair he had brought his little leather purse from his pocket, and was swinging it violently back and forth. "You may not know it, but you're the only thing left in the world that hasn't stopped!"

The purse, like a little pendulum, slowed down in his hand. He stared at her intently, and then his working mouth drooped, and he stood there holding the purse as still as possible in his palms.

But Marjorie sat as undismayed as anyone could ever be, there on the trunk, looking with her head to one side. Her fullness seemed never to have touched his body. Away at his distance, backed against the wall, he regarded her world of sureness and fruitfulness and comfort, grown forever apart, safe and hopeful in pregnancy, as if he thought it strange that this world, too, should not suffer.

"Have you had anything to eat?" she was asking him.

He was astonished at her; he hated her, then. Inquiring out of her safety into his hunger and weakness! He flung the purse violently to the floor, where it struck softly like the body of a shot bird. It was empty.

Howard walked unsteadily about and came to the stove. He picked up a small clean bent saucepan, and put it down again. They had taken it with them wherever they had moved, from room to room. His hand went to the objects on the shelf as if he were blind. He got hold of the butcher knife. Holding it gently, he turned toward Marjorie.

"Howard, what are you going to do?" she murmured in a patient, lullaby-like voice, as she had asked him so many times.

They were now both far away, remote from each other, detached. Like a flash of lightning he changed his hold on the knife and thrust it under her breast.

The blood ran down the edge of the handle and dripped regularly into her open hand which she held in her lap. How strange! he thought wonderingly. She still leaned back on her other arm, but she must have borne down too heavily upon it, for before long her head bowed slowly over, and her forehead touched the window sill. Her hair began to blow from the back of her head and after a few minutes it was all turned the other way. Her arm that had rested on the window sill in a raised position was just as it was before. Her fingers were relaxed, as if she had just let something fall. There were little white cloudy markings on her nails. It was perfect balance, Howard thought, staring at her arm. That was why Marjorie's arm did not fall. When he finally looked down there was blood everywhere; her lap was like a bowl.

Yes, of course, he thought; for it had all been impossible. He went to wash his hands. The clock ticked dreadfully, so he threw it out the window. Only after a long time did he hear it hit the courtyard below.

His head throbbing in sudden pain, he stooped and picked up his purse. He went out, after closing the door behind him gently.

There in the city the sun slanted onto the streets. It lay upon a thin gray cat watching in front of a barber's pole; as Howard passed, she licked herself over-neatly, staring after him. He set his hat on straight and walked through a crowd of children who surged about a jumping rope, chanting and jumping around him with their lips hanging apart. He crossed a street and a messenger boy banged into him with the wheel of his bicycle, but it never hurt at all.

He walked up Sixth Avenue under the shade of the L, and kept setting his hat on straight. The little spurts of wind tried to take it off and blow it away. How far he would have had to chase it! . . . He reached a crowd of people who were watching a machine behind a window; it made doughnuts very slowly. He went to the next door, where he saw another window full of colored prints of the Virgin Mary and nearly all kinds of birds and animals, and down below these a shelf of little gray pasteboard boxes in which were miniature toilets and night jars to be used in playing jokes, and in the middle box a bulb attached to a long tube, with a penciled sign, "Palpitator—the Imitation Heart. Show her you Love her." An organ grinder immediately removed his hat and played "Valencia."

He went on and in a doorway watched how the auctioneer

leaned out so intimately and waved a pair of gold candlesticks at some men who puffed smoke straight up against the brims of their hats. He passed another place, with the same pictures of the Virgin Mary pinned with straight pins to the door facing, in case they had not been seen the first time. On a dusty table near his hand was a glass-ball paperweight. He reached out with shy joy and touched it, it was so small and round. There was a little scene inside made of bits of colored stuff. That was a bright land under the glass; he would like to be there. It made him smile: it was like everything made small and illuminated and flowering, not too big now. He turned the ball upside down with a sort of instinct, and in shocked submission and pity saw the landscape deluged in a small fury of snow. He stood for a moment fascinated, and then, suddenly aware of his great size, he put the paperweight back where he had found it, and stood shaking in the door. A man passing by dropped a dime into his open hand.

Then he found himself in the tunnel of a subway. All along the tile wall was written, "God sees me, God sees me, God sees me, God sees me"—four times where he walked by. He read the signs, "Entrance" and "Exit Only," and where someone had printed "Nuts!" under both words. He looked at himself in a chewing-gum-machine mirror and straightened his hat before entering the train.

In the car he looked above the heads of the people at the pictures on the advertisements, and saw many couples embracing and smiling. A beggar came through with a cane and sang "Let Me Call You Sweetheart" like a blind man, and he too was given a dime. As Howard left the car a guard told him to watch his step. He clutched his hat. The wind blew underground, too, whistling down the tracks after the trains. He went up the stairs between two old warm Jewish women.

Up above, he went into a bar and had a drink of whisky, and though he could not pay for that, he had a nickel left over from the subway ride. In the back he heard a slot machine being played. He moved over and stood for a while between two friendly men and then put in the nickel. The many nickels that poured spurting and clanging out of the hole sickened him; they fell all over his legs, and he backed up against the dusty red curtain. His hat slid off onto the floor. They all rushed to pick it up, and some of them gave him handfuls of nickels to hold and bought him drinks with the rest. One of them said, "Fella, you ought not to let all hell loose that way." It was a Southern man. Howard agreed that they should all have drinks around and that his fortune belonged to them all.

But after he had walked around outside awhile he still had nowhere in his mind to go. He decided to try the W.P.A. office and Miss Ferguson. Miss Ferguson knew him. There was an old habit he used to have of going up to see her.

He went into the front office. He could see Miss Ferguson through the door, typing the same as ever.

"Oh, Miss Ferguson!" he called softly, leaning forward in all his confidence. He reached up, ready to remove his hat, but she went on typing.

"Oh, Miss Ferguson!"

A woman who did not know him at all came into the room.

"Did you receive a card to call?" she asked.

"Miss Ferguson," he repeated, peering around her red arm to keep his eye on the typewriter.

"Miss Ferguson is busy," said the red-armed woman.

If he could only tell Miss Ferguson everything, everything in his life! Howard was thinking. Then it would come clear, and Miss Ferguson would write a note on a little card and hand it to him, tell him exactly where he could go and what he could do.

When the red-armed woman walked out of the office, Howard tried to win Miss Ferguson over. She could be very sympathetic.

"Somebody told me you could type!" he called softly, in complimentary tones.

Miss Ferguson looked up. "Yes, that's right, I can type," she said, and went on typing.

"I got something to tell you," Howard said. He smiled at her.

"Some other time," replied Miss Ferguson over the sound of the keys. "I'm busy now. You'd better go home and sleep it off, h'm?"

Howard dropped his arm. He waited, and tried desperately to think of an answer to that. He was gazing into the water cooler, in which minute air bubbles swam. But he could think of nothing.

He lifted his hat with a strange jauntiness which may have stood for pride.

"Good-by, Miss Ferguson!"

And he was back on the street.

He walked further and further. It was late when he turned into a large arcade, and when he followed someone through a free turnstile, a woman marched up to him and said, "You are the ten millionth person to enter Radio City, and you will broadcast over a nationwide red-and-blue network tonight at six o'clock, Eastern standard time. What is your name, address, and phone number? Are you married? Accept these roses and the key to the city."

She gave him a great heavy key and an armful of bright red roses. He tried to give them back to her at first, but she had not waited a moment. A ring of men with hawklike faces aimed cameras at him and all took his picture, to the flashing of lights.

"What is your occupation?"

"Are you married?"

Almost in his face a large woman with feathery furs and a small brown wire over one tooth was listening, and others were waiting behind her.

He watched for an opening, and when they were not looking he broke through and ran.

He ran down Sixth Avenue as fast as he could, ablaze with horror, the roses nodding like heads in his arm, the key prodding his side. With his free hand he held determinedly to his hat. Doorways and intersections blurred past. All shining within was a restaurant beside him, but now it was too late to be hungry. He wanted only to get home. He could not see easily, but traffic seemed to stop softly when he ran thundering by; horses under the L drew up, and trucks kindly contracted, as if on a bellows, in front of him. People seemed to melt out of his way. He thought that maybe he was dead, and now in the end everything and everybody was afraid of him.

When he reached his street his breath was gone. There were the children playing. They were afraid of him and let him by. He ran into the courtyard, and stopped still.

There on the walk was the clock.

It lay on its face, and scattered about it in every direction were wheels and springs and bits of glass. He bent over and looked at the tiny little pieces.

At last he climbed the stairs. Somehow he tried to unlock the door with the key to the city. But the door was not locked at all, and when he got inside, he looked over to the window and there was Marjorie on the little trunk. Then the roses gave out deep waves of fragrance. He stroked their soft leaves. Marjorie's arm had fallen down; the balance was gone, and now her hand hung out the window as if to catch the wind.

Then Howard knew for a fact that everything had stopped. It was just as he had feared, just as he had dreamed. He had had a dream to come true.

He backed away slowly, until he was out of the room. Then he ran down the stairs.

On the street corner the first person he saw was a policeman watching pigeons flying.

Howard went up and stood for a little while beside him.

"Do you know what's up there in that room?" he asked finally. He was embarrassed to be asking anything of a policeman and to be holding such beautiful flowers.

"What is that?" asked the policeman.

Howard bent his head and buried his eyes, nose, and mouth in the roses. "A dead woman. Marjorie is dead."

Although the street-intersection sign was directly over their heads, and in the air where the pigeons flew the chimes of a clock were striking six, even the policeman did not seem for a moment to be sure of the time and place they were in, but had to consult his own watch and pocket effects.

"Oh!" and "So!" the policeman kept saying, while Howard in perplexity turned his head from side to side. He looked at him steadily, memorizing for all time the nondescript, dusty figure with the wide gray eyes and the sandy hair. "And I don't suppose the red drops on your pants are rose petals, are they?"

He grasped the staring man finally by the arm.

"Don't be afraid, big boy. *I'll* go up with you," he said.

They turned and walked back side by side. When the roses slid from Howard's fingers and fell on their heads all along the sidewalk, the little girls ran stealthily up and put them in their hair.

A Curtain of Green

EVERY DAY one summer in Larkin's Hill, it rained a little. The rain was a regular thing, and would come about two o'clock in the afternoon.

One day, almost as late as five o'clock, the sun was still shining. It seemed almost to spin in a tiny groove in the polished sky, and down below, in the trees along the street and in the rows of flower gardens in the town, every leaf reflected the sun from a hardness like a mirror surface. Nearly all the women sat in the windows of their houses, fanning and sighing, waiting for the rain.

Mrs Larkin's garden was a large, densely grown plot running downhill behind the small white house where she lived alone now, since the death of her husband. The sun and the rain that beat down so heavily that summer had not kept her from working there daily. Now the intense light like a tweezers picked out her clumsy, small figure in its old pair of men's overalls rolled up at the sleeves and trousers, separated it from the thick leaves, and made it look strange and yellow as she worked with a hoe—over-vigorous, disreputable, and heedless.

Within its border of hedge, high like a wall, and visible only from the upstairs windows of the neighbors, this slanting, tangled garden, more and more overabundant and confusing, must have become so familiar to Mrs Larkin that quite possibly by now she was unable to conceive of any other place. Since the accident in which her husband was killed, she had never once been seen anywhere else. Every morning she might be observed walking slowly, almost timidly, out of the white house, wearing a pair of the untidy overalls, often with her hair streaming and tangled where she had neglected to comb it. She would wander about for a little while at first, uncertainly, deep among the plants and wet with their dew, and yet not quite putting out her hand to touch anything. And then a sort of sturdiness would possess her—stabilize her; she would stand still for a moment, as if a blindfold were being removed; and then she would kneel in the flowers and begin to work.

She worked without stopping, almost invisibly, submerged all day among the thick, irregular, sloping beds of plants. The servant would call her at dinnertime, and she would obey; but it was not until it was completely dark that she would truthfully give up her labor and with a drooping, submissive walk appear at the house, slowly opening the small low door at the back. Even the rain would bring only a pause to her. She would move to the shelter of the pear tree, which in mid-April hung heavily almost to the ground in brilliant full leaf, in the center of the garden.

It might seem that the extreme fertility of her garden formed at once a preoccupation and a challenge to Mrs Larkin. Only by ceaseless activity could she cope with the rich blackness of this soil. Only by cutting, separating, thinning and tying back in the clumps of flowers and bushes and vines could she have kept them from overreaching their boundaries and multiplying out of all reason. The daily summer rains could only increase her vigilance and her already excessive energy. And yet, Mrs Larkin rarely cut, separated, tied back. . . . To a certain extent, she seemed not to seek for order, but to allow an overflowering, as if she consciously ventured forever a little farther, a little deeper, into her life in the garden.

She planted every kind of flower that she could find or order from a catalogue—planted thickly and hastily, without stopping to think, without any regard for the ideas that her neighbors might elect in their club as to what constituted an appropriate vista, or an effect of restfulness, or even harmony of color. Just to what end Mrs Larkin worked so strenuously in her garden, her neighbors could not see. She certainly never sent a single one of her fine flowers to any of them. They might get sick and die, and she would never send a flower. And if she thought of *beauty* at all (they regarded her stained overalls, now almost of a color with the leaves), she certainly did not strive for it in her garden. It was impossible to enjoy looking at such a place. To the neighbors gazing down from their upstairs windows it had the appearance of a sort of jungle, in which the slight, heedless form of its owner daily lost itself.

At first, after the death of Mr Larkin—for whose father, after all, the town had been named—they had called upon the widow with decent frequency. But she had not appreciated it, they said to one another. Now, occasionally, they looked down from their bedroom windows as they brushed studiously at their hair in the morning; they found her place in the garden, as they might have run their fingers toward a city on a map of a foreign country, located her from their distance almost in curiosity, and then forgot her.

Early that morning they had heard whistling in the Larkin garden. They had recognized Jamey's tune, and had seen him kneeling in the flowers at Mrs Larkin's side. He was only the colored boy who worked in the neighborhood by the day. Even Jamey, it was said, Mrs Larkin would tolerate only now and then. . . .

Throughout the afternoon she had raised her head at intervals to see how fast he was getting along in his transplanting. She had to make him finish before it began to rain. She was busy with the hoe, clearing one of the last patches of uncultivated ground for some new shrubs. She bent under the sunlight, chopping in blunt, rapid, tireless strokes. Once she raised her head far back to stare at the flashing sky. Her eyes were dull and puckered, as if from long impatience or bewilderment. Her mouth was a sharp line. People said she never spoke.

But memory tightened about her easily, without any prelude of warning or even despair. She would see promptly, as if a curtain had been jerked quite unceremoniously away from a little scene, the front porch of the white house, the shady street in front, and the blue automobile in which her husband approached, driving home from work. It was a summer day, a day from the summer before. In the freedom of gaily turning her head, a motion she was now forced by memory to repeat as she hoed the ground, she could see again the tree that was going to fall. There had been no warning. But there was the enormous tree, the fragrant chinaberry tree, suddenly tilting, dark and slow like a cloud, leaning down to her husband.

From her place on the front porch she had spoken in a soft voice to him, never so intimate as at that moment, "You can't be hurt." But the tree had fallen, had struck the car exactly so as to crush him to death. She had waited there on the porch for a time afterward, not moving at all—in a sort of recollection—as if to reach under and bring out from obliteration her protective words and to try them once again . . . so as to change the whole happening. It was accident that was incredible, when her love for her husband was keeping him safe.

She continued to hoe the breaking ground, to beat down the juicy weeds. Presently she became aware that hers was the only motion to continue in the whole slackened place. There was no wind at all now. The cries of the birds had hushed. The sun seemed clamped to the side of the sky. Everything had stopped once again, the stillness had mesmerized the stems of the plants, and all the leaves went suddenly into thickness. The shadow of the pear tree in the center of the garden lay callous on the ground. Across the yard, Jamey knelt, motionless.

"Jamey!" she called angrily.

But her voice hardly carried in the dense garden. She felt all at once terrified, as though her loneliness had been pointed out by some outside force whose finger parted the hedge. She drew her hand for an instant to her breast. An obscure fluttering there frightened her, as though the force babbled to her, *The bird that flies within your heart could not divide this cloudy air* . . . She stared without expression at the garden. She was clinging to the hoe, and she stared across the green leaves toward Jamey.

A look of docility in the Negro's back as he knelt in the plants began to infuriate her. She started to walk toward him, dragging the hoe vaguely through the flowers behind her. She forced herself to look at him, and noticed him closely for the first time—the way he looked like a child. As he turned his head a little to one side and negligently stirred the dirt with his yellow finger, she saw, with a sort of helpless suspicion and hunger, a soft, rather deprecating smile on his face; he was lost in some impossible dream of his own while he was transplanting the little shoots. He was not even whistling; even that sound was gone.

She walked nearer to him—he must have been deaf!—almost stealthily bearing down upon his laxity and his absorption, as if that glimpse of the side of his face, that turned-away smile, were a teasing, innocent, flickering and beautiful vision—some mirage to her strained and wandering eyes.

Yet a feeling of stricture, of a responding hopelessness almost approaching ferocity, grew with alarming quickness about her. When she was directly behind him she stood quite still for a moment, in the queer sheathed manner she had before beginning her gardening in the morning. Then she raised the hoe above her head; the clumsy sleeves both fell back, exposing the thin, unsunburned whiteness of her arms, the shocking fact of their youth.

She gripped the handle tightly, tightly, as though convinced that the wood of the handle could feel, and that all her strength could indent its surface with pain. The head of Jamey, bent there below her, seemed witless, terrifying, wonderful, almost inaccessible to her, and yet in its explicit nearness meant surely for destruction, with its clustered hot woolly hair, its intricate, glistening ears, its small brown branching streams of sweat, the bowed head holding so obviously and so deafly its ridiculous dream.

Such a head she could strike off, intentionally, so deeply did she know, from the effect of a man's danger and death, its cause in oblivion; and so helpless was she, too helpless to defy the workings of accident, of life and death, of unaccountability. . . . Life and death, she thought, gripping the heavy hoe, life and death, which now meant nothing to her but which she was compelled continually to wield with both her hands, ceaselessly asking, Was it not possible to compensate? to punish? to protest? Pale darkness turned for a moment through the sunlight, like a narrow leaf blown through the garden in a wind.

In that moment, the rain came. The first drop touched her upraised arm. Small, close sounds and coolness touched her.

Sighing, Mrs Larkin lowered the hoe to the ground and laid it carefully among the growing plants. She stood still where she was, close to Jamey, and listened to the rain falling. It was so gentle. It was so full—the sound of the end of waiting.

In the light from the rain, different from sunlight, everything appeared to gleam unreflecting from within itself in its quiet arcade of identity. The green of the small zinnia shoots was very pure, almost burning. One by one, as the rain reached them, all the individual little plants shone out, and then the branching vines. The pear tree gave a soft rushing noise, like the wings of a bird alighting. She could sense behind her, as if a lamp were lighted in the night, the signal-like whiteness of the house. Then Jamey, as if in the shock of realizing the rain had come, turned his full face toward her, questions and delight intensifying his smile, gathering up his aroused, stretching body. He stammered some disconnected words, shyly.

She did not answer Jamey or move at all. She would not feel anything now except the rain falling. She listened for its scattered soft drops between Jamey's words, its quiet touching of the spears of the iris leaves, and a clear sound like a bell as it began to fall into a pitcher the cook had set on the doorstep.

Finally, Jamey stood there quietly, as if waiting for his money, with his hand trying to brush his confusion away from before his face. The rain fell steadily. A wind of deep wet fragrance beat against her.

Then as if it had swelled and broken over a daily levee, tenderness tore and spun through her sagging body.

It has come, she thought senselessly, her head lifting and her eyes looking without understanding at the sky which had begun to move, to fold nearer in softening, dissolving clouds. It was almost dark. Soon the loud and gentle night of rain would come. It would pound upon the steep roof of the white house. Within, she would lie in her bed and hear the rain. On and on it would fall, beat and fall. The day's work would be over in the garden. She would lie in bed, her arms tired at her sides and in motionless peace: against that which was inexhaustible, there was no defense.

Then Mrs Larkin sank in one motion down into the flowers and lay there, fainting and streaked with rain. Her face was fully upturned, down among the plants, with the hair beaten away from her forehead and her open eyes closing at once when the rain touched them. Slowly her lips began to part.

She seemed to move slightly, in the sad adjustment of a sleeper.

Jamey ran jumping and crouching about her, drawing in his breath alternately at the flowers breaking under his feet and at the shapeless, passive figure on the ground. Then he became quiet, and stood back at a little distance and looked in awe at the unknowing face, white and rested under its bombardment. He remembered how something had filled him with stillness when he felt her standing there behind him looking down at him, and he would not have turned around at that moment for anything in the world. He remembered all the while the oblivious crash of the windows next door being shut when the rain started. . . . But now, in this unseen place, it was he who stood looking at poor Mrs Larkin.

He bent down and in a horrified, piteous, beseeching voice he began to call her name until she stirred.

"Miss Lark'! Miss Lark'!"

Then he jumped nimbly to his feet and ran out of the garden.

A Visit of Charity

IT WAS mid-morning—a very cold, bright day. Holding a potted plant before her, a girl of fourteen jumped off the bus in front of the Old Ladies' Home, on the outskirts of town. She wore a red coat, and her straight yellow hair was hanging down loose from the pointed white cap all the little girls were wearing that year. She stopped for a moment beside one of the prickly dark shrubs with which the city had beautified the Home, and then proceeded slowly toward the building, which was of whitewashed brick and reflected the winter sunlight like a block of ice. As she walked vaguely up the steps she shifted the small pot from hand to hand; then she had to set it down and remove her mittens before she could open the heavy door.

"I'm a Campfire Girl. . . . I have to pay a visit to some old lady," she told the nurse at the desk. This was a woman in a white uniform who looked as if she were cold; she had close-cut hair which stood up on the very top of her head exactly like a sea wave. Marian, the little girl, did not tell her that this visit would give her a minimum of only three points in her score.

"Acquainted with any of our residents?" asked the nurse. She lifted one eyebrow and spoke like a man.

"With any old ladies? No—but—that is, any of them will do," Marian stammered. With her free hand she pushed her hair behind her ears, as she did when it was time to study Science.

The nurse shrugged and rose. "You have a nice *multiflora cineraria* there," she remarked as she walked ahead down the hall of closed doors to pick out an old lady.

There was loose, bulging linoleum on the floor. Marian felt as if she were walking on the waves, but the nurse paid no attention to it. There was a smell in the hall like the interior of a clock. Everything was silent until, behind one of the doors, an old lady of some kind cleared her throat like a sheep bleating. This decided the nurse. Stopping in her tracks, she first extended her arm, bent her elbow, and leaned forward from the hips—all to examine the watch strapped to her wrist; then she gave a loud double-rap on the door.

"There are two in each room," the nurse remarked over her shoulder.

"Two what?" asked Marian without thinking. The sound like a sheep's bleating almost made her turn around and run back.

One old woman was pulling the door open in short, gradual jerks, and when she saw the nurse a strange smile forced her old face dangerously awry. Marian, suddenly propelled by the strong, impatient arm of the nurse, saw next the side-face of another old woman, even older, who was lying flat in bed with a cap on and a counterpane drawn up to her chin.

"Visitor," said the nurse, and after one more shove she was off up the hall.

Marian stood tongue-tied; both hands held the potted plant. The old woman, still with that terrible, square smile (which was a smile of welcome) stamped on her bony face, was waiting. . . . Perhaps she said something. The old woman in bed said nothing at all, and she did not look around.

Suddenly Marian saw a hand, quick as a bird claw, reach up in the air and pluck the white cap off her head. At the same time, another claw to match drew her all the way into the room, and the next moment the door closed behind her.

"My, my, my," said the old lady at her side.

Marian stood enclosed by a bed, a washstand and a chair; the tiny room had altogether too much furniture. Everything smelled wet—even the bare floor. She held onto the back of the chair, which was wicker and felt soft and damp. Her heart beat more and more slowly, her hands got colder and colder, and she could not hear whether the old women were saying anything or not. She could not see them very clearly. How dark it was! The window shade was down, and the only door was shut. Marian looked at the ceiling. . . . It was like being caught in a robbers' cave, just before one was murdered.

"Did you come to be our little girl for a while?" the first robber asked.

Then something was snatched from Marian's hand—the little potted plant.

"Flowers!" screamed the old woman. She stood holding the pot in an undecided way. "Pretty flowers," she added.

Then the old woman in bed cleared her throat and spoke. "They are not pretty," she said, still without looking around, but very distinctly.

Marian suddenly pitched against the chair and sat down in it.

"Pretty flowers," the first old woman insisted. "Pretty— pretty . . ."

Marian wished she had the little pot back for just a moment—she had forgotten to look at the plant herself before giving it away. What did it look like?

"Stinkweeds," said the other old woman sharply. She had a bunchy white forehead and red eyes like a sheep. Now she turned them toward Marian. The fogginess seemed to rise in her throat again, and she bleated, "Who—are—you?"

To her surprise, Marian could not remember her name. "I'm a Campfire Girl," she said finally.

"Watch out for the germs," said the old woman like a sheep, not addressing anyone.

"One came out last month to see us," said the first old woman.

A sheep or a germ? wondered Marian dreamily, holding onto the chair.

"Did not!" cried the other old woman.

"Did so! Read to us out of the Bible, and we enjoyed it!" screamed the first.

"Who enjoyed it!" said the woman in bed. Her mouth was unexpectedly small and sorrowful, like a pet's.

"We enjoyed it," insisted the other. "You enjoyed it—I enjoyed it."

"We all enjoyed it," said Marian, without realizing that she had said a word.

The first old woman had just finished putting the potted plant high, high on the top of the wardrobe, where it could hardly be seen from below. Marian wondered how she had ever succeeded in placing it there, how she could ever have reached so high.

"You mustn't pay any attention to old Addie," she now said to the little girl. "She's ailing today."

"Will you shut your mouth?" said the woman in bed. "I am not."

"You're a story."

"I can't stay but a minute—really, I can't," said Marian suddenly. She looked down at the wet floor and thought that if she were sick in here they would have to let her go.

With much to-do the first old woman sat down in a rocking chair—still another piece of furniture!—and began to rock. With the fingers of one hand she touched a very dirty cameo pin on her chest. "What do you do at school?" she asked.

"I don't know . . ." said Marian. She tried to think but she could not.

"Oh, but the flowers are beautiful," the old woman whispered. She seemed to rock faster and faster; Marian did not see how anyone could rock so fast.

"Ugly," said the woman in bed.

"If we bring flowers——" Marian began, and then fell silent. She had almost said that if Campfire Girls brought flowers to the Old Ladies' Home, the visit would count one extra point, and if they took a Bible with them on the bus and read it to the old ladies, it counted double. But the old woman had not listened, anyway; she was rocking and watching the other one, who watched back from the bed.

"Poor Addie is ailing. She has to take medicine—see?" she said, pointing a horny finger at a row of bottles on the table, and rocking so high that her black comfort shoes lifted off the floor like a little child's.

"I am no more sick than you are," said the woman in bed.

"Oh yes you are!"

"I just got more sense than you have, that's all," said the other old woman, nodding her head.

"That's only the contrary way she talks when *you all* come," said the first old lady with sudden intimacy. She stopped the rocker with a neat pat of her feet and leaned toward Marian. Her hand reached over—it felt like a petunia leaf, clinging and just a little sticky.

"Will you hush! Will you hush!" cried the other one.

Marian leaned back rigidly in her chair.

"When I was a little girl like you, I went to school and all," said the old woman in the same intimate, menacing voice. "Not here—another town. . . ."

"Hush!" said the sick woman. "You never went to school. You never came and you never went. You never were anywhere—only here. You never were born! You don't know anything. Your head is empty, your heart and hands and your old black purse are all empty, even that little old box that you brought with you you brought empty—you showed it to me. And yet you talk, talk, talk, talk, talk all the time until I think I'm losing my mind! Who are you? You're a stranger—a perfect stranger! Don't you know you're a stranger? Is it possible that they have actually done a thing like this to anyone—sent them in a stranger to talk, and rock, and tell away her whole long rigmarole? Do they seriously suppose that I'll be able to keep it up, day in, day out, night in, night out, living in the same room with a terrible old woman—forever?"

Marian saw the old woman's eyes grow bright and turn toward her. This old woman was looking at her with despair and calculation in her face. Her small lips suddenly dropped apart, and exposed a half circle of false teeth with tan gums.

"Come here, I want to tell you something," she whispered. "Come here!"

Marian was trembling, and her heart nearly stopped beating altogether for a moment.

"Now, now, Addie," said the first old woman. "That's not polite. Do you know what's really the matter with old Addie today?" She, too, looked at Marian; one of her eyelids drooped low.

"The matter?" the child repeated stupidly. "What's the matter with her?"

"Why, she's mad because it's her birthday!" said the first old woman, beginning to rock again and giving a little crow as though she had answered her own riddle.

"It is not, it is not!" screamed the old woman in bed. "It is not my birthday, no one knows when that is but myself, and will you please be quiet and say nothing more, or I'll go straight out of my mind!" She turned her eyes toward Marian again, and presently she said in the soft, foggy voice, "When the worst comes to the worst, I ring this bell, and the nurse comes." One of her hands was drawn out from under the patched counterpane—a thin little hand with enormous black freckles. With a finger which would not hold still she pointed to a little bell on the table among the bottles.

"How old are you?" Marian breathed. Now she could see the old woman in bed very closely and plainly, and very abruptly, from all sides, as in dreams. She wondered about her—she wondered for a moment as though there was nothing else in the world to wonder about. It was the first time such a thing had happened to Marian.

"I won't tell!"

The old face on the pillow, where Marian was bending over it, slowly gathered and collapsed. Soft whimpers came out of the small open mouth. It was a sheep that she sounded like—a little lamb. Marian's face drew very close, the yellow hair hung forward.

"She's crying!" She turned a bright, burning face up to the first old woman.

"That's Addie for you," the old woman said spitefully.

Marian jumped up and moved toward the door. For the second time, the claw almost touched her hair, but it was not quick enough. The little girl put her cap on.

"Well, it was a real visit," said the old woman, following Marian through the doorway and all the way out into the hall. Then from behind she suddenly clutched the child with her sharp little fingers. In an affected, high-pitched whine she cried, "Oh, little girl, have you a penny to spare for a poor old woman that's not got anything of her own? We don't have a thing in the world—not a penny for candy—not a thing! Little girl, just a nickel—a penny——"

Marian pulled violently against the old hands for a moment before she was free. Then she ran down the hall, without looking behind her and without looking at the nurse, who was reading *Field & Stream* at her desk. The nurse, after another triple motion to consult her wrist watch, asked automatically the question put to visitors in all institutions: "Won't you stay and have dinner with *us*?"

Marian never replied. She pushed the heavy door open into the cold air and ran down the steps.

Under the prickly shrub she stooped and quickly, without being seen, retrieved a red apple she had hidden there.

Her yellow hair under the white cap, her scarlet coat, her bare knees all flashed in the sunlight as she ran to meet the big bus rocketing through the street.

"Wait for me!" she shouted. As though at an imperial command, the bus ground to a stop.

She jumped on and took a big bite out of the apple.

Death of a Traveling Salesman

R. J. BOWMAN, who for fourteen years had traveled for a shoe company through Mississippi, drove his Ford along a rutted dirt path. It was a long day! The time did not seem to clear the noon hurdle and settle into soft afternoon. The sun, keeping its strength here even in winter, stayed at the top of the sky, and every time Bowman stuck his head out of the dusty car to stare up the road, it seemed to reach a long arm down and push against the top of his head, right through his hat—like the practical joke of an old drummer, long on the road. It made him feel all the more angry and helpless. He was feverish, and he was not quite sure of the way.

This was his first day back on the road after a long siege of influenza. He had had very high fever, and dreams, and had become weakened and pale, enough to tell the difference in the mirror, and he could not think clearly. . . . All afternoon, in the midst of his anger, and for no reason, he had thought of his dead grandmother. She had been a comfortable soul. Once more Bowman wished he could fall into the big feather bed that had been in her room. . . . Then he forgot her again.

This desolate hill country! And he seemed to be going the wrong way—it was as if he were going back, far back. There was not a house in sight. . . . There was no use wishing he were back in bed, though. By paying the hotel doctor his bill he had proved his recovery. He had not even been sorry when the pretty trained nurse said good-by. He did not like illness, he distrusted it, as he distrusted the road without signposts. It angered him. He had given the nurse a really expensive bracelet, just because she was packing up her bag and leaving.

But now—what if in fourteen years on the road he had never been ill before and never had an accident? His record was broken, and he had even begun almost to question it. . . . He had gradually put up at better hotels, in the bigger towns, but weren't they all, eternally, stuffy in summer and drafty in winter? Women? He could only remember little rooms within little rooms, like a nest of Chinese paper boxes, and if he thought of one woman he saw the worn loneliness that the furniture of that room seemed built of. And he himself—he was a man who always wore rather wide-brimmed black hats, and in the wavy hotel mirrors had looked something like a bullfighter, as he paused for that inevitable instant on the landing, walking downstairs to supper. . . . He leaned out of the car again, and once more the sun pushed at his head.

Bowman had wanted to reach Beulah by dark, to go to bed and sleep off his fatigue. As he remembered, Beulah was fifty miles away from the last town, on a graveled road. This was only a cow trail. How had he ever come to such a place? One hand wiped the sweat from his face, and he drove on.

He had made the Beulah trip before. But he had never seen this hill or this petering-out path before—or that cloud, he thought shyly, looking up and then down quickly—any more than he had seen this day before. Why did he not admit he was simply lost and had been for miles? . . . He was not in the habit of asking the way of strangers, and these people never knew where the very roads they lived on went to; but then he had not even been close enough to anyone to call out. People standing in the fields now and then, or on top of the haystacks, had been too far away, looking like leaning sticks or weeds, turning a little at the solitary rattle of his car across their countryside, watching the pale sobered winter dust where it chunked out behind like big squashes down the road. The stares of these distant people had followed him solidly like a wall, impenetrable, behind which they turned back after he had passed.

The cloud floated there to one side like the bolster on his grandmother's bed. It went over a cabin on the edge of a hill, where two bare chinaberry trees clutched at the sky. He drove through a heap of dead oak leaves, his wheels stirring their weightless sides to make a silvery melancholy whistle as the car passed through their bed. No car had been along this way ahead of him. Then he saw that he was on the edge of a ravine that fell away, a red erosion, and that this was indeed the road's end.

He pulled the brake. But it did not hold, though he put all

his strength into it. The car, tipped toward the edge, rolled a little. Without doubt, it was going over the bank.

He got out quietly, as though some mischief had been done him and he had his dignity to remember. He lifted his bag and sample case out, set them down, and stood back and watched the car roll over the edge. He heard something—not the crash he was listening for, but a slow, unuproarious crackle. Rather distastefully he went to look over, and he saw that his car had fallen into a tangle of immense grapevines as thick as his arm, which caught it and held it, rocked it like a grotesque child in a dark cradle, and then, as he watched, concerned somehow that he was not still inside it, released it gently to the ground.

He sighed.

Where am I? he wondered with a shock. Why didn't I do something? All his anger seemed to have drifted away from him. There was the house, back on the hill. He took a bag in each hand and with almost childlike willingness went toward it. But his breathing came with difficulty, and he had to stop to rest.

It was a shotgun house, two rooms and an open passage between, perched on the hill. The whole cabin slanted a little under the heavy heaped-up vine that covered the roof, light and green, as though forgotten from summer. A woman stood in the passage.

He stopped still. Then all of a sudden his heart began to behave strangely. Like a rocket set off, it began to leap and expand into uneven patterns of beats which showered into his brain, and he could not think. But in scattering and falling it made no noise. It shot up with great power, almost elation, and fell gently, like acrobats into nets. It began to pound profoundly, then waited irresponsibly, hitting in some sort of inward mockery first at his ribs, then against his eyes, then under his shoulder blades, and against the roof of his mouth when he tried to say, "Good afternoon, madam." But he could not hear his heart—it was as quiet as ashes falling. This was rather comforting; still, it was shocking to Bowman to feel his heart beating at all.

Stock-still in his confusion, he dropped his bags, which

seemed to drift in slow bulks gracefully through the air and to cushion themselves on the gray prostrate grass near the doorstep.

As for the woman standing there, he saw at once that she was old. Since she could not possibly hear his heart, he ignored the pounding and now looked at her carefully, and yet in his distraction dreamily, with his mouth open.

She had been cleaning the lamp, and held it, half blackened, half clear, in front of her. He saw her with the dark passage behind her. She was a big woman with a weather-beaten but unwrinkled face; her lips were held tightly together, and her eyes looked with a curious dulled brightness into his. He looked at her shoes, which were like bundles. If it were summer she would be barefoot. . . . Bowman, who automatically judged a woman's age on sight, set her age at fifty. She wore a formless garment of some gray coarse material, rough-dried from a washing, from which her arms appeared pink and unexpectedly round. When she never said a word, and sustained her quiet pose of holding the lamp, he was convinced of the strength in her body.

"Good afternoon, madam," he said.

She stared on, whether at him or at the air around him he could not tell, but after a moment she lowered her eyes to show that she would listen to whatever he had to say.

"I wonder if you would be interested——" He tried once more. "An accident—my car . . ."

Her voice emerged low and remote, like a sound across a lake. "Sonny he ain't here."

"Sonny?"

"Sonny ain't here now."

Her son—a fellow able to bring my car up, he decided in blurred relief. He pointed down the hill. "My car's in the bottom of the ditch. I'll need help."

"Sonny ain't here, but he'll be here."

She was becoming clearer to him and her voice stronger, and Bowman saw that she was stupid.

He was hardly surprised at the deepening postponement and tedium of his journey. He took a breath, and heard his voice speaking over the silent blows of his heart. "I was sick. I am not strong yet. . . . May I come in?"

He stooped and laid his big black hat over the handle on his bag. It was a humble motion, almost a bow, that instantly struck him as absurd and betraying of all his weakness. He looked up at the woman, the wind blowing his hair. He might have continued for a long time in this unfamiliar attitude; he had never been a patient man, but when he was sick he had learned to sink submissively into the pillows, to wait for his medicine. He waited on the woman.

Then she, looking at him with blue eyes, turned and held open the door, and after a moment Bowman, as if convinced in his action, stood erect and followed her in.

Inside, the darkness of the house touched him like a professional hand, the doctor's. The woman set the half-cleaned lamp on a table in the center of the room and pointed, also like a professional person, a guide, to a chair with a yellow cowhide seat. She herself crouched on the hearth, drawing her knees up under the shapeless dress.

At first he felt hopefully secure. His heart was quieter. The room was enclosed in the gloom of yellow pine boards. He could see the other room, with the foot of an iron bed showing, across the passage. The bed had been made up with a red-and-yellow pieced quilt that looked like a map or a picture, a little like his grandmother's girlhood painting of Rome burning.

He had ached for coolness, but in this room it was cold. He stared at the hearth with dead coals lying on it and iron pots in the corners. The hearth and smoked chimney were of the stone he had seen ribbing the hills, mostly slate. Why is there no fire? he wondered.

And it was so still. The silence of the fields seemed to enter and move familiarly through the house. The wind used the open hall. He felt that he was in a mysterious, quiet, cool danger. It was necessary to do what? . . . To talk.

"I have a nice line of women's low-priced shoes . . ." he said.

But the woman answered, "Sonny 'll be here. He's strong. Sonny 'll move your car."

"Where is he now?"

"Farms for Mr Redmond."

Mr Redmond. Mr Redmond. That was someone he would never have to encounter, and he was glad. Somehow the name did not appeal to him. . . . In a flare of touchiness and anxiety, Bowman wished to avoid even mention of unknown men and their unknown farms.

"Do you two live here alone?" He was surprised to hear his old voice, chatty, confidential, inflected for selling shoes, asking a question like that—a thing he did not even want to know.

"Yes. We are alone."

He was surprised at the way she answered. She had taken a long time to say that. She had nodded her head in a deep way too. Had she wished to affect him with some sort of premonition? he wondered unhappily. Or was it only that she would not help him, after all, by talking with him? For he was not strong enough to receive the impact of unfamiliar things without a little talk to break their fall. He had lived a month in which nothing had happened except in his head and his body—an almost inaudible life of heartbeats and dreams that came back, a life of fever and privacy, a delicate life which had left him weak to the point of—what? Of begging. The pulse in his palm leapt like a trout in a brook.

He wondered over and over why the woman did not go ahead with cleaning the lamp. What prompted her to stay there across the room, silently bestowing her presence upon him? He saw that with her it was not a time for doing little tasks. Her face was grave; she was feeling how right she was. Perhaps it was only politeness. In docility he held his eyes stiffly wide; they fixed themselves on the woman's clasped hands as though she held the cord they were strung on.

Then, "Sonny's coming," she said.

He himself had not heard anything, but there came a man passing the window and then plunging in at the door, with two hounds beside him. Sonny was a big enough man, with his belt slung low about his hips. He looked at least thirty. He had a hot, red face that was yet full of silence. He wore muddy blue pants and an old military coat stained and patched. World War? Bowman wondered. Great God, it was a Confederate coat. On the back of his light hair he had a wide filthy black hat which seemed to insult Bowman's own.

He pushed down the dogs from his chest. He was strong, with dignity and heaviness in his way of moving. . . . There was the resemblance to his mother.

They stood side by side. . . . He must account again for his presence here.

"Sonny, this man, he had his car to run off over the prec'pice an' wants to know if you will git it out for him," the woman said after a few minutes.

Bowman could not even state his case.

Sonny's eyes lay upon him.

He knew he should offer explanations and show money—at least appear either penitent or authoritative. But all he could do was to shrug slightly.

Sonny brushed by him going to the window, followed by the eager dogs, and looked out. There was effort even in the way he was looking, as if he could throw his sight out like a rope. Without turning Bowman felt that his own eyes could have seen nothing: it was too far.

"Got me a mule out there an' got me a block an' tackle," said Sonny meaningfully. "I *could* catch me my mule an' git me my ropes, an' before long I'd git your car out the ravine."

He looked completely around the room, as if in meditation, his eyes roving in their own distance. Then he pressed his lips firmly and yet shyly together, and with the dogs ahead of him this time, he lowered his head and strode out. The hard earth sounded, cupping to his powerful way of walking—almost a stagger.

Mischievously, at the suggestion of those sounds, Bowman's heart leapt again. It seemed to walk about inside him.

"Sonny's goin' to do it," the woman said. She said it again, singing it almost, like a song. She was sitting in her place by the hearth.

Without looking out, he heard some shouts and the dogs barking and the pounding of hoofs in short runs on the hill. In a few minutes Sonny passed under the window with a rope, and there was a brown mule with quivering, shining, purple-looking ears. The mule actually looked in the window. Under its eyelashes it turned target-like eyes into his. Bowman averted his head and saw the woman looking serenely back at the mule, with only satisfaction in her face.

She sang a little more, under her breath. It occurred to him, and it seemed quite marvelous, that she was not really talking to him, but rather following the thing that came about with words that were unconscious and part of her looking.

So he said nothing, and this time when he did not reply he felt a curious and strong emotion, not fear, rise up in him.

This time, when his heart leapt, something—his soul—seemed to leap too, like a little colt invited out of a pen. He stared at the woman while the frantic nimbleness of his feeling made his head sway. He could not move; there was nothing he could do, unless perhaps he might embrace this woman who sat there growing old and shapeless before him.

But he wanted to leap up, to say to her, I have been sick and I found out then, only then, how lonely I am. Is it too late? My heart puts up a struggle inside me, and you may have heard it, protesting against emptiness. . . . It should be full, he would rush on to tell her, thinking of his heart now as a deep lake, it should be holding love like other hearts. It should be flooded with love. There would be a warm spring day . . . Come and stand in my heart, whoever you are, and a whole river would cover your feet and rise higher and take your knees in whirlpools, and draw you down to itself, your whole body, your heart too.

But he moved a trembling hand across his eyes, and looked at the placid crouching woman across the room. She was still as a statue. He felt ashamed and exhausted by the thought that he might, in one more moment, have tried by simple words and embraces to communicate some strange thing—something which seemed always to have just escaped him . . .

Sunlight touched the furthest pot on the hearth. It was late afternoon. This time tomorrow he would be somewhere on a good graveled road, driving his car past things that happened to people, quicker than their happening. Seeing ahead to the next day, he was glad, and knew that this was no time to embrace an old woman. He could feel in his pounding temples the readying of his blood for motion and for hurrying away.

"Sonny's hitched up your car by now," said the woman. "He'll git it out the ravine right shortly."

"Fine!" he cried with his customary enthusiasm.

•

Yet it seemed a long time that they waited. It began to get dark. Bowman was cramped in his chair. Any man should know enough to get up and walk around while he waited. There was something like guilt in such stillness and silence.

But instead of getting up, he listened. . . . His breathing restrained, his eyes powerless in the growing dark, he listened uneasily for a warning sound, forgetting in wariness what it would be. Before long he heard something—soft, continuous, insinuating.

"What's that noise?" he asked, his voice jumping into the dark. Then wildly he was afraid it would be his heart beating so plainly in the quiet room, and she would tell him so.

"You might hear the stream," she said grudgingly.

Her voice was closer. She was standing by the table. He wondered why she did not light the lamp. She stood there in the dark and did not light it.

Bowman would never speak to her now, for the time was past. I'll sleep in the dark, he thought, in his bewilderment pitying himself.

Heavily she moved on to the window. Her arm, vaguely white, rose straight from her full side and she pointed out into the darkness.

"That white speck's Sonny," she said, talking to herself.

He turned unwillingly and peered over her shoulder; he hesitated to rise and stand beside her. His eyes searched the dusky air. The white speck floated smoothly toward her finger, like a leaf on a river, growing whiter in the dark. It was as if she had shown him something secret, part of her life, but had offered no explanation. He looked away. He was moved almost to tears, feeling for no reason that she had made a silent declaration equivalent to his own. His hand waited upon his chest.

Then a step shook the house, and Sonny was in the room. Bowman felt how the woman left him there and went to the other man's side.

"I done got your car out, mister," said Sonny's voice in the dark. "She's settin' a-waitin' in the road, turned to go back where she come from."

"Fine!" said Bowman, projecting his own voice to loudness. "I'm surely much obliged—I could never have done it myself—I was sick. . . ."

"I could do it easy," said Sonny.

Bowman could feel them both waiting in the dark, and he could hear the dogs panting out in the yard, waiting to bark when he should go. He felt strangely helpless and resentful. Now that he could go, he longed to stay. From what was he being deprived? His chest was rudely shaken by the violence of his heart. These people cherished something here that he could not see, they withheld some ancient promise of food and warmth and light. Between them they had a conspiracy. He thought of the way she had moved away from him and gone to Sonny, she had flowed toward him. He was shaking with cold, he was tired, and it was not fair. Humbly and yet angrily he stuck his hand into his pocket.

"Of course I'm going to pay you for everything——"

"We don't take money for such," said Sonny's voice belligerently.

"I want to pay. But do something more . . . . Let me stay—tonight. . . ." He took another step toward them. If only they could see him, they would know his sincerity, his real need! His voice went on, "I'm not very strong yet, I'm not able to walk far, even back to my car, maybe, I don't know—I don't know exactly where I am——"

He stopped. He felt as if he might burst into tears. What would they think of him!

Sonny came over and put his hands on him. Bowman felt them pass (they were professional too) across his chest, over his hips. He could feel Sonny's eyes upon him in the dark.

"You ain't no revenuer come sneakin' here, mister, ain't got no gun?"

To this end of nowhere! And yet *he* had come. He made a grave answer. "No."

"You can stay."

"Sonny," said the woman, "you'll have to borry some fire."

"I'll go git it from Redmond's," said Sonny.

"What?" Bowman strained to hear their words to each other.

"Our fire, it's out, and Sonny's got to borry some, because it's dark an' cold," she said.

"But matches—I have matches——"

"We don't have no need for 'em," she said proudly. "Sonny's goin' after his own fire."

"I'm goin' to Redmond's," said Sonny with an air of importance, and he went out.

After they had waited a while, Bowman looked out the window and saw a light moving over the hill. It spread itself out like a little fan. It zigzagged along the field, darting and swift, not like Sonny at all. . . . Soon enough, Sonny staggered in, holding a burning stick behind him in tongs, fire flowing in his wake, blazing light into the corners of the room.

"We'll make a fire now," the woman said, taking the brand.

When that was done she lit the lamp. It showed its dark and light. The whole room turned golden-yellow like some sort of flower, and the walls smelled of it and seemed to tremble with the quiet rushing of the fire and the waving of the burning lampwick in its funnel of light.

The woman moved among the iron pots. With the tongs she dropped hot coals on top of the iron lids. They made a set of soft vibrations, like the sound of a bell far away.

She looked up and over at Bowman, but he could not answer. He was trembling. . . .

"Have a drink, mister?" Sonny asked. He had brought in a chair from the other room and sat astride it with his folded arms across the back. Now we are all visible to one another, Bowman thought, and cried, "Yes sir, you bet, thanks!"

"Come after me and do just what I do," said Sonny.

It was another excursion into the dark. They went through the hall, out to the back of the house, past a shed and a hooded well. They came to a wilderness of thicket.

"Down on your knees," said Sonny.

"What?" Sweat broke out on his forehead.

He understood when Sonny began to crawl through a sort of tunnel that the bushes made over the ground. He followed, startled in spite of himself when a twig or a thorn touched him gently without making a sound, clinging to him and finally letting him go.

Sonny stopped crawling and, crouched on his knees, began to dig with both his hands into the dirt. Bowman shyly struck matches and made a light. In a few minutes Sonny pulled up a jug. He poured out some of the whisky into a bottle from his coat pocket, and buried the jug again. "You never know who's liable to knock at your door," he said, and laughed. "Start back," he said, almost formally. "Ain't no need for us to drink outdoors, like hogs."

At the table by the fire, sitting opposite each other in their chairs, Sonny and Bowman took drinks out of the bottle, passing it across. The dogs slept; one of them was having a dream.

"This is good," said Bowman. "This is what I needed." It was just as though he were drinking the fire off the hearth.

"He makes it," said the woman with quiet pride.

She was pushing the coals off the pots, and the smells of corn bread and coffee circled the room. She set everything on the table before the men, with a bone-handled knife stuck into one of the potatoes, splitting out its golden fiber. Then she stood for a minute looking at them, tall and full above them where they sat. She leaned a little toward them.

"You all can eat now," she said, and suddenly smiled.

Bowman had just happened to be looking at her. He set his cup back on the table in unbelieving protest. A pain pressed at his eyes. He saw that she was not an old woman. She was young, still young. He could think of no number of years for her. She was the same age as Sonny, and she belonged to him. She stood with the deep dark corner of the room behind her, the shifting yellow light scattering over her head and her gray formless dress, trembling over her tall body when it bent over them in its sudden communication. She was young. Her teeth were shining and her eyes glowed. She turned and walked slowly and heavily out of the room, and he heard her sit down on the cot and then lie down. The pattern on the quilt moved.

"She's goin' to have a baby," said Sonny, popping a bite into his mouth.

Bowman could not speak. He was shocked with knowing what was really in this house. A marriage, a fruitful marriage. That simple thing. Anyone could have had that.

Somehow he felt unable to be indignant or protest, although some sort of joke had certainly been played upon him.

There was nothing remote or mysterious here—only something private. The only secret was the ancient communication between two people. But the memory of the woman's waiting silently by the cold hearth, of the man's stubborn journey a mile away to get fire, and how they finally brought out their food and drink and filled the room proudly with all they had to show, was suddenly too clear and too enormous within him for response. . . .

"You ain't as hungry as you look," said Sonny.

The woman came out of the bedroom as soon as the men had finished, and ate her supper while her husband stared peacefully into the fire.

Then they put the dogs out, with the food that was left.

"I think I'd better sleep here by the fire, on the floor," said Bowman.

He felt that he had been cheated, and that he could afford now to be generous. Ill though he was, he was not going to ask them for their bed. He was through with asking favors in this house, now that he understood what was there.

"Sure, mister."

But he had not known yet how slowly he understood. They had not meant to give him their bed. After a little interval they both rose and looking at him gravely went into the other room.

He lay stretched by the fire until it grew low and dying. He watched every tongue of blaze lick out and vanish. "There will be special reduced prices on all footwear during the month of January," he found himself repeating quietly, and then he lay with his lips tight shut.

How many noises the night had! He heard the stream running, the fire dying, and he was sure now that he heard his heart beating, too, the sound it made under his ribs. He heard breathing, round and deep, of the man and his wife in the room across the passage. And that was all. But emotion swelled patiently within him, and he wished that the child were his.

He must get back to where he had been before. He stood weakly before the red coals and put on his overcoat. It felt too heavy on his shoulders. As he started out he looked and saw that the woman had never got through with cleaning the lamp. On some impulse he put all the money from his billfold under its fluted glass base, almost ostentatiously.

Ashamed, shrugging a little, and then shivering, he took his bags and went out. The cold of the air seemed to lift him bodily. The moon was in the sky.

On the slope he began to run, he could not help it. Just as he reached the road, where his car seemed to sit in the moonlight like a boat, his heart began to give off tremendous explosions like a rifle, bang bang bang.

He sank in fright onto the road, his bags falling about him. He felt as if all this had happened before. He covered his heart with both hands to keep anyone from hearing the noise it made.

But nobody heard it.

Powerhouse

POWERHOUSE is playing!

He's here on tour from the city—"Powerhouse and His Keyboard"—"Powerhouse and His Tasmanians"—think of the things he calls himself! There's no one in the world like him. You can't tell what he is. "Nigger man"?—he looks more Asiatic, monkey, Jewish, Babylonian, Peruvian, fanatic, devil. He has pale gray eyes, heavy lids, maybe horny like a lizard's, but big glowing eyes when they're open. He has African feet of the greatest size, stomping, both together, on each side of the pedals. He's not coal black—beverage colored—looks like a preacher when his mouth is shut, but then it opens—vast and obscene. And his mouth is going every minute: like a monkey's when it looks for something. Improvising, coming on a light and childish melody—*smooch*—he loves it with his mouth.

Is it possible that he could be this! When you have him there performing for you, that's what you feel. You know people on a stage—and people of a darker race—so likely to be marvelous, frightening.

This is a white dance. Powerhouse is not a show-off like the Harlem boys, not drunk, not crazy—he's in a trance; he's a person of joy, a fanatic. He listens as much as he performs, a look of hideous, powerful rapture on his face. Big arched eyebrows that never stop traveling, like a Jew's—wandering-Jew eyebrows. When he plays he beats down piano and seat and wears them away. He is in motion every moment—what could be more obscene? There he is with his great head, fat stomach, and little round piston legs, and long yellow-sectioned strong big fingers, at rest about the size of bananas. Of course you know how he sounds—you've heard him on records—but still you need to see him. He's going all the time, like skating around the skating rink or rowing a boat. It makes everybody crowd around, here in this shadowless steel-trussed hall with the rose-like posters of Nelson Eddy and the testimonial for the mind-reading horse in handwriting magnified five hundred times. Then all quietly he lays his finger on a key with the promise and serenity of a sibyl touching the book.

Powerhouse is so monstrous he sends everybody into oblivion. When any group, any performers, come to town, don't people always come out and hover near, leaning inward about them, to learn what it is? What is it? Listen. Remember how it was with the acrobats. Watch them carefully, hear the least word, especially what they say to one another, in another language—don't let them escape you; it's the only time for hallucination, the last time. They can't stay. They'll be somewhere else this time tomorrow.

Powerhouse has as much as possible done by signals. Everybody, laughing as if to hide a weakness, will sooner or later hand him up a written request. Powerhouse reads each one, studying with a secret face: that is the face which looks like a mask—anybody's; there is a moment when he makes a decision. Then a light slides under his eyelids, and he says, "92!" or some combination of figures—never a name. Before a number the band is all frantic, misbehaving, pushing, like children in a schoolroom, and he is the teacher getting silence. His hands over the keys, he says sternly, "You-all ready? You-all ready to do some serious walking?"—waits—then, STAMP. Quiet. STAMP, for the second time. This is absolute. Then a set of rhythmic kicks against the floor to communicate the tempo. Then, O Lord! say the distended eyes from beyond the boundary of the trumpets, Hello and good-by, and they are all down the first note like a waterfall.

This note marks the end of any known discipline. Powerhouse seems to abandon them all—he himself seems lost—down in the song, yelling up like somebody in a whirlpool—not guiding them—hailing them only. But he knows, really. He cries out, but he must know exactly. "Mercy! . . . What I say! . . . Yeah!" And then drifting, listening—"Where that skin beater?"—wanting drums, and starting up and pouring it out in the greatest delight and brutality. On the sweet pieces such a leer for everybody! He looks down so benevolently upon all our faces and whispers the lyrics to us. And if you could hear him at this moment on "Marie, the Dawn is Breaking"! He's going up the keyboard with a few fingers in some very derogatory triplet-routine, he gets higher and higher, and then he looks over the end of the piano, as if over a cliff. But not in a show-off way—the song makes him do it.

He loves the way they all play, too—all those next to him. The far section of the band is all studious, wearing glasses, every one—they don't count. Only those playing around Powerhouse are the real ones. He has a bass fiddler from Vicksburg, black as pitch, named Valentine, who plays with his eyes shut and talking to himself, very young: Powerhouse has to keep encouraging him. "Go on, go on, give it up, bring it on out there!" When you heard him like that on records, did you know he was really pleading?

He calls Valentine out to take a solo.

"What you going to play?" Powerhouse looks out kindly from behind the piano; he opens his mouth and shows his tongue, listening.

Valentine looks down, drawing against his instrument, and says without a lip movement, " 'Honeysuckle Rose.' "

He has a clarinet player named Little Brother, and loves to listen to anything he does. He'll smile and say, "Beautiful!" Little Brother takes a step forward when he plays and stands at the very front, with the whites of his eyes like fishes swimming. Once when he played a low note, Powerhouse muttered in dirty praise, "He went clear downstairs to get that one!"

After a long time, he holds up the number of fingers to tell the band how many choruses still to go—usually five. He keeps his directions down to signals.

It's a bad night outside. It's a white dance, and nobody dances, except a few straggling jitterbugs and two elderly couples. Everybody just stands around the band and watches Powerhouse. Sometimes they steal glances at one another, as if to say, Of course, you know how it is with *them*—Negroes—band leaders—they would play the same way, giving all they've got, for an audience of one. . . . When somebody, no matter who, gives everything, it makes people feel ashamed for him.

Late at night they play the one waltz they will ever consent to play—by request, "Pagan Love Song." Powerhouse's head rolls and sinks like a weight between his waving shoulders. He groans, and his fingers drag into the keys heavily, holding on to the notes, retrieving. It is a sad song.

"You know what happened to me?" says Powerhouse.

Valentine hums a response, dreaming at the bass.

"I got a telegram my wife is dead," says Powerhouse, with wandering fingers.

"Uh-huh?"

His mouth gathers and forms a barbarous O while his fingers walk up straight, unwillingly, three octaves.

"Gypsy? Why how come her to die, didn't you just phone her up in the night last night long distance?"

"Telegram say—here the words: Your wife is dead." He puts 4/4 over the 3/4.

"Not but four words?" This is the drummer, an unpopular boy named Scoot, a disbelieving maniac.

Powerhouse is shaking his vast cheeks. "What the hell was she trying to do? What was she up to?"

"What name has it got signed, if you got a telegram?" Scoot is spitting away with those wire brushes.

Little Brother, the clarinet player, who cannot now speak, glares and tilts back.

"Uranus Knockwood is the name signed." Powerhouse lifts his eyes open. "Ever heard of him?" A bubble shoots out on his lip like a plate on a counter.

Valentine is beating slowly on with his palm and scratching the strings with his long blue nails. He is fond of a waltz, Powerhouse interrupts him.

"I don't know him. Don't know who he is." Valentine shakes his head with the closed eyes.

"Say it agin."

"Uranus Knockwood."

"That ain't Lenox Avenue."

"It ain't Broadway."

"Ain't ever seen it wrote out in any print, even for horse racing."

"Hell, that's on a star, boy, ain't it?" Crash of the cymbals.

"What the hell was she up to?" Powerhouse shudders. "Tell me, tell me, tell me." He makes triplets, and begins a new chorus. He holds three fingers up.

"You say you got a telegram." This is Valentine, patient and sleepy, beginning again.

Powerhouse is elaborate. "Yas, the time I go out, go way downstairs along a long cor-ri-dor to where they puts us: coming back along the cor-ri-dor: steps out and hands me a telegram: Your wife is dead."

"Gypsy?" The drummer like a spider over his drums.

"Aaaaaaaaa!" shouts Powerhouse, flinging out both powerful arms for three whole beats to flex his muscles, then kneading a dough of bass notes. His eyes glitter. He plays the piano like a drum sometimes—why not?

"Gypsy? Such a dancer?"

"Why you don't hear it straight from your agent? Why it ain't come from headquarters? What you been doing, getting telegrams in the *corridor*, signed nobody?"

They all laugh. End of that chorus.

"What time is it?" Powerhouse calls. "What the hell place is this? Where is my watch and chain?"

"I hang it on you," whimpers Valentine. "It still there."

There it rides on Powerhouse's great stomach, down where he can never see it.

"Sure did hear some clock striking twelve while ago. Must be *midnight*."

"It going to be intermission," Powerhouse declares, lifting up his finger with the signet ring.

He draws the chorus to an end. He pulls a big Northern hotel towel out of the deep pocket in his vast, special-cut tux pants and pushes his forehead into it.

"If she went and killed herself!" he says with a hidden face. "If she up and jumped out that window!" He gets to his feet, turning vaguely, wearing the towel on his head.

"Ha, ha!"

"Sheik, sheik!"

"She wouldn't do that." Little Brother sets down his clarinet like a precious vase, and speaks. He still looks like an East Indian queen, implacable, divine, and full of snakes. "You ain't going to expect people doing what they says over long distance."

"Come on!" roars Powerhouse. He is already at the back

door, he has pulled it wide open, and with a wild, gathered-up face is smelling the terrible night.

Powerhouse, Valentine, Scoot and Little Brother step outside into the drenching rain.

"Well, they emptying buckets," says Powerhouse in a mollified voice. On the street he holds his hands out and turns up the blanched palms like sieves.

A hundred dark, ragged, silent, delighted Negroes have come around from under the eaves of the hall, and follow wherever they go.

"Watch out Little Brother don't shrink," says Powerhouse. "You just the right size now, clarinet don't suck you in. You got a dry throat, Little Brother, you in the desert?" He reaches into the pocket and pulls out a paper of mints. "Now hold 'em in your mouth—don't chew 'em. I don't carry around nothing without limit."

"Go in that joint and have beer," says Scoot, who walks ahead.

"Beer? Beer? You know what beer is? What do they say is beer? What's beer? Where I been?"

"Down yonder where it say World Café—that do?" They are in Negrotown now.

Valentine patters over and holds open a screen door warped like a sea shell, bitter in the wet, and they walk in, stained darker with the rain and leaving footprints. Inside, sheltered dry smells stand like screens around a table covered with a red-checkered cloth, in the center of which flies hang onto an obelisk-shaped ketchup bottle. The midnight walls are checkered again with admonishing "Not Responsible" signs and black-figured, smoky calendars. It is a waiting, silent, limp room. There is a burned-out-looking nickelodeon and right beside it a long-necked wall instrument labeled "Business Phone, Don't Keep Talking." Circled phone numbers are written up everywhere. There is a worn-out peacock feather hanging by a thread to an old, thin, pink, exposed light bulb, where it slowly turns around and around, whoever breathes.

A waitress watches.

"Come here, living statue, and get all this big order of beer we fixing to give."

"Never seen you before anywhere." The waitress moves and comes forward and slowly shows little gold leaves and tendrils over her teeth. She shoves up her shoulders and breasts. "How I going to know who you might be? Robbers? Coming in out of the black of night right at midnight, setting down so big at my table?"

"Boogers," says Powerhouse, his eyes opening lazily as in a cave.

The girl screams delicately with pleasure. O Lord, she likes talk and scares.

"Where you going to find enough beer to put out on this here table?"

She runs to the kitchen with bent elbows and sliding steps.

"Here's a million nickels," says Powerhouse, pulling his hand out of his pocket and sprinkling coins out, all but the last one, which he makes vanish like a magician.

Valentine and Scoot take the money over to the nickelodeon, which looks as battered as a slot machine, and read all the names of the records out loud.

"Whose 'Tuxedo Junction'?" asks Powerhouse.

"You know whose."

"Nickelodeon, I request you please to play 'Empty Bed Blues' and let Bessie Smith sing."

Silence: they hold it like a measure.

"Bring me all those nickels on back here," says Powerhouse. "Look at that! What you tell me the name of this place?"

"White dance, week night, raining, Alligator, Mississippi, long ways from home."

"Uh-huh."

"Sent for You Yesterday and Here You Come Today" plays.

The waitress, setting the tray of beer down on a back table, comes up taut and apprehensive as a hen. "Says in the kitchen, back there putting their eyes to little hole peeping out, that you is Mr Powerhouse. . . . They knows from a picture they seen."

"They seeing right tonight, that is him," says Little Brother.

"You him?"

"That is him in the flesh," says Scoot.

"Does you wish to touch him?" asks Valentine. "Because he don't bite."

"You passing through?"

"Now you got everything right."

She waits like a drop, hands languishing together in front.

"Little-Bit, ain't you going to bring the beer?"

She brings it, and goes behind the cash register and smiles, turning different ways. The little fillet of gold in her mouth is gleaming.

"The Mississippi River's here," she says once.

Now all the watching Negroes press in gently and bright-eyed through the door, as many as can get in. One is a little boy in a straw sombrero which has been coated with aluminum paint all over.

Powerhouse, Valentine, Scoot and Little Brother drink beer, and their eyelids come together like curtains. The wall and the rain and the humble beautiful waitress waiting on them and the other Negroes watching enclose them.

"Listen!" whispers Powerhouse, looking into the ketchup bottle and slowly spreading his performer's hands over the damp, wrinkling cloth with the red squares. "Listen how it is. My wife gets missing me. Gypsy. She goes to the window. She looks out and sees you know what. Street. Sign saying Hotel. People walking. Somebody looks up. Old man. She looks down, out the window. Well? . . . *Sssst! Plooey!* What she do? Jump out and bust her brains all over the world."

He opens his eyes.

"That's it," agrees Valentine. "You gets a telegram."

"Sure she misses you," Little Brother adds.

"No, it's night time." How softly he tells them! "Sure. It's the night time. She say, What do I hear? Footsteps walking up the hall? That him? Footsteps go on off. It's not me. I'm in Alligator, Mississippi, she's crazy. Shaking all over. Listens till her ears and all grow out like old music-box horns but still she can't hear a thing. She says, All right! I'll jump out the window then. Got on her nightgown. I know that nightgown, and her thinking there. Says, Ho hum, all right, and jumps out the window. Is she mad at me! Is she crazy! She don't leave *nothing* behind her!"

"Ya! Ha!"

"Brains and insides everywhere, Lord, Lord."

All the watching Negroes stir in their delight, and to their higher delight he says affectionately, "Listen! Rats in here."

"That must be the way, boss."

"Only, naw, Powerhouse, that ain't true. That sound too *bad*."

"Does? I even know who finds her," cries Powerhouse. "That no-good pussyfooted crooning creeper, that creeper that follow around after me, coming up like weeds behind me, following around after me everything I do and messing around on the trail I leave. Bets my numbers, sings my songs, gets close to my agent like a Betsy-bug; when I going out he just coming in. I got him now! I got my eye on him."

"Know who he is?"

"Why it's that old Uranus Knockwood!"

"Ya! Ha!"

"Yeah, and he coming now, he going to find Gypsy. There he is, coming around that corner, and Gypsy kadoodling down, oh-oh, watch out! *Sssst! Plooey!* See, there she is in her little old nightgown, and her insides and brains all scattered round."

A sigh fills the room.

"Hush about her brains. Hush about her insides."

"Ya! Ha! You talking about her brains and insides—old Uranus Knockwood," says Powerhouse, "look down and say Jesus! He say, Look here what I'm walking round in!"

They all burst into halloos of laughter. Powerhouse's face looks like a big hot iron stove.

"Why, he picks her up and carries her off!" he says.

"Ya! Ha!"

"Carries her *back* around the corner. . . ."

"Oh, Powerhouse!"

"You know him."

"Uranus Knockwood!"

"Yeahhh!"

"He take our wives when we gone!"

"He come in when we goes out!"

"Uh-huh!"

"He go out when we comes in!"

"Yeahhh!"

"He standing behind the door!"

"Old Uranus Knockwood."

"You know him."

"Middle-size man."

"Wears a hat."

"That's him."

Everybody in the room moans with pleasure. The little boy in the fine silver hat opens a paper and divides out a jelly roll among his followers.

And out of the breathless ring somebody moves forward like a slave, leading a great logy Negro with bursting eyes, and says, "This here is Sugar-Stick Thompson, that dove down to the bottom of July Creek and pulled up all those drownded white people fall out of a boat. Last summer, pulled up fourteen."

"Hello," says Powerhouse, turning and looking around at them all with his great daring face until they nearly suffocate.

Sugar-Stick, their instrument, cannot speak; he can only look back at the others.

"Can't even swim. Done it by holding his breath," says the fellow with the hero.

Powerhouse looks at him seekingly.

"I his half brother," the fellow puts in.

They step back.

"Gypsy say," Powerhouse rumbles gently again, looking at *them*, " 'What is the use? I'm gonna jump out so far—so far. . . .' *Ssssst—!*"

"Don't, boss, don't do it agin," says Little Brother.

"It's awful," says the waitress. "I hates that Mr Knockwoods. All that the truth?"

"Want to see the telegram I got from him?" Powerhouse's hand goes to the vast pocket.

"Now wait, now wait, boss." They all watch him.

"It must be the real truth," says the waitress, sucking in her lower lip, her luminous eyes turning sadly, seeking the windows.

"No, babe, it ain't the truth." His eyebrows fly up, and he

begins to whisper to her out of his vast oven mouth. His hand stays in his pocket. "Truth is something worse, I ain't said what, yet. It's something hasn't come to me, but I ain't saying it won't. And when it does, then want me to tell you?" He sniffs all at once, his eyes come open and turn up, almost too far. He is dreamily smiling.

"Don't, boss, don't, Powerhouse!"

"Oh!" the waitress screams.

"Go on git out of here!" bellows Powerhouse, taking his hand out of his pocket and clapping after her red dress.

The ring of watchers breaks and falls away.

"*Look* at that! Intermission is up," says Powerhouse.

He folds money under a glass, and after they go out, Valentine leans back in and drops a nickel in the nickelodeon behind them, and it lights up and begins to play "The Goona Goo." The feather dangles still.

"Take a telegram!" Powerhouse shouts suddenly up into the rain over the street. "Take a answer. Now what was that name?"

They get a little tired.

"Uranus Knockwood."

"You ought to know."

"Yas? Spell it to me."

They spell it all the ways it could be spelled. It puts them in a wonderful humor.

"Here's the answer. I got it right here. 'What in the hell you talking about? Don't make any difference: I gotcha.' Name signed: Powerhouse."

"That going to reach him, Powerhouse?" Valentine speaks in a maternal voice.

"Yas, yas."

All hushing, following him up the dark street at a distance, like old rained-on black ghosts, the Negroes are afraid they will die laughing.

Powerhouse throws back his vast head into the steaming rain, and a look of hopeful desire seems to blow somehow like a vapor from his own dilated nostrils over his face and bring a mist to his eyes.

"Reach him and come out the other side."

"That's it, Powerhouse, that's it. You got him now."

Powerhouse lets out a long sigh.

"But ain't you going back there to call up Gypsy long distance, the way you did last night in that other place? I seen a telephone. . . . Just to see if she there at home?"

There is a measure of silence. That is one crazy drummer that's going to get his neck broken some day.

"No," growls Powerhouse. "No! How many thousand times tonight I got to say No?"

He holds up his arm in the rain.

"You sure-enough unroll your voice some night, it about reach up yonder to her," says Little Brother, dismayed.

They go on up the street, shaking the rain off and on them like birds.

Back in the dance hall, they play "San" (99). The jitterbugs start up like windmills stationed over the floor, and in their orbits—one circle, another, a long stretch and a zigzag—dance the elderly couples with old smoothness, undisturbed and stately.

When Powerhouse first came back from intermission, no doubt full of beer, they said, he got the band tuned up again in his own way. He didn't strike the piano keys for pitch—he simply opened his mouth and gave falsetto howls—in A, D and so on—they tuned by him. Then he took hold of the piano, as if he saw it for the first time in his life, and tested it for strength, hit it down in the bass, played an octave with his elbow, lifted the top, looked inside, and leaned against it with all his might. He sat down and played it for a few minutes with outrageous force and got it under his power—a bass deep and coarse as a sea net—then produced something glimmering and fragile, and smiled. And who could ever remember any of the things he says? They are just inspired remarks that roll out of his mouth like smoke.

They've requested "Somebody Loves Me," and he's already done twelve or fourteen choruses, piling them up nobody knows how, and it will be a wonder if he ever gets through. Now and then he calls and shouts, " 'Somebody loves me! Somebody loves me, I wonder who!' " His mouth gets to be nothing but a volcano. "I wonder who!"

"Maybe . . ." He uses all his right hand on a trill.

"Maybe . . ." He pulls back his spread fingers, and looks out upon the place where he is. A vast, impersonal and yet furious grimace transfigures his wet face.

". . . Maybe it's you!"

A Worn Path

IT WAS December—a bright frozen day in the early morning. Far out in the country there was an old Negro woman with her head tied in a red rag, coming along a path through the pinewoods. Her name was Phoenix Jackson. She was very old and small and she walked slowly in the dark pine shadows, moving a little from side to side in her steps, with the balanced heaviness and lightness of a pendulum in a grandfather clock. She carried a thin, small cane made from an umbrella, and with this she kept tapping the frozen earth in front of her. This made a grave and persistent noise in the still air, that seemed meditative like the chirping of a solitary little bird.

She wore a dark striped dress reaching down to her shoe tops, and an equally long apron of bleached sugar sacks, with a full pocket: all neat and tidy, but every time she took a step she might have fallen over her shoelaces, which dragged from her unlaced shoes. She looked straight ahead. Her eyes were blue with age. Her skin had a pattern all its own of numberless branching wrinkles and as though a whole little tree stood in the middle of her forehead, but a golden color ran underneath, and the two knobs of her cheeks were illumined by a yellow burning under the dark. Under the red rag her hair came down on her neck in the frailest of ringlets, still black, and with an odor like copper.

Now and then there was a quivering in the thicket. Old Phoenix said, "Out of my way, all you foxes, owls, beetles, jack rabbits, coons and wild animals! . . . Keep out from under these feet, little bob-whites. . . . Keep the big wild hogs out of my path. Don't let none of those come running my direction. I got a long way." Under her small black-freckled hand her cane, limber as a buggy whip, would switch at the brush as if to rouse up any hiding things.

On she went. The woods were deep and still. The sun made the pine needles almost too bright to look at, up where the wind rocked. The cones dropped as light as feathers. Down in the hollow was the mourning dove—it was not too late for him.

The path ran up a hill. "Seem like there is chains about my feet, time I get this far," she said, in the voice of argument old people keep to use with themselves. "Something always take a hold of me on this hill—pleads I should stay."

After she got to the top she turned and gave a full, severe look behind her where she had come. "Up through pines," she said at length. "Now down through oaks."

Her eyes opened their widest, and she started down gently. But before she got to the bottom of the hill a bush caught her dress.

Her fingers were busy and intent, but her skirts were full and long, so that before she could pull them free in one place they were caught in another. It was not possible to allow the dress to tear. "I in the thorny bush," she said. "Thorns, you doing your appointed work. Never want to let folks pass, no sir. Old eyes thought you was a pretty little *green* bush."

Finally, trembling all over, she stood free, and after a moment dared to stoop for her cane.

"Sun so high!" she cried, leaning back and looking, while the thick tears went over her eyes. "The time getting all gone here."

At the foot of this hill was a place where a log was laid across the creek.

"Now comes the trial," said Phoenix.

Putting her right foot out, she mounted the log and shut her eyes. Lifting her skirt, leveling her cane fiercely before her, like a festival figure in some parade, she began to march across. Then she opened her eyes and she was safe on the other side.

"I wasn't as old as I thought," she said.

But she sat down to rest. She spread her skirts on the bank around her and folded her hands over her knees. Up above her was a tree in a pearly cloud of mistletoe. She did not dare to close her eyes, and when a little boy brought her a plate with a slice of marble-cake on it she spoke to him. "That would be acceptable," she said. But when she went to take it there was just her own hand in the air.

So she left that tree, and had to go through a barbed-wire fence. There she had to creep and crawl, spreading her knees and stretching her fingers like a baby trying to climb the steps.

But she talked loudly to herself: she could not let her dress be torn now, so late in the day, and she could not pay for having her arm or her leg sawed off if she got caught fast where she was.

At last she was safe through the fence and risen up out in the clearing. Big dead trees, like black men with one arm, were standing in the purple stalks of the withered cotton field. There sat a buzzard.

"Who you watching?"

In the furrow she made her way along.

"Glad this not the season for bulls," she said, looking sideways, "and the good Lord made his snakes to curl up and sleep in the winter. A pleasure I don't see no two-headed snake coming around that tree, where it come once. It took a while to get by him, back in the summer."

She passed through the old cotton and went into a field of dead corn. It whispered and shook and was taller than her head. "Through the maze now," she said, for there was no path.

Then there was something tall, black, and skinny there, moving before her.

At first she took it for a man. It could have been a man dancing in the field. But she stood still and listened, and it did not make a sound. It was as silent as a ghost.

"Ghost," she said sharply, "who be you the ghost of? For I have heard of nary death close by."

But there was no answer—only the ragged dancing in the wind.

She shut her eyes, reached out her hand, and touched a sleeve. She found a coat and inside that an emptiness, cold as ice.

"You scarecrow," she said. Her face lighted. "I ought to be shut up for good," she said with laughter. "My senses is gone. I too old. I the oldest people I ever know. Dance, old scarecrow," she said, "while I dancing with you."

She kicked her foot over the furrow, and with mouth drawn down, shook her head once or twice in a little strutting way. Some husks blew down and whirled in streamers about her skirts.

Then she went on, parting her way from side to side with

the cane, through the whispering field. At last she came to the end, to a wagon track where the silver grass blew between the red ruts. The quail were walking around like pullets, seeming all dainty and unseen.

"Walk pretty," she said. "This the easy place. This the easy going."

She followed the track, swaying through the quiet bare fields, through the little strings of trees silver in their dead leaves, past cabins silver from weather, with the doors and windows boarded shut, all like old women under a spell sitting there. "I walking in their sleep," she said, nodding her head vigorously.

In a ravine she went where a spring was silently flowing through a hollow log. Old Phoenix bent and drank. "Sweet-gum makes the water sweet," she said, and drank more. "Nobody know who made this well, for it was here when I was born."

The track crossed a swampy part where the moss hung as white as lace from every limb. "Sleep on, alligators, and blow your bubbles." Then the track went into the road.

Deep, deep the road went down between the high green-colored banks. Overhead the live-oaks met, and it was as dark as a cave.

A black dog with a lolling tongue came up out of the weeds by the ditch. She was meditating, and not ready, and when he came at her she only hit him a little with her cane. Over she went in the ditch, like a little puff of milkweed.

Down there, her senses drifted away. A dream visited her, and she reached her hand up, but nothing reached down and gave her a pull. So she lay there and presently went to talking. "Old woman," she said to herself, "that black dog come up out of the weeds to stall you off, and now there he sitting on his fine tail, smiling at you."

A white man finally came along and found her—a hunter, a young man, with his dog on a chain.

"Well, Granny!" he laughed. "What are you doing there?"

"Lying on my back like a June-bug waiting to be turned over, mister," she said, reaching up her hand.

He lifted her up, gave her a swing in the air, and set her down. "Anything broken, Granny?"

"No sir, them old dead weeds is springy enough," said Phoenix, when she had got her breath. "I thank you for your trouble."

"Where do you live, Granny?" he asked, while the two dogs were growling at each other.

"Away back yonder, sir, behind the ridge. You can't even see it from here."

"On your way home?"

"No sir, I going to town."

"Why, that's too far! That's as far as I walk when I come out myself, and I get something for my trouble." He patted the stuffed bag he carried, and there hung down a little closed claw. It was one of the bob-whites, with its beak hooked bitterly to show it was dead. "Now you go on home, Granny!"

"I bound to go to town, mister," said Phoenix. "The time come around."

He gave another laugh, filling the whole landscape. "I know you old colored people! Wouldn't miss going to town to see Santa Claus!"

But something held old Phoenix very still. The deep lines in her face went into a fierce and different radiation. Without warning, she had seen with her own eyes a flashing nickel fall out of the man's pocket onto the ground.

"How old are you, Granny?" he was saying.

"There is no telling, mister," she said, "no telling."

Then she gave a little cry and clapped her hands and said, "Git on away from here, dog! Look! Look at that dog!" She laughed as if in admiration. "He ain't scared of nobody. He a big black dog." She whispered, "Sic him!"

"Watch me get rid of that cur," said the man. "Sic him, Pete! Sic him!"

Phoenix heard the dogs fighting, and heard the man running and throwing sticks. She even heard a gunshot. But she was slowly bending forward by that time, further and further forward, the lids stretched down over her eyes, as if she were doing this in her sleep. Her chin was lowered almost to her knees. The yellow palm of her hand came out from the fold of her apron. Her fingers slid down and along the ground under the piece of money with the grace and care they would have in lifting an egg from under a setting hen. Then she slowly straightened up, she stood erect, and the nickel was in her apron pocket. A bird flew by. Her lips moved. "God watching me the whole time. I come to stealing."

The man came back, and his own dog panted about them. "Well, I scared him off that time," he said, and then he laughed and lifted his gun and pointed it at Phoenix.

She stood straight and faced him.

"Doesn't the gun scare you?" he said, still pointing it.

"No, sir, I seen plenty go off closer by, in my day, and for less than what I done," she said, holding utterly still.

He smiled, and shouldered the gun. "Well, Granny," he said, "you must be a hundred years old, and scared of nothing. I'd give you a dime if I had any money with me. But you take my advice and stay home, and nothing will happen to you."

"I bound to go on my way, mister," said Phoenix. She inclined her head in the red rag. Then they went in different directions, but she could hear the gun shooting again and again over the hill.

She walked on. The shadows hung from the oak trees to the road like curtains. Then she smelled wood-smoke, and smelled the river, and she saw a steeple and the cabins on their steep steps. Dozens of little black children whirled around her. There ahead was Natchez shining. Bells were ringing. She walked on.

In the paved city it was Christmas time. There were red and green electric lights strung and crisscrossed everywhere, and all turned on in the daytime. Old Phoenix would have been lost if she had not distrusted her eyesight and depended on her feet to know where to take her.

She paused quietly on the sidewalk where people were passing by. A lady came along in the crowd, carrying an armful of red-, green- and silver-wrapped presents; she gave off perfume like the red roses in hot summer, and Phoenix stopped her.

"Please, missy, will you lace up my shoe?" She held up her foot.

"What do you want, Grandma?"

"See my shoe," said Phoenix. "Do all right for out in the country, but wouldn't look right to go in a big building."

"Stand still then, Grandma," said the lady. She put her packages down on the sidewalk beside her and laced and tied both shoes tightly.

"Can't lace 'em with a cane," said Phoenix. "Thank you, missy. I doesn't mind asking a nice lady to tie up my shoe, when I gets out on the street."

Moving slowly and from side to side, she went into the big building, and into a tower of steps, where she walked up and around and around until her feet knew to stop.

She entered a door, and there she saw nailed up on the wall the document that had been stamped with the gold seal and framed in the gold frame, which matched the dream that was hung up in her head.

"Here I be," she said. There was a fixed and ceremonial stiffness over her body.

"A charity case, I suppose," said an attendant who sat at the desk before her.

But Phoenix only looked above her head. There was sweat on her face, the wrinkles in her skin shone like a bright net.

"Speak up, Grandma," the woman said. "What's your name? We must have your history, you know. Have you been here before? What seems to be the trouble with you?"

Old Phoenix only gave a twitch to her face as if a fly were bothering her.

"Are you deaf?" cried the attendant.

But then the nurse came in.

"Oh, that's just old Aunt Phoenix," she said. "She doesn't come for herself—she has a little grandson. She makes these trips just as regular as clockwork. She lives away back off the Old Natchez Trace." She bent down. "Well, Aunt Phoenix, why don't you just take a seat? We won't keep you standing after your long trip." She pointed.

The old woman sat down, bolt upright in the chair.

"Now, how is the boy?" asked the nurse.

Old Phoenix did not speak.

"I said, how is the boy?"

But Phoenix only waited and stared straight ahead, her face very solemn and withdrawn into rigidity.

"Is his throat any better?" asked the nurse. "Aunt Phoenix,

don't you hear me? Is your grandson's throat any better since the last time you came for the medicine?"

With her hands on her knees, the old woman waited, silent, erect and motionless, just as if she were in armor.

"You mustn't take up our time this way, Aunt Phoenix," the nurse said. "Tell us quickly about your grandson, and get it over. He isn't dead, is he?"

At last there came a flicker and then a flame of comprehension across her face, and she spoke.

"My grandson. It was my memory had left me. There I sat and forgot why I made my long trip."

"Forgot?" The nurse frowned. "After you came so far?"

Then Phoenix was like an old woman begging a dignified forgiveness for waking up frightened in the night. "I never did go to school, I was too old at the Surrender," she said in a soft voice. "I'm an old woman without an education. It was my memory fail me. My little grandson, he is just the same, and I forgot it in the coming."

"Throat never heals, does it?" said the nurse, speaking in a loud, sure voice to old Phoenix. By now she had a card with something written on it, a little list. "Yes. Swallowed lye. When was it?—January—two-three years ago——"

Phoenix spoke unasked now. "No, missy, he not dead, he just the same. Every little while his throat begin to close up again, and he not able to swallow. He not get his breath. He not able to help himself. So the time come around, and I go on another trip for the soothing medicine."

"All right. The doctor said as long as you came to get it, you could have it," said the nurse. "But it's an obstinate case."

"My little grandson, he sit up there in the house all wrapped up, waiting by himself," Phoenix went on. "We is the only two left in the world. He suffer and it don't seem to put him back at all. He got a sweet look. He going to last. He wear a little patch quilt and peep out holding his mouth open like a little bird. I remembers so plain now. I not going to forget him again, no, the whole enduring time. I could tell him from all the others in creation."

"All right." The nurse was trying to hush her now. She

THE WIDE NET

and Other Stories

TO MY MOTHER,

CHESTINA ANDREWS WELTY

Contents

First Love

WHATEVER happened, it happened in extraordinary times, in a season of dreams, and in Natchez it was the bitterest winter of them all. The north wind struck one January night in 1807 with an insistent penetration, as if it followed the settlers down by their own course, screaming down the river bends to drive them further still. Afterwards there was the strange drugged fall of snow. When the sun rose the air broke into a thousand prisms as close as the flash-and-turn of gulls' wings. For a long time afterwards it was so clear that in the evening the little companion-star to Sirius could be seen plainly in the heavens by travelers who took their way by night, and Venus shone in the daytime in all its course through the new transparency of the sky.

The Mississippi shuddered and lifted from its bed, reaching like a somnambulist driven to go in new places; the ice stretched far out over the waves. Flatboats and rafts continued to float downstream, but with unsignalling passengers submissive and huddled, mere bundles of sticks; bets were laid on shore as to whether they were alive or dead, but it was impossible to prove it either way.

The coated moss hung in blue and shining garlands over the trees along the changed streets in the morning. The town of little galleries was all laden roofs and silence. In the fastness of Natchez it began to seem then that the whole world, like itself, must be in a transfiguration. The only clamor came from the animals that suffered in their stalls, or from the wildcats that howled in closer rings each night from the frozen cane. The Indians could be heard from greater distances and in greater numbers than had been guessed, sending up placating but proud messages to the sun in continual ceremonies of dancing. The red percussion of their fires could be seen night and day by those waiting in the dark trance of the frozen town. Men were caught by the cold, they dropped in its snare-like silence. Bands of travelers moved closer together, with intenser caution, through the glassy tunnels of the Trace, for all proportion went away, and they followed one another like insects going at dawn through the heavy grass. Natchez people turned silently to look when a solitary man that no one had ever seen before was found and carried in through the streets, frozen the way he had crouched in a hollow tree, gray and huddled like a squirrel, with a little bundle of goods clasped to him.

Joel Mayes, a deaf boy twelve years old, saw the man brought in and knew it was a dead man, but his eyes were for something else, something wonderful. He saw the breaths coming out of people's mouths, and his dark face, losing just now a little of its softness, showed its secret desire. It was marvelous to him when the infinite designs of speech became visible in formations on the air, and he watched with awe that changed to tenderness whenever people met and passed in the road with an exchange of words. He walked alone, slowly through the silence, with the sturdy and yet dreamlike walk of the orphan, and let his own breath out through his lips, pushed it into the air, and whatever word it was it took the shape of a tower. He was as pleased as if he had had a little conversation with someone. At the end of the street, where he turned into the Inn, he always bent his head and walked faster, as if all frivolity were done, for he was boot-boy there.

He had come to Natchez some time in the summer. That was through great worlds of leaves, and the whole journey from Virginia had been to him a kind of childhood wandering in oblivion. He had remained to himself: always to himself at first, and afterwards too—with the company of Old Man McCaleb who took him along when his parents vanished in the forest, were cut off from him, and in spite of his last backward look, dropped behind. Arms bent on destination dragged him forward through the sharp bushes, and leaves came toward his face which he finally put his hands out to stop. Now that he was a boot-boy, he had thought little, frugally, almost stonily, of that long time . . . until lately Old Man McCaleb had reappeared at the Inn, bound for no telling where, his tangled beard like the beards of old men in dreams; and in the act of cleaning his boots, which were uncommonly heavy and burdensome with mud, Joel came upon a little part of the old adventure, for there it was, dark and crusted . . . came back to it, and went over it again. . . .

He rubbed, and remembered the day after his parents had left him, the day when it was necessary to hide from the Indians. Old Man McCaleb, his stern face lighting in the most unexpected way, had herded them, the whole party alike, into the dense cane brake, deep down off the Trace—the densest part, where it grew as thick and locked as some kind of wild teeth. There they crouched, and each one of them, man, woman, and child, had looked at all the others from a hiding place that seemed the least safe of all, watching in an eager wild instinct for any movement or betrayal. Crouched by his bush, Joel had cried; all his understanding would desert him suddenly and because he could not hear he could not see or touch or find a familiar thing in the world. He wept, and Old Man McCaleb first felled the excited dog with the blunt end of his axe, and then he turned a fierce face toward him and lifted the blade in the air, in a kind of ecstasy of protecting the silence they were keeping. Joel had made a sound. . . . He gasped and put his mouth quicker than thought against the earth. He took the leaves in his mouth. . . . In that long time of lying motionless with the men and women in the cane brake he had learned what silence meant to other people. Through the danger he had felt acutely, even with horror, the nearness of his companions, a speechless embrace of which he had had no warning, a powerful, crushing unity. The Indians had then gone by, followed by an old woman—in solemn, single file, careless of the inflaming arrows they carried in their quivers, dangling in their hands a few strings of catfish. They passed in the length of the old woman's yawn. Then one by one McCaleb's charges had to rise up and come out of the hiding place. There was little talking together, but a kind of shame and shuffling. As soon as the party reached Natchez, their little cluster dissolved completely. The old man had given each of them one long, rather forlorn look for a farewell, and had gone away, no less preoccupied than he had ever been. To the man who had saved his life Joel lifted the gentle, almost indifferent face of the child who has asked for nothing. Now he remembered the white gulls flying across the sky behind the old man's head.

Joel had been deposited at the Inn, and there was nowhere else for him to go, for it stood there and marked the foot of the long Trace, with the river back of it. So he remained. It was a noncommittal arrangement: he never paid them anything for his keep, and they never paid him anything for his work. Yet time passed, and he became a little part of the place where it passed over him. A small private room became his own; it was on the ground floor behind the saloon, a dark little room paved with stones with its ceiling rafters curved not higher than a man's head. There was a fireplace and one window, which opened on the courtyard filled always with the tremor of horses. He curled up every night on a highbacked bench, when the weather turned cold he was given a collection of old coats to sleep under, and the room was almost excessively his own, as it would have been a stray kitten's that came to the same spot every night. He began to keep his candlestick carefully polished, he set it in the center of the puncheon table, and at night when it was lighted all the messages of love carved into it with a knife in Spanish words, with a deep Spanish gouging, came out in black relief, for anyone to read who came knowing the language.

Late at night, nearer morning, after the travelers had all certainly pulled off their boots to fall into bed, he waked by habit and passed with the candle shielded up the stairs and through the halls and rooms, and gathered up the boots. When he had brought them all down to his table he would sit and take his own time cleaning them, while the firelight would come gently across the paving stones. It seemed then that his whole life was safely alighted, in the sleep of everyone else, like a bird on a bough, and he was alone in the way he liked to be. He did not despise boots at all—he had learned boots; under his hand they stood up and took a good shape. This was not a slave's work, or a child's either. It had dignity: it was dangerous to walk about among sleeping men. More than once he had been seized and the life half shaken out of him by a man waking up in a sweat of suspicion or nightmare, but he dealt nimbly as an animal with the violence and quick frenzy of dreamers. It might seem to him that the whole world was sleeping in the lightest of trances, which the least movement would surely wake; but he only walked softly, stepping around and over, and got back to his room. Once a rattlesnake had shoved its head from a boot as he stretched out his hand; but that was not likely to happen again in a thousand years.

It was in his own room, on the night of the first snowfall, that a new adventure began for him. Very late in the night, toward morning, Joel sat bolt upright in bed and opened his eyes to see the whole room shining brightly, like a brimming lake in the sun. Boots went completely out of his head, and he was left motionless. The candle was lighted in its stick, the fire was high in the grate, and from the window a wild tossing illumination came, which he did not even identify at first as the falling of snow. Joel was left in the shadow of the room, and there before him, in the center of the strange multiplied light, were two men in black capes sitting at his table. They sat in profile to him, tall under the little arch of the rafters, facing each other across the good table he used for everything, and talking together. They were not of Natchez, and their names were not in the book. Each of them had a white glitter upon his boots—it was the snow; their capes were drawn together in front, and in the blackness of the folds, snowflakes were just beginning to melt.

Joel had never been able to hear the knocking at a door, and still he knew what that would be; and he surmised that these men had never knocked even lightly to enter his room. When he found that at some moment outside his knowledge or consent two men had seemingly fallen from the clouds onto the two stools at his table and had taken everything over for themselves, he did not keep the calm heart with which he had stood and regarded all men up to Old Man McCaleb, who snored upstairs.

He did not at once betray the violation that he felt. Instead, he simply sat, still bolt upright, and looked with the feasting the eyes do in secret—at their faces, the one eye of each that he could see, the cheeks, the half-hidden mouths—the faces each firelit, and strange with a common reminiscence or speculation. . . . Perhaps he was saved from giving a cry by knowing it could be heard. Then the gesture one of the men made in the air transfixed him where he waited.

One of the two men lifted his right arm—a tense, yet gentle

and easy motion—and made the dark wet cloak fall back. To Joel it was like the first movement he had ever seen, as if the world had been up to that night inanimate. It was like the signal to open some heavy gate or paddock, and it did open to his complete astonishment upon a panorama in his own head, about which he knew first of all that he would never be able to speak—it was nothing but brightness, as full as the brightness on which he had opened his eyes. Inside his room was still another interior, this meeting upon which all the light was turned, and within that was one more mystery, all that was being said. The men's heads were inclined together against the blaze, their hair seemed light and floating. Their elbows rested on the boards, stirring the crumbs where Joel had eaten his biscuit. He had no idea of how long they had stayed when they got up and stretched their arms and walked out through the door, after blowing the candle out.

When Joel woke up again at daylight, his first thought was of Indians, his next of ghosts, and then the vision of what had happened came back into his head. He took a light beating for forgetting to clean the boots, but then he forgot the beating. He wondered for how long a time the men had been meeting in his room while he was asleep, and whether they had ever seen him, and what they might be going to do to him, whether they would take him each by the arm and drag him on further, through the leaves. He tried to remember everything of the night before, and he could, and then of the day before, and he rubbed belatedly at a boot in a long and deepening dream. His memory could work like the slinging of a noose to catch a wild pony. It reached back and hung trembling over the very moment of terror in which he had become separated from his parents, and then it turned and started in the opposite direction, and it would have discerned some shape, but he would not let it, of the future. In the meanwhile, all day long, everything in the passing moment and each little deed assumed the gravest importance. He divined every change in the house, in the angle of the doors, in the height of the fires, and whether the logs had been stirred by a boot or had only fallen in an empty room. He was seized and possessed by mystery. He waited for night. In his own room the candlestick now stood on the table covered with the wonder of having been touched by unknown hands in his absence and seen in his sleep.

It was while he was cleaning boots again that the identity of the men came to him all at once. Like part of his meditations, the names came into his mind. He ran out into the street with this knowledge rocking in his head, remembering then the tremor of a great arrival which had shaken Natchez, caught fast in the grip of the cold, and shaken it through the lethargy of the snow, and it was clear now why the floors swayed with running feet and unsteady hands shoved him aside at the bar. There was no one to inform him that the men were Aaron Burr and Harman Blennerhassett, but he knew. No one had pointed out to him any way that he might know which was which, but he knew that: it was Burr who had made the gesture.

They came to his room every night, and indeed Joel had not expected that the one visit would be the end. It never occurred to him that the first meeting did not mark a beginning. It took a little time always for the snow to melt from their capes—for it continued all this time to snow. Joel sat up with his eyes wide open in the shadows and looked out like the lone watcher of a conflagration. The room grew warm, burning with the heat from the little grate, but there was something of fire in all that happened. It was from Aaron Burr that the flame was springing, and it seemed to pass across the table with certain words and through the sudden nobleness of the gesture, and touch Blennerhassett. Yet the breath of their speech was no simple thing like the candle's gleam between them. Joel saw them still only in profile, but he could see that the secret was endlessly complex, for in two nights it was apparent that it could never be all told. All that they said never finished their conversation. They would always have to meet again. The ring Burr wore caught the firelight repeatedly and started it up again in the intricate whirlpool of a signet. Quicker and fuller still was his eye, darting its look about, but never at Joel. Their eyes had never really seen his room . . . the fine polish he had given the candlestick, the clean boards from which he had scraped the crumbs, the wooden bench where he was himself, from which he put outward—just a little, carelessly—his hand. . . . Everything in the room was conquest, all was a dream of delights and powers beyond its walls. . . . The light-filled hair fell over Burr's sharp forehead, his cheek grew taut, his smile was sudden, his lips drove the breath through. The other man's face, with its quiet mouth, for he was the listener, changed from ardor to gloom and back to ardor. . . . Joel sat still and looked from one man to the other.

At first he believed that he had not been discovered. Then he knew that they had learned somehow of his presence, and that it had not stopped them. Somehow that appalled him. . . . They were aware that if it were only before him, they could talk forever in his room. Then he put it that they accepted him. One night, in his first realization of this, his defect seemed to him a kind of hospitality. A joy came over him, he was moved to gaiety, he felt wit stirring in his mind, and he came out of his hiding place and took a few steps toward them. Finally, it was too much: he broke in upon the circle of their talk, and set food and drink from the kitchen on the table between them. His hands were shaking, and they looked at him as if from great distances, but they were not surprised, and he could smell the familiar black wetness of travelers' clothes steaming up from them in the firelight. Afterwards he sat on the floor perfectly still, with Burr's cloak hanging just beside his own shoulder. At such moments he felt a dizziness as if the cape swung him about in a great arc of wonder, but Aaron Burr turned his full face and looked down at him only with gravity, the high margin of his brows lifted above tireless eyes.

There was a kind of dominion promised in his gentlest glance. When he first would come and throw himself down to talk and the fire would flame up and the reflections of the snowy world grew bright, even the clumsy table seemed to change its substance and to become a part of a ceremony. He might have talked in another language, in which there was nothing but evocation. When he was seen so plainly, all his movements and his looks seemed part of a devotion that was curiously patient and had the illusion of wisdom all about it. Lights shone in his eyes like travelers' fires seen far out on the river. Always he talked, his talking was his appearance, as if there were no eyes, nose, or mouth to remember; in his face there was every subtlety and eloquence, and no features, no kindness, for there was no awareness whatever of the present. Looking up from the floor at his speaking face, Joel knew all at once some secret of temptation and an anguish that would reach out after it like a closing hand. He would allow Burr to take him with him wherever it was that he meant to go.

Sometimes in the nights Joel would feel himself surely under their eyes, and think they must have come; but that would be a dream, and when he sat up on his bench he often saw nothing more than the dormant firelight stretched on the empty floor, and he would have a strange feeling of having been deserted and lost, not quite like anything he had ever felt in his life. It was likely to be early dawn before they came.

When they were there, he sat restored, though they paid no more attention to him than they paid the presence of the firelight. He brought all the food he could manage to give them; he saved a little out of his own suppers, and one night he stole a turkey pie. He might have been their safety, for the way he sat up so still and looked at them at moments like a father at his playing children. He never for an instant wished for them to leave, though he would so long for sleep that he would stare at them finally in bewilderment and without a single flicker of the eyelid. Often they would talk all night. Blennerhassett's wide vague face would grow out of devotion into exhaustion. But Burr's hand would always reach across and take him by the shoulder as if to rouse him from a dull sleep, and the radiance of his own face would heighten always with the passing of time. Joel sat quietly, waiting for the full revelation of the meetings. All his love went out to the talkers. He would not have known how to hold it back.

In the idle mornings, in some morning need to go looking at the world, he wandered down to the Esplanade and stood under the trees which bent heavily over his head. He frowned out across the ice-covered racetrack and out upon the river. There was one hour when the river was the color of smoke, as if it were more a thing of the woods than an element and a power in itself. It seemed to belong to the woods, to be gentle and watched over, a tethered and grazing pet of the forest, and then when the light spread higher and color stained the world, the river would leap suddenly out of the shining ice around, into its full-grown torrent of life, and its strength and its churning passage held Joel watching over it like the spell unfolding by night in his room. If he could not speak to the river, and he could not, still he would try to read in the river's blue and violet skeins a working of the momentous event. It was hard to understand. Was any scheme a man had, however secret and intact, always broken upon by the very current of its working? One day, in anguish, he saw a raft torn apart in midstream and the men scattered from it. Then all that he felt move in his heart at the sight of the inscrutable river went out in hope for the two men and their genius that he sheltered.

It was when he returned to the Inn that he was given a notice to paste on the saloon mirror saying that the trial of Aaron Burr for treason would be held at the end of the month at Washington, capitol of Mississippi Territory, on the campus of Jefferson College, where the crowds might be amply accommodated. In the meanwhile, the arrival of the full, armed flotilla was being awaited, and the price of whisky would not be advanced in this tavern, but there would be a slight increase in the tariff on a bed upstairs, depending on how many slept in it.

The month wore on, and now it was full moonlight. Late at night the whole sky was lunar, like the surface of the moon brought as close as a cheek. The luminous ranges of all the clouds stretched one beyond the other in heavenly order. They seemed to be the streets where Joel was walking through the town. People now lighted their houses in entertainments as if they copied after the sky, with Burr in the center of them always, dancing with the women, talking with the men. They followed and formed cotillion figures about the one who threatened or lured them, and their minuets skimmed across the nights like a pebble expertly skipped across water. Joel would watch them take sides, and watch the arguments, all the frilled motions and the toasts, and he thought they were to decide whether Burr was good or evil. But all the time, Joel believed, when he saw Burr go dancing by, that did not touch him at all. Joel knew his eyes saw nothing there and went always beyond the room, although usually the most beautiful woman there was somehow in his arms when the set was over. Sometimes they drove him in their carriages down to the Esplanade and pointed out the moon to him, to end the evening. There they sat showing everything to Aaron Burr, nodding with a magnificence that approached fatigue toward the reaches of the ice that stretched over the river like an impossible bridge, some extension to the West of the Natchez Trace; and a radiance as soft and near as rain fell on their hands and faces, and on the plumes of the breaths from the horses' nostrils, and they were as gracious and as grand as Burr.

Each day that drew the trial closer, men talked more hotly on the corners and the saloon at the Inn shook with debate; every night Burr was invited to a finer and later ball; and Joel waited. He knew that Burr was being allotted, by an almost specific consent, this free and unmolested time till dawn, to meet in conspiracy, for the sake of continuing and perfecting the secret. This knowledge Joel gathered to himself by being, himself, everywhere; it decreed his own suffering and made it secret and filled with private omens.

One day he was driven to know everything. It was the morning he was given a little fur cap, and he set it on his head and started out. He walked through the dark trodden snow all the way up the Trace to the Bayou Pierre. The great trees began to break that day. The pounding of their explosions filled the subdued air; to Joel it was as if a great foot had stamped on the ground. And at first he thought he saw the fulfillment of all the rumor and promise—the flotilla coming around the bend, and he did not know whether he felt terror or pride. But then he saw that what covered the river over was a chain of great perfect trees floating down, lying on their sides in postures like slain giants and heroes of battle, black cedars and stone-white sycamores, magnolias with their leavy leaves shining as if they were in bloom, a long procession. Then it was terror that he felt.

He went on. He was not the only one who had made the pilgrimage to see what the original flotilla was like, that had been taken from Burr. There were many others: there was Old Man McCaleb, at a little distance. . . . In care not to show any excitement of expectation, Joel made his way through successive little groups that seemed to meditate there above the encampment of militia on the snowy bluff, and looked down at the water.

There was no galley there. There were nine small flatboats tied to the shore. They seemed so small and delicate that he was shocked and distressed, and looked around at the faces of the others, who looked coolly back at him. There was no sign of a weapon about the boats or anywhere, except in the hands of the men on guard. There were barrels of molasses and whisky, rolling and knocking each other like drowned men, and stowed to one side of one of the boats, in a dark place, a strange little collection of blankets, a silver bridle with bells, a book swollen with water, and a little flute with a narrow ridge of snow along it. Where Joel stood looking down upon them, the boats floated in clusters of three, as small as water-lilies on a still bayou. A canoe filled with crazily wrapped-up Indians passed at a little distance, and with severe open mouths the Indians all laughed.

But the soldiers were sullen with cold, and very grave or angry, and Old Man McCaleb was there with his beard flying and his finger pointing prophetically in the direction of upstream. Some of the soldiers and all the women nodded their heads, as though they were the easiest believers, and one woman drew her child tightly to her. Joel shivered. Two of the young men hanging over the edge of the bluff flung their arms in sudden exhilaration about each other's shoulders, and a look of wildness came over their faces.

Back in the streets of Natchez, Joel met part of the militia marching and stood with his heart racing, back out of the way of the line coming with bright guns tilted up in the sharp air. Behind them, two of the soldiers dragged along a young dandy whose eyes glared at everything. There where they held him he was trying over and over again to make Aaron Burr's gesture, and he never convinced anybody.

Joel went in all three times to the militia's encampment on the Bayou Pierre, the last time on the day before the trial was to begin. Then out beyond a willow point a rowboat with one soldier in it kept laconic watch upon the north.

Joel returned on the frozen path to the Inn, and stumbled into his room, and waited for Burr and Blennerhassett to come and talk together. His head ached. . . . . All his walking about was no use. Where did people learn things? Where did they go to find them? How far?

Burr and Blennerhassett talked across the table, and it was growing late on the last night. Then there in the doorway with a fiddle in her hand stood Blennerhassett's wife, wearing breeches, come to fetch him home. The fiddle she had simply picked up in the Inn parlor as she came through, and Joel did not think she bothered now to speak at all. But she waited there before the fire, still a child and so clearly related to her husband that their sudden movements at the encounter were alike and made at the same time. They stood looking at each other there in the firelight like creatures balancing together on a raft, and then she lifted the bow and began to play.

Joel gazed at the girl, not much older than himself. She leaned her cheek against the fiddle. He had never examined a fiddle at all, and when she began to play it she frightened and dismayed him by her almost insect-like motions, the pensive antennae of her arms, her mask of a countenance. When she played she never blinked her eye. Her legs, fantastic in breeches, were separated slightly, and from her bent knees she swayed back and forth as if she were weaving the tunes with her body. The sharp odor of whisky moved with her. The slits of her eyes were milky. The songs she played seemed to him to have no beginnings and no endings, but to be about many hills and valleys, and chains of lakes. She, like the men, knew of a place. . . . All of them spoke of a country.

And quite clearly, and altogether to his surprise, Joel saw a sight that he had nearly forgotten. Instead of the fire on the hearth, there was a mimosa tree in flower. It was in the little back field at his home in Virginia and his mother was leading him by the hand. Fragile, delicate, cloud-like it rose on its pale trunk and spread its long level arms. His mother pointed to it. Among the trembling leaves the feathery puffs of sweet bloom filled the tree like thousands of paradisical birds all alighted at an instant. He had known then the story of the Princess Labam, for his mother had told it to him, how she was so radiant that she sat on the roof-top at night and lighted the city. It seemed to be the mimosa tree that lighted the garden, for its brightness and fragrance overlaid all the rest. Out of its graciousness this tree suffered their presence and shed its splendor upon him and his mother. His mother pointed again, and its scent swayed like the Asiatic princess moving up and down the pink steps of its branches. Then the vision was gone. Aaron Burr sat in front of the fire, Blennerhassett faced him, and Blennerhassett's wife played on the violin.

There was no compassion in what this woman was doing, he knew that—there was only a frightening thing, a stern allurement. Try as he might, he could not comprehend it, though it was so calculated. He had instead a sensation of pain, the ends of his fingers were stinging. At first he did not realize that he had heard the sounds of her song, the only thing he had ever heard. Then all at once as she held the lifted bow still for a moment he gasped for breath at the interruption, and he did not care to learn her purpose or to wonder any longer, but bent his head and listened for the note that she would fling down upon them. And it was so gentle then, it touched him with surprise; it made him think of animals sleeping on their cushioned paws.

For a moment his love went like sound into a myriad life and was divided among all the people in his room. While they listened, Burr's radiance was somehow quenched, or theirs was raised to equal it, and they were all alike. There was one thing that shone in all their faces, and that was how far they were from home, how far from everywhere that they knew. Joel put his hand to his own face, and hid his pity from them while they listened to the endless tunes.

But she ended them. Sleep all at once seemed to overcome her whole body. She put down the fiddle and took Blennerhassett by both hands. He seemed tired too, more tired than talking could ever make him. He went out when she led him. They went wrapped under one cloak, his arm about her.

Burr did not go away immediately. First he walked up and down before the fire. He turned each time with diminishing violence, and light and shadow seemed to stream more softly with his turning cloak. Then he stood still. The firelight threw its changes over his face. He had no one to talk to. His boots smelled of the fire's closeness. Of course he had forgotten

Joel, he seemed quite alone. At last with a strange naturalness, almost with a limp, he went to the table and stretched himself full length upon it.

He lay on his back. Joel was astonished. That was the way they laid out the men killed in duels in the Inn yard; and that was the table they laid them on.

Burr fell asleep instantly, so quickly that Joel felt he should never be left alone. He looked at the sleeping face of Burr, and the time and the place left him, and all that Burr had said that he had tried to guess left him too—he knew nothing in the world except the sleeping face. It was quiet. The eyes were almost closed, only dark slits lay beneath the lids. There was a small scar on the cheek. The lips were parted. Joel thought, I could speak if I would, or I could hear. Once I did each thing. . . . Still he listened . . . and it seemed that all that would speak, in this world, was listening. Burr was silent; he demanded nothing, nothing. . . . A boy or a man could be so alone in his heart that he could not even ask a question. In such silence as falls over a lonely man there is childlike supplication, and all arms might wish to open to him, but there is no speech. This was Burr's last night: Joel knew that. This was the moment before he would ride away. Why would the heart break so at absence? Joel knew that it was because nothing had been told. The heart is secret even when the moment it dreamed of has come, a moment when there might have been a revelation. . . . Joel stood motionless; he lifted his gaze from Burr's face and stared at nothing. . . . If love does a secret thing always, it is to reach backward, to a time that could not be known—for it makes a history of the sorrow and the dream it has contemplated in some instant of recognition. What Joel saw before him he had a terrible wish to speak out loud, but he would have had to find names for the places of the heart and the times for its shadowy and tragic events, and they seemed of great magnitude, heroic and terrible and splendid, like the legends of the mind. But for lack of a way to tell how much was known, the boundaries would lie between him and the others, all the others, until he died.

Presently Burr began to toss his head and to cry out. He talked, his face drew into a dreadful set of grimaces, which it followed over and over. He could never stop talking. Joel was afraid of these words, and afraid that eavesdroppers might listen to them. Whatever words they were, they were being taken by some force out of his dream. In horror, Joel put out his hand. He could never in his life have laid it across the mouth of Aaron Burr, but he thrust it into Burr's spread-out fingers. The fingers closed and did not yield; the clasp grew so fierce that it hurt his hand, but he saw that the words had stopped.

As if a silent love had shown him whatever new thing he would ever be able to learn, Joel had some wisdom in his fingers now which only this long month could have brought. He knew with what gentleness to hold the burning hand. With the gravity of his very soul he received the furious pressure of this man's dream. At last Burr drew his arm back beside his quiet head, and his hand hung like a child's in sleep, released in oblivion.

The next morning, Joel was given a notice to paste on the saloon mirror that conveyances might be rented at the Inn daily for the excursion to Washington for the trial of Mr. Burr, payment to be made in advance. Joel went out and stood on a corner, and joined with a group of young boys walking behind the militia.

It was warm—a "false spring" day. The little procession from Natchez, decorated and smiling in all they owned or whatever they borrowed or chartered or rented, moved grandly through the streets and on up the Trace. To Joel, somewhere in the line, the blue air that seemed to lie between the high banks held it all in a mist, softly colored, the fringe waving from a carriage top, a few flags waving, a sword shining when some gentleman made a flourish. High up on their horses a number of the men were wearing their Revolutionary War uniforms, as if to reiterate that Aaron Burr fought once at their sides as a hero.

Under the spreading live-oaks at Washington, the trial opened like a festival. There was a theatre of benches, and a promenade; stalls were set out under the trees and glasses of whisky, and colored ribbons, were sold. Joel sat somewhere among the crowds. Breezes touched the yellow and violet of dresses and stirred them, horses pawed the ground, and the people pressed upon him and seemed more real than those in dreams, and yet their pantomime was like those choruses and companies whose movements are like the waves running together. A hammer was then pounded, there was sudden attention from all the spectators, and Joel felt the great solidifying of their silence.

He had dreaded the sight of Burr. He had thought there might be some mark or disfigurement that would come from his panic. But all his grace was back upon him, and he was smiling to greet the studious faces which regarded him. Before their bright façade others rose first, declaiming men in turn, and then Burr.

In a moment he was walking up and down with his shadow on the grass and the patches of snow. He was talking again, talking now in great courtesy to everybody. There was a flickering light of sun and shadow on his face.

Then Joel understood. Burr was explaining away, smoothing over all that he had held great enough to have dreaded once. He walked back and forth elegantly in the sun, turning his wrist ever so airily in its frill, making light of his dream that had terrified him. And it was the deed they had all come to see. All around Joel they gasped, smiled, pressed one another's arms, nodded their heads; there were tender smiles on the women's faces. They were at Aaron Burr's feet at last, learning their superiority. They loved him now, in their condescension. They leaned forward in delight at the parading spectacle he was making. And when it was over for the day, they shook each other's hands, and Old Man McCaleb could be seen spitting on the ground, in the anticipation of another day as good as this one.

Blennerhassett did not come that night.

Burr came very late. He walked in the door, looked down at Joel where he sat among his boots, and suddenly stooped and took the dirty cloth out of his hand. He put his face quickly into it and pressed and rubbed it against his skin. Joel saw that all his clothes were dirty and ragged. The last thing he did was to set a little cap of turkey feathers on his head. Then he went out.

Joel followed him along behind the dark houses and

through a ravine. Burr turned toward the Halfway Hill. Joel turned too, and he saw Burr walk slowly up and open the great heavy gate.

He saw him stop beside a tall camellia bush as solid as a tower and pick up one of the frozen buds which were shed all around it on the ground. For a moment he held it in the palm of his hand, and then he went on. Joel, following behind, did the same. He held the bud, and studied the burned edges of its folds by the pale half-light of the East. The bud came apart in his hand, its layers like small velvet shells, still iridescent, the shriveled flower inside. He held it tenderly and yet timidly, in a kind of shame, as though all disaster lay pitifully disclosed now to the eyes.

He knew the girl Burr had often danced with under the rings of tapers when she came out in a cloak across the shadowy hill. Burr stood, quiet and graceful as he had always been as her partner at the balls. Joel felt a pain like a sting while she first merged with the dark figure and then drew back. The moon, late-risen and waning, came out of the clouds. Aaron Burr made the gesture there in the distance, toward the West, where the clouds hung still and red, and when Joel looked at him in the light he saw as she must have seen the absurdity he was dressed in, the feathers on his head. With a curious feeling of revenge upon her, he watched her turn, draw smaller within her own cape, and go away.

Burr came walking down the hill, and passed close to the camellia bush where Joel was standing. He walked stiffly in his mock Indian dress with the boot polish on his face. The youngest child in Natchez would have known that this was a remarkable and wonderful figure that had humiliated itself by disguise.

Pausing in an open space, Burr lifted his hand once more and a slave led out from the shadows a majestic horse with silver trappings shining in the light of the moon. Burr mounted from the slave's hand in all the clarity of his true elegance, and sat for a moment motionless in the saddle. Then he cut his whip through the air, and rode away.

Joel followed him on foot toward the Liberty Road. As he walked through the streets of Natchez he felt a strange mourning to know that Burr would never come again by that way. If he had left in disguise, the thirst that was in his face was the same as it had ever been. He had eluded judgment, that was all he had done, and Joel was glad while he still trembled. Joel would never know now the true course, or the true outcome of any dream: this was all he felt. But he walked on, in the frozen path into the wilderness, on and on. He did not see how he could ever go back and still be the boot-boy at the Inn.

He did not know how far he had gone on the Liberty Road when the posse came riding up behind and passed him. He walked on. He saw that the bodies of the frozen birds had fallen out of the trees, and he fell down and wept for his father and mother, to whom he had not said goodbye.

The Wide Net

This Story is for John Fraiser Robinson

WILLIAM WALLACE JAMIESON'S wife Hazel was going to have a baby. But this was October, and it was six months away, and she acted exactly as though it would be tomorrow. When he came in the room she would not speak to him, but would look as straight at nothing as she could, with her eyes glowing. If he only touched her she stuck out her tongue or ran around the table. So one night he went out with two of the boys down the road and stayed out all night. But that was the worst thing yet, because when he came home in the early morning Hazel had vanished. He went through the house not believing his eyes, balancing with both hands out, his yellow cowlick rising on end, and then he turned the kitchen inside out looking for her, but it did no good. Then when he got back to the front room he saw she had left him a little letter, in an envelope. That was doing something behind someone's back. He took out the letter, pushed it open, held it out at a distance from his eyes. . . . After one look he was scared to read the exact words, and he crushed the whole thing in his hand instantly, but what it had said was that she would not put up with him after that and was going to the river to drown herself.

"Drown herself. . . . But she's in mortal fear of the water!"

He ran out front, his face red like the red of the picked cotton field he ran over, and down in the road he gave a loud shout for Virgil Thomas, who was just going in his own house, to come out again. He could just see the edge of Virgil, he had almost got in, he had one foot inside the door.

They met half-way between the farms, under the shade-tree.

"Haven't you had enough of the night?" asked Virgil. There they were, their pants all covered with dust and dew, and they had had to carry the third man home flat between them.

"I've lost Hazel, she's vanished, she went to drown herself."

"Why, that ain't like Hazel," said Virgil.

William Wallace reached out and shook him. "You heard me. Don't you know we have to drag the river?"

"Right this minute?"

"You ain't got nothing to do till spring."

"Let me go set foot inside the house and speak to my mother and tell her a story, and I'll come back."

"This will take the wide net," said William Wallace. His eyebrows gathered, and he was talking to himself.

"How come Hazel to go and do that way?" asked Virgil as they started out.

William Wallace said, "I reckon she got lonesome."

"That don't argue—drown herself for getting lonesome. My mother gets lonesome."

"Well," said William Wallace. "It argues for Hazel."

"How long is it now since you and her was married?"

"Why, it's been a year."

"It don't seem that long to me. A year!"

"It was this time last year. It seems longer," said William Wallace, breaking a stick off a tree in surprise. They walked along, kicking at the flowers on the road's edge. "I remember the day I seen her first, and that seems a long time ago. She was coming along the road holding a little frying-size chicken from her grandma, under her arm, and she had it real quiet. I spoke to her with nice manners. We knowed each other's names, being bound to, just didn't know each other to speak to. I says, 'Where are you taking the fryer?' and she says, 'Mind your manners,' and I kept on till after while she says, 'If you want to walk me home, take littler steps.' So I didn't lose time. It was just four miles across the field and full of blackberries, and from the top of the hill there was Dover below, looking sizeable-like and clean, spread out between the two churches like that. When we got down, I says to her, 'What kind of water's in this well?' and she says, 'The best water in the world.' So I drew a bucket and took out a dipper and she drank and I drank. I didn't think it was that remarkable, but I didn't tell her."

"What happened that night?" asked Virgil.

"We ate the chicken," said William Wallace, "and it was

tender. Of course that wasn't all they had. The night I was trying their table out, it sure had good things to eat from one end to the other. Her mama and papa sat at the head and foot and we was face to face with each other across it, with I remember a pat of butter between. They had real sweet butter, with a tree drawed down it, elegant-like. Her mama eats like a man. I had brought her a whole hat-ful of berries and she didn't even pass them to her husband. Hazel, she would leap up and take a pitcher of new milk and fill up the glasses. I had heard how they couldn't have a singing at the church without a fight over her."

"Oh, she's a pretty girl, all right," said Virgil. "It's a pity for the ones like her to grow old, and get like their mothers."

"Another thing will be that her mother will get wind of this and come after me," said William Wallace.

"Her mother will eat you alive," said Virgil.

"She's just been watching her chance," said William Wallace. "Why did I think I could stay out all night."

"Just something come over you."

"First it was just a carnival at Carthage, and I had to let them guess my weight . . . and after that . . ."

"It was nice to be sitting on your neck in a ditch singing," prompted Virgil, "in the moonlight. And playing on the harmonica like you can play."

"Even if Hazel did sit home knowing I was drunk, that wouldn't kill her," said William Wallace. "What she knows ain't ever killed her yet. . . . She's smart, too, for a girl," he said.

"She's a lot smarter than her cousins in Beulah," said Virgil. "And especially Edna Earle, that never did get to be what you'd call a heavy thinker. Edna Earle could sit and ponder all day on how the little tail of the 'C' got through the 'L' in a Coca-Cola sign."

"Hazel *is* smart," said William Wallace. They walked on. "You ought to see her pantry shelf, it looks like a hundred jars when you open the door. I don't see how she could turn around and jump in the river."

"It's a woman's trick."

"I always behaved before. Till the one night—last night."

"Yes, but the one night," said Virgil. "And she was waiting to take advantage."

"She jumped in the river because she was scared to death of the water and that was to make it worse," he said. "She remembered how I used to have to pick her up and carry her over the oak-log bridge, how she'd shut her eyes and make a dead-weight and hold me round the neck, just for a little creek. I don't see how she brought herself to jump."

"Jumped backwards," said Virgil. "Didn't look."

When they turned off, it was still early in the pink and green fields. The fumes of morning, sweet and bitter, sprang up where they walked. The insects ticked softly, their strength in reserve; butterflies chopped the air, going to the east, and the birds flew carelessly and sang by fits and starts, not the way they did in the evening in sustained and drowsy songs.

"It's a pretty *day* for sure," said William Wallace. "It's a pretty *day* for it."

"I don't see a sign of her ever going along here," said Virgil.

"Well," said William Wallace. "She wouldn't have dropped anything. I never saw a girl to leave less signs of where she's been."

"Not even a plum seed," said Virgil, kicking the grass.

In the grove it was so quiet that once William Wallace gave a jump, as if he could almost hear a sound of himself wondering where she had gone. A descent of energy came down on him in the thick of the woods and he ran at a rabbit and caught it in his hands.

"Rabbit . . . Rabbit . . ." He acted as if he wanted to take it off to himself and hold it up and talk to it. He laid a palm against its pushing heart. "Now . . . There now . . ."

"Let her go, William Wallace, let her go." Virgil, chewing on an elderberry whistle he had just made, stood at his shoulder: "What do you want with a live rabbit?"

William Wallace squatted down and set the rabbit on the ground but held it under his hand. It was a little, old, brown rabbit. It did not try to move. "See there?"

"Let her go."

"She can go if she wants to, but she don't want to."

Gently he lifted his hand. The round eye was shining at him sideways in the green gloom.

"Anybody can freeze a rabbit, that wants to," said Virgil. Suddenly he gave a far-reaching blast on the whistle, and the rabbit went in a streak. "Was you out catching cotton-tails, or was you out catching your wife?" he said, taking the turn to the open fields. "I come along to keep you on the track."

"Who'll we get, now?" They stood on top of a hill and William Wallace looked critically over the countryside. "Any of the Malones?"

"I was always scared of the Malones," said Virgil. "Too many *of* them."

"This is my day with the net, and they would have to watch out," said William Wallace. "I reckon some Malones, and the Doyles, will be enough. The six Doyles and their dogs, and you and me, and two little nigger boys is enough, with just a few Malones."

"That ought to be enough," said Virgil, "no matter what."

"I'll bring the Malones, and you bring the Doyles," said William Wallace, and they separated at the spring.

When William Wallace came back, with a string of Malones just showing behind him on the hilltop, he found Virgil with the two little Rippen boys waiting behind him, solemn little towheads. As soon as he walked up, Grady, the one in front, lifted his hand to signal silence and caution to his brother Brucie who began panting merrily and untrustworthily behind him.

Brucie bent readily under William Wallace's hand-pat, and gave him a dreamy look out of the tops of his round eyes, which were pure green-and-white like clover tops. William Wallace gave him a nickel. Grady hung his head; his white hair lay in a little tail in the nape of his neck.

"Let's let them come," said Virgil.

"Well, they can come then, but if we keep letting everybody come it is going to be too many," said William Wallace.

"They'll appreciate it, those little-old boys," said Virgil. Brucie held up at arm's length a long red thread with a bent pin tied on the end; and a look of helpless and intense interest gathered Grady's face like a drawstring—his eyes, one bright with a sty, shone pleadingly under his white bangs, and he snapped his jaw and tried to speak. . . . "Their papa was drowned in the Pearl River," said Virgil.

There was a shout from the gully.

"Here come all the Malones," cried William Wallace. "I asked four of them would they come, but the rest of the family invited themselves."

"Did you ever see a time when they didn't," said Virgil. "And yonder from the other direction comes the Doyles, still with biscuit crumbs on their cheeks, I bet, now it's nothing to do but eat as their mother said."

"If two little niggers would come along now, or one big nigger," said William Wallace. And the words were hardly out of his mouth when two little Negro boys came along, going somewhere, one behind the other, stepping high and gay in their overalls, as though they waded in honeydew to the waist.

"Come here, boys. What's your names?"

"Sam and Robbie Bell."

"Come along with us, we're going to drag the river."

"You hear that, Robbie Bell?" said Sam.

They smiled.

The Doyles came noiselessly, their dogs made all the fuss. The Malones, eight giants with great long black eyelashes, were already stamping the ground and pawing each other, ready to go. Everybody went up together to see Doc.

Old Doc owned the wide net. He had a house on top of the hill and he sat and looked out from a rocker on the front porch.

"Climb the hill and come in!" he began to intone across the valley. "Harvest's over . . . slipped up on everybody . . . cotton's picked, gone to the gin . . . hay cut . . . molasses made around here. . . . Big explosion's over, supervisors elected, some pleased, some not. . . . We're hearing talk of war!"

When they got closer, he was saying, "Many's been saved at revival, twenty-two last Sunday including a Doyle, ought to counted two. Hope they'll be a blessing to Dover community besides a shining star in Heaven. Now what?" he asked, for they had arrived and stood gathered in front of the steps.

"If nobody is using your wide net, could we use it?" asked William Wallace.

"You just used it a month ago," said Doc. "It ain't your turn."

Virgil jogged William Wallace's arm and cleared his throat. "This time is kind of special," he said. "We got reason to think William Wallace's wife Hazel is in the river, drowned."

"What reason have you got to think she's in the river drowned?" asked Doc. He took out his old pipe. "I'm asking the husband."

"Because she's not in the house," said William Wallace.

"Vanished?" and he knocked out the pipe.

"Plum vanished."

"Of course a thousand things could have happened to her," said Doc, and he lighted the pipe.

"Hand him up the letter, William Wallace," said Virgil. "We can't wait around till Doomsday for the net while Doc sits back thinkin'."

"I tore it up, right at the first," said William Wallace. "But I know it by heart. It said she was going to jump straight in the Pearl River and that I'd be sorry."

"Where do you come in, Virgil?" asked Doc.

"I was in the same place William Wallace sat on his neck in, all night, and done as much as he done, and come home the same time."

"You-all were out cuttin' up, so Lady Hazel has to jump in the river, is that it? Cause and effect? Anybody want to argue with me? Where do these others come in, Doyles, Malones, and what not?"

"Doc is the smartest man around," said William Wallace, turning to the solidly waiting Doyles, "but it sure takes time."

"These are the ones that's collected to drag the river for her," said Virgil.

"Of course I am not going on record to say so soon that *I* think she's drowned," Doc said, blowing out blue smoke.

"Do you think . . ." William Wallace mounted a step, and his hands both went into fists. "Do you think she was *carried off*?"

"Now that's the way to argue, see it from all sides," said Doc promptly. "But who by?"

Some Malone whistled, but not so you could tell which one.

"There's no booger around the Dover section that goes around carrying off young girls that's married," stated Doc.

"She was always scared of the Gypsies." William Wallace turned scarlet. "She'd sure turn her ring around on her finger if she passed one, and look in the other direction so they couldn't see she was pretty and carry her off. They come in the end of summer."

"Yes, there are the Gypsies, kidnappers since the world began. But was it to be you that would pay the grand ransom?" asked Doc. He pointed his finger. They all laughed then at how clever old Doc was and clapped William Wallace on the back. But that turned into a scuffle and they fell to the ground.

"Stop it, or you can't have the net," said Doc. "You're scaring my wife's chickens."

"It's time we was gone," said William Wallace.

The big barking dogs jumped to lean their front paws on the men's chests.

"My advice remains, Let well enough alone," said Doc. "Whatever this mysterious event will turn out to be, it has kept one woman from talking a while. However, Lady Hazel is the prettiest girl in Mississippi, you've never seen a prettier one and you never will. A golden-haired girl." He got to his feet with the nimbleness that was always his surprise, and said, "I'll come along with you."

The path they always followed was the Old Natchez Trace. It took them through the deep woods and led them out down below on the Pearl River, where they could begin dragging it upstream to a point near Dover. They walked in silence around William Wallace, not letting him carry anything, but the net dragged heavily and the buckets were full of clatter in a place so dim and still.

Once they went through a forest of cucumber trees and came up on a high ridge. Grady and Brucie who were running ahead all the way stopped in their tracks; a whistle had blown and far down and far away a long freight train was passing. It seemed like a little festival procession, moving with the slowness of ignorance or a dream, from distance to distance, the tiny pink and gray cars like secret boxes. Grady was counting the cars to himself, as if he could certainly see each one clearly, and Brucie watched his lips, hushed and cautious, the way he would watch a bird drinking. Tears suddenly came to Grady's eyes, but it could only be because a tiny man walked along the top of the train, walking and moving on top of the moving train.

They went down again and soon the smell of the river spread over the woods, cool and secret. Every step they took among the great walls of vines and among the passion-flowers started up a little life, a little flight.

"We're walking along in the changing-time," said Doc. "Any day now the change will come. It's going to turn from hot to cold, and we can kill the hog that's ripe and have fresh meat to eat. Come one of these nights and we can wander down here and tree a nice possum. Old Jack Frost will be pinching things up. Old Mr. Winter will be standing in the door. Hickory tree there will be yellow. Sweet-gum red, hickory yellow, dogwood red, sycamore yellow." He went along rapping the tree trunks with his knuckle. "Magnolia and live-oak never die. Remember that. Persimmons will all get fit to eat, and the nuts will be dropping like rain all through the woods here. And run, little quail, run, for we'll be after you too."

They went on and suddenly the woods opened upon light, and they had reached the river. Everyone stopped, but Doc talked on ahead as though nothing had happened. "Only today," he said, "today, in October sun, it's all gold—sky and tree and water. Everything just before it changes looks to be made of gold."

William Wallace looked down, as though he thought of Hazel with the shining eyes, sitting at home and looking straight before her, like a piece of pure gold, too precious to touch.

Below them the river was glimmering, narrow, soft, and skin-colored, and slowed nearly to stillness. The shining willow trees hung round them. The net that was being drawn out, so old and so long-used, it too looked golden, strung and tied with golden threads.

Standing still on the bank, all of a sudden William Wallace, on whose word they were waiting, spoke up in a voice of surprise. "What is the name of this river?"

They looked at him as if he were crazy not to know the name of the river he had fished in all his life. But a deep frown was on his forehead, as if he were compelled to wonder what people had come to call this river, or to think there was a mystery in the name of a river they all knew so well, the same as if it were some great far torrent of waves that dashed through the mountains somewhere, and almost as if it were a river in some dream, for they could not give him the name of that.

"Everybody knows Pearl River is named the Pearl River," said Doc.

A bird note suddenly bold was like a stone thrown into the water to sound it.

"It's deep here," said Virgil, and jogged William Wallace. "Remember?"

William Wallace stood looking down at the river as if it were still a mystery to him. There under his feet which hung over the bank it was transparent and yellow like an old bottle lying in the sun, filling with light.

Doc clattered all his paraphernalia.

Then all of a sudden all the Malones scattered jumping and tumbling down the bank. They gave their loud shout. Little Brucie started after them, and looked back.

"Do you think she jumped?" Virgil asked William Wallace.

II

Since the net was so wide, when it was all stretched it reached from bank to bank of the Pearl River, and the weights would hold it all the way to the bottom. Jug-like sounds filled the air, splashes lifted in the sun, and the party began to move upstream. The Malones with great groans swam and pulled near the shore, the Doyles swam and pushed from behind with Virgil to tell them how to do it best; Grady and Brucie with his thread and pin trotted along the sandbars hauling buckets and lines. Sam and Robbie Bell, naked and bright, guided the old oarless rowboat that always drifted at the shore, and in it, sitting up tall with his hat on, was Doc—he went along without ever touching water and without ever taking his eyes off the net. William Wallace himself did everything but most of the time he was out of sight, swimming about under water or diving, and he had nothing to say any more.

The dogs chased up and down, in and out of the water, and in and out of the woods.

"Don't let her get too heavy, boys," Doc intoned regularly, every few minutes, "and she won't let nothing through."

"She won't let nothing through, she won't let nothing through," chanted Sam and Robbie Bell, one at his front and one at his back.

The sandbars were pink or violet drifts ahead. Where the light fell on the river, in a wandering from shore to shore, it was leaf-shaped spangles that trembled softly, while the dark of the river was calm. The willow trees leaned overhead under muscadine vines, and their trailing leaves hung like waterfalls in the morning air. The thing that seemed like silence must have been the endless cry of all the crickets and locusts in the world, rising and falling.

Every time William Wallace took hold of a big eel that slipped the net, the Malones all yelled, "Rassle with him, son!"

"Don't let her get too heavy, boys," said Doc.

"This is hard on catfish," William Wallace said once.

There were big and little fishes, dark and bright, that they caught, good ones and bad ones, the same old fish.

"This is more shoes than I ever saw got together in any store," said Virgil when they emptied the net to the bottom. "Get going!" he shouted in the next breath.

The little Rippens who had stayed ahead in the woods stayed ahead on the river. Brucie, leading them all, made small jumps and hops as he went, sometimes on one foot, sometimes on the other.

The winding river looked old sometimes, when it ran wrinkled and deep under high banks where the roots of trees hung down, and sometimes it seemed to be only a young creek, shining with the colors of wildflowers. Sometimes sandbars in the shapes of fishes lay nose to nose across, without the track of even a bird.

"Here comes some alligators," said Virgil. "Let's let them by."

They drew out on the shady side of the water, and three big alligators and four middle-sized ones went by, taking their own time.

"Look at their great big old teeth!" called a shrill voice. It was Grady making his only outcry, and the alligators were not showing their teeth at all.

"The better to eat folks with," said Doc from his boat, looking at him severely.

"Doc, you are bound to declare all you know," said Virgil. "Get going!"

When they started off again the first thing they caught in the net was the baby alligator.

"That's just what we wanted!" cried the Malones.

They set the little alligator down on a sandbar and he squatted perfectly still; they could hardly tell when it was he started to move. They watched with set faces his incredible mechanics, while the dogs after one bark stood off in inquisitive humility, until he winked.

"He's ours!" shouted all the Malones. "We're taking him home with us!"

"He ain't nothing but a little-old baby," said William Wallace.

The Malones only scoffed, as if he might be only a baby but he looked like the oldest and worst lizard.

"What are you going to do with him?" asked Virgil.

"Keep him."

"I'd be more careful what I took out of this net," said Doc.

"Tie him up and throw him in the bucket," the Malones were saying to each other, while Doc was saying, "Don't come running to me and ask me what to do when he gets big."

They kept catching more and more fish, as if there was no end in sight.

"Look, a string of lady's beads," said Virgil. "Here, Sam and Robbie Bell."

Sam wore them around his head, with a knot over his forehead and loops around his ears, and Robbie Bell walked behind and stared at them.

In a shadowy place something white flew up. It was a heron, and it went away over the dark treetops. William Wallace followed it with his eyes and Brucie clapped his hands, but Virgil gave a sigh, as if he knew that when you go looking for what is lost, everything is a sign.

An eel slid out of the net.

"Rassle with him, son!" yelled the Malones. They swam like fiends.

"The Malones are in it for the fish," said Virgil.

It was about noon that there was a little rustle on the bank.

"Who is that yonder?" asked Virgil, and he pointed to a little undersized man with short legs and a little straw hat with a band around it, who was following along on the other side of the river.

"Never saw him and don't know his brother," said Doc.

Nobody had ever seen him before.

"Who invited you?" cried Virgil hotly. "Hi . . . !" and he made signs for the little undersized man to look at him, but he would not.

"Looks like a crazy man, from here," said the Malones.

"Just don't pay any attention to him and maybe he'll go away," advised Doc.

But Virgil had already swum across and was up on the other bank. He and the stranger could be seen exchanging a word apiece and then Virgil put out his hand the way he would pat a child and patted the stranger to the ground. The little man got up again just as quickly, lifted his shoulders, turned around, and walked away with his hat tilted over his eyes.

When Virgil came back he said, "Little-old man claimed he was harmless as a baby. I told him to just try horning in on this river and anything in it."

"What did he look like up close?" asked Doc.

"I wasn't studying how he looked," said Virgil. "But I don't like anybody to come looking at me that I am not familiar with." And he shouted, "Get going!"

"Things are moving in too great a rush," said Doc.

Brucie darted ahead and ran looking into all the bushes, lifting up their branches and looking underneath.

"Not one of the Doyles has spoke a word," said Virgil.

"That's because they're not talkers," said Doc.

All day William Wallace kept diving to the bottom. Once he dived down and down into the dark water, where it was so still that nothing stirred, not even a fish, and so dark that it was no longer the muddy world of the upper river but the dark clear world of deepness, and he must have believed this was the deepest place in the whole Pearl River, and if she was not here she would not be anywhere. He was gone such a long time that the others stared hard at the surface of the water, through which the bubbles came from below. So far down and all alone, had he found Hazel? Had he suspected down there, like some secret, the real, the true trouble that Hazel had fallen into, about which words in a letter could not speak . . . how (who knew?) she had been filled to the brim with that elation that they all remembered, like their own secret, the elation that comes of great hopes and changes, sometimes simply of the harvest time, that comes with a little course of its own like a tune to run in the head, and there was nothing she could do about it—they knew—and so it had turned into this? It could be nothing but the old trouble that William Wallace was finding out, reaching and turning in the gloom of such depths.

"Look down yonder," said Grady softly to Brucie.

He pointed to the surface, where their reflections lay colorless and still side by side. He touched his brother gently as though to impress him.

"That's you and me," he said.

Brucie swayed precariously over the edge, and Grady caught him by the seat of his overalls. Brucie looked, but showed no recognition. Instead, he backed away, and seemed all at once unconcerned and spiritless, and pressed the nickel William Wallace had given him into his palm, rubbing it into his skin. Grady's inflamed eyes rested on the brown water. Without warning he saw something . . . perhaps the image in the river seemed to be his father, the drowned man—with arms open, eyes open, mouth open. . . . Grady stared and blinked, again something wrinkled up his face.

And when William Wallace came up it was in an agony from submersion, which seemed an agony of the blood and of the very heart, so woeful he looked. He was staring and glaring around in astonishment, as if a long time had gone by, away from the pale world where the brown light of the sun and the river and the little party watching him trembled before his eyes.

"What did you bring up?" somebody called—was it Virgil?

One of his hands was holding fast to a little green ribbon of plant, root and all. He was surprised, and let it go.

It was afternoon. The trees spread softly, the clouds hung wet and tinted. A buzzard turned a few slow wheels in the sky, and drifted upwards. The dogs promenaded the banks.

"It's time we ate fish," said Virgil.

On a wide sandbar on which seashells lay they dragged up the haul and built a fire.

Then for a long time among clouds of odors and smoke, all half-naked except Doc, they cooked and ate catfish. They ate until the Malones groaned and all the Doyles stretched out on their faces, though for long after, Sam and Robbie Bell sat up to their own little table on a cypress stump and ate on and on. Then they all were silent and still, and one by one fell asleep.

"There ain't a thing better than fish," muttered William Wallace. He lay stretched on his back in the glimmer and shade of trampled sand. His sunburned forehead and cheeks seemed to glow with fire. His eyelids fell. The shadow of a willow branch dipped and moved over him. "There is nothing in the world as good as . . . fish. The fish of Pearl River." Then slowly he smiled. He was asleep.

But it seemed almost at once that he was leaping up, and one by one up sat the others in their ring and looked at him, for it was impossible to stop and sleep by the river.

"You're feeling as good as you felt last night," said Virgil, setting his head on one side.

"The excursion is the same when you go looking for your sorrow as when you go looking for your joy," said Doc.

But William Wallace answered none of them anything, for he was leaping all over the place and all over them and the feast and the bones of the feast, trampling the sand, up and down, and doing a dance so crazy that he would die next. He took a big catfish and hooked it to his belt buckle and went up and down so that they all hollered, and the tears of laughter streaming down his cheeks made him put his hand up, and the two days' growth of beard began to jump out, bright red.

But all of a sudden there was an even louder cry, something almost like a cheer, from everybody at once, and all pointed fingers moved from William Wallace to the river. In the center of three light-gold rings across the water was lifted first an old hoary head ("It has whiskers!" a voice cried) and then in an undulation loop after loop and hump after hump of a long dark body, until there were a dozen rings of ripples, one behind the other, stretching all across the river, like a necklace.

"The King of the Snakes!" cried all the Malones at once, in high tenor voices and leaning together.

"The King of the Snakes," intoned old Doc in his profound bass.

"He looked you in the eye."

William Wallace stared back at the King of the Snakes with all his might.

It was Brucie that darted forward, dangling his little thread with the pin tied to it, going toward the water.

"That's the King of the Snakes!" cried Grady, who always looked after him.

Then the snake went down.

The little boy stopped with one leg in the air, spun around on the other, and sank to the ground.

"Git up," Grady whispered. "It was just the King of the Snakes. He went off whistling. Git up. It wasn't a thing but the King of the Snakes."

Brucie's green eyes opened, his tongue darted out, and he sprang up; his feet were heavy, his head light, and he rose like a bubble coming to the surface.

Then thunder like a stone loosened and rolled down the bank.

They all stood unwilling on the sandbar, holding to the net. In the eastern sky were the familiar castles and the round towers to which they were used, gray, pink, and blue, growing darker and filling with thunder. Lightning flickered in the sun along their thick walls. But in the west the sun shone with such a violence that in an illumination like a long-prolonged glare of lightning the heavens looked black and white; all color left the world, the goldenness of everything was like a memory, and only heat, a kind of glamor and oppression, lay on their heads. The thick heavy trees on the other side of the river were brushed with mile-long streaks of silver, and a wind touched each man on the forehead. At the same time there was a long roll of thunder that began behind them, came up and down mountains and valleys of air, passed over their heads, and left them listening still. With a small, near noise a mocking-bird followed it, the little white bars of its body flashing over the willow trees.

"We are here for a storm now," Virgil said. "We will have to stay till it's over."

They retreated a little, and hard drops fell in the leathery leaves at their shoulders and about their heads.

"Magnolia's the loudest tree there is in a storm," said Doc.

Then the light changed the water, until all about them the woods in the rising wind seemed to grow taller and blow inward together and suddenly turn dark. The rain struck heavily. A huge tail seemed to lash through the air and the river broke in a wound of silver. In silence the party crouched and stooped beside the trunk of the great tree, which in the push of the storm rose full of a fragrance and unyielding weight. Where they all stared, past their tree, was another tree, and beyond that another and another, all the way down the bank of the river, all towering and darkened in the storm.

"The outside world is full of endurance," said Doc. "Full of endurance."

Robbie Bell and Sam squatted down low and embraced each other from the start.

"Runs in our family to get struck by lightnin'," said Robbie Bell. "Lightnin' drawed a pitchfork right on our grandpappy's cheek, stayed till he died. Pappy got struck by some bolts of lightnin' and was dead three days, dead as that-there axe."

There was a succession of glares and crashes.

"This'n's goin' to be either me or you," said Sam. "Here come a little bug. If he go to the left, be me, and to the right, be you."

But at the next flare a big tree on the hill seemed to turn into fire before their eyes, every branch, twig, and leaf, and a purple cloud hung over it.

"Did you hear that crack?" asked Robbie Bell. "That were its bones."

"Why do you little niggers talk so much!" said Doc. "Nobody's profiting by this information."

"We always talks this much," said Sam, "but now everybody so quiet, they hears us."

The great tree, split and on fire, fell roaring to earth. Just at its moment of falling, a tree like it on the opposite bank split wide open and fell in two parts.

"Hope they ain't goin' to be no balls of fire come rollin' over the water and fry all the fishes with they scales on," said Robbie Bell.

The water in the river had turned purple and was filled with sudden currents and whirlpools. The little willow trees bent almost to its surface, bowing one after another down the bank and almost breaking under the storm. A great curtain of wet leaves was borne along before a blast of wind, and every human being was covered.

"Now us got scales," wailed Sam. "Us is the fishes."

"Hush up, little-old colored children," said Virgil. "This isn't the way to act when somebody takes you out to drag a river."

"Poor lady's-ghost, I bet it is scareder than us," said Sam.

"All I hoping is, us don't find her!" screamed Robbie Bell.

William Wallace bent down and knocked their heads together. After that they clung silently in each other's arms, the two black heads resting, with wind-filled cheeks and tight-closed eyes, one upon the other until the storm was over.

"Right over yonder is Dover," said Virgil. "We've come all the way. William Wallace, you have walked on a sharp rock and cut your foot open."

III

In Dover it had rained, and the town looked somehow like new. The wavy heat of late afternoon came down from the watertank and fell over everything like shiny mosquito-netting. At the wide place where the road was paved and patched with tar, it seemed newly embedded with Coca-Cola tops. The old circus posters on the store were nearly gone, only bits, the snowflakes of white horses, clinging to its side. Morning-glory vines started almost visibly to grow over the roofs and cling round the ties of the railroad track, where bluejays lighted on the rails, and umbrella chinaberry trees hung heavily over the whole town, dripping intermittently upon the tin roofs.

Each with his counted fish on a string the members of the river-dragging party walked through the town. They went toward the town well, and there was Hazel's mother's house, but no sign of her yet coming out. They all drank a dipper of the water, and still there was not a soul on the street. Even the bench in front of the store was empty, except for a little corn-shuck doll.

But something told them somebody had come, for after one moment people began to look out of the store and out of the postoffice. All the bird dogs woke up to see the Doyle dogs and such a large number of men and boys materialize suddenly with such a big catch of fish, and they ran out barking. The Doyle dogs joyously barked back. The bluejays flashed up and screeched above the town, whipping through their tunnels in the chinaberry trees. In the café a nickel clattered inside a music box and a love song began to play. The whole town of Dover began to throb in its wood and tin, like an old tired heart, when the men walked through once more, coming around again and going down the street carrying the fish, so drenched, exhausted, and muddy that no one could help but admire them.

William Wallace walked through the town as though he did not see anybody or hear anything. Yet he carried his great string of fish held high where it could be seen by all. Virgil came next, imitating William Wallace exactly, then the modest Doyles crowded by the Malones, who were holding up their alligator, tossing it in the air, even, like a father tossing his child. Following behind and pointing authoritatively at the ones in front strolled Doc, with Sam and Robbie Bell still chanting in his wake. In and out of the whole little line Grady and Brucie jerked about. Grady, with his head ducked, and stiff as a rod, walked with a springy limp; it made him look forever angry and unapproachable. Under his breath he was whispering, "Sty, sty, git out of my eye, and git on somebody passin' by." He traveled on with narrowed shoulders, and kept his eye unerringly upon his little brother, wary and at the same time proud, as though he held a flying June-bug on a string. Brucie, making a twanging noise with his lips, had shot forth again, and he was darting rapidly everywhere at once, delighted and tantalized, running in circles around William Wallace, pointing to his fish. A frown of pleasure like the print of a bird's foot was stamped between his faint brows, and he trotted in some unknown realm of delight.

"Did you ever see so many fish?" said the people in Dover.

"How much are your fish, mister?"

"Would you sell your fish?"

"Is that all the fish in Pearl River?"

"How much you sell them all for? Everybody's?"

"Three dollars," said William Wallace suddenly, and loud.

The Malones were upon him and shouting, but it was too late.

And just as William Wallace was taking the money in his hand, Hazel's mother walked solidly out of her front door and saw it.

"You can't head her mother off," said Virgil. "Here she comes in full bloom."

But William Wallace turned his back on her, that was all, and on everybody, for that matter, and that was the breaking-up of the party.

Just as the sun went down, Doc climbed his back steps, sat in his chair on the back porch where he sat in the evenings, and lighted his pipe. William Wallace hung out the net and came back and Virgil was waiting for him, so they could say good evening to Doc.

"All in all," said Doc, when they came up, "I've never been on a better river-dragging, or seen better behavior. If it took catching catfish to move the Rock of Gibraltar, I believe this outfit could move it."

"Well, we didn't catch Hazel," said Virgil.

"What did you say?" asked Doc.

"He don't really pay attention," said Virgil. "I said, 'We didn't catch Hazel.'"

"Who says Hazel was to be caught?" asked Doc. "She wasn't in there. Girls don't like the water—remember that. Girls don't just haul off and go jumping in the river to get back at their husbands. They got other ways."

"Didn't you ever think she was in there?" asked William Wallace. "The whole time?"

"Nary once," said Doc.

"He's just smart," said Virgil, putting his hand on William Wallace's arm. "It's only because we didn't find her that he wasn't looking for her."

"I'm beholden to you for the net, anyway," said William Wallace.

"You're welcome to borry it again," said Doc.

On the way home Virgil kept saying, "Calm down, calm down, William Wallace."

"If he wasn't such an old skinny man I'd have wrung his neck for him," said William Wallace. "He had no business coming."

"He's too big for his britches," said Virgil. "Don't nobody know everything. And just because it's his net. Why does it have to be his net?"

"If it wasn't for being polite to old men, I'd have skinned him alive," said William Wallace.

"I guess he don't really know nothing about wives at all, his wife's so deaf," said Virgil.

"He don't know Hazel," said William Wallace. "I'm the only man alive knows Hazel: would she jump in the river or not, and I say she would. She jumped in because I was sitting on the back of my neck in a ditch singing, and that's just what she ought to done. Doc ain't got no right to say one word about it."

"Calm down, calm down, William Wallace," said Virgil.

"If it had been you that talked like that, I'd have broke every bone in your body," said William Wallace. "Just let you talk like that. You're my age and size."

"But I ain't going to talk like that," said Virgil. "What have I done the whole time but keep this river-dragging going straight and running even, without no hitches? You couldn't have drug the river a foot without me."

"What are you talking about! Without who!" cried William Wallace. "This wasn't your river-dragging! It wasn't your wife!" He jumped on Virgil and they began to fight.

"Let me up." Virgil was breathing heavily.

"Say it was my wife. Say it was my river-dragging."

"Yours!" Virgil was on the ground with William Wallace's hand putting dirt in his mouth.

"Say it was my net."

"Your net!"

"Get up then."

They walked along getting their breath, and smelling the honeysuckle in the evening. On a hill William Wallace looked down, and at the same time there went drifting by the sweet sounds of music outdoors. They were having the Sacred Harp Sing on the grounds of an old white church glimmering there at the crossroads, far below. He stared away as if he saw it minutely, as if he could see a lady in white take a flowered cover off the organ, which was set on a little slant in the shade, dust the keys, and start to pump and play. . . . He smiled faintly, as he would at his mother, and at Hazel, and at the singing women in his life, now all one young girl standing up to sing under the trees the oldest and longest ballads there were.

Virgil told him good night and went into his own house and the door shut on him.

When he got to his own house, William Wallace saw to his surprise that it had not rained at all. But there, curved over the roof, was something he had never seen before as long as he could remember, a rainbow at night. In the light of the moon, which had risen again, it looked small and of gauzy material, like a lady's summer dress, a faint veil through which the stars showed.

He went up on the porch and in at the door, and all exhausted he had walked through the front room and through the kitchen when he heard his name called. After a moment, he smiled, as if no matter what he might have hoped for in his wildest heart, it was better than that to hear his name called out in the house. The voice came out of the bedroom.

"What do you want?" he yelled, standing stock-still.

Then she opened the bedroom door with the old complaining creak, and there she stood. She was not changed a bit.

"How do you feel?" he said.

"I feel pretty good. Not too good," Hazel said, looking mysterious.

"I cut my foot," said William Wallace, taking his shoe off so she could see the blood.

"How in the world did you do that?" she cried, with a step back.

"Dragging the river. But it don't hurt any longer."

"You ought to have been more careful," she said. "Supper's ready and I wondered if you would ever come home, or if it would be last night all over again. Go and make yourself fit to be seen," she said, and ran away from him.

After supper they sat on the front steps a while.

"Where were you this morning when I came in?" asked William Wallace when they were ready to go in the house.

"I was hiding," she said. "I was still writing on the letter. And then you tore it up."

"Did you watch me when I was reading it?"

"Yes, and you could have put out your hand and touched me, I was so close."

But he bit his lip, and gave her a little tap and slap, and then turned her up and spanked her.

"Do you think you will do it again?" he asked.

"I'll tell my mother on you for this!"

"Will you do it again?"

"No!" she cried.

"Then pick yourself up off my knee."

It was just as if he had chased her and captured her again. She lay smiling in the crook of his arm. It was the same as any other chase in the end.

"I will do it again if I get ready," she said. "Next time will be different, too."

Then she was ready to go in, and rose up and looked out from the top step, out across their yard where the China tree was and beyond, into the dark fields where the lightning-bugs flickered away. He climbed to his feet too and stood beside her, with the frown on his face, trying to look where she looked. And after a few minutes she took him by the hand and led him into the house, smiling as if she were smiling down on him.

A Still Moment

LORENZO DOW rode the Old Natchez Trace at top speed upon a race horse, and the cry of the itinerant Man of God, "I must have souls! And souls I must have!" rang in his own windy ears. He rode as if never to stop, toward his night's appointment.

It was the hour of sunset. All the souls that he had saved and all those he had not took dusky shapes in the mist that hung between the high banks, and seemed by their great number and density to block his way, and showed no signs of melting or changing back into mist, so that he feared his passage was to be difficult forever. The poor souls that were not saved were darker and more pitiful than those that were, and still there was not any of the radiance he would have hoped to see in such a congregation.

"Light up, in God's name!" he called, in the pain of his disappointment.

Then a whole swarm of fireflies instantly flickered all around him, up and down, back and forth, first one golden light and then another, flashing without any of the weariness that had held back the souls. These were the signs sent from God that he had not seen the accumulated radiance of saved souls because he was not able, and that his eyes were more able to see the fireflies of the Lord than His blessed souls.

"Lord, give me the strength to see the angels when I am in Paradise," he said. "Do not let my eyes remain in this failing proportion to my loving heart always."

He gasped and held on. It was that day's complexity of horse-trading that had left him in the end with a Spanish race horse for which he was bound to send money in November from Georgia. Riding faster on the beast and still faster until he felt as if he were flying he sent thoughts of love with matching speed to his wife Peggy in Massachusetts. He found it effortless to love at a distance. He could look at the flowering trees and love Peggy in fullness, just as he could see his visions and love God. And Peggy, to whom he had not spoken until he could speak fateful words ("Would she accept of such an object as him?"), Peggy, the bride, with whom he had spent a few hours of time, showing of herself a small round handwriting, declared all in one letter, her first, that she felt the same as he, and that the fear was never of separation, but only of death.

Lorenzo well knew that it was Death that opened underfoot, that rippled by at night, that was the silence the birds did their singing in. He was close to death, closer than any animal or bird. On the back of one horse after another, winding them all, he was always riding toward it or away from it, and the Lord sent him directions with protection in His mind.

Just then he rode into a thicket of Indians taking aim with their new guns. One stepped out and took the horse by the bridle, it stopped at a touch, and the rest made a closing circle. The guns pointed.

"Incline!" The inner voice spoke sternly and with its customary lightning-quickness.

Lorenzo inclined all the way forward and put his head to the horse's silky mane, his body to its body, until a bullet meant for him would endanger the horse and make his death of no value. Prone he rode out through the circle of Indians, his obedience to the voice leaving him almost fearless, almost careless with joy.

But as he straightened and pressed ahead, care caught up with him again. Turning half-beast and half-divine, dividing himself like a heathen Centaur, he had escaped his death once more. But was it to be always by some metamorphosis of himself that he escaped, some humiliation of his faith, some admission to strength and argumentation and not frailty? Each time when he acted so it was at the command of an instinct that he took at once as the word of an angel, until too late, when he knew it was the word of the devil. He had roared like a tiger at Indians, he had submerged himself in water blowing the savage bubbles of the alligator, and they skirted him by. He had prostrated himself to appear dead, and deceived bears. But all the time God would have protected him in His own way, less hurried, more divine.

Even now he saw a serpent crossing the Trace, giving out knowing glances.

He cried, "I know you now!", and the serpent gave him

one look out of which all the fire had been taken, and went away in two darts into the tangle.

He rode on, all expectation, and the voices in the throats of the wild beasts went, almost without his noticing when, into words. "Praise God," they said. "Deliver us from one another." Birds especially sang of divine love which was the one ceaseless protection. "Peace, in peace," were their words so many times when they spoke from the briars, in a courteous sort of inflection, and he turned his countenance toward all perched creatures with a benevolence striving to match their own.

He rode on past the little intersecting trails, letting himself be guided by voices and by lights. It was battlesounds he heard most, sending him on, but sometimes ocean sounds, that long beat of waves that would make his heart pound and retreat as heavily as they, and he despaired again in his failure in Ireland when he took a voyage and persuaded with the Catholics with his back against the door, and then ran away to their cries of "Mind the white hat!" But when he heard singing it was not the militant and sharp sound of Wesley's hymns, but a soft, tireless and tender air that had no beginning and no end, and the softness of distance, and he had pleaded with the Lord to find out if all this meant that it was wicked, but no answer had come.

Soon night would descend, and a camp-meeting ground ahead would fill with its sinners like the sky with its stars. How he hungered for them! He looked in prescience with a longing of love over the throng that waited while the flames of the torches threw change, change, change over their faces. How could he bring them enough, if it were not divine love and sufficient warning of all that could threaten them? He rode on faster. He was a filler of appointments, and he filled more and more, until his journeys up and down creation were nothing but a shuttle, driving back and forth upon the rich expanse of his vision. He was homeless by his own choice, he must be everywhere at some time, and somewhere soon. There hastening in the wilderness on his flying horse he gave the night's torch-lit crowd a premature benediction, he could not wait. He spread his arms out, one at a time for safety, and he wished, when they would all be gathered in by his tin horn blasts and the inspired words would go out over their heads, to brood above the entire and passionate life of the wide world, to become its rightful part.

He peered ahead. "Inhabitants of Time! The wilderness is your souls on earth!" he shouted ahead into the treetops. "Look about you, if you would view the conditions of your spirit, put here by the good Lord to show you and afright you. These wild places and these trails of awesome loneliness lie nowhere, nowhere, but in your heart."

A dark man, who was James Murrell the outlaw, rode his horse out of a cane brake and began going along beside Lorenzo without looking at him. He had the alternately proud and aggrieved look of a man believing himself to be an instrument in the hands of a power, and when he was young he said at once to strangers that he was being used by Evil, or sometimes he stopped a traveler by shouting, "Stop! I'm the Devil!" He rode along now talking and drawing out his talk, by some deep control of the voice gradually slowing the speed of Lorenzo's horse down until both the horses were softly trotting. He would have wondered that nothing he said was heard, not knowing that Lorenzo listened only to voices of whose heavenly origin he was more certain.

Murrell riding along with his victim-to-be, Murrell riding, was Murrell talking. He told away at his long tales, with always a distance and a long length of time flowing through them, and all centered about a silent man. In each the silent man would have done a piece of evil, a robbery or a murder, in a place of long ago, and it was all made for the revelation in the end that the silent man was Murrell himself, and the long story had happened yesterday, and the place *here*—the Natchez Trace. It would only take one dawning look for the victim to see that all of this was another story and he himself had listened his way into it, and that he too was about to recede in time (to where the dread was forgotten) for some listener and to live for a listener in the long ago. Destroy the present!—that must have been the first thing that was whispered in Murrell's heart—the living moment and the man that lives in it must die before you can go on. It was his habit to bring the journey—which might even take days—to a close with a kind of ceremony. Turning his face at last into the face of the victim, for he had never seen him before now, he would tower up with the sudden height of a man no longer the tale teller but the speechless protagonist, silent at last, one degree nearer the hero. Then he would murder the man.

But it would always start over. This man going forward was going backward with talk. He saw nothing, observed no world at all. The two ends of his journey pulled at him always and held him in a nowhere, half asleep, smiling and witty, dangling his predicament. He was a murderer whose final stroke was over-long postponed, who had to bring himself through the greatest tedium to act, as if the whole wilderness, where he was born, were his impediment. But behind him and before him he kept in sight a victim, he saw a man fixed and stayed at the point of death—no matter how the man's eyes denied it, a victim, hands spreading to reach as if for the first time for life. Contempt! That is what Murrell gave that man.

Lorenzo might have understood, if he had not been in haste, that Murrell in laying hold of a man meant to solve his mystery of being. It was as if other men, all but himself, would lighten their hold on the secret, upon assault, and let it fly free at death. In his violence he was only treating of enigma. The violence shook his own body first, like a force gathering, and now he turned in the saddle.

Lorenzo's despair had to be kindled as well as his ecstasy, and could not come without that kindling. Before the awe-filled moment when the faces were turned up under the flares, as though an angel hand tipped their chins, he had no way of telling whether he would enter the sermon by sorrow or by joy. But at this moment the face of Murrell was turned toward him, turning at last, all solitary, in its full, and Lorenzo would have seized the man at once by his black coat and shaken him like prey for a lost soul, so instantly was he certain that the false fire was in his heart instead of the true fire. But Murrell, quick when he was quick, had put his own hand out, a restraining hand, and laid it on the wavelike flesh of the Spanish race horse, which quivered and shuddered at the touch.

They had come to a great live-oak tree at the edge of a low marsh-land. The burning sun hung low, like a head lowered on folded arms, and over the long reaches of violet trees the evening seemed still with thought. Lorenzo knew the place from having seen it among many in dreams, and he stopped readily and willingly. He drew rein, and Murrell drew rein, he dismounted and Murrell dismounted, he took a step, and Murrell was there too; and Lorenzo was not surprised at the closeness, how Murrell in his long dark coat and over it his dark face darkening still, stood beside him like a brother seeking light.

But in that moment instead of two men coming to stop by the great forked tree, there were three.

From far away, a student, Audubon, had been approaching lightly on the wilderness floor, disturbing nothing in his lightness. The long day of beauty had led him this certain distance. A flock of purple finches that he tried for the first moment to count went over his head. He made a spelling of the soft *pet* of the ivory-billed woodpecker. He told himself always: remember.

Coming upon the Trace, he looked at the high cedars, azure and still as distant smoke overhead, with their silver roots trailing down on either side like the veins of deepness in this place, and he noted some fact to his memory—this earth that wears but will not crumble or slide or turn to dust, they say it exists in one other spot in the world, Egypt—and then forgot it. He walked quietly. All life used this Trace, and he liked to see the animals move along it in direct, oblivious journeys, for they had begun it and made it, the buffalo and deer and the small running creatures before man ever knew where he wanted to go, and birds flew a great mirrored course above. Walking beneath them Audubon remembered how in the cities he had seen these very birds in his imagination, calling them up whenever he wished, even in the hard and glittering outer parlors where if an artist were humble enough to wait, some idle hand held up promised money. He walked lightly and he went as carefully as he had started at two that morning, crayon and paper, a gun, and a small bottle of spirits disposed about his body. (*Note: "The mocking birds so gentle that they would scarcely move out of the way."*) He looked with care; great abundance had ceased to startle him, and he could see things one by one. In Natchez they had told him of many strange and marvelous birds that were to be found here. Their descriptions had been exact, complete, and wildly varying, and he took them for inventions and believed that like all the worldly things that came out of Natchez, they would be disposed of and shamed by any man's excursion into the reality of Nature.

In the valley he appeared under the tree, a sure man, very sure and tender, as if the touch of all the earth rubbed upon him and the stains of the flowery swamp had made him so.

Lorenzo welcomed him and turned fond eyes upon him. To transmute a man into an angel was the hope that drove him all over the world and never let him flinch from a meeting or withhold good-byes for long. This hope insistently divided his life into only two parts, journey and rest. There could be no night and day and love and despair and longing and satisfaction to make partitions in the single ecstasy of this alternation. All things were speech.

"God created the world," said Lorenzo, "and it exists to give testimony. Life is the tongue: speak."

But instead of speech there happened a moment of deepest silence.

Audubon said nothing because he had gone without speaking a word for days. He did not regard his thoughts for the birds and animals as susceptible, in their first change, to words. His long playing on the flute was not in its origin a talking to himself. Rather than speak to order or describe, he would always draw a deer with a stroke across it to communicate his need of venison to an Indian. He had only found words when he discovered that there is much otherwise lost that can be noted down each item in its own day, and he wrote often now in a journal, not wanting anything to be lost the way it had been, all the past, and he would write about a day, "Only sorry that the Sun Sets."

Murrell, his cheated hand hiding the gun, could only continue to smile at Lorenzo, but he remembered in malice that he had disguised himself once as an Evangelist, and his final words to this victim would have been, "One of my disguises was what you are."

Then in Murrell Audubon saw what he thought of as "acquired sorrow"—that cumbrousness and darkness from which the naked Indian, coming just as he was made from God's hand, was so lightly free. He noted the eyes—the dark kind that loved to look through chinks, and saw neither closeness nor distance, light nor shade, wonder nor familiarity. They were narrowed to contract the heart, narrowed to make an averting plan. Audubon knew the finest-drawn tendons of the body and the working of their power, for he had touched them, and he supposed then that in man the enlargement of the eye to see started a motion in the hands to make or do, and that the narrowing of the eye stopped the hand and contracted the heart. Now Murrell's eyes followed an ant on a blade of grass, up the blade and down, many times in the single moment. Audubon had examined the Cave-In Rock where one robber had lived his hiding life, and the air in the cave was the cavelike air that enclosed this man, the same odor, flinty and dark. O secret life, he thought—is it true that the secret is withdrawn from the true disclosure, that man is a cave man, and that the openness I see, the ways through forests, the rivers brimming light, the wide arches where the birds fly, are dreams of freedom? If my origin is withheld from me, is my end to be unknown too? Is the radiance I see closed into an interval between two darks, or can it not illuminate them both and discover at last, though it cannot be spoken, what was thought hidden and lost?

In that quiet moment a solitary snowy heron flew down not far away and began to feed beside the marsh water.

At the single streak of flight, the ears of the race horse lifted, and the eyes of both horses filled with the soft lights of sunset, which in the next instant were reflected in the eyes of the men too as they all looked into the west toward the heron, and all eyes seemed infused with a sort of wildness.

Lorenzo gave the bird a triumphant look, such as a man may bestow upon his own vision, and thought, Nearness is near, lighted in a marsh-land, feeding at sunset. Praise God, His love has come visible.

Murrell, in suspicion pursuing all glances, blinking into a haze, saw only whiteness ensconced in darkness, as if it were a little luminous shell that drew in and held the eyesight. When he shaded his eyes, the brand "H.T." on his thumb thrust itself into his own vision, and he looked at the bird with the whole plan of the Mystic Rebellion darting from him as if in rays of the bright reflected light, and he stood looking proudly, leader as he was bound to become of the slaves, the brigands and outcasts of the entire Natchez country, with plans, dates, maps burning like a brand into his brain, and he saw himself proudly in a moment of prophecy going down rank after rank of successively bowing slaves to unroll and flaunt an awesome great picture of the Devil colored on a banner.

Audubon's eyes embraced the object in the distance and he could see it as carefully as if he held it in his hand. It was a snowy heron alone out of its flock. He watched it steadily, in his care noting the exact inevitable things. When it feeds it muddies the water with its foot. . . . It was as if each detail about the heron happened slowly in time, and only once. He felt again the old stab of wonder—what structure of life bridged the reptile's scale and the heron's feather? That knowledge too had been lost. He watched without moving. The bird was defenseless in the world except for the intensity of its life, and he wondered, how can heat of blood and speed of heart defend it? Then he thought, as always as if it were new and unbelievable, it has nothing in space or time to prevent its flight. And he waited, knowing that some birds will wait for a sense of their presence to travel to men before they will fly away from them.

Fixed in its pure white profile it stood in the precipitous moment, a plumicorn on its head, its breeding dress extended in rays, eating steadily the little water creatures. There was a little space between each man and the others, where they stood overwhelmed. No one could say the three had ever met, or that this moment of intersection had ever come in their lives, or its promise fulfilled. But before them the white heron rested in the grasses with the evening all around it, lighter and more serene than the evening, flight closed in its body, the circuit of its beauty closed, a bird seen and a bird still, its motion calm as if it were offered: Take my flight. . . .

What each of them had wanted was simply *all.* To save all souls, to destroy all men, to see and to record all life that filled this world—all, all—but now a single frail yearning seemed to go out of the three of them for a moment and to stretch toward this one snowy, shy bird in the marshes. It was as if three whirlwinds had drawn together at some center, to find there feeding in peace a snowy heron. Its own slow spiral of flight could take it away in its own time, but for a little it held them still, it laid quiet over them, and they stood for a moment unburdened. . . .

Murrell wore no mask, for his face was that, a face that was aware while he was somnolent, a face that watched for him, and listened for him, alert and nearly brutal, the guard of a planner. He was quick without that he might be slow within, he staved off time, he wandered and plotted, and yet his whole desire mounted in him toward the end (was this the end—the sight of a bird feeding at dusk?), toward the instant of confession. His incessant deeds were thick in his heart now, and flinging himself to the ground he thought wearily, when all these trees are cut down, and the Trace lost, then my Conspiracy that is yet to spread itself will be disclosed, and all the stone-loaded bodies of murdered men will be pulled up, and all everywhere will know poor Murrell. His look pressed upon Lorenzo, who stared upward, and Audubon, who was taking out his gun, and his eyes squinted up to them in pleading, as if to say, "How soon may I speak, and how soon will you pity me?" Then he looked back to the bird, and he thought if it would look at him a dread penetration would fill and gratify his heart.

Audubon in each act of life was aware of the mysterious origin he half-concealed and half-sought for. People along the way asked him in their kindness or their rudeness if it were true, that he was born a prince, and was the Lost Dauphin, and some said it was his secret, and some said that that was what he wished to find out before he died. But if it was his identity that he wished to discover, or if it was what a man had to seize beyond that, the way for him was by endless examination, by the care for every bird that flew in his path and every serpent that shone underfoot. Not one was enough; he looked deeper and deeper, on and on, as if for a particular beast or some legendary bird. Some men's eyes persisted in looking outward when they opened to look inward, and to their delight, there outflung was the astonishing world under the sky. When a man at last brought himself to face some mirror-surface he still saw the world looking back at him, and if he continued to look, to look closer and closer, what then? The gaze that looks outward must be trained without rest, to be indomitable. It must see as slowly as Murrell's ant in the grass, as exhaustively as Lorenzo's angel of God, and then, Audubon dreamed, with his mind going to his pointed brush, it must see like this, and he tightened his hand on the trigger of the gun and pulled it, and his eyes went closed. In memory the heron was all its solitude, its total beauty. All its whiteness could be seen from all sides at once, its pure feathers were as if counted and known and their array one upon the other would never be lost. But it was not from that memory that he could paint.

His opening eyes met Lorenzo's, close and flashing, and it was on seeing horror deep in them, like fires in abysses, that he recognized it for the first time. He had never seen horror in its purity and clarity until now, in bright blue eyes. He went and picked up the bird. He had thought it to be a female, just as one sees the moon as female; and so it was. He put it in his bag, and started away. But Lorenzo had already gone on, leaning a-tilt on the horse which went slowly.

Murrell was left behind, but he was proud of the dispersal, as if he had done it, as if he had always known that three men in simply being together and doing a thing can, by their obstinacy, take the pride out of one another. Each must go away alone, each send the others away alone. He himself had purposely kept to the wildest country in the world, and would have sought it out, the loneliest road. He looked about with satisfaction, and hid. Travelers were forever innocent, he believed: that was his faith. He lay in wait; his faith was in innocence and his knowledge was of ruin; and had these things been shaken? Now, what could possibly be outside his grasp? Churning all about him like a cloud about the sun was the great folding descent of his thought. Plans of deeds made his thoughts, and they rolled and mingled about his ears as if he heard a dark voice that rose up to overcome the wilderness voice, or was one with it. The night would soon come; and he had gone through the day.

Audubon, splattered and wet, turned back into the wilderness with the heron warm under his hand, his head still light in a kind of trance. It was undeniable, on some Sunday mornings, when he turned over and over his drawings they seemed beautiful to him, through what was dramatic in the conflict of life, or what was exact. What he would draw, and what he had seen, became for a moment one to him then. Yet soon enough, and it seemed to come in that same moment, like Lorenzo's horror and the gun's firing, he knew that even the sight of the heron which surely he alone had appreciated, had not been all his belonging, and that never could any vision, even any simple sight, belong to him or to any man. He knew that the best he could make would be, after it was apart from his hand, a dead thing and not a live thing, never the essence, only a sum of parts; and that it would always meet with a stranger's sight, and never be one with the beauty in any other man's head in the world. As he had seen the bird most purely at its moment of death, in some fatal way, in his care for looking outward, he saw his long labor most revealingly at the point where it met its limit. Still carefully, for he was trained to see well in the dark, he walked on into the deeper woods, noting all sights, all sounds, and was gentler than they as he went.

In the woods that echoed yet in his ears, Lorenzo riding slowly looked back. The hair rose on his head and his hands began to shake with cold, and suddenly it seemed to him that God Himself, just now, thought of the Idea of Separateness. For surely He had never thought of it before, when the little white heron was flying down to feed. He could understand God's giving Separateness first and then giving Love to follow and heal in its wonder; but God had reversed this, and given Love first and then Separateness, as though it did not matter to Him which came first. Perhaps it was that God never counted the moments of Time; Lorenzo did that, among his tasks of love. Time did not occur to God. Therefore—did He even know of it? How to explain Time and Separateness back to God, Who had never thought of them, Who could let the whole world come to grief in a scattering moment?

Lorenzo brought his cold hands together in a clasp and stared through the distance at the place where the bird had been as if he saw it still; as if nothing could really take away what had happened to him, the beautiful little vision of the feeding bird. Its beauty had been greater than he could account for. The sweat of rapture poured down from his forehead, and then he shouted into the marshes.

"Tempter!"

He whirled forward in the saddle and began to hurry the horse to its high speed. His camp ground was far away still, though even now they must be lighting the torches and gathering in the multitudes, so that at the appointed time he would duly appear in their midst, to deliver his address on the subject of "In that day when all hearts shall be disclosed."

Then the sun dropped below the trees, and the new moon, slender and white, hung shyly in the west.

Asphodel

IT WAS a cloudless day—a round hill where the warm winds blew. It was noon, and without a shadow the line of columns rose in perfect erectness from the green vines. There was a quiver of birdsong. A little company of three women stood fixed on the slope before the ruin, holding wicker baskets between them. They were not young. There were identical looks of fresh mourning on their faces. A wind blew down from the columns, and the white dimity fluttered about their elbows.

"Look—"

"Asphodel."

It was a golden ruin: six Doric columns, with the entablature unbroken over the first two, full-facing the approach. The sky was pure, transparent, and round like a shell over this hill.

The three women drew nearer, in postures that were still from ministrations, and that came from a mourning procession.

"This is Asphodel," they repeated, looking modestly upward to the frieze of maidens that was saturated with sunlight and seemed to fill with color, and before which the branch of a leafy tree was trembling.

"If there's one place in the solid world where Miss Sabina would never look for us, it's Asphodel," they said. "She forbade it," they said virtuously. "She would never tolerate us to come, to Mr. Don McInnis's Asphodel, or even to say his name."

"Her funeral was yesterday, and we've cried our eyes dry," said one of the three. "And as for saying Mr. Don's name out loud, of course he is dead too." And they looked from one to the other—Cora, Phoebe, and Irene, all old maids, in hanging summer cottons, carrying picnic baskets. The way was so narrow they had come in a buggy, then walked.

There was not a shadow. It was high noon. A honey locust bent over their heads, sounding with the bees that kept at its bee-like flowers.

"This is the kind of day I could just *eat*!" cried Cora ardently.

They were another step forward. A little stream spread from rock to rock and over the approach. Then their shoes were off, and their narrow maiden feet hung trembling in the rippling water. The wind had shaken loose their gray and scanty hair. They smiled at one another.

"I used to be scared of little glades," said Phoebe. "I used to think something, something wild, would come and carry me off."

Then they were laughing freely all at once, drying their feet on the other side of the stream. The mocking-birds seemed to imitate flutes in the midday air. The horse they had unhitched champed on the hill, always visible—an old horse that seemed about to run, his mane fluttering in the light and his tail flaunted like a decoration he had only just put on.

Then the baskets were opened, the cloth was spread with the aromatic ham and chicken, spices and jellies, fresh breads and a cake, peaches, bananas, figs, pomegranates, grapes, and a thin dark bottle of blackberry cordial.

"There's one basket left in the buggy," said Irene, always the last to yield. "I like to have a little something saved back."

The women reclined before the food, beside the warm and weighty pedestal. Above them the six columns seemed to be filled with the inhalations of summer and to be suspended in the resting of noon.

They pressed at the pomegranate stains on their mouths. And then they began to tell over Miss Sabina's story, their voices serene and alike: how she looked, the legend of her beauty when she was young, the house where she was born and what happened in it, and how she came out when she was old, and her triumphal way, and the pitiful end when she toppled to her death in a dusty place where she was a stranger, that she had despised and deplored.

"Miss Sabina's house stood on the high hill," Cora said, but the lips of the others moved with hers. It was like an old song they carried in their memory, the story of the two houses separated by a long, winding, difficult, untravelled road—a curve of the old Natchez Trace—but actually situated almost back to back on the ring of hills, while completely hidden from each other, like the reliefs on opposite sides of a vase.

"It commanded the town that came to be at its foot. Her house was a square of marble and stone, the front was as dark as pitch under the magnolia trees. Not one blade of grass grew in the hard green ground, but in some places a root stuck up like a serpent. Inside, the house was all wood, dark wood carved and fluted, long hallways, great staircases of walnut, ebony beds that filled a room, even mahogany roses in the ceilings, where the chandeliers hung down like red glass fruit. There was one completely dark inside room. The house was a labyrinth set with statues—Venus, Hermes, Demeter, and with singing ocean shells on draped pedestals.

"Miss Sabina's father came bringing Mr. Don McInnis home, and proposed the marriage to him. She was no longer young for suitors; she was instructed to submit. On the marriage night the house was ablaze, and lighted the town and the wedding guests climbing the hill. We were there. The presents were vases of gold, gold cups, statues of Diana. . . . And the bride . . . We had not forgotten it yesterday when we drew it from the chest—the stiff white gown she wore! It never made a rustle when she gave him her hand. It was spring, the flowers in the baskets were purple hyacinths and white lilies that wilted in the heat and showed their blue veins. Ladies fainted from the scent; the gentlemen were without exception drunk, and Mr. Don McInnis, with his head turning quickly from side to side, like an animal's, opened his mouth and laughed."

Irene said: "A great, profane man like all the McInnis men of Asphodel, Mr. Don McInnis. He was the last of his own, just as she was the last of hers. The hope was in him, and he knew it. He had a sudden way of laughter, like a rage, that pointed his eyebrows that were yellow, and changed his face. That night he stood astride . . . astride the rooms, the guests, the flowers, the tapers, the bride and her father with his purple face. 'What, Miss Sabina?' he would roar, though she had never said a word, not one word . . . waiting in the stiffened gown that took then its odor of burning wax. We remembered that, that roar, that 'What, Miss Sabina?' and we whispered it among ourselves later when we embroidered together, as though it were a riddle that young ladies could not answer. He seemed never to have said any other thing to her. He was dangerous that first night, swaying with drink, trampling the scattered flowers, led up to a ceremony there before all our eyes, Miss Sabina so rigid by his side. He was a McInnis, a man that would be like a torch carried into a house."

The three old maids, who lay like a faded garland at the foot of the columns, paused in peaceful silence. When the story was taken up again, it was in Phoebe's delicate and gentle way, for its narrative was only part of memory now, and its beginning and ending might seem mingled and freed in the blue air of the hill.

"She bore three children, two boys and a girl, and one by one they died as they reached maturity. There was Minerva and she was drowned—before her wedding day. There was Theo, coming out from the university in his gown of the law, and killed in a fall off the wild horse he was bound to ride. And there was Lucian the youngest, shooting himself publicly on the courthouse steps, drunk in the broad daylight.

"Who can tell what will happen in this world!" said Phoebe, and she looked placidly up into the featureless sky overhead.

"It all served to make Miss Sabina prouder than ever," Irene said. "She was born grand, with a will to impose, and now she had only Mr. Don left, to impose it upon. But he was a McInnis. He had the wildness we all worshipped that first night, since he was not to be ours to love. He was unfaithful—maybe always—maybe once—"

"We told the news," said Cora. "We went in a body up the hill and into the house, weeping and wailing, hardly daring to name the name or the deed."

"It was in the big hall by the statues of the Seasons, and she stood up to listen to us all the way through," Irene murmured. "She didn't move—she didn't blink her eye. We stood there in our little half-circle not daring to come closer. Then she reached out both her arms as though she would embrace us all, and made fists with her hands, with the sharp rings cutting into her, and called down the curse of heaven on everybody's head—his, and the woman's, and the dead children's, and ours. Then she walked out, and the door of her bedroom closed."

"We ran away," said Phoebe languidly. "We ran down the steps and in and out of the boxwood garden, around the fountain, all clutching one another as though we were pursued, and away through the street, crying. She never shed a tear, whatever happened, but we shed enough for everybody."

Cora said: "By that time, her father was dead and there was no one to right the wrong. And Mr. Don—he only flourished. He wore white linen suits summer and winter. She declared the lightning would strike him for the destruction he had brought on her, but it never struck. She never closed her eyes a single night, she was so outraged and so undone. She would not eat a bite for anybody. We carried things up to her—soups, birds, wines, frozen surprises, cold shapes, one after the other. She only pushed them away. It could have been thought that life with the beast was the one thing in the living world to be pined after. But 'How can I hate him enough?' she said over and over. 'How can I show him the hate I have for him?' She implored us to tell her."

"We heard he was running away to Asphodel," said Irene, "and taking the woman. And when we went and told Miss Sabina, she would not wait any longer for an act of God to punish him, though we took her and held her till she pushed us from her side."

"She drove Mr. Don out of the house," said Cora, to whom the cordial was now passed. "Drove him out with a whip, in the broad daylight. It was a day like this, in summer—I remember the magnolias that made the air so heavy and full of sleep. It was just after dinner time and all the population came out and stood helpless to see, as if in a dream. Like a demon she sprang from the door and rushed down the long iron steps, driving him before her with the buggy whip, that had a purple tassel. He walked straight ahead as if to humor her, with his white hat lifted and held in his hand."

"We followed at a little distance behind her, in case she should faint," said Phoebe. "But we were the ones who were near to fainting, when she set her feet in the gateway after driving him through, and called at the top of her voice for the woman to come forward. She longed to whip her there and then. But no one came forward. She swore that we were hiding and protecting some wretched creature, that we were all in league. Miss Sabina put a great blame on the whole town."

"When Asphodel burned that night," said Cora, "and we all saw the fire raging on the sky, we ran and told her, and she was gratified—but from that moment remote from us and grand. And she laid down the law that the name of Don McInnis and the name of Asphodel were not to cross our lips again. . . ."

The prodigious columns shone down and appeared tremulous with the tender light of summer which enclosed them all around, in equal and shadowless flame. They seemed to flicker with the flight of birds.

"Miss Sabina," said Irene, "for the rest of her life was proceeding through the gateway and down the street, and all her will was turned upon the population."

"She was painted to be beautiful and terrible in the face, all dark around the eyes," said Phoebe, "in the way of grand ladies of the South grown old. She wore a fine jet-black wig of great size, for she had lost her hair by some illness or violence. She went draped in the heavy brocades from her family trunks, which she hung about herself in some bitter disregard. She would do no more than pin them and tie them into place. Through such a weight of material her knees pushed slowly, her progress was hampered but she came on. Her look was the challenging one when looks met, though only Miss Sabina knew why there had to be any clangor of encounter among peaceable people. *We* knew she had been beautiful. Her hands were small, and as hot to the touch as a child's under the sharp diamonds. One hand, the right one, curved round and clenched an ebony stick mounted with the gold head of a lion."

"She took her stick and went down the street proclaiming and wielding her power," said Cora. "Her power reached over the whole population—white and black, men and women, children, idiots, and animals—even strangers. Her law was laid over us, her riches were distributed upon us; we were given a museum and a statue, a waterworks. And we stood in fear of her, old and young and like ourselves. At the May Festival when she passed by, all the maypoles became hopelessly tangled, one by one. Her good wish and her censure could be as clearly told apart as a white horse from a black one. All news was borne to her first, and she interrupted every newsbearer. 'You don't have to tell me: I know. The woman is dead. The child is born. The man is proved a thief.' There would be a time when she appeared at the door of every house on the street, pounding with her cane. She dominated every ceremony, set the times for weddings and for funerals, even for births, and she named the children. She ordered lives about and moved people from one place to another in the town, brought them together or drove them apart, with the mystical and rigorous devotion of a priestess in a story; and she prophesied all the things beforehand. She foretold disaster, and was ready with hot breads and soups to send by running Negroes to every house the moment it struck. And she expected her imparted recipes to be used forever after, and no other. We are eating Miss Sabina's cake now. . . ."

"But at the end of the street there was one door where Miss Sabina had never entered," said Phoebe. "The door of the post office. She acted as if the post office had no existence in the world, or else she called it a dirty little room with the door standing wide open to the flies. All the hate she had left in her when she was old went out to a little four-posted whitewashed building, the post office. It was beyond her domain. For there we might still be apart in a dream, and she did not know what it was."

"But in the end, she came in," said Irene.

"We were there," she said. "It was mail time, and we each had a letter in our hands. We heard her come to the end of the street, the heavy staggering figure coming to the beat of the cane. We were silent all at once. When Miss Sabina is at the door, there is no other place in the world but where you stand, and no other afternoon but that one, past or future. We held onto our letters as onto all far-away or ephemeral things at that moment, to our secret hope or joy and our despair too, which she might require of us."

"When she entered," said Cora, "and took her stand in the center of the floor, a little dog saw who it was and trotted out, and alarm like the vibration from the firebell trembled in the motes of the air, and the crowded room seemed to shake, to totter. We looked at one another in greater fear of her than ever before in our lives, and we would have run away or spoken to her first, except for a premonition that this time was the last, this demand the final one."

"It was as if the place of the smallest and the longest-permitted indulgence, the little common green, were to be invaded when the time came for the tyrant to die," said Phoebe.

The three old maids sighed gently. The grapes they held upon their palms were transparent in the light, so that the little black seeds showed within.

"But when Miss Sabina spoke," said Irene, "she said, 'Give me my letter.' And Miss Sabina never got a letter in her life. She never knew a soul beyond the town. We told her there was no letter for her, but she cried out again, 'Give me my letter!' We told her there was none, and we went closer and tried to gather her to us. But she said, 'Give me that.' And she took our letters out of our hands. 'Your lovers!' she said, and tore them in two. We let her do just as she would. But she was not satisfied. 'Open up!' she said to the postmistress, and she beat upon the little communicating door. So the postmistress had to open up, and Miss Sabina went in to the inner part. We all drew close. We glanced at one another with our eyes grown bright, like people under a spell, for she was bent upon destruction."

"A fury and a pleasure seemed to rise inside her, that went out like lightning through her hands," said Cora. "She threw down her stick, she advanced with her bare hands. She seized upon everything before her, and tore it to pieces. She dragged the sacks about, and the wastebaskets, and the contents she scattered like snow. Even the ink pad she flung against the wall, and it left a purple mark like a grape stain that will never wear off.

"She was possessed then, before our eyes, as she could never have been possessed. She raged. She rocked from side to side, she danced. Miss Sabina's arms moved like a harvester's in the field, to destroy all that was in the little room. In her frenzy she tore all the letters to pieces, and even put bits in her mouth and appeared to eat them.

"Then she stood still in the little room. She had finished.

We had not yet moved when she lay toppled on the floor, her wig fallen from her head and her face awry like a mask.

" 'A stroke.' That is what we said, because we did not know how to put a name to the end of her life. . . ."

Here in the bright sun where the three old maids sat beside their little feast, Miss Sabina's was an old story, closed and complete. In some intoxication of the time and the place, they recited it and came to the end. Now they lay stretched on their sides on the ground, their summer dresses spread out, little smiles forming on their mouths, their eyes half-closed, Phoebe with a juicy green leaf between her teeth. Above them like a dream rested the bright columns of Asphodel, a dream like the other side of their lamentations.

All at once there was a shudder in the vines growing up among the columns. Out into the radiant light with one foot forward had stepped a bearded man. He stood motionless as one of the columns, his eyes bearing without a break upon the three women. He was as rude and golden as a lion. He did nothing, and he said nothing while the birds sang on. But he was naked.

The white picnic cloth seemed to have stirred of itself and spilled out the half-eaten fruit and shattered the bottle of wine as the three old maids first knelt, then stood, and with a cry clung with their arms upon one another. As if they heard a sound in the vibrant silence, they were compelled to tarry in the very act of flight. In a soft little chorus of screams they waited, looking back over their shoulders, with their arms stretched before them. Then their shoes were left behind them, and the three made a little line across the brook, and across the field in an aisle that opened among the mounds of wild roses. With the suddenness of birds they had all dropped to earth at the same moment and as if by magic risen on the other side of the fence, beside a "No Trespassing" sign.

They stood wordless together, brushing and plucking at their clothes, while quite leisurely the old horse trotted towards them across this pasture that was still, for him, unexplored.

The bearded man had not moved once.

Cora spoke. "That was Mr. Don McInnis."

"It was not," said Irene. "It was a vine in the wind."

Phoebe was bent over to pull a thorn from her bare foot. "But we thought he was dead."

"That was just as much Mr. Don as this is I," said Cora, "and I would swear to that in a court of law."

"He was naked," said Irene.

"He was buck-naked," said Cora. "He was as naked as an old goat. He must be as old as the hills."

"I didn't look," declared Phoebe. But there at one side she stood bowed and trembling as if from a fateful encounter.

"No need to cry about it, Phoebe," said Cora. "If it's Mr. Don, it's Mr. Don."

They consoled one another, and hitched the horse, and then waited still in their little cluster, looking back.

"What Miss Sabina wouldn't have given to see him!" cried Cora at last. "What she wouldn't have told him, what she wouldn't have done to him!"

But at that moment, as their gaze was fixed on the ruin, a number of goats appeared between the columns of Asphodel, and with a little leap started down the hill. Their nervous little hooves filled the air with a shudder and palpitation.

"Into the buggy!"

Tails up, the goats leapt the fence as if there was nothing they would rather do.

Cora, Irene, and Phoebe were inside the open buggy, the whip was raised over the old horse.

"There are more and more coming still," cried Irene.

There were billy-goats and nanny-goats, old goats and young, a whole thriving herd. Their little beards all blew playfully to the side in the wind of their advancement.

"They are bound to catch up," cried Irene.

"Throw them something," said Cora, who held the reins.

At their feet was the basket that had been saved out, with a napkin of biscuits and bacon on top.

"Here, billy-goats!" they cried.

Leaning from the sides of the buggy, their sleeves fluttering, each one of them threw back biscuits with both hands.

"Here, billy-goats!" they cried, but the little goats were prancing so close, their inquisitive noses were almost in the spokes of the wheels.

"It won't stop them," said Phoebe. "They're not satisfied in the least, it only makes them curious."

Cora was standing up in the open buggy, driving it like a chariot. "Give them the little baked hen, then," she said, and they threw it behind.

The little goats stopped, with their heads flecked to one side, and then their horns met over the prize.

There was a turn, and Asphodel was out of sight. The road went into a ravine and wound into the shade. . . .

"We escaped," said Cora.

"I am thankful Miss Sabina did not live to see us then," said Irene. "She would have been ashamed of us—barefooted and running. She would never have given up the little basket we had saved back."

"He ought not to be left at liberty," cried Cora. She spoke soothingly to the old horse whose haunches still trembled, and then said, "I have a good mind to report him to the law!"

There was the great house where Miss Sabina had lived, high on the coming hill.

But Phoebe laughed aloud as they made the curve. Her voice was soft, and she seemed to be still in a tender dream and an unconscious celebration—as though the picnic were not already set rudely in the past, but were the enduring and intoxicating present, still the phenomenon, the golden day.

The Winds

WHEN Josie first woke up in the night she thought the big girls of the town were having a hay-ride. Choruses and cries of what she did not question to be joy came stealing through the air. At once she could see in her mind the source of it, the Old Natchez Trace, which was at the edge of her town, an old dark place where the young people went, and it was called both things, the Old Natchez Trace and Lover's Lane. An excitement touched her and she could see in her imagination the leaning wagon coming, the long white-stockinged legs of the big girls hung down in a fringe on one side of the hay—then as the horses made a turn, the boys' black stockings stuck out the other side.

But while her heart rose longingly to the pitch of their delight, hands reached under her and she was lifted out of bed.

"Don't be frightened," said her father's voice into her ear, as if he told her a secret.

Am I old? Am I invited? she wondered, stricken.

The chorus seemed to envelop her, but it was her father's thin nightshirt she lay against in the dark.

"I still say it's a shame to wake them up." It was her mother's voice coming from the doorway, though strangely argumentative for so late in the night.

Then they were all moving in the stirring darkness, all in their nightgowns, she and Will being led by their mother and father, and they in turn with their hands out as if they were being led by something invisible. They moved off the sleeping porch into the rooms of the house. The calls and laughter of the older children came closer, and Josie thought that at any moment their voices would all come together, and they would sing their favorite round, "Row, row, row your boat, gently down the stream—merrily, merrily, merrily, merrily—"

"Don't turn on the lights," said her father, as if to keep the halls and turnings secret within. They passed the front bedroom; she knew it by the scent of her mother's verbena sachet and the waist-shape of the mirror which showed in the dark. But they did not go in there. Her father put little coats about them, not their right ones. In her sleep she seemed to have dreamed the sounds of all the windows closing, upstairs and down. Coming out of the guest-room was a sound like a nest of little mice in the hay; in a flash of pride and elation Josie discovered it to be the empty bed rolling around and squeaking on its wheels. Then close beside them was a small musical tinkle against the floor, and she knew the sound; it was Will's Tinker-Toy tower coming apart and the wooden spools and rods scattering down.

"Oh boy!" cried Will, spreading his arms high in his sleep and beginning to whirl about. "The house is falling down!"

"Hush," said their mother, catching him.

"Never mind," said their father, smoothing Josie's hair but speaking over her head. "Downstairs."

The hour had never seemed so late in their house as when they made this slow and unsteady descent. Josie thought again of Lover's Lane. The stairway gave like a chain, the pendulum shivered in the clock.

They moved into the living room. The summer matting was down on the floor, cracked and lying in little ridges under their sandals, smelling of its stains and dust, of thin green varnish, and of its origin in China. The sheet of music open on the piano had caved in while they slept, and gleamed faintly like a shell in the shimmer and flow of the strange light. Josie's drawing of the plaster-cast of Joan of Arc, which it had taken her all summer to do for her mother, had rolled itself tightly up on the desk like a diploma. Were they all going away and leave that? They wandered separately for a moment looking like strangers at the wicker chairs. The cretonne pillows smelled like wet stones. Outside the beseeching cries rose and fell, and drew nearer. The curtains hung almost still, like poured cream, down the windows, but on the table the petals shattered all at once from a bowl of roses. Then the chorus of wildness and delight seemed to come almost into their street, though still it held its distance, exactly like the wandering wagon filled with the big girls and boys at night.

Will in his little shirt was standing straight up with his eyes closed, erect as a spinning top.

"He'll sleep through it," said their mother. "You take him,

and I'll take the girl." With a little push, she divided the children; she was unlike herself. Then their mother and father sat down opposite each other in the wicker chairs. They were waiting.

"Is it a moonlight picnic?" asked Josie.

"It's a storm," said her father. He answered her questions formally in a kind of deep courtesy always, which did not depend on the day or night. "This is the equinox."

Josie gave a leap at that and ran to the front window and looked out.

"Josie!"

She was looking for the big girl who lived in the double-house across the street. There was a strange fluid lightning which she now noticed for the first time to be filling the air, violet and rose, and soundless of thunder; and the eyes of the double-house seemed to open and shut with it.

"Josie, come back."

"I see Cornella. I see Cornella in the equinox, there in her high-heeled shoes."

"Nonsense," said her father. "Nonsense, Josie."

But she stood with her back to all of them and looked, saying, "I see Cornella."

"How many times have I told you that you need not concern yourself with—Cornella!" The way her mother said her name was not diminished now.

"I see Cornella. She's on the outside, Mama, outside in the storm, and she's in the equinox."

But her mother would not answer.

"Josie, don't you understand—I want to keep us close together," said her father. She looked back at him. "Once in an equinoctial storm," he said cautiously over the sleeping Will, "a man's little girl was blown away from him into a haystack out in a field."

"The wind will come after Cornella," said Josie.

But he called her back.

The house shook as if a big drum were being beaten down the street.

Her mother sighed. "Summer is over."

Josie drew closer to her, with a sense of consolation. Her mother's dark plait was as warm as her arm, and she tugged at it. In the coming of these glittering flashes and the cries and the calling voices of the equinox, summer was turning into the past. The long ago . . .

"What is the equinox?" she asked.

Her father made an explanation. "A seasonal change, you see, Josie—like the storm we had in winter. You remember that."

"No, sir," she said. She clung to her mother.

"She couldn't remember it next morning," said her mother, and looked at Will, who slept up against his father with his hands in small fists.

"You mustn't be frightened, Josie," said her father again. "You have my word that this is a good strong house." He had built it before she was born. But in the equinox Josie stayed with her mother, though the lightning stamped the pattern of her father's dressing gown on the room.

With the pulse of the lightning the wide front window was oftener light than dark, and the persistence of illumination seemed slowly to be waking something that slept longer than Josie had slept, for her trembling body turned under her mother's hand.

"Be still," said her mother. "It's soon over."

They looked at one another, parents and children, as if through a turning wheel of light, while they waited in their various attitudes against the wicker arabesques and the flowered cloth. When the wind rose still higher, both mother and father went all at once silent, Will's eyes lifted open, and all their gazes confronted one another. Then in a single flickering, Will's face was lost in sleep. The house moved softly like a boat that has been stepped into.

Josie lay drifting in the chair, and where she drifted was through the summertime, the way of the past. . . .

It seemed to her that there should have been more time for the monkey-man—for the premonition, the organ coming from the distance, the crisis in the house, "Is there a penny upstairs or down?", the circle of following children, their downcast looks of ecstasy, and for the cold imploring hand of the little monkey.

She woke only to hunt for signs of the fairies, and counted

nothing but a footprint smaller than a bird-claw. All of the sand pile went into a castle, and it was a rite to stretch on her stomach and put her mouth to the door. "O my Queen!" and the coolness of the whisper would stir the grains of sand within. Expectant on the floor were spread the sycamore leaves, Will's fur rugs with the paws, head, and tail. "I am thine eternally, my Queen, and will serve thee always and I will be enchanted with thy love forever." It was delicious to close both eyes and wait a length of time. Then, supposing a mocking-bird sang in the tree, "I ask for my first wish, to be made to understand the tongue of birds." They called her back because they had no memory of magic. Even a June-bug, if he were caught and released, would turn into a being, and this was forgotten in the way people summoned one another.

Polishing the dark hall clock as though it was through her tending that the time was brought, the turbaned cook would be singing, "Dere's a Hole in de Bottom of de Sea." "How old will I get to be, Johanna?" she would ask as she ran through the house. "Ninety-eight." "How old is Will going to be?" "Ninety-nine." Then she was out the door. Her bicycle was the golden Princess, the name in a scroll in front. She would take her as early as possible. So as to touch nothing, to make no print on the earliness of the day, she rode with no hands, no feet, touching nowhere but the one place, moving away into the leaves, down the swaying black boards of the dewy alley. They called her back. She hung from and circled in order the four round posts, warm and filled with weight, on the porch. Green arched ferns, like great exhalations, spread from the stands. The porch was deep and wide and painted white with a blue ceiling, and the swing, like three sides of a box, was white too under its long quiet chains. She ran and jumped, secure that the house was theirs and identical with them—the pale smooth house seeming not to yield to any happening, with the dreamlike arch of the roof over the entrance like the curve of their upper lips.

All the children came running and jumping out. She went along chewing nasturtium stems and sucking the honey from four-o'clock flowers, out for whatever figs and pomegranates came to hand. She floated a rose petal dry in her mouth, and sucked on the spirals of honeysuckle and the knobs of purple clover. She wore crowns. She added flower necklaces as the morning passed, then bracelets, and applied transfer-pictures to her forehead and arms and legs—a basket of roses, a windmill, Columbus's ships, ruins of Athens. But always oblivious, off in the shade, the big girls reclined or pressed their flowers in a book, or filled whole baking-powder cans with four-leaf-clovers they found.

And watching it all from the beginning, the morning going by, was the double-house. This worn old house was somehow in disgrace, as if it had been born into it and could not help it. Josie was sorry, and sorry that it looked like a face, with its wide-apart upper windows, the nose-like partition between the two sagging porches, the chimneys rising in listening points at either side, and the roof across which the birds sat. It watched, and by not being what it should have been, the house was inscrutable. There was always some noise of disappointment to be heard coming from within—a sigh, a thud, something dropped. There were eight children in all that came out of it—all sizes, and all tow-headed, as if they might in some way all be kin under that roof, and they had a habit of arranging themselves in the barren yard in a little order, like an octave, and staring out across the street at the rest of the neighborhood—as if to state, in their rude way, "This is us." Everyone was cruelly prevented from playing with the children of the double-house, no matter how in their humility they might change—in the course of the summer they would change to an entirely new set, with the movings in and out, though somehow there were always exactly eight. Cornella, being nearly grown and being transformed by age, was not to be counted simply as a forbidden playmate—yet sometimes, as if she wanted to be just that, she chased after them, or stood in the middle while they ran a ring around her.

In the morning was Cornella's time of preparation. She was forever making ready. Big girls are usually idle, but Cornella, as occupied as a child, vigorously sunned her hair, or else she had always just washed it and came out busily to dry it. It was bright yellow, wonderfully silky and long, and she would bend her neck and toss her hair over her head before her face like a waterfall. And her hair was as constant a force as a waterfall to Josie, under whose eyes alone it fell. Cornella, Cornella, let down thy hair, and the King's son will come climbing up.

Josie watched her, for there was no one else to see, how she shook it and played with it and presently began to brush it, over and over, out in public. But always through the hiding hair she would be looking out, steadily out, over the street. Josie, who followed her gaze, felt the emptiness of their street too, and could not understand why at such a moment no one could be as pitiful as only the old man driving slowly by in the cart, and no song could be as sad as his song,

> "Milk, milk,
> Buttermilk!
> Sweet potatoes—Irish potatoes—green peas—
> And buttermilk!"

But Cornella, instead of being moved by this sad moment, in which Josie's love began to go toward her, stamped her foot. She was angry, angry. To see her then, oppression touched Josie and held her quite still. Called in to dinner before she could understand, she felt a conviction: I will never catch up with her. No matter how old I get, I will never catch up with Cornella. She felt that daring and risking everything went for nothing; she would never take a poison wild strawberry into her mouth again in the hope of finding out the secret and the punishment of the world, for Cornella, whom she might love, had stamped her foot, and had as good as told her, "You will never catch up." All that she ran after in the whole summer world came to life in departure before Josie's eyes and covered her vision with wings. It kept her from eating her dinner to think of all that she had caught or meant to catch before the time was gone—June-bugs in the banana plants to fly before breakfast on a thread, lightning-bugs that left a bitter odor in the palms of the hands, butterflies with their fierce and haughty faces, bees in a jar. A great tempest of droning and flying seemed to have surrounded her as she ran, and she seemed not to have moved without putting her hand out after something that flew ahead. . . .

"There! I thought you were asleep," said her father.

She turned in her chair. The house had stirred.

"Show me their tracks," muttered Will. "Just show me their tracks."

As though the winds were changed back into songs, Josie seemed to hear "Beautiful Ohio" slowly picked out in the key of C down the hot afternoon. That was Cornella. Through the tied-back curtains of parlors the other big girls, with rats in their hair and lace insertions in their white dresses, practiced forever on one worn little waltz, up and down the street, for they took lessons.

"Come spend the day with me." "See who can eat a banana down without coming up to breathe." That was Josie and her best friend, smirking at each other.

They wandered at a trot, under their own parasols. In the vacant field, in the center of summer, was a chinaberry tree, as dark as a cloud in the middle of the day. Its frail flowers or its bitter yellow balls lay trodden always over the whole of the ground. There was a little path that came through the hedge and went its way to this tree, and there was an old low seat built part-way around the trunk, on which was usually lying an abandoned toy of some kind. Here beside the nurses stood the little children, whose level eyes stared at the rosettes on their garters.

"How do you do?"

"How do you do?"

"I remembers you. Where you all think you goin'?"

"We don't have to answer."

They went to the drugstore and treated each other. It was behind the latticed partition. How well she knew its cut-out pasteboard grapes whose color was put on a little to one side. Her elbows slid smoothly out on the cold damp marble that smelled like hyacinths. "You say first." "No, you. First you love me last you hate me." When they were full of sweets it was never too late to take the long way home. They ran through the park and drank from the fountain. Moving slowly as sunlight over the grass were the broad and dusty backs of pigeons. They stopped and made a clover-chain and hung it on a statue. They groveled in the dirt under the bandstand hunting for lost money, but when they found a dead bird with its feathers cool as rain, they ran out in the sun. Old Biddy

Felix came to make a speech, he stood up and shouted with no one to listen—"The time flies, the time flies!"—and his arm and hand flew like a bat in the ragged sleeve. Walking the see-saw she held her breath for him. They floated magnolia leaves in the horse trough, themselves taking the part of the wind and waves, and suddenly remembering who they were. They closed in upon the hot tamale man, fixing their frightened eyes on his lantern and on his scars.

Josie never came and she never went without touching the dragon—the Chinese figure in the garden on the corner that in biting held rain water in the cavern of its mouth. And never did it seem so still, so utterly of stone, as when all the children said goodbye as they always did on that corner, and she was left alone with it. Stone dragons opened their mouths and begged to swallow the day, they loved to eat the summer. It was painful to think of even pony-rides gobbled, the way they all went, the children, every one (except from the double-house) crammed into the basket with their heads stuck up like candy-almonds in a treat. She backed all the way home from the dragon.

But she had only to face the double-house in her meditations, and then she could invoke Cornella. Thy name is Corn, and thou art like the ripe corn, beautiful Cornella. And before long the figure of Cornella would be sure to appear. She would dart forth from one old screen door of the double-house, trailed out by the nagging odor of cabbage cooking. She would have just bathed and dressed, for it took her so long, and her bright hair would be done in puffs and curls with a bow behind.

Cornella was not even a daughter in her side of the house, she was only a niece or cousin, there only by the frailest indulgence. She would come out with this frailty about her, come without a hat, without anything. Between the double-house and the next house was the strongest fence that could be built, and no ball had ever come back that went over it. It reached all the way out to the street. So Cornella could never see if anyone might be coming, unless she came all the way out to the curb and leaned around the corner of the fence. Josie knew the way it would happen, and yet it was like new always. At the opening of the door, the little towheads would scatter, dash to the other side of the partition, disappear as if by consent. Then lightly down the steps, down the walk, Cornella would come, in some kind of secrecy swaying from side to side, her skirts swinging round, and the sidewalk echoing smally to her pumps with the Baby Louis heels. Then, all alone, Cornella would turn and gaze away down the street, as if she could see far, far away, in a little pantomime of hope and apprehension that would not permit Josie to stir.

But the moment came when without meaning to she lifted her hand softly, and made a sign to Cornella. She almost said her name.

And Cornella—what was it she had called back across the street, the flash of what word, so furious and yet so frail and thin? It was more furious than even the stamping of her foot, only a single word.

Josie took her hand down. In a seeking humility she stood there and bore her shame to attend Cornella. Cornella herself would stand still, haughtily still, waiting as if in pride, until a voice old and cracked would call her too, from the upper window, "Cornella, Cornella!" And she would have to turn around and go inside to the old woman, her hair ribbon and her sash in pale bows that sank down in the back.

Then for Josie the sun on her bangs stung, and the pity for ribbons drove her to a wild capering that would end in a tumble.

Will woke up with a yell like a wild Indian.

"Here, let me hold him," said his mother. Her voice had become soft; time had passed. She took Will on her lap.

Josie opened her eyes. The lightning was flowing like the sea, and the cries were like waves at the door. Her parents' faces were made up of hundreds of very still moments.

"Tomahawks!" screamed Will.

"Mother, don't let him—" Josie said uneasily.

"Never mind. You talk in your sleep too," said her mother.

She experienced a kind of shock, a small shock of detachment, like the time in the picture-show when a little blurred moment of the summer's May Festival had been thrown on the screen and there was herself, ribbon in hand, weaving once in and once out, a burning and abandoned look in the flicker of her face as though no one in the world would ever see her.

Her mother's hand stretched to her, but Josie broke away. She lay with her face hidden in the pillow. . . . The summer day became vast and opalescent with twilight. The calming and languid smell of manure came slowly to meet her as she passed through the back gate and went out to the pasture among the mounds of wild roses. "Daisy," she had only to say once, in her quietest voice, for she felt very near to the cow. There she walked, not even eating—Daisy, the small tender Jersey with her soft violet nose, walking and presenting her warm side. Josie bent to lean her forehead against her. Here the tears from her eyes could go rolling down Daisy's shining coarse hairs, and Daisy did not move or speak but held patient, richly compassionate and still. . . .

"You're not frightened any more, are you, Josie?" asked her father.

"No, sir," she said, with her face buried. . . . She thought of the evening, the sunset, the stately game played by the flowering hedge when the vacant field was theirs. "Here comes the duke a-riding, riding, riding . . . What are you riding here for, here for?" while the hard iron sound of the Catholic Church bell tolled at twilight for unknown people. "The fairest one that I can see . . . London Bridge is falling down . . . Lady Moon, Lady Moon, show your shoe . . . I measure my love to show you . . ." Under the fiery windows, how small the children were. "Fox in the morning!—Geese in the evening!—How many have you got?—More than you can ever catch!" The children were rose-colored too. Fading, rolling shouts cast long flying shadows behind them, and to watch them she stood still. Above everything in the misty blue dome of the sky was the full white moon. So it is, for a true thing, round, she thought, and where she waited a hand seemed to reach around and take her under the loose-hanging hair, and words in her thoughts came shaped like grapes in her throat. She felt lonely. She would stop a runner. "Did you know the moon was round?" "I did. Annie told me last summer." The game went on. But I must find out everything about the moon, Josie thought in the solemnity of evening.

The moon and tides. O moon! O tides! I ask thee. I ask thee. Where dost thou rise and fall? As if it were this knowledge which she would allow to enter her heart, for which she had been keeping room, and as if it were the moon, known to be round, that would go floating through her dreams forever and never leave her, she looked steadily up at the moon. The moon looked down at her, full with all the lonely time to go.

When night was about to fall, the time came to bring out her most precious possession, the steamboat she had made from a shoe-box. In all boats the full-moon, half-moon, and new moon were cut out of each side for the windows, with tissue-paper through which shone the unsteady candle inside. She knew this journey ahead of time as if it were long ago, the hushing noise the boat made being dragged up the brick walk by the string, the leap it had to take across the three-cornered missing place over the big root, the spreading smell of warm wax in the evening, and the remembered color of the daylight turning. Coming to meet the boat was another boat, shining and gliding as if by itself.

Children greeted each other dreamily at twilight.

"Choo-choo!"

"Choo-choo!"

And something made her turn after that and see how Cornella stood and looked across at them, all dressed in gauze, looking as if the street were a river flowing along between, and she did not speak at all. Josie understood: she *could* not. It seemed to her as she guided her warm boat under the brightening moon that Cornella would have turned into a tree if she could, there in the front yard of the double-house, and that the center of the tree would have to be seen into before her heart was bared, so undaunted and so filled with hope. . . .

"I'll shoot you dead!" screamed Will.

"Hush, hush," said their mother.

Her father held up his hand and said, "Listen."

Then their house was taken to the very breast of the storm.

Josie lay as still as an animal, and in panic thought of the future . . . the sharp day when she would come running out of the field holding the ragged stems of the quick-picked goldenrod and the warm flowers thrust out for a present for somebody. The future was herself bringing presents, the season of gifts. When would the day come when the wind would fall and they would sit in silence on the fountain rim, their play done, and the boys would crack the nuts under their heels? If they would bring the time around once more, she would lose nothing that was given, she would hoard the nuts like a squirrel.

For the first time in her life she thought, might the same wonders never come again? Was each wonder original and alone like the falling star, and when it fell did it bury itself beyond where you hunted it? Should she hope to see it snow twice, and the teacher running again to open the window, to hold out her black cape to catch it as it came down, and then going up and down the room quickly, quickly, to show them the snowflakes? . . .

"Mama, where is my muff that came from Marshall Field's?"

"It's put away, it was your grandmother's present." (But it came from those far fields.) "Are you dreaming?" Her mother felt of her forehead.

"I want my little muff to hold." She ached for it. "Mother, give it to me."

"Keep still," said her mother softly.

Her father came over and kissed her, and as if a new kiss could bring a memory, she remembered the night. . . . It was that very night. How could she have forgotten and nearly let go what was closest of all? . . .

The whole way, as they walked slowly after supper past the houses, and the wet of sprinkled lawns was rising like a spirit over the streets, the locusts were filling the evening with their old delirium, the swell that would rise and die away.

In the Chautauqua when they got there, there was a familiar little cluster of stars beyond the hole in the top of the tent, but the canvas sides gave off sighs and stirred, and a knotted rope knocked outside. It was war time where there were grown people, and the vases across the curtained stage held little bunches of flags on sticks which drooped and wilted like flowers before their eyes. Josie and Will sat waiting on the limber board in the front row, their feet hanging into the spice-clouds of sawdust. The curtains parted. Waiting with lifted hands was a company with a sign beside them saying "The Trio." All were ladies, one in red, one in white, and one in blue, and after one smile which touched them all at the same instant, like a match struck in their faces, they began to play a piano, a cornet, and a violin.

At first, in the hushed disappointment which filled the Chautauqua tent in beginning moments, the music had been sparse and spare, like a worn hedge through which the hiders can be seen. But then, when hope had waned, there had come a little transition to another key, and the woman with the cornet had stepped forward, raising her instrument.

If morning-glories had come out of the horn instead of those sounds, Josie would not have felt a more astonished delight. She was pierced with pleasure. The sounds that so tremulously came from the striving of the lips were welcome and sweet to her. Between herself and the lifted cornet there was no barrier, there was only the stale, expectant air of the old shelter of the tent. The cornetist was beautiful. There in the flame-like glare that was somehow shadowy, she had come from far away, and the long times of the world seemed to be about her. She was draped heavily in white, shaded with blue, like a Queen, and she stood braced and looking upward like the figurehead on a Viking ship. As the song drew out, Josie could see the slow appearance of a little vein in her cheek. Her closed eyelids seemed almost to whir and yet to rest motionless, like the wings of a humming-bird, when she reached the high note. The breaths she took were fearful, and a little medallion of some kind lifted each time on her breast. Josie listened in mounting care and suspense, as if the performance led in some direction away—as if a destination were being shown her.

And there not far away, with her face all wild, was Cornella, listening too, and still alone. In some alertness Josie turned and looked back for her parents, but they were far back in the crowd; they did not see her, they were not listening. She was let free, and turning back to the cornetist, who was transfixed beneath her instrument, she bent gently forward and closed her hands together over her knees.

"Josie!" whispered Will, prodding her.

"That's my name." But she would not talk to him.

She had come home tired, in a dream. But after the light had been turned out on the sleeping porch, and the kisses of her family were put on her cheek, she had not fallen asleep. She could see out from the high porch that the town was dark, except where beyond the farthest rim of trees the old cotton-seed mill with its fiery smokestack and its lights forever seemed an inland boat that waited for the return of the sea. It came over her how the beauty of the world had come with its sign and stridden through their town that night; and it seemed to her that a proclamation had been made in the last high note of the lady trumpeteer when her face had become set in its passion, and that after that there would be no more waiting and no more time left for the one who did not take heed and follow. . . .

There was a breaking sound, the first thunder.

"You see!" said her father. He struck his palms together, and it thundered again. "It's over."

"Back to bed, every last one of you," said her mother, as if it had all been something done to tease her, and now her defiance had won. She turned a light on and off.

"Pow!" cried Will, and then toppled into his father's arms, and was carried up the stairs.

From then on there was only the calm steady falling of rain.

Josie was placed in her winter-time bed. They would think her asleep, for they had all kissed one another in a kind of triumph to do for the rest of the night. The rain was a sleeper's sound. She listened for a time to a tapping that came at her window, like a plea from outside. . . . From whom? She could not know. Cornella, sweet summertime, the little black monkey, poor Biddy Felix, the lady with the horn whose lips were parted? Had they after all asked something of her? There, outside, was all that was wild and beloved and estranged, and all that would beckon and leave her, and all that was beautiful. She wanted to follow, and by some metamorphosis she would take them in—all—every one. . . .

The first thing next morning Josie ran outdoors to see what signs the equinox had left. The sun was shining. Will was already out, gruffly exhorting himself, digging in his old hole to China. The double-house across the street looked as if its old age had come upon it at last. Nobody was to be seen at the windows, and not a child was near. The whole façade drooped and gave way in the soft light, like the face of an old woman fallen asleep in church. In all the trees in all the yards the leaves were slowly dropping, one by one, as if in breath after breath.

There at Josie's foot on the porch was something. It was a folded bit of paper, wet and pale and thin, trembling in the air and clinging to the pedestal of the column, as though this were the residue of some great wave that had rolled upon the rock and then receded for another time. It was a fragment of a letter. It was written not properly in ink but in indelible pencil, and so its message had not been washed away as it might have been.

Josie knelt down and took the paper in both hands, and without moving read all that was there. Then she went to her room and put it into her most secret place, the little drawstring bag that held her dancing shoes. The name Cornella was on it, and it said, "O my darling I have waited so long when are you coming for me? Never a day or a night goes by that I do not ask When? When? When?" . . .

The Purple Hat

IT WAS in a bar, a quiet little hole in the wall. It was four o'clock in the afternoon. Beyond the open door the rain fell, the heavy color of the sea, in air where the sunlight was still suspended. Its watery reflection lighted the room, as a room might have lighted a mouse-hole. It was in New Orleans.

There was a bartender whose mouth and eyes curved downward from the divide of his baby-pink nose, as if he had combed them down, like his hair; he always just said nothing. The seats at his bar were black oilcloth knobs, worn and smooth and as much alike as six pebbles on the beach, and yet the two customers had chosen very particularly the knobs they would sit on. They had come in separately out of the wet, and had each chosen an end stool, and now sat with the length of the little bar between them. The bartender obviously did not know either one; he rested his eyes by closing them. . . .

The fat customer, with a rather affable look about him, said he would have a rye. The unshaven young man with the shaking hands, though he had come in first, only looked fearfully at a spot on the counter before him until the bartender, as if he could hear silent prayer, covered the spot with a drink.

The fat man swallowed, and began at once to look a little cosy and prosperous. He seemed ready to speak, if the moment came. . . .

There was a calm roll of thunder, no more than a shifting of the daily rain clouds over Royal Street.

Then—"Rain or shine," the fat man spoke, "she'll be there."

The bartender stilled his cloth on the bar, as if mopping up made a loud noise, and waited.

"Why, at the Palace of Pleasure," said the fat man. He was really more heavy and solid than he was simply fat.

The bartender leaned forward an inch on his hand.

"The lady will be at the Palace of Pleasure," said the fat man in his drowsy voice. "The lady with the purple hat."

Then the fat man turned on the black knob, put his elbow on the counter, and rested his cheek on his hand, where he could see all the way down the bar. For a moment his eyes seemed dancing there, above one of those hands so short and so plump that you are always counting the fingers . . . really helpless-looking hands for so large a man.

The young man stared back without much curiosity, looking at the affable face much the way you stare out at a little station where your train is passing through. His hand alone found its place on his small glass.

"Oh, the hat she wears is a creation," said the fat man, almost dreamily, yet not taking his eyes from the young man. It was strange that he did not once regard the bartender, who after all had done him the courtesy of asking a polite question or two, or at least the same as asked. "A great and ancient and bedraggled purple hat."

There was another rumble overhead. Here they seemed to inhabit the world that was just beneath the thunder. The fat man let it go by, lifting his little finger like a pianist. Then he went on.

"Sure, she's one of those thousands of middle-aged women who come every day to the Palace, would not be kept away by anything on earth. . . . Most of them are dull enough, drab old creatures, all of them, walking in with their big black purses held wearily by the handles like suitcases packed for a trip. No one has ever been able to find out how all these old creatures can leave their lives at home like that to gamble . . . what their husbands think . . . who keeps the house in order . . . who pays. . . . At any rate, she is one like the rest, except for the hat, and except for the young man that always meets her there, from year to year. . . . And I think she is a ghost."

"Ghost!" said the bartender—noncommittally, just as he might repeat an order.

"For this reason," said the fat man.

A reminiscent tone came into his voice which seemed to put the silent thin young man on his guard. He made the beginning of a gesture toward the bottle. The bartender was already filling his glass.

"In thirty years she has not changed," said the fat man.

"Neither has she changed her hat. Dear God, how the moths must have hungered for that hat. But she has kept it in full bloom on her head, that monstrosity—purple, too, as if she were beautiful in the bargain. She has not aged, but she keeps her middle-age. The young man, on the other hand, must change—I'm sure he's not always the same young man. For thirty years," he said, "she's met a young man at the dice table every afternoon, rain or shine, at five o'clock, and gambles till midnight and tells him goodbye, and still it looks to be always the same young man—always young, but a little stale, a little tired . . . the smudge of a sideburn. . . . She finds them, she does. She picks them. Where I don't know, unless New Orleans, as I've always had a guess, is the birthplace of ready-made victims."

"Who are you?" asked the young man. It was the sort of idle voice in which the greatest wildness sometimes speaks out at last in a quiet bar.

"In the Palace of Pleasure there is a little catwalk along beneath the dome," said the fat man. His rather small, mournful lips, such as big men often have, now parted in a vague smile. "I am the man whose eyes look out over the gambling room. I am the armed man that everyone knows to be watching, at all they do. I don't believe my position is dignified by a title." Nevertheless, he looked rather pleased. "I have watched her every day for thirty years and I think she is a ghost. I have seen her murdered twice," said the fat man.

The bartender's enormous sad black eyebrows raised, like hoods on baby-carriages, and showed his round eyes.

The fat man lifted his other fat little hand and studied, or rather showed off, a ruby ring that he wore on his little finger. "That carpet, if you have ever been there, in the Palace of Pleasure, is red, but from up above, it changes and gives off light between the worn criss-crossing of the aisles like the facets of a well-cut ruby," he said, speaking in a declarative manner as if he had been waiting for a chance to deliver this enviable comparison. "The tables and chandeliers are far down below me, points in its interior. . . . Life in the ruby. And yet somehow all that people do is clear and lucid and authentic there, as if it were magnified in the red lens, not made smaller. I can see everything in the world from my cat-walk. You mustn't think I brag. . . ." He looked all at once from his ring straight at the young man's face, which was as drained and white as ever, expressionless, with a thin drop of whisky running down his cheek where he had blundered with his glass.

"I have seen this old and disgusting creature in her purple hat every night, quite plainly, for thirty years, and to my belief she has been murdered twice. I suppose it will take the third time." He himself smoothly tossed down a drink.

The bartender leaned over and filled the young man's glass.

"It's within the week, within the month, that she comes back. Once she was shot point-blank—that was the first time. The young man was hotheaded then. I saw her carried out bleeding from the face. We hush those things, you know, at the Palace. There are no signs afterwards, no trouble. . . . The soft red carpet . . . Within the month she was back—with her young man meeting her at the table just after five."

The bartender put his head to one side.

"The only good of shooting her was, it made a brief period of peace there," said the fat man. "I wouldn't scoff, if I were you." He did seem the least bit fretted by that kind of interruption.

"The second time took into account the hat," he went on. "And I do think her young man was on his way toward the right idea that time, the secret. I think he had learned something. Or he wanted it all kept more quiet, or he was a new one. . . ." He looked at the young man at the other end of the bar with a patient, compassionate expression, or it may have been the inevitably tender contour of his round cheeks. "It is time that I told you about the hat. It is quite a hat. A great, wide, deep hat such as has no fashion and never knew there was fashion and change. It serves her to come out in winter and summer. Those are old plush flowers that trim it—roses? Poppies? A man wouldn't know easily. And you would never know if you only met her wearing the hat that a little glass vial with a plunger helps decorate the crown. You would have to see it from above. . . . Or you would need to be the young man sitting beside her at the gambling table when, at some point in the evening, she takes the hat off and lays it carefully in her lap, under the table. . . . Then you might notice the little vial, and be attracted to it and wish to take it out and examine it at your pleasure off in the washroom—to admire the handle, for instance, which is red glass, like the petal of an artificial flower."

The bartender suddenly lifted his hand to his mouth as if it held a glass, and yawned into it. The thin young man hit the counter faintly with his tumbler.

"She does more than just that, though," said the fat man with a little annoyance in his soft voice. "Perhaps I haven't explained that she is a lover, too, or did you know that she would be? It is hard to make it clear to a man who has never been out to the Palace of Pleasure, but only serves drinks all day behind a bar. You see . . ." And now, lowering his voice a little, he deliberately turned from the young man and would not look at him any more. But the young man looked at him, without lifting his drink—as if there were something hypnotic and irresistible even about his side face with the round, hiding cheek.

"Try to imagine," the fat man was saying gently to the bartender, who looked back at him. "At some point in the evening she always takes off the purple hat. Usually it is very late . . . when it is almost time for her to go. The young man who has come to the rendezvous watches her until she removes it, watches her hungrily. Is it in order to see her hair? Well, most ghosts that are lovers, and lovers that are ghosts, have the long thick black hair that you would expect, and hers is no exception to the rule. It is pinned up, of course—in her straggly vague way. But the young man doesn't look at it after all. He is enamoured of her hat—her ancient, battered, outrageous hat with the awful plush flowers. She lays it down below the level of the table there, on her shabby old lap, and he caresses it. . . . Well, I suppose in this town there are stranger forms of love than that, and who are any of us to say what ways people may not find to love? She herself, you know, seems perfectly satisfied with it. And yet she must not be satisfied, being a ghost. . . . Does it matter how she seeks her desire? I am sure she speaks to him, in a sort of purr, the purr that is used for talking in that room, and the young man does not know what she seeks of him, and she is leading him on, all the time. What does she say? I do not know. But believe me . . . . she leads him on. . . ."

The bartender leaned on one hand. He had an oddly cheerful look by this time, as if with strange and sad things to come his way his outlook became more vivacious.

"To look at, she has a large-sized head," said the fat man, pushing his lip with his short finger. "Well, it is more that her face spreads over such a wide area. Like the moon's. . . . Much as I have studied her, I can only say that all her features seem to have moved further apart from each other—expanded, if you see what I mean." He brought his hands together and parted them.

The bartender leaned over closer, staring at the fat man's face interestedly.

"But I can never finish telling you about the hat!" the fat man cried, and there was a little sigh somewhere in the room, very young, like a child's. "Of course, to balance the weight of the attractive little plunger, there is an object to match on the other side of this marvelous old hat—a jeweled hatpin, no less. Of course the pin is there to keep the hat safe! Each time she takes off the hat, she has first to remove the hatpin. You can see her do it every night of the world. It comes out a regular little flashing needle, ten or twelve inches long, and after she has taken the hat off, she sticks the pin back through."

The bartender pursed his lips.

"What about the second time she was murdered? Have you wondered how that was done?" The fat man turned back to face the young fellow, whose feet drove about beneath the stool. "The young lover had learned something, or come to some conclusion, you see," he said. "It was obvious all the time, of course, that by spinning the brim ever so easily as it rested on the lady's not over-sensitive old knees, it would be possible to remove the *opposite* ornament. There was not the slightest fuss or outcry when the pin entered between the ribs and pierced the heart. No one saw it done . . . except for me, naturally—I had been watching for it, more or less. The old creature, who had been winning at that, simply folded all softly in on herself, like a circus tent being taken down after the show, if you've ever seen the sight. I saw her carried out again. It takes three big boys every time, she is so heavy, and one of them always has the presence of mind to cover her piously with her old purple hat for the occasion."

The bartender shut his eyes distastefully.

"If you had ever been to the Palace of Pleasure, you'd know it all went completely as usual—people at the tables never turn around," said the fat man.

The bartender ran his hand down the side of his sad smooth hair.

"The trouble lies, you see," said the fat man, "with the young lover. You are he, let us say. . . ." But he turned from the drinking young man, and it was the bartender who was asked to be the lover for the moment. "After a certain length of time goes by, and love has blossomed, and the hat, the purple hat, is thrilling to the touch of your hand—you can no longer be sure about the little vial. There in privacy you may find it to be empty. It is her coquettishness, you see. She leads you on. You are never to know whether . . ."

The chimes of St. Louis Cathedral went somnambulantly through the air. It was five o'clock. The young man had risen somehow to his feet. He moved out of the bar and disappeared in the rain of the alley. On the floor where his feet had been were old cigarette stubs that had been kicked and raked into a little circle—a rosette, a clock, a game wheel, or something. . . .

The bartender put a cork in the bottle.

"I have to go myself," said the fat man.

Once more the bartender raised his great hooded brows. For a moment their eyes met. The fat man pulled out an enormous roll of worn bills. He paid in full for all drinks and added a nice tip.

"Up on the catwalk you get the feeling now and then that you could put out your finger and make a change in the universe." His great shoulders lifted.

The bartender, with his hands full of cash, leaned confidentially over the bar. "Is she a real ghost?" he asked, in a real whisper.

There was a pause, which the thunder filled.

"I'll let you know tomorrow," said the fat man.

Then he too was gone.

Livvie

SOLOMON carried Livvie twenty-one miles away from her home when he married her. He carried her away up on the Old Natchez Trace into the deep country to live in his house. She was sixteen—an only girl, then. Once people said he thought nobody would ever come along there. He told her himself that it had been a long time, and a day she did not know about, since that road was a traveled road with *people* coming and going. He was good to her, but he kept her in the house. She had not thought that she could not get back. Where she came from, people said an old man did not want anybody in the world to ever find his wife, for fear they would steal her back from him. Solomon asked her before he took her, "Would she be happy?"—very dignified, for he was a colored man that owned his land and had it written down in the courthouse; and she said, "Yes, sir," since he was an old man and she was young and just listened and answered. He asked her, if she was choosing winter, would she pine for spring, and she said, "No indeed." Whatever she said, always, was because he was an old man . . . while nine years went by. All the time, he got old, and he got so old he gave out. At last he slept the whole day in bed, and she was young still.

It was a nice house, inside and outside both. In the first place, it had three rooms. The front room was papered in holly paper with green palmettos from the swamp spaced at careful intervals over the walls. There was fresh newspaper cut with fancy borders on the mantel-shelf, on which were propped photographs of old or very young men printed in faint yellow—Solomon's people. Solomon had a houseful of furniture. There was a double settee, a tall scrolled rocker and an organ in the front room, all around a three-legged table with a pink marble top, on which was set a lamp with three gold feet, besides a jelly glass with pretty hen feathers in it. Behind the front room, the other room had the bright iron bed with the polished knobs like a throne, in which Solomon slept all day. There were snow-white curtains of wiry lace at the window, and a lace bed-spread belonged on the bed. But what old Solomon slept so sound under was a big feather-stitched piece-quilt in the pattern "Trip Around the World," which had twenty-one different colors, four hundred and forty pieces, and a thousand yards of thread, and that was what Solomon's mother made in her life and old age. There was a table holding the Bible, and a trunk with a key. On the wall were two calendars, and a diploma from somewhere in Solomon's family, and under that Livvie's one possession was nailed, a picture of the little white baby of the family she worked for, back in Natchez before she was married. Going through that room and on to the kitchen, there was a big wood stove and a big round table always with a wet top and with the knives and forks in one jelly glass and the spoons in another, and a cut-glass vinegar bottle between, and going out from those, many shallow dishes of pickled peaches, fig preserves, watermelon pickles and blackberry jam always sitting there. The churn sat in the sun, the doors of the safe were always both shut, and there were four baited mouse-traps in the kitchen, one in every corner.

The outside of Solomon's house looked nice. It was not painted, but across the porch was an even balance. On each side there was one easy chair with high springs, looking out, and a fern basket hanging over it from the ceiling, and a dish-pan of zinnia seedlings growing at its foot on the floor. By the door was a plow-wheel, just a pretty iron circle, nailed up on one wall and a square mirror on the other, a turquoise-blue comb stuck up in the frame, with the wash stand beneath it. On the door was a wooden knob with a pearl in the end, and Solomon's black hat hung on that, if he was in the house.

Out front was a clean dirt yard with every vestige of grass patiently uprooted and the ground scarred in deep whorls from the strike of Livvie's broom. Rose bushes with tiny blood-red roses blooming every month grew in threes on either side of the steps. On one side was a peach tree, on the other a pomegranate. Then coming around up the path from the deep cut of the Natchez Trace below was a line of bare crape-myrtle trees with every branch of them ending in a colored bottle, green or blue. There was no word that fell from Solomon's lips to say what they were for, but Livvie knew that there could be a spell put in trees, and she was familiar from the time she was born with the way bottle trees kept evil spirits from coming into the house—by luring them inside the colored bottles, where they cannot get out again. Solomon had made the bottle trees with his own hands over the nine years, in labor amounting to about a tree a year, and without a sign that he had any uneasiness in his heart, for he took as much pride in his precautions against spirits coming in the house as he took in the house, and sometimes in the sun the bottle trees looked prettier than the house did.

It was a nice house. It was in a place where the days would go by and surprise anyone that they were over. The lamplight and the firelight would shine out the door after dark, over the still and breathing country, lighting the roses and the bottle trees, and all was quiet there.

But there was nobody, nobody at all, not even a white person. And if there had been anybody, Solomon would not have let Livvie look at them, just as he would not let her look at a field hand, or a field hand look at her. There was no house near, except for the cabins of the tenants that were forbidden to her, and there was no house as far as she had been, stealing away down the still, deep Trace. She felt as if she waded a river when she went, for the dead leaves on the ground reached as high as her knees, and when she was all scratched and bleeding she said it was not like a road that went anywhere. One day, climbing up the high bank, she had found a graveyard without a church, with ribbon-grass growing about the foot of an angel (she had climbed up because she thought she saw angel wings), and in the sun, trees shining like burning flames through the great caterpillar nets which enclosed them. Scarey thistles stood looking like the prophets in the Bible in Solomon's house. Indian paint brushes grew over her head, and the mourning dove made the only sound in the world. Oh for a stirring of the leaves, and a breaking of the nets! But not by a ghost, prayed Livvie, jumping down the bank. After Solomon took to his bed, she never went out, except one more time.

Livvie knew she made a nice girl to wait on anybody. She fixed things to eat on a tray like a surprise. She could keep from singing when she ironed, and to sit by a bed and fan away the flies, she could be so still she could not hear herself breathe. She could clean up the house and never drop a thing, and wash the dishes without a sound, and she would step outside to churn, for churning sounded too sad to her, like sobbing, and if it made her home-sick and not Solomon, she did not think of that.

But Solomon scarcely opened his eyes to see her, and scarcely tasted his food. He was not sick or paralyzed or in any pain that he mentioned, but he was surely wearing out in the body, and no matter what nice hot thing Livvie would bring him to taste, he would only look at it now, as if he were past seeing how he could add anything more to himself. Before she could beg him, he would go fast asleep. She could not surprise him any more, if he would not taste, and she was afraid that he was never in the world going to taste another thing she brought him—and so how could he last?

But one morning it was breakfast time and she cooked his eggs and grits, carried them in on a tray, and called his name. He was sound asleep. He lay in a dignified way with his watch beside him, on his back in the middle of the bed. One hand drew the quilt up high, though it was the first day of spring. Through the white lace curtains a little puffy wind was blowing as if it came from round cheeks. All night the frogs had sung out in the swamp, like a commotion in the room, and he had not stirred, though she lay wide awake and saying "Shh, frogs!" for fear he would mind them.

He looked as if he would like to sleep a little longer, and so she put back the tray and waited a little. When she tiptoed and stayed so quiet, she surrounded herself with a little reverie, and sometimes it seemed to her when she was so stealthy that the quiet she kept was for a sleeping baby, and that she had a baby and was its mother. When she stood at Solomon's bed and looked down at him, she would be thinking, "He sleeps so well," and she would hate to wake him up. And in some other way, too, she was afraid to wake him up because even in his sleep he seemed to be such a strict man.

Of course, nailed to the wall over the bed—only she would forget who it was—there was a picture of him when he was young. Then he had a fan of hair over his forehead like a king's crown. Now his hair lay down on his head, the spring had gone out of it. Solomon had a lightish face, with eyebrows scattered but rugged, the way privet grows, strong eyes, with second sight, a strict mouth, and a little gold smile. This was the way he looked in his clothes, but in bed in the daytime he looked like a different and smaller man, even when he was wide awake, and holding the Bible. He looked like somebody kin to himself. And then sometimes when he lay in sleep and she stood fanning the flies away, and the light came in, his face was like new, so smooth and clear that it was like a glass of jelly held to the window, and she could almost look through his forehead and see what he thought.

She fanned him and at length he opened his eyes and spoke her name, but he would not taste the nice eggs she had kept warm under a pan.

Back in the kitchen she ate heartily, his breakfast and hers, and looked out the open door at what went on. The whole day, and the whole night before, she had felt the stir of spring close to her. It was as present in the house as a young man would be. The moon was in the last quarter and outside they were turning the sod and planting peas and beans. Up and down the red fields, over which smoke from the brush-burning hung showing like a little skirt of sky, a white horse and a white mule pulled the plow. At intervals hoarse shouts came through the air and roused her as if she dozed neglectfully in the shade, and they were telling her, "Jump up!" She could see how over each ribbon of field were moving men and girls, on foot and mounted on mules, with hats set on their heads and bright with tall hoes and forks as if they carried streamers on them and were going to some place on a journey—and how as if at a signal now and then they would all start at once shouting, hollering, cajoling, calling and answering back, running, being leaped on and breaking away, flinging to earth with a shout and lying motionless in the trance of twelve o'clock. The old women came out of the cabins and brought them the food they had ready for them, and then all worked together, spread evenly out. The little children came too, like a bouncing stream overflowing the fields, and set upon the men, the women, the dogs, the rushing birds, and the wave-like rows of earth, their little voices almost too high to be heard. In the middle distance like some white and gold towers were the haystacks, with black cows coming around to eat their edges. High above everything, the wheel of fields, house, and cabins, and the deep road surrounding like a moat to keep them in, was the turning sky, blue with long, far-flung white mare's-tail clouds, serene and still as high flames. And sound asleep while all this went around him that was his, Solomon was like a little still spot in the middle.

Even in the house the earth was sweet to breathe. Solomon had never let Livvie go any farther than the chicken house and the well. But what if she would walk now into the heart of the fields and take a hoe and work until she fell stretched out and drenched with her efforts, like other girls, and laid her cheek against the laid-open earth, and shamed the old man with her humbleness and delight? To shame him! A cruel wish could come in uninvited and so fast while she looked out the back door. She washed the dishes and scrubbed the table. She could hear the cries of the little lambs. Her mother, that she had not seen since her wedding day, had said one time, "I rather a man be anything, than a woman be mean."

So all morning she kept tasting the chicken broth on the stove, and when it was right she poured off a nice cup-ful. She carried it in to Solomon, and there he lay having a dream. Now what did he dream about? For she saw him sigh gently as if not to disturb some whole thing he held round in his mind, like a fresh egg. So even an old man dreamed about something pretty. Did he dream of her, while his eyes were shut and sunken, and his small hand with the wedding ring curled close in sleep around the quilt? He might be dreaming of what time it was, for even through his sleep he kept track of it like a clock, and knew how much of it went by, and waked up knowing where the hands were even before he consulted the silver watch that he never let go. He would sleep with the watch in his palm, and even holding it to his cheek like a child that loves a plaything. Or he might dream of journeys and travels on a steamboat to Natchez. Yet she thought he dreamed of her; but even while she scrutinized him, the rods of the foot of the bed seemed to rise up like a rail fence between them, and she could see that people never could be sure of anything as long as one of them was asleep and the other awake. To look at him dreaming of her when he might be going to die frightened her a little, as if he might carry her with him that way, and she wanted to run out of the room. She took hold of the bed and held on, and Solomon opened his eyes and called her name, but he did not want anything. He would not taste the good broth.

Just a little after that, as she was taking up the ashes in the front room for the last time in the year, she heard a sound. It was somebody coming. She pulled the curtains together and looked through the slit.

Coming up the path under the bottle trees was a white lady. At first she looked young, but then she looked old. Marvelous to see, a little car stood steaming like a kettle out in the field-track—it had come without a road.

Livvie stood listening to the long, repeated knockings at the door, and after a while she opened it just a little. The lady came in through the crack, though she was more than middle-sized and wore a big hat.

"My name is Miss Baby Marie," she said.

Livvie gazed respectfully at the lady and at the little suitcase she was holding close to her by the handle until the proper moment. The lady's eyes were running over the room, from palmetto to palmetto, but she was saying, "I live at home . . . out from Natchez . . . and get out and show these pretty cosmetic things to the white people and the colored people both . . . all around . . . years and years. . . . Both shades of powder and rouge. . . . It's the kind of work a girl can do and not go clear 'way from home . . ." And the harder she looked, the more she talked. Suddenly she turned up her nose and said, "It is not Christian or sanitary to put feathers in a vase," and then she took a gold key out of the front of her dress and began unlocking the locks on her suitcase. Her face drew the light, the way it was covered with intense white and red, with a little patty-cake of white between the wrinkles by her upper lip. Little red tassels of hair bobbed under the rusty wires of her picture-hat, as with an air of triumph and secrecy she now drew open her little suitcase and brought out bottle after bottle and jar after jar, which she put down on the table, the mantel-piece, the settee, and the organ.

"Did you ever see so many cosmetics in your life?" cried Miss Baby Marie.

"No'm," Livvie tried to say, but the cat had her tongue.

"Have you ever applied cosmetics?" asked Miss Baby Marie next.

"No'm," Livvie tried to say.

"Then look!" she said, and pulling out the last thing of all, "Try this!" she said. And in her hand was unclenched a golden lipstick which popped open like magic. A fragrance came out of it like incense, and Livvie cried out suddenly, "Chinaberry flowers!"

Her hand took the lipstick, and in an instant she was carried away in the air through the spring, and looking down with a half-drowsy smile from a purple cloud she saw from above a chinaberry tree, dark and smooth and neatly leaved, neat as a guinea hen in the dooryard, and there was her home that she had left. On one side of the tree was her mama holding up her heavy apron, and she could see it was loaded with ripe figs, and on the other side was her papa holding a fish-pole over the pond, and she could see it transparently, the little clear fishes swimming up to the brim.

"Oh, no, not chinaberry flowers—secret ingredients," said Miss Baby Marie. "My cosmetics have secret ingredients—not chinaberry flowers."

"It's purple," Livvie breathed, and Miss Baby Marie said, "Use it freely. Rub it on."

Livvie tiptoed out to the wash stand on the front porch and before the mirror put the paint on her mouth. In the wavery surface her face danced before her like a flame. Miss Baby Marie followed her out, took a look at what she had done, and said, "That's it."

Livvie tried to say "Thank you" without moving her parted lips where the paint lay so new.

By now Miss Baby Marie stood behind Livvie and looked in the mirror over her shoulder, twisting up the tassels of her hair. "The lipstick I can let you have for only two dollars," she said, close to her neck.

"Lady, but I don't have no money, never did have," said Livvie.

"Oh, but you don't pay the first time. I make another trip, that's the way I do. I come back again—later."

"Oh," said Livvie, pretending she understood everything so as to please the lady.

"But if you don't take it now, this may be the last time I'll call at your house," said Miss Baby Marie sharply. "It's far away from anywhere, I'll tell you that. You don't live close to anywhere."

"Yes'm. My husband, he keep the *money*," said Livvie, trembling. "He is strict as he can be. He don't know *you* walk in here—Miss Baby Marie!"

"Where is he?"

"Right now, he in yonder sound asleep, an old man. I wouldn't ever ask him for anything."

Miss Baby Marie took back the lipstick and packed it up. She gathered up the jars for both black and white and got them all inside the suitcase, with the same little fuss of triumph with which she had brought them out. She started away.

"Goodbye," she said, making herself look grand from the back, but at the last minute she turned around in the door. Her old hat wobbled as she whispered, "Let me see your husband."

Livvie obediently went on tiptoe and opened the door to the other room. Miss Baby Marie came behind her and rose on her toes and looked in.

"My, what a little tiny old, old man!" she whispered, clasping her hands and shaking her head over them. "What a beautiful quilt! What a tiny old, old man!"

"He can sleep like that all day," whispered Livvie proudly.

They looked at him awhile so fast asleep, and then all at once they looked at each other. Somehow that was as if they had a secret, for he had never stirred. Livvie then politely, but all at once, closed the door.

"Well! I'd certainly like to leave you with a lipstick!" said Miss Baby Marie vivaciously. She smiled in the door.

"Lady, but I told you I don't have no money, and never did have."

"And never will?" In the air and all around, like a bright halo around the white lady's nodding head, it was a true spring day.

"Would you take eggs, lady?" asked Livvie softly.

"No, I have plenty of eggs—plenty," said Miss Baby Marie.

"I still don't have no money," said Livvie, and Miss Baby Marie took her suitcase and went on somewhere else.

Livvie stood watching her go, and all the time she felt her heart beating in her left side. She touched the place with her hand. It seemed as if her heart beat and her whole face flamed from the pulsing color of her lips. She went to sit by Solomon and when he opened his eyes he could not see a change in her. "He's fixin' to die," she said inside. That was the secret. That was when she went out of the house for a little breath of air.

She went down the path and down the Natchez Trace a way, and she did not know how far she had gone, but it was not far, when she saw a sight. It was a man, looking like a vision—she standing on one side of the Old Natchez Trace and he standing on the other.

As soon as this man caught sight of her, he began to look himself over. Starting at the bottom with his pointed shoes, he began to look up, lifting his peg-top pants the higher to see fully his bright socks. His coat long and wide and leaf-green he opened like doors to see his high-up tawny pants and his pants he smoothed downward from the points of his collar, and he wore a luminous baby-pink satin shirt. At the end, he reached gently above his wide platter-shaped round hat, the color of a plum, and one finger touched at the feather, emerald green, blowing in the spring winds.

No matter how she looked, she could never look so fine as he did, and she was not sorry for that, she was pleased.

He took three jumps, one down and two up, and was by her side.

"My name is Cash," he said.

He had a guinea pig in his pocket. They began to walk along. She stared on and on at him, as if he were doing some daring spectacular thing, instead of just walking beside her. It was not simply the city way he was dressed that made her look at him and see hope in its insolence looking back. It was not only the way he moved along kicking the flowers as if he could break through everything in the way and destroy anything in the world, that made her eyes grow bright. It might be, if he had not appeared the way he did appear that day she would never have looked so closely at him, but the time people come makes a difference.

They walked through the still leaves of the Natchez Trace, the light and the shade falling through trees about them, the white irises shining like candles on the banks and the new ferns shining like green stars up in the oak branches. They came out at Solomon's house, bottle trees and all. Livvie stopped and hung her head.

Cash began whistling a little tune. She did not know what it was, but she had heard it before from a distance, and she had a revelation. Cash was a field hand. He was a transformed field hand. Cash belonged to Solomon. But he had stepped out of his overalls into this. There in front of Solomon's house he laughed. He had a round head, a round face, all of him was young, and he flung his head up, rolled it against the mare's-tail sky in his round hat, and he could laugh just to see Solomon's house sitting there. Livvie looked at it, and there was Solomon's black hat hanging on the peg on the front door, the blackest thing in the world.

"I been to Natchez," Cash said, wagging his head around against the sky. "*I* taken a trip, *I* ready for Easter!"

How was it possible to look so fine before the harvest? Cash must have stolen the money, stolen it from Solomon. He stood in the path and lifted his spread hand high and brought it down again and again in his laughter. He kicked up his heels. A little chill went through her. It was as if Cash was bringing that strong hand down to beat a drum or to rain blows upon a man, such an abandon and menace were in his laugh. Frowning, she went closer to him and his swinging arm drew her in at once and the fright was crushed from her body, as a little match-flame might be smothered out by what it lighted. She gathered the folds of his coat behind him and fastened her red lips to his mouth, and she was dazzled by herself then, the way he had been dazzled at himself to begin with.

In that instant she felt something that could not be told—that Solomon's death was at hand, that he was the same to her as if he were dead now. She cried out, and uttering little cries turned and ran for the house.

At once Cash was coming, following after, he was running behind her. He came close, and half-way up the path he laughed and passed her. He even picked up a stone and sailed it into the bottle trees. She put her hands over her head, and sounds clattered through the bottle trees like cries of outrage. Cash stamped and plunged zigzag up the front steps and in at the door.

When she got there, he had stuck his hands in his pockets and was turning slowly about in the front room. The little guinea pig peeped out. Around Cash, the pinned-up palmettos looked as if a lazy green monkey had walked up and down and around the walls leaving green prints of his hands and feet.

She got through the room and his hands were still in his pockets, and she fell upon the closed door to the other room and pushed it open. She ran to Solomon's bed, calling "Solomon! Solomon!" The little shape of the old man never moved at all, wrapped under the quilt as if it were winter still.

"Solomon!" She pulled the quilt away, but there was another one under that, and she fell on her knees beside him. He made no sound except a sigh, and then she could hear in the silence the light springy steps of Cash walking and walking in the front room, and the ticking of Solomon's silver watch, which came from the bed. Old Solomon was far away in his sleep, his face looked small, relentless, and devout, as if he were walking somewhere where she could imagine the snow falling.

Then there was a noise like a hoof pawing the floor, and the door gave a creak, and Cash appeared beside her. When she looked up, Cash's face was so black it was bright, and so bright and bare of pity that it looked sweet to her. She stood up and held up her head. Cash was so powerful that his presence gave her strength even when she did not need any.

Under their eyes Solomon slept. People's faces tell of things and places not known to the one who looks at them while they sleep, and while Solomon slept under the eyes of Livvie and Cash his face told them like a mythical story that all his life he had built, little scrap by little scrap, respect. A beetle could not have been more laborious or more ingenious in the task of its destiny. When Solomon was young, as he was in his picture overhead, it was the infinite thing with him, and he could see no end to the respect he would contrive and keep in a house. He had built a lonely house, the way he would make a cage, but it grew to be the same with him as a great monumental pyramid and sometimes in his absorption of getting it erected he was like the builder-slaves of Egypt who forgot or never knew the origin and meaning of the thing to which they gave all the strength of their bodies and used up all their days. Livvie and Cash could see that as a man might rest from a life-labor he lay in his bed, and they could hear how, wrapped in his quilt, he sighed to himself comfortably in sleep, while in his dreams he might have been an ant, a beetle, a bird, an Egyptian, assembling and carrying on his back and building with his hands, or he might have been an old man of India or a swaddled baby, about to smile and brush all away.

Then without warning old Solomon's eyes flew wide open under the hedge-like brows. He was wide awake.

And instantly Cash raised his quick arm. A radiant sweat stood on his temples. But he did not bring his arm down—it stayed in the air, as if something might have taken hold.

It was not Livvie—she did not move. As if something said "Wait," she stood waiting. Even while her eyes burned under motionless lids, her lips parted in a stiff grimace, and with her arms stiff at her sides she stood above the prone old man and the panting young one, erect and apart.

Movement when it came came in Solomon's face. It was an old and strict face, a frail face, but behind it, like a covered light, came an animation that could play hide and seek, that would dart and escape, had always escaped. The mystery flickered in him, and invited from his eyes. It was that very mystery that Cash with his quick arm would have to strike, and that Livvie could not weep for. But Cash only stood holding his arm in the air, when the gentlest flick of his great strength, almost a puff of his breath, would have been enough, if he had known how to give it, to send the old man over the obstruction that kept him away from death.

If it could not be that the tiny illumination in the fragile and ancient face caused a crisis, a mystery in the room that would not permit a blow to fall, at least it was certain that Cash, throbbing in his Easter clothes, felt a pang of shame that the vigor of a man would come to such an end that he could not be struck without warning. He took down his hand and stepped back behind Livvie, like a round-eyed schoolboy on whose unsuspecting head the dunce cap has been set.

"Young ones can't wait," said Solomon.

Livvie shuddered violently, and then in a gush of tears she stooped for a glass of water and handed it to him, but he did not see her.

"So here come the young man Livvie wait for. Was no prevention. No prevention. Now I lay eyes on young man and it come to be somebody I know all the time, and been knowing since he were born in a cotton patch, and watched grow up year to year, Cash McCord, growed to size, growed up to come in my house in the end—ragged and barefoot."

Solomon gave a cough of distaste. Then he shut his eyes vigorously, and his lips began to move like a chanter's.

"When Livvie married, her husband were already somebody. He had paid great cost for his land. He spread sycamore leaves over the ground from wagon to door, day he brought her home, so her foot would not have to touch ground. He carried her through his door. Then he growed old and could not lift her, and she were still young."

Livvie's sobs followed his words like a soft melody repeating each thing as he stated it. His lips moved for a little without sound, or she cried too fervently, and unheard he might have been telling his whole life, and then he said, "God forgive Solomon for sins great and small. God forgive Solomon for carrying away too young girl for wife and keeping her away from her people and from all the young people would clamor for her back."

Then he lifted up his right hand toward Livvie where she stood by the bed and offered her his silver watch. He dangled it before her eyes, and she hushed crying; her tears stopped. For a moment the watch could be heard ticking as it always did, precisely in his proud hand. She lifted it away. Then he took hold of the quilt; then he was dead.

Livvie left Solomon dead and went out of the room. Stealthily, nearly without noise, Cash went beside her. He was like a shadow, but his shiny shoes moved over the floor in spangles, and the green downy feather shone like a light in his hat. As they reached the front room, he seized her deftly as a long black cat and dragged her hanging by the waist round and round him, while he turned in a circle, his face bent down to hers. The first moment, she kept one arm and its hand stiff and still, the one that held Solomon's watch. Then the fingers softly let go, all of her was limp, and the watch fell somewhere on the floor. It ticked away in the still room, and all at once there began outside the full song of a bird.

They moved around and around the room and into the brightness of the open door, then he stopped and shook her once. She rested in silence in his trembling arms, unprotesting as a bird on a nest. Outside the redbirds were flying and criss-crossing, the sun was in all the bottles on the prisoned trees, and the young peach was shining in the middle of them with the bursting light of spring.

At the Landing

THE NIGHT that Jenny's grandfather died, he dreamed of high water.

He came in his dream and stood just outside the door of her room, his little chin that was like a chicken's clean breastbone tilting upwards.

"It has come," the old man said, and he made a complaint of it.

Jenny in her bed lay still, waking more still than in the sleep of a moment before.

"The river has come back. That Floyd came to tell me. The sun was shining full on the face of the church, and that Floyd came around it with his wrist hung with a great long catfish. 'It's coming,' he said. 'It's the river.' Oh, it came then! Like a head and arm. Like a horse. A mane of cedar trees tossing over the top. It has borne down, and it has closed us in. That Floyd was right."

He reached as if to lift an obstacle that he thought was stretched there—the bar that crossed the door in her mother's time. It seemed beyond his strength, she tried to cry out, and he came in through the doorway. The cord and tassel of his brocade robe—for he had put it on—seemed to weigh upon his fragile walking like a chain, and yet it could have been by inexorable will that he wore it, so set were his little steps, in such duty he dragged it.

"Like poor people who have learned to fly at last," he said, walking, dragging, the fine deprecation in his voice, "all the people in The Landing, all kinds and conditions of people, are gliding off and upward to darkness. The little mandolin that my daughter used to play—it's rising like a bubble, and filling with water."

"Grandpa!" cried Jenny, and then she was up and taking her grandfather by his tiny adamant shoulders. It was moonlight. She saw his open eyes. "Wake up, Grandpa!"

"That Floyd's catfish has gone loose and free," he said gently, as if breaking news to someone. "And all of a sudden, my dear—my dears, it took its river life back, and shining so brightly swam through the belfry of the church, and downstream." At that his mouth clamped tight shut.

She held out both arms and he fell trembling against her. With beating heart she carried him through the dark halls to his room and put him down into his bed. He lay there in the moonlight, which moved and crept across him as it would a little fallen withered leaf, and he never moved or spoke any more, but lay softly, as if he were floating, being carried away, drawn by the passing moon; and Jenny's heart beat on and on, sharp as birdsong in the night, under her breast, until day.

Under the shaggy bluff the bottomlands lay in a river of golden haze. The road dropped like a waterfall from the ridge to the town at its foot and came to a grassy end there. It was spring. One slowly moving figure that was a man with a fishing pole passed like a dreamer through the empty street and on through the trackless haze toward the river. The town was still called The Landing. The river had gone, three miles away, beyond sight and smell, beyond the dense trees. It came back only in flood, and boats ran over the houses.

Up the light-scattered hill, in the house with the galleries, the old man and his granddaughter had always lived. They were the people least seen in The Landing. The grandfather was too old, and the girl was too shy of the world, and they were both too good—the old ladies said—to come out, and so they stayed inside.

For all her life the shy Jenny could look, if she stayed in the parlor, back and forth between her mother's two paintings, "The Bird Fair" and "The Massacre at Fort Rosalie." Or if she went in the dining room she could walk around the table or sit on one after the other of eight needle-point pieces, each slightly different, which her mother had worked and sewn to the chairs, or she could count the plates that stood on their rims in the closet. In the library she could circle an entirely bare floor and make up a dance to a song she made up, all silently, or gaze at the backs of the books without titles—books that had been on ships and in oxcarts and through fire and water, and were singed and bleached and swollen and shrunken, and arranged up high and nearly unreachable, like objects of beauty. Wherever she went she almost touched a prism. The house was full of prisms. They hung everywhere in the shadow of the halls and in the sunlight of the rooms, stirring under the hanging lights, dangling and circling where they were strung in the window curtains. They gave off the faintest of musical notes when air stirred in any room or when only herself passed by, and they touched. It was her way not to touch them herself, but to let the touch be magical, a stir of the curtain by the outer air, that would also make them rainbows. Vases with landscapes on them stood in the halls and were reflected endlessly rising in front of her when she passed quickly between the two mirrors. She might stop and touch all things, trace their little pictures with her finger, and put them back again; it was not forbidden; but her touch that dared not break would have been transparent as a spirit's on the objects. She was calm the way a child is calm, with never the calmness of a spirit. But like distant lightning that silently bathes a whole shimmering sky, one awareness was always trembling about her: one day she would be free to come and go. Nothing now held her in her own room, with the great wardrobe in which she had sometimes longed to hide, and the great box-like canopied bed and the little picture on the wall of her mother with upturned eyes. Jenny could go from room to room, and out at the door. But at the door her grandfather would call her back, with his little murmur.

At sunset the old man and his granddaughter would take their supper in the pavilion on the knoll, that had been a gazebo when the river ran before it. There a little breeze came all the way from the river still. All about the pavilion was an ancient circling thorny rose, like the initial letter in a poetry book. The cook came out and served with exaggerated dignity, as though she scolded in the house. A little picture might be preserved then in all their heads. The old man and the young girl looked across the round table leaf-shadowed under the busy black hands, and smiled by long habit at each other. But her grandfather could not look at her without speculation in his eyes, and the gaze that went so fondly between them held and stretched tight the memory of Jenny's mother. It seemed strange that her mother had been dead now for so many years and yet the wild desire that had torn her seemed still fresh and still a small thing. It was a desire to get to Natchez. People said Natchez was a nice little town on Saturdays with a crowd filling it and moving around.

The grandfather stirred his black coffee and smiled at Jenny. He deprecated raving simply as raving, as a force of Nature and so beneath notice or mention. And yet—even now, too late—if Jenny could plead . . . ! In a heat wave one called the cook to bring a fan, and in his daughter's first raving he rang a bell and told the cook to take her off and sit by her until she had done with it, but in the end she died of it. But Jenny could not plead for her.

Her grandfather, frail as a little bird, would say when it was time to go in. He would rise slowly in the brocade gown he wore to study in, and put his weight, which was the terrifying weight of a claw, on Jenny's arm. Jenny was obedient to her grandfather and would have been obedient to anybody, to a stranger in the street if there could be one. She never performed any act, even a small act, for herself, she would not touch the prisms. It might seem that nothing began in her own heart.

Nothing ever happened, to be seen from the gazebo, except that Billy Floyd went through the town. He was almost unknown, and one to himself. If he came at all, he would come at this time of day. In the long shadows below they could see his figure with the gleaming fish he carried move clear as a candle over the road that he had to himself, and out to the blue distance. In The Landing, every person that moved was watched out of sight, and it made a little pause in every life. And if in each day a moment of hope must come, in Jenny's day the moment was when the rude wild Floyd walked through The Landing carrying the big fish he had caught.

Under the blue sky, skirting the ravine, a half-ring of twenty cedar trees stood leading to the cemetery, their bleached trunks the colors of red and white roses. Jenny, given permission, would walk up there to visit the grave of her mother.

The cemetery was a dark shelf above the town, on the site of the old landing place when the ships docked from across the world a hundred years ago, and its brink was marked by an old table-like grave with its top ajar where the woodbine grew. Everywhere there, the hanging moss and the upthrust stones were in that strange graveyard shade where, by the light they give, the moss seems made of stone, and the stone of moss.

On one of the days, while she sat there on a stile, Jenny looked across the ravine and there was Floyd, standing still in a sunny pasture. She could watch between the grapevines, which hung and held back like ropes on either side to clear her view. Floyd had a head of straight light-colored hair and it hung over his forehead, for he never was near a comb. He stood facing her in a tall squared posture of silence and rest, while a rusty-red horse that belonged to the Lockharts cropped loudly beside him in the wild-smelling pasture.

It was said by the old ladies that he slept all morning for he fished all night. Stiff and stern, Jenny sat there with her feet planted just so on the step below, in the posture of a child who is appalled at the stillness and unsurrender of the still and unsurrendering world.

At last she sighed, and when she took up her skirt to go, as if she were dreaming she saw Floyd coming across the pasture toward her. When he reached the ravine and leaped down into it with widespread arms as though he jumped into something dangerous, she stood still on the stile to watch. He moved up near to her now, his feet on the broken ferns at the spring. The wind whipped his hair, almost making a noise.

"Go back," she said. She wanted to watch him a while longer first, before he got to her.

He stopped and looked full at her, his strong neck bending to one side as if yielding in pleasure to the wind. His arms went down and his fists opened. But for her, his eyes were as bright and unconsumed as stars up in the sky. Then she wanted to catch him and see him close, but not to touch him. He stood watching her, though, as if to prevent it. They were as still and rigid as two mocking-birds that were about to strike their beaks and dance.

She waited, but he smiled, and then knelt and cupped both hands to his face in the spring water. He drank for a long time, while she stood there with her skirt whipping in the wind, and waited on him to see how long he could drink without lifting his face. When he had drunk that much, he went back to the field and threw himself yawning down into the grass. The grass was so deep there that she could see only the one arm flung out in the torn sleeve, straight, sun-blacked and motionless.

The day she watched him in the woods, she felt it come to her dimly that her innocence had left her, since she could watch his. She could only sink down onto the step of the stile, and lay her heavy forehead in her hand. But if innocence had left, she still did not know what was to come. She would wait and see him come awake.

But he slept and slept like the dead, and defeated her. She went to her grandfather and left Floyd sleeping.

Another day, they walked for a little near together, each picking some berry or leaf to hold in the mouth, on their opposite sides of the little spring. The pasture, the sun and the grazing horse were on his side, the graves on hers, and they each looked across at the other's. The whole world seemed filled with butterflies. At each step they took, two black butterflies over the flowers were whirring just alike, suspended in the air, one circling the other rhythmically, or both moving from side to side in a gentle wave-like way, one above the other. They were blue-black and moving their wings faster than Jenny's eye could follow, always together, like each other's shadows, beautiful each one with the other. Jenny could see to start with that no kiss had ever brought love tenderly enough from mouth to mouth.

Jenny and Floyd stopped and looked for a little while at all the butterflies and they never touched each other. When Jenny did touch Floyd, touch his sleeve, he started.

He went alert in the field like a listening animal. The horse came near and when he touched it, stood with lifted ears beside him, then broke away. But over all The Landing there was not a sound that she could hear. It could only be that Floyd missed nothing in the world, and could hear innumerable outward things. He suddenly flung up his head. She knew he was smiling. And a smile was always a barrier.

She said his name, for she was so close by. It was the first time.

He stayed motionless, and she knew that he lived apart in delight. That could make a strange glow fall over the field where he was, and the world go black for her, left behind. She felt terrified, as if at a pitiless thing.

Floyd lifted his foot and stamped on the ground, and held out his careless arms to catch the horse he had excited. Then he was jumping on its bare back and riding into a gallop, shouting to frighten and amaze whoever listened. She threw herself down into the grass. Never had she known that the Lockhart horse could run like that. Floyd went at a racing speed and he seemed somehow in his tattered shirt—as she watched from beneath her arm—to stream with the wind, and he circled the steep field three times, and with flying yellow hair and a diminishing shout rode up into the woods.

If she could have followed and found him then, she would have started on foot. But she knew what she would find when she would come to him. She would find him equally real with herself—and could not touch him then. As she was living and inviolate, so of course was he, and when that gave him delight, how could she bring a question to him? She walked in the woods and around the graves in it, and knew about love, how it would have a different story in the world if it could lose the moral knowledge of a mystery that is in the other heart. Nothing in Floyd frightened her that drew her near, but at once she had the knowledge come to her that a fragile mystery was in everyone and in herself, since there it was in Floyd, and that whatever she did, she would be bound to ride over and hurt, and the secrecy of life was the terror of it. When Floyd rode the red horse, she lay in the grass. He might even have jumped across her. But the vaunting and prostration of love told her nothing—nothing at all.

The very next day Jenny waited on the stile and she saw Floyd come walking up the road in the morning, with drenched hair. He might have come and found her, but he came to the Lockhart house first.

The Lockhart house stood between two of the empty stretches along the road. It was wide, low, and twisted. Its roof, held up at the corners by the two chimneys, sagged like a hammock, and was mended with bark and small colored signs. The black high-water mark made a belt around the house and that alone seemed to tighten it and hold it together. Floyd stood gazing in at the doorway, as if what might not come out? And it was a beautiful doorway to see, with its fanlight and its sidelights, though they were blind with silt. The door was shut and the squirrels were asleep on the floor of the long cage across the front wall. Under the forward-tilting porch the clay-colored hens were sitting in twos in the old rowboat. And while Floyd looked, out came Mag.

And the next thing, he was playing with Mag Lockhart, that was an albino. Mag's short white hair would stream out from her head when she crouched nodding over her flowers in the yard, tending them with a jack-knife all day, and she would give a splitting laugh to see anyone come. Jenny from the stile watched them wrestle and play. The treadmill ran under the squirrels' quick feet.

Mag's voice came a long distance through the still day. "You are not!" "It is not!" "I am not!" she would scream, and she would jump away.

Floyd would turn on his heel and whirl old Mag off the ground. Mag ran and she snapped at him, she struggled and she crackled like a green wood fire, and he laughed and caught her. She pointed and sent him for the water, and he went and clattered and banged the buckets for her at the well until she begged him to stop. He went straight off and old Mag sat down on her front steps with the hens and rubbed at her flame-pink arms.

And then suddenly Mag was gone.

Jenny put her hands over her forehead, and then rubbed at her own arms. She believed Mag had been there, because she had felt whatever Mag had felt. If this was a vision, it was the first. And it did not frighten her; she knew it only came because she had felt what was in another heart besides her own. But it had been Mag's heart that grew clear to her, while Floyd ran away.

She lay down in the grass, which whispered in her ear. If desperation were only a country, it would be at the bottom of the well. She wanted to get there, to arrive graceful and airy in some strange other country and walk along its level land beneath its secret sky. She thought she could see herself, fleet as a mirror-image, rising up in a breath of astonished farewell and walking to the well of old Mag. It was built so that it had steps like a stile. She saw herself walk up them, stand on top, look about, and then go into the dark passage.

But my grandfather, she thought, even while she sank so deeply, will call me back. I will have to go back. He will ask me if I have put flowers on my mother's grave. And she looked over at the stone on the grave of her mother, with her married name of Lockhart cut into it.

She clutched the thing in her hand, a blade of grass, and held on. There she was, sitting up in the sun, with the blade of grass stretched between her thumbs and held to her mouth, for the calling back that was in the world. She blew on the grass. It made a thoughtless reedy sound, and she blew again.

II

The morning after her grandfather's death, Jenny put on a starched white dress and went down the hill into The Landing. A little crocheted bag hung by a ribbon over her wrist, and she had taken a nickel to put in it. Her good black strapped slippers moved lightly in the dust. She was going to tell the news of her grandfather, whom the old ladies had said would die suddenly—like *that*. And looking about with every step she took, she saw what a lonesome place it was for all of this to happen in.

She passed a house that only the mice inhabited. She passed a black boarded-up store where an owl used to live and maintain its nocturnal habits. And there, a young calf belonging to the Lockharts used to nose through the grassy rooms, before the walls were carried away by the Negroes and burned in a winter for firewood. In front of the row of Negro cabins was one long fence, made of lumber from old boats, built there to delay the river for one more moment when it came, the same as they would have delayed a giant bent on destruction by some foolish pretext.

Across the end of the road, crumbling under her eyes, was a two-story building with a remnant of gallery, and that was Jenny's destination. The store and the postoffice were in the one used room. Across the tin awning hung the moss icicles with which the postmaster had decorated for Christmas. Over the door was the shriveled mistletoe, and the gun that had shot it down still standing in the corner. Tipped back against the front wall sat five old men in their chairs, with one holding the white cat. On the step, Son Alford was playing his mandolin that had been Jenny's mother's and given away. He was singing his fast song.

"Ain't she cute
Ain't she smart
Don't look twice
It'll break my heart
Everybody loves my gal."

All nodded to her, but they knew she was not supposed to speak to them.

She went inside, and the first thing she saw was Billy Floyd. He was standing in the back of the room with the postmaster saying to him, "Reckon we're going to have water this year?"

She had never seen the man between walls and under a roof and somehow it made him a different man after the one in the field. He stood in the dim and dingy store with a row of filmy glass lamps and a pair of boots behind his head, and there was something close, gathering-close, and used and worldly about him.

"That slime, that's just as slick! You know how a fish is, I expect," the postmaster was saying affably to them both, just as if they were in any way together. "That's the way a house is, been under water. It's a sight to see those niggers try to clean this place out, falling down to slide from here to the front door and back. You have to get the slime off right away too, or you never can. Sure would make the best paint in the world." He laughed.

There was something handled and used about Floyd, something strong as an odor, the odor of the old playing cards that the old men of The Landing shuffled every day over their table in the street.

"Reckon we're going to have water this year?" the postmaster asked again. He looked from one of them to the other.

Floyd said nothing, he only held a penny. For a moment Jenny thought he was going to drop his high head at being trapped in the confined place, with her between him and the door, which would be the same as telling it out, before a third person, that he could be known in time if he were caught and cornered in a little store.

"What would you like today, Miss Jenny?" asked the postmaster. "Posy seeds?"

But she could not think what she would like. She held her little bag quite still, the strings drawn tight.

All the time, Floyd was giving her a glaring look.

"Well, it makes you think sometimes, to see the water come over all the world," said the postmaster. "I took everything I could out of here last time. Then I come down from the hill and peeked in the door and what did I see? My showcases commencing to float loose. What a sight that did make! I wouldn't have thought I sold some of them things. Carried the showcases out on the hill, but nowhere much to take them. Could you believe I could carry everything out of my store in twenty minutes but my safe? Couldn't lift that. Left the door to it open and went off and left it. So as it wouldn't rust shut, Floyd, Miss Jenny. Took me a long time to scrape the river out of that thing."

All three waited a moment, and then the postmaster spoke again in a softer, intimate voice, smilingly. "Some stranger lost through here says, 'Why don't you all move away?' Move away?" He laughed, and pointed a finger at Jenny. "Did you hear that, Miss Jenny—why don't we move away? Because we live here, don't we, Miss Jenny?"

Then she knew it was a challenge Floyd made with his hard look, and she lost to him. She walked out and left him where he held his solid stand. And when the postmaster had pointed his finger at her, she remembered that she was never to speak to Billy Floyd, by the order of her grandfather.

Outside the door, she stopped still. The weight of the nickel swung in her little bag, and she felt as if she had forgotten Doomsday. She took a step back toward the challenging Floyd. Then in a kind of haste she whispered to the five old men, separately, and even to Son Alford, and each time nearer to tears for her grandfather that died in the night. Then they gathered round her, and hurried her to the old women, and so back home.

But Floyd's face glared before her eyes all the way, it was

like something in her vision that kept her from seeing. It was brighter than the glare of death. He might have been buying a box of matches with his penny, which was what his going cost. He would go. The danger of flood was her grandfather's dream, and the postmaster's storekeeper wit. These were bright days and clear nights; and so Floyd would not wait long in The Landing. That was what the old ladies said, and asked that their words be marked.

But on a later day, Jenny took a walk and met Floyd by the little river that came out of the spring and went to the Mississippi beyond. She sat down and made a clover chain that would never get long because the cloverheads slipped out, and while she made it she kept looking with assuring looks into his illuminated eyes that went over the landscape and searched the sky for clouds. She could hold his look for a moment and then it would get away. She did not say a thing to him, for nobody can say, "It is a heavy heart that makes me clumsy." Nobody can say anything so true and apologetic. Nobody can say, "Forgive the heavy heart that loves more than the tongue can say or the hands can do. Look back at me every time I look at you and never feel pity, for what my heart holds this minute is better than what you offer the least bit less." Her eyes were telling him this but if he knew it or felt a threat in it, he never gave a sign. "My heart loves more than I can say or do, but feel no pity, only have a little vision too, of all clumsiness fallen away." She guessed that all grace belongs to the future. But he never had anything to say to her thought or her guess. He stood above her with his feet planted down and looked out over the landscape from within that moment. Level with him now, all The Landing spread under his eyes. Not knowing the world around, she could not know how The Landing looked set down in it. All she knew was that he would leave it when his patience gave out, and that this little staving moment by the river would reach its limit and go first.

Her eyes descended slowly, as if adorned with flowers, from his light blowing hair and his gathering brows down, down him, past his clever hands that caught and trapped so delicately away from her side, softly down to the ground that was a sandy shore. A hidden mussel was blowing bubbles like a spring through the sand where his boot was teasing the water. It was the little pulse of bubbles and not himself or herself that was the moment for her then; and he could have already departed and she could have already wept, and it would have been the same, as she stared at the little fountain rising so gently out of the shimmering sand. A clear love is *in the world*—this came to her as insistently as the mussel's bubbles through the water. There it was, existing there where they came and were beside it now. It is in the bubble in the water in the river, and it has its own changing and its mysteries of days and nights, and it does not care how we come and go.

But when the moment ended, he went. And as soon as he left The Landing, the rain began to fall.

Each day the storm clouds were opening like great purple flowers and pouring out their dark thunder. Each nightfall, the storm was laid down on their houses like a burden the day had carried. The noise of rain, of the gullies filling, of the little river leaping up and running in waves filled all The Landing.

And when at last the river came, it did come like a hand and arm, and pushed black trees before it, but it was at dawn. Jenny went with the others, behind Mag Lockhart, onto the hill and the water followed, whirling and bobbing the young dead animals around on its roaring breast. The clouds lowered and broke again and the rain put out the lanterns. Boat whistles began crying as faint as baby cries in that rainy dark.

Jenny had not spoken for a day and a night on the hill when she told someone that she was sleepy. It was Billy Floyd that she told it to. He put her in his boat, that she had never seen. Jenny looked in Floyd's shining eyes and saw how they held the whole flood, as the flood held its triumph in its whirlpools, and it was a vast and unsuspected thing.

It was on the high hill of the cemetery, when the water was at its peak. They came in Floyd's boat where the river lapped around the dark cedar tops, and monuments like pillars to bear them up scraped their passage, and she knew they rode over the grave of her grandfather and the grave of her mother. Muscadine vines spread under the water rippling their leaves like schools of fishes. It was always the same darkness. Fires burned somewhere, but in the distance, red and blue.

"I . . ." she began, and stopped.

He scowled.

She knew at once that there was nothing in her life past or even now in the flood that would make anything to tell. He already knew that he had saved her life, for that had taken up his time in the time of danger. Yet she might confess it. It came to her lips. He scowled on. Still, it was not any kind of confession that she would finally wish to make. She would like to tell him some strange beautiful thing, if she could speak at all, something to make him speak. Communication would be telling something that is all new, so as to have more of the new told back. The dream of that held her spellbound, with the things possible that hung in the air like clouds over the world, and she smiled in pure belief, for they were beautiful.

"I . . ." She looked softly at him as if from a distance down a little road or a little tether he sent her on.

He took hold of her, put her out of the boat into a little place he made that was dry and green and smelled good, and she went to sleep. After a time that could have been long or short, she thought she heard him say, "Wake up."

When her eyes were open and clear upon him, he violated her and still he was without care or demand and as gay as if he were still clanging the bucket at the well. With the same thoughtlessness of motion, that was a kind of grace, he next speared a side of wild meat from an animal he had killed and had ready in his boat, and cooked it over a fire he had burning on the ground. All the water lapped around. Over its sound she whispered something, but his movement and his task went on firmly about his leaping fire. People who had been there in other floods had put their initials on the tree. Her words came a little louder and in shyness she changed them from words of love to words of wishing, but still he did not look around. "I wish you and I could be far away. I wish for a little house." But ideas of any different thing from what was in his circle of fire might never have reached his ears, for all the attention he paid to her remarks.

He had fishes ready too, wrapped and cooking in a hole scooped in the ground. When she ate it was in obedience to him, though he did not say "Eat" or say anything, he only smiled at the fire, and for him it was all a taking freely of what was free. She knew from him nevertheless that what people ate in the world was earth, river, wildness and litheness, fire and ashes. People took the fresh death and the hot fire into their mouths and got their own life. She ate greedily as long as he ate, and took what he took. She ate eagerly, looking up at him while her teeth bit, to show him herself, her proud hunger, as if to please and flatter him with her original and now lost starvation. But she could make him neither sorry nor proud. When she was sick afterwards, he walked away and waited apart from her shame, as he had left her in his delight.

The dream of love, that made her hold as still in her life as if she heard music, had never carried her yet to the first country of which it told. But there was a country, as surely as there was herself. When she saw the moon come up that night and grow bright as it went above the flood and the boats in it, she was not as sorrowful as she might have been, now that they floated so high, that no threads hung down from the moon, no tender ladder all at once caught light and drifted down. There was a need in all dreams for something to stay far, far away, never to torment with the rest, and the bright moon now was that.

III

When the water was down, Jenny went back below and Floyd went down the river in his boat. They parted with the clumsiest of touches. Down through the exhausted and still dripping trees she made her way, again behind Mag, following the tracks and signs of others, and the mud sticking to her. Ashes sifted through the air and she saw them touch her skin but did not feel them. She came to the stile where she could look at the world below. The sun was going down and a wind blew following after the river, and the little town had turned the color of river water and the trees in their shame of refuse rattled like yellow pebbles and the houses sank below them scuffed and small. The smoky band of woods that lay in the distance toward the retreating river still seemed to waver and slide.

In The Landing the houses had turned a little, like people whose skirts are pulled. Where the front of the Lockhart house had been pulled away, the furniture, that had been carried out of the corners by the river and rocked about, stood in the middle of the floor and showed down its back the curly yellow grain, like its long hair. One old store had been carried clean away, after it was closed so long, and in its foundations were the old men standing around poking for money with little sticks. Money could have fallen through the cracks for many years. Fifteen cents and twenty cents and a Spanish piece were found, and the old fellows poking with their sticks were laughing like women.

Jenny came to her house. It stood as before, except that in the yellow and windy light it seemed to draw its galleries to itself, to return to its cave of night and trees, crouched like a child going backwards to the womb.

But once inside, she took one step and was into a whole new ecstasy, an ecstasy of cleaning, to wash the river out. She ran as if driven, carrying buckets and mops. She scrubbed and pried and shook the river away. Even the pages of books seemed to have been opened and written on again by muddy fingers. In the long days when she stretched and dried white curtains and sheets, rubbed the rust off knives and made them shine, and wiped the dark river from all the prisms, she forgot even love, to clean.

But the shock of love had brought a trembling to her fingers that made her drop what she touched, and made her stumble on the stair, though all the time she was driven on. And when the house was clean again she felt that there was no place to hide in it, not one room. She even opened the small door of her mother's last room, but when she looked in she thought of her mother who was kept guard on there, who struggled unweariedly and all in loneliness, and it was not a hiding place.

If in all The Landing she could have found a place to feel alone and out of sight, she would have gone there. One old lady or another would always call to her when she went by, to tell her something, and if she walked out in the road she brushed up against the old men sitting at their cards, and they spoke to her. She did not like to see faces, which were ugly, or flowers, which were beautiful and smelled sweet.

But at last the trembling left and dull strength came back, as if a wound had ceased to flow its blood. And then one day in summer she could look at a bird flying in the air, its tiny body like a fist opening and closing, and did not feel daze or pain, and then she was healed of the shock of love.

Then whenever she thought that Floyd was in the world, that his life lived and had this night and day, it was like discovery once more and again fresh to her, and if it was night and she lay stretched on her bed looking out at the dark, a great radiant energy spread intent upon her whole body and fastened her heart beneath its breath, and she would wonder almost aloud, "Ought I to sleep?" For it was love that might always be coming, and she must watch for it this time and clasp it back while it clasped, and while it held her never let it go.

Then the radiance touched at her heart and her brain, moving within her. Maybe some day she could become bright and shining all at once, as though at the very touch of another with herself. But now she was like a house with all its rooms dark from the beginning, and someone would have to go slowly from room to room, slowly and darkly, leaving each one lighted behind, before going to the next. It was not caution or distrust that was in herself, it was only a sense of journey, of something that might happen. She herself did not know what might lie ahead, she had never seen herself. She looked outward with the sense of rightful space and time within her, which must be traversed before she could be known at all. And what she would reveal in the end was not herself, but the way of the traveler.

In The Landing much was known about all kinds of love that had happened there, and wisdom traveled, when it left the porches, in the persons of three old women. The day the old women would come to see Jenny, it would be to celebrate her ruin that they trudged through the sun in their bonnets. They would come up the hill to say, "Why don't you run after him?" and to say, "Now you won't love him any more," for they always did pay a visit to say those words.

Now only Mag came sidling up, and brought a bouquet of amaryllis to present with blushes to Jenny. Jenny blushed too.

"Some people that don't speak to other people don't grow the prettiest flowers!" Mag cried victoriously as Jenny took them. Her baby hair blew down and her sharp smile cut back into her long dry cheek.

"I speak to you, Mag," said Jenny.

When she walked she heard them talk—the three old ladies. About her they said, "She'll follow her mother to her mother's grave." About Floyd they had more to say. They called him "the wild man" because they had never been told quite who he was or where he had come from. The sun had burned his skin dark and his hair light, till he was golden in the road, and they freely considered his walking by again, as if they could take his life up into their fingers with their sewing and sew it or snip it on their laps. They always went back to saying that at any rate he caught enormous fish wherever he fished in the river, and always had a long wet thing slung over his wrist when he went by, ugh! One old lady thought he was a Gipsy and had called "Gipsy!" after him when he went by her front porch once too often. One lady said she did not care what he was or if she ever knew what he was, and whether he lived or died it was all the same to her. But the third old lady had books, though she was the one that was a little crazy, and she waited till the others had done and then explained that Floyd had the blood of a Natchez Indian, though the Natchez might be supposed to be all gone, massacred. The Natchez, she said—and she nodded toward her books, "The Queen's Library," high on the shelf—were the people from the lost Atlantis, had they heard of that? and took their pride in the escape from that flood, when the island went under. And there was something all Indians knew, about never letting the last spark of fire go out. What did the other ladies think of that?

They were shocked. They had thought all the time he was really the bastard of one of the old checker-players, that had been let grow up away in the woods until he got big enough to come back and make trouble. They said he was half-wild like one family they could name, and half of the time he did not know what he was doing, like another family. All in his own right he could scent coming things like an animal and in some of his ways, just like all men, he was something of an animal. But they said it was the way he was.

"Why don't you run after him?"—"Now you won't love him any more."

Jenny wondered what more love would be like. Then of course she knew. More love would be quiet. She would never be so quiet as she wished until she was quiet with her love. In the center of everything, in the center of thunder, there was a precious piece of quiet, and into quiet her love would go. The Landing was filled with clangor, it seemed to her, until her love was filled with quiet. It seemed to her that she had been the same as in many places in the world, traveling and traveling, always with quiet to give. It had been enough to make her desperate in her heart, the long search for Billy Floyd to give quiet to.

But if Floyd had a search, what was it?

She was holding the amber beads they used to give her mother to play with. She looked at the lump of amber, and looked through to its core. Nobody could ever know about the difference between the radiance that was the surface and the radiance that was inside. There were the two worlds. There was no way at all to put a finger on the center of light. And if there were a mountain, the cloud over it could not touch its heart when it traveled over, and if there were an island out in the sea, the waves at its shore would never come over the place in the middle of the island. She looked in her very dreams at Floyd who had such clear eyes shining at her, and knew his heart lay clearer still, safe and deep in his innocence, safe and away from the outside, deeper than quiet. What she remembered was that when her hand started out to touch him in delight, he smiled and turned away—not from her, but toward something. . . .

Was it toward one thing, toward some one thing alone?

But it was when love was of the one for the one, that it seemed to hold all that was multitudinous and nothing was single any more. She had one love and that was all, but she dreamed that she lined up on both sides of the road to see her love come by in a procession. She herself was more people than there were people in The Landing, and her love was enough to pass through the whole night, never lifting the same face.

It was July when Jenny left The Landing. The grass was tall and gently ticking between the tracks of the road. The stupor of air, the quiet of the river that now went behind a veil, the sheen of heat and the gray sheen of summering trees, and the silence of day and night seemed all to touch, to bathe and administer to The Landing. The little town took a languor and a kind of beauty from the treatment of time and place. It stretched and swooned, and when two growing boys knelt in the road and caught the sun rays in a bit of glass and got fire, they seemed to tease a sleeper, and when they said "Hooray!" they sounded like adventurers in a dream.

Pears lying on the ground warmed and soured, bees gathered at the figs, birds put their little holes of possession in each single fruit in the world that they could fly to. The scent of lilies rolled sweetly from their heavy cornucopias and trickled down by shady paths to fill the golden air of the valley. The mourning dove called its three notes, kept its short silence—which was its mourning?—and called three more.

Jenny had known the most when she knew Floyd rode the horse in the field of butterflies while she was still; and she had known something when she watched him cook the meat and had eaten it for him under his eye; and now once more, in the dream of July, she knew very little, she was lost in wonder again. If she could find him now, or even find the place where he had last passed through, she would gain the next wisdom. It was a following after, now—it was too late to find any way alone.

The sun was going down when she went. The red eyes of the altheas were closing, and the lizards ran on the wall. The last lily buds hung green and glittering, pendulant in the heat. The crape-myrtle trees were beginning to fill with light for they drank the last of it every day, and gave off their white and flame in the evening that filled with the throb of cicadas. There was an old mimosa closing in the ravine—the ancient fern, as old as life, the tree that shrank from the touch, grotesque in its tenderness. All nearness and darkness affected it, even clouds going by, but for Jenny that left it no tree ever gave such allurement of fragrance anywhere.

She looked behind her for the last time as she went down under the trees. As if it were made of shells and pearls and treasures from the sea, the house glinted in the sunset, tinted with the drops of light that seemed to fall slowly through the vaguely stirring leaves. Tenderly as seaweed the long moss swayed. The chimney branched like coral in the upper blue.

Then green branches closed it over, and with her next step trumpet and muscadine vines and the great big-leaved vines made pillars about the trunks of the trees and arches and buttresses all among them. Passion flowers bloomed with their white and purple rays about her shoulders and under her feet. She walked on into the streaming hot shade of the wilderness, and put out her hands between the hanging vines. She feared the snakes in the sudden cool. Like thousands of silver bells the frogs rang her through the swamp, which then closed behind her.

All at once the whole open sky could be seen—she had come to the river. A quiet fire burned on the bluff and moving as far outward as she could see was the cold blur of water. A great spiraled net lay on its side and its circles twinkled faintly on the sky. Veil behind veil of long drying nets hung on all sides, dropping softly and blue-colored in the low wind and the place was folded in by them. All things, river, sky, fire, and air, seemed the same color, the color that is seen behind the closed eyelids, the color of day when vision and despair are the same thing.

Some fishermen came around her and when she named Billy Floyd they nodded their heads. They said, what with the rains, they waited for the racing of the waters to slow down, but that he went out on them. They said he was out on them now, but would come back to the camp, if he did not turn over and drown first. She asked the fishermen to let her wait there with them, since it was to them that he would return. They said it did not matter to them how long she waited, or where.

She stood by the nets. A little distance away men and women were cooking and eating and she smelled the fish and the wild meat. The river went by immeasurable under the sky, moving and dimly catching and snagging itself, freeing itself without effort, heavy with its great waves of drift, deep with stirring fish.

But after a certain length of time, the men that had been throwing knives at the tree by the last light put her inside a grounded houseboat on the plank of which chickens were standing. The willow branches hung down over and dragged softly back and forth across the roof. There were noises and fires all around. There were pigs in the wood.

One by one the men came in to her. She actually spoke to the first one that entered between the dozing chickens, for now she could speak to everyone, in a vague stir of welcome or in the humility that moved now deep in her spirit. About them all and closer to them than their own breath was the smell of trees that had bled to the knives they wore.

When she called out, she did not call any name; it was a cry with a rising sound, as if she said "Go back," or asked a question, and then at the last protested. A rude laugh covered her cry, and somehow both the harsh human sounds could easily have been heard as rejoicing, going out over the river in the dark night. By the fire, little boys were slapped crossly by their mothers—as if they knew that the original smile now crossed Jenny's face, and hung there no matter what was done to her, like a bit of color that kindles in the sky after the light has gone.

"Is she asleep? Is she in a spell? Or is she dead?" asked a little old bright-eyed woman who went and looked in the door, and crept up to the now meditating men outside. She was so precise in her question that she even held up three rheumatic fingers when she asked.

"She's waiting for Billy Floyd," they said.

The old woman nodded, and nodded out to the flowing river, with the firelight following her face and showing its dignity. The younger boys separated and took their turns throwing knives with a dull *pit* at the tree.

THE GOLDEN APPLES

To Rosa Farrar Wells
and Frank Hallam Lyell

Contents

The town of Morgana and the county of MacLain, Mississippi, are fictitious; all their inhabitants, as well as the characters placed in San Francisco, and their situations are products of the author's imagination and are not intended to portray real people or real situations.

Main Families in Morgana, Mississippi

King MacLain
Mrs. MacLain (nee Miss Snowdie Hudson)
Ran and Eugene

Comus Stark
Mrs. Stark (nee Miss Lizzie Morgan)
Jinny Love

Wilbur Morrison
Mrs. Morrison
Cassie and Loch

Mr. Carmichael
Mrs. Carmichael (Miss Nell)
Nina

Felix Spights
Mrs. Spights (Miss Billy Texas)
Woodrow, Missie, and Little Sister

Old Man Moody
Mrs. Moody (Miss Jefferson)
Parnell

Miss Perdita Mayo
Miss Hattie Mayo

Fate Rainey
Mrs. Fate Rainey (Miss Katie)
Victor and Virgie

Also Loomises, Carlyles, Holifields, Nesbitts, Bowleses, Sissums *and* Sojourners. *Also* Plez, Louella, and Tellie Morgan, Elberta, Twosie, *and* Exum McLane; Blackstone *and* Juba, *colored.*

I.

Shower of Gold

THAT WAS Miss Snowdie MacLain.

She comes after her butter, won't let me run over with it from just across the road. Her husband walked out of the house one day and left his hat on the banks of the Big Black River.—That could have started something, too.

We might have had a little run on doing that in Morgana, if it had been so willed. What King did, the copy-cats always might do. Well, King MacLain left a new straw hat on the banks of the Big Black and there are people that consider he headed West.

Snowdie grieved for him, but the decent way you'd grieve for the dead, more like, and nobody wanted to think, around her, that he treated her that way. But how long can you humor the humored? Well, always. But I could almost bring myself to talk about it—to a passer-by, that will never see her again, or me either. Sure I can churn and talk. My name's Mrs. Rainey.

You seen she wasn't ugly—and the little blinky lines to her eyelids comes from trying to see. She's an albino but nobody would ever try to call her ugly around here—with that tender, tender skin like a baby. Some said King figured out that if the babies started coming, he had a chance for a nestful of little albinos, and that swayed him. No, I don't say it. I say he was just willful. *He* wouldn't think ahead.

Willful and outrageous, to some several. Well: he married Snowdie.

Lots of worse men wouldn't have: no better sense. Them Hudsons had more than MacLains, but none of 'em had enough to count or worry over. Not by then. Hudson money built that house, and built it for *Snowdie* . . . they prayed over that. But take King: marrying must have been some of his showing off—like man never married at all till *he* flung in, then had to show the others how he could go right on acting. And like, "Look, everybody, this is what I think of Morgana and MacLain Courthouse and all the way between"—further, for all I know—"marrying a girl with pink eyes." "I swan!" we all say. Just like he wants us to, scoundrel. And Snowdie as sweet and gentle as you find them. Of course gentle people aren't the ones you lead best, he had that to find out, so know-all. No, sir, she'll beat him yet, balking. In the meantime children of his growing up in the County Orphan's, so say several, and children known and unknown, scattered-like. When he does come, he's just as nice as he can be to Snowdie. Just as courteous. Was from the start.

Haven't you noticed it prevail, in the world in general? Beware of a man with manners. He never raised his voice to her, but then one day he walked out of the house. Oh, I don't mean once!

He went away for a good spell before he come back that time. She had a little story about him needing the waters. Next time it was more than a year, it was two—oh, it was three. I had two children myself, enduring his being gone, and one to die. Yes, and that time he sent her word ahead: "Meet me in the woods." No, he more invited her than told her to come—"Suppose you meet me in the woods." And it was night time he supposed to her. And Snowdie met him without asking "What for?" which I would want to know of Fate Rainey. After all, they were married—they had a right to sit inside and talk in the light and comfort, or lie down easy on a good goosefeather bed, either. I would even consider he might not be there when I came. Well, if Snowdie went without a question, then I can tell it without a question as long as I love Snowdie. Her version is that in the woods they met and both decided on what would be best.

Best for him, of course. We could see the writing on the wall.

"The woods" was Morgan's Woods. We would any of us know the place he meant, without trying—I could have streaked like an arrow to the very oak tree, one there to itself and all spready: a real shady place by *day*, is all I know. Can't you just see King MacLain leaning his length against that tree by the light of the moon as you come walking through Morgan's Woods and you hadn't seen him in three years? "Suppose you meet me in the woods." My foot. Oh, I don't know how poor Snowdie stood it, crossing the distance.

Then, twins.

That was where I come in, I could help when things got to there. I took her a little churning of butter with her milk and we took up. I hadn't been married long myself, and Mr. Rainey's health was already a little delicate so he'd thought best to quit heavy work. We was both hard workers fairly early.

I always thought twins might be nice. And might have been for them, by just the sound of it. The MacLains first come to Morgana bride and groom from MacLain and went into that new house. He was educated off, to practice law—well needed here. Snowdie was Miss Lollie Hudson's daughter, well known. Her father was Mr. Eugene Hudson, a storekeeper down at Crossroads past the Courthouse, but he was a lovely man. Snowdie was their only daughter, and they give her a nice education. And I guess people more or less expected her to teach school: not marry. She couldn't see all that well, was the only thing in the way, but Mr. Comus Stark here and the supervisors overlooked that, knowing the family and Snowdie's real good way with Sunday School children. Then before the school year even got a good start, she got took up by King MacLain all of a sudden. I think it was when jack-o'-lanterns was pasted on her window I used to see his buggy roll up right to the schoolhouse steps and wait on her. He courted her in Morgana and MacLain too, both ends, didn't skip a day.

It was no different—no quicker and no slower—than the like happens every whipstitch, so I don't need to tell you they got married in the MacLain Presbyterian Church before you could shake a stick at it, no matter how surprised people were going to be. And once they dressed Snowdie all in white, you know she was whiter than your dreams.

So—he'd been educated in the law and he traveled for somebody, that was the first thing he did—I'll tell you in a minute what he sold, and she stayed home and cooked and kept house. I forget if she had a Negro, she didn't know how to tell one what to do if she had. And she put her eyes straight out, almost, going to work and making curtains for every room and all like that. So busy. At first it didn't look like they would have any children.

So it went the way I told you, slipped into it real easy,

people took it for granted mighty early—him leaving and him being welcomed home, him leaving and him sending word, "Meet me in the woods," and him gone again, at last leaving the hat. I told my husband I was going to quit keeping count of King's comings and goings, and it wasn't long after that he did leave the hat. I don't know yet whether he meant it kind or cruel. Kind, I incline to believe. Or maybe she was winning. Why do I try to figure? Maybe because Fate Rainey ain't got a surprise in him, and proud of it. So Fate said, "Well now, let's have the women to settle down and pay attention to homefolks a while." That was all he could say about it.

So, you wouldn't have had to wait long. Here come Snowdie across the road to bring the news. I seen her coming across my pasture in a different walk, it was the way somebody comes down an aisle. Her sunbonnet ribbons was jumping around her: springtime. Did you notice her little dainty waist she has still? I declare it's a mystery to think about her having the strength once. Look at me.

I was in the barn milking, and she come and took a stand there at the head of the little Jersey, Lady May. She had a quiet, picked-out way to tell news. She said, "I'm going to have a baby too, Miss Katie. Congratulate me."

Me and Lady May both had to just stop and look at her. She looked like more than only the news had come over her. It was like a shower of something had struck her, like she'd been caught out in something bright. It was more than the day. There with her eyes all crinkled up with always fighting the light, yet she was looking out bold as a lion that day under her brim, and gazing into my bucket and into my stall like a visiting somebody. Poor Snowdie. I remember it was Easter time and how the pasture was all spotty there behind her little blue skirt, in sweet clover. He sold tea and spices, that's what it was.

It was sure enough nine months to the day the twins come after he went sallying out through those woods and fields and laid his hat down on the bank of the river with "King MacLain" on it.

I wish I'd seen him! I don't guess *I'd* have stopped him. I can't tell you why, but I wish I'd seen him! But nobody did.

For Snowdie's sake—here they come bringing the hat, and a hullaballoo raised—they drug the Big Black for nine miles down, or was it only eight, and sent word to Bovina and on, clear to Vicksburg, to watch out for anything to wash up or to catch in the trees in the river. Sure, there never was anything—just the hat. They found everybody else that ever honestly drowned along the Big Black in this neighborhood. Mr. Sissum at the store, he drowned later on and they found him. I think with the hat he ought to have laid his watch down, if he wanted to give it a better look.

Snowdie kept just as bright and brave, she didn't seem to give in. She must have had her thoughts and they must have been one of two things. One that he was dead—then why did her face have the glow? It had a glow—and the other that he left her and meant it. And like people said, if she smiled *then*, she was clear out of reach. I didn't know if I liked the glow. Why didn't she rage and storm a little—to me, anyway, just Mrs. Rainey? The Hudsons all hold themselves in. But it didn't seem to me, running in and out the way I was, that Snowdie had ever got a real good look at life, maybe. Maybe from the beginning. Maybe she just doesn't know the *extent*. Not the kind of look I got, and away back when I was twelve year old or so. Like something was put to my eye.

She just went on keeping house, and getting fairly big with what I told you already was twins, and she seemed to settle into her content. Like a little white kitty in a basket, making you wonder if she just mightn't put up her paw and scratch, if anything was, after all, to come near. At her house it was like Sunday even in the mornings, every day, in that cleaned-up way. She was taking a joy in her fresh untracked rooms and that dark, quiet, real quiet hall that runs through her house. And I love Snowdie. I love her.

Except none of us felt very *close* to her all the while. I'll tell you what it was, what made her different. It was the not waiting any more, except where the babies waited, and that's not but one story. We were mad at her and protecting her all at once, when we couldn't be close to her.

And she come out in her pretty clean shirt waists to water the ferns, and she had remarkable flowers—she had her mother's way with flowers, of course. And give just as many away, except it wasn't like I or you give. She was by her own self. Oh, her mother was dead by then, and Mr. Hudson fourteen miles down the road away, crippled up, running his store in a cane chair. We was every bit she had. Everybody tried to stay with her as much as they could spare, not let a day go by without one of us to run in and speak to her and say a word about an ordinary thing. Miss Lizzie Stark let her be in charge of raising money for the poor country people at Christmas that year, and like that. Of course we made all her little things for her, stitches like that was way beyond her. It was a good thing she got such a big stack.

The twins come the first day of January. Miss Lizzie Stark—she hates all men, and is real important: across yonder's her chimney—made Mr. Comus Stark, her husband, hitch up and drive to Vicksburg to bring back a Vicksburg doctor in her own buggy the night before, instead of using Dr. Loomis here, and stuck him in a cold room to sleep at her house; she said trust any doctor's buggy to break down on those bridges. Mrs. Stark stayed right by Snowdie, and of course several, and I, stayed too, but Mrs. Stark was not budging and took charge when pains commenced. Snowdie had the two little boys and neither one albino. They were both King all over again, if you want to know it. Mrs. Stark had so hoped for a girl, or two *girls.* Snowdie clapped the names on them of Lucius Randall and Eugene Hudson, after her own father and her mother's father.

It was the only sign she ever give Morgana that maybe she didn't think the name King MacLain had stayed beautiful. But not much of a sign; some women don't name after their husbands, until they get down to nothing else left. I don't think with Snowdie even *two* other names meant she had changed yet, not towards King, that scoundrel.

Time goes like a dream no matter how hard you run, and all the time we heard things from out in the world that we listened to but that still didn't mean we believed them. You know the kind of things. Somebody's cousin saw King MacLain. Mr. Comus Stark, the one the cotton and timber belongs to, he goes a little, and he claimed three or four times he saw his back, and once saw him getting a haircut in Texas.

Those things you will hear forever when people go off, to keep up a few shots in the woods. They might mean something—might not.

Till the most outrageous was the time my husband went up to Jackson. He saw a man that was the spit-image of King in the parade, my husband told me in his good time, the inauguration of Governor Vardaman. He was right up with the big ones and astride a fine animal. Several from here went but as Mrs. Spights said, why wouldn't they be looking at the Governor? Or the New Capitol? But King MacLain could steal anyone's glory, so he thought.

When I asked the way he looked, I couldn't get a thing out of my husband, except he lifted his feet across the kitchen floor like a horse and man in one, and I went after him with my broom. I knew, though. If it was King, he looked like, "Hasn't everybody been wondering, though, been out of their minds to know, where I've been keeping myself!" I told my husband it reasoned to me like it was up to Governor Vardaman to get hold of King and bring something out of him, but my husband said why pick on one man, and besides a parade was going on and what all. Men! I said if I'd been Governor Vardaman and spied King MacLain from Morgana marching in my parade as big as I was and no call for it, I'd have had the whole thing brought to a halt and called him to accounts. "Well, what good would it have done you?" my husband said. "A plenty," I said. I was excited at the time it happened. "That was just as good a spot as any to show him forth, right in front of the New Capitol in Jackson with the band going, and just as good a man to do it."

Well, sure, men like that need to be shown up before the world, I guess—not that any of us would be surprised. "Did you go and find him after the Governor got inaugurated to suit you then?" I asked my husband. But he said no, and reminded me. He went for me a new bucket; and brought me the wrong size. Just like the ones at Holifield's. But he said he saw King or his twin. What twin!

Well, through the years, we'd hear of him here or there—maybe two places at once, New Orleans and Mobile. That's people's careless way of using their eyes.

I believe he's been to California. Don't ask me why. But I picture him there. I see King in the West, out where it's gold and all that. Everybody to their own visioning.

II.

Well, what happened turned out to happen on Hallowe'en. Only last week—and seems already like something that couldn't happen at all.

My baby girl, Virgie, swallowed a button that same day—later on—and that *happened*, it seems like still, but not this. And not a word's been spoke out loud, for Snowdie's sake, so I trust the rest of the world will be as careful.

You can talk about a baby swallowing a button off a shirt and having to be up-ended and her behind pounded, and it sounds reasonable if you can just see the baby—there she runs—but get to talking about something that's only a kind of *near* thing—and hold your horses.

Well, Hallowe'en, about three o'clock, I was over at Snowdie's helping her cut out patterns—she's kept on sewing for those boys. Me, I have a little girl to sew for—she was right there, asleep on the bed in the next room—and it hurts my conscience being that lucky over Snowdie too. And the twins wouldn't play out in the yard that day but had hold of the scraps and the scissors and the paper of pins and all, and there underfoot they were dressing up and playing ghosts and boogers. Uppermost in their little minds was Hallowe'en.

They had on their masks, of course, tied on over their Buster Brown bobs and pressing a rim around the back. I was used to how they looked by then—but I don't like masks. They both come from Spights' store and cost a nickel. One was the Chinese kind, all yellow and mean with slant eyes and a dreadful thin mustache of black horsy hair. The other one was a lady, with an almost scary-sweet smile on her lips. I never did take to that smile, with all day for it. Eugene Hudson wanted to be the Chinaman and so Lucius Randall had to be the lady.

So they were making tails and do-lollies and all kinds of foolishness, and sticking them on to their little middles and behinds, snatching every scrap from the shirts and flannels me and Snowdie was cutting out on the dining room table. Sometimes we could grab a little boy and baste something up on him whether or no, but we didn't really pay them much mind, we was talking about the prices of things for winter, and the funeral of an old maid.

So we never heard the step creak or the porch give, at all. That was a blessing. And if it wasn't for something that come from outside us all to tell about it, I wouldn't have the faith I have that it come about.

But happening along our road—like he does every day—was a real trustworthy nigger. He's one of Mrs. Stark's mother's niggers, Old Plez Morgan everybody calls him. Lives down beyond me. The real old kind, that knows everybody since time was. He knows more folks than I do, who they are, and all the *fine* people. If you wanted anybody in Morgana that wouldn't be likely to make a mistake in who a person is, you would ask for Old Plez.

So he was making his way down the road, by stages. He still has to do a few people's yards won't let him go, like Mrs. Stark, because he don't pull up things. He's no telling how old and starts early and takes his time coming home in the evening—always stopping to speak to people to ask after their health and tell them good evening all the way. Only that day, he said he didn't see a soul *else*—besides you'll hear who in a minute—on the way, not on porches or in the yards. I can't tell you why, unless it was those little gusts of north wind that had started blowing. Nobody likes that.

But yonder ahead of him was walking a man. Plez said it was a white man's walk and a walk he knew—but it struck him it was from away in another year, another time. It wasn't just the walk of anybody supposed to be going along the road to MacLain right at that *time*—and yet it was too—and if it was, he still couldn't think what business that somebody would be up to. That was the careful way Plez was putting it to his mind.

If you saw Plez, you'd know it was him. He had some roses stuck in his hat that day, I saw him right after it happened. Some of Miss Lizzie's fall roses, big as a man's fist and red as blood—they were nodding side-to-side out of the band of his old black hat, and some other little scraps out of the garden laid around the brim, throwed away by Mrs. Stark; he'd been cleaning out her beds that day, it was fixing to rain.

He said later he wasn't in any great hurry, or he would have maybe caught up and passed the man. Up yonder ahead he went, going the same way Plez was going, and not much more interested in a race. And a real familiar stranger.

So Plez says presently the familiar stranger paused. It was in front of the MacLains'—and sunk his weight on one leg and just stood there, posey as statues, hand on his hip. Ha! Old Plez says, according, he just leaned himself against the Presbyterian Church gate and waited a while.

Next thing, the stranger—oh, it was King! By then Plez was calling him Mr. King to himself—went up through the yard and then didn't go right in like anybody else. First he looked around. He took in the yard and summerhouse and skimmed from cedar to cedar along the edge of where he lived, and under the fig tree at the back and under the wash (if he'd counted it!) and come close to the front again, sniffy like, and Plez said though he couldn't swear to seeing from the Presbyterian Church exactly what Mr. King was doing, he knows as good as seeing it that he looked through the blinds. He would have looked in the dining room—have mercy. We shut the West out of Snowdie's eyes of course.

At last he come full front again, around the flowers under the front bedroom. Then he settled himself nice and started up the front steps.

The middle step sings when it's stepped on, but we didn't hear it. Plez said, well, he had on fine tennis shoes. So he got across the front porch and what do you think he's fixing to do but knock on that door? Why wasn't he satisfied with outdoors?

On his own front door. He makes a little shadow knock, like trying to see how it would look, and then puts his present behind his coat. Of course he had something there in a box for her. You know he constitutionally brought home the kind of presents that break your heart. He stands there with one leg out pretty, to surprise them. And I bet a nice smile on his face. Oh, don't ask me to go on!

Suppose Snowdie'd took a notion to glance down the hall—the dining room's at the end of it, and the folding-doors pushed back—and seen him, all "Come-kiss-me" like that. I don't know if she could have seen that good—but *I* could. I was a fool and didn't look.

It was the twins seen him. Through those little bitty mask holes, those eagle eyes! There ain't going to be no stopping those twins. And he didn't get to knock on the door, but he had his hand raised the second time and his knuckles sticking up, and out come the children on him, hollering "Boo!" and waving their arms up and down the way it would scare you to death, or it ought to, if you wasn't ready for them.

We heard them charge out, but we thought it was just a nigger that was going by for them to scare, if we thought anything.

Plez says—allowing for all human mistakes—he seen on one side of King come rolling out Lucius Randall all dressed up, and on the other side, Eugene Hudson all dressed up. Could I have forgotten to speak of their being on skates? Oh, that was all afternoon. They're real good skaters, the little fellows, not to have a sidewalk. They sailed out the door and circled around their father, flying their arms and making their fingers go scarey, and those little Buster Brown bobs going in a circle.

Lucius Randall, Plez said, had on something pink, and he did, the basted flannelette teddy-bears we had tried on on top of his clothes and he got away. And said Eugene was a Chinaman, and that was what he was. It would be hard to tell which would come at you the more outrageous of the two, but to me it would be Lucius Randall with the girl's face and the big white cotton gloves falling off his fingers, and oh! he had on *my hat.* This one I milk in.

And they made a tremendous uproar with their skates, Plez said, and that was no mistake, because I remember what a hard time Snowdie and me had hearing what each other had to say all afternoon.

Plez said King stood it a minute—he got to turning around too. They were skating around him and saying in high birdie voices, "How do you do, Mister Booger?" You know if children *can* be monkeys, they're going to be them. (Without the masks, though, those two children would have been more polite about it—there's enough Hudson in them.) Skating around and around their papa, and just as ignorant! Poor little fellows. After all, they'd had nobody to scare all day for Hallowe'en, except one or two niggers that went by, and the Y. & M. V. train whistling through at two-fifteen, they scared that.

But monkeys—! Skating around their papa. Plez said if those children had been black, he wouldn't hesitate to say they would remind a soul of little nigger cannibals in the jungle. When they got their papa in their ring-around-a-rosy and he couldn't get out, Plez said it was enough to make an onlooker a little uneasy, and he called once or twice on the Lord. And after they went around high, they crouched down and went around low, about his knees.

The minute come, when King just couldn't get out quick enough. Only he had a hard time, and took him more than one try. He gathered himself together and King is a man of six foot height and weighs like a horse, but he was confused, I take it. But he got aloose and up and out like the Devil was after him—or in him—finally. Right up over the bannister and the ferns, and down the yard and over the ditch and gone. He plowed into the rough toward the Big Black, and the willows waved behind him, and where he run then, Plez don't know and I don't and don't nobody.

Plez said King passed right by him, that time, but didn't seem to know him, and the opportunity had gone by then to speak. And where he run then, nobody knows.

He should have wrote another note, instead of coming.

Well then, the children, I reckon, just held openmouth behind him, and then something got to mounting up after it was all over, and scared them. They come back in the dining room. There were innocent ladies visiting with each other. The little boys had to scowl and frown and drag their skates over the carpet and follow us around the table where we was cutting out Eugene Hudson's underbody, and pull on our skirts till we saw.

"Well, speak," said their mother, and they told her a booger had come up on the front porch and when they went out to see him he said, "I'm going. You stay," so they chased him down the steps and run him off. "But he looked back like this!" Lucius Randall said, lifting off his mask and showing us on his little naked face with the round blue eyes. And Eugene

Hudson said the booger took a handful of pecans before he got through the gate.

And Snowdie dropped her scissors on the mahogany, and her hand just stayed in the air as still, and she looked at me, a look a minute long. And first she caught her apron to her and then started shedding it in the hall while she run to the door—so as not to be caught in it, I suppose, if anybody was still there. She run and the little glass prisms shook in the parlor—I don't remember another time, from *her*. She didn't stop at the door but run on through it and out on the porch, and she looked both ways and was running down the steps. And she run out in the yard and stood there holding to the tree, looking towards the country, but I could tell by the way her head held there wasn't nobody.

When I got to the steps—I didn't like to follow right away—there was nobody at all but old Plez, who was coming by raising his hat.

"Plez, did you see a gentleman come up on my porch just now?" I heard Snowdie call, and there was Plez, just ambling by with his hat raised, like he was just that minute passing, like we thought. And Plez, of course, he said, "No'm, Mistis, I don't recollect one soul pass me, whole way from town."

The little fellows held on to me, I could feel them tugging. And my little girl slept through it all, inside, and then woke up to swallow that button.

Outdoors the leaves was rustling, different from when I'd went in. It was coming on a rain. The day had a two-way look, like a day will at change of the year—clouds dark and the gold air still in the road, and the trees lighter than the sky was. And the oak leaves scuttling and scattering, blowing against old Plez and brushing on him, the old man.

"You're real positive, I guess, Plez?" asks Snowdie, and he answers comforting-like to her, "*You* wasn't looking for nobody to come today, was you?"

It was later on that Mrs. Stark got hold of Plez and got the truth out of him, and I heard it after a while, through her church. But of course he wasn't going to let Miss Snowdie MacLain get hurt now, after we'd all watched her so long. So he fabricated.

After he'd gone by, Snowdie just stood there in the cool

without a coat, with her face turned towards the country and her fingers pulling at little threads on her skirt and turning them loose in the wind, making little kind deeds of it, till I went and got her. She didn't cry.

"Course, could have been a ghost," Plez told Mrs. Stark, "but a ghost—I believe—if he had come to see the lady of the house, would have waited to have word with her."

And he said he had nary doubt in his mind, that it was Mr. King MacLain, starting home once more and thinking better of it. Miss Lizzie said to the church ladies, "I, for one, trust the Negro. I trust him the way you trust me, old Plez's mind has remained clear as a bell. I trust his story implicitly," she says, "because that's just what *I know* King MacLain'd do—run." And that's one time I feel in agreement about something with Miss Lizzie Stark, though she don't know about it, I guess.

And I live and hope *he* hit a stone and fell down running, before he got far off from here, and took the skin off his handsome nose, the devil.

And so that's why Snowdie comes to get her butter now, and won't let me bring it to her any longer. I think she kind of holds it against me, because I was there that day when he come; and she don't like my baby any more.

And you know, Fate says maybe King did know it was Hallowe'en. Do you think he'd go that far for a prank? And his own come back to him? Fate's usually more down to earth than that.

With men like King, your thoughts are bottomless. He was going like the wind, Plez swore to Miss Lizzie Stark; though he couldn't swear to the direction—so he changed and said.

But I bet my little Jersey calf King tarried long enough to get him a child somewhere.

What makes me say a thing like that? I wouldn't say it to my husband, you mind you forget it.

2.

June Recital

LOCH WAS in a tempest with his mother. She would keep him in bed and make him take Cocoa-Quinine all summer, if she had her way. He yelled and let her wait holding the brimming spoon, his eyes taking in the whole ironclad pattern, the checkerboard of her apron—until he gave out of breath, and took the swallow. His mother laid her hand on his pompadour cap, wobbled his scalp instead of kissing him, and went off to her nap.

"Louella!" he called faintly, hoping she would come upstairs and he could devil her into running to Loomis's and buying him an ice cream cone out of her pocket, but he heard her righteously bang a pot to him in the kitchen. At last he sighed, stretched his toes—so clean he despised the very sight of his feet—and brought himself up on his elbow to the window.

Next door was the vacant house.

His family would all be glad if it burned down; he wrapped it with the summer's love. Beyond the hackberry leaves of their own tree and the cedar row and the spready yard over there, it stretched its weathered side. He let his eyes rest or go flickering along it, as over something very well known indeed. Its left-alone contour, its careless stretching away into that deep backyard he knew by heart. The house's side was like a person's, if a person or giant would lie sleeping there, always sleeping.

A red and bottle-shaped chimney held up all. The roof spread falling to the front, the porch came around the side leaning on the curve, where it hung with bannisters gone, like a cliff in a serial at the Bijou. Instead of cowboys in danger, Miss Jefferson Moody's chickens wandered over there from across the way, flapped over the edge, and found the shade cooler, the dust fluffier to sit in, and the worms thicker under that blackening floor.

In the side of the house were six windows, two upstairs and four down, and back of the chimney a small stair window shaped like a keyhole—one made never to open; they had one like it. There were green shades rolled up to various levels, but not curtains. A table showed in the dining room, but no chairs. The parlor window was in the shadow of the porch and of thin, vibrant bamboo leaves, clear and dark as a pool he knew in the river. There was a piano in the parlor. In addition there were little fancy chairs, like Sunday School chairs or children's drug store chairs, turned this way and that, and the first strong person trying to sit down would break them one after the other. Instead of a door into the hall there was a curtain; it was made of beads. With no air the curtain hung still as a wall and yet you could see through it, if anybody should pass the door.

In that window across from his window, in the back upper room, a bed faced his. The foot was gone, and a mattress had partly slid down but was holding on. A shadow from a tree, a branch and its leaves, slowly traveled over the hills and hollows of the mattress.

In the front room there, the window was dazzling in afternoon; it was raised. Except for one tall post with a hat on it, that bed was out of sight. It was true, there was one person in the house—Loch would recall him sooner or later—but it was only Mr. Holifield. He was the night watchman down at the gin, he always slept all day. A framed picture could be seen hanging on the wall, just askew enough so that it looked straightened every now and then. Sometimes the glass in the picture reflected the light outdoors and the flight of birds between branches of trees, and while it reflected, Mr. Holifield was having a dream.

Loch could look across through cedars that missed one, in the line, and in a sweeping glance see it all—as if he possessed it—from its front porch to its shedlike back and its black-shadowed summerhouse—which was an entirely different love, odorous of black leaves that crumbled into soot; and its shade of four fig trees where he would steal the figs if July ever came. And above all the shade, which was dark as a boat, the blue sky flared—shooting out like a battle, and hot as fire. The hay riders his sister went with at night (went with against their father's will, slipped out by their mother's connivance) would ride off singing, "Oh, It Ain't Gonna Rain No More."

Even under his shut eyelids, that light and shade stayed divided from each other, but reversed.

Some whole days at a time, often in his dreams day and night, he would seem to be living next door, wild as a cowboy, absolutely by himself, without his mother or father coming in to feel his skin, or run a finger up under his cap—without one parent to turn on the fan and the other to turn it off, or them both together to pin a newspaper around the light at night to shade him out of their talk. And there was where Cassie could never bring him books to read, miserable girls' books and fairy tales.

It was the leaky gutter over there that woke Loch up, back in the spring when it rained. Splashy as a waterfall in a forest, it shook him with that agony of being *made* to wake up from a sound sleep to be taken away somewhere, made to go. It made his heart beat fast.

They could do what they wanted to to him but they could not take his pompadour cap off him or take his house away. He reached down under the bed and pulled up the telescope.

It was his father's telescope and he was allowed to look through it unmolested as long as he ran a temperature. It was what they gave him instead of his nigger-shooter and cap pistol. Smelling of brass and the drawer of the library table where it came from, it was an object hitherto brought out in the family group for eclipses of the moon; and the day the airplane flew over with a lady in it, and they all waited for it all day, wry and aching up at the sky, the telescope had been gripped in his father's hand like a big stick, some kind of protective weapon for what was to come.

Loch fixed the long brass tubes and shot the telescope out the window, propping the screen outward and letting more mosquitoes in, the way he was forbidden. He examined the size of the distant figs: like marbles yesterday, wine-balls today. Getting those would not be the same as stealing. On the other side of fury at confinement a sweet self-indulgence could visit him in his bed. He moved the glass lovingly toward the house and touched its roof, with the little birds on it cocking their heads.

With the telescope to his eye he even smelled the house

strongly. Morgana was extra deep in smell this afternoon; the magnolias were open all over the tree at the last corner. They glittered like lights in the dense tree that loomed in the shape of a cave opening at the brought-up-close edge of the Carmichael roof. He looked at the thrush's nest, Woodrow Spights' old ball on the roof, the drift of faded election handbills on the porch—the vacant house again, the half of a china plate deep in the weeds; the chickens always went to that plate, and it was dry.

Loch trained the telescope to the back and caught the sailor and the girl in the moment they jumped the ditch. They always came the back way, swinging hands and running low under the leaves. The girl was the piano player at the picture show. Today she was carrying a paper sack from Mr. Wiley Bowles' grocery.

Loch squinted; he was waiting for the day when the sailor took the figs. And see what the girl would hurry him into. Her name was Virgie Rainey. She had been in Cassie's room all the way through school, so that made her sixteen; she would ruin any nice idea. She looked like a tomboy but it was not the truth. She had let the sailor pick her up and carry her one day, with her fingers lifting to brush the leaves. It was she that had showed the sailor the house to begin with, she that started him coming. They were rusty old fig trees but the figs were the little sweet blue. When they cracked open their pink and golden flesh would show, their inside flowers, and golden bubbles of juice would hang, to touch your tongue to first. Loch gave the sailor time, for it was he, Loch, who was in command of leniency here; he was giving him day after day.

He swayed on his knees and saw the sailor and Virgie Rainey in a clear blue-and-white small world run sparkling to the back door of the empty house.

And next would come the old man going by in the blue wagon, up as far as the Starks' and back to the Carmichaels' corner.

"Milk, milk,
Buttermilk.
Fresh dewberries and—
Buttermilk."

That was Mr. Fate Rainey and his song. He would take a long time to pass. Loch could study through the telescope the new flower in his horse's hat each day. He would go past the Starks' and circle the cemetery and niggertown, and come back again. His cry, with a song's tune, would come near, then far, and near again. Was it an echo—was an echo that? Or was it, for the last time, the call of somebody seeking about in a deep cave, "Here—here! Oh, here am I!"

There was a sound that might have been a blue jay scolding, and that was the back door; they were just now going in off the back porch. When he saw the door prized open—the stretched screen billowing from being too freely leaned against—and let the people in, Loch felt the old indignation rise up. But at the same time he felt joy. For while the invaders did not see him, he saw them, both with the naked eye and through the telescope; and each day that he kept them to himself, they were his.

Louella appeared below on their steps and with a splash threw out the dirty dish water in the direction of the empty house. But she would never speak, and he would never speak. He had not shared anybody in his life even with Louella.

After the door fell to at the sailor's heel, and the upstairs window had been forced up and propped, then silence closed over the house next door. It closed over just as silence did in their house at this time of day; but like the noisy waterfall it kept him awake—fighting sleep.

In the beginning, before he saw anyone, he would just as soon have lain there and thought of wild men holding his house in thrall, or of a giant crouched double behind the window that corresponded to his own. The big fig tree was many times a magic tree with golden fruit that shone in and among its branches like a cloud of lightning bugs—a tree twinkling all over, burning, on and off, off and on. The sweet golden juice to come—in his dream he put his tongue out, and then his mother would be putting that spoon in his mouth.

More than once he dreamed it was inside that house that the cave had moved, and the buttermilk man went in and out the rooms driving his horse with its red rose and berating its side with a whip that unfurled of itself; in the dream he was not singing. Or the horse itself, a white and beautiful one, was on its way over, approaching to ask some favor of him, a request called softly and intelligibly upward—which he was not decided yet whether to grant or deny. This call through the window had not yet happened—not quite. But someone had come.

He turned away. "Cassie!" he cried.

Cassie came to his room. She said, "Didn't I tell you what you could do? Trim up those Octagon Soap coupons and count them good if you want that jack-knife." Then she went off again and slammed her door. He seemed to see her belatedly. She had been dressed up for whatever she was doing in her room like somebody in the circus, with colored spots on her, and hardly looked like his sister.

"You looked silly when you came in!" he called.

But over at the empty house was a stillness not of going off and leaving him but of coming nearer. Something was coming very close to him, there was something he had better keep track of. He had the feeling that something was being counted. Then he too must count. He could be wary enough that way, counting by ones, counting by fives, by tens. Sometimes he threw his arm across his eyes and counted without moving his lips, imagining that when he got to a certain amount he might give a yell, like "Coming, ready or not!" and go down by the hackberry limb. He never had yelled, and his arm was a heavy weight across his face. Often that was the way he fell asleep. He woke up drenched with the afternoon fever breaking. Then his mother pulled him and pushed him as she put cool pillow cases on the pillows and pushed him back straight. She was doing it now.

"Now your powder."

His mother, dressed up for a party, tilted the little pinked paper toward his stuck-out, protesting tongue, and guided the glass of water into his groping hand. Every time he got a powder swallowed, she said calmly, "Dr. Loomis only gives you these to satisfy me you're getting medication." His father, when he came home from the office, would say, "Well, if you've got malaria, son . . ." (kissing him) ". . . you've got malaria, that's all there is to it. Ha! Ha! Ha!"

"I've made you some junket, too," she said with a straight face.

He made a noise calculated to sicken her, and she smiled at him.

"When I come back from Miss Nell Carlisle's I'll bring you all the news of Morgana."

He could not help but smile at her—lips shut. She was almost his ally. She swung her little reticule at him and went off to the Rook party. By leaning far out he could see a lackadaisical, fluttery kind of parade, the ladies of Morgana under their parasols, all trying to keep cool while they walked down to Miss Nell's. His mother was absorbed into their floating, transparent colors. Miss Perdita Mayo was talking, and they were clicking their summery heels and drowning out—drowning out something. . . .

A little tune was playing on the air, and it was coming from the piano in the vacant house.

The tune came again, like a touch from a small hand that he had unwittingly pushed away. Loch lay back and let it persist. All at once tears rolled out of his eyes. He opened his mouth in astonishment. Then the little tune seemed the only thing in the whole day, the whole summer, the whole season of his fevers and chills, that was accountable: it was personal. But he could not tell why it was so.

It came like a signal, or a greeting—the kind of thing a horn would play out in the woods. He halfway closed his eyes. It came and trailed off and was lost in the neighborhood air. He heard it and then wondered how it went.

It took him back to when his sister was so sweet, to a long time ago. To when they loved each other in a different world, a boundless, trustful country all its own, where no mother or father came, either through sweetness or impatience—different altogether from his solitary world now, where he looked out all eyes like Argus, on guard everywhere.

A spoon went against a dish, three times. In her own room Cassie was carrying on some girls' business that, at least, smelled terrible to him, as bad as when she painted a hair-receiver with rosebuds and caught it on fire drying it. He heard Louella talking to herself in the lower hall. "Louella!" he called, flat on his back, and she called up for him to favor her with some rest or she would give up the ghost right then. When he drew up to the window again, the first thing he saw was someone new, coming along the walk out front.

Here came an old lady. No, she was an old woman, round and unsteady-looking—unsteady the way he felt himself when he got out of bed—not on her way to a party. She must have walked in from out in the country. He saw her stop in front of the vacant house, turn herself, and go up the front walk.

Something besides countriness gave her her look. Maybe it came from her having nothing in her hands, no reticule or fan. She looked as if she could even be the one who lived in the house and had just stepped outside for a moment to see if it was going to rain and now, matter-of-factly, a little toilsomely with so much to do, was going back in.

But when she began to hasten, Loch got the idea she might be the sailor's mother come after her son. The sailor didn't belong in Morgana anyhow. Whoever she was, she climbed the steps and crossed the wobbly porch and put her hand to the front door, which she opened just as easily as Virgie Rainey had opened the back door. She went inside, and he saw her through the beady curtain, which made her outline quiver for a moment.

Suppose doors with locks and keys were ever locked—then nothing like this would have the chance to happen. The nearness of missing things, and the possibility of preventing them, made Loch narrow his eyes.

Three party ladies who were late and puffing, all hurrying together in a duck-like line, now passed. They just missed sight of the old woman—Miss Jefferson Moody, Miss Mamie Carmichael, and Miss Billy Texas Spights. They would have stopped everything. Then in the middle of the empty air behind everybody, butterflies suddenly crossed and circled each other, their wings digging and flashing like duelers' swords in the vacuum.

Though Loch was gratified with the outrage mounting—three people now were in the vacant house—and could consider whether the old woman might have come to rout out the other two and give them her tirade, he was puzzled when the chandelier lighted up in the parlor. He ran the telescope out the window again and put his frowning eye to it. He discovered the old woman moving from point to point all around the parlor, in and out of the little chairs, sidling along the piano. He could not see her feet; she behaved a little like a wind-up toy on wheels, rolling into the corners and edges of objects and being diverted and sent on, but never out of the parlor.

He moved his eye upstairs, up an inch on the telescope. There on a mattress delightfully bare—where he would love, himself, to lie, on a slant and naked, to let the little cottony tufts annoy him and to feel the mattress like billows bouncing beneath, and to eat pickles lying on his back—the sailor and the piano player lay and ate pickles out of an open sack between them. Because of the down-tilt of the mattress, the girl had to keep watch on the sack, and when it began to slide down out of reach that was when they laughed. Sometimes they held pickles stuck in their mouths like cigars, and turned to look at each other. Sometimes they lay just alike, their legs in an M and their hands joined between them, exactly like the paper dolls his sister used to cut out of folded newspaper and unfold to let him see. If Cassie would come in now, he would point out the window and she would remember.

And then, like the paper dolls sprung back together, they folded close—the real people. Like a big grasshopper lighting, all their legs and arms drew in to one small body, deadlike, with protective coloring.

He leaned back and bent his head against the cool side of the pillow and shut his eyes, and felt tired out. He clasped the cool telescope to his side, and with his fingernail closed its little eye.

"Poor old Telescope," he said.

When he looked out again, everybody next door was busier.

Upstairs, the sailor and Virgie Rainey were running in circles around the room, each time jumping with outstretched arms over the broken bed. Who chased whom had nothing to do with it because they kept the same distance between them. They went around and around like the policeman and Charlie Chaplin, both intending to fall down.

Downstairs, the sailor's mother was doing something just as fanciful. She was putting up decorations. (Cassie would be happy to see that.) As if she were giving a party that day, she was dressing up the parlor with ribbons of white stuff. It was newspaper.

The old woman left the parlor time and time again and reappeared—in and out through the beads in the doorway—each time with an armful of old *Bugles* that had lain on the back porch in people's way for a long time. And from her gestures of eating crumbs or pulling bits of fluff from her bosom, Loch recognized that mother-habit: she had pins there. She pinned long strips of the newspaper together, first tearing them carefully and evenly as a school teacher. She made ribbons of newspaper and was hanging them all over the parlor, starting with the piano where she weighted down the ends with a statue.

When Loch grew tired of watching one animated room he watched the other. How the two playing would whirl and jump over the old woman's head! That was the way the bed fell to begin with.

As Loch leaned his chin in his palm at the window and watched, it seemed strangely as if he had seen this whole thing before. The old woman was decorating the piano until it rayed out like a Christmas tree or a Maypole. Maypole ribbons of newspaper and tissue paper streamed and crossed each other from the piano to the chandelier and festooned again to the four corners of the room, looped to the backs of chairs here and there. When would things begin?

Soon everything seemed fanciful and beautiful enough to Loch; he thought she could stop. But the old woman kept on. This was only a part of something in her head. And in the splendor she fixed and pinned together she was all alone. She was not connected with anything else, with anybody. She was one old woman in a house not bent on dealing punishment. Though once when Woody Spights and his sister came by on skates, of course she came out and ran them away.

Once she left the house, to come right back. With her unsteady but purposeful walk, as if she were on a wheel that misguided her, she crossed the road to the Carmichael yard and came back with some green leaves and one bloom from the magnolia tree—carried in her skirt. She pulled the corners of her skirt up like a girl, and she was thin beneath in her old legs. But she zigzagged across the road—such a show-off, carefree way for a mother to behave, but mothers sometimes did. She lifted her elbows—as if she might skip! But nobody saw her: his forehead was damp. He heard a scream from the Rook party up at Miss Nell's—it sounded like Miss Jefferson Moody shooting-the-moon. Nobody saw the old woman but Loch, and he told nothing.

She brought the bunch of green into the parlor and put it on the piano, where the Maypole crown would go. Then she took a step back and was as admiring as if somebody else had done it—nodding her head.

But after she had the room all decorated to suit her, she kept on, and began to stuff the cracks. She brought in more paper and put it in all the cracks at the windows. Now Loch realized that the windows in the parlor were both down, it was tight as a box, and she had been inside in the suffocating heat. A wave of hotness passed over his body. Furthermore, she made her way with a load of *Bugles* to the blind part of the wall where he knew the fireplace was. All the load went into the fireplace.

When she went out of the parlor again she came back slowly indeed. She was pushing a big square of matting along on its side; she wove and bent and struggled behind it, like a spider with something bigger than he can eat, pushing it into the parlor. Loch was suddenly short of breath and pressed forward, cramped inside, checkerboarding his forehead and nose against the screen. He both wanted the plot to work and wanted it to fail. In another moment he was shed of all the outrage and the possessiveness he had felt for the vacant house. This house was something the old woman intended to burn down. And Loch could think of a thousand ways she could do it better.

She could fetch a mattress—that would burn fine. Suppose she went upstairs now for the one they played on? Or pulled the othei one, sheet and all, from under Mr. Holifield (whose hat had imperceptibly turned on the bedpost; it changed like a weathercock)? If she went out of sight for a minute, he watched at the little stair window, but she did not go up.

She brought in an old quilt that the dogs there once slept on, that had hung over the line on the back porch until it was half light-colored and half dark. She climbed up on the piano stool, the way women climb, death-defying, and hung the quilt over the front window. It fell down. Twice more she climbed up with it and the third time it stayed. If only she did not block the window toward him! But if she meant to, she forgot. She kept putting her hand to her head.

Everything she did was wrong, after a certain point. She had got off the track. What she really wanted was a draft. Instead, she was keeping air away, and let her try to make fire burn in an airless room. That was the conceited thing girls and women would try.

But now she went to the blind corner of the parlor and when she came out she had a new and mysterious object in her hands.

At that moment Loch heard Louella climbing the back stairs, coming to peep in at him. He flung himself on his back, stretched out one arm, his hand on his heart and his mouth agape, as he did when he played dead in battle. He forgot to shut his eyes. Louella stood there a minute and then tiptoed off.

Loch then leapt to his knees, crawled out the window under the pushed-out screen, onto the hackberry branch, and let himself into the tree the old way.

He went out on a far-extending limb that took him nearest the vacant house. With him at their window the sailor and girl saw him and yet did not see him. He descended further. He found his place in the tree, a rustling, familiar old crotch where he used to sit and count up his bottle tops. He hung watching, sometimes by the hands and sometimes by the knees and feet.

The old woman was dirty. Standing still she shook a little—her hanging cheeks and her hands. He could see well now what she was holding there like a lamp. But he could not tell what it was—a small brown wooden box, shaped like the Obelisk. It had a door—she opened it. It made a mechanical sound. He heard it plainly through the boxed room which was like a sounding board; it was ticking.

She set the obelisk up on the piano, there in the crown of leaves; she pushed a statue out of the way. He listened to it ticking on and his hopes suddenly rose for her. Holding by the knees and diving head down, then swaying in the sweet open free air and dizzy as an apple on a tree, he thought: the box is where she has the dynamite.

He opened his arms and let them hang outward, and flickered his lashes in the June light, watching house, sky, leaves, a flying bird, all and nothing at all.

Little Sister Spights, aged two, that he had not seen cross the street since she was born, wandered under him dragging a skate.

"Hello, little bitty old sweet thing," he murmured from the leaves. "Better go back where you came from."

And then the old woman stuck out a finger and played the tune.

He hung still as a folded bat.

II.

Für Elise.

In her bedroom when she heard the gentle opening, the little phrase, Cassie looked up from what she was doing and said in response, "Virgie Rainey, *danke schoen.*"

In surprise, but as slowly as in regret, she stopped stirring the emerald green. She got up from where she had been squatting in the middle of the floor and stepped over the dishes which were set about on the matting rug. She went quietly to her south window, where she lifted a curtain, spotting it with her wet fingers. There was not a soul in sight at the MacLain house but Old Man Holifield asleep with his gawky hightop shoes on and his stomach full as a robin's. His presence—he was the Holifield who was night watchman at the gin and slept here by day—never kept Cassie's mother from going right ahead and calling the MacLain house "the vacant house."

Whatever you called it, the house was something you saw

without seeing it—it was part of the world again. That unpainted side changed passively with the day and the season, the way a natural place like the river bank changed. In cooler weather its windows would turn like sweetgum leaves, maroon when the late sun came up, and in winter it was bare and glinty, more exposed and more lonesome even than now. In summer it was an overgrown place. Leaves and their shadows pressed up to it, arc-light sharp and still as noon all day. It showed at all times that no woman kept it.

That rainless, windless June the bright air and the town of Morgana, life itself, sunlit and moonlit, were composed and still and china-like. Cassie felt that now. Yet in the shade of the vacant house, though all looked still, there was agitation. Some life stirred through. It may have been *old* life.

Ever since the MacLains had moved away, that roof had stood (and leaked) over the heads of people who did not really stay, and a restless current seemed to flow dark and free around it (there would be some sound or motion to startle the birds), a life quicker than the Morrisons' life, more driven probably, thought Cassie uneasily.

Was it Virgie Rainey in there now? Where was she hiding, if she sneaked in and touched that piano? When did she come? Cassie felt teased. She doubted for a moment that she had heard *Für Elise*—she doubted herself, so easily, and she struck her chest with her fist, sighing, the way Parnell Moody always struck hers.

A line of poetry tumbled in her ears, or started to tumble.

"Though I am old with wandering . . ."

She banged her hands on her hipbones, enough to hurt, flung around, and went back to her own business. On one bare foot with the other crossed over it, she stood gazing down at the pots and dishes in which she had enough colors stirred up to make a sunburst design. She was shut up in here to tie-and-dye a scarf. "Everybody stay out!!!" said an envelope pinned to her door, signed with skull and crossbones.

You took a square of crepe de Chine, you made a point of the goods and tied a string around it in hard knots. You kept on gathering it in and tying it. Then you hung it in the different dyes. The strings were supposed to leave white lines in the colors, a design like a spiderweb. You couldn't possibly have any idea what you would get when you untied your scarf; but Missie Spights said there had never been one yet that didn't take the breath away.

Für Elise. This time there were two phrases, the *E* in the second phrase very flat.

Cassie edged back to the window, while her heart sank, praying that she would not catch sight of Virgie Rainey or, especially, that Virgie Rainey would not catch sight of her.

Virgie Rainey worked. Not at teaching. She played the piano for the picture show, both shows every night, and got six dollars a week, and was not popular any more. Even in her last year in consolidated high school—just ended—she worked. But when Cassie and she were little, they used to take music together in the MacLain house next door, from Miss Eckhart. Virgie Rainey played *Für Elise* all the time. And Miss Eckhart used to say, "Virgie Rainey, *danke schoen*." Where had Miss Eckhart ever gone? She had been Miss Snowdie MacLain's roomer.

"Cassie!" Loch was calling again.

"What!"

"Come here!"

"I can't!"

"Got something to show you!"

"I *ain't got time*!"

Her bedroom door had been closed all afternoon. But first her mother had opened it and come in, only to exclaim and not let herself be touched, and to go out leaving the smell of rose geranium behind for the fan to keep bringing at her. Then Louella had moved right in on her without asking and for ages was standing over her rolling up her hair on newspaper to make it bushy for the hayride that night. "I cares if you don't."

With her gaze at a judicious distance from the colors she dipped in, Cassie was now for a little time far away, perhaps up in September in college, where, however, tie-and-dye scarves would be out-of-uniform, though something to unfold and show.

But with *Für Elise* the third time, her uncritical self of the crucial present, this Wednesday afternoon, slowly came forward—as if called on. Cassie saw herself without even facing the mirror, for her small, solemn, unprotected figure was emerging staring-clear inside her mind. There she was now, standing scared at the window again in her petticoat, a little of each color of the rainbow dropped on her—bodice and flounce—in spite of reasonable care. Her pale hair was covered and burdened with twisty papers, like a hat too big for her. She balanced her head on her frail neck. She was holding a spoon up like a mean switch in her right hand, and her feet were bare. She had seemed to be favored and happy and she stood there pathetic—homeless-looking—horrible. Like a wave, the gathering past came right up to her. Next time it would be too high. The poetry was all around her, pellucid and lifting from side to side,

> "Though I am old with wandering
> Through hollow lands and hilly lands,
> I will find out where she has gone . . ."

Then the wave moved up, towered, and came drowning down over her stuck-up head.

Through the years Cassie had come just before Virgie Rainey for her music lesson, or, at intervals, just after her. To start with, Cassie was so poor in music and Virgie so good (the opposite of themselves in other things!) that Miss Eckhart with her methodical mind might have coupled them on purpose. They went on Mondays and Thursdays at 3:30 and 4:00 and after school was out and up until the recital, at 9:30 and 10:00 in the morning. So punctual and so formidable was Miss Eckhart that all the little girls passed, one going and one coming, through the beaded curtains mincing like strangers. Only Virgie would let go the lights of mockery from her eyes.

Though she was tireless as a spider, Miss Eckhart waited so unbudgingly for her pupils that from the back she appeared asleep in her studio. How much later had it occurred to Cassie that "the studio" itself, the only one ever heard of in Morgana, was nothing more than a room that was rented? Rented because poor Miss Snowdie MacLain needed the money?

Then it seemed a dedicated place. The black-painted floor was bare even of matting, so as not to deaden any sound of music. There was in the very center a dark squarish piano (ebony, they all thought) with legs twisted like elephant legs, bearing many pounds of sheet music on its back—just to look heavy there, Cassie thought, for whose music was it? The yellow keys, some split and others in the bass coffee-colored, always had a little film of sweat. There was a stool spun up high, with a seat worn away like a bowl. Beside it, Miss Eckhart's chair was the kind of old thing most people placed by their telephones.

There were gold chairs, their legs brittle and set the way pulled candy was, sliding across the floor at a touch, and forbidden—they were for the recital audience; their fragility was intentional. There were taboret tables with little pink statuettes and hydrangea-colored, horny shells. Beaded curtains in the doorway stirred and clicked now and then during a lesson, as if someone were coming, but it signified no more than the idle clicking redbirds made in the free outdoors, if it was not time for a pupil. (The MacLains lived largely upstairs, except for the kitchen, and came in at the side.) The beads were faintly sweet-smelling, and made you think of long strings of wine-balls and tiny candy bottles filled with violet liquid, and licorice sticks. The studio was in some ways like the witch's house in *Hansel and Gretel*, Cassie's mother said, "including the witch." On the right-hand corner of the piano stood a small, mint-white bust of Beethoven, all softened around the edges with the nose smoothed down, as if a cow had licked it.

Miss Eckhart, a heavy brunette woman whose age was not known, sat during the lessons on the nondescript chair, which her body hid altogether, in apparent disregard for body and chair alike. She was alternately very quiet and very alert, and sometimes that seemed to be because she hated flies. She held a swatter in her down-inclined lap, gracefully and tenderly as a fan, her hard, round, short fingers surprisingly forgetful-looking. All at once as you played your piece, making errors or going perfectly it did not matter, smack down would come the fly swatter on the back of your hand. No words would be passed, of triumph or apology on Miss Eckhart's part or of surprise or pain on yours. It did hurt. Virgie, her face hardening under the progress of her advancing piece, could manage the most oblivious look of all, though Miss Eckhart might strike harder and harder at the persistent flies. All her pupils let the flies in, when they trailed in and out for their lessons; not to speak of the MacLain boys, who left their door wide open to the universe when they went out to play.

Miss Eckhart might also go abruptly to her little built-on kitchen—she and her mother had no Negro and didn't use Miss Snowdie's; she did not say "Excuse me," or explain what was on the stove. And there were times, perhaps on rainy days, when she walked around and around the studio, and you felt her pause behind you. Just as you thought she had forgotten you, she would lean over your head, you were under her bosom like a traveler under a cliff, her penciled finger would go to your music, and above the bar you were playing she would slowly write "Slow." Or sometimes, precipitant above you, she would make a curly circle with a long tail, as if she might draw a cat, but it would be her "P" and the word would turn into "Practice!!"

When you could once play a piece, she paid scant attention, and made no remark; her manners were all very unfamiliar. It was only time for a new piece. Whenever she opened the cabinet, the smell of new sheet music came out swift as an imprisoned spirit, something almost palpable, like a pet coon; Miss Eckhart kept the music locked up and the key down her dress, inside the collar. She would seat herself and with a dipped pen add "$.25" to the bill on the spot. Cassie could see the bills clearly, in elaborate handwriting, the "z" in Mozart with an equals-sign through it and all the "y's" so heavily tailed they went through the paper. It took a whole lesson for those tails to dry.

What was it she did when you played without a mistake? Oh, she went over and told the canary something, tapping the bars of his cage with her finger. "Just listen," she told him. "Enough from *you* for today," she would call to you over her shoulder.

Virgie Rainey would come through the beads carrying a magnolia bloom which she had stolen.

She would ride over on a boy's bicycle (her brother Victor's) from the Raineys' with sheets of advanced music rolled naked (girls usually had portfolios) and strapped to the boy's bar which she straddled, the magnolia broken out of the Carmichaels' tree and laid bruising in the wire basket on the handlebars. Or sometimes Virgie would come an hour late, if she had to deliver the milk first, and sometimes she came by the back door and walked in peeling a ripe fig with her teeth; and sometimes she missed her lesson altogether. But whenever she came on the bicycle she would ride it up into the yard and run the front wheel bang into the lattice, while Cassie was playing the "Scarf Dance." (In those days, the house looked nice, with latticework and plants hiding the foundation, and a three-legged fern stand at the turn in the porch to discourage skaters and defeat little boys.) Miss Eckhart would put her hand to her breast, as though she felt the careless wheel shake the very foundation of the studio.

Virgie carried in the magnolia bloom like a hot tureen, and offered it to Miss Eckhart, neither of them knowing any better: magnolias smelled too sweet and heavy for right after breakfast. And Virgie handled everything with her finger stuck out; she was conceited over a musician's cyst that appeared on her fourth finger.

Miss Eckhart took the flower but Virgie might be kept waiting while Cassie recited on her catechism page. Sometimes Miss Eckhart checked the questions missed, sometimes the questions answered; but every question she did check got a heavy "V" that crossed the small page like the tail of a comet. She would draw her black brows together to see Cassie forgetting, unless it was to remember some nearly forgotten thing herself. At the exact moment of the hour (the alarm clock had a green and blue waterfall scene on its face) she would dismiss Cassie and incline her head toward Virgie, as though she was recognizing her only now, when she was ready for her; yet all this time she had held the strong magnolia flower in her hand, and its scent was filling the room.

Virgie would drift over to the piano, spread out her music, and make sure she was sitting just the way she wanted to be upon the stool. She flung her skirt behind her, with a double swimming motion. Then without a word from Miss Eckhart she would start to play. She played firmly, smoothly, her face at rest, the musician's cyst, of which she was in idleness so proud, perched like a ladybug, riding the song. She went now gently, now forcibly, never loudly.

And when she was finished, Miss Eckhart would say, "Virgie Rainey, *danke schoen.*"

Cassie, so still her chest cramped, not daring to walk on the creaky floor down the hall, would wait till the end to run out of the house and home. She would whisper while she ran, with the sound of an engine, *"Danke schoen, danke schoen, danke schoen."* It wasn't the meaning that propelled her; she didn't know then what it meant.

But then nobody knew for years (until the World War) what Miss Eckhart meant by *"Danke Schoen"* and *"Mein lieber Kind"* and the rest, and who would dare ask? It was like belling the cat. Only Virgie had the nerve, only she could have found out for the others. Virgie said she did not know and did not care. So they just added that onto Virgie's name in the school yard. She was Virgie Rainey *Danke Schoen* when she jumped hot pepper or fought the boys, when she had to sit down the very first one in the spelling match for saying "E-a-r, ear, r-a-k-e, rake, ear-ache." She was named for good. Sometimes even in the Bijou somebody cat-called that to her as she came in her high heels down the steep slant of the board aisle to switch on the light and open the piano. When she was grown she would tilt up her chin. Calm as a marble head, defamed with a spit-curl, Virgie's head would be proudly carried past the banner on the wall, past every word of "It's Cool at the Bijou, Enjoy Typhoons of Alaskan Breezes," which was tacked up under the fan. Rats ran under her feet, most likely, too; the Bijou was once Spights' Livery Stable.

"Virgie brings me good luck!" Miss Eckhart used to say, with a round smile on her face. Luck that might not be good was something else that was a new thought to them all.

Virgie Rainey, when she was ten or twelve, had naturally curly hair, silky and dark, and a great deal of it—uncombed. She was not sent to the barber shop often enough to suit the mothers of other children, who said it was probably dirty hair too—what could the children see of the back of her neck, poor Katie Rainey being so rushed for time? Her middy blouse was trimmed in a becoming red, her anchor was always loose, and her red silk lacers were actually ladies' shoestrings dipped in pokeberry juice. She was full of the airs of wildness, she swayed and gave way to joys and tempers, her own and other people's with equal freedom—except never Miss Eckhart's, of course.

School did not lessen Virgie's vitality; once on a rainy day when recess was held in the basement, she said she was going to butt her brains out against the wall, and the teacher, old Mrs. McGillicuddy, had said, "Beat them out, then," and she had really tried. The rest of the fourth grade stood around expectant and admiring, the smell of open thermos bottles sweetly heavy in the close air. Virgie came with strange kinds of sandwiches—everybody wanted to swap her—stewed peach, or perhaps banana. In the other children's eyes she was as exciting as a gypsy would be.

Virgie's air of abandon that was so strangely endearing made even the Sunday School class think of her in terms of the future—she would go somewhere, somewhere away off, they said then, talking with their chins sunk in their hands—she'd be a missionary. (Parnell Moody used to be wild and now *she* was pious.) Miss Lizzie Stark's mother, old Mrs. Sad-Talking Morgan, said Virgie would be the first lady governor of Mississippi, that was where she would go. It sounded worse than the infernal regions. To Cassie, Virgie was a secret love, as well as her secret hate. To Cassie she looked like an illustration by Reginald Birch for a serial in Etta Carmichael's *St. Nicholas Magazine* called "The Lucky Stone." Her inky hair fell in the same loose locks—because it was dirty. She often took the very pose of that inventive and persecuted little heroine who coped with people she thought were witches and ogres (alas! they were not)—feet apart, head aslant, eyes glancing up sideways, ears cocked; but you could not tell whether Virgie would boldly interrupt her enemies or run off to her own devices with a forgetful smile on her lips.

And she smelled of flavoring. She drank vanilla out of the bottle, she told them, and it didn't burn her a bit. She did that because she knew they called her mother Miss Ice Cream Rainey, for selling cones at speakings.

Für Elise was always Virgie Rainey's piece. For years Cassie thought Virgie wrote it, and Virgie never did deny it. It was a kind of signal that Virgie had burst in; she would strike that little opening phrase off the keys as she passed anybody's piano—even the one in the café. She never abandoned *Für Elise*; long after she went on to the hard pieces, she still played that.

Virgie Rainey was gifted. Everybody said that could not be denied. To show her it was not denied, she was allowed to play all through school for the other children to march in and to play for Wand Drill. Sometimes they drilled to "Dorothy, an Old English Dance," and sometimes to *Für Elise*—everybody out of kilter.

"I guess they scraped up the money for music lessons somehow," said Cassie's mother. Cassie, when she heard Virgie running her scales next door, would see a vision of the Rainey dining room—an interior which in life she had never seen, for she didn't go home from school with the Raineys—and sitting around the table Miss Katie Rainey and Old Man Fate Rainey and Berry and Bolivar Mayhew, some cousins, and Victor who was going to be killed in the war, and Virgie waiting; with Miss Katie scraping up nickels and pennies with an old bone-handled knife, patting them into shape like her butter, and each time—as the scale went up—just barely getting enough or—as it went down—not quite.

Cassie was Miss Eckhart's first pupil, the reason she "took" being that she lived right next door, but she never had any glory from it. When Virgie began "taking," she was the one who made things evident about Miss Eckhart, her lessons, and all. Miss Eckhart, for all her being so strict and inexorable, in spite of her walk, with no give whatsoever, had a timid spot in her soul. There was a little weak place in her, vulnerable, and Virgie Rainey found it and showed it to people.

Miss Eckhart worshiped her metronome. She kept it, like the most precious secret in the teaching of music, in a wall safe. Jinny Love Stark, who was only seven or eight years old but had her tongue, did suggest that this was the only thing Miss Eckhart owned of the correct size to lock up there. Why there had ever been a real safe built into the parlor nobody seemed to know; Cassie remembered Miss Snowdie saying the Lord knew, in His infinite workings and wisdom, and some day, somebody would come riding in to Morgana and have need of that safe, after she was gone.

Its door looked like a tin plate there in the wall, the closed-up end of an old flue. Miss Eckhart would go toward it with measured step. Technically the safe was hidden, of course, and only she knew it was there, since Miss Snowdie rented it; even Miss Eckhart's mother, possibly, had no expectations of getting in. Yes, her mother lived with her.

Cassie, out of nice feeling, looked the other way when it was time for the morning opening of the safe. It seemed awful, and yet imminent, that because she was the first pupil she, Cassie Morrison, might be the one to call logical attention to the absurdity of a safe in which there were no jewels, in which there was the very opposite of a jewel. Then Virgie, one day when the metronome was set going in front of her—Cassie was just leaving—announced simply that she would not play another note with that thing in her face.

At Virgie's words, Miss Eckhart quickly—it almost seemed that was what she'd wanted to hear—stopped the hand and slammed the little door, bang. The metronome was never set before Virgie again.

Of course all the rest of them still got it. It came out of the safe every morning, as regularly as the canary was uncovered in his cage. Miss Eckhart had made an exception of Virgie Rainey; she had first respected Virgie Rainey, and now fell humble before her impudence.

A metronome was an infernal machine, Cassie's mother said when Cassie told on Virgie. "Mercy, you have to keep moving, with that infernal machine. I want a song to *dip*."

"What do you mean, dip? Could you have played the piano, Mama?"

"Child, I could have *sung*," and she threw her hand from her, as though all music might as well now go jump off the bridge.

As time went on, Virgie Rainey showed her bad manners to Miss Eckhart still more, since she had won about the metronome. Once she had a little *Rondo* her way, and Miss Eckhart was so beset about it that the lesson was not like a real lesson at all. Once she unrolled the new *Étude* and when it kept rolling back up, as the *Étude* always did, she threw it on the floor and jumped on it, before Miss Eckhart had even seen it; that was heartless. After such showing off, Virgie would push her hair behind her ears and then softly lay her hands on the keys, as she would take up a doll.

Miss Eckhart would sit there blotting out her chair in the same way as ever, but inside her she was listening to every note. Such listening would have made Cassie forget. And half the time, the piece was only *Für Elise*, which Miss Eckhart could probably have played blindfolded and standing up with her back to the keys. Anybody could tell that Virgie was doing something to Miss Eckhart. She was turning her from a teacher into something lesser. And if she was not a teacher, what was Miss Eckhart?

At times she could not bring herself to swat a summer fly. And as little as Virgie, of them all, cared if her hand was rapped, Miss Eckhart would raise her swatter and try to bring it down and could not. You could see torment in her regard of the fly. The smooth clear music would move on like water, beautiful and undisturbed, under the hanging swatter and Miss Eckhart's red-rimmed thumb. But even boys hit Virgie, because she liked to fight.

There were times when Miss Eckhart's Yankeeness, if not her very origin, some last quality to fade, almost faded. Before some caprice of Virgie's, her spirit drooped its head. The child had it by the lead. Cassie saw Miss Eckhart's spirit as a terrifyingly gentle water-buffalo cow in the story of "Peasie and Beansie" in the reader. And sooner or later, after taming her teacher, Virgie was going to mistreat her. Most of them expected some great scene.

There was in the house itself, soon, a daily occurrence to distress Miss Eckhart. There was now a second roomer at Miss Snowdie's. While Miss Eckhart listened to a pupil, Mr. Voight would walk over their heads and come down to the turn of the stairs, open his bathrobe, and flap the skirts like an old turkey gobbler. They all knew Miss Snowdie never suspected she housed a man like that: he was a sewing machine salesman. When he flapped his maroon-colored bathrobe, he wore no clothes at all underneath.

It would be plain to Miss Eckhart or to anybody that he

wanted, first, the music lesson to stop. They could not close the door, there was no door, there were beads. They could not tell Miss Snowdie even that he objected; she would have been agonized. All the little girls and the one little boy were afraid of Mr. Voight's appearance at every lesson and felt nervous until it had happened and got over with. The one little boy was Scooter MacLain, the twin that took the free lessons; he kept mum.

Cassie saw that Miss Eckhart, who might once have been formidable in particular to any Mr. Voights, was helpless toward him and his antics—as helpless as Miss Snowdie MacLain would have been, helpless as Miss Snowdie was, toward her own little twin sons—all since she had begun giving in to Virgie Rainey. Virgie kept the upper hand over Miss Eckhart even at the moment when Mr. Voight came out to scare them. She only played on the stronger and clearer, and never pretended he had not come out and that she did not know it, or that she might not tell it, no matter how poor Miss Eckhart begged.

"Tell a soul what you have seen, I'll beat your hands until you scream," Miss Eckhart had said. Her round eyes opened wide, her mouth went small. This was all she knew to say. To Cassie it was as idle as a magic warning in a story; she criticized the rhyme. She herself had told all about Mr. Voight at breakfast, stood up at the table and waved her arms, only to have her father say he didn't believe it; that Mr. Voight represented a large concern and covered seven states. He added his own threat to Miss Eckhart's: no picture show money.

Her mother's laugh, which followed, was as usual soft and playful but not illuminating. Her laugh, like the morning light that came in the window each summer breakfast time around her father's long head, slowly made it its solid silhouette where he sat against the day. He turned to his paper like Douglas Fairbanks opening big gates; it was indeed his; he published the *Morgana-MacLain Weekly Bugle* and Mr. Voight had no place in it.

"Live and let live, Cassie," her mother said, meaning it mischievously. She showed no repentance, such as Cassie felt, for her inconsistencies. She had sometimes said passionately, "Oh, I hate that old MacLain house next door to me! I hate having it there all the time. I'm worn out with Miss Snowdie's cross!" Later on, when Miss Snowdie finally had to sell the house and move away, her mother said, "Well, I see Snowdie gave up." When she told bad news, she wore a perfectly blank face and her voice was helpless and automatic, as if she repeated a lesson.

Virgie told on Mr. Voight too, but she had nobody to believe her, and so Miss Eckhart did not lose any pupils by that. Virgie did not know how to tell anything.

And for what Mr. Voight did there were no ready words—what would you call it? "Call it spontaneous combustion," Cassie's mother said. Some performances of people stayed partly untold for lack of a name, Cassie believed, as well as for lack of believers. Mr. Voight before so very long—it happened during a sojourn home of Mr. MacLain, she remembered—was transferred to travel another seven states, ending the problem; and yet Mr. Voight had done something that amounted to more than going naked under his robe and calling alarm like a turkey gobbler, it was more belligerent; and the least describable thing of all had been a look on his face; that was strange. Thinking of it now, and here in her room, Cassie found she had bared her teeth and set them, trying out the frantic look. She could not now, any more than then, really describe Mr. Voight, but without thinking she could *be* Mr. Voight, which was more frightening still.

Like a dreamer dreaming with reservations, Cassie moved over and changed the color for her scarf and moved back to the window. She reached behind her for a square of heavenly-hash in its platter and bit down on the marshmallow.

There was another man Miss Eckhart had been scared of, up until the last. (Not Mr. King MacLain. They always passed without touching, like two stars, perhaps they had some kind of eclipse-effect on each other.) She had been sweet on Mr. Hal Sissum, who clerked in the shoe department of Spights' store.

Cassie remembered him—who didn't know Mr. Sissum and all the Sissums? His sandy hair, parted on the side, shook over his ear like a toboggan cap when he ambled forward, in his long lazy step, to wait on people. He teased people that came to buy shoes, as though that took the prize for the vainest, most outlandish idea that could ever come over human beings.

Miss Eckhart had pretty ankles for a heavy lady like herself. Mrs. Stark said what a surprise it was for Miss Eckhart, of all people, to turn up with such pretty ankles, which made it the same as if she didn't have them. When she came in she took her seat and put her foot earnestly up on Mr. Sissum's stool like any other lady in Morgana and he spoke to her very nicely. He generally invited the bigger ladies, like Miss Nell Loomis or Miss Gert Bowles, to sit in the children's chair, but he held back, with Miss Eckhart, and spoke very nicely to her about her feet and treated them as a real concern; he even brought out a choice of shoes. To most ladies he brought out one box and said, "There's your shoe," as though shoes were something predestined. He knew them all so well.

Miss Eckhart might have come over to his aisle more often, but she had an incomprehensible habit of buying shoes two or even four pairs at a time, to save going back, or to take precaution against never finding them again. She didn't know how to do about Mr. Sissum at all.

But what could they either one have done? They couldn't go to church together; the Sissums were Presbyterians from the beginning of time and Miss Eckhart belonged to some distant church with a previously unheard-of name, the Lutheran. She could not go to the picture show with Mr. Sissum because he was already at the picture show. He played the music there every evening after the store closed—he had to; this was before the Bijou afforded a piano, and he could play the cello. He could not have refused Mr. Syd Sissum who bought the stable and built the Bijou.

Miss Eckhart used to come to the political speakings in the Starks' yard when Mr. Sissum played with the visiting band. Anybody could see him all evening then, high on the fresh plank platform behind his cello. Miss Eckhart, the true musician, sat on the damp night grass and listened. Nobody ever saw them really together any more than that. How did they know she was sweet on Mr. Sissum? But they did.

Mr. Sissum was drowned in the Big Black River one summer—fell out of his boat, all alone.

Cassie would rather remember the sweet soft speaking-nights in the Starks' yard. Before the speakings began, while the music was playing, Virgie and her older brother Victor ran wild all over everywhere, assaulting the crowd, where couples and threes and fives of people joined hands like paperdoll strings and wandered laughing and turning under the blossoming China trees and the heavy crape myrtles that were wound up in honeysuckle. How delicious it all smelled! Virgie let herself go completely, as anyone would like to do. Jinny Love Stark's swing was free to anybody and Virgie ran under the swingers, or jumped on behind, booting and pumping. She ran under sweethearts' twining arms, and nobody, even her brother, could catch her. She rolled the country people's watermelons away. She caught lightning bugs and tore out their lights for jewelry. She never rested as long as the music played except at last to throw herself hard and panting on the ground, her open mouth smiling against the trampled clover. Sometimes she made Victor climb up on the Starks' statue. Cassie remembered him, white face against dark leaves, a baseball cap turned backwards with the bill behind, and long black-stockinged legs wound over the snowy limbs of the goddess, and slowly, proudly sliding down.

But Virgie would not even watch him. She whirled in one direction till she fell down drunk, or turned about more slowly when they played *Vienna Woods.* She pushed Jinny Love Stark into her own lily bed. And all the time, she was eating. She ate all the ice cream she wanted. Now and then, in the soft parts of *Carmen* or before the storm in *William Tell*—even during dramatic pauses in the speaking—Mrs. Ice Cream Rainey's voice could be heard quickly calling, "Ice cream?" She had brought a freezer or two on Mr. Rainey's wagon to the foot of the yard. This time of year it might be fig. Sometimes Virgie whirled around with a fig ice cream cone in each hand, held poised like daggers.

Virgie would run closer and closer circles around Miss Eckhart who sat alone (her mother never came out that far) on a *Bugle*, all four pages unfolded on the grass, listening. Up above, Mr. Sissum—who bent over his cello in the Bijou every night like an old sewing woman over the machine, like a shoe clerk over another foot to fit—shone in a palm beach coat and played straight-backed in the visiting band, and as fast as they did. The lock of hair was no longer hiding his eyes and nose; like the candidate for supervisor, he looked out.

Virgie put a loop of clover chain down over Miss Eckhart's head, her hat—her one hat—and all. She hung Miss Eckhart with flowers, while Mr. Sissum plucked the strings up above her. Miss Eckhart sat on, perfectly still and submissive. She gave no sign. She let the clover chain come down and lie on her breast.

Virgie laughed delightedly and with her long chain in her hand ran around and around her, binding her up with clovers. Miss Eckhart let her head roll back, and then Cassie felt that the teacher was filled with terror, perhaps with pain. She found it so easy—ever since Virgie showed her—to feel terror and pain in an outsider; in someone you did not know at all well, pain made you wonderfully sorry. It was not so easy to be sorry about it in the people close to you—it came unwillingly; and how strange—in yourself, on nights like this, pain—even a moment's pain—seemed inconceivable.

Cassie's whole family would be at the speakings, of course, her father moving at large through the crowd or sometimes sitting on the platform with Mr. Carmichael and Mr. Comus Stark with the rolling head and Mr. Spights. Cassie would try to stay in sight of her mother, but no matter how slightly she strayed, only to follow Virgie around the backyard and find croquet balls in the grass, or down the hill to get a free cone, when she got back to their place her mother would be gone. She always lost her mother. She would find Loch there, rolled in a ball asleep in his sailor suit, his cheek holding down the ribbon of her softly removed hat. When she was back again, "I've just been through yonder to speak to my candidate," she said. "It's you that vanishes, Lady Bug, you that gets away."

It appeared to Cassie that only the figure of Miss Eckhart, off there like a vast receptacle in its island of space, did not move or sway when the band played *Tales of Hoffmann.*

One time Mr. Sissum gave Miss Eckhart something, a Billikin. The Billikin was a funny, ugly doll that Spights' store gave free to children with every pair of Billikin shoes. Never had Miss Eckhart laughed so hard, and with such an unfamiliar sound, as she laughed to see Mr. Sissum's favor. Tears ran down her bright, distorted cheeks every time one of the children coming into the studio picked the Billikin up. When her laughter was exhausted she would sigh faintly and ask for the doll, and then soberly set it down on a little minaret table, as if it were a vase of fresh red roses. Her old mother took it one day and cracked it across her knee.

When Mr. Sissum was drowned, Miss Eckhart came to his funeral like everybody else. The Loomises invited her to ride with them. She looked exactly the same as ever, round and solid, her back a ramrod in her dress that was the wrong season's length and her same hat, the home-made one with cambric flowers sticking up on it. But when the coffin was lowered into Mr. Sissum's place in the Sissum lot under a giant magnolia tree, and Mr. Sissum's preacher, Dr. Carlyle, said burial service, Miss Eckhart broke out of the circle.

She pressed to the front, through Sissums from everywhere and all the Presbyterians, and went close to get a look; and if Dr. Loomis had not caught her she would have gone headlong into the red clay hole. People said she might have thrown herself upon the coffin if they'd let her; just as, later, Miss Katie Rainey did on Victor's when he was brought back from France. But Cassie had the impression that Miss Eckhart simply wanted to see—to see what was being done with Mr. Sissum.

As she struggled, her round face seemed stretched wider than it was long by a feeling that failed to match the feelings of everybody else. It was not the same as sorrow. Miss Eckhart, a stranger to their cemetery, where none of her people lay, pushed forward with her unstylish, winter purse swinging on her arm, and began to nod her head—sharply, to one side and then the other. She appeared almost little under the tree, but Mr. Comus Stark and Dr. Loomis looked more shrunken still by the side of her as they—sent by ladies—reached for her elbows. Her vigorous nods included them too, increasing in urgency. It was the way she nodded at pupils to bring up their rhythm, helping out the metronome.

Cassie remembered how Miss Snowdie MacLain's grip tightened on her hand and stayed tightened until Miss Eckhart got over it. But Cassie remembered her manners better than to seem to watch Miss Eckhart after one look; she stared down at her Billikin shoes. And her mother had slipped away.

It was strange that in Mr. Sissum's life Miss Eckhart, as everybody said, had never known what to do; and now she did this. Her sharp nodding was like something to encourage them all—to say that she knew now, to do this, and that nobody need speak to her or touch her unless, if they thought best, they could give her this little touch at the elbows, the steer of politeness.

"Pizzicato."

Once, Miss Eckhart gave out the word to define in the catechism lesson.

"*Pizzicato* is when Mr. Sissum played the cello before he got drowned."

That was herself: Cassie heard her own words. She had tried—she was as determined as if she'd been dared—to see how that sounded, spoken out like that to Miss Eckhart's face. She remembered how Miss Eckhart listened to her and did nothing but sit still as a statue, as she sat when the flowers came down over her head.

After the way she cried in the cemetery—for they decided it must have been crying she did—some ladies stopped their little girls from learning any more music; Miss Jefferson Moody stopped Parnell.

Cassie heard noises—a thump next door, the antiquated sound of thunder. There was nothing she could see—only Old Man Holifield's hat that idly made a half-turn on the bedpost, as if something, by a long grapevine, had jolted it.

One summer morning, a sudden storm had rolled up and three children were caught at the studio—Virgie Rainey, little Jinny Love Stark, and Cassie—though the two bigger girls might have run their short way home with newspapers over their hair.

Miss Eckhart, without saying what she was going to do, poked her finger solidly along the pile of music on top of the piano, pulled out a piece, and sat down on her own stool. It was the only time she ever performed in Cassie's presence except when she took the other half in duets.

Miss Eckhart played as if it were Beethoven; she struck the

music open midway and it was in soft yellow tatters like old satin. The thunder rolled and Miss Eckhart frowned and bent forward or she leaned back to play; at moments her solid body swayed from side to side like a tree trunk.

The piece was so hard that she made mistakes and repeated to correct them, so long and stirring that it soon seemed longer than the day itself had been, and in playing it Miss Eckhart assumed an entirely different face. Her skin flattened and drew across her cheeks, her lips changed. The face could have belonged to someone else—not even to a woman, necessarily. It was the face a mountain could have, or what might be seen behind the veil of a waterfall. There in the rainy light it was a sightless face, one for music only—though the fingers kept slipping and making mistakes they had to correct. And if the sonata had an origin in a place on earth, it was the place where Virgie, even, had never been and was not likely ever to go.

The music came with greater volume—with fewer halts—and Jinny Love tiptoed forward and began turning the music. Miss Eckhart did not even see her—her arm struck the child, making a run. Coming from Miss Eckhart, the music made all the pupils uneasy, almost alarmed; something had burst out, unwanted, exciting, from the wrong person's life. This was some brilliant thing too splendid for Miss Eckhart, piercing and striking the air around her the way a Christmas firework might almost jump out of the hand that was, each year, inexperienced anew.

It was when Miss Eckhart was young that she had learned this piece, Cassie divined. Then she had almost forgotten it. But it took only a summer rain to start it again; she had been pricked and the music came like the red blood under the scab of a forgotten fall. The little girls, all stationed about the studio with the rushing rain outside, looked at one another, the three quite suddenly on some equal footing. They were all wondering—thinking—perhaps about escape. A mosquito circled Cassie's head, singing, and fastened on her arm, but she dared not move.

What Miss Eckhart might have told them a long time ago was that there was more than the ear could bear to hear or the eye to see, even in her. The music was too much for Cassie

Morrison. It lay in the very heart of the stormy morning—there was something almost too violent about a storm in the morning. She stood back in the room with her whole body averted as if to ward off blows from Miss Eckhart's strong left hand, her eyes on the faintly winking circle of the safe in the wall. She began to think of an incident that had happened to Miss Eckhart instead of about the music she was playing; that was one way.

One time, at nine o'clock at night, a crazy nigger had jumped out of the school hedge and got Miss Eckhart, had pulled her down and threatened to kill her. That was long ago. She had been walking by herself after dark; nobody had told her any better. When Dr. Loomis made her well, people were surprised that she and her mother did not move away. They wished she had moved away, everybody but poor Miss Snowdie; then they wouldn't always have to remember that a terrible thing once happened to her. But Miss Eckhart stayed, as though she considered one thing not so much more terrifying than another. (After all, nobody knew why she came!) It was because she was from so far away, at any rate, people said to excuse her, that she couldn't comprehend; Miss Perdita Mayo, who took in sewing and made everybody's trousseaux, said Miss Eckhart's *differences* were why shame alone had not killed her and killed her mother too; that differences were reasons.

Cassie thought as she listened, had to listen, to the music that perhaps more than anything it was the nigger in the hedge, the terrible fate that came on her, that people could not forgive Miss Eckhart. Yet things divined and endured, spectacular moments, hideous things like the black nigger jumping out of the hedge at nine o'clock, all seemed to Cassie to be by their own nature rising—and so alike—and crossing the sky and setting, the way the planets did. Or they were more like whole constellations, turning at their very centers maybe, like Perseus and Orion and Cassiopeia in her Chair and the Big Bear and Little Bear, maybe often upside down, but terribly recognizable. It was not just the sun and moon that traveled. In the deepening of the night, the rising sky lifted like a cover when Louella let it soar as she made the bed.

All kinds of things would rise and set in your own life, you could begin now to watch for them, roll back your head and feel their rays come down and reach your open eyes.

Performing, Miss Eckhart was unrelenting. Even when the worst of the piece was over, her fingers like foam on rocks pulled at the spent-out part with unstilled persistence, insolence, violence.

Then she dropped her hands.

"Play it again, Miss Eckhart!" they all cried in startled recoil, begging for the last thing they wanted, looking at her great lump of body.

"No."

Jinny Love Stark gave them a grown-up look and closed the music. When she did, the other two saw it wasn't the right music at all, for it was some bound-together songs of Hugo Wolf.

"What were you playing, though?"

That was Miss Snowdie MacLain, standing in the door, holding streams of bead curtains in both hands.

"I couldn't say," Miss Eckhart said, rising. "I have forgotten."

The pupils all ran out in the slackening rain without another word, scattering in three directions by the mimosa tree, its flowers like wet fur, which once grew in the yard of the now-vacant house.

Für Elise. It came again, but in a labored, foolish way. Was it a man, using one finger?

Virgie Rainey had gone straight from taking music to playing the piano in the picture show. With her customary swiftness and lightness she had managed to skip an interval, some world-in-between where Cassie and Missie and Parnell were, all dyeing scarves. Virgie had gone direct into the world of power and emotion, which was beginning to seem even bigger than they had all thought. She belonged now with the Gish and the Talmadge sisters. With her yellow pencil she hit the tin plate when the tent opened where Valentino lived.

Virgie sat nightly at the foot of the screen ready for all that happened at the Bijou, and keeping pace with it. Nothing proved too much for her or ever got too far ahead, as it certainly got ahead of Mr. Sissum. When the dam broke everywhere at once, or when Nazimova cut off both feet with a saber rather than face life with Sinji, Virgie was instantly playing *Kamennoi-Ostrow.* Missie Spights said only one thing was wrong with having Virgie to play at the Bijou. She didn't work hard enough. Some evenings, she would lean back in her chair and let a whole forest fire burn in dead silence on the screen, and then when the sweethearts had found each other, she would switch on her light with a loud click and start up with creeping, minor runs—perhaps *Anitra's Dance.* But that had nothing to do with working hard.

The only times she played *Für Elise* now were for the advertisements; she played it moodily while the slide of the big white chicken on the watermelon-pink sky came on for Bowles' Gro., or the yellow horn on the streaky blue sky flashed on for the *Bugle*, with Cassie's father's picture as a young man inserted in the wavy beam of noise. *Für Elise* never got finished any more; it began, went a little way, and was interrupted by Virgie's own clamorous hand. She could do things with "You've Got to See Mama Every Night," and "Avalon."

By now, it was not likely she could play the opening movement of her Liszt concerto. That was the piece none of the rest of them could ever hope to play. Virgie would be heard from in the world, playing that, Miss Eckhart said, revealing to children with one ardent cry her lack of knowledge of the world. How could Virgie be heard from, in the world? And "the world"! Where did Miss Eckhart think she was now? Virgie Rainey, she repeated over and over, had a gift, and she must go away from Morgana. From them all. From her studio. In the world, she must study and practice her music for the rest of her life. In repeating all this, Miss Eckhart suffered.

And all the time, it was on Miss Eckhart's piano that Virgie had to do her practicing. The Raineys' old borrowed piano was butted and half-eaten by the goats one summer day; something that could only happen at the Raineys'. But they had all known Virgie would never go, or study, or practice anywhere, never would even have her own piano, because it wouldn't be like her. They felt no less sure of that when they heard, every recital, every June, Virgie Rainey playing better and better something that was harder and harder, or watched this fill Miss Eckhart with stiff delight, curious anguish. The very place to prove Miss Eckhart crazy was on her own subject, piano playing: she didn't know what she was talking about.

When the Raineys, after their barn got blown away in a big wind, had no more money to throw away on piano lessons, Miss Eckhart said she would teach Virgie free, because she must not stop learning. But later she made her pick the figs off the trees in the backyard in summer and the pecans off the ground in the front yard in winter, for her lessons. Virgie said Miss Eckhart never gave her a one. Yet she always had nuts in her pocket.

Cassie heard a banging and a running next door, the obvious sound of falling. She shut her eyes.

"Virgie Rainey, *danke schoen.*" Once that was said in a dreadful voice, condemning. There were times in the studio when Miss Eckhart's mother would roll in; she had a wheelchair. The first years, she had kept to herself, rolling around no closer than the dining room, round and round with a whining wheel. She was old, and fair as a doll. Up close, her yellowish hair was powdery like goldenrod that had gone forgotten in a vase, turned white in its curls like Miss Snowdie's. She had wasting legs that showed knifelike down her long skirt, and clumsy-shaped, suffering feet that she placed just so out in front of her on the step of her chair, as if she wanted you to think they were pretty.

The mother rolled in to the studio whenever she liked, as time went on; with her shepherdess curls she bobbed herself through the beads that opened to her easier than a door. She would roll a certain distance into the room, then stop the wheels and wait there. She was not so much listening to the lesson as watching it, and though she was not keeping time, it was all the more noticeable the way her hands would tip, tap against her chair; she had a brass thimble on one finger.

Ordinarily, Miss Eckhart never seemed disturbed by her mother's abrupt visits. She appeared gentler, more bemused than before, when old Mrs. Eckhart made Parnell Moody cry, just by looking at Parnell too hard. Should daughters *forgive* mothers (with mothers under their heel)? Cassie would rather look at the two of them at night, separated by the dark and the distance between. For when from your own table you saw the Eckharts through their window in the light of a lamp, and Miss Eckhart with a soundless ebullience bouncing up to wait on her mother, sometimes you could imagine them back far away from Morgana, before they had troubles and before they had come to you—plump, bright, and sweet somewhere.

Once when Virgie was practicing on Miss Eckhart's piano, and before she was through, the old mother screamed, *"Danke schoen, danke schoen, danke schoen!"* Cassie heard and saw her.

She screamed with a shy look still on her face, as though through Virgie Rainey she would scream at the whole world, at least at all the music in the world and wasn't that all right? Then she sat there looking out the front window, half smiling, having mocked her daughter. Virgie, of course, kept on practicing—it was a Schumann "forest piece." She had a pomegranate flower (the marbelized kind, from the Moodys') stuck in her breast-pin, and it did not even move.

But when the song was smoothly finished, Miss Eckhart made her way among the little tables and chairs across the studio. Cassie thought she was going for a drink of water, or something for herself. When she reached her mother, Miss Eckhart slapped the side of her mouth. She stood there a moment more, leaning over the chair—while it seemed to Cassie that it must, after all, have been the mother that slapped the daughter—with the key from her bosom, slipped out, beginning to swing on its chain, back and forth, catching the light.

Then Miss Eckhart, with her back turned, asked Cassie and Virgie to stay for dinner.

Enveloping all that the pupils did—entering the house, parting the curtains, turning the music page, throwing up the wrist for a "rest"—was the smell of cooking. But the smell was wrong, as the pitch of a note could be wrong. It was the smell of food nobody else had ever tasted.

Cabbage was cooked there by no Negro and by no way it was ever cooked in Morgana. With wine. The wine was brought on foot by Dago Joe, and to the front door. Some nice mornings the studio smelled like a spiced apple. But it was known from Mr. Wiley Bowles, the grocer, that Miss Eckhart and her mother (whose mouth was still held crooked after the slap) ate pigs' brains. Poor Miss Snowdie!

Cassie yearned—she did want to taste the cabbage—that was really the insurmountable thing, and even the brains of a pig she would have put in her mouth that day. With that, Missie Spights might be flouted. But when Miss Eckhart said, "Please—please, will you stay to dinner?" Virgie and Cassie twined arms and said "No" together.

The war came and all through it and even after 1918 people said Miss Eckhart was a German and still wanted the Kaiser to win, and that Miss Snowdie could get along without her. But the old mother died, and Miss Snowdie said Miss Eckhart needed a friendly roof more than she did herself. Miss Eckhart raised the price of her lessons to six dollars a month. Miss Mamie Carmichael stopped her girls from taking, for this or for one thing or another, and then Miss Billy Texas Spights stopped Missie to be like her. Virgie stopped taking her free lessons when her brother Victor was killed in France, but that might have been coincidence, for Virgie had a birthday: she was fourteen. It might have been Virgie's stopping that took away Miss Eckhart's luck for good.

And when she stopped, Virgie's hand lost its touch—that was what they said. Perhaps nobody wanted Virgie Rainey to be anything in Morgana any more than they had wanted Miss Eckhart to be, and they were the two of them still linked together by people's saying that. How much might depend on people's being linked together? Even Miss Snowdie had a little harder time than she had had already with Ran and Scooter, her bad boys, by being linked with roomers and music lessons and Germans.

The time came when Miss Eckhart had almost no pupils at all. Then she had only Cassie.

Her mother, Cassie had long known in her heart, could not help but despise Miss Eckhart. It was just for living so close to her, or maybe just for living, a poor unwanted teacher and unmarried. And Cassie's instinct told her her mother despised herself for despising. That was why she kept Cassie taking just a little longer after Miss Eckhart had been deserted by all the other mothers. It was more that than the money, which would go to Miss Snowdie on the rent bill. The child had to make up for her mother's abhorrence, to keep her mother as kind as she really was. While Miss Snowdie could stay kind through always being far away in her heart.

Cassie herself was well applauded when she played a piece. The recital audience always clapped more loudly for her than they did for Virgie; but then they clapped more loudly still for little Jinny Love Stark. It was Cassie who was awarded the Presbyterian Church's music scholarship that year to go to college—not Virgie. It made Cassie feel "natural"; winning the scholarship over Virgie did not surprise her too much. The only reason for that which she put into words, to be self-effacing, was that the Raineys were Methodists; and yet she did not, basically, understand a slight. And now stretching ahead of her, as far as she could see, were those yellow Schirmer books: all the rest of her life.

But Miss Eckhart sent for Virgie and gave her a present that Cassie for many days could close her eyes and see. It was a little butterfly pin made of cut-out silver, like silver lace, to wear on her shoulder; the safety-catch wasn't any good.

But that didn't make Virgie say she loved Miss Eckhart or go on practicing as she told her. Miss Eckhart gave Virgie an armful of books that were written in German about the lives of the masters, and Virgie couldn't read a word; and Mr. Fate Rainey tore out the Venusberg pictures and fed them to the pigs. Miss Eckhart tried all those things and was strict to the last in the way she gave all her love to Virgie Rainey and none to anybody else, the way she was strict in music; and for Miss Eckhart love was just as arbitrary and one-sided as music teaching.

Her love never did anybody any good.

Then one day, Miss Eckhart had to move out.

The trouble was that Miss Snowdie had had to sell the house. She moved with her two boys back to MacLain where she came from, seven miles away, and where her husband's people came from too. She sold the house to Mrs. Vince Murphy. And soon Miss Eckhart was put out, with Mrs. Vince

Murphy retaining the piano and anything Miss Eckhart had or that Miss Snowdie had left for Miss Eckhart.

It was not long before Mrs. Vince Murphy was struck by lightning and left the house to Miss Francine, who always kept meaning to fix up the house and take boarders, but had a beau then. She temporized by putting Mr. Holifield in to see that nobody ran off with the bathtubs and what furniture there was. And the house "ran down"—as they said alike of houses and clocks, thought Cassie, to put the seal on inferiority and carelessness and fainting hopes alike, and for ever.

Then stories began to be told of what Miss Eckhart had really done to her old mother. People said the old mother had been in pain for years, and nobody was told. What kind of pain they did not say. But they said that during the war, when Miss Eckhart lost pupils and they did not have very much to eat, she would give her mother paregoric to make sure she slept all night and not wake the street with noise or complaint, for fear still more pupils would be taken away. Some people said Miss Eckhart killed her mother with opium.

Miss Eckhart, in a room out at the old Holifields' on Morgan's Wood Road, got older and weaker, though not noticeably thinner, and would be seen from time to time walking into Morgana, up one side of the street and down the other and home. People said you could look at her and see she had broken. Yet she still had authority. She could still stop young, unknowing children like Loch on the street and ask them imperative questions, "Where were you throwing that ball?" "Are you trying to break that tree?" . . . Of course her only associates from first to last were children; not counting Miss Snowdie.

Where did Miss Eckhart come from, and where in the end did she go? In Morgana most destinies were known to everybody and seemed to go without saying. It was unlikely that anybody except Miss Perdita Mayo had asked Miss Eckhart where the Eckharts came from, where exactly in the world, and so received the answer. And Miss Perdita was so undependable: she couldn't tell you now, to save her life. And Miss Eckhart had gone down out of sight.

Once on a Sunday ride, Cassie's father said he bet a nickel that was old lady Eckhart hoeing peas out there on the

County Farm, and he bet another nickel she could still do the work of ten nigger men.

Wherever she was, she had no people. Surely, by this time, she had nobody at all. The only one she had ever wanted to have for "people" was Virgie Rainey *Danke Schoen.*

Missie Spights said that if Miss Eckhart had allowed herself to be called by her first name, then she would have been like other ladies. Or if Miss Eckhart had belonged to a church that had ever been heard of, and the ladies would have had something to invite her to belong to . . . Or if she had been married to anybody at all, just the awfullest man—like Miss Snowdie MacLain, that everybody could feel sorry for.

Cassie knelt, and with hurrying hands untied all the knots in her scarf. She held it out in a square. Though she was not thinking of her scarf, it did surprise her; she didn't see indeed how she had ever made it. They had told her so. She hung it over the two posts of a chair to dry and as it fell softly over the ladder of the back she thought that somewhere, even up to the last, there could have been for Miss Eckhart a little opening wedge—a crack in the door. . . .

But if I had been the one to see it open, she thought slowly, I might have slammed it tight for ever. I might.

Her eyes lifted to the window where she saw a thin gray streak go down, like the trail of a match. The humming-bird! She knew him, one that came back every year. She stood and looked down at him. He was a little emerald bobbin, suspended as always before the opening four-o'clocks. Metallic and misty together, tangible and intangible, splendid and fairy-like, the haze of his invisible wings mysterious, like the ring around the moon—had anyone ever tried to catch him? Not she. Let him be suspended there for a moment each year for a hundred years—incredibly thirsty, greedy for every drop in every four-o'clock trumpet in the yard, as though he had them numbered—then dart.

"Like a military operation."

Cassie's father always said the recital was planned that way, in all its tactics and dress. The preparations went on for many hot, secret weeks—all of May. "You're not to tell anyone what the program is to be," Miss Eckhart warned at every lesson and rehearsal, as if there were other music teachers, other classes, rivaling, and as if every year the program didn't begin with "The Stubborn Rocking Horse" by the one boy and end with *"Marche Militaire"* for eight hands. What Virgie played in the recital one year, Cassie (gradually improving) would come to the next, and Missie Spights had it one more step in the future.

Miss Eckhart decided early in the spring what color each child should wear, with what color sash and hair ribbon, and sent written word to the mother. She explained to the children that it was important which color followed which. "Think of God's rainbow and its order," and she would shake her pencil in abrupt little beats in an arch overhead; but they had to think of Spights' store. The quartet, with four dresses in view at one time and in close conjunction, pushing one another, made Miss Eckhart especially apprehensive.

Account was kept in a composition book of each child's assigned color; Miss Eckhart made a little "v" beside the name in token of the mother's agreement and regarded it as a promise. When the dress was reported finished, starched, and ironed, a line was drawn through that name.

In general, mothers were scared of Miss Eckhart then. Miss Lizzie Stark laughed about it, but she was as scared as anybody else. Miss Eckhart assumed that there would be a new dress for every pupil for the recital night, that Miss Perdita Mayo would make it, or if not Miss Perdita, who even with her sister could not make them all, then the pupil's own mother. The dress must be made with the fingers and the edges of bertha and flounce picoted, the sash as well; and—whatever happened—the costume must be saved for recital night. And this was the kind of thing that both Miss Perdita and most mothers understood immediately.

And it could seldom be worn again; certainly not to another recital—by then an "old" dress. A recital dress was fuller and had more trimming than a Sunday dress. It was like a flower girl's dress in a wedding; once little Nina Carmichael's *was* a flower girl's dress, after Etta's wedding, but this was special dispensation. The dress should be organdie, with ruffles on skirt, bertha, and sleeves; it called for a satin or taffeta sash tied in a back bow with long tails, pointed like the tails of arrows, to hang over the stool and, if it could be afforded, to reach the floor.

All through May, Miss Eckhart would ask how far along the dresses had come. Cassie was uneasy, for her mother's way was to speak too late for Miss Perdita's list and plan to run the dress up herself at the last minute; but Cassie had to encourage Miss Eckhart. "She's just evening my hem," she would report, when the material would still be lying folded up with the newspaper-pattern borrowed from Miss Jefferson Moody, in the *armoire*.

As for the program, that was no problem; it existed ready-made without discussion. Far back in the winter, Virgie Rainey would have been allotted a piece that was the most difficult Miss Eckhart could find in the music cabinet. Sometimes it was not as showy a thing as Teensie Loomis always had to have (before she got old and stopped taking), but always it was the hardest piece of all. It would be the test of what Virgie could do, to learn it; an ordeal was set for her each year and each year it was accomplished, with no yielding sign from Virgie that she had struggled. The rest of the program would lead up to this, and did not matter enough to be altered seriously from one year to the next. Just so everybody had a piece to play, and a new dress finished in time, and kept the secrets, there was nothing to do but endure May.

A week ahead of the night, the gold chairs were set in a solid row across the room, to look as if all were gold, and the extra chairs would appear one by one behind them until the room was filled. Miss Eckhart must have carried them in from the dining room first, and then, as she could get hold of them, from elsewhere. She carried them downstairs from Miss Snowdie's freely, of course, and then even from Mr. Voight's, for no matter what Miss Eckhart thought of Mr. Voight, she wouldn't hesitate to go in and take his chairs for the recital.

A second piano had to be rented from the Presbyterian Sunday School (through the Starks), hauled over in time for rehearsing the quartet all together, and of course tuned. There were programs to be printed (through the Morrisons), elaborate enough to include the opus numbers, the first, middle, and last name of each pupil, and flowing across the top in a script which resembled, as if for a purpose, Miss Eckhart's writing in the monthly bills, the full name of Miss Lotte Elisabeth Eckhart. Some little untalented Maloney would give the programs out at the door from a pink fruit plate.

On the day, gladiolas or carnations in princess-baskets were expected to arrive for each child, duly ordered from some Loomis florist-connections in Vicksburg and kept in buckets of water on the MacLains' shady back porch. They would be presented at the proper time—immediately after the bow—by Miss Eckhart. The pupil could hold the basket for the count of three—this had been rehearsed, using a black umbrella—then present it back to Miss Eckhart, who had in mind a crescent moon design on the floor which she would fill in basket by basket on the night. Jinny Love Stark always received a bouquet of Parma violets in a heart of leaves, and had to be allowed to keep it. She said, "Ta-ta." She never did give it up a single year, which hurt the effect.

For the recital was, after all, a ceremony. Better than school's being let out—for that presupposed examinations—or the opening political fireworks—the recital celebrated June. Both dread and delight were to come down on little girls that special night, when only certain sashes and certain flowers could possibly belong, and with only smart, pretty little girls to carry things out.

And Miss Eckhart pushed herself to quite another level of life for it. A blushing sensitivity sprang up in her every year at the proper time like a flower of the season, like the Surprise Lilies that came up with no leaves and overnight in Miss Nell's yard. Miss Eckhart stirred here and there utterly carried away by matters that at other times interested her least—dresses and sashes, prominence and precedence, smiles and bows. It was strange, exciting. She called up the pictures on those little square party invitations, the brown bear in a frill and the black poodle standing on a chair to shave at a mirror . . .

With recital night over, the sensitivity and the drive too would be over and gone. But then all trials would be ended. The limitless part of vacation would have come. Girls and boys could go barefooted alike in the mornings.

The night of the recital was always clear and hot; everyone came. The prospective audience turned out in full oppression.

Miss Eckhart and her pupils were not yet to be visible. It was up to Miss Snowdie MacLain to be at the door, and she was at the door, staunchly, as if she'd been in on things the whole time. She welcomed all female Morgana there in perfect innocence. By eight o'clock the studio was packed.

Miss Katie Rainey would always come early. She trembled with delight, like a performer herself, and she had milked with that hat on. She laughed with pleasure as she grew accustomed to it all, and through the recital she would stay much in evidence, the first to clap when a piece was over, and pleased equally with the music she listened to and the gold chair she sat on. And Old Man Fate Rainey, the buttermilk man, was the only father who came. He remained standing. Miss Perdita Mayo, who had made most of the recital dresses, was always on the front row to see that the bastings had all been pulled out after the dresses got home, and beside her was Miss Hattie Mayo, her quiet sister who helped her.

As the studio filled, Cassie, peeping around the sheet curtain (*they* were all herded in the dining room), bore the dread that her mother might not come at all. She was always late, perhaps because she lived so near. Miss Lizzie Stark, the most important mother there, who was just waiting for Jinny Love to get a little older to play better, would turn around in her chair down front to spot each of the other mothers. Knowing that too, and dressed beautifully in a becoming flowery dress just right for a mother on recital night, Cassie's mother could not walk across the two yards on time to save her life. And Cassie's *Rustle of Spring*, for instance, was very hard, harder than Missie Spights' piece; but it appeared that everything Miss Eckhart planned for, Cassie's mother could let go for nothing.

In the studio decorated like the inside of a candy box, with "material" scalloping the mantel shelf and doilies placed under every movable object, now thus made immovable, with streamers of white ribbons and nosegays of pink and white Maman Cochet roses and the last MacLain sweetpeas dividing and re-dividing the room, it was as hot as fire. No matter that this was the first night of June; no electric fans were to whir around while music played. The metronome, ceremoniously closed, stood on the piano like a vase. There was no piece of music anywhere in sight.

When the first unreasoning hush—there was the usual series—fell over the audience, the room seemed to shake with the agitation of palmetto and feather fans alone, plus the occasional involuntary tick of the metronome within its doors. There was the mixture together of agitation and decoration which could make every little forthcoming child turn pale with a kind of ultimate dizziness. Whoever might look up at the ceiling for surcease would be floundered within a paper design stemming out of the chandelier, as complicated and as unavailing as a cut-out paper snowflake.

Now Miss Eckhart came into the room all changed, with her dark hair pulled low on her brow, and gestured for silence. She was wearing her recital dress which made her look larger and closer-to than she looked at any other times. It was an old dress: Miss Eckhart disregarded her own rules. People would forget that dress between times and then she would come out in it again, the untidy folds not quite spotlessly clean, gathered about her bosom and falling heavy as a coat to the sides; it was a tawny crepe-back satin. There was a bodice of browning lace. It was as rich and hot and deep-looking as a furskin. The unexpected creamy flesh on her upper arms gave her a look of emerging from it.

Miss Eckhart, achieving silence, stood in the shadowy spot directly under the chandelier. Her feet, white-shod, shod by Mr. Sissum for good, rested in the chalk circle previously marked on the floor and now, she believed, perfectly erased. One hand, with its countable little muscles so hard and ready, its stained, blue nails, went to the other hand and they folded quite still, holding nothing, until they lost their force by lying on her breast and made a funny little house with peaks and gables. Standing near the piano but not near enough to help, she presided but not with her whole heart on guard against disaster; while disaster was what remained on the minds of the little girls. Starting with the youngest, she called them out.

So they played, and except Virgie, all played their worst. They shocked themselves. Parnell Moody burst into tears on schedule. But Miss Eckhart never seemed to notice or to care. How forgetful she seemed at exactly the moments she should have been agonized! You expected the whip, almost, for forgetting to repeat before the second ending, or for failing to count ten before you came around the curtain at all; and instead you received a strange smile. It was as though Miss Eckhart, at the last, were grateful to you for *anything*.

When Hilda Ray Bowles' turn came and Miss Eckhart herself was to bend down and move the stool out twelve inches, she did it in a spirit of gentle, uninterrupted abstraction. She might be not moving a stool out for an overgrown girl at all, but performing some gentle ministration to someone else, someone who was not there; perhaps it was Beethoven, who wrote Hilda Ray's piece, and perhaps not.

Cassie played, and her mother—not betraying her, after all—was seated among the rest. At the end, she had creased her program into a little hat, for which Cassie could have fallen at her feet.

But recital night was Virgie's night, whatever else it was. The time Virgie Rainey was most wonderful in her life, to Cassie, was when she came out—her turn was just before the quartet—wearing a Christmas-red satin band in her hair with rosettes over the ears, held on by a new elastic across the back; she had a red sash drawn around under the arms of a starched white swiss dress. She was thirteen. She played the *Fantasia on Beethoven's Ruins of Athens*, and when she finished and got up and made her bow, the red of the sash was all over the front of her waist, she was wet and stained as if she had been stabbed in the heart, and a delirious and enviable sweat ran down from her forehead and cheeks and she licked it in with her tongue.

Cassie, who had slipped around to the front, was spellbound still when Miss Katie Rainey put a hand on her sash and to her pure terror said, "Oh, but I wish Virgie had a sister!"

Then there was only the quartet, and with the last chord—sudden disintegration itself—laughter and teasing broke loose. All the children got a kiss or a token spank in congratulation and then ran free. Ladies waved and beckoned with their fans, conversation opened up. Flowers were lifted high, shown off, thrown, given, and pulled to giddy pieces by fingers freed for the summer. The MacLain twins, now crashing restraint, rushed downstairs in identical cowboy suits, pointing and even firing cap pistols. Two fans were set rumbling and walking on the floor, from which the dropped programs flew up like a flock of birds, while the decorations whipped and played all over. Neither piano was gone near except for punching out "Sally in Her Shimmie Tail." Little Jinny Stark, after all, fell, skinned her knee and bled profusely. It was like any other party.

"Punch and *kuchen*!" Miss Eckhart came announcing.

The big MacLain dining room at the back, where Miss Snowdie only wintered her flowers for the most part, was thrown open tonight. Punch was being served from the MacLain punch bowl, one of Miss Snowdie's gifts from her husband—served impromptu by Miss Billy Texas Spights who sprang for the ladle, and they drank it out of the twenty-four MacLain cups and the twelve Loomis. The little cakes that Miss Eckhart tirelessly brought out were sweet, light, and warm, their tops sprinkled with colored "shot" that came (or so they'd thought) only out of glass pistols sold on trains. When the plate was empty you saw it was decorated with slipping flower garlands and rowdy babies, sprinkled with gold and now with golden crumbs.

Miss Eckhart's cheeks flooded with color as the guests accepted her sugar cookies and came back to lift their punch cups, with the drowned fruit in the bottom, again to her quick, brimming ladle. ("*I'll* give you more punch!" she cried, when Miss Billy Texas started counting.) Her hair was as low on her forehead as Circe's, on the fourth grade wall feeding her swine. She smiled, not on any particular one but on everyone, everywhere she looked and everywhere she went—for the party had spread out—from studio to dining room and back and out on the porch, where she called, "What is this out here? You little girls come back inside and stay till you eat my *kuchen* all up! The last crumb!" It made them laugh to hear her, when strictness was only a pretense.

Miss Lizzie Stark, although she had occasionally referred to Miss Eckhart as "Miss Do-daddle," did not spare herself from wearing her most elaborate hat, one resembling a large wreath or a wedding cake, and it was constantly in the vision, turned this way and that like a floating balloon at a fair over the heads of the crowd. The canary sang; his cover was lifted off. Gradually the Maman Cochets bowed their little green stems over the vase's edge.

At the close of the evening, saying goodnight, people congratulated Miss Eckhart and her mother. Old Mrs. Eckhart had sat near the door during the whole evening—had sat by Miss Snowdie at the door, when she welcomed them in. She wore a dark dress too, but it was sprigged. In the path of the talking and laughing mothers and the now wild children she sat blinking her eyes, but amenable, like a baby when he is wheeled out into the sunlight. While Miss Snowdie watched her kindly, she would hold her mouth in one evening-long smile; she was letting herself be looked at and herself, at the end, be thanked.

Miss Eckhart, breasting the pushing, departing children, moving among the swinging princess-baskets and the dropped fans of the suddenly weakened mothers, would be heard calling, "Virgie Rainey? Virgie Rainey?" Then she would look down ceremoniously at the sleepiest and smallest child, who had only played "Playful Kittens" that night. All her pupils on that evening partook of the grace of Virgie Rainey. Miss Eckhart would catch them running out the door, speaking German to them and holding them to her. In the still night air her dress felt damp and spotted, as though she had run a long way.

Cassie listened, but *Für Elise* was not repeated. She took up her ukulele from the foot of the bed. She screwed it into tune and played it, slurring the chords expertly and fanning with her fingers. She strolled around her scarf hanging up to dry, playing a chorus or two, and then wandered back to the window.

There she saw Loch go hanging on all fours like a monkey down the hackberry limb. Far on the other side of the tree he hung by his hands, perfectly still, diver-like—not going into any of his tricks. That was the way he stayed in bed taking quinine.

He was concerned not with tricks but with watching something inside the vacant house. Loch could see in. Cassie opened her mouth to cry out, but the cry wouldn't come.

Except for once, she had not answered Loch all day when he called her, and now the sight of his spread-eagled back in the white night drawers seemed as far from her as the morning star. It was gone from her, any way to shield his innocence, when his innocence was out there shining at her, cavorting—for Loch calmly reversed himself and hung by his knees; plunged upside down, he looked in at the old studio window, with his pompadour cap falling to earth and his hair spiking out all over his young boy's head.

Once Loch wandered over their house in a skirt, beating on a christening cup with a pencil. "Mama, do you think I can ever play music too?" "Why, of course, dear heart. You're *my* child. Just you bide your time." (He was her favorite.) And he never could—bide or play. How Cassie had adored him! He didn't know one tune from another. "Is this *Jesus Loves Me*?" he'd ask, interrupting his own noise. She looked out at him now as stricken as if she saw him hurt, from long ago, and silently performing tricks to tell her. She stood there at her window. Softly she was playing and singing, "By the light, light, light, light, light of the silvery moon," her favorite song.

She could never go for herself, never creep out on the shimmering bridge of the tree, or reach the dark magnet there that drew you inside, kept drawing you in. She could not see herself do an unknown thing. She was not Loch, she was not Virgie Rainey; she was not her mother. She was Cassie in her room, seeing the knowledge and torment beyond her reach, standing at her window singing—in a voice soft, rather full today, and halfway thinking it was pretty.

III.

After a moment of blackness, upside down, Loch opened his eyes. Nothing had happened. The house he watched was all silence but for the progressing tick-tock that was different from a clock's. There were outer sounds. His sister was practicing on her ukulele again so she could sing to the boys. He heard from up the street the water-like sounds of the ladies' party, and off through the trees where the big boys were playing, sounds of the ball being knocked out—gay and removed as birdsong. But the tick-tock was sharper and clearer than all he could hear just now in the world, and at moments seemed to ring close, the way his own heartbeat rang against the bed he came out of.

His mother, had it been she in the vacant house, would have stopped those two Negroes straggling home with their unsold peas and made them come in off the street and do all that for her, and finish up in no time. But the sailor's mother was doing her work alone. She wanted things to suit herself, nobody else would have been able to please her; and she was taking her own sweet time. She was building a bonfire of her own in the piano and would set off the dynamite when she was ready and not before.

Loch knew from her actions that the contrivance down in the wires—the piano front had been taken away—was a kind of nest. She was building it like a thieving bird, weaving in every little scrap that she could find around her. He saw in two places the mustached face of Mr. Drewsie Carmichael, his father's candidate for mayor—she found the circulars in the door. The litter on his bed, the Octagon Soap coupons, would have pleased her at that moment, and he would have turned them over to her.

Then Loch almost gave a yell; pride filled him, like a second yell, that he did not. Here down the street came Old Man Moody, the marshal, and Mr. Fatty Bowles with him. They had taken the day off to go fishing in Moon Lake and came carrying their old fishing canes but no fish. Their pants and shoes were heavy with mud. They were cronies of old Mr. Holifield and often came to wake him up, this time of day, and hound him off to the gin.

Loch skinned the cat over the limb and waited head down as they came tramping, sure enough, across the yard. In his special vision he saw that they could easily be lying on their backs in the blue sky and waving their legs pleasantly around, having nothing to do with law and order.

Old Man Moody and Mr. Fatty Bowles divided at the pecan stump, telling a joke, joined, said "Bread and butter," and then clogged up the steps. The curtain at the front window flapped signaling in their faces. They looked at each other anew. Their bodies and their faces grew smooth as fishes. They floated around the porch and flattened like fishes to nose at the window. There were round muddy spots on the seats of their pants; they squatted.

Well, there it is, thought Loch—the houseful. Two upstairs, one downstairs, and the two on the porch. And on the piano sat the ticking machine. . . . Directly below Loch a spotted thrush walked noisily in the weeds, pointing her beak ahead of her straight as a gun, just as busy in the world as people.

He held his own right hand ever so still as the old woman, unsteady as the Christmas angel in Mrs. McGillicuddy's fourth-grade pageant, came forward with a lighted candle in her hand. It was a kitchen tallow candle; she must have taken it out of Mr. Holifield's boxful against all the times the lights went out in Morgana. She came so slowly and held the candle so high that he could have popped it with a nigger-shooter from where he was. Her hair, he saw, was cropped and white and lighted up all around. From the swaying, farthest length of a branch that would hold his weight, he could see how bright her big eyes were under their black circling brows, and how seldom they blinked. They were owl eyes.

She bent over, painfully, he felt, and laid the candle in the paper nest she had built in the piano. He too drew his breath in, protecting the flame, and as she pulled her aching hand back he pulled his. The newspaper caught, it was ablaze, and the old woman threw in the candle. Hands to thighs, she raised up, her work done.

Flames arrowed out so noiselessly. They ran down the streamers of paper, as double-quick as freshets from a loud gully-washer of rain. The room was criss-crossed with quick, dying yellow fire, there were pinwheels falling and fading from the ceiling. And up above, on the other side of the ceiling, they, the first two, were as still as mice.

The law still squatted. Mr. Fatty's and Old Man Moody's necks stretched sideways, the fat and the thin. Loch could have dropped a caterpillar down onto either of their heads, which rubbed together like mother's and child's.

"So help me. She *done* it," Mr. Fatty Bowles said in a natural voice. He lifted his arm, that had been hugging Old Man Moody's shoulders, and transferred to his own back pocket a slap that would have cracked Old Man Moody's bones. "Bless her heart! She done it before our eyes. What would you have bet?"

"Not a thing," said Old Man Moody. "Watch. If it catches them old dried-out squares of matting, Booney Holifield's going to feel a little warm ere long."

"Booney! Why, I done forgot him!"

Old Man Moody laughed explosively with shut lips.

"Wouldn't you say it's done caught now," said Mr. Fatty, pointing into the room with his old fishing knife.

"The house is on fire!" Loch cried at the top of his voice. He was riding his limb up and down and shaking the leaves.

Old Man Moody and Mr. Fatty might have heard, for, a little as if they were insulted, they raised up, moved their fishing poles along, and deliberately chose the dining room window instead of the parlor window to get to work on.

They lifted the screen out, and Mr. Fatty accidentally stepped through it. They inched the sash up with a sound that made them draw high their muck-coated heels. They could go in now: they opened their mouths and guffawed silently. They were so used to showing off, they almost called up Morgana then and there.

Mr. Fatty Bowles started to squeeze himself over the sill into the room, but Old Man Moody was ready for that, pulled him back by the suspenders, and went first. He leap-frogged it. Inside, they both let go a holler.

"Look out! You're caught in the act!"

In the parlor, the old lady backed herself into the blind corner.

Old Man Moody and Mr. Fatty made a preliminary run around the dining room table to warm up, and then charged the parlor. They trod down the barrier of sparky matting and stomped in. They boxed at the smoke, hit each other, and ran to put up the window. Then Loch heard their well-known coughs and the creep and crack of fire inside the room. The smoke mostly stayed inside, contained and still.

Loch skinned the cat again. Here came somebody else. It was a fine day! Presently he thought he knew the golden Panama hat, and the elastic spareness of the man under it. He used to live in that vacant house and had at that time promised to bring Loch a talking bird, one that could say "Rabbits!" He had left and never returned. After all the years, Loch still wanted a bird like that. It was to his taste today.

"Nobody lives there now!" Loch called out of the leaves in an appropriate voice, for Mr. Voight turned in just like home at the vacant house. "If you go in, you'll blow up."

There was no talking bird on his shoulder yet. It was a long time ago that Mr. Voight had promised it. (And how often, Loch thought now with great surprise, he had remembered and cherished the promise!)

Mr. Voight shook his head rapidly as though a far-away voice from the leaves bothered him only for a moment. He ran up the steps with a sound like a green stick along a fence. He, though, instead of running into the flapping barrier over the door, drifted around the porch to the side and leisurely took a look through the window. Everything made his shout alarming.

"Will you please tell me why you're trespassing here?"

"So help me!" said Mr. Fatty Bowles, who was looking right at him, holding a burning hat.

Old Man Moody only said, "*Good* evening. Now I don't speak to you."

"Answer me! Trespassing, are you?"

"Whoa. Your house is afire."

"If my house is afire, then where's my folks gone?"

"Oh, *'tain't* your house no more, I forgot. It's Miss Francine Murphy's house. You're late, Captain."

"What antics are these? Get out of my house. Put that fire out behind you. Tell me where they went. Never mind, I know where they went. All right, burn it down, who's to stop you?"

He slapped his hands on the boarding of the house, fanfare like, and must have glared at them between, at the window. He had inserted himself between Loch and what happened, and to tell the truth he made one too many.

Old Man Moody and Mr. Fatty, exchanging murderous looks, ran hopping about the parlor, clapping their hats at the skittering flames, working in a team mad at itself, the way two people try to head off chickens in a yard. They jumped up and knocked at the same flame. They kicked and rubbed under their feet a spark they found by themselves, sometimes imaginary. Maybe because they'd let the fire almost go out, or because Mr. Voight had come to criticize, they pretended this fire was bigger than it had ever been. They bit their underlips tightly as old people do in carrying out acts of rudeness. They didn't speak.

Mr. Voight shook all over. He was laughing, Loch discovered. Now he watched the room like a show. "That's it! That's it!" he said.

Old Man Moody and Mr. Bowles together beat out the fire in the piano, fighting over it hard, banging and twanging the strings. Old Man Moody, no matter how his fun had been spoiled, enjoyed jumping up and down on the fierce-burning magnolia leaves. So they put the fire out, every spark, even the matting, which twinkled all over time and again before it went out for good. When a little tongue of flame started up for the last time, they quenched it together; and with a whistle and one more stamp each, they dared it, and it stayed out.

"That's it, boys," said Mr. Voight.

Then the old woman came out of the blind corner. "Now who's this?" cried Mr. Voight. In the center of the room she stopped. Without the law to stand over her, she might have clasped her empty hands and turned herself this way and that. But she did not; she was more desperate still. Loch hollered out again, riding the tree, his branch in both fists.

"Why don't you step on in, Captain?" called Mr. Fatty Bowles, and he beckoned the old lady to him.

"Down to business here. Now I'd appreciate knowing why you done this, lady," Old Man Moody said, rubbing his eyes and rimming them with black. "Putting folks to all this trouble. Now what you got against us?"

"Cat's got her tongue," said Mr. Fatty.

"I'm an old man. But you're an old woman. *I* don't know why you done it. Unless of course it was for pure lack of good sense."

"Where you come from?" asked Mr. Fatty in his little tenor voice.

"You clowns."

Mr. Voight, who said that, now went lightly as a dragonfly around the porch and entered the house by the front door: it was not locked. He might have been waiting until all the beating about had been done by others—clowns—or perhaps he thought he was so valuable that he could burn up in too big a hurry.

Loch saw him step, with rather a flare, through the beads at the hall door and come into the parlor. He gazed serenely about the walls, pausing for a moment first, as though something had happened to them not that very hour but a long time ago. He was there and not there, for he alone was not at his wit's end. He went picking his feet carefully among the frills and flakes of burned paper, and wrinkled up his sharp nose; not from the smell, it seemed, but from wider, dissolving things. Now he stood at the window. His eyes rolled. Would he foam at the mouth? He did once. If he did not, Loch might not be sure about him; he remembered Mr. Voight best as foaming.

"Do you place her, Captain?" asked Old Man Moody in a cautious voice. "Who's this here firebug? You been places."

Mr. Voight was strolling about the room, and taking the poker he poked among the ashes. He picked up a seashell. The old lady advanced on him and he put it back, and as he came up he took off his hat. It looked more than polite. There close to the old lady's face he cocked his head, but she looked through him, a long way through Mr. Voight. She could have been a lady on an opposite cliff, far away, out of eye range and earshot, but about to fall.

The tick-tock was very loud then. Just as Mr. Fatty had forgotten Mr. Booney Holifield, Loch had forgotten the dynamite. Now he could go back to expecting a blast. The fire had had a hard time, but fire could manage to connect itself with an everlasting little mechanism that could pound like that, right along, right in the room.

("Do you hear something, Mr. Moody?" Loch could cry out right now. "Mr. Voight, listen."—"All right, say—do you want your bird this minute?" might be the reply. "We'll call everything off.")

"Man, what's that?" asked Mr. Fatty Bowles, and "Fatty boy, do you hear something ugly?" Old Man Moody asked at the same instant. At last they cocked their ears at the ticking that had been there in the room with them all this time. They looked at each other and then with hunched shoulders paraded around looking for the source of it.

"It's a rattlesnake! No, it ain't! But it's close," said Mr. Fatty.

They looked high and low all over the room but they couldn't see it right in front of their eyes and up just a little, on top of the piano. That was honestly not a fair place, not where most people would put a thing. They looked at each other harder and hurried faster, but all they did was run on each other's heels and tip the chairs over. One of the chair legs snapped like a chicken bone.

Mr. Voight only got in their way, since he did not move an inch. He was still standing before the eyes of the sailor's mother, looking at her with lips puckered. It could be indeed that he knew her from his travels. He looked tired from these same travels now.

At last Old Man Moody, the smarter one of those two, spied what they were looking for, the obelisk with its little moving part and its door open. Once seen, that thing was so surely *it* that he merely pointed it out to Mr. Fatty. Mr. Fatty tiptoed over and picked the obelisk up and set it down again quickly. So Old Man Moody stumped over and picked it up and held it up on the diagonal, posing, like a fisherman holding a funny-looking fish to have come out of Moon Lake.

The old woman lifted her head and walked around Mr. Voight to Old Man Moody. She reached up and took the ticking thing right out of his hand, and he turned it loose agreeably; Old Man Moody seemed not taken by surprise by women.

The old woman held her possession to her, drawn to her big gray breast. Her eyesight returned from far to close by. Then she stood looking at the three people fixedly, as if she showed them her insides, her live heart.

And then a little whir of her own voice: "See . . . See, Mr. MacLain."

Nothing blew up, but Mr. Voight (but she called him MacLain) groaned.

"No, boys. I never saw her in my life," he said.

He walked stiffly out of the room. He walked out of the house and cater-cornered across the yard toward the MacLain

Road. As he reached the road itself, he put his hat on, and then he did not look as shabby, or as poor.

Loch clasped a leafy armful of the tree and sank his head in the green cool.

"Let *me* see your play-pretty," Mr. Fatty Bowles was saying with his baby-smile. He took the obelisk away from the old woman, and with a sudden change on his face threw it with all his might out the open window. It came straight toward Loch, and fell into the weeds below him. And still it ticked.

"You could have been a little too quick there, Fatty boy," said Old Man Moody. "Flinging evidence."

"You ought to think about us. Listen and you'll hear it blow up. I'd rather have it blow up your wife's chickens."

"Well, I wouldn't."

And while they talked, the poor old woman tried it again. She was down on her knees cradling the lump of candle and the next moment had it lighted. She rose up, agitated now, and went running about the room, holding the candle above her, evading the men each time they tried to head her off.

This time, the fire caught her own hair. The little short white frill turned to flame.

Old Man Moody was so quick that he caught her. He came up with a big old rag from somewhere, and ran after the old woman with it. They both ran extraordinarily fast. He had to make a jump. He brought the cloth down over her head from behind, grimacing, as if all people on earth had to do acts of shame, some time. He hit her covered-up head about with the flat of his hand.

Old Man Moody and Mr. Bowles brought the old woman between them out on the porch of the vacant house. She was quiet now, with the scorched black cloth covering her head; she herself held it on with both hands.

"Know what I'm going to have to do with you?" Old Man Moody was saying gently and conversationally, but she only stood there, all covered in wrinkled cloth with her little hands up, clawed, the way a locust shell would be found clinging to that empty door in August.

"It don't signify nothing what your name is now, or what you intended, old woman," Mr. Bowles told her as he got the fishing canes. "We know where you belong at, and that's Jackson."

"Come on ladylike. I'm sure you know how," Old Man Moody said.

She came along but she did not answer either man anything.

"Maybe she aimed mischief at King MacLain after all," said Mr. Fatty Bowles. "She's a she, ain't she?"

"That'll be enough out of you for the rest of the day," said Old Man Moody.

Among the leaves, Loch watched them come down the walk and head towards town. They went slowly, for the old woman took short, hesitant steps. Where would they take her now? Not later, to Jackson, but now? After they passed, he let go his hands and jumped out of the tree. It made a good noise when he hit ground. He turned a forward and a backward somersault and started walking on his hands around the tree trunk. He made noises like a goat, and a bobwhite, like the silly Moody chickens, and like a lion.

On his hands he circled the tree and the obelisk waited in the weeds, upright. He stood up and looked at it. Its ticker was outside it.

He felt charmed like a bird, for the ticking stick went like a tail, a tongue, a wand. He picked the box up in his hands.

"Now go on. Blow up."

When he examined it, he saw the beating stick to be a pendulum that instead of hanging down stuck upwards. He touched it and stopped it with his finger. He felt its pressure, and the weight of the obelisk, which seemed about two pounds. He released the stick, and it went on beating.

Then he turned a little key in the side of the box, and that controlled it. The stick stopped and he poked it into place within the box, and shut the door of the thing.

It might not be dynamite: especially since Mr. Fatty thought it was.

What was it?

He opened his shirt and buttoned it in. He thought he might take it up to his room. It was this; not a bird that knew how to talk.

The sand pile was before him now. He planed away the hot

top layer and sat down. He held still for a while, while nothing was ticking. Nothing but the crickets. Nothing but the train going through, ticking its two cars over the Big Black bridge.

IV.

Cassie moved to the front window, where she could see Old Man Moody and Mr. Fatty Bowles carrying off the old woman. The old woman was half sick or dazed. She held on her head some nameless kitchen rag; she had no purse. In a gray housedress prophetic of an institution she was making her way along, about to be touched, prodded, any minute, but not worrying about it. She wore shoes without stockings—and she had such white, white ankles. When she saw the ankles, Cassie flung herself in full view at the window and gave a cry.

No head lifted. Cassie rushed out of her room, down the stairs and out the front door.

To Loch's amazement his sister Cassie came running barefooted down the front walk in her petticoat and in full awareness turned toward town, crying, "You can't take her! Miss Eckhart!"

She was too late for anybody to hear her, of course, but he creaked up out of the sand pile and ran out after her as if they had heard. He caught up with her and pulled at her petticoat. She turned, with her head still swimming high in the air, and cried softly, "Oh, Mother!"

They looked at each other.

"Crazy."

"Crazy yourself."

"Back yonder," said Loch presently, "I can show you how ripe the figs are." They withdrew as far as the tree. But it was only in time to see the sailor and Virgie Rainey run out, trying to escape by the back way. Virgie and the sailor saw them. Back into the house they ran, and then, in utter recklessness, out the front, the sailor first. The Morrisons had nowhere to go.

Old Man Moody's party was only now progressing again, for the old woman had fallen down and they had to hold her on her feet. Further along, the ladies' Rook party was coming out of Miss Nell's with a pouring sound. The sailor faced both these ranks.

The marshal tagged him but he ran straight on into the wall of ladies, most of whom cried "Why, Kewpie Moffitt!"—an ancient nickname he had outgrown. He whirled about-face and ran the other way, and since he was carrying his blouse and was naked from the waist up, his collar stood out behind him like the lowest-hung wings. At the Carmichael corner, he tried east and took west, and ran into the shadows of the short-cut to the river, where he would just about meet with Mr. King MacLain, if he was not too late.

"Look at that!" Miss Billy Texas Spights called clearly. "I see you, Virgie Rainey!"

"Mother!" Cassie called, just as clearly. She and Loch found themselves out in front again.

The front door of the empty house fell to with a frail sound behind Virgie Rainey. A haze of the old smoke lifted unhurryingly over her, brushed and hid her for a moment like a gauzy cloud. She was coming right out, though, in a homemade dress of apricot voile, carrying a mesh bag on a chain. She ran down the steps and walked clicking her heels out to the sidewalk—always Virgie clicked her heels as if nothing had happened in the past or behind her, as if she were free, whatever else she might be. The ladies hushed, holding onto their prizes and folded parasols. Virgie faced them as she turned toward town.

It was the hour, of course, for her to go to work. Once past the next corner, she could drink a Coca-Cola and eat a box of cakes at Loomis's drug store, as she did every evening for her supper; then she could vanish inside the Bijou.

She passed Cassie and Loch, cutting them, and kept going and caught up, as she had to, with the marshal, Fatty Bowles, and the old woman.

"You're running the wrong way!" Miss Billy Texas Spights called loudly. "Better run after that sailor boy!"

"Isn't he visiting the Flewellyns out in the country?" Miss Perdita Mayo was pleading to everybody. "What ever became of his mother? I'd forgotten all about him!"

Pinning Loch tightly by the arms in front of her, Cassie could only think: we were spies too. And nobody else was surprised at anything—it was only we two. People saw things like this as they saw Mr. MacLain come and go. They only hoped to place them, in their hour or their street or the name of their mothers' people. Then Morgana could hold them, and at last they were this and they were that. And when ruin was predicted all along, even if people had forgotten it was on the way, even if they mightn't have missed it if it hadn't appeared, still they were never surprised when it came.

"She'll stop for Miss Eckhart," breathed Cassie.

Virgie went by. There was a meeting of glances between the teacher and her old pupil, that Cassie knew. She could not be sure that Miss Eckhart's eyes closed once in recall—they had looked so wide-open at everything alike. The meeting amounted only to Virgie Rainey's passing by, in plain fact. She clicked by Miss Eckhart and she clicked straight through the middle of the Rook party, without a word or the pause of a moment.

Old Man Moody and Fatty Bowles, dirty, their faces shining like the fish they didn't catch, took advantage of the path Virgie cut through the ladies and walked Miss Eckhart, unprotesting, on. Then the ladies brought their ranks safely to, and Miss Billy Texas, suddenly beside herself, cried once more, "He went the *other* way, Virgie!"

"That's enough, Billy Texas," said Miss Lizzie Stark. "As if her mother didn't have enough on her, just burying her son."

The noise of tin pans being beaten came from the distance, then little children's and Negro nurses' cries, "Crazy! Crazy!"

Cassie turned on Loch, pulled him to her and shook him by the shoulders. He was wet as a dishrag. A row of those big salt-and-pepper-colored mosquitoes perched all along his forehead. "What were you doing out of your bed, anyway?" she asked in a matter-of-fact, scolding voice. Loch gave her a long, gratified look. "What have you got there inside your nighties, crazy?"

"None of your business."

"Give it to me."

"It's mine."

"It is not. Let go."

"You make me."

"All right, I know what it is."

"What is it? You do not."

"You can't have that."

"Get away from me."

"I'll tell Mama and Papa.—You hit me! You hit a girl where she's tender."

"Well, you know you can't have it."

"All right then—did you see Mr. MacLain? He's been gone since you were born."

"Why, sure," said Loch. "I saw Mr. MacLain."

"Oh, Loch, why don't you beat off those mosquitoes!" She wept. "Mother!" Even Loch flew from her, at once.

"Well, here I am," said her mother.

"Oh!" After a moment she raised her head to say, "And Mr. King MacLain was here, and now he's gone."

"Well. You've seen him before," said her mother after a moment, breaking from her. "That's no excuse for coming outdoors in your petticoat to cry."

"You knew it would be this way, you were with them!"

There was no answer then either, and Cassie trudged through the yard. Loch stood near the sandpile. His lips clamped down, he held his bulging nightie and regarded it. She ran him back under the tree and into the house by the back door.

"What orphan-lookin' children is these here?" said Louella. "Where yawl orphan come from? Yawl don't live here, yawl live at County Orphan. Gawn back."

Cassie pushed Loch through the kitchen and then pulled him to a stop in the back hall. It was their father coming home.

"What's going on here! The house is on fire, the MacLain house! I see smoke!"

They could see him coming up the front walk, waving the rolled-up *Bugle* he brought home every night.

"Holifield! Holifield!"

Mr. Holifield must have come to the window, for they heard, "Did I hear my name called?" and they sighed with foreboding.

"It's gone out, Wilbur," said their mother at the door.

"That house has been on fire *and* gone out, sir." Their

father was speaking loudly as he did from the platform at election time. "You can read about it in tomorrow's *Bugle*."

"Come in, Wilbur."

They could see her finger tracing a little pattern on the screen door as she stood there in her party dress. "Cassie says King MacLain was here and gone. That's as interesting as twenty fires."

Cassie shivered.

"Maybe this will bestir Francine Murphy to take a step. *There's* a public guardian for you: Booney Holifield."

Cassie was glad her father kept on. If there was anything that unsettled him it was for people not to be on the inside what their outward semblances led you to suppose. "MacLain came to the wrong place this time. It might have caught *our* house: Booney Holifield!"

Their mother laughed. "That old monkey," she said. As far as she was concerned, the old man next door had just come alive, redeemed himself a little from being a Holifield.

The six-o'clock summer light shone just as usual on their father and mother meeting at the door.

"Come on."

Cassie and Loch running up the back stairs heard the sigh of the door and the old, muffled laugh that came between their parents at this moment. No matter what had happened, or had started to happen, around them, they could come in the house and laugh about the old thing. Theirs was a laugh that hinted of some small but interesting object, a thing even their deliberate father could find—something that might be seizable and holdable as well as findable, as ridiculous and forbidden to children, as alive, as a stray kitten or a rabbit.

The children kept on going up the steep dark backstairs, so close on each other they prodded and nudged each other, both punishing and petting.

"Get back in bed like you were never out," Cassie advised. "Pull the beggarlice off you."

"But I think Mother saw me," he said over his shoulder, going.

Cassie didn't answer.

She shivered and walked into her room. There was the scarf. It was an old friend, part enemy. She brought it to her face, touched her lips to it, breathed its smoky dye-smell, and passed it up her cheeks and over her eyes. She pressed it against her forehead. She might have lost it, might have run out with it . . . for she had visions of poor Miss Eckhart wearing it away over her head; of Virgie waving it, brazenly, in the air of the street; of too-knowing Jinny Love Stark asking, "Couldn't you keep it?"

"Listen and I'll tell you what Miss Nell served at the party," Loch's mother said softly, with little waits in her voice. She was just a glimmer at the foot of his bed.

"Ma'am."

"An orange scooped out and filled with orange juice, with the top put back on and decorated with icing leaves, a straw stuck in. A slice of pineapple with a heap of candied sweet potatoes on it, and a little handle of pastry. A cup made out of toast, filled with creamed chicken, fairly warm. A sweet peach pickle with flower petals around it of different-colored cream cheese. A swan made of a cream puff. He had whipped cream feathers, a pastry neck, green icing eyes. A pastry biscuit the size of a marble with a little date filling." She sighed abruptly.

"Were you hungry, Mama?" he said.

It was not really to him that his mother would be talking, but it was he who tenderly let her, as they watched and listened to the swallows just at dark. It was always at this hour that she spoke in this voice—not to him or to Cassie or Louella or to his father, or to the evening, but to the wall, more nearly. She bent seriously over him and kissed him hard, and swayed out of the room.

There was singing in the street. He saw Cassie, a lesser but similar gleam, go past his door. The hay wagon was coming up the street to get her. He heard the girls and boys hail her, and her greeting the same as theirs, as if nothing had happened up until now, heard them pull her up. Ran MacLain from MacLain Courthouse, or was it his brother Eugene, always called to Mrs. Morrison, teasing, "Come on! You come with us!" Did they really want to take her? He heard the wagon creak away. They were singing and playing on their ukuleles, some song of which he couldn't be sure.

Presently Loch lifted up and gazed through the same old leaves, dark once more, and saw the vacant house looking the same as it ever did. A cloud lighted anew, low in the deep sky, a single long wing. The mystery he had felt like a golden and aimless bird had waited until now to fly over. Until now, when all else had been driven out. His body shook. Perhaps the fever would go now, and the chill come.

But Louella brought him his supper, and waited while he ate it, sitting quietly. She had made him chicken broth that sparkled like diamonds in the evening light, and then there would be the junket he hated, turning to water under his tongue.

"Louella, I don't want junket tonight. Louella, listen. Do you hear a thing ticking?"

"Hear it plain."

She took his tray and sat down again, and he lay on his back, looking upward. High in the sky the quarter moon was bright. "Reckon it's going to blow up in the night? You can see it. Look on the washstand." All by itself, of its own accord, it might let fly its little door and start up. He thought he heard it now. Or was it his father's watch in the next room, already laid on the dresser for the night?

"I 'spec' it will, Loch, if you wants it to," she said readily, and sat on in the dark. She added, "Blow up? If it do, I'll wrang your neck. Next time you scoot down that tree and come back draggin' sompm. Listen that big bullfrog in the swamp, you want to listen to sompm might blow up."

He listened, lying stretched and pointed in the four directions. His heart pumping the secret anticipation that parted his lips, he fell into space and floated. Even floating, he felt the pressure of his frown and heard his growling voice and the gnashing of his teeth. He dreamed close to the surface, and his dreams were filled with a color and a fury that the daytime that summer never held.

Later, in her moonlit bed, Cassie lay thinking. Her hair and the inner side of her arms still smelled of hay; she tasted the sweet summer dryness in her mouth. In the distances of her mind the wagon still rocked, rocking its young girls' burden, the teasing anxiety, the singing, the moon and stars and the moving roof of leaves, Moon Lake brimming and the boat on it, the smiling drowse of boys, and the way she herself had let nobody touch even her hand. And she thought back to the sailor beginning to run down the street, as strange a sight with his clothes partly missing as a mer-man from the lake, and around again to Miss Eckhart and Virgie coming together on the deadquiet sidewalk. What she was certain of was the distance those two had gone, as if all along they had been making a trip (which the sailor was only starting). It had changed them. They were deliberately terrible. They looked at each other and neither wished to speak. They did not even horrify each other. No one could touch them now, either.

Danke schoen. . . . That much was out in the open. Gratitude—like rescue—was simply no more. It was not only past; it was outworn and cast away. Both Miss Eckhart and Virgie Rainey were human beings terribly at large, roaming on the face of the earth. And there were others of them—human beings, roaming, like lost beasts.

Into her head flowed the whole of the poem she had found in that book. It ran perfectly through her head, vanishing as it went, one line yielding to the next, like a torch race. All of it passed through her head, through her body. She slept, but sat up in bed once and said aloud, "*'Because a fire was in my head.'*" Then she fell back unresisting. She did not see except in dreams that a face looked in; that it was the grave, unappeased, and radiant face, once more and always, the face that was in the poem.

3.
Sir Rabbit

He looked around first one side of the tree and then the other. And not a word!

"Oh-oh. I know you, Mr. King MacLain!" Mattie Will cried, but the impudence—which still seemed marvelous to her since she'd never laid eyes on him close or thought of opening her mouth to him—all the impudence was carried off on the batting spring wind. "I know the way you do." When it came down to it, scared or not, she wanted to show him she'd heard all about King MacLain and his way. And scared or not, the air made her lightheaded.

If it was Mr. King, he was, suddenly, looking around both sides of the tree at once—two eyes here and two eyes there, two little Adam's apples, and all those little brown hands. She shut her eyes, then her mouth. She planted her hoe in front of her toes and stood her ground by the bait can, too old—fifteen—to call out now that something was happening, but she took back what she'd said.

Then as she peeped, it was two MacLains that came out from behind the hickory nut tree. Mr. MacLain's twins, his sons of course. Who would have believed they'd grown up?—or almost; for they were scared. They must be as old as herself, thought Mattie Will. People aren't prepared for twins having to grow up like ordinary people but see them always miniature and young somewhere. And here they were coming—the very spit of Mr. King their father.

Mattie Will waited on them. She yawned—strangely, for she felt at that moment as though somewhere a little boat was going out on a lake, never to come back—to see two little meanies coming now that she'd never dreamed of, instead of the one that would have terrified her for the rest of her days.

Those twins were town boys. They had their own pop stand by the post office stile on Saturdays in summer. Out here in the country they had undone their knee buckles and came jingling. Their fair bangs lifted and fell in the soft downy light under the dark tree, with its flowers so few you could still count them, it was so early in spring. They trotted down and up through the little gully like a pony pair that could keep time to music in the Ringling Brothers', touching shoulders until the last.

They made a tinkling circle around her. They didn't give her a chance to begin her own commotion, only lifted away her hoe that she stretched out and leaned it on the big vines. They didn't have one smile between them; instead, little matching frowns were furring their foreheads, so that she wanted to press them out with the flat of her finger.

One of the twins took hold of her by the apron sash and the other one ran under and she was down. One of them pinned her arms and the other one jumped her bare, naked feet. Biting their lips, they sat on her. One small hand, smelling of a recent lightning-bug (so early in the year?), blindfolded her eyes. The strong fresh smell of the place—which she had found first—came up and they rolled over on the turned-up mold, where the old foolish worms were coming out in their blindness.

At moments the sun would take hold of their arms with a bold dart of light, or rest on their wetted, shaken hair, or splash over their pretty clothes like the torn petals of a sunflower. She felt the soft and babylike heads, and the nuzzle of little cool noses. Whose nose was whose? She might have felt more anger than confusion, except that to keep twins straight had fallen her lot. And it seemed to her that from now on, having a visit go the visitor's way would come before giving trouble. She who had kicked Old Man Flewellyn out of the dewberry patch, an old smiling man! She had set her teeth in a small pointed ear that had the fuzz of a peach, and did not bite. Then she rolled her head and dared the other twin, with her teeth at his ear, since they were all in this together, all in here equally now, where it had been quiet as moonrise to her, and now while one black crow after another beat his wings across a turned-over field no distance at all beyond.

When they sat up in a circle with their skinned knees propped up in the playing light that came down like a fountain, she and the MacLain twins ate candy—as many sticks of candy as they felt like eating out of one paper sack for three people. The MacLain twins had brought the sack away out here with them and had put it in a safe place ahead of time, as far from the scene as the pin oak—needlessly far. Their forethought cast a pall on all three as they sucked and held their candy in their mouths like old men's pipes. One crow hollered over their heads and they all got to their feet as though a clock struck.

"Now."

What did it matter which twin said that word, like a little bark? It was the parting word. There was her hoe held up in a grandfather vine, gone a little further in its fall, and there was her bucket. After they'd walked away from her—backwards for a piece—then she, jumping at them to chase them off, screamed into the veil of leaves, "I just did it because your mama's a poor albino!"

She would think afterwards, married, when she had the time to sit down—churning, for instance—"Who had the least sense and the least care, for fifteen? They did. I did. But it wasn't fair to tease me. To try to make me dizzy, and run a ring around me, or make me think that first minute I was going to be carried off by their pa. Teasing because I had to open my mouth about Mr. King MacLain before I knew what was coming."

Tumbling on the wet spring ground with the goody-goody MacLain twins was something Junior Holifield would have given her a licking for, just for making such a story up, supposing, after she married Junior, she had put anything in words. Or he would have said he'd lick her for it if she told it *again*.

Poor Junior!

II.

"Oh, good afternoon, sir. Don't shoot me, it's King MacLain. I'm in the habit of hunting these parts."

Junior had just knocked off a dead, double-headed pine cone and Blackstone was aiming at the telephone wire when the light voice with the fast words running together came out of the trees above the gully.

"Thought I'd see if the birds around here still tasted as

sweet as they used to." And there he was—that is, he showed for a minute and then was gone behind a reddening sweetgum tree.

But fall coming or not, poor little quails weren't any of his business, with him darting around tree trunks in a starched white suit, even if he did carry a gun for looks, Mattie Will thought. She studied the empty arch between two trees with a far-sighted look. If that was Mr. King MacLain, nobody was ever going to shoot him. Shoot *him*? Let him go on ahead in his Sunday best from one tree to another without giving warning or being so fussy about wild shots from the low scrub. He was Mr. King, all right. Up there back of the leaves his voice laughed and made fun this minute.

Junior looked up and said, "Well, we come out to use up some old ammunition." He lifted his upper lip. He had another pine cone on his mind. He pinged it.

"You hear me?" said the voice.

"It sure did look like Mr. MacLain to me, Junior," Mattie Will whispered, pretending to be as slow as Junior was. She squinted against the small sun points that came at her cheeks through the braid of her hat. Then she pushed her way around her husband.

"Well. And we come out to shoot up some old ammunition on Saturday," Junior told her. "This *is* Saturday." He pulled her back.

"You boys been sighting any birds this way?" the white glimmer asked courteously, and then it passed behind another tree. "Seen my dog, then?" And the invisible mouth whistled, from east right around to west, they could hear the clean round of it. Mr. King even *whistled* with manners. And with familiarity. And what two men in the world whistle the same? Mattie Will believed she must have heard him and seen him closer-to than she thought. Nobody could have *told* her how sweet the old rascal whistled, but it didn't surprise her.

Wilbur, the Holifield dog, flailed his tail and took a single bound toward the bank. Of course he had been barking the whole time, answered tolerantly by some dogs in town who—as certainly as if you could see them—were lying in front of the barbershop.

"Sighted e'er bird? Just one cuckoo," Junior said now, with

his baby-mouth drawn down as if he would cry, which meant he was being funny, and so Blackstone, his distance behind in the plum thicket, hopped on one foot for Junior, but Junior said, "Be still, Blackstone, no call for you to start cutting up yet."

"No, sir. Never pass by these parts without bringing down a few plump, juicy birds for my supper," said the voice. It was far-away for the moment; Mr. MacLain must have turned and looked at the view from the hilltop. You could see all Morgana from there, and he could have picked out his own house.

"My name is Holifield. We was just out using up some old ammunition on Saturday, me and a nigger. And as long as you don't get no closer to us, we ain't liable to hit you," said Junior.

That echoed a little. They both happened to get behind gum trees just then, Mr. MacLain and Junior. *Junior* was behind a tree! And she was between them. Mattie Will put her hand over her laughing mouth. Blackstone in the thicket broke a stick and chunked the pieces in the air. "And we won't pay no attention what you do in your part of the woods," Junior said, a dignified gaze on the falling chips.

"Suits me, sir!"

"Truth is—" Junior always kept right on! Just as he would do eating, at the table, and to his sorrow. "I ain't prepared to believe you come after birds, hardly, Mr. MacLain, if it is you. *We* are the ones come after what birds they is, if they is any birds. You're trespassing."

"Trespassing," said the voice presently. "Well—don't shoot me for that."

"Oho ho, Mr. Junior! Know what? *He* gawn shoot *us*! Shoot us!" In the ecstasy of knowing the end of it ahead of time, Blackstone flew out in the open and sang it like a bird, and beat his pants.

"You hush up, or if he don't shoot you, I will," Junior said. "Look, what happened to your gun, you lost it agin?"

Mr. MacLain was moving waywardly along, and sometimes got as completely hidden by even a skinny little wild cherry as if he'd melted into it.

Ping!

"One more redbird!" sighed Mattie Will.

"Ain't we two hunting men letting each other by and about their own business?" asked Mr. MacLain, suddenly loud upon them. They saw part of him, looking out there at the head of the gully, one hand on a knee. "Look—this is the stretch of woods I always did like the best. Why don't you try a different stretch?"

"See there?"

Mr. MacLain laughed agreeably at accusation.

"There's something else ain't what you think," Junior said in his most Holifield way. "Ain't e'er young lady folling after me, that you can catch a holt of—white or black."

Wilbur spraddled right up the bank to Mr. MacLain suddenly, before they knew it, and fawned on him before they got him back. He was named Wilbur after Mr. Morrison, who had printed Mattie Will's and Junior's marriage in the newspaper.

Mr. MacLain withdrew, and Junior was patting Wilbur, hammer-like.

"Junior," Mattie Will called softly through the cup of her hand. "Looks like you really scared that man away. Wonder who he was?"

"Bless God. Come out in the open, young lady. I can hear you but not see you," Mr. MacLain called, appearing immediately from the waist up.

So poor Junior had got one thing right. Mr. MacLain had been counting on it all the time—that young girl-wives not tied down yet could generally be found following after their husbands, if the husbands went out with a .22 on a nice enough day in October.

"Won't you come out and explain something mysterious to me, young lady?"

But it sounded as if he'd just thought of it, and called it mysterious.

Mattie Will, who was crouched to her knees, bent her head. She took a June bug off a leaf, a late June bug. She was thinking to herself, Mr. MacLain must be up in years, and they said he never did feel constrained to live in Morgana like other people and just visited Mrs. MacLain a little now and then. He roamed the country end on end, living up north and where-all, on funds; and might at any time appear and then, over night, disappear. Who could have guessed today he was this close?

"Show yourself, young lady. Are you a Holifield too? I don't think you are. Come out here and let me ask you something." But he went bobbing on to another tree while he was cajoling, bright as a lantern that swayed in a wind.

"Show yourself and I'll brain you directly, Mattie Will," Junior said. "You heard who he said he was and you done heard what he was, all your life, or you ain't a girl." Junior squeezed up to his .22 and trained it, immediately changing his voice to a little high singsong. "He's the one gits ever'thing he wants shootin' from around trees, like the MacLains been doing since Time. Killed folks trespassin' when he was growin' up, or his pa did, if it so pleased him. MacLains begun killin' when they begun settlin'. And don't nobody know how many chirren he has. Don't let him git no closer to me than he is now, you all."

Mattie Will ran the June bug up and down her arm and remembered once when she was little and her mother and father had both been taken with the prevalent sickness, and it was Mrs. MacLain from Morgana—who before that was known only by sight to her—who had come out to the farm and nursed and cooked for them, since there was nobody. She served them light-bread toast, and not biscuit, and didn't believe in molasses. She was not afraid of all the mud. She was in the congregation, always, a sweet-looking Presbyterian albino lady. Nothing was her fault. Mrs. MacLain came by herself to church, without boy or man, her lace collar fastened down by a cluster-pearl pin just like a little ice cream spoon, loaded. Going down the aisle she held up her head for the benefit of them all, while they considered Mr. MacLain a thousand miles away. And when they sang in church with her, they might as well have sung,

> "A thousand miles away.
> A thousand miles away."

It made church holier.

"I'll just start up that little bank till I see what he's after, Junior," Mattie Will said, rising.

Junior just looked at her stubbornly.

She pinched him. "Didn't you hear him ask me a question? Don't be so country: I'm going to answer it. And who's trespassing, if it's not us all three and a nigger? These whole woods belongs to you know who, Old Lady Stark. She'd like to see us all in Coventry this minute." She pointed overhead, without looking, where the signs said,

Posted.
No Pigs With or Without Rings.
No Hunting.
This Means You.
STARK

While he looked at those, and even Mr. MacLain looked at them, Mattie Will made her way up the bank.

"You see?" Junior cried again. "Yonder comes Mattie Will. It's just a good thing I got my gun too, Mr. MacLain. You're so smart. I didn't even know you was near enough to flush out, Mr. MacLain. You back to stay? Come on, Blackstone, let's me and you shoot him right now if he budges to catch a holt of Mattie Will, don't care what happens to us or who we hit, whether we both go to the 'lectric chair or not."

Mr. MacLain then looked out from a pin oak and fired a load of buckshot down, the way he'd throw a bone. Mattie Will's tongue ran out too, to show Junior how he'd acted in public.

Blackstone was howling out from his plum thicket, "Now it be's our turn and I found my old gun and we done used up every bit of ammunition we had on turtles an' trash! You see, you see."

Mattie Will looked up at Mr. MacLain and he beamed at her. He sent another load out, this one down over her where she held to some roots on the bank, and right over Junior's head.

It peppered his hat. Baby holes shamed it all over, blush-like, Junior threw away his gun.

Big red hand spread out on his shirt (he would always think he was shot through the heart if anybody's gun but his went off), Junior rose in the air and got a holler out. And then—he seemed determined about the way to come down, like Mister Holifield down from a ladder; no man more set in his ways than he, even Mister Holifield—he kicked and came down backwards. There was a fallen tree, a big fresh-cut magnolia some good-for-nothing had amused himself chopping down. Across that Junior decided to light, instead of on green moss—head and body on one side of the tree, feet and legs on the other. Then he went limp from the middle out, before their eyes. He was dead to the world; as immune as if asleep in his pew, but bent the opposite way.

Mr. MacLain appeared on top of the gully, wearing a yellowy Panama hat and a white linen suit with the sleeves as ridgy as two washboards. He looked like the preternatural month of June. He came light of foot and let his gunstock trail carefree through the periwinkle, which would bind it a little and then let go.

He went to Junior first, taking the bank in three or four knee-deep steps down.

He bent over and laid his ear to Junior. He thumped him, like a melon he tested, and let him lie—too green. As if lighting a match from his side, he drew a finger down Junior's brown pants leg, and stepped away. Mr. MacLain's linen shoulders, white as a goose's back in the sun, shrugged and twinkled in the glade.

To his back, he was not so very big, not so flashy and splendid as, for example, some brand-new evangelist come into the midst. He turned around and threw off his hat, and showed a thatch of straight, biscuit-colored hair. He smiled. His puckered face was like a little boy's, with square brown teeth.

Mattie Will slid down the bank. Mr. MacLain stood with head cocked while the wind swelled and blew across the top of the ridge, turning over the green and gold leaves high up around them all, stirring along suspicions of burning leaves and gunpowder smoke and the juice of the magnolia, and then he dropped his gun flat in the vines. Mattie Will saw he was coming now.

"Turn *your* self around and start picking plums!" she called, joining her hands, and Blackstone turned around, just in time.

When she laid eyes on Mr. MacLain close, she staggered, he had such grandeur, and then she was caught by the hair and brought down as suddenly to earth as if whacked by an unseen shillelagh. Presently she lifted her eyes in a lazy dread and saw those eyes above hers, as keenly bright and unwavering and apart from her life as the flowers on a tree.

But he put on her, with the affront of his body, the affront of his sense too. No pleasure in that! She had to put on what he knew with what he did—maybe because he was so grand it was a thorn to him. Like submitting to another way to talk, she could answer to his burden now, his whole blithe, smiling, superior, frantic existence. And no matter what happened to her, she had to remember, disappointments are not to be borne by Mr. MacLain, or he'll go away again.

Now he clasped her to his shoulder, and her tongue tasted sweet starch for the last time. Her arms dropped back to the mossiness, and she was Mr. MacLain's Doom, or Mr. MacLain's Weakness, like the rest, and neither Mrs. Junior Holifield nor Mattie Will Sojourner; now she was something she had always heard of. She did not stir.

Then when he let her fall and walked off, when he was out of hearing in the woods, and the birds and woods-sounds and the wood-chopping throbbed clearly, she lay there on one elbow, wide awake. A dove feather came turning down through the light that was like golden smoke. She caught it with a dart of the hand, and brushed her chin; she was never displeased to catch anything. Nothing more fell.

But she moved. She was the mover in the family. She jumped up. Besides, she heard plums falling into the bucket—sounds of pure complaint by this time. She threw Blackstone a glance. He picked plums and had a lizard to play with, and his cap unretrieved from his first sailing delight still hung in a tree. The Holifield dog licked Blackstone on the seat patch and then trotted over and licked Junior on the stone-like hand, and looked back over his shoulder with the expression of a lady soloist to whose song nobody has really listened. For ages he might have been making a little path back and forth between Junior and Blackstone, but she could not think of his name, or would not, just as Junior would not wake up.

She wasn't going to call a one of them, man or dog, to his senses. There was Junior suspended dead to the world over a tree that was big enough around for two of him half as willful. He was hooped in the middle like the bridge over Little

Chunky. Fools could set foot on him, walk over him. Even a young mule could run across him, the one he wanted to buy. His old brown pants hung halfway up his legs, and there in his poky middle pitifully gleamed the belt buckle anybody would know him by, even in a hundred years. J for Junior. A pang reached her and she took a step. It could be he was scared more than half to death—but no, not with that sleeping face, still with its look of "How come?", or its speckled lashes, quiet as the tails of sitting birds, in the shade of his brow.

"Let the church bells wake him!" said Mattie Will to Wilbur. "Ain't tomorrow Sunday? Blackstone, you have your cap to climb up after."

In the woods she heard sounds, the dry creek beginning to run or a strange man calling, one or the other, she thought, but she walked right up on Mr. MacLain again, asleep—snoring. He slept sitting up with his back against a tree, his head pillowed in the luminous Panama, his snorting mouth drawn round in a perfect heart open to the green turning world around him.

She stamped her foot, nothing happened, then she approached softly, and down on hands and knees contemplated him. Her hair fell over her eyes and she steadily blew a part in it; her head went back and forth appearing to say "No." Of course she was not denying a thing in this world, but now had time to look at anything she pleased and study it.

With her almost motherly sway of the head and arms to help her, she gazed at the sounding-off, sleeping head, and the neck like a little porch column in town, at the one hand, the other hand, the bent leg and the straight, all those parts looking no more driven than her man's now, or of any more use than a heap of cane thrown up by the mill and left in the pit to dry. But they were, and would be. He snored as if all the frogs of spring were inside him—but to him an old song. Or to him little balls, little bells for the light air, that rose up and sank between his two hands, never to be let fall.

His coat hung loosely out from him, and a letter suddenly dropped a little way out from a pocket—whiter than white.

Mattie Will subsided forward onto her arms. Her rear stayed up in the sky, which seemed to brush it with little feathers. She lay there and listened to the world go round.

But presently Mr. MacLain leaped to his feet, bolt awake, with a flourish of legs. He looked horrified—that he had been seen asleep? and by Mattie Will? And he did not know that there was nothing she could or would take away from him —Mr. King MacLain?

> In the night time,
> At the right time,
> So I've understood,
> 'Tis the habit of Sir Rabbit
> To dance in the wood—

That was all that went through Mattie Will's head.

"What you doing here, girl?" Mr. MacLain beat his snowy arms up and down. "Go on! Go on off! Go to Guinea!"

She got up and skedaddled.

She pressed through a haw thicket and through the cherry trees. With a tree-high seesawing of boughs a squirrel chase ran ahead of her through the woods—Morgan's Woods, as it used to be called. Fat birds were rocking on their perches. A little quail ran on the woods floor. Down an arch, some old cedar lane up here, Mattie Will could look away into the big West. She could see the drift of it all, the stretched land below the little hills, and the Big Black, clear to MacLain's Courthouse, almost, the Stark place plain and the fields, and their farm, everybody's house above trees, the MacLains'—the white floating peak—and even Blackstone's granny's cabin, where there had been a murder one time. And Morgana all in rays, like a giant sunflower in the dust of Saturday.

But as she ran down through the woods and vines, this side and that, on the way to get Junior home, it stole back into her mind about those two gawky boys, the MacLain twins. They were soft and jumpy! That day, with their brown, bright eyes popping and blinking, and their little aching Adam's apples—they were like young deer, or even remoter creatures . . . kangaroos. . . . For the first time Mattie Will thought they were mysterious and sweet—gamboling now she knew not where.

4.
Moon Lake

FROM THE BEGINNING his martyred presence seriously affected them. They had a disquieting familiarity with it, hearing the spit of his despising that went into his bugle. At times they could hardly recognize what he thought he was playing. Loch Morrison, Boy Scout and Life Saver, was under the ordeal of a week's camp on Moon Lake with girls.

Half the girls were county orphans, wished on them by Mr. Nesbitt and the Men's Bible Class after Billy Sunday's visit to town; but all girls, orphans and Morgana girls alike, were the same thing to Loch; maybe he threw in the two councilors too. He was hating every day of the seven. He hardly spoke; he never spoke first. Sometimes he swung in the trees; Nina Carmichael in particular would hear him crashing in the foliage somewhere when she was lying rigid in siesta.

While they were in the lake, for the dip or the five-o'clock swimming period in the afternoon, he stood against a tree with his arms folded, jacked up one-legged, sitting on his heel, as absolutely tolerant as an old fellow waiting for the store to open, being held up by the wall. Waiting for the girls to get out, he gazed upon some undisturbed part of the water. He despised their predicaments, most of all their not being able to swim. Sometimes he would take aim and from his right cheek shoot an imaginary gun at something far out, where they never were. Then he resumed his pose. He had been roped into this by his mother.

At the hours too hot for girls he used Moon Lake. He dived high off the crosspiece nailed up in the big oak, where the American Legion dived. He went through the air rocking and jerking like an engine, splashed in, climbed out, spat, climbed up again, dived off. He wore a long bathing suit which stretched longer from Monday to Tuesday and from Tuesday to Wednesday and so on, yawning at the armholes toward infinity, and it looked black and formal as a minstrel suit as he stood skinny against the clouds as on a stage.

He came and got his food and turned his back and ate it

all alone like a dog and lived in a tent by himself, apart like a nigger, and dived alone when the lake was clear of girls. That way, he seemed able to bear it; that would be his life. In early evening, in moonlight sings, the Boy Scout and Life Saver kept far away. They would sing "When all the little ships come sailing home," and he would be roaming off; they could tell about where he was. He played taps for them, invisibly then, and so beautifully they wept together, whole tentfuls some nights. Off with the whip-poor-wills and the coons and the owls and the little bobwhites—down where it all sloped away, he had pitched his tent, and slept there. Then at reveille, how he would spit into that cornet.

Reveille was his. He harangued the woods when the little minnows were trembling and running wizardlike in the water's edge. And how lovely and altered the trees were then, weighted with dew, leaning on one another's shoulders and smelling like big wet flowers. He blew his horn into their presence—trees' and girls'—and then watched the Dip.

"Good morning, Mr. Dip, Dip, Dip, with your water just as cold as ice!" sang Mrs. Gruenwald hoarsely. She took them for the dip, for Miss Moody said she couldn't, simply couldn't.

The orphans usually hung to the rear, and every other moment stood swayback with knees locked, the shoulders of their wash dresses ironed flat and stuck in peaks, and stared. For swimming they owned no bathing suits and went in in their underbodies. Even in the water they would stand swayback, each with a fist in front of her over the rope, looking over the flat surface as over the top of a tall mountain none of them could ever get over. Even at this hour of the day, they seemed to be expecting little tasks, something more immediate—little tasks that were never given out.

Mrs. Gruenwald was from the North and said "dup." "Good morning, Mr. Dup, Dup, Dup, with your water just as cold as ice!" sang Mrs. Gruenwald, fatly capering and leading them all in a singing, petering-out string down to the lake. She did a sort of little rocking dance in her exhortation, broad in her bathrobe. From the tail end of the line she looked like a Shredded Wheat Biscuit box rocking on its corners.

Nina Carmichael thought, There is nobody and nothing

named Mr. Dip, it is not a good morning until you have had coffee, and the water is the temperature of a just-cooling biscuit, thank Goodness. I hate this little parade of us girls, Nina thought, trotting fiercely in the center of it. It ruins the woods, all right. "Gee, we think you're mighty nice," they sang to Mr. Dip, while the Boy Scout, waiting at the lake, watched them go in.

"Watch out for mosquitoes," they called to one another, lyrically because warning wasn't any use anyway, as they walked out of their kimonos and dropped them like the petals of one big scattered flower on the bank behind them, and exposing themselves felt in a hundred places at once the little pangs. The orphans ripped their dresses off over their heads and stood in their underbodies. Busily they hung and piled their dresses on a cedar branch, obeying one of their own number, like a whole flock of ferocious little birds with pale topknots building themselves a nest. The orphan named Easter appeared in charge. She handed her dress wrong-side-out to a friend, who turned it and hung it up for her, and waited standing very still, her little fingers locked.

"Let's let the orphans go in the water first and get the snakes stirred up, Mrs. Gruenwald," Jinny Love Stark suggested first off, in the cheerful voice she adopted toward grown people. "Then they'll be chased away by the time *we* go in."

That made the orphans scatter in their pantie-waists, outwards from Easter; the little gauzes of gnats they ran through made them beat their hands at the air. They ran back together again, to Easter, and stood excitedly, almost hopping.

"I think we'll all go in in one big bunch," Mrs. Gruenwald said. Jinny Love lamented and beat against Mrs. Gruenwald, Mrs. Gruenwald's solid, rope-draped stomach all but returning her blows. "All take hands—march! Into the water! *Don't* let the stobs and cypress roots break your legs! *Do* your best! Kick! Stay on top if you can and hold the rope if necessary!"

Mrs. Gruenwald abruptly walked away from Jinny Love, out of the bathrobe, and entered the lake with a vast displacing. She left them on the bank with her Yankee advice.

The Morgana girls might never have gone in if the orphans hadn't balked. Easter came to a dead stop at Moon Lake and looked at it squinting as though it floated really on the Moon. And mightn't it be on the Moon?—it was a strange place, Nina thought, unlikely—and three miles from Morgana, Mississippi, all the time. The Morgana girls pulled the orphans' hands and dragged them in, or pushed suddenly from behind, and finally the orphans took hold of one another and waded forward in a body, singing "Good Morning" with their stiff, chip-like lips. None of them could or would swim, ever, and they just stood waist-deep and waited for the dip to be over. A few of them reached out and caught the struggling Morgana girls by the legs as they splashed from one barky post to another, to see how hard it really was to stay up.

"Mrs. Gruenwald, look, they want to drown us."

But Mrs. Gruenwald all this time was rising and sinking like a whale, she was in a sea of her own waves and perhaps of self-generated cold, out in the middle of the lake. She cared little that Morgana girls who learned to swim were getting a dollar from home. She had deserted them, no, she had never really been with them. Not only orphans had she deserted. In the water she kept so much to the profile that her single pushing-out eyeball looked like a little bottle of something. It was said she believed in evolution.

While the Boy Scout in the rosy light under the green trees twirled his horn so that it glittered and ran a puzzle in the sun, and emptied the spit out of it, he yawned, snappingly—as if he would bite the day, as quickly as Easter had bitten Deacon Nesbitt's hand on Opening Day.

"Gee, we think you're mighty nice," they sang to Mr. Dip, gasping, pounding their legs in him. If they let their feet go down, the invisible bottom of the lake felt like soft, knee-deep fur. The sharp hard knobs came up where least expected. The Morgana girls of course wore bathing slippers, and the mud loved to suck them off. The alligators had been beaten out of this lake, but it was said that water snakes—pilots—were swimming here and there; they would bite you but not kill you; and one cottonmouth moccasin was still getting away from the niggers—if the niggers were still going after him; he would kill you. These were the chances of getting sucked under, of being bitten, and of dying three miles away from home.

The brown water cutting her off at the chest, Easter looked directly before her, wide awake, unsmiling. Before she could hold a stare like that, she would have had to swallow something big—so Nina felt. It would have been something so big that it didn't matter to her what the inside of a snake's mouth was lined with. At the other end of her gaze the life saver grew almost insignificant. Her gaze moved like a little switch or wand, and the life saver scratched himself with his bugle, raked himself, as if that eased him. Yet the flick of a bluebottle fly made Easter jump.

They swam and held to the rope, hungry and waiting. But they had to keep waiting till Loch Morrison blew his horn before they could come out of Moon Lake. Mrs. Gruenwald, who capered before breakfast, believed in evolution, and put her face in the water, was quarter of a mile out. If she said anything, they couldn't hear her for the frogs.

II.

Nina and Jinny Love, with the soles of their feet shocked from the walk, found Easter ahead of them down at the spring.

For the orphans, from the first, sniffed out the way to the spring by themselves, and they could get there without stops to hold up their feet and pull out thorns and stickers, and could run through the sandy bottoms and never look down where they were going, and could grab hold with their toes on the sharp rutted path up the pine ridge and down. They clearly could never get enough of skimming over the silk-slick needles and setting prints of their feet in the bed of the spring to see them dissolve away under their eyes. What was it to them if the spring was muddied by the time Jinny Love Stark got there?

The one named Easter could fall flat as a boy, elbows cocked, and drink from the cup of her hand with her face in the spring. Jinny Love prodded Nina, and while they looked on Easter's drawers, Nina was opening the drinking cup she had brought with her, then collapsing it, feeling like a lady with a fan. That way, she was going over a thought, a fact: Half the people out here with me are orphans. Orphans. Orphans. She yearned for her heart to twist. But it didn't, not in time. Easter was through drinking—wiping her mouth and flinging her hand as if to break the bones, to get rid of the drops, and it was Nina's turn with her drinking cup.

Nina stood and bent over from the waist. Calmly, she held her cup in the spring and watched it fill. They could all see how it spangled like a cold star in the curling water. The water tasted the silver cool of the rim it went over running to her lips, and at moments the cup gave her teeth a pang. Nina heard her own throat swallowing. She paused and threw a smile about her. After she had drunk she wiped the cup on her tie and collapsed it, and put the little top on, and its ring over her finger. With that, Easter, one arm tilted, charged against the green bank and mounted it. Nina felt her surveying the spring and all from above. Jinny Love was down drinking like a chicken, kissing the water only.

Easter was dominant among the orphans. It was not that she was so bad. The one called Geneva stole, for example, but Easter was dominant for what she was in herself—for the way she held still, sometimes. All orphans were at once wondering and stoic—at one moment loving everything too much, the next folding back from it, tightly as hard green buds growing in the wrong direction, closing as they go. But it was as if Easter signaled them. Now she just stood up there, watching the spring, with the name Easter—tacky name, as Jinny Love Stark was the first to say. She was medium size, but her hair seemed to fly up at the temples, being cropped and wiry, and this crest made her nearly as tall as Jinny Love Stark. The rest of the orphans had hair paler than their tanned foreheads—straight and tow, the greenish yellow of cornsilk that dimmed black at the roots and shadows, with burnt-out-looking bangs like young boys' and old men's hair; that was from picking in the fields. Easter's hair was a withstanding gold. Around the back of her neck beneath the hair was a dark band on her skin like the mark a gold bracelet leaves on the arm. It came to the Morgana girls with a feeling of elation: the ring was pure dirt. They liked to look at it, or to remember, too late, what it was—as now, when Easter had already lain down for a drink and left the spring. They liked to walk behind her and see her back, which seemed spectacular from crested gold head to hard, tough heel. Mr. Nesbitt, from the Bible Class, took Easter by the wrist and turned her around to him and looked just as hard at her front. She had started her breasts. What Easter did was to bite his right hand, his collection hand. It was wonderful to have with them someone dangerous but not, so far, or provenly, bad. When Nina's little lead-mold umbrella, the size of a clover, a Crackerjack prize, was stolen the first night of camp, that was Geneva, Easter's friend.

Jinny Love, after wiping her face with a hand-made handkerchief, pulled out a deck of cards she had secretly brought in her middy pocket. She dropped them down, bright blue, on a sandy place by the spring. "Let's play cassino. Do they call you *Easter*?"

Down Easter jumped, from the height of the bank. She came back to them. "Cassino, what's that?"

"All right, what do *you* want to play?"

"All right, I'll play you mumblety-peg."

"I don't know how you play that!" cried Nina.

"Who would ever want to know?" asked Jinny Love, closing the circle.

Easter flipped out a jack-knife and with her sawed fingernail shot out three blades.

"Do you carry that in the orphan asylum?" Jinny Love asked with some respect.

Easter dropped to her scarred and coral-colored knees. They saw the dirt. "Get down if you want to play me mumblety-peg," was all she said, "and watch out for your hands and faces."

They huddled down on the piney sand. The vivid, hurrying ants were everywhere. To the squinted eye they looked like angry, orange ponies as they rode the pine needles. There was Geneva, skirting behind a tree, but she never came close or tried to get in the game. She pretended to be catching doodlebugs. The knife leaped and quivered in the sandy arena smoothed by Easter's hand.

"I may not know how to play, but I bet I win," Jinny Love said.

Easter's eyes, lifting up, were neither brown nor green nor cat; they had something of metal, flat ancient metal, so that you could not see into them. Nina's grandfather had possessed a box of coins from Greece and Rome. Easter's eyes could have come from Greece or Rome that day. Jinny Love stopped short of apprehending this, and only took care to watch herself when Easter pitched the knife. The color in Easter's eyes could have been found somewhere, away—away, under lost leaves—strange as the painted color of the ants. Instead of round black holes in the center of her eyes, there might have been women's heads, ancient.

Easter, who had played so often, won. She nodded and accepted Jinny Love's barrette and from Nina a blue jay feather which she transferred to her own ear.

"I wouldn't be surprised if you cheated, and don't know what you had to lose if you lost," said Jinny Love thoughtfully but with an admiration almost fantastic in her.

Victory with a remark attached did not crush Easter at all, or she scarcely listened. Her indifference made Nina fall back and listen to the spring running with an endless sound and see how the July light like purple and yellow birds kept flickering under the trees when the wind blew. Easter turned her head and the new feather on her head shone changeably. A black funnel of bees passed through the air, throwing a funneled shadow, like a visitor from nowhere, another planet.

"We have to play again to see whose the drinking cup will be," Easter said, swaying forward on her knees.

Nina jumped to her feet and did a cartwheel. Against the spinning green and blue her heart pounded as heavily as she touched lightly.

"You ruined the game," Jinny Love informed Easter. "You don't know Nina." She gathered up her cards. "You'd think it was made of fourteen-carat gold, and didn't come out of the pocket of an old suitcase, that cup."

"I'm sorry," said Nina sincerely.

As the three were winding around the lake, a bird flying above the opposite shore kept uttering a cry and then diving deep, plunging into the trees there, and soaring to cry again.

"Hear him?" one of the niggers said, fishing on the bank; it was Elberta's sister Twosie, who spoke as if a long, long conversation had been going on, into which she would intrude only the mildest words. "Know why? Know why, in de sky, he say 'Spirit? Spirit?' And den he dive *boom* and say 'GHOST'?"

"Why does he?" said Jinny Love, in a voice of objection.

"Yawl knows. *I* don't know," said Twosie, in her little high, helpless voice, and she shut her eyes. They couldn't seem to get on by her. On fine days there is danger of some sad meeting, the positive danger of it. "*I* don't know what he say dat for." Twosie spoke pitifully, as though accused. She sighed. "Yawl sho ain't got yo' eyes opem good, yawl. Yawl don't know what's out here in woods wid you."

"Well, what?"

"Yawl walk right by mans wid great big gun, could jump out at yawl. Yawl don't eem smellim."

"You mean Mr. Holifield? That's a flashlight he's got." Nina looked at Jinny Love for confirmation. Mr. Holifield was their handy man, or rather simply "the man to be sure and have around the camp." He could be found by beating for a long time on the porch of the American Legion boat house—he slept heavily. "He hasn't got a gun to jump out with."

"I know who you mean. I hear those boys. Just some big boys, like the MacLain twins or somebody, and who cares about them?" Jinny Love, with her switch indented the thick mat of hair on Twosie's head and prodded and stirred it gently. She pretended to fish in Twosie's woolly head. "Why ain't *you* scared, then?"

"I is."

Twosie's eyelids fluttered. Already she seemed to be fishing in her night's sleep. While they gazed at her crouched, devoted figure, from which the long pole hung, so steady and beggarlike and ordained an appendage, all their passions flew home again and went huddled and soft to roost.

Back at the camp, Jinny Love told Miss Moody about the great big jack-knife. Easter gave it up.

"I didn't mean you couldn't *drink* out of my cup," Nina said, waiting for her. "Only you have to hold it carefully, it leaks. It's engraved."

Easter wouldn't even try it, though Nina dangled it on its ring right under her eyes. She didn't say anything, not even

"It's pretty." Was she even thinking of it? Or if not, what did she think about?

"Sometimes orphans act like deaf-and-dumbs," said Jinny Love.

III.

"Nina!" Jinny Love whispered across the tent, during siesta. "What do you think you're reading?"

Nina closed *The Re-Creation of Brian Kent.* Jinny Love was already coming directly across the almost-touching cots to Nina's, walking on her knees and bearing down over Gertrude, Etoile, and now Geneva.

With Jinny Love upon her, Geneva sighed. Her sleeping face looked as if she didn't want to. She slept as she swam, in her pantie-waist, she was in running position and her ribs went up and down frantically—a little box in her chest that expanded and shut without a second's rest between. Her cheek was pearly with afternoon moisture and her kitten-like teeth pearlier still. As Jinny Love hid her and went over, Nina seemed to see her still; even her vaccination mark looked too big for her.

Nobody woke up from being walked over, but after Jinny Love had fallen in bed with Nina, Easter gave a belated, dreaming sound. She had not even been in the line of march; she slept on the cot by the door, curved shell-like, both arms forward over her head. It was an inward sound she gave—now it came again—of such wholehearted and fateful concurrence with the thing dreamed, that Nina and Jinny Love took hands and made wry faces at each other.

Beyond Easter's cot the corona of afternoon flared and lifted in an intensity that came through the eyelids. There was nothing but light out there. True, the black Negroes inhabited it. Elberta moved slowly through it, as if she rocked a baby with her hips, carrying a bucket of scraps to throw in the lake—to get hail Columbia for it later. Her straw hat spiraled rings of orange and violet, like a top. Far, far down a vista of intolerable light, a tiny daub of black cotton, Twosie had stationed herself at the edge of things, and slept and fished.

Eventually there was Exum wandering with his fish pole—he could dance on a dime, Elberta said, he used to work for a blind man. Exum was smart for twelve years old; too smart. He found that hat he wore—not a sign of the owner. He had a hat like new, filled out a little with peanut shells inside the band to correct the size, and he like a little black peanut in it. It stood up and away from his head all around, and seemed only following him—on runners, perhaps, like those cartridges for change in Spights' store.

Easter's sighs and her prolonged or half-uttered words now filled the tent, just as the heat filled it. Her words fell in threes, Nina observed, like the mourning-dove's call in the woods.

Nina and Jinny Love lay speechless, doubling for themselves the already strong odor of Sweet Dreams Mosquito Oil, in a trance of endurance through the hour's siesta. Entwined, they stared—orphan-like themselves—past Easter's cot and through the tent opening as down a long telescope turned on an incandescent star, and saw the spiral of Elberta's hat return, and saw Exum jump over a stick and on the other side do a little dance in a puff of dust. They could hear the intermittent crash, splash of Loch Morrison using their lake, and Easter's voice calling again in her sleep, her unintelligible words.

But however Nina and Jinny Love made faces at they knew not what, Easter concurred; she thoroughly agreed.

The bugle blew for swimming. Geneva jumped so hard she fell off her cot. Nina and Jinny Love were indented with each other, like pressed leaves, and jumped free. When Easter, who had to be shaken, sat up drugged and stupid on her cot, Nina ran over to her.

"Listen. Wake up. Look, you can go in in my bathing shoes today."

She felt her eyes glaze with this plan of kindness as she stretched out her limp red shoes that hung down like bananas under Easter's gaze. But Easter dropped back on the cot and stretched her legs.

"Never mind your shoes. I don't have to go in the lake if I don't want to."

"You do. I never heard of that. Who picked you out? You do," they said, all gathering.

"You make me."

Easter yawned. She fluttered her eyes and rolled them back—she loved doing that. Miss Moody passed by and beamed in at them hovered around Easter's passive and mutinous form. All along she'd been afraid of some challenge to her counselorship, from the way she hurried by now, almost too daintily.

"Well, *I* know," Jinny Love said, sidling up. "I know as much as you know, Easter." She made a chant, which drove her hopping around the tent pole in an Indian step. "You don't have to go, if you don't want to go. And if it ain't so, you still don't have to go, if you don't want to go." She kissed her hand to them.

Easter was silent—but if she groaned when she waked, she'd only be imitating herself.

Jinny Love pulled on her bathing cap, which gave way and came down over her eyes. Even in blindness, she cried, "So you needn't think you're the only one, Easter, not always. What do you say to that?"

"I should worry, I should cry," said Easter, lying still, spread-eagled.

"Let's us run away from basket weaving," Jinny Love said in Nina's ear, a little later in the week.

"Just as soon."

"Grand. They'll think we're drowned."

They went out the back end of the tent, barefooted; their feet were as tough as anybody's by this time. Down in the hammock, Miss Moody was reading *The Re-Creation of Brian Kent* now. (Nobody knew whose book that was, it had been found here, the covers curled up like side combs. Perhaps anybody at Moon Lake who tried to read it felt cheated by the title, as applying to camp life, as Nina did, and laid it down for the next person.) Cat, the niggers' cat, was sunning on a post and when they approached jumped to the ground like something poured out of a bottle, and went with them, in front.

They trudged down the slope past Loch Morrison's tent and took the track into the swamp. There they moved single file between two walls; by lifting their arms they could have touched one or the other pressing side of the swamp. Their toes exploded the dust that felt like the powder clerks pump into new kid gloves, as Jinny Love said twice. They were eye to eye with the finger-shaped leaves of the castor bean plants, put out like those gypsy hands that part the curtains at the back of rolling wagons, and wrinkled and coated over like the fortune-teller's face.

Mosquitoes struck at them; Sweet Dreams didn't last. The whining lifted like a voice, saying "I don't want . . ." At the girls' shoulders Queen Anne's lace and elderberry and blackberry thickets, loaded heavily with flower and fruit and smelling with the melony smell of snake, overhung the ditch to touch them. The ditches had dried green or blue bottoms, cracked and glazed—like a dropped vase. "I hope we don't meet any nigger men," Jinny Love said cheerfully.

Sweet bay and cypress and sweetgum and live oak and swamp maple closing tight made the wall dense, and yet there was somewhere still for the other wall of vine; it gathered itself on the ground and stacked and tilted itself in the trees; and like a table in the tree the mistletoe hung up there black in the zenith. Buzzards floated from one side of the swamp to the other, as if choice existed for them—raggedly crossing the sky and shadowing the track, and shouldering one another on the solitary limb of a moon-white sycamore. Closer to the ear than lips could begin words came the swamp sounds—closer to the ear and nearer to the dreaming mind. They were a song of hilarity to Jinny Love, who began to skip. Periods of silence seemed hoarse, or the suffering from hoarseness, otherwise inexplicable, as though the world could stop. Cat was stalking something at the black edge of the ditch. The briars didn't trouble Cat at all, it was they that seemed to give way beneath that long, boatlike belly.

The track serpentined again, and walking ahead was Easter. Geneva and Etoile were playing at her side, edging each other out of her shadow, but when they saw who was coming up behind them, they turned and ran tearing back towards camp, running at angles, like pullets, leaving a cloud of dust as they passed by.

"Wouldn't you know!" said Jinny Love.

Easter was going unconcernedly on, her dress stained green behind; she ate something out of her hand as she went.

"We'll soon catch up—don't hurry."

The reason orphans were the way they were lay first in nobody's watching them, Nina thought, for she felt obscurely like a trespasser. They, they were not answerable. Even on being watched, Easter remained not answerable to a soul on earth. Nobody cared! And so, in this beatific state, something came out of *her*.

"Where are you going?"

"Can we go with you, Easter?"

Easter, her lips stained with blackberries, replied, "It ain't my road."

They walked along, one on each side of her. Though they automatically stuck their tongues out at her, they ran their arms around her waist. She tolerated the closeness for a little while; she smelled of orphan-starch, but she had a strange pure smell of sweat, like a sleeping baby, and in her temple, so close then to their eyes, the skin was transparent enough for a little vein to be seen pounding under it. She seemed very tender and very small in the waist to be trudging along so doggedly, when they had her like that.

Vines, a magnificent and steamy green, covered more and more of the trees, played over them like fountains. There were stretches of water below them, blue-black, netted over with half-closed waterlilies. The horizontal limbs of cypresses grew a short, pale green scruff like bird feathers.

They came to a tiny farm down here, the last one possible before the muck sucked it in—a patch of cotton in flower, a house whitewashed in front, a cleanswept yard with a little iron pump standing in the middle of it like a black rooster. These were white people—an old woman in a sunbonnet came out of the house with a galvanized bucket, and pumped it full in the dooryard. That was an excuse to see people go by.

Easter, easing out of the others' clasp, lifted her arm halfway and turning for an instant, gave two waves of the hand. But the old woman was prouder than she.

Jinny Love said, "How would you all like to live there?"

Cat edged the woods onward, and at moments vanished into a tunnel in the briars. Emerging from other tunnels, he—or she—glanced up at them with a face more mask-like than ever.

"There's a short-cut to the lake." Easter, breaking and darting ahead, suddenly went down on her knees and slid under a certain place in the barbed wire fence. Rising, she took a step inward, sinking down as she went. Nina untwined her arm from Jinny Love's and went after her.

"I might have known you'd want us to go through a barbed wire fence." Jinny Love sat down where she was, on the side of the ditch, just as she would take her seat on a needlepoint stool. She jumped up once, and sat back. "Fools, fools!" she called. "Now I think you've made me turn my ankle. Even if I wanted to track through the mud, I couldn't!"

Nina and Easter, dipping under a second, unexpected fence, went on, swaying and feeling their feet pulled down, reaching to the trees. Jinny Love was left behind in the heartless way people and incidents alike are thrown off in the course of a dream, like the gratuitous flowers scattered from a float—rather in celebration. The swamp was now all-enveloping, dark and at the same time vivid, alarming—it was like being inside the chest of something that breathed and might turn over.

Then there was Moon Lake, a different aspect altogether. Easter climbed the slight rise ahead and reached the pink, grassy rim and the innocent open. Here it was quiet, until, fatefully, there was one soft splash.

"You see the snake drop off in the water?" asked Easter.

"Snake?"

"Out of that tree."

"You can have him."

"There he is: coming up!" Easter pointed.

"That's probably a different one," Nina objected in the voice of Jinny Love.

Easter looked both ways, chose, and walked on the pink sandy rim with its purpled lip, her blue shadow lolling over it. She went around a bend, and straight to an old gray boat. Did she know it would be there? It was in some reeds, looking mysterious to come upon and yet in place, as an old boat will. Easter stepped into it and hopped to the far seat that was over the water, and dropping to it lay back with her toes hooked up. She looked falling over backwards. One arm lifted, curved over her head, and hung till her finger touched the water.

The shadows of the willow leaves moved gently on the sand,

deep blue and narrow, long crescents. The water was quiet, the color of pewter, marked with purple stobs, although where the sun shone right on it the lake seemed to be in violent agitation, almost boiling. Surely a little chip would turn around and around in it. Nina dropped down on the flecked sandbar. She fluttered her eyelids, half closed them, and the world looked struck by moonlight.

"Here I come," came Jinny Love's voice. It hadn't been long. She came twitching over their tracks along the sandbar, her long soft hair blowing up like a skirt in a play of the breeze in the open. "But I don't choose to sit myself in a leaky boat," she was calling ahead. "I choose the land."

She took her seat on the very place where Nina was writing her name. Nina moved her finger away, drawing a long arrow to a new place. The sand was coarse like beads and full of minute shells, some shaped exactly like bugles.

"Want to hear about my ankle?" Jinny Love asked. "It wasn't as bad as I thought. I must say you picked a queer place, I saw an *owl*. It smells like the school basement to me—peepee and old erasers." Then she stopped with her mouth a little open, and was quiet, as though something had been turned off inside her. Her eyes were soft, her gaze stretched to Easter, to the boat, the lake—her long oval face went vacant.

Easter was lying rocked in the gentle motion of the boat, her head turned on its cheek. She had not said hello to Jinny Love anew. Did she see the drop of water clinging to her lifted finger? Did it make a rainbow? Not to Easter: her eyes were rolled back, Nina felt. Her own hand was writing in the sand. Nina, Nina, Nina. Writing, she could dream that her self might get away from her—that here in this faraway place she could tell her self, by name, to go or to stay. Jinny Love had begun building a sand castle over her foot. In the sky clouds moved no more perceptibly than grazing animals. Yet with a passing breeze, the boat gave a knock, lifted and fell. Easter sat up.

"Why aren't we out in the boat?" Nina, taking a strange and heady initiative, rose to her feet. "Out there!" A picture in her mind, as if already furnished from an eventual and appreciative distance, showed the boat floating where she pointed, far out in Moon Lake with three girls sitting in the three spaces. "We're coming, Easter!"

"Just as I make a castle. *I'm* not coming," said Jinny Love. "Anyway, there's stobs in the lake. We'd be upset, ha ha."

"What do I care, I can swim!" Nina cried at the water's edge.

"You can just swim from the first post to the second post. And that's in front of camp, not here."

Firming her feet in the sucking, minnowy mud, Nina put her weight against the boat. Soon her legs were half hidden, the mud like some awful kiss pulled at her toes, and all over she tautened and felt the sweat start out of her body. Roots laced her feet, knotty and streaming. Under water, the boat was caught too, but Nina was determined to free it. She saw that there was muddy water in the boat too, which Easter's legs, now bright pink, were straddling. Suddenly all seemed easy.

"It's coming loose!"

At the last minute, Jinny Love, who had extracted her foot from the castle with success, hurried over and climbed to the middle seat of the boat, screaming. Easter sat up swaying with the dip of the boat; the energy seemed all to have gone out of her. Her lolling head looked pale and featureless as a pear beyond the laughing face of Jinny Love. She had not said whether she wanted to go or not—yet surely she did; she had been in the boat all along, she had discovered the boat.

For a moment, with her powerful hands, Nina held the boat back. Again she thought of a pear—not the everyday gritty kind that hung on the tree in the backyard, but the fine kind sold on trains and at high prices, each pear with a paper cone wrapping it alone—beautiful, symmetrical, clean pears with thin skins, with snow-white flesh so juicy and tender that to eat one baptized the whole face, and so delicate that while you urgently ate the first half, the second half was already beginning to turn brown. To all fruits, and especially to those fine pears, something happened—the process was so swift, you were never in time for them. It's not the flowers that are fleeting, Nina thought, it's the fruits—it's the time when things are ready that they don't stay. She even went through the rhyme, "Pear tree by the garden gate, How much longer must

I wait?"—thinking it was the pears that asked it, not the picker.

Then she climbed in herself, and they were rocking out sideways on the water.

"Now what?" said Jinny Love.

"This is all right for me," said Nina.

"Without oars?—Ha ha."

"Why didn't you tell me, then!—But I don't care now."

"You never are as smart as you think."

"Wait till you find out where we get to."

"I guess you know Easter can't swim. She won't even touch water with her foot."

"What do you think a *boat*'s for?"

But a soft tug had already stopped their drifting. Nina with a dark frown turned and looked down.

"A chain! An old mean chain!"

"That's how smart you are."

Nina pulled the boat in again—of course nobody helped her!—burning her hands on the chain, and kneeling outward tried to free the other end. She could see now through the reeds that it was wound around and around an old stump, which had almost grown over it in places. The boat had been chained to the bank since maybe last summer.

"No use hitting it," said Jinny Love.

A dragonfly flew about their heads. Easter only waited in her end of the boat, not seeming to care about the disappointment either. If this was their ship, she was their figurehead, turned on its back, sky-facing. She wouldn't be their passenger.

"You thought we'd all be out in the middle of Moon Lake by now, didn't you?" Jinny Love said, from her lady's seat. "Well, look where we are."

"Oh, Easter! Easter! I wish you still had your knife!"

"—But let's don't go back yet," Jinny Love said on shore. "I don't think they've missed us." She started a sand castle over her other foot.

"You make me sick," said Easter suddenly.

"Nina, let's pretend Easter's not with us."

"But that's what *she* was pretending."

Nina dug into the sand with a little stick, printing "Nina" and then "Easter."

Jinny Love seemed stunned, she let sand run out of both fists. "But how could you ever know what Easter was pretending?"

Easter's hand came down and wiped her name clean; she also wiped out "Nina." She took the stick out of Nina's hand and with a formal gesture, as if she would otherwise seem to reveal too much, wrote for herself. In clear, high-waisted letters the word "Esther" cut into the sand. Then she jumped up.

"Who's that?" Nina asked.

Easter laid her thumb between her breasts, and walked about.

"Why, I call that 'Esther.' "

"Call it 'Esther' if you want to, I call it 'Easter.' "

"Well, sit down. . . ."

"And I named myself."

"How could you? Who let you?"

"I let myself name myself."

"Easter, I believe you," said Nina. "But I just want you to spell it right. Look—E-A-S—"

"I should worry, I should cry."

Jinny Love leaned her chin on the roof of her castle to say, "I was named for my maternal grandmother, so my name's Jinny Love. It couldn't be anything else. Or anything better. You see? Easter's just not a real name. It doesn't matter how she spells it, Nina, nobody ever had it. Not around here." She rested on her chin.

"I have it."

"Just see how it looks spelled right." Nina lifted the stick from Easter's fingers and began to print, but had to throw herself bodily over the name to keep Easter from it. "Spell it right and it's real!" she cried.

"But right or wrong, it's tacky," said Jinny Love. "You can't get me mad over it. All I can concentrate on out here is missing the figs at home."

" 'Easter' is real beautiful!" Nina said distractedly. She suddenly threw the stick into the lake, before Easter could grab it, and it trotted up and down in a crucible of sun-filled water.

"I thought it was the day you were found on a doorstep," she said sullenly—even distrustfully.

Easter sat down at last and with slow, careful movements of her palms rubbed down the old bites on her legs. Her crest of hair dipped downward and she rocked a little, up and down, side to side, in a rhythm. Easter never did intend to explain anything unless she had to—or to force your explanations. She just had hopes. She hoped never to be sorry. Or did she?

"I haven't got no father. I never had, he ran away. I've got a mother. When I could walk, then my mother took me by the hand and turned me in, and I remember it. I'm going to be a singer."

It was Jinny Love, starting to clear her throat, who released Nina. It was Jinny Love, escaping, burrowing her finger into her castle, who was now kind, pretending Easter had never spoken. Nina banged Jinny Love on the head with her fist. How good and hot her hair was! Like hot glass. She broke the castle from her tender foot. She wondered if Jinny Love's head would break. Not at all. You couldn't learn anything through the head.

"Ha, ha, ha!" yelled Jinny Love, hitting back.

They were fighting and hitting for a moment. Then they lay quiet, tilted together against the crumbled hill of sand, stretched out and looking at the sky where now a white tower of cloud was climbing.

Someone moved; Easter lifted to her lips a piece of cross-vine cut back in the days of her good knife. She brought up a kitchen match from her pocket, lighted up, and smoked.

They sat up and gazed at her.

"If you count much on being a singer, that's not a very good way to start," said Jinny Love. "Even boys, it stunts their growth."

Easter once more looked the same as asleep in the dancing shadows, except for what came out of her mouth, more mysterious, almost, than words.

"Have some?" she asked, and they accepted. But theirs went out.

Jinny Love's gaze was fastened on Easter, and she dreamed and dreamed of telling on her for smoking, while the sun, even through leaves, was burning her pale skin pink, and she looked the most beautiful of all: she felt temptation. But what she said was, "Even after all this is over, Easter, I'll always remember you."

Off in the thick of the woods came a fairy sound, followed by a tremulous silence, a holding apart of the air.

"What's that?" cried Easter sharply. Her throat quivered, the little vein in her temple jumped.

"That's Mister Loch Morrison. Didn't you know he had a horn?"

There was another fairy sound, and the pried-apart, gentle silence. The woods seemed to be moving after it, running—the world pellmell. Nina could see the boy in the distance, too, and the golden horn tilted up. A few minutes back her gaze had fled the present and this scene; now she put the horn blower into his visionary place.

"Don't blow that!" Jinny Love cried out this time, jumping to her feet and stopping up her ears, stamping on the shore of Moon Lake. "You shut up! We can hear!—Come on," she added prosaically to the other two. "It's time to go. I reckon they've worried enough." She smiled. "Here comes Cat."

Cat always caught something; something was in his—or her—mouth, a couple of little feet or claws bouncing under the lifted whiskers. Cat didn't look especially triumphant; just through with it.

They marched on away from their little boat.

IV.

One clear night the campers built a fire up above the spring, cooked supper on sticks around it, and after stunts, a recitation of "How They Brought the Good News from Ghent to Aix" by Gertrude Bowles, and the ghost story about the bone, they stood up on the ridge and poured a last song into the woods—"Little Sir Echo."

The fire was put out and there was no bright point to look into, no circle. The presence of night was beside them—a beast in gossamer, with no shine of outline, only of ornament—rings, earrings. . . .

"March!" cried Mrs. Gruenwald, and stamped down the trail for them to follow. They went single file on the still-warm pine needles, soundlessly now. Not far away there were crackings of twigs, small, regretted crashes; Loch Morrison, supperless for all they knew, was wandering around by himself, sulking, alone.

Nobody needed light. The night sky was pale as a green grape, transparent like grape flesh over each tree. Every girl saw moths—the beautiful ones like ladies, with long legs that were wings—and the little ones, mere bits of bark. And once against the night, just before Little Sister Spights' eyes, making her cry out, hung suspended a spider—a body no less mysterious than the grape of the air, different only a little.

All around swam the fireflies. Clouds of them, trees of them, islands of them floating, a lower order of brightness—one could even get into a tent by mistake. The stars barely showed their places in the pale sky—small and far from this bright world. And the world would be bright as long as these girls held awake, and could keep their eyes from closing. And the moon itself shone—taken for granted.

Moon Lake came in like a flood below the ridge; they trailed downward. Out there Miss Moody would sometimes go in a boat; sometimes she had a late date from town, "Rudy" Spights or "Rudy" Loomis, and then they could be seen drifting there after the moon was up, far out on the smooth bright surface. ("And she lets him hug her out there," Jinny Love had instructed them. "Like this." She had seized, of all people, Etoile, whose name rhymed with tinfoil. "Hands off," said Etoile.) Twice Nina had herself seen the silhouette of the canoe on the bright water, with the figures at each end, like a dark butterfly with wings spread open and still. Not tonight!

Tonight, it was only the niggers, fishing. But their boat must be full of silver fish! Nina wondered if it was the slowness and near-fixity of boats out on the water that made them so magical. Their little boat in the reeds that day had not been far from this one's wonder, after all. The turning of water and sky, of the moon, or the sun, always proceeded, and there was this magical hesitation in their midst, of a boat. And in the boat, it was not so much that they drifted, as that in the presence of a boat the world drifted, forgot. The dreamed-about changed places with the dreamer.

Home from the wild moonlit woods, the file of little girls wormed into the tents, which were hot as cloth pockets. The candles were lighted by Miss Moody, dateless tonight, on whose shelf in the flare of nightly revelation stood her toothbrush in the glass, her hand-painted celluloid powder box, her Honey and Almond cream, her rouge and eyebrow tweezers, and at the end of the line the bottle of Compound, containing true and false unicorn and the life root plant.

Miss Moody, with a fervent frown which precluded interruption, sang in soft tremolo as she rubbed the lined-up children with "Sweet Dreams."

"Forgive me
O please forgive me
I didn't mean to make
You cry!
I love you and I need you—"

They crooked and bent themselves and lifted nightgowns to her silently while she sang. Then when she faced them to her they could look into the deep tangled rats of her puffed hair and at her eyebrows which seemed fixed for ever in that elevated line of adult pleading.

"Do anything but don't say good-bye!"

And automatically they almost said, "Good-bye!" Her hands rubbed and cuffed them while she sang, pulling to her girls all just alike, as if girlhood itself were an infinity, but a commodity. ("I'm ticklish," Jinny Love informed her every night.) Her look of pleading seemed infinitely perilous to them. Her voice had the sway of an aerialist crossing the high wire, even while she sang out of the nightgown coming down over her head.

There were kisses, prayers. Easter, as though she could be cold tonight, got into bed with Geneva. Geneva like a little June bug hooked onto her back. The candles were blown. Miss Moody ostentatiously went right to sleep. Jinny Love cried into her pillow for her mother, or perhaps for the figs.

Just outside their tent, Citronella burned in a saucer in the weeds—Citronella, like a girl's name.

Luminous of course but hidden from them, Moon Lake streamed out in the night. By moonlight sometimes it seemed to run like a river. Beyond the cry of the frogs there were the sounds of a boat moored somewhere, of its vague, clumsy reaching at the shore, those sounds that are recognized as being made by something sightless. When did boats have eyes—once? Nothing watched that their little part of the lake stayed roped off and protected; was it there now, the rope stretched frail-like between posts that swayed in mud? That rope was to mark how far the girls could swim. Beyond lay the deep part, some bottomless parts, said Moody. Here and there was the quicksand that stirred your footprint and kissed your heel. All snakes, harmless and harmful, were freely playing now; they put a trailing, moony division between weed and weed—bright, turning, bright and turning.

Nina still lay dreamily, or she had waked in the night. She heard Gertrude Bowles gasp in a dream, beginning to get her stomach ache, and Etoile begin, slowly, her snore. She thought: Now I can think, in between them. She could not even feel Miss Moody fretting.

The orphan! she thought exultantly. The other way to live. There were secret ways. She thought, Time's really short, I've been only thinking like the others. It's only interesting, only worthy, to try for the fiercest secrets. To slip into them all—to change. To change for a moment into Gertrude, into Mrs. Gruenwald, into Twosie—into a boy. To *have been* an orphan.

Nina sat up on the cot and stared passionately before her at the night—the pale dark roaring night with its secret step, the Indian night. She felt the forehead, the beaded stars, look in thoughtfully at her.

The pondering night stood rude at the tent door, the opening fold would let it stoop in—it, him—he had risen up inside. Long-armed, or long-winged, he stood in the center there where the pole went up. Nina lay back, drawn quietly from him. But the night knew about Easter. All about her. Geneva had pushed her to the very edge of the cot. Easter's hand hung down, opened outward. Come here, night, Easter might say, tender to a giant, to such a dark thing. And the night, obedient and graceful, would kneel to her. Easter's calloused hand hung open there to the night that had got wholly into the tent.

Nina let her own arm stretch forward opposite Easter's. Her hand too opened, of itself. She lay there a long time motionless, under the night's gaze, its black cheek, looking immovably at her hand, the only part of her now which was not asleep. Its gesture was like Easter's, but Easter's hand slept and her own hand knew—shrank and knew, yet offered still.

"Instead . . . me instead. . . ."

In the cup of her hand, in her filling skin, in the fingers' bursting weight and stillness, Nina felt it: compassion and a kind of competing that were all one, a single ecstasy, a single longing. For the night was not impartial. No, the night loved some more than others, served some more than others. Nina's hand lay open there for a long time, as if its fingers would be its eyes. Then it too slept. She dreamed her hand was helpless to the tearing teeth of wild beasts. At reveille she woke up lying on it. She could not move it. She hit it and bit it until like a cluster of bees it stung back and came to life.

V.

They had seen, without any idea of what he would do—and yet it was just like him—little old Exum toiling up the rough barky ladder and dreaming it up, clinging there monkeylike among the leaves, all eyes and wrinkled forehead.

Exum was apart too, boy and nigger to boot; he constantly moved along an even further fringe of the landscape than Loch, wearing the man's stiff straw hat brilliant as a snowflake. They would see Exum in the hat bobbing along the rim of the swamp like a fisherman's cork, elevated just a bit by the miasma and illusion of the landscape he moved in. It was Exum persistent as a little bug, inching along the foot of the swamp wall, carrying around a fishing cane and minnow can, fishing around the bend from their side of the lake, catching all kinds of things. Things, things. He claimed all he caught, gloating—dangled it and loved it, clasped it with suspicious glee—wouldn't a soul dispute him that? The Boy Scout asked him if he could catch an electric eel and Exum promised it readily—a gift; the challenge was a siesta-long back-and-forth across the water.

Now all rolling eyes, he hung on the ladder, too little to count as looking—too everything-he-was to count as anything.

Beyond him on the diving-board, Easter was standing—high above the others at their swimming lesson. She was motionless, barefooted, and tall with her outgrown, printed dress on her and the sky under her. She had not answered when they called things up to her. They splashed noisily under her calloused, coral-colored foot that hung over.

"How are you going to get down, Easter!" shouted Gertrude Bowles.

Miss Moody smiled understandingly up at Easter. How far, in the water, could Miss Parnell Moody be transformed from a schoolteacher? They had wondered. She wore a canary yellow bathing cap lumpy over her hair, with a rubber butterfly on the front. She wore a brassiere and bloomers under her bathing suit because, said Jinny Love, that was exactly how good she was. She scarcely looked for trouble, immediate trouble—though this was the last day at Moon Lake.

Exum's little wilted black fingers struck at his lips as if playing a tune on them. He put out a foolishly long arm. He held a green willow switch. Later they every one said they saw him—but too late. He gave Easter's heel the tenderest, obscurest little brush, with something of nigger persuasion about it.

She dropped like one hit in the head by a stone from a sling. In their retrospect, her body, never turning, seemed to languish upright for a moment, then descend. It went to meet and was received by blue air. It dropped as if handed down all the way and was let into the brown water almost on Miss Moody's crown, and went out of sight at once. There was something so positive about its disappearance that only the instinct of caution made them give it a moment to come up again; it didn't come up. Then Exum let loose a girlish howl and clung to the ladder as though a fire had been lighted under it.

Nobody called for Loch Morrison. On shore, he studiously

hung his bugle on the tree. He was enormously barefooted. He took a frog dive and when he went through the air they noticed that the powdered-on dirt gave him lavender soles. Now he swam destructively into the water, cut through the girls, and began to hunt Easter where all the fingers began to point.

They cried while he hunted, their chins dropping into the brown buggy stuff and their mouths sometimes swallowing it. He didn't give a glance their way. He stayed under as though the lake came down a lid on him, at each dive. Sometimes, open-mouthed, he appeared with something awful in his hands, showing not them, but the world, or himself—long ribbons of green and terrible stuff, shapeless black matter, nobody's shoe. Then he would up-end and go down, hunting her again. Each dive was a call on Exum to scream again.

"Shut up! Get out of the way! You stir up the lake!" Loch Morrison yelled once—blaming them. They looked at one another and after one loud cry all stopped crying. Standing in the brown that cut them off where they waited, ankle-deep, waist-deep, knee-deep, chin-deep, they made a little V, with Miss Moody in front and partly obscuring their vision with her jerky butterfly cap. They felt his insult. They stood so still as to be almost carried away, in the pictureless warm body of lake around them, until they felt the weight of the currentless water pulling anyhow. Their shadows only, like the curled back edges of a split drum, showed where they each protruded out of Moon Lake.

Up above, Exum howled, and further up, some fulsome, vague clouds with uneasy hearts blew peony-like. Exum howled up, down, and all around. He brought Elberta, mad, from the cook tent, and surely Mrs. Gruenwald was dead to the world—asleep or reading—or she would be coming too, by now, capering down her favorite trail. It was Jinny Love, they realized, who had capered down, and now stood strangely signaling from shore. The painstaking work of Miss Moody, white bandages covered her arms and legs; poison ivy had appeared that morning. Like Easter, Jinny Love had no intention of going in the lake.

"Ahhhhh!" everybody said, long and drawn out, just as he found her.

Of course he found her, there was her arm sliding through his hand. They saw him snatch the hair of Easter's head, the way a boy will snatch anything he wants, as if he won't have invisible opponents snatching first. Under the water he joined himself to her. He spouted, and with engine-like jerks brought her in.

There came Mrs. Gruenwald. With something like a skip, she came to a stop on the bank and waved her hands. Her middy blouse flew up, showing her loosened corset. It was red. They treasured that up. But her voice was pre-emptory.

"This minute! Out of the lake! Out of the lake, out-out! Parnell! Discipline! March them out."

"One's drowned!" shrieked poor Miss Moody.

Loch stood over Easter. He sat her up, folding, on the shore, wheeled her arm over, and by that dragged her clear of the water before he dropped her, a wrapped bundle in the glare. He shook himself in the sun like a dog, blew his nose, spat, and shook his ears, all in a kind of leisurely trance that kept Mrs. Gruenwald off—as though he had no notion that he was interrupting things at all. Exum could now be heard shrieking for Miss Marybelle Steptoe, the lady who had had the camp last year and was now married and living in the Delta.

Miss Moody and all her girls now came out of the lake. Tardy, drooping, their hair heavy-wet and their rubber shoes making wincing sounds, they edged the shore.

Loch returned to Easter, spread her out, and then they could all get at her, but they watched the water lake in her lap. The sun like a weight fell on them. Miss Moody wildly ran and caught up Easter's ankle and pushed on her, like a lady with a wheelbarrow. The Boy Scout looped Easter's arms like sashes on top of her and took up his end, the shoulders. They carried her, looking for shade. One arm fell, touching ground. Jinny Love, in the dazzling bandages, ran up and scooped Easter's arm in both of hers. They proceeded, zigzag, Jinny Love turning her head toward the rest of them, running low, bearing the arm.

They put her down in the only shade on earth, after all, the table under the tree. It was where they ate. The table was itself still mostly tree, as the ladder and diving board were half tree too; a camp table had to be round and barky on the underside, and odorous of having been chopped down. They knew that splintery surface, and the ants that crawled on it. Mrs. Gruenwald, with her strong cheeks, blew on the table, but she might have put a cloth down. She stood between table and girls; her tennis shoes, like lesser corsets, tied her feet solid there; and they did not go any closer, but only to where they could see.

"I got her, please ma'am."

In the water, the life saver's face had held his whole impatience; now it was washed pure, blank. He pulled Easter his way, away from Miss Moody—who, however, had got Easter's sash ends wrung out—and then, with a turn, hid her from Mrs. Gruenwald. Holding her folded up to him, he got her clear, and the next moment, with a spread of his hand, had her lying there before him on the table top.

They were silent. Easter lay in a mold of wetness from Moon Lake, on her side; sharp as a flatiron her hipbone pointed up. She was arm to arm and leg to leg in a long fold, wrong-colored and pressed together as unopen leaves are. Her breasts, too, faced together. Out of the water Easter's hair was darkened, and lay over her face in long fern shapes. Miss Moody laid it back.

"You can tell she's not breathing," said Jinny Love.

Easter's nostrils were pinched-looking like an old country woman's. Her side fell slack as a dead rabbit's in the woods, with the flowers of her orphan dress all running together in some antic of their own, some belated mix-up of the event. The Boy Scout had only let her go to leap onto the table with her. He stood over her, put his hands on her, and rolled her over; they heard the distant-like knock of her forehead on the solid table, and the knocking of her hip and knee.

Exum was heard being whipped in the willow clump; then they remembered Elberta was his mother. "You little black son-a-bitch!" they heard her yelling, and he howled through the woods.

Astride Easter the Boy Scout lifted her up between his legs and dropped her. He did it again, and she fell on one arm. He nodded—not to them.

There was a sigh, a Morgana sigh, not an orphans'. The

orphans did not press forward, or claim to own or protect Easter any more. They did nothing except mill a little, and yet their group was delicately changed. In Nina's head, where the world was still partly leisurely, came a recollected scene: birds on a roof under a cherry tree; they were drunk.

The Boy Scout, nodding, took Easter's hair and turned her head. He left her face looking at them. Her eyes were neither open nor altogether shut but as if her ears heard a great noise, back from the time she fell; the whites showed under the lids pale and slick as watermelon seeds. Her lips were parted to the same degree; her teeth could be seen smeared with black mud.

The Boy Scout reached in and gouged out her mouth with his hand, an unbelievable act. She did not alter. He lifted up, screwed his toes, and with a groan of his own fell upon her and drove up and down upon her, into her, gouging the heels of his hands into her ribs again and again. She did not alter except that she let a thin stream of water out of her mouth, a dark stain down the fixed cheek. The children drew together. Life-saving was much worse than they had dreamed. Worse still was the carelessness of Easter's body.

Jinny Love volunteered once more. She would wave a towel over things to drive the mosquitoes, at least, away. She chose a white towel. Her unspotted arms lifted and criss-crossed. She faced them now; her expression quietened and became ceremonious.

Easter's body lay up on the table to receive anything that was done to it. If *he* was brutal, her self, her body, the withheld life, was brutal too. While the Boy Scout as if he rode a runaway horse clung momently to her and arched himself off her back, dug his knees and fists into her and was flung back careening by his own tactics, she lay there.

Let him try and try!

The next thing Nina knew was a scent of home, an adult's thumb in her shoulder, and a cry, "Now what?" Miss Lizzie Stark pushed in front of her, where her hips and black purse swung to a full stop, blotting out everything. She was Jinny Love's mother and had arrived on her daily visit to see how the camp was running.

They never heard the electric car coming, but usually they saw it, watched for it in the landscape, as out of place as a piano rocking over the holes and taking the bumps, making a high wall of dust.

Nobody dared tell Miss Lizzie; only Loch Morrison's grunts could be heard.

"Some orphan get too much of it?" Then she said more loudly, "But what's *he* doing to her? Stop that."

The Morgana girls all ran to her and clung to her skirt.

"Get off me," she said. "Now look here, everybody. I've got a weak heart. You all know that.—Is that *Jinny Love*?"

"Leave me alone, Mama," said Jinny Love, waving the towel.

Miss Lizzie, whose hands were on Nina's shoulders, shook Nina. "Jinny Love Stark, come here to me, Loch Morrison, get off that table and shame on you."

Miss Moody was the one brought to tears. She walked up to Miss Lizzie holding a towel in front of her breast and weeping. "He's our life saver, Miss Lizzie. Remember? Our Boy Scout. Oh, mercy, I'm thankful you've come, he's been doing that a long time. Stand in the shade, Miss Lizzie."

"Boy Scout? Why, he ought to be—he ought to be—I can't stand it, Parnell Moody."

"Can't any of us help it, Miss Lizzie. Can't any of us. It's what he came for." She wept.

"That's Easter," Geneva said. "That is."

"He ought to be put out of business," Miss Lizzie Stark said. She stood in the center of them all, squeezing Nina uncomfortably for Jinny Love, who flouted her up in front, and Nina could look up at her. The white rice powder which she used on the very front of her face twinkled on her faint mustache. She smelled of red pepper and lemon juice—she had been making them some mayonnaise. She was valiantly trying to make up for all the Boy Scout was doing by what she was thinking of him: that he was odious. Miss Lizzie's carelessly flung word to him on sight—the first day—had been, "You little rascal, I bet you run down and pollute the spring, don't you?" "Nome" the Boy Scout had said, showing the first evidence of his gloom.

"Tears won't help, Parnell," Miss Lizzie said. "Though

some don't know what tears are." She glanced at Mrs. Gruenwald, who glanced back from another level; she had brought herself out a chair. "And our last afternoon. I'd thought we'd have a treat."

They looked around as here came Marvin, Miss Lizzie's yard boy, holding two watermelons like a mother with twins. He came toward the table and just stood there.

"Marvin. You can put those melons down, don't you see the table's got somebody on it?" Miss Lizzie said. "Put 'em down and wait."

Her presence made this whole happening seem more in the nature of things. They were glad Miss Lizzie had come! It was somehow for this that they had given those yells for Miss Lizzie as Camp Mother. Under her gaze the Boy Scout's actions seemed to lose a good deal of significance. He was reduced almost to a nuisance—a mosquito, with a mosquito's proboscis. "Get him off her," Miss Lizzie repeated, in her rich and yet careless, almost humorous voice, knowing it was no good. "Ah, get him off her." She stood hugging the other little girls, several of them, warmly. Her gaze only hardened on Jinny Love; they hugged her all the more.

She loved them. It seemed the harder it was to get out here and the harder a time she found them having, the better she appreciated them. They remembered now—while the Boy Scout still drove up and down on Easter's muddy back—how they were always getting ready for Miss Lizzie; the tents even now were straight and the ground picked up and raked for her, and the tea for supper was already made and sitting in a tub in the lake; and sure enough, the niggers' dog had barked at the car just as always, and now here she was. She could have stopped everything; and she hadn't stopped it. Even her opening protests seemed now like part of things—what she was supposed to say. Several of the little girls looked up at Miss Lizzie instead of at what was on the table. Her powdered lips flickered, her eyelids hooded her gaze, but she was there.

On the table, the Boy Scout spat, and took a fresh appraisal of Easter. He reached for a hold on her hair and pulled her head back. No longer were her lips faintly parted—her mouth was open. It gaped. So did his. He dropped her, the head with its suddenness bowed again on its cheek, and he started again.

"Easter's dead! Easter's d—" cried Gertrude Bowles in a rowdy voice, and she was slapped rowdily across the mouth to cut off the word, by Miss Lizzie's hand.

Jinny Love, with a persistence they had not dreamed of, deployed the towel. Could it be owing to Jinny Love's always being on the right side that Easter mustn't dare die and bring all this to a stop? Nina thought, It's I that's thinking. Easter's not thinking at all. And while not thinking, she is not dead, but unconscious, which is even harder to be. Easter had come among them and had held herself untouchable and intact. Of course, for one little touch could smirch her, make her fall so far, so deep.—Except that by that time they were all saying the nigger deliberately poked her off in the water, meant her to drown.

"Don't touch her," they said tenderly to one another.

"Give up! Give up! Give up!" screamed Miss Moody—she who had rubbed them all the same, as if she rubbed chickens for the frying pan. Miss Lizzie without hesitation slapped her too.

"Don't touch her."

For they were crowding closer to the table all the time.

"If Easter's dead, I get her coat for winter, all right," said Geneva.

"Hush, orphan."

"Is she then?"

"You shut up." The Boy Scout looked around and panted at Geneva. "You can ast *me* when I ast you to ast me."

The niggers' dog was barking again, had been barking.

"Now who?"

"A big boy. It's old Ran MacLain and he's coming."

"He would."

He came right up, wearing a cap.

"Get away from me, Ran MacLain," Miss Lizzie called toward him. "You and dogs and guns, keep away. We've already got all we can put up with out here."

She put her foot down on his asking any questions, getting up on the table, or leaving, now that he'd come. Under his cap bill, Ran MacLain set his gaze—he was twenty-three, his seasoned gaze—on Loch and Easter on the table. He could not be prevented from considering them all. He moved under the tree. He held his gun under his arm. He let two dogs run loose, and almost imperceptibly, he chewed gum. Only Miss Moody did not move away from him.

And pressing closer to the table, Nina almost walked into Easter's arm flung out over the edge. The arm was turned at the elbow so that the hand opened upward. It held there the same as it had held when the night came in and stood in the tent, when it had come to Easter and not to Nina. It was the one hand, and it seemed the one moment.

"Don't touch her."

Nina fainted. She woke up to the cut-onion odor of Elberta's under-arm. She was up on the table with Easter, foot to head. There was so much she loved at home, but there was only time to remember the front yard. The silver, sweet-smelling paths strewed themselves behind the lawn mower, the four-o'clocks blazed. Then Elberta raised her up, she got down from the table, and was back with the others.

"Keep away. Keep away, I told you you better keep away. Leave me alone," Loch Morrison was saying with short breaths. "I dove for her, didn't I?"

They hated him, Nina most of all. Almost, they hated Easter.

They looked at Easter's mouth and at the eyes where they were contemplating without sense the back side of the light. Though she had bullied and repulsed them earlier, they began to speculate in another kind of allurement: was there danger that Easter, turned in on herself, might call out to them after all, from the other, worse, side of it? Her secret voice, if soundless then possibly visible, might work out of her terrible mouth like a vine, preening and sprung with flowers. Or a snake would come out.

The Boy Scout crushed in her body and blood came out of her mouth. For them all, it was like being spoken to.

"Nina, you! Come stand right here in my skirt," Miss Lizzie called. Nina went and stood under the big bosom that started down, at the neck of her dress, like a big cloven white hide.

Jinny Love was catching her mother's eye. Of course she had stolen brief rests, but now her white arms lifted the white towel and whipped it bravely. She looked at them until she caught their eye—as if in the end the party was for *her*.

Marvin had gone back to the car and brought two more melons, which he stood holding.

"Marvin. We aren't ready for our watermelon. I told you."

"Oh, Ran. How could you? Oh, Ran."

That was Miss Moody in still a third manifestation.

By now the Boy Scout seemed for ever part of Easter and she part of him, he in motion on the up-and-down and she stretched across. He was dripping, while her skirt dried on the table; so in a manner they had changed places too. Was time moving? Endlessly, Ran MacLain's dogs frisked and played, with the niggers' dog between.

Time was moving because in the beginning Easter's face—the curve of her brow, the soft upper lip and the milky eyes—partook of the swoon of her fall—the almost forgotten fall that bathed her so purely in blue for that long moment. The face was set now, and ugly with that rainy color of seedling petunias, the kind nobody wants. Her mouth surely by now had been open long enough, as long as any gape, bite, cry, hunger, satisfaction lasts, any one person's grief, or even protest.

Not all the children watched, and their heads all were beginning to hang, to nod. Everybody had forgotten about crying. Nina had spotted three little shells in the sand she wanted to pick up when she could. And suddenly this seemed to her one of those moments out of the future, just as she had found one small brief one out of the past; this was far, far ahead of her—picking up the shells, one, another, another, without time moving any more, and Easter abandoned on a little edifice, beyond dying and beyond being remembered about.

"I'm so tired!" Gertrude Bowles said. "And hot. Ain't you tired of Easter, laying up there on that table?"

"My arms are about to break, you all," and Jinny Love stood and hugged them to her.

"I'm so tired of Easter," Gertrude said.

"Wish she'd go ahead and die and get it over with," said Little Sister Spights, who had been thumb-sucking all afternoon without a reprimand.

"I give up," said Jinny Love.

Miss Lizzie beckoned, and she came. "I and Nina and Easter all went out in the woods, and I was the only one that came back with poison ivy," she said, kissing her mother.

Miss Lizzie sank her fingers critically into the arms of the girls at her skirt. They all rose on tiptoe. Was Easter dead then?

Looking out for an instant from precarious holds, they took in sharply for memory's sake that berated figure, the mask formed and set on the face, one hand displayed, one jealously clawed under the waist, as if a secret handful had been groveled for, the spread and spotted legs. It was a betrayed figure, the betrayal was over, it was a memory. And then as the blows, automatic now, swung down again, the figure itself gasped.

"Get back. Get back." Loch Morrison spoke between cruel, gritted teeth to them, and crouched over.

And when they got back, her toes webbed outward. Her belly arched and drew up from the board under her. She fell, but she kicked the Boy Scout.

Ridiculously, he tumbled backwards off the table. He fell almost into Miss Lizzie's skirt; she halved herself on the instant, and sat on the ground with her lap spread out before her like some magnificent hat that has just got crushed. Ran MacLain hurried politely over to pick her up, but she fought him off.

"Why don't you go home—now!" she said.

Before their eyes, Easter got to her knees, sat up, and drew her legs up to her. She rested her head on her knees and looked out at them, while she slowly pulled her ruined dress downward.

The sun was setting. They felt it directly behind them, the warmth flat as a hand. Easter leaned slightly over the table's edge, as if to gaze down at what might move, and blew her nose; she accomplished that with the aid of her finger, like people from away in the country. Then she sat looking out again; in another moment her legs dropped and hung down. The girls looked back at her, through the yellow and violet streams of dust—just now reaching them from Ran MacLain's flivver—the air coarse as sacking let down from the tree branches. Easter lifted one arm and shaded her eyes, but the arm fell in her lap like a clod.

There was a sighing sound from them. For the first time they noticed there was an old basket on the table. It held their knives, forks, tin cups and plates.

"Carry me." Easter's words had no inflection. Again, "Carry me."

She held out her arms to them, stupidly.

Then Ran MacLain whistled to his dogs.

The girls ran forward all together. Mrs. Gruenwald's fists rose in the air as if she lifted—no, rather had lowered—a curtain and she began with a bleating sound, "Pa-a-ack—"

> "—up your troubles in your old kit bag
> And smile, smile, smile!"

The Negroes were making a glorious commotion, all of them came up now, and then Exum escaped them all and ran waving away to the woods, dainty as a loosened rabbit.

"Who was he, that big boy?" Etoile was asking Jinny Love.

"Ran MacLain, slow-poke."

"What did he want?"

"He's just waiting on the camp. *They're* coming out tomorrow, hunting. I heard all he said to Miss Moody."

"Did Miss Moody *know* him?"

"Anybody knows him, and his twin brother too."

Nina, running up in the front line with the others, sighed—the sigh she gave when she turned in her examination papers at school. Then with each step she felt a defiance of her own. She screamed, "Easter!"

In that passionate instant, when they reached Easter and took her up, many feelings returned to Nina, some joining and some conflicting. At least what had happened to Easter was out in the world, like the table itself. There it remained—mystery, if only for being hard and cruel and, by something Nina felt inside her body, murderous.

Now they had Easter and carried her up to the tent, Mrs. Gruenwald still capering backwards and leading on,

"—in your old kit bag!
Smile, girls-instead-of-boys, that's the style!"

Miss Lizzie towered along darkly, groaning. She grabbed hold of Little Sister Spights, and said, "Can *you* brush me off!" She would be taking charge soon, but for now she asked for a place to sit down and a glass of cold water. She did not speak to Marvin yet; he was shoving the watermelons up onto the table.

Their minds could hardly capture it again, the way Easter was standing free in space, then handled and turned over by the blue air itself. Some of them looked back and saw the lake, rimmed around with its wall-within-walls of woods, into which the dark had already come. There were the water wings of Little Sister Spights, floating yet, white as a bird. "I know another Moon Lake," one girl had said yesterday. "Oh, my child, Moon Lakes are all over the world," Mrs. Gruenwald had interrupted. "I know of one in Austria . . ." And into each fell a girl, they dared, now, to think.

The lake grew darker, then gleamed, like the water of a rimmed well. Easter was put to bed, they sat quietly on the ground outside the tent, and Miss Lizzie sipped water from Nina's cup. The sky's rising clouds lighted all over, like one spread-out blooming mimosa tree that could be seen from where the trunk itself should rise.

VI.

Nina and Jinny Love, wandering down the lower path with arms entwined, saw the Boy Scout's tent. It was after the watermelon feast, and Miss Lizzie's departure. Miss Moody, in voile and tennis shoes, had a date with old "Rudy" Loomis, and Mrs. Gruenwald was trying to hold the girls with a sing before bedtime. Easter slept; Twosie watched her.

Nina and Jinny Love could hear the floating songs, farewell-like, the cheers and yells between. An owl hooted in a tree, closer by. The wind stirred.

On the other side of the tent wall the slats of the Boy Scout's legs shuttered open and shut like a fan when he moved back and forth. He had a lantern in there, or perhaps only a candle. He finished off his own shadow by opening the flap of his tent. Jinny Love and Nina halted on the path, quiet as old campers.

The Boy Scout, little old Loch Morrison, was undressing in his tent for the whole world to see. He took his time wrenching off each garment; then he threw it to the floor as hard as he would throw a ball; yet that seemed, in him, meditative.

His candle—for that was all it was—jumping a little now, he stood there studying and touching his case of sunburn in a Kress mirror like theirs. He was naked and there was his little tickling thing hung on him like the last drop on the pitcher's lip. He ceased or exhausted study and came to the tent opening again and stood leaning on one raised arm, with his weight on one foot—just looking out into the night, which was clamorous.

It seemed to them he had little to do!

Hadn't he surely, just before they caught him, been pounding his chest with his fists? Bragging on himself? It seemed to them they could still hear in the beating air of night the wild tattoo of pride he must have struck off. His silly, brief, overriding little show they could well imagine there in his tent of separation in the middle of the woods, in the night. Minnowy thing that matched his candle flame, naked as he was with that, he thought he shone forth too. Didn't he?

Nevertheless, standing there with the tent slanting over him and his arm knobby as it reached up and his head bent a little, he looked rather at loose ends.

"We can call like an owl," Nina suggested. But Jinny Love thought in terms of the future. "I'll tell on him, in Morgana tomorrow. He's the most conceited Boy Scout in the whole troop; and's bowlegged.

"You and I will always be old maids," she added.

Then they went up and joined the singing.

5.

The Whole World Knows

FATHER, I wish I could talk to you, wherever you are right now.

Mother said, *Where have you been, son?*—Nowhere, Mother.—*I wish you wouldn't sound so unhappy, son. You could come back to MacLain and live with me now.*—I can't do that, Mother. You know I have to stay in Morgana.

When I slammed the door of the bank I rolled down my sleeves and stood for some time looking out at the cotton field behind Mr. Wiley Bowles' across the street, until it nearly put me to sleep and then woke me up like a light turned on in my face. Woodrow Spights had been gone a few minutes or so. I got in my car and drove up the street, turned around at the foot of Jinny's driveway (yonder went Woody) and drove down again. I turned around in our old driveway, where Miss Francine had the sprinkler running, and made the same trip. The thing everybody does every day, except not by themselves.

There was Maideen Sumrall on the drugstore step waving a little green handkerchief. When I didn't remember to stop I saw the handkerchief pulled down. I turned again, to pick her up, but she'd caught her ride with Red Ferguson.

So I went to my room. Bella, Miss Francine Murphy's little dog, panted all the time—she was sick. I always went out in the backyard and spoke to her. Poor Bella, how do you do, lady? Is it hot, do they leave you alone?

Mother said on the phone, *Have you been out somewhere, son?*—Just to get a little air.—*I can tell you're all peaked. And you keep things from me, I don't understand. You're as bad as Eugene Hudson. Now I have two sons keeping things from me.*—I haven't been anywhere, where would I go?—*If you came back with me, to MacLain Courthouse, everything would be all right. I know you won't eat at Miss Francine's table, not her biscuit.*—It's as good as Jinny's, Mother.

But Eugene's safe in California, that's what we think.

•

When the bank opened, Miss Perdita Mayo came up to my window and hollered, "Randall, when are you going back to your precious wife? You forgive her, now you hear? That's no way to do, bear grudges. Your mother never bore your father a single grudge in her life, and he made her life right hard. I tell you, how do you suppose he made her life? She don't bear him a grudge. We're all human on earth. Where's little old Woodrow this morning, late to work or you done something to him? I still think of him a boy in knee britches and Buster Brown bob, riding that pony, that extravagant pony, cost a hundred dollars. Woodrow: a little common but so smart. Felix Spights never overcharged a customer, and Miss Billy Texas amounted to a good deal before she got like she is now; and Missie could always play the piano better than average; Little Sister too young to tell yet. Ah, I'm a woman that's been clear around the world in my rocking chair, and I tell you we all get surprises now and then. But you march on back to your wife, Ran MacLain. You hear? It's a thing of the flesh not the spirit, it'll pass. Jinny'll get over this in three four months. You hear me? And you go back *nice*."

"Still hotter today, isn't it?"

I picked up Maideen Sumrall and we rode up and down the street. She was from the Sissum community. She was eighteen years old. "Look! Citified," she said, and pushed both hands at me; she had new white cotton gloves on. Maideen would ride there by me and talk about things I didn't mind hearing about—the Seed and Feed where she clerked and kept the books, Old Man Moody that she worked for, the way working in Morgana seemed after the country and junior college. Her first job: her mother still didn't like the idea. And people could be so nice: getting a ride home with me sometimes like this, instead of with Red Ferguson in the Coca-Cola truck. So she told me now. "And I didn't think you were going to see me at first, Ran. I saved my gloves to wear riding home in a car."

I told her my eyes had gone bad. She said she was sorry. She was country-prim and liked to have something to put in words that she could be sorry about. I drove, idling along, up and down a few times more. Mr. Steptoe was dragging the mail sack into the postoffice—he and Maideen waved. In the Presbyterian church Missie Spights was playing "Will There Be Any Stars in My Crown?", and Maideen listened. And on the street the same ones stood in doorways or rode in their cars, and waved at my car. Maideen's little blue handkerchief was busy waving back. She waved at them as she did at me.

"I wouldn't be surprised if it *wasn't* hard on the eyes, to be cooped up and just count money all day, Ran"—to say something to me.

She knew what anybody in Morgana told her; and for four or five afternoons after the first one I picked her up and took her up and down the street a few turns, bought her a coke at Johnny Loomis's, and drove her home out by Old Forks and let her out, and she never said a word except a kind one, like about counting money. She was kind; her company was the next thing to being alone.

I drove her home and then drove back to Morgana to the room I had at Miss Francine Murphy's.

Next time, there at the end of the pavement, I turned up the cut to the Starks'. I couldn't stand it any longer.

Maideen didn't say a word till we reached the head of the drive and stopped.

"Ran?" she said. She wasn't asking anything. She meant just to remind me I had company, but that was what I knew. I got out and went around and opened her door.

"You want to take me in yonder?" she said. "Please, I'd just as soon you wouldn't." Her head hung. I saw the extra-white part in her hair.

I said, "Sure. Let's go in and see Jinny. Why not?"

I couldn't stand it any longer, that was why.

"I'm going and taking you."

It wasn't as if Mr. Drewsie Carmichael didn't say to me every afternoon, "Come on home with me, boy"—argue, while he banged that big Panama—like yours, Father—down on his head, "no sense in your not sleeping cool, with one of our fans turned on you. Mamie's mad at you for roasting in that room across the street from us—you could move in five minutes. Well, Ran, look: Mamie has something to say to you:

I don't." And he'd wait a minute in the door before he left. He'd stand and hold his cane—the one Woody Spights and I had bought him together when he was elected Mayor—up by his head, to threaten me with comfort, till I answered him, "No thanks, sir."

Maideen was at my side. We walked across the Starks' baked yard to the front porch, passing under the heavy heads of those crape myrtles, the too bright blooms that hang down like fruits that might drop. My wife's mother—Miss Lizzie Morgan, Father—put her face to her bedroom window first thing. She'd know it first if I came back, all right. Parting her curtains with a steel crochet hook, she looked down at Randall MacLain coming to her door, and bringing who-on-earth with him.

"What are you doing here, Ran MacLain?"

When I didn't look up, she rapped on the window sill with her hook.

"I've never been inside the Stark home," Maideen said, and I began to smile. I felt curiously light-hearted. Lilies must have been in bloom somewhere near, and I took a full breath of their ether smell: consciousness could go or not. I pulled open the screen door. From above, inside somewhere, Miss Lizzie was calling, "Jinny Love!" like Jinny had a date.

Jinny—not out playing croquet—stood with her legs apart, cutting off locks of her hair at the hall mirror. The locks fell at her feet. She had on straw sandals, the kind that would have to be ordered, boy's shorts. She looked up at me, short range, and said "Just in time, to tell me when to stop." She'd cut bangs. Her smile reminded me of the way a child will open its mouth all right, but not let out the cry till it sees the right person.

And turning to the mirror she cut again. "Obey that impulse—" She had seen Maideen then, and she went right on cutting her hair with those stork-shaped scissors. "Come in *too*, take off your gloves."

That's right: she would know, with her quickness like foreknowledge, first that I would come back when the summer got too much for me, and second that I'd just as soon bring a stranger if I could find one, somebody who didn't know any better, to come in the house with me when I came.

Father, I wished I could go back.

I looked at Jinny's head with the ragged points all over it, and there was Miss Lizzie coming down; she had just stopped to change her shoes, of course. For the kind that came down stairs like a march. As we all fell in together, we were leaving where we met too, starting down the hall with nobody pairing, and over each other's names or whatever we said, Jinny's voice hollered at Tellie for cokes. She counted us with her finger. That lightness came right back. Just to step on the matting, that billows a little anyway, and with Jinny's hair scattered like feathers on it, I could have floated, risen and floated.

In rockers—we sat on the back porch—we were all not rocking. The chairs, white wicker, had a new coat of paint—their thousandth-and-first, but one new coat since I left Jinny. The outside—a sheet of white light—was in my eyes. The ferns close around us were hushing on their stands, they had just been watered. I could listen to women and hear pieces of the story, of what happened to us, of course—but I listened to the ferns.

No matter, it was being told. Not in Miss Lizzie's voice, which wouldn't think of it, certainly not in Jinny's, but in the clear voice of Maideen where it had never existed—all the worse for the voice not even questioning what it said—just repeating, just rushing, old—the town words.

Telling what she was told she saw, repeating what she listened to—young girls are outlandish little birds that talk. They can be taught, some each day, to sing a song *people* have made. . . . Even Miss Lizzie put her head on one side, to let Maideen be.

He walked out on her and took his clothes down to the other end of the street. Now everybody's waiting to see how soon he'll go back. They say Jinny MacLain invites Woody out there to eat, a year younger than she is, remember when they were born. Invites, under her mama's nose. Sure, it's Woodrow Spights she invites. Who else in Morgana would there be for Jinny Stark after Ran, with even Eugene MacLain gone? She's kin to the Nesbitts. They don't say when it started, can anybody tell? At the Circle, at Miss Francine's, at Sunday School, they say, they say she will marry Woodrow: Woodrow'd jump at it but Ran will kill somebody first. And there's Ran's papa and the way he was and is, remember, remember? And Eugene gone that could sometimes hold him down. Poor Snowdie, it's her burden. He used to be sweet but too much devil in him from Time was, that's Ran. He'll do something bad. He won't divorce Jinny but he'll do something bad. Maybe kill them all. They say Jinny's not scared of that. Maybe she drinks and hides the bottle, you know her father's side. And just as prissy as ever on the street. And oh, don't you know, they run into each other every day of the world, all three. Sure, how could they help it if they wanted to help it, how could you get away from it, right in Morgana? You can't get away in Morgana. Away from anything at all, you know that.

Father! You didn't listen.

And Tellie was mad at all of us. She still held the tray, she held it about an inch and a half too high. When Maideen took her coke in her white glove, she said to Miss Lizzie, "I look too tacky and mussed when I work in the store all day to be coming in anybody's strange house."

"You're by far the freshest one here, my dear."

Who else had Maideen ever known to talk about but herself?

But she looked like Jinny. She was a child's copy of Jinny. Jinny's first steady look at me, coming just then, made that plain all at once. (Oh, her look always made contamination plain. Or plainer.) That resemblance I knew *post-mortem*, so to speak—and it made me right pleased with myself. I don't mean there was any mockery in Maideen's little face—no—but there was something of Maideen in Jinny's, that went back early—to whatever I knew my Jinny would never be now.

The slow breeze from that ceiling fan—its old white blades frosted like a cake, with the flies riding on it—lifted the girls' hair like one passing hand, Maideen's brown hair shoulder-long and Jinny's brown hair short, ruined—she ruined it herself, as she liked doing. Maideen was even more polite than she'd ever been to me, and making intervals in the quiet, like the ferns dripping, she talked about herself and the Seed and Feed; but she glowed with something she didn't know about, yet, there in the room with Jinny. And Jinny sat not rocking, yet, with her clever, not-listening smile.

I looked from Jinny to Maideen and back to Jinny, and almost listened for some compliment—a compliment from somewhere—Father!—for my good eyes, my vision. It took me, after all, to bring it out. There was nothing but time between them.

There were those annoying sounds keeping on out there—people and croquet. We finished the cokes. Miss Lizzie just sat there—hot. She still held the crochet hook, straight up like a ruler, and nobody was rapped, done to death. Jinny was on her feet, inviting us out to play croquet.

But it had been long enough.

They were slowly moving across the shade of the far backyard—Woody, Johnnie and Etta Loomis, Nina Carmichael and Jinny's cousin Junior Nesbitt, and the fourteen-year-old child that they let play—with Woody Spights knocking his ball through a wicket. He was too young for me—I'd never really looked at him before this year; he was coming up in the world. I looked down through the yard and the usual crowd seemed to have dwindled a little, I could not think who was out. Jinny went down there. It was myself.

Mother said, *Son, you're walking around in a dream.*

Miss Perdita came and said, "I hear you went back yesterday and wouldn't open your mouth, left again. Might as well not go at all. But no raring up now and doing anything we'll all be sorry to hear about. I know you won't. I knew your father, was crazy about your father, glad to see him come every time, sorry to see him go, and love your mother. Sweetest people in the world, most happily mated people in the world, long as he was home. Tell your mother I said so, next time you see her. And you march back to that precious wife. March back and have you some chirren. My Circle declares Jinny's going to divorce you, marry Woodrow. I said, Why? Thing of the flesh, I told my Circle, won't last. Sister said you'd kill him, and I said Sister, who are you talking about? If it's Ran MacLain that *I* knew in his buggy, I said, he's not at all likely to take on to that extent. And little Jinny. Who's going to tell Lizzie to spank her, though? I couldn't help but laugh at Jinny: she says, It's my own business! We was in Hardware, old Holifield just scowling his head off. I says, How did it happen, Jinny, tell old Miss Perdita, you monkey, and she says, Oh, Miss Perdita, do like *me*. Do like *me*, she says, and just go on like nothing's happened. I declare, and she says I have to write my checks on the Morgana bank, and Woody Spights works in it, there's just him and Ran, so I go up to Woody and cash them. And I says, Child—how could you all get away from each other if you tried? You couldn't. It's a pity you had to run to a Spights, though. Oh, if there'd just been some Carmichael *boys*, I often say! No matter who you are, though, it's an endless circle. That's what a thing of the flesh is, endless circle. And you won't get away from that in Morgana. Even our little town.

"All right, I said to Old Man Moody while ago, look. Jinny was unfaithful to Ran—that's the up-and-down of it. There you have what it's all *about*. That's the brunt of it. Face it, I told Dave Moody. Like Lizzie Stark does, she's brave. Though she's seven miles south of here, Snowdie MacLain's another brave one. Poor Billy Texas Spights is beyond knowing. You're just a seed and feed man and the marshal here, you don't form opinions enough to suit me.

"Jinny was never scared of the Devil himself as a growing girl, so she certainly shouldn't be now, she's twenty-five. She's Lizzie's own. And Woodrow Spights won't ever quit at the bank, will he? It's so much cleaner than the store, and he'll get the store too. So it's up to you, Ran, looks like.

"And I'd go back to my lawful spouse!" Miss Perdita puts both hands on the bars of my cage and raises her voice. "You or I or the Man in the Moon got no business sleeping in that little hot upstairs room with a western exposure at Miss Francine Murphy's for all the pride on earth, not in August! And even if it is the house you grew up in, it's a different room. And listen here to me. Don't you ruin a *country* girl in the bargain. Make what you will of that."

She backs away leaving her hands out, pulling-like at the air, like I'm floating on my ear suspended, hypnotized, and she can leave. But she just goes as far as the next window—Woody Spights'.

I went back to the room I had at Miss Francine Murphy's. Father, it used to be the trunk room. It had Mother's pieced quilts and her wedding dress and all the terrible accumulation of a long time you wouldn't have known about.

After work I would cut the grass or something in Miss Francine's backyard so it would be cooler for Bella. It kept the fleas away from her to some extent. It didn't do much good. The heat held on.

I tried going to Jinny's a little later in the afternoon. The men were playing, still playing croquet with a little girl, and the women had taken off to themselves, on the porch. I tried without Maideen.

It was the long Mississippi evening, the waiting till it was cool enough to eat. The voice of Miss Lizzie carried. Like the hum of the gin, it was there, but the evening was still quiet, still very hot and quiet.

Somebody called to me, "You're dead on Woody." It was just a little Williams girl in pigtails.

I may have answered with a joke. I felt light-headed, not serious at all, really doing it for a child when I lifted my mallet—the one with the red band that had always been mine. But I brought Woody Spights down with it. He toppled and shook the ground. I felt the air rush up. Then I beat on him. I went over his whole length, and cracked his head apart with that soft girl's hair and all the ideas, beat on him without stopping till every bone, all the way down to the numerous little bones in the foot, was cracked in two. I didn't have done with Woody Spights till then. And I proved the male human body—it has a too positive, too special shape, you know, not to be hurt—it could be finished up pretty fast. It just takes one good loud blow after another—Jinny should be taught that.

I looked at Woodrow down there. And his blue eyes were just as unharmed. Just as unharmed as bubbles a child blows, the most impervious things—you've seen grass blades go through bubbles and they still reflect the world, give it back unbroken. Woodrow Spights I declare was dead. "Now you watch," he said.

He spoke with no sign of pain. Just that edge of competition was in his voice. He was ever the most ambitious fool. To me ambition's always been a mystery, but now it was his try to deceive us—me and him both. I didn't know how it could open again, the broken jawbone of Woody Spights, but it could. I heard him say, "Now you watch."

He was dead on the ruined grass. But he had risen up. Just to call attention to it, he gave the fat little Williams girl a spank. I could see the spank, but I couldn't hear it—the most familiar sound in the world.

And I should have called out *then*—All is disgrace! Human beings' cries could swell if locusts' could, in the last of evening like this, and cross the grass in a backyard, if only they enough of them cried. At our feet the shadows faded out light into no shadows left and the locusts sang in long waves, O-E, O-E, and the gin ran on. Our grass in August is like the floor of the sea, and we walk on it slowly playing, and the sky turns green before dark, Father, as you know. The sweat ran over my back and down my arms and legs, branching, like an upside-down tree.

Then, "You all come in!" They were calling from the porch—the well-known lamps suddenly all went on. They called us in their calling women's voices, of disguise, all but Jinny. "Fools, you're playing in the dark!" she said. "Supper's ready, if anybody cares."

The bright porch across the dark was like a boat on the river to me; an excursion boat I wasn't going on. I was going to Miss Francine Murphy's, as everybody knew.

Each evening to avoid Miss Francine and the three school teachers, I ran through the porch and hall both like a man through a burning building. In the backyard, with fig trees black, otherwise moonlit, Bella opened her eyes and looked at me. Her eyes both showed the moon. If she drank water, she vomited it up—yet she went with effort to her pan and drank again, for me. I held her. Poor Bella. I thought she suffered from a tumor, and stayed with her most of the night.

Mother said, *Son, I was glad to see you but I noticed that old pistol of your father's in your nice coat pocket, what do you want with that? Your father never cared for it, went off and left it. Not any robbers coming to the Morgana bank that I know of. Son, if you'd just saved your money you could take a little trip to the coast. I'd go with you. They always have a breeze at Gulfport, nearly always.*

Where the driveway ends at Jinny's, there are Spanish daggers and the bare front yard with the forked tree with the seat around it—like some old playground of a consolidated school, with the school back out of sight. Just the sharp, overgrown Spanish daggers, and the spiderwebs draped over them like clothes-rags. You can go under trees to the house by going all around the yard and opening the old gate by the summerhouse. Somewhere back in the shade there's a statue from Morgan days, of a dancing girl with her finger to her chin, all pockmarked, with some initials on her legs.

Maideen liked the statue but she said, "Are you taking me back in? I thought maybe now you weren't going to."

I saw my hand on the gate and said, "Now you wait. I've lost a button." I held out my sleeve to Maideen. All at once I felt so unlike myself I was ready to shed tears.

"A button? Why, I'll sew you one on, if you come on and take me home," Maideen said. That's what I wanted her to say, but she touched my sleeve. A chameleon ran up a leaf, and held there panting. "Then Mama can meet you. She'd be glad to have you stay to supper."

I unlatched the little old gate. I caught a whiff of the sour pears on the ground, the smell of August. I'd never told Maideen I was coming to supper, at any time, or would see her mama, of course; but also I kept forgetting about the old ways, the eternal politeness of the people you hope not to know.

"Oh, Jinny can sew it on now," I said.

"Oh, I can?" Jinny said. She'd of course been listening all the time from the summerhouse. She came out, alone, with the old broken wicker basket full of speckled pears. She didn't say go back and shut the gate.

I carried the rolling basket for her and we went ahead of Maideen but I knew she was coming behind; she wouldn't know very well how not to. There in the flower beds walked the same robins. The sprinkler dripped now. Once again we went into the house by the back door. Our hands touched. We had stepped on Tellie's patch of mint. The yellow cat was waiting to go in with us, the door handle was as hot as the hand, and on the step, getting under the feet of two people who went in together, the Mason jars with the busy cuttings in water— "Watch out for Mama's—!" A thousand times we'd gone in like that. As a thousand bees had droned and burrowed in the pears that lay on the ground.

Miss Lizzie shrank with a cry and started abruptly up the back stairs—bosom lifted—her shadow trotted up the boarding beside her like a bear with a nose. But she couldn't get to the top; she turned. She came down, carefully, and held up a finger at me. She needed to be careful. That stairs was the one Mr. Comus Stark fell down and broke his neck on one night, going up the back way drunk. Did I call it to attention?—Jinny got away.

"Randall. I can't help but tell you about a hand I held yesterday. My partner was Mamie Carmichael and you know she always plays her own hand with no more regard for her partner than you have. Well, she opened with a spade and Etta Loomis doubled. I held: a singleton spade, five clubs to the king-queen, five hearts to the king, and two little diamonds. I said two clubs. Parnell Moody said two diamonds, Mamie two spades, all passed. And when I laid down my hand Mamie said, Oh, *partner*! Why didn't you bid your hearts! I said, Hardly. At the level of three with the opponents doubling for a takeout. It developed of course she was two-suited—six spades to the ace-jack and four hearts to the ace-jack-ten, also my ace of clubs. Now, Randall. It would have been just as easy for Mamie to bid three hearts on that second go-round. But no! She could see only her own hand and took us down two, and we could have made five hearts. Now do *you* say I should have bid three hearts?"

I said, "You were justified not to, Miss Lizzie."

She began to cry on the stairs. Tears stood on her powdered face. "You men. You got us beat in the end. May be I'm getting old. Oh no, that's not it. Because I can tell you where you got us beat. We'd know you through and through except we never know what ails you. Don't you look at me like that. Of course I see what Jinny's doing, the fool, but you ailed first. You just got her answer to it, Ran." Then she glared again, turned, and went back upstairs.

And what ails me I don't know, Father, unless maybe you know. All through what she had to say I stood holding the cooking-pears. Then I set the basket on the table.

Jinny was in the little back study, "Mama's office," with the landscape wallpaper and Mr. Comus's old desk full-up with U.D.C. correspondence and plat maps that cracked like thunder when the fan blew them. She was yelling at Tellie. Tellie came in with the workbasket and then just waited, eyeing her.

"Put it down, Tellie, I'll use it when I get ready. Now you go on. Pull your mouth in, you hear?"

Tellie put down the basket and Jinny flicked it open and fished in it. The stork scissors fell out. She found a button that belonged to me, and waited on Tellie.

"I hear you's a mess." Tellie went out.

Jinny looked at me and didn't mind. I minded. I fired point-blank at Jinny—more than once. It was close range—there was barely room between us suddenly for the pistol to come up. And she only stood frowning at the needle I had forgotten the reason for. Her hand never deviated, never shook from the noise. The dim clock on the mantel was striking—the pistol hadn't drowned that out. I was watching Jinny and I saw her pouting childish breasts, excuses for breasts, sprung full of bright holes where my bullets had gone. But Jinny didn't feel it. She threaded her needle. She made her little face of success. Her thread always went straight in the eye.

"Will you hold still."

She far from acknowledged pain—anything but sorrow and pain. When I couldn't give her something she wanted she would hum a little tune. In our room, her voice would go low and soft to complete disparagement. Then I loved her a lot. The little cheat. I waited on, while she darted the needle and pulled at my sleeve, the sleeve to my helpless hand. It was like counting my breaths. I let out my fury and breathed the pure disappointment in: that she was not dead on earth. She bit the thread—magnificently. When she took her mouth away I nearly fell. The cheat.

I didn't dare say good-bye to Jinny any more. "All right, now you're ready for croquet," she told me. She went upstairs too.

Old Tellie spat a drop of nothing into the stove and clanged the lid down as I went out through the kitchen. Maideen was out in the swing, sitting. I told her to come on down to the croquet yard, where we all played Jinny's game, without Jinny.

Going to my room, I saw Miss Billy Texas Spights outdoors in her wrapper, whipping the flowers to make them bloom.

Father! Dear God wipe it clean. Wipe it clean, wipe it out. Don't let it be.

At last Miss Francine caught hold of me in the hall. "Do me a favor, Ran. Do me a favor and put Bella out of her misery. None of these school teachers any better at it than I'd be. And my friend coming to supper too tenderhearted. You do it. Just do it and don't tell us about it, hear?"

Where have you been, Son, it's so late.—Nowhere, Mother, nowhere.—*If you were back under my roof,* Mother said, *if Eugene hadn't gone away too. He's gone and you won't listen to anybody.*—It's too hot to sleep, Mother.—*I stayed awake by the telephone. The Lord never meant us all to separate. To go and be cut off. One from the other, off in some little room.*

"I remember your wedding," old Miss Jefferson Moody said at my window, nodding on the other side of the bars. "Never knew it would turn out like this, the prettiest and longest wedding I ever saw. Look! If all that money belonged to you, you could leave town."

And I was getting tired, oh so tired, of Maideen waiting on me. I felt cornered when she told me, still as kind as ever, about the Seed and Feed. Because ever since I was born, Old Man Moody lined his sidewalk with pie pans full of shelled corn and stuff like bird-shot. The window used to be so clouded up it looked like stained glass. She'd scrubbed it for him, and exposed the barrels and cannisters and the sacks and bins of stuff inside, and Old Man Moody in an eyeshade sitting on a stool, making cat's-cradles; and her poking food at the bird. There were cotton blooms across the window and door, and then it would be sugar-cane, and she told me she was thinking already about the Christmas tree. No telling what she was going to string on Old Man Moody's Christmas tree. And now I was told her mother's maiden name. God help me, the name Sojourner was laid on my head like the top teetering crown of a pile of things to remember. Not to forget, never to forget the name of Sojourner.

And then always having to take the little Williams girl home at night. She was the bridge player. That was a game Maideen had never learned to play. Maideen: I never kissed her.

But the Sunday came when I took her to Vicksburg.

Already on the road I began to miss my bridge. We could get our old game now, Jinny, Woody, myself, and either Nina Carmichael or Junior Nesbitt, or both and sit in. Miss Lizzie of course would walk out on us now, never be our fourth, holding no brief for what a single one of us had done; she couldn't stand the Nesbitts to begin with. I always won—Nina used to win, but anybody could see she was pressed too much about Nesbitt to play her cards, and sometimes she didn't come to play at all, or Nesbitt either, and we had to go get the little Williams girl and take her home.

Maideen never put in a word to our silence now. She sat holding some women's magazine. Every now and then she'd turn over a page, moistening her finger first, like my mother. When she lifted her eyes to me, I didn't look up. Every night I would take their money. Then at Miss Francine's I would be sick, going outdoors so the teachers wouldn't wonder.

"Now you really must get these two home. Their mothers will be wondering." Jinny's voice.

Maideen would stand up with the little Williams girl to leave, and I thought whatever I let her in for, I could trust her.

She would get stupefied for sleep. She would lean farther and farther over in the Starks' chair. She would never have a rum and coke with us, but would be simply dead for sleep. She slept sitting up in the car going home, where her mama, now large-eyed, maiden name Sojourner, sat up listening. I'd wake Maideen and tell her where we were. The little Williams girl would be chatting away in the back seat, there and as far as her house wide awake as an owl.

Vicksburg: nineteen miles over the gravel and the thirteen little bridges and the Big Black. And suddenly all sensation returned.

Morgana I had looked at too long. Till the street was a pencil mark on the sky. The street was there just the same, red-brick scallops, two steeples and the water tank and the branchy trees, but if I saw it, it was not with love, it was a pencil mark on the sky that jumped with the shaking of the gin. If some indelible red false-fronts joined one to the other like a little toy train went by, I didn't think of my childhood any more. I saw Old Man Holifield turn his back, his suspenders looked cross, very cross.

In Vicksburg, I stopped my car at the foot of the street under the wall, by the canal. There was that dazzling light, water-marked light. I woke Maideen and asked her if she was thirsty. She smoothed her dress and lifted her head at the sounds of a city, the traffic on cobblestones just behind the wall. I watched the water taxi come to get us, chopping over the canal strip, babyish as a rocking horse.

"Duck your head," I told Maideen.

"In here?"

It was sunset. The island was very near across the water—a waste of willows, yellow and green strands loosely woven together, like a basket that let the light spill out uncontrollably. We all stood up and bent our heads under the ceiling in the tiny cabin, and shaded our eyes. The Negro who ran the put-put never said a word, "Get in" or "Get out." "Where is this we're going?" Maideen said. In two minutes we were touching the barge.

Nobody was inside but the barkeep—a silent, relegated place like a barn, old and tired. I let him bring some rum cokes out to the card table on the back where the two cane chairs were. It was open back there. The sun was going down on the island side while we sat, and making Vicksburg all picked out on the other. East and West were in our eyes.

"Don't make me drink it. I don't want to drink it," Maideen said.

"Go on and drink it."

"You drink it if you like it. Don't make me drink it."

"You drink it too."

I looked at her take some of it, and sit shading her eyes. There were wasps dipping from a nest over the old screen door and skimming her hair. There was a smell of fish and of the floating roots fringing the island, and of the oilcloth top of our table, and endless deals. A load of Negroes came over on the water taxi and stepped out sulphur-yellow all over, coated with cottonseed meal. They disappeared in the colored barge at the other end, in single file, carrying their buckets, like they were sentenced to it.

"Sure enough, I don't want to drink it."

"Look, you drink it and then tell me if it tastes bad, and I'll pour 'em both in the river."

"It will be too late."

Through the screen door I could see into the dim saloon. Two men with black cocks under their arms had come in. Without noise they each set a muddy boot on the rail and drank, the cocks absolutely still. They got off the barge on the island side and were lost in a minute in a hot blur of willow trees. They might never be seen again.

The heat shook on the water and on the other side shook along the edges of the old white buildings and the concrete slabs and the wall. From the barge Vicksburg looked like an image of itself in some old mirror—like a portrait at a sad time of life.

A short cowboy and his girl came in, walking alike. They dropped a nickel in the nickelodeon, and came together.

There weren't any waves visible, yet the water did tremble under our chairs. I was aware of it like the sound of a winter fire in the room.

"You don't ever dance, do you," Maideen said.

It was a long time before we left. A good many people had come out to the barge. There was old Gordon Nesbitt, dancing. When we left, the white barge and the nigger barge had both filled up, and it was good-dark.

The lights were far between on shore—sheds and warehouses, long walls that needed propping. High up on the ramparts of town some old iron bells were ringing.

"Are you a Catholic?" I asked her suddenly, and she shook her head.

Nobody was a Catholic but I looked at her—I made it plain she disappointed some hope of mine, and she had, standing there with a foreign bell ringing on the air.

"We're all Baptists. Why, are you a Catholic? Is that what you are?"

Without touching her except by accident with my knee I walked her ahead of me up the steep uneven way to where my car was parked listing downhill. Inside, she couldn't shut her door. I stood outside and waited, the door hung heavily and she had drunk all I had made her drink. Now she couldn't shut her door.

"Shut it."

"I'll fall out. I'll fall in your arms. If I fall, catch me."

"No. Shut it. You have to shut it. I can't. All your might."

At last. I leaned against her shut door, and held on for a moment.

I grated up the steep hills, turned and followed the river road along the bluff, turned again off into a deep rutted dirt way under shaggy banks, Father, dark and circling and rushing down.

"Don't lean on me," I said. "Better to sit up and get air."

"Don't want to."

"Pull up your head." I could hardly understand what she said any more. "You want to lie down?"

"Don't want to lie down."

"You get some air."

"Don't want to do a thing, Ran, do we, from now and on till evermore."

We circled down. The sounds of the river tossing and teasing its great load, its load of trash, I could hear through the dark now. It made the noise of a moving wall, and up it fishes and reptiles and uprooted trees and man's throw-aways played and climbed all alike in a splashing like innocence. A great wave of smell beat at my face. The track had come down here deep as a tunnel. We were on the floor of the world. The trees met and their branches matted overhead, the cedars came together, and through them the stars of Morgana looked sifted and fine as seed, so high, so far. Away off, there was the sound of a shot.

"Yonder's the river," she said, and sat up. "I see it—the Mississippi River."

"You don't see it. You only hear it."

"I see it, I see it."

"Haven't you ever seen the river before? You baby."

"I thought we were on it on the boat. Where's this?"

"The road's ended. You can see that."

"Yes, I can. Why does it come this far and stop?"

"How should I know?"

"What do they come down here for?"

"There're all kinds of people in the world." Far away, somebody was burning something.

"You mean bad people? Niggers?"

"Oh, fishermen. River men. See, you're waked up."

"I think we're lost," she said.

Mother said, *If I thought you'd ever go back to that Jinny Stark, I couldn't stand it.*—No, Mother, I'm not going back.—*The whole world knows what she did to you. It's different from when it's the man.*

"You dreamed we're lost. That's all right, you can lie down a little."

"You can't get lost in Morgana."

"After you lie down a little you'll be all right again. We'll go somewhere where you can lie down good."

"Don't want to lie down."

"Did you know my car would back up a hill as steep as this?"

"You'll be killed."

"I bet nobody ever saw such a crazy thing. Do you think anybody ever saw such a crazy thing?"

We were almost straight up and down, Father, hanging on the wall of the bluff, and the rear end of the car bumping and rising like something that wanted to fly, lifting and dropping us. At last we backed back over the brink, like a bee pulling out of a flower cup, and skidded a little. Without that last drink, maybe I wouldn't have made it at all.

We drove a long way then. All through the dark park, the same old statues and stances, the stone rifles at point again and again on the hills, lost and the same. The towers they've condemned, the lookout towers, lost and the same.

Maybe I didn't have my bearings, but I looked for the

moon, due to be in the last quarter. There she was. The air wasn't darkness but faint light and floating sound. It was the breath of all the people in the world who were breathing out into the late night looking at the moon, knowing her quarter. And all along I knew I rode in the open world and took bearings by the stars.

We rode in wildernesses under the lifting moon. Maideen was awake because I heard her sighing faintly, as if she longed for something for herself. A coon, white as a ghost, pressed low like an enemy, crossed over the road.

We crossed a highway and there a light burned in a white-washed tree. Under hanging moss it showed a half-circle of whitewashed cabins, dark, and all along it a fence of pale palings. A little nigger boy leaned on the gate where our lights moved on him; he was wearing a train engineer's cap. Sunset Oaks.

The little nigger hopped on the runningboard, and I paid. I guided Maideen by the shoulders. She had been asleep after all.

"One step up," I told her at the door.

We fell dead asleep in our clothes across the iron bed.

The naked light hung far down into the room and our sleep, a long cord with the strands almost untwisted. Maideen got up after some time and turned the light off, and the night descended like a bucket let down a well, and I woke up. It was never dark enough, the enormous sky flashing with August light rushing into the emptiest rooms, the loneliest windows. The month of falling stars. I hate the time of year this is, Father.

I saw Maideen taking her dress off. She bent over all tender toward it, smoothing its skirt and shaking it and laying it, at last, on the room's chair; and tenderly like it was any chair, not that one. I propped myself up against the rods of the bed with my back pressing them. I was sighing—deep sigh after deep sigh. I heard myself. When she turned back to the bed, I said, "Don't come close to me."

And I showed I had the pistol. I said, "I want the whole bed." I told her she hadn't needed to be here. I got down in the bed and pointed the pistol at her, without much hope, the way I used to lie cherishing a dream in the morning, and she the way Jinny would come pull me out of it.

Maideen came into the space before my eyes, plain in the lighted night. She held her bare arms. She was disarrayed. There was blood on her, blood and disgrace. Or perhaps there wasn't. For a minute I saw her double. But I pointed the gun at her the best I could.

"Don't come close to me," I said.

Then while she spoke to me I could hear all the noises of the place we were in—the frogs and nightbirds of Sunset Oaks, and the little idiot nigger running up and down the fence, up and down, as far as it went and back, sounding the palings with his stick.

"Don't, Ran. Don't do that, Ran. Don't do it, please don't do it." She came closer, but when she spoke I wasn't hearing what she said. I was reading her lips, the conscientious way people do through train windows. Outside, I thought the little nigger at the gate would keep that up for ever, no matter what I did, or what anyone did—running a stick along the fence, up and then down, to the end and back again.

Then that stopped. I thought, he's still running. The fence stopped, and he ran on without knowing it.

I drew back the pistol, and turned it. I put the pistol's mouth to my own. My instinct is always quick and ardent and hungry and doesn't lose any time. There was Maideen still, coming, coming in her petticoat.

"Don't do it, Ran. Please don't do it." Just the same.

I made it—made the awful sound.

And *she* said, "Now you see. It didn't go off. Give me that. Give that old thing to me, I'll take care of it."

She took it from me. Dainty as she always was, she carried it over to the chair; and prissy as she was, like she knew some long-tried way to deal with a gun, she folded it in her dress. She came back to the bed again, and dropped down on it.

In a minute she put her hand out again, differently, and laid it cold on my shoulder. And I had her so quick.

I could have been asleep then. I was lying there.

"You're so stuck up," she said.

I lay there and after a while I heard her again. She lay there by the side of me, weeping for herself. The kind of soft, patient, meditative sobs a child will venture long after punishment.

So I slept.

How was I to know she would go and hurt herself? She cheated, she cheated too.

Father, Eugene! What you went and found, was it better than this?

And where's Jinny?

6.

Music from Spain

ONE MORNING at breakfast Eugene MacLain was opening his paper and without the least idea of why he did it, when his wife said some innocent thing to him—"Crumb on your chin" or the like—he leaned across the table and slapped her face. They were in their forties, married twelve years—she was the older: she was looking it now.

He waited for her to say "Eugene MacLain!" The oven roared behind her—the second pan of toast was under the flame. Almost leisurely—that is, he sighed—Eugene rose and walked out of the kitchen, holding on to his paper; usually he put it in Emma's hand as he gave her the good-bye kiss.

He listened for "Eugene?" to follow him into the chill of the hall and wait for "Yes, dear?" He saw his face go past the mirror with a smile on it; that was a memory of little Fan's fly-away habit of answering her mother—and the sticking out of her two pigtails behind her as she ran off, the fair hair screwed up to the first tightenings of vanity—"That's my name." She had now been dead a year.

He put on his raincoat and hat, and secured his paper flat under his arm. Emma was still sitting propped back in her chair between table and stove, with the parrot-tailed housecoat just now settling in a series of puffs about her, and her too small, fat feet, as if *they* had been the most outraged, propped out before her. He knew the way Emma was looking in the kitchen behind him not because he had ever struck anyone before but because, with her, it was like having eyes in the back of his head. (*Only* in the back of his head!) Why, now, drawing her breath fast in the only warm room, she sat self-hypnotized in her own domain, with her "Get-out-of-my-kitchen" and "Come-here-do-you-realize-what-you've-done," all her stiffening and wifely glaze running sweet and finespun as sugar threads over her.

But Eugene went down the hall—now he heard like an echo her wounded cry and the shriek of the toast-pan—and pulled the apartment door locked behind him. He never could bear the sound of his own name called out in public, and she could still fling open the door and cry "Eugene Hudson MacLain, come here to me!" down the stairs.

A tremor ran through his arm as it struggled with the front door, and he stepped through to the outside and the perfectly still, foggy morning. He let his breath out, and there it was: he could see it. The air, the street, a sea gull, all the same soft gray, were in the same degree visible and seemed to him suddenly as pure as his own breath was.

The sea gull like a swinging pearl came walking across Jones Street as if to join him. "Our sea gulls have become so immured to San Francisco life," he would remark on walking in Bertsingers'—for you came in to work with a humorous remark—"they even cross the streets at the intersections now." He couldn't have hurt Emma. There couldn't be a mark on her.

She was stronger than he was, 150 pounds to 139, he could inform old Mr. Bertsinger Senior, who liked to press for figures. He and Emma MacLain could at any time be printed in the paper where all could see, side by side naked and compared, in those testimonial silhouettes; maybe had been. Emma knew he hadn't hurt her; better than he knew, Emma knew.

He sighed gently. By now—for she did take things in slowly—the rosy mole might be riding the pulse in her throat as it did long after the telephone rang late in the night and was the wrong number—"Why, it might have been a *thousand* things." Pretty soon, with her middle finger she would start touching her hairpins, one by one, going over her head as though in finishing her meditations she was sewing some precautionary cap on.

Eugene was walking down the habitual hills to Bertsingers', Jewelers, and with sharp sniffs that as always rather pained him after breakfast he was taking note of the day, its temperature, fog condition, and prospects of clearing and warming up, all of which would be asked him by Mr. Bertsinger Senior who would then tell him if he was right. Why, in the name of all reason, had he struck Emma? His act—with that, proving it had been a part of him—slipped loose from him, turned around and looked at him in the form of a question. At Sacramento Street it skirted through traffic beside him in sudden dependency, almost like a comedian pretending to be an old man.

If Eugene had not known he could do such a thing as strike Emma, he was even less prepared for having done it. Down hill the eucalyptus trees seemed bigger in the fog than when the sun shone through them, they had the fluffiness of birds in the cold; he had the utterly strange and unamiable notion that he could hear their beating hearts. Walking down a very steep hill was an act of holding back; he had never seen it like that or particularly noticed himself reflected in these people's windows. His head and neck jerked in motions like a pigeon's; he looked down, and when he saw the fallen and purple eucalyptus leaves underfoot, his shoes suddenly stamped them hard as hooves.

A quarrel couldn't even grow between him and Emma. And she would be unfair, beg the question, if a quarrel did spring up; she would cry. That was a thing a stranger might feel on being introduced to Emma, even though Emma never proved it to anybody: she had a waterfall of tears back there. He walked on. The sun, smaller than the moon, rolled like a little wheel through the fog but gave no light yet.

Why strike her even softly? They weren't very lovingly inclined these days, with the heart taken out of them by sorrow; violence was out of place to begin with. *Why not strike her? And if she thought he would stay around only to hear her start tuning up, she had another think coming. Let her take care and go about her business, he might do it once more and not so kindly.*

If he had had time to think about it, he might simply have refused to eat his breakfast. He knew that she minded. Ever since Emma was a landlady calling "Come on quick, Mr. MacLain!" and he was an anxious roomer, he had known where she was *sensitive.* Actually, of course, he wouldn't have dared not eat—under any circumstances. If he had wanted to kill her, he would have had to eat everything on her table first, and praise it. She had had a first husband, the mighty Mr. Gaines, and she would love forever a compliment on her food. "Sit down and tell me what you see" was what Emma would say.

The present fact was that she'd said something innocent—innocent but personal, personal but not dear—to him, which she might have said a thousand times in twelve years of marriage, and simply taking the perogative of a wife was leaning over to remove some offense of his with her own motherly finger, and he had slapped her face today. Why slap her today? The question prodded him locally now, in the back of one knee as nearly as he could tell. It accommodated itself like the bang of a small bell to the stiff pull of his shanks.

He struck her because she was a fat thing. Absurd, she had always been fat, at least plump ("Your little landlady's forever busy with something nice!"), plump when he married her. *Always was is no reason for its being absurd even yet to—* But couldn't it be his reason for hitting her, and not hers? *He struck her because he wanted another love. The forties. Psychology.*

Nevertheless a face from nowhere floated straight into that helpless irony and contemplated the world of his inward gaze, a dark full-face, obscure and obedient-looking as a newsprint face, looking outward from its cap of dark hair and a dark background—all shadow and softness, like a blurred spot on Jones Street. *Miss Dimdummie Dumwiddie,* he could the same as read underneath, in the italics of poetry. A regardful look. Should he suspect? She had died, was that the story? *Then too late to love you now. Too late to verify this story of yours* . . . in the paper, though he was carrying the paper for any such possible reference, pinned there by his right arm. This morning it had become too late to love the young and dead Miss Dumwiddie, and he had struck his wife with the flat of his hand.

Eugene slowed his step obediently here; at the jobbing butcher's he was habitually caught. Without warning red and white beeves were volleyed across the sidewalk on hooks, out of a van. The butchers, stepped outside for a moment in their bloody aprons, made a pause for ladies sometimes, but never for men. The beeves were moving across, all right, and on the other side a tramp leaned on a cane to watch, leering like a dandy at each one of the carcasses as it went by; it could have been some haughty and spurning woman he kept catching like that.

At the go-ahead from the butcher, made with a knife, Eugene took one step, but stopped suddenly. It was out of the question—that was all of a sudden beautifully clear—that he should go to work that day.

And things were a great deal more serious than he had thought.

Delicately and slowly as if he had been dared, Eugene felt with his hand under his raincoat, touching coat and vest and silver pencil. He clung to one small revelation: that today he was not able to take those watches apart.

He had only reached California Street. He stood without moving at the brink of the great steepness, looking down. He had struck Emma and when he struck, her face had met his blow with blankness, a wide-open eye. It had been like kissing the cheek of the dead.

She could still bite his finger, couldn't she? and some mischievous, teasing spirit looked at him, mouthing joy before darting ahead. But he looked down at the steepness, shocked and almost numb. A passerby gave him a silent margin. The slap had been like kissing the cheek of the dead.

What would Mr. Bertsinger Senior, down at the shop, have to say about this, Eugene wondered, what lengthy thing? His watch opened in the palm of his hand, and then he was walking on again with protest and speed down the hill, the street like the sag of a rope that disappeared into fog. The world was the old man's subject, but he knew yours.

II.

Below in Market Street the fog ran high overhead and the bustle of life was revealed. Eugene could imitate his hurry. Could it seem at all sad or absurd to the others, he wondered—with his head seeming to float above his long steps—that Market had with the years become a street of trusses, pads, braces, false bosoms, false teeth, and glass eyes? And of course of jewelry stores. He passed the health food store where the shark liver oil pellets were displayed (really attractively, to tell the truth) on a paper lacy as a Valentine. How amazing it all was. Wasn't it? A sailor in the penny arcade was having his girl photographed in the arms of a stuffed gorilla. Eugene would like to show that to somebody.

He read the second story level of signs across the street, Joltz Nature System, Honest John Trusses, No Toothless Days. A lady carrying a street-car transfer slip and a bunch of daisies wrapped in newspaper was coming down the stairs from the No Toothless Days door; would she dare smile, supposing she heard of a little joke, horseplay, would there be any use in telling her?

In the flyblown window of a bookstore a dark photograph that looked at first glance like Emma (Emma, he could bet, still sat on at the table composing herself, as carefully as if she had been up to the ceiling and back) was, he read below, Madame Blavatsky. Every other store on Market Street was, pursuing some necessity, a jewelry store; so that if you wore a Strictform No Give Brace you could wear at the same time a butterfly breast pin or a Joy watch band, "Nothing but Gold to Touch the Flesh." It could all make a man feel shame. The kind of shame one had to jump up in the air, kick his heels, to express—whirl around!

Just on the other side of Bertsingers' there was a crowded market. Eugene could hear all day as he worked at his meticulous watches the glad mallet of the man who cracked the crabs. He could hear it more plainly now, mixed with the street noises, like the click and caw of a tropical bird, and the doorway there shimmered with the blue of Dutch iris and the mixed pink and white of carnations in tubs, and the bright clash of the pink, red, and orange azaleas lined up in pots. Oh, to have been one step further on, and grown flowers!

There was Bertsingers'.

Compunction gave Eugene a little elderly-like rap, and he recognized that Bertsingers' was more respectable than most of the jewelry stores: Mr. Bertsinger Senior was on hand. Bertsingers' did carry its brand of the rhinestone Pegasus and ruby swordfish, its tray of charms; and the diamond rings filling the window did each bear a neat card saying "With Full Trade-in Privilege." But the cards were in Mr. Bertsinger Senior's handwriting—fine and with shaded loops. And Bertsingers' never had a neon sign over his cage in the repair department.

There was some dignity left to everything, if you knew where to find it. And Eugene passed by the door.

Bertie Junior was up front and on the lookout for what he might miss, of course—Eugene took a chance. Bertie Junior's thumbs bent softly back, he had little ducktails at the back of his head, he looked privileged as well as young. He'd put a chip diamond in his Army discharge button, for the hell of it—he said. Even in the dark rear of the shop his gleam and his eagerness could be detected from the street, and there was an equal chance he might detect Eugene going by, his target on any occasion. But he came to the door with head lifted high at that moment, watching a fist fight come out of a barber shop. He gleamed even to the sideways glance, wearing two fountain pens, their clips forking tongue-like out of his still-soldierly breast. Eugene got by.

He was not called back, either, or discovered pausing so near, at the market. The fish windows were decorated like a holiday show. There was a double row of salmon steaks placed fan-wise on a tray, and filets of sole fixed this way and that down another tray as in a plait, like cut-off golden hair. When Eugene set his eyes on an arrangement of amber-red caviar in the shape of a large anchor, "They are fish eggs, sir," a young, smocked clerk said, "and personally I think it's a perfect *pity* that they should be allowed to take them." He stood arms akimbo in the market entrance and did not recognize Mr. MacLain who had repaired his watch at all, *that* little drudge. A yearning for levity took hold of the little drudge, he tipped his hat and bowed like a Southerner, to the fish eggs.

There was a soft gleam. Above, blue slides of sky were cutting in on the fog. The sun, as with a spurt of motion, came out. The streetcars, taking on banana colors, drove up and down, the line of movie houses fluttered streamers and flags as if they were going to sea. Eugene moved into the central crowd, which seemed actually to increase its jostling with the sunshine, like the sea with wind.

A little old tramp woke up on the street, and rubbed his eyes. He began scattering crumbs to the descending pigeons and sea gulls. They walked about him fussing like barnyard chickens, and he stood as if flattered by their transformation and their greed, pressing his knees together in the posture of a saint or a lady of the house and looking up to smile at the world. Eugene walked among crumbs and pigeons and crossed over the wide trashy street and when he looked to the right he could see, quite clearly just now, the twin brown-green peaks at the end of the view, the houses bright in their sides, while the lifted mass of blue and gray fog swayed as gently over them as a shade tree.

The lift of fog in the city, that daily act of revelation, brought him a longing now like that of vague times in the past, of long ago in Mississippi, to see the world—there were places he longed for the sight of whose names he had forgotten. And while now it was doubtful that he would ever see the Seven Wonders of the World, he had suggested to Emma that they take a simple little pleasure trip—modestly, on the bus—down the inexpensive side of the Peninsula; but it had been his luck to mention it on the anniversary of Fan's death and she had slammed the door in his face.

It was womanlike; he understood it now. The inviolable grief she had felt for a great thing only widened her capacity to take little things hard. Mourning over the same thing she mourned, he was not to be let in. For letting in was something else. How cold to the living hour grief could make you! Her eye was quite marble-like at the door crack.

There had been a time, too, when she was a soft woman, just as he had been a kind man, soft unto innocence—soft like little Fan, and he saw the child at bedtime letting her hair ripple down and all around, with it almost meeting under her chin like a little golden rain hat, and he wanted to say, "Oh, stay, wait." Just as the other thing was there too: Fan from the age she could walk to it was standing with her back to the fire (they kept an open fireplace then) and with that gesture like a curtsey was lifting up her gown to warm her backside, like any woman in the world.

Now, too late when the city opened out so softly in beauty and to such distances, it awoke a longing for that careless, patched land of Mississippi winter, trees in their rusty wrappers, slow-grown trees taking their time, the lost shambles of old cane, the winter swamp where his own twin brother, he supposed, still hunted. Eugene looked askance at a flower seller: where had the seasons gone? Too cheap, bewilderingly massed together, the summerlike, winterlike, springlike flowers tied up in bunches made him glance disparately at the old man marking down the price on a jug of tulips, and at three turbaned Hindus who bought nothing but in calm turn smelled the bouquets until they stood there with all their six eyes closed, translated into still another world.

"Open the door, Richard!" sang a hoarse, nigger voice from a pitch-black bar. A small Chinese girl, all by herself, with her hair up in aluminum curlers, went around Eugene, swinging a little silky purse. He all but put out a staying hand. When a stocky boy with a black pompadour went by him wearing taps on his shoes, some word waited unspoken on Eugene's lips. His chance for speaking tapped rhythmically by. He frowned in the street, the more tantalized, somehow, by seeing at the last minute that the stranger was tattooed with a butterfly on the inner side of his wrist; an intimate place, the wrist appeared to be. Eugene saw the butterfly plainly enough to recognize it again, when this unfamiliar, calloused hand of San Francisco put a flame to a bitten cigarette. In blue ink the double wings spanned the veins and the two feelers reached into the fold at the base of the hand; the spots were so deep they seemed to have come perilously near to piercing the skin.

It was then that Eugene—withdrawing one step in his thoughts, to where old Mr. Bertsinger Senior in his jeweler's glass doddered around, the most critical and slowest to appraise of men, and Bertie Junior waited, knowing without being told (nobody surer than a young man)—felt sure in some absolute way that no familiar person could do him any good. After the step he had taken, the thing he had done, he couldn't stop at all, he had to go on, go in this new direction. Friends: no help there.

In panic—and, it struck him, in exultation—seek a stranger. *Hi, mate. Just lammed the little wifey over the puss.—Hooray!—That's what I did.—Sure, not a bad idea once ever so often. Take it easy.* They would be perched up at a bar having a beer together. And the other man would turn out to have done a whole lot worse; in fact, something should be done about *him.*

A tortoise-shell cat pillowed in apples gazed at him from a grocer's window. She pulled her round eyes closed as on little drawstrings. Eugene recollected that one street back a plaster bull dog, cerise with blue rings around the eyes, which ordinarily sat in the ground floor window of a hotel between the drawn shade and the glass, had this morning been taken away. Eugene had missed it—been cheated of it. As the cat opened her eyes again he had a moment of believing he would know anything that happened, anything that threatened the moral way, or transformed it, even, in the city of San Francisco that day: as if he and the city were watching each other—without accustomed faith. But with interest . . . boldness . . . recklessness, almost.

III.

Eugene proceeded down Market, his stride as brisk, businesslike, and concealing as though he had not already left Bertsingers' far behind. Bright mist bathed this end of the street and hid the tower of the Ferry Building; but as he walked he saw, going ahead of him and in the same direction, a tall and distinct figure that he recognized. It was the Spaniard he had heard play the guitar at Aeolian Hall the evening before. Imagine him walking along here! And as far as Eugene could make out over the heads of people intervening, he was walking along by himself.

Eugene had no doubts about that identity. Last night—though it seemed long enough ago now to make the recognition clever—Emma had come out with Eugene to a music hall, and it had turned out that this Spaniard performed, in solo recital. (No, she would not go with him to Half Moon Bay, but she would consent to a little music in one of the smaller halls, she said, and added, "Though you don't appreciate music." He patted her shoulder; they must have been thinking it together: his failure to respect music was part of the past, a night with little Fan at the Symphony, her treat. When the music began the child had held out her little arms, saying Pierre Monteaux came out of *Babar* and she wanted him down here and would spank him. Emma, honestly shocked, had pulled down her daughter's arms, and Eugene had laughed out loud, not then but in the middle of the next piece.) . . . He could not think of the Spaniard's name, but it was pretty observant the way he recognized the man at this distance and from the back, after seeing him only the one time and then over the bird of a lady's hat.

He was alluring, up ahead—the perfect being to catch up with. Eugene walked steadily and looked steadily at him, a stranger and yet not a stranger, going along measuredly and sedately before, the only black-clad figure on this Western street, head and shoulders above all the rest.

And the very next moment, something terrible almost happened.

The guitarist reached the curb and in entering the traffic —really, he was quite provocatively slow, moving through this city street—he almost walked beneath the wheels of an automobile.

With the other's sudden danger, a gate opened to Eugene. That was all there was to it. He did not have time to think, but sprang forward as if to protect his own. His paper flew away from him piecemeal and as he ran he felt his toes pointing out behind him. This did not surprise him, for he had been noted for his running when he was a boy back home; in Morgana, Mississippi, he was still little old Scooter MacLain.

He seized hold of the Spaniard's coat—which had him weighing it, smelling it, and feeling the sun warm on it—and pulled. So out of breath he was laughing, he pulled in the big Spaniard—who for all his majestic weight proved light on his feet, like a big woman who turns graceful once she's on the dance floor. For a moment Eugene kept him at tow there, on the safe curb, breathing his faint smoke-smell or travel-smell; but he could not think of that long Spanish name, and he didn't say a word.

Well, what did that matter, when he was so relieved, so delighted, that he had reached the big old person in time— as delighted as with the surprise of a gift? Eugene drew both hands away lightly, as if he were publicly disclosing something, unveiling a huge statue. But in the next moment, rescuer and rescuee shook hands, and even in that self-conscious greeting

Eugene discovered something that made him want to turn his back and say "Damn it all!" The Spaniard could not speak English.

At least he smiled and *did* not. Proof, wasn't it? Eugene felt overwhelmed, cut off—disappointed in the man's very life. He pumped the substantial arm, taking an extra moment to recover himself, not to appear quite this disconcerted, or so rejected; he had entirely surprised himself.

Then the order of things seemed to be that the two men should stroll on together down the street. That came out of the very helplessness of not being able to speak—to thank or to deprecate. As he walked, Eugene sent out shy, still respectful glances, those of a man not quite sure his new pet knows who has just come into possession. Now that he thought back, the big fellow had walked out in front of the automobile almost tempting it to try and get him, with all the aplomb of—certainly, a bull fighter. There was another kind of Spaniard! Eugene looked up at his prize again, quite closely. The artist, who now smoked a cigarette, was wholly as imperturbable, if not quite as large bodily, as he had seemed on the Aeolian Hall stage the evening before.

At that time, he appeared carrying ahead of him a guitar, majestic and seeming in his walk years older than his thick black hair would show. He walked across the stage without a glance at the audience—an enormous man in an abundant dress suit with long, heavy tails. As he reached the center front of the stage and turned gravely—he seemed serious as a doctor—his head looked weighty too, long and broad together, with black-rimmed glasses circling his eyes and his hair combed back to hang behind him almost to his shoulders, like an Indian, or the old senator from back home.

He lowered himself to the straight chair that was the only furnishing of the stage except for an oblong object covered in black cloth that had been placed before it. Then he sat there like a mountain. This was just the sort of preliminary to-do that Emma liked; Eugene felt her draw herself up in the kind of bodily indignation that was her quickest expression of pleasure when she was out in public.

The guitarist began to play only after many tender and prolonged attentions to his instrument. He tuned it so softly that only he could hear. Then he gave some care to his extended right foot, which the black oblong object was there to accommodate as a rest, and care most of all to his fingers—flexing all ten of them, stretching them leisurely upon his thighs like a cat testing her claws on a cushion.

His face in the stage light, dark-skinned, smooth, with two deep folds from his nose down the sides of his mouth, was unmoved or even affronted in its stage expression. It did not change while he played or during the applause that came after each song. Only at the very last of the applause after the last song, a smile was seen to have come on his face—and to be enjoying itself there; it had the enchanted presence of a smile on the face of a beast. It lasted just so long, like an act of strength—as long as a strong man might hold a lifted weight. Yet it had been as clear and gradual a change as the light goes through at sunset. It hinted of ordeal, but the smile showed that like the audience, after all, he loved the extraordinary thing. His fingernails were painted bright red.

"Red fingernails," Eugene had whispered, just at the moment when Emma turned her head and gave him a look. It was meant to be a meaningful look from under the brim of the blue hat in which she had that night emerged from public-mourning.

The blueness of the hat even in the light of the dim hall ("Emma's blue," her sister called it) and the blank shine of her new glasses which hid her eyes, and her cheek with a little tear offered on it, all held his head turned toward her as though she had bidden it, but did not distract him from a deep lull in his spirit that was as enfolding as love. He turned his head gently back toward the stage, where an encore was being played. A most unexpected kind of music was being struck off the guitar.

He felt a lapse of all knowledge of Emma as his wife, and of comprehending the future, in some visit to a vast present-time. The lapse must have endured for a solid minute or two, and afterwards he could recollect it. It was as positively there and as defined at the edges as a spot or stain, and it affected him like a secret.

Now out here in the everyday and the open, Eugene was

aware, as at the racing of the pulse, of the dark face by his, the Spaniard going beside him, his life actually owing to him, Eugene MacLain. Again he felt fleet of foot, at the very heels of a secret in the day. Was it so strange, the way things are flung out at us, like the apples of Atalanta perhaps, once we have begun a certain onrush? With his hand, which could have stormed a gate, he touched the Spaniard's elbow. It responded like a swinging weight, a balance, in the calm black sleeve. Eugene's touch, his push, now seemed judicious; and he pushed forthrightly to propel the old fellow across the street at the next crossing.

Once, waiting for a traffic light to change, they stood beside a woman on whom Eugene let his gaze rest. There was such strange beauty about her that he did not realize for a few moments that she was birth-marked and would be considered disfigured by most people—by himself, ordinarily. She was a Negro or a Polynesian and marked as a butterfly is, over all her visible skin. Curves, scrolls, dark brown areas on light brown, were beautifully placed on her body, as if by design, with pools about the eyes, at the nape of her neck, at the wrist, and about her legs too, like fawn spots, visible through her stockings. She had the look of waiting in leafy shade.

She was dressed in humble brown, but her hat was an exotic one, with curving bright feathers about her head. Eugene felt an almost palpable aura of a disgrace or sadness that had to be as ever-present as the skin is, of hiding and flaunting together. It was so strong an aura that by softly whistling Eugene pretended to people around that the woman was not there, and tried to keep the Spaniard from seeing her. For he might pounce upon her; something made him afraid of the Spaniard at that moment.

After a little it seemed something of a favor, a privilege, to be unable to communicate any more than by smiles and signs. They strolled along together. The Spaniard appeared content enough to walk along in the soft, mild sun with the little man who undertook to pull him out of the way of wheels. He did not object. He neither hurried nor revealed a plan.

Three pink neon arrows flickered toward a bar. Where were

they going, thought Eugene, he and his Spaniard? They were still walking down Market Street past the shoddy, catch-eye stores. And just now they were approaching a shabby spot only too familiar to Eugene; he had to pass it every day, since it was between Bertsingers' and the cafeteria where he daily ate lunch.

A side-show had opened to take its turn in the rundown building where previously some gypsies had been telling fortunes. There were posters in the dirty windows and a languid, enthroned man offering tickets and intoning all day long the words, "Have—you—seen—Em-ma?" in a voice so tired it gave the effect of downright menace. Bertie Junior thought it was terribly funny, with old MacLain's wife being named Emma. He came along with Eugene to lunch now, so he could hear it, and every morning he too asked, "Have—you—seen—Emma?" as Eugene came in, before he could get past.

An enlarged photograph showed the side-show Emma—enormously fat, blown, her small features bunched like a paper of violets in the center of her face. But in the crushed, pushed-together countenance there was a look; it was accusation, of course. The sight of a person to whom other people have been cruel can be the most formidable of all, Eugene thought as he was ready to pass it again. And it is so recognizable, the glance that meets all glances and holds, like a mother's: they done me wrong.

The photograph showed Emma as wearing lace panties, and opposite it a real pair of panties—faded red with no lace—was exhibited hung up by clothespins, vast and sagging, limp with dust and travel. In his childhood, Eugene recalled, there was a Thelma that he had paid his Sunday School collection money to see. Thelma was an optical illusion, a woman's head on top of a stepladder; and she had been golden-haired and young, and had smiled invitingly.

Eugene all at once felt himself the host. Should he invite the Spaniard to take a look at Emma, inside? It gave him an appalling moment.

But the Spaniard, cocking his head at Emma's full-sailed manifestation, simply pointed to his own breadth and opened his eyes on Eugene with one warm, brimming question of his own.

It was midday. The street beggars knew it, they sat light-drenched, the blind accordion player with his eyes wide open and his lips formed in a kiss.

"Come on. I'm inviting you, all right. We'll eat," Eugene said, and tipping his finger to his companion's elbow turned him right around.

IV.

Eugene thought—as if in the nick of time—that only a good restaurant would do. Besides, though the cafeteria was economical and healthy, just now it had begun to be infested by those wiry, but unlucky, old men forever reading racing forms as they drank coffee; one particularly, in a belligerent pea-green sweater with yellow bands, seemed to change the whole tone of the place simply by always occupying the table anybody else would want. With a suitable indication of where they were going, perhaps, in his smile, Eugene pulled open the door to a restaurant in Maiden Lane.

The Spaniard, with the merest lift of his black brows, walked in shaking the floor around him and proceeded up the staircase, shaking it, to the little upper dining room, where Eugene, as a matter of fact, had never been in his life.

This Spaniard everywhere seemed to be too much at home. He placed his hat, a big floppy black one, carefully on the radiator in the upper hall, not only as if he was perfectly aware without testing it that there was no heat in the pipes, but also as if the radiator existed not to heat others but to hold his hat.

The head waiter couldn't have seated them more showily. They were given a table by the curtained window; its own lamp was instantly flicked on. Huge menus were set up like tents on a camp field between them.

To Eugene the room was somehow old-fashioned and boxy, like a scene in some old silent movie. The gesturing people, who seemed actually to be turning artificial smiles upon them, were enclosed by walls papered in an intrusive design of balls and bubbles, lights behind poppy shades. Filipinos wearing their boys' belts ran around in a constant, silent double-time looking like twins-on-twins themselves, clearing tables, laying cloths, smiling.

The guitar player with something like a false expression of grief on his face meditated upon what he would, or would not, eat. With his finger he caressed the air; he decided; and it was probably in French that he responded (like a worshiper in the Catholic Church) to the waiter.

When the food was brought, and then still brought, Eugene sat up straight, still pleased but shocked to some extent at all the Spanish guest had commanded. Was he so great? How great was he, how great did he think he was? How well did he think he played the guitar? These things, in fact, made real mysteries.

Eugene, who got veal, began to count up mentally the money in his billfold, only to lose track, start over, and get lost again. He chewed steadily on his veal in another wonder where he lost himself still further.

Last night, he had not been able to keep from wondering at moments all through the music: what would the artist be doing if he weren't performing? After the songs were finished, then would he be alone, for instance? Those things were not such idle questions. . . . The fact was, Eugene thought now, he had had speculations about a man on the stage exactly as if he had known he would meet him in closer fashion afterward. As if he had known that by morning he himself would have struck his wife that blow and found out something new, something entirely different about life.

Eugene had been easily satisfied of one thing—the formidable artist was free. There was no one he loved, to tell him anything, to lay down the law.

The Spaniard tossed a clam shell out of his plate and Eugene at once bent expectantly toward him. He was glad to feel himself in the role of companion and advisor to the artist —just as he had felt, in that prophetic way, his only audience last night. Now he would undertake to put forward an idea or two—suggest something they might do together.

Eugene lifted one hand, vaguely caressing the air in front

of the Spaniard. He tried to bring up a woman before him. Perhaps the Spaniard could produce a beautiful mistress he had somewhere, one he enjoyed and always went straight to, while in San Francisco: the strangely marked Negress, wouldn't she exactly do? And Eugene envisioned some silent (and this time, foreign) movie with that never spoken-in-love word, "enjoy," dancing for an instant upon the bouquet of flowers he'd be taking her. His own hand held an invisible bouquet, but the Spaniard looked right through it.

Eugene sank his cheek on his hand and looked across at his guest, who was good-humoredly spitting out a bone. It was more probable that the artist remained alone at night, aware of being too hard to please—and practicing on his guitar.

Yet these moments seemed so precious!

Why waste them? Why not visit a gambling house? A game of chance would be very interesting. With those red-nailed fingers (only—and Eugene's hope fell—they were not red now) the Spaniard would be able to place their chips on lucky numbers, and with his sharp and shaming ear listen to the delicate, cheating click of the ball in the wheel. Eugene usually only pressed his lips together—to part them—at the idea of such places, but with the Spaniard along—! For them, as for young, unattached, dashing boys, or renegade old men far gone, the roulette wheel all evening in some smoke-filled but ascetic room . . . how would it be?

Suppose he, Eugene, found himself in San Francisco for only a day and a night, say, and not for the rest of his life? Suppose he was still in the process of leaving Mississippi—not stopped here, but simply an artist, touring through. Or, if he chanced not to play the guitar or something, simply out looking: not for anyone in particular; on the track, say, of his old man? (God forbid he'd find him! Old Papa King MacLain was an old goat, a black name *he* had.)

From right here, himself stopped in San Francisco, Eugene could have told the artist something. This city . . . often it looked open and free, down through its long-sighted streets, all in the bright, washing light. But hill and hill, cloud and cloud, all shimmering one back of the other like purities or transparencies of clear idleness and blue smoke, lifting and going down like the fire-sirens that forever curved through the place, and traveling water-bright one upon the other—they were any man's walls still.

And at the same time it would be terrifying if walls, even the walls of Emma's and his room, the walls of whatever room it was that closed a person in in the evening, would go soft as curtains and begin to tremble. If like the curtains of the aurora borealis the walls of rooms would give even the illusion of lifting—if they would threaten to go up. That would be repeating the Fire—of course. That could happen any time to San Francisco. It was a special threat out here. But the thing he thought of wasn't really physical. . . .

Eugene slowly buttered the last crust of bread. There was nothing to change his mind about the Spaniard—to make him think that this sedate man, installed on the lighted stage with his foot on a rest the way he liked to present himself, hadn't a secret practice of going out to a dark and shady place on his own, and wouldn't seek out as a further preoccupation in his life some stranger's disgrace or necessity, some marked, designated house. For it was natural to suppose, supposed Eugene, that the solidest of artists were chameleons.

What mightn't this Spaniard be capable of?

Eugene felt untoward visions churning, the Spaniard with his great knees bent and his black slippers turning as if on a wheel's rim, dancing in a red smoky place with a lead-heavy alligator. The Spaniard turning his back, with his voluminous coat-tails sailing, and his feet off the ground, floating bird-like up into the pin-point distance. The Spaniard with his finger on the page of a book, looking over his shoulder, as did the framed Sibyl on the wall in his father's study—no! then, it was old Miss Eckhart's "studio"—where he was muscular, but in a story-like way womanly. And the Spaniard with horns on his head—waiting—or advancing! And always the one, dark face, though momently fire from his nostrils brimmed over, with that veritable *waste* of life!

Eugene, unaccustomed to visions of people as they were not, as unaccustomed as he was to the presence of the Spaniard as he was, choked abruptly on his crust. He had even forgotten all about old Miss Eckhart in Mississippi, and the lessons he and not Ran had had on her piano, though perhaps it was natural that he should remember her now, within the aura of music. Experimentally he let down one by one the touchy, nimble fingers of his left hand on the table, then little finger and thumb see-sawed. The Spaniard as if through a curtain still seemed about to breathe fire. Across the table his incessant cigarette smoke came out of his nostrils in a double spout. It was this that was smelling so sweet . . . Eugene seemed to hear the extending cadence of "The Stubborn Rocking Horse," a piece of his he always liked, and could play very well. He saw the window and the yard, with the very tree. The thousands of mimosa flowers, little puffs, blue at the base like flames, seemed not to hold quite steady in this heat and light. His "Stubborn Rocking Horse" was transformed into drops of light, plopping one, two, three, four, through sky and trees to earth, to lie there in the pattern opposite to the shade of the tree. He could feel his forehead bead with drops and the pleasure run like dripping juice through each plodding finger, at such an hour, on such a day, in such a place. Mississippi. A humming bird, like a little fish, a little green fish in the hot air, had hung for a moment before his gaze, then jerked, vanishing, away.

He held his glass again to the Filipino's pitcher. Eugene saw himself for a moment as the kneeling Man in the Wilderness in the engraving in his father's remnant geography book, who hacked once at the Traveler's Tree, opened his mouth, and the water came pouring in. What did Eugene MacLain really care about the life of an artist, or a foreigner, or a wanderer, all the same thing—to have it all brought upon him now? That engraving itself, he had once believed, represented his father, King MacLain, in the flesh, the one who had never seen him or wanted to see him.

A Filipino dropped a dish which broke to pieces on the floor and sent the food spilling. Eugene felt his face growing pointed with derogatory, yet pitying, truly pitying sounds. He was laughing at the Filipino; and all the time, out of the whole room, perhaps, only he knew how excruciating this small mishap probably was.

But he had got his money mentally counted up. He found he could pay for this affair, almost exactly, with a few pennies left over. It made the awe of the thing settle a little and go down.

The Spaniard had attracted some attention from the room, spitting out the bones of his special dish, breaking the bread and clamping it in his teeth with the sound of firecrackers. His black eyes were amiably following a little fly now. Dishes, hats, ladies' noses, curtains at the window, were his little fly's lighting places, his little choices. The Spaniard seemed to be playing the mildest little game with himself.

This was what he was like when he was not playing the guitar. Yet—he was not so bad. When the waiter came with the bill, Eugene paid for the extravagance quite eagerly. The sight, the memory now, of the aloof and ravenous face opposite his, dark in the pearly window light, and the sorrowful mouth devouring the very best food until all had disappeared except for a pile of bones and a frill of paper—this filled him with a glow that began to increase while they smilingly nodded and rose. Like a peacock's tail the papered wall seemed lazily to extend now from the table at which they had sat. As they walked among the tables to leave, the Spaniard reaching out and gently taking a number of match packets, in a breeze of succession the women in their large hats leaned toward one another, the flowery brims touching, and murmured some name, and glanced. Eugene looked back at them and frowned in a deaf, possessive fashion.

They came out into the flat light of day and the noise, like a deception or a concealment of rage, of the ordinary afternoon stir. As they paused on the walk, a streetcar not far away roared down a crowded street. With the air of a fool or a traitor, so the crowd felt all together—there was a feeling like a concussion in the air—a dumpy little woman tripped forward on high heels in the street, swung her purse like a hatful of flowers, spilling everything, and sank in an outrageous-looking pink color in the streetcar's path. In a moment the streetcar struck her. She was pitched about, thrown ahead on the tracks, then let alone; she was not run over by the car, but she was dead. Eugene could tell that, as they all could, by the slow swinging walk of the pair of policemen who saw everything and now had to take charge. This pair saw no use in the world to hurry now.

"Accident!" Eugene said—repeated, that is. His voice must

have told the Spaniard that this should be of special interest to him. The big man stood planted, his lower lip jutted out under his cigarette, his eyes squinting. It was unquestionably a very horrible thing. Nobody hurried.

"She's dead, I'm pretty sure," Eugene said, but determined to keep his single voice a cautious one. Other voices close by were speaking. The Spaniard was shaking his head.

"Why don't the ambulance come?"

"Look at the motorman. His fault."

"She had gray hair."

Shake of the head.

"Somebody ought to pick up all those things and get them back in her purse."

"Don't they cover them up?"

"I wonder who she was."

"Who will they know to tell?"

Shake of the head.

The Spaniard shook his head.

"Let's go." Two girls spoke, turning. "I'm ready when you are."

But an inner group, a hollow square of people, hid the victim. They flanked her, and not all the time, but at moments, looked down at her. They held their ranks closed, like valuable persons. They were going to have been there. The group, business men, lady shoppers and children, seemed to consider themselves gently floating like the passengers on a raft, a little way out. One youth, hand on hip, looked with deep, idle, inward gaze at a street-sparrow by his foot, and then, beside the sparrow's little foot was the dead woman's open purse.

"Well—!"

They went around the corner, the Spaniard still shaking his head at moments. At a glance he looked as if he thought the place couldn't be any good, really.

Eugene led him to a big hotel. They entered the glitter and perfume of the lobby and through its entire maze before Eugene could discover the men's room, feeling the responsibility of the big black Spaniard like a parade he was leading.

As they stood in their caves with the echoing partition between, Eugene's head nodded and rolled once or twice, rhythmically. . . .

Well, the music last night had not been what he had thought it would be. In prophesying that, Emma had known what she was talking about. It was not at all throbbing—and of course not nigger. It had not a great many chords, it was never loud. The Spaniard's songs were old—ancient, his program said; some of them were written for organs and for lutes; and yet, he, So-and-So, the guitarist, played them. Were the difficulties and challenges what he had sought for most? Vain old person. Yes, it is the *guitar* I am playing. Yes, I am a *guitar player.* What did you think I was?

He was in as overwhelming a degree as if he announced it from the stage—in English—an extremely careful old person, an extremely careful artist.

Eugene suddenly felt both impatient and offended with him. Not bothering to conceal his own absorption in what he was playing, the man took no notice or care that he pleased anyone else either. . . . No! And Eugene had not been carried away altogether by the Spaniard's music. Not by any means. Only when the man at last played very softly some unbearably rapid or subtle songs of his own country, so soft as to be almost without sound, only a beating on the air like a fast wing—then was Eugene moved. Sometimes the sounds seemed shaken out, not struck, with the unearthly faint crash of a tambourine.

In love songs as in the rest, the artist himself remained remote, as a conscientious black cloud from a summer day. He only loomed. He ended the recital with a formal bow—as though it had been taken for granted by then that passion was the thing he had in hand, love was his servant, and even despair was a little tamed animal trotting about in plain view. The bow had been consummate with grace, and when he lifted up, he was so big he looked very close to the eyes.

When Eugene came out, the Spaniard was weighing himself. The arrow trembled, the Spaniard gently regarding it, filling himself with a sigh to make it shake. Eugene frowned at the figure. Only 240. He had supposed the Spaniard would weigh more than that—250 or 255.

His guest looked at him as bright and fresh as a daisy. "Where shall we go now?" he meant, as plain as day.

Eugene ushered him to the street. On the step was a band of sunlight soft and level as little Fan's hair when she would go flying before him. The men began walking, the Spaniard with spirit—was this exercise? The square shone, and the façade of a steep street like a great gray accordion spread over a knee seemed about to stutter into the air.

V.

They walked city squares in the sun until some meditative mood between them bound them like consenting speech. At a corner two old fellows, twins, absurdly dressed alike in plaid jackets, the same size and together still, were helping each other onto the crowded step of a streetcar. Eugene and the Spaniard noticed them at the same moment and casting each other amused glances, they stepped up too, as the car began moving, and rode off on the step. It was like surf-boarding on waves. Behind them, the cow-catcher was a big basketful of children.

A Negro, his fan of hair so coarse as to look grainy, immediately rammed his head between Eugene's and the Spaniard's. His pop-eyes watched. The streetcar climbed, rolled, and descended, rocking through warming and ever-crowding streets, and finally turned straight into the West. Eugene, with his head turned away from the Negro's, tried to close his ears against the cries of the children, and read the tattered street signs to himself as they passed.

The conductor was a big fat Negro woman who yelled out all the street names with joy. "Divisadero! I say Divisadero!" At The Bug Used Records and Shoe Massage Parlor, and from the steep, fancy-fronted, engraved-looking houses with all the paint worn away—like the solitary houses over railroad cuts seen once—the conductor's friends hollered at her as they went by. Swinging out of the car she often called back. "Off at two A.M.!" "See you at the Cat!"

The Negro head between Eugene and the Spaniard rolled its eyes. Once Eugene caught a glimpse of the Spaniard *smiling* as he traveled. Niggers would think he comprehended all their nigger-business—that he himself might be at the Cat at two. The basket of children swarmed over.

Eugene managed to reach the bell. He got the Spaniard off the streetcar, actually having to pull him by the waist to extricate him backwards. It was too much. They continued their direction on foot, still into the sun and still up into the last rim of hills.

It was by rights a sleepy hour, for people who didn't have to work. The city was so ugly at close quarters and so beautiful down its long distances. The hills, hills after hills that they walked over, the increasing freshness of the air, the warmth of the nearer sun, all made Eugene feel as if he were falling asleep. Because the very silence between the men was—at last—replete and dreamlike, the hills were to Eugene increasingly like those stairs he climbed in dreams.

The hills with their uniform, unseparated houses repeated over and over again his hill on Jones Street; the houses occurred over and over—all built on the same day, all one age. There was all one destiny. Suppose another Fire were to rack San Francisco and topple it and he, Eugene MacLain out of Mississippi, had to put it all back together again. His eyes half closed upon the mountains of houses not wall-like, as houses were in other places, but swollen like bee-hives, and one hive succeeding another, mounting into tremendous steps of stairs—and alive inside, inwardly contriving. How could he put a watch back together?

Here came the old woman down the hill—there was always one. In tippets and tapping their canes they slowly came down to meet you. Sometimes it seemed to Eugene that all the women in San Francisco were walking those hills all their lives, with canes before they knew it, and when they got old, instead of dying they used two canes, or crutches. Emma's feet were dainty, but the round flesh came all the way down her legs like pantalettes. She said it had only been there since the birth of the child: she blamed little Fan with it. Out of the middle of her grief she could rise and put her unanswerable pink finger on Woman's Sacrifice.

"Your little girl," Eugene remarked aloud, "said, 'Mama, my throat hurts me,' and she was dead in three days. You expected her mother would watch a fever, while you were at the office, not go talk to Mrs. Herring. But you never spoke of it, did you. Never did."

Each rounded house contained a stair. Every form had its spiral or its tendril, outward or concealed. Outside were fire escapes. He gazed up at the intricacies of those things; sea gulls were sitting at their heads. How could he make a fire-escape if he were required to? The laddered, tricky fire-escapes, the mesh of unguarded traffic, coiling springs, women's lace, the nests in their purses—he thought how the making and doing of daily life mazed a man about, eyes, legs, ladders, feet, fingers, like a vine. It twined a man in, the very doing and dying and daring of the world, the citified world. He could not set about making a fire-escape to his flat in Jones Street, given all the parts and the whole day off and the right instruments, if Mr. Bertsinger and Emma too told him to go ahead, and that his life depended on it. Should he be ashamed?

"Open the door, Richard. *Ouvrez la fenêtre, Paul ou Jacques,*" the demoniac voice of the comedian sang on the record, and Eugene waited to hear it again. He remembered away back: there was an old Negro and everybody in Morgana knew when he was in trouble at home; he walked into the store and asked them to play him a record—"Rocks in My Bed Number Two," by Blind Boy Fuller. Through a basement window he saw an upright piano and a big colored woman plying the keys. She looked like a long way from home. He could not hear her, and realized that there was much noise outside here, in the streets.

"*I* don't get the sun in *my* eyes," said a little boy, looking up at Eugene, who was holding one hand slanted before his face.

"You don't, sonnie?" said Eugene gently. With one hand he took away the other, as if the little boy had asked him to stop using it. The boy gave him a sweet, cocksure smile, which jumped with many suns in Eugene's vision.

They were on a numbered avenue not far, now, from the ocean. Seasoned with light like old invalids the young bungalows looked into the West. The Spaniard rather unexpectedly lunged forward, swung his big body around, and gazed for himself at the world behind and below where they had come. He tenderly swept an arm. The whole arena was alight with a fairness and blueness at this hour of afternoon; all the gray was blue and the white was blue—the laid-out city looked soft, brushed over with some sky-feather. Then he dropped his hand, as though the city might retire; and lifted it again, as though to bring it back for a second time. He was really wonderful, with his arm raised.

They walked on, until the sky ahead was brilliant enough to keep the eyes dazzled. On the next hill two nuns in a sea of wind looked destructible as smokestacks on a flaming roof.

"Chances are"—Eugene had begun speaking again—"you didn't know you had it in you—to strike a woman. Did you?"

The Spaniard threw him a dark glance. But it was as if Eugene had said, "You are a guitar player" or "This is Presidio Avenue." Calmly he set his steps over a sprawled old winehead sleeping up here far away from his kind. Quite unheeding of legs overhead, the sleeper was stretched out of a little garden with his head in the anemones and the gray beard shining like spittle on his face.

"You wouldn't mind finding yourself like that," Eugene said, walking in the Spaniard's exact steps over the fallen legs.

And Eugene felt all at once an emotion that visited him inexplicably at times—the overwhelming, secret tenderness toward his twin, Ran MacLain, whom he had not seen for half his life, that he might have felt toward a lover. Was all well with Ran? How little we know! For considering that he might have done some reprehensible thing, then he would need the gravest and tenderest handling. Eugene's eyes nearly closed and he half fainted upon the body of the city, the old veins, the mottled skin of pavement. Perhaps the soft grass in which little daisies opened would hold his temples and put its eyes to his. He heard the murmuring slit of the cable track.

The Spaniard was holding him by the arm. His large face overhead flowed over with commiseration and pleasure. As if he were saying, "Why, of course. This is what we came for!" Eugene was half-lifted across the street. Then the Spaniard, still with a look of interest, made a gesture of examining him, patted him and straightened him up, gave him a little finishing shake, a cuff.

And rain fell on them. In the air a fine, caressing "precipitation" was shining. An open-eyed baby in his cart extended his little hands and held his thumbs and forefingers tight-shut: a hold on the bright mist. On the hill a cable car slid to a perch on the crest and sat there, home-like as a lawn swing, gay with girls' and boys' legs. Above, over cleared ground where a tree-cutting and excavation went on in the old graveyard—the Spanish tombs—two home-made kites in the sky jumped at each other and nodded like gossips. A sea wind blew the scent of alyssum from all the waste spaces. It waved the wispy white beard of an old Chinese gentleman who was running with the abandon of a school child for the car, which waited on him. This hilltop wind passed over Eugene with the refreshment that sometimes comes of a gentle sloughing off of a daydream or desire which takes even its memory with it. He looked up at his Spaniard and drew a breath also, perhaps not really a sympathetic one, but he seemed to increase in size. Eugene watched his great fatherly barrel of chest move, and had a momentary glimpse of his suspenders, which were pink trimmed in silver with little bearded animal faces on the buckles.

His face with its expression that might be solicitude still—and at the same time, meditation, amusement, sleepiness, or implacability when the whole was seen at such close quarters with the black circles, the shell rims, around the eyes—was directed for a round moment on Eugene. Then his head swung and with the long black hair bobbing behind, nodded a fraction at something. It struck Eugene that he looked like that Doctor Caligari in the old silent movie days, ringing his bell on the sideshow platform.

For he had nodded up at the undestroyed part of the embankment, where some of the old graves, still to be ransacked by the shovels, stood here and there under the olive trees. In the foreground was a cat. In the deep grass she held a motionless and time-honored pose.

Her head was three-quarters turned toward them where they stood. It seemed to have womanly eyebrows. Her gaze came out of her face with the whole of animal comprehension;

whether it was menace or alarm in the full-open eyes, her face made a burning-glass of looking. Her eyes seemed after so long a time to be holding her herself in their power. She crouched rigid with the devotion and intensity of her vision, and if she had caught fire there, still she could not, Eugene felt, have stirred out of the seizure. She would have been consumed twice over before she disregarded either what she was looking at or her own frenzy.

On the untidy embankment something else—the object of the gaze—presently showed itself by a motion in the grass. As if the sight pricked him to move, Eugene darted for a heavy pine twig with cones and threw it at the cat; it struck her side. She seemed not to feel it, since she did not waver.

He exclaimed. And all the while the Spaniard was standing there in a relaxed posture looking on—he might have been over in Paris, looking at the Seine! And yet that detachment, Eugene was not unaware, and it gave him some bitterness, had been the outer semblance of what passion in his music last night! Eugene watched stubbornly, and even felt his excitement grow as the whirring of a wing or the pulsing of a tongue, whatever it was, came at less frequent intervals. It was still too rapid for the eye to tell what made it. Which was happening: was the whirring spending itself out, or was the lure, on its side, becoming an old thing, taken for granted? This had a beginning and end.

"What's in the grass, a bird or a snake? What do you bet?" Eugene said softly.

But the Spaniard stood patiently planted there, while the terrible gaze ran fast as a humming wire between the cat and the other creature. Didn't it matter which poor, avid life took the gaze and which gave it? The cat's eyes big as watches shone tearlessly. Eugene thought all at once, It's all the same—it's a bestial thing, all of it, I don't care to know, thank you.

But he waited. The next minute he threw a stone, this time in the direction of the fluttering in the grass. It excited him; this, indeed, made the cat spit drily and tremble all over.

The Spaniard, when Eugene looked to him, was making a

hideous face over the lighting of another cigarette. The muscles of his face grouped themselves in hideous luxuriousness, rippled once, then all cleared. His lips were grape-colored, and the smoke smelled sweet.

"Come on," Eugene said to him, and took his arm and pulled. "Come on, you Dago."

VI.

They had come down at the end to the beach: great emptiness. At first it seemed no one was there, so late on this uncertain day. Then crossing the middle distance toward the sea appeared a student with his pants rolled up, reading as he walked, and a man, who looked like a hermit, rather gracefully shouldering wood. Farther away still in the pale expanse two middle-aged ladies in steadily threatened hats materialized; they looked at their watches: waiting for sunset. One battered, sand-colored auto was in sight; it had been left by the sea wall gate, one door open, a horse's bleached skull hanging on the face of the radiator. A little dog sat inside. Black smoke moved on the air, fading; the day's casual fires along the beach had gone out, and a ship was disclosed at sea. Some sea gulls perched on the roller-coaster humps, some stood short-necked and unmoving in front of the shuttered-down food stands, and the blackbirds like little ladies walked about at their feet, keeping busy.

How could it have seemed so silent, because it was deserted? Just the way it had seemed deserted, at first, because the noise hadn't been taken in. There was actually a steady tinkling where the carousel went around, with no child riding, and there was the excited and unrelieved sound of laughter filling the midway. Eugene knew its source and pointed it out to the Spaniard, who swayed each way and smiled faintly. The shouting mechanical dummy of a woman, larger than life, dressed up and with a feather in her hat, stood beckoning on the upper gallery of the House of Mirth and producing her wound-up laughter. In every way she called for the attention; the motions of her head with its feather, and of her arms and hips, were as raucous and hilarious as the sound that was played in her insides. The boom of the ocean seemed to be bearing that small sound, too, on its back, supporting this one extra little chip.

Eugene walked down to the sands where the wind beat the laughter to pieces and the ripping sound of his own hat filled his ears. The Spaniard was already at the shore, facing the waves, and so immovably established that the esthetic ladies had withdrawn. Only a pair of lovers lay close by the wall—motionless also. His solid tracks in the sand were the only straight line on the beach, butting through wood gatherers', students', ladies', lovers', and all the vanished children's and dogs'. Eugene's now went around his, light and toeing out. Sea onions littered the beach; what night had the storm been? Now and then the crashing reach of water came to the European points of the other man's shoes, advancing at the last instant with pure little tongues, that minutely kissed and withdrew.

Eugene gently pulled the Spaniard's arm, and pointed up the beach to the cliffs there. "Land's End!" he shouted, while the waves' sound drowned him out. He pulled gently.

The Spaniard looked affirmative, but first disengaged himself and made water toward the sea, throwing up a rampart, a regular castle, in the sand.

So they turned and their walk could still go on along shore, past the black pits of fires and the ubiquitous, ugly, naked sea onions, until they reached rocks; then it led up to the overlooking wall. A little boy up there on a velocipede with his yellow hair blown in points came riding dreamily between the men, even he with a tied-on sea onion tail dragging six feet behind him. The Spaniard soberly bent over and gave the tail a carefree, lariat-like swing. The little boy looked back, eyes and mouth all round, and the next instant screamed with delighted outrage, as if he saw himself mocked. Beyond the car barn was a black scraggly wood, and then there was something of a road that followed along the cliff interminably, or once there had been.

For there had been an occasion when Eugene and Emma had come this far, and picnicked here. They had drunk several bottles of red wine and gone to sleep in the hot sun on the rocks, lying on their backs, knees up, heads tipped together.

Emma's fair skin had turned pink as a rose. Where was little Fan then? That hadn't bothered them that day.

The men walked and climbed along this road with the sea exploding straight under them at times—no beach now, only the brown rocks. From time to time another rock would move a little, or there would be a little rain of pebbly sound somewhere. Occasional paths wandered off down the sharp slopes through grass or over the bare rock to the boulders at the water's edge. The little bushes whipped, and the Spaniard's black coat leaped and danced. Eugene felt the Pacific wind like a fortification, he could storm it or lean onto it, just the same; it could stop his breath and keep him from falling too.

It blew the sea gulls back. A flock of them, collected points of light halfway up the sky, made a turn all at one time, and showed the facets of their flight clear as a diamond. Eugene sucked in the air—now it was rapture. He watched the birds fly out, blow back.

(Down at the wharf, down out of the high heavens, they stood solid as housewives, one large plump one to each little fishing boat, almost moral-looking, ready to pronounce judgment. It seemed sometimes that all sea gulls could not be the same, that they must be two varieties of birdkind, or the birds themselves must have two lives. Was it the sun or the fog, the time of day, that most often changed things, by changing their appearances? He supposed he had a horror of closed-in places and of being shut in, but in late afternoon he had seen Alcatraz light as a lady's hat afloat on the water, looking inviting, and he would almost wish to go to that island himself, and say to people, "Convicts are Christ," or the like.)

"Will you go in front, or behind?" he asked, but the Spaniard was already going in front.

"You know what you did," Eugene said. "You assaulted your wife. Do you say you didn't know you had it in you?"

The Spaniard up ahead made his way forward without turning around. By now the path had grown wild and narrow; it made slow going, or rather, the Spaniard's leisurely gaining of the cliff set the pace, not Eugene's backslidings and precarious scramblings.

All the while, as if they were borne independently of legs of any kind beneath, the heads of the two men kept turning calmly outward, eyes traveling over the view. But as if to mock that too, once the Spaniard's hands met on top of his head to clamp his hat, his elbows bent outward. It was the lumpy pose of a woman, a "nude reclining."

The deepening sky was divided in half as it often was at this hour, by a kind of spinal cloud. Ahead, the north was clear and the south behind was thickened with white. Under the clear portion of sky the sea rushed in dark to greenness and blackness, the lips of the waves livid. ("Flounder, flounder in the sea," he heard his mother read.) Under the cloudy portion the sea burned silver and at moments entirely white, and the waves coming in held their form until the last minute and appeared still and limitless as snow. The beach and the city where they had walked were crossed with dust and mist, the scene flickered like the banners and flying sand of distant battle or a tumult in the past. Ahead, the extending rocks were unqualifiedly clear, hard, and azure.

The steepness increased, the path after a certain point appeared entirely out of use. Here and there a boulder had lately fallen and lay in their path wet within its fissures as if it began to live, and secrete, and they had to climb around it, holding to brush. Where there were not rocks it was sandy and grassy and very wild. A fault of course lay all through the land.

Sometimes Eugene was aware that he jerked like a pigeon or rocked like a sailor, going down, or sagged like an old poodle, going up; it was all the same. Once he leaped, and almost without a care. His tiltings, projections, slidings, working to keep up, all were painless now, and a progress he kept to himself. When pain did not hurt, and the world did, things had got very strange—different.

The sun was low, and some of the fog bank had detached itself in narrow clouds thin and delicate as bone, with the red light beginning to come through. The Spaniard went as sedately as ever along the edge he walked; had he been here before too? When he jumped in his slick black shoes, his footing was sure. It was he who took the choice of paths, and the choice was always a clever and difficult one. Paths ran everywhere now, a network of threads over waste and rock, with dancing, graybeard bushes to hold to. Below, the wet boulders were now faintly covered with light. Bathers in the distance, or porpoises, rose and sank sky-colored; there are always strangers who swim at sunset time.

Eugene went where the Spaniard went, but not always everywhere he went. There were caves where the paths dropped to the sea, and the Spaniard went on his own to inspect them. Eugene ceased crying directions, for it made him feel like a lost lamb bleating. The huge fellow let himself down the steep rocks and with hands and knees peered into the caves, like a dentist into alluring mouths. Rats ran up the bald surfaces. They were big rats—a size not of any habitation anywhere but of away out here, of unvisited geographical parts—as the world's wild dogs and wild horses are unseen and sizeless. The Spaniard glanced after the rats with his head inclined to one side. Even he could not light his cigarettes in this wind.

As it grew later the men made their way on, and piercing the sound of the wind the little dark birds that lived for neatness about the edge of the sea began to fill the air with twitterings, like birds ready to nest in leafy trees in a little springtime town. There had evidently been, without their knowing it, a loss of the wish to go back. Perhaps this wish had expired. Eugene, who had once nearly drowned, remembered his discovery of the death of volition to stay up in the water. Such things were always found out no telling how long after it was too late.

The sun was dropping. It looked wetter than water, then not so much a bright body as a red body. It dropped and was gone in the blue mist that was coming in over the sea. For a brief period the water, brighter than air, turned smooth and calm and the fog with wings spreading sank over it and was skimming at Eugene's face.

"You heard me, all the time," he said.

But the Spaniard bent over with his back to Eugene, and was peering at some blotched wild lilies that grew in the coarse grass there. He touched the tips of his fingers deliberately under the soft pale petals and examined their hairy hearts. Eugene was waiting behind him as he turned with a flower in his hand. All at once the Spanish eyes looked wide awake, and the man smiled—like someone waking from a deep dream, the sleep of a month. He put up his little flower, and regarded it.

"Mariposa," he said, making each syllable clearly distinct. He held up the little wild waving spotted thing, the common mariposa lily. *"Mariposa?"* He repeated the word encouragingly, even sweetly, making the sound of it beautiful.

"You assaulted your wife," Eugene said loudly.

The Spaniard still held his eyes open wide. If the staring smile was a slight, at the same time he was presenting his stupid flower.

"But in your heart," Eugene said, and then he was lost. It was a lifelong trouble, he had never been able to express himself at all when it came to the very moment. And now, on a cliff, in a wind, to . . .

Eugene thrust both hands forward and took hold of the other man, not half compassing the vast waist. But he recognized the weight that was so light on its feet, and he had only to make one move more, to unsettle that weight and let it go. Under his watchful eyes the flower went out of the other's loosening, softening hand: it lay on the wind, and sank. One more move and the man would go too, drop out of sight. He would go down below and it took only a touch.

Eugene clung to the Spaniard now, almost as if he had waited for him a long time with longing, almost as if he loved him, and had found a lasting refuge. He could have caressed the side of the massive face with the great pores in the loose, hanging cheek. The Spaniard closed his eyes.

Then a bullish roar opened out of him. He wagged his enormous head. What seemed to be utterances of the wildest order came from the wide mouth, together with the dinner's old reek. Eugene half expected more bones. He could see everything more than plainly. The Spaniard's eyes also were open to the widest, and his nostrils had the hairs raised erect in them.

Eugene suddenly lost his balance and nearly fell, so that he had to pull himself back by helplessly seizing hold of the big man. He listened on, perforce, to the voice that did not stop.

It was a terrible recital. Eugene drew back as far as possible and presently began to glare at him—a man laying himself altogether bare like that, with no shame, no respect. . . . What was he digging up to confess to, making such a spectacle? To whom did he think he prayed for relief? Eugene's hands waited nerveless moment after moment, while his ears were beaten upon, his whole body, indeed.

Abruptly—and causing silence as with a stopper—the Spaniard's broad-brimmed hat shot up in the wind and was blown—to sea? Landward. Eugene felt compelled to: he let go the Spaniard and ran hurrying to catch the hat and bring it back. Now it lifted ahead, turned over, clung to a wall, flew up again. Eugene had to climb a rather difficult part of the cliff. He saw the hat, and reached it where it danced about a bush, and got it in his hand.

Eugene lost his own hat in the chase; but inspiration was with him now, and he put on the Spaniard's. Knees bent on the pinnacle, raincoat whipping, he reached up and set it on his head. It stayed on, and at the same time it shadowed him. The band inside was warm and fragrant still. Elation ran all through his body, like the first runner that ever knew the way to it. His hands shaking with extreme care, as particularly as if he could see himself again in Emma's mirror with the little snapshot stuck in the corner, he set the brim just so.

He returned over the rocks and placed himself and looked back at the other man, eyes protected. It was in all confidence that he took fresh hold of him, but this time—how cruel!—he could not move him. He could not budge him an inch. He stood there with his hands in appeal on the Spaniard's silent arms. But this time the Spaniard had hold of him. It was a hold of hard, calloused fingers like prongs.

And the Spaniard would have looked small down there, all the way down below. Suppose there were a little guitar, no bigger than a watch. Eugene stood waiting there as if he listened to sirens. Then within himself he felt a strange sensation, strange in itself but, alas, he recognized it. He had felt it before—always before when very tired, and always when lying in bed at night, with Emma asleep beside him. Something round would be in his mouth. But its size was the thing that was strange.

It was as if he were trying to swallow a cherry but found he was only the size of the stem of the cherry. His mouth received and was explored by some immensity. It became more and more immense while he waited. All knowledge of the rest of his body and the feeling in it would leave him; he would not find it possible to describe his position in the bed, where his legs were or his hands; his mouth alone felt and it felt enormity. Only the finest, frailest thread of his own body seemed to exist, in order to provide the mouth. He seemed to have the world on his tongue. And it had no taste—only size.

He held onto the Spaniard and once more, feebly, with an arm or a leg, he tried to move him, to break away. The fog flowed into his throat and made him laugh. His laugh was repeated, an uncertain distance away. Eugene heard, then by chance saw, a man and girl moving along by their own light, a flashlight, skirting the brink just above, ahead of the night falling. They circled near. He heard them laugh, and in the dusk he flung back his head and could look up into the gleam of their teeth—was that happiness? Teeth bared like the rats', the same as in hunger or stress?

As he gasped, the sweet and the salt, the alyssum and the sea affected him as a single scent. It lulled him slightly, blurring the moment. The now calming ocean, the pounding of a thousand gentlenesses, went on into darkness and obscurity. He felt himself lifted up in the strong arms of the Spaniard, up above the bare head of the other man. Now the second hat blew away from him too. He was without a burden in the world.

Pillowed on great strength, he was turned in the air. It was greatest comfort. It was too bad that circling in his mind the daylong foreboding had to return, that he had yet to open the door and climb the stairs to Emma. There she waited in the front room, shedding her tears standing up, like a bride, with the white curtains of the bay window hanging heavy all around her.

When his body was wheeled another turn, the foreboding like a spinning ball was caught again. This time the vision—some niche of clarity, some future—was Emma MacLain turning around and coming part way to meet him on the stairs. Still like a rumble, her light and young-like tread, that could cause his whole body to be shaken with tenderness and mystery, crossed the floor. She lifted both arms in the wide, aroused sleeves and brought them together around him. He had to sink upon the frail hall chair intended for the coats and hats. And she was sinking upon him and on his mouth putting kisses like blows, returning him awesome favors in full vigor, with not the ghost of the salt of tears.

If he could have spoken! It was out of this relentlessness, not out of the gush of tears, that there would be a child again. Could it be possible that everything now could wait? If he could have stopped everything, until that pulse, far back, far inside, far within now, could shake like the little hard red fist of the first spring leaf!

He was brought over and held by the knees in the posture of a bird, his body almost upright and his forearms gently spread. In his nostrils and relaxing eyes and around his naked head he could feel the reach of fine spray or the breath of fog. He was upborne, open-armed. He was only thinking, My dear love comes.

He heard a loud, emotional cry—a bellow—from some other throat than his own, and heard it sink to the deepest rumbling. That was his Spaniard.

And the next moment—"Oh, is he going to throw him over?" a feminine voice with some eagerness in it was crying. The sweethearts were coming, on a lower road. "Aren't you ashamed of yourself, teasing a little fellow like that, scaring him?" the girl's voice continued. "Put him down and pick up one your own size, or Billy will teach you."

Then, or even before then, Eugene was lowered and set down again. His dangling heels, one of which had gone to sleep, kicked at the rock and then his feet stood on it. In the purple of night there was struck a little pasteboard match. Two big common toothy sweethearts stood there in its light, and the next moment vanished in the fog looking pleased with each other.

The mask face of the Spaniard, with hair swirling about it, was left shining there by matchlight. It turned one way and the other, looked up and down. It exuded sweat.

VII.

So now, the Spaniard took hold of Eugene's arm and guided him carefully by the instant's light of one match after another and the emergent light of the wreathed, racing moon. The world was not dark, but pale. The mist flowed from their fingers and rolled behind their heels. They looked together for the thread of the way back. They seized hands at perilous places and took mistaken hold of streaming thorn bushes with a chorus of outcries. They retreated at points and tried the way again. They both jumped at scuttling sounds, though the Spaniard made some inimitable Spanish noise that sounded as though it might have, before now, made rats go back. When was it they came to the easy part of the path, then to the road? Next, the whole sound of the sea faded behind the windbreak of trees, which in the wet fog smelled of black pepper.

When the trees opened out and they reached pavement, some city corner and its streetlight, they were so cold it was foregone they should go in the nearest café for coffee.

Eugene pulled away, combed back his hair, and led the way now.

"Two coffees!" he said loudly to the bare room when they were seated at the counter.

It was warm here. The Spaniard began to smoke, and sat with eyes shut, even when the waitress came out.

Large, middle-aged, big-boned, she moved up in a loose, grand style. Her face was large. All her features were made to seem bigger than life by paint, a pinkish mouth painted over her real mouth, eyebrows put on with brown grease in bands half an inch wide with perfect curves. Her eyes were small, so that with the mascara and the shadows painted on their lids they looked like flopping black butterflies. She had hennaed hair, somewhat greasy. She wore jewelry worth about eleven dollars and a quarter all together, Eugene saw—hoops of gold in her ears, a lavalier around her neck, four bracelets, and rings on both hands. There on her one body the illusions of gold, of silver, and of diamonds were all gone.

"One coffee with milk," Eugene said to her, "one black," and she turned from him. Her way of response was dramatic—soliloquy, and with an accent.

"Meelk, meelk, there is one who wants meelk," she said, striding up and then down behind the counter but not going away or looking at her customers or consulting further.

"And pastry."

"Oh, no. Pastry is no more." She had a resonant, brooding voice—there was something likeable and understandable about her, with her unbelievable accent. "A long time too you will wait for sandwiches." She shook her head. "All people here tonight waiting, waiting.—If sandwiches, what kind of bread, too? It is imporrrtant for me to know this."

"Two coffees. One with milk," Eugene said. He nodded at her.

When the waitress brought the coffees, cups swimming in their saucers, she marched off without bringing any sugar. Eugene, remembering the three lumps the Spaniard used, glanced at him.

The Spaniard met his glance, and his great black brows slowly lifted and his eyes implored like the eyes of a dog. The shell-rimmed glasses, sanded and smeared, he took off and held in his hand a moment, then put back on. He gave another imploring look. But Eugene only sat there. The Spaniard tried to bring back the waitress with his Spanish, then with a wave of the arm. And at first she only looked at him dreamily without moving, there at the back with her arm propped against the curtain. But then, swinging her hips weightily, she came. He had clapped his hands together; it woke her right up, like applause. She brought in a sugar jar with a spout.

"It was *sugar* you wanted," she said to the Spaniard, with baby-talk on top of her accent, as though it had been sugar, sugar for a long time. She patted him on the head. "Go to hell," she said resonantly to Eugene. "In my country I have a husband. He too is a little man, and sits up as small as you. When he is bad, I peek him up, I stand him on the mantelpiece." She held out her palm; Eugene could not help but peek in it. He paid—his last penny; there was a streetcar token left—one.

"Well, that will be all," Eugene said, to nobody.

The Spaniard had crumbs, sand, sugar, and ashes on him.

Outside, back on the corner, the two men turned to each other almost formally. Eugene could only think, in their parting moment, Suppose there had been pastry, would the Spaniard finally have lowered himself to pay? Then he flew out to catch a streetcar.

The Spaniard was left waiting, for what one never would know, alone in the night on a dark corner at the edge of the city. Perhaps he was not so proud now! At the last glance, he seemed to be looking in the sky for the little moon.

Eugene raced up the stairs to the flat and opened the door. There was the smell of strong hot chowder. Emma was in the kitchen but there was feminine talking-away—her great friend, Mrs. Herring from next door, had evidently come to stay for supper. Right away he thought he might as well not tell them anything.

"You've left your hat somewhere," Emma told him. "I'll be burying you next from pneumonia." Then, with a stamp of her foot, she showed him—and also Mrs. Herring, who was evidently seeing it for the second or third time—where the hot grease had splattered on her hand today.

There couldn't have been a peep out of Mr. Bertsinger, it occurred to Eugene as he threw off his raincoat. Maybe he was dead!

They sat on at the table after the big meal. Sawing idly at the cheese and to interrupt Mrs. Herring (in honor of Mrs. Herring, who had returned from a trip, they even had a little wine), Eugene felt called on to make one remark.

"Saw Long-Hair, the guitar player, today, saw him walking along the street just like you or me. What was his name, anyway?" he asked, as if he wondered now for the first time.

"Bartolome Montalbano," Emma said and popped a grape onto her extended tongue. She added, "I have the feeling he suffers from indigestion," and drummed her breast while she swallowed. ". . . He's a Spaniard."

"A Spaniard? There was a Spaniard at early church this morning," Mrs. Herring offered, "that needed a haircut. He was next to a woman and he was laughing with her out loud—bad taste, *we* thought. It was before service began, it's true.

He laughed first and then slapped her leg, there in Peter and Paul directly in front of me home from my trip."

Eugene tilted back in his chair, and watched Emma pop the grapes in.

"That would be him," said Emma.

7.

The Wanderers

HOW COME you weren't here yesterday?" old Mrs. Stark asked her maid, looking up from her solitaire board —inlaid wood that gave off pistol-like reports under the blows of her shuffling cards. It was September and here in the hall she imagined she could feel October at her back.

"I didn' get back from my sisters' in the country."

"And poor Miss Katie Rainey dead. What were you so busy doing?"

"Showin' my teef."

Mrs. Stark raised her voice. "Only thing I can do for people any more, in joy or sorrow, is send 'em you. You know how Miss Jinny and Mr. Ran back out on me, then you go off. Now it's here next day. Fix my breakfast and yours and go on down there. Get in the kitchen and clean it up for Miss Virgie, don't pay any attention to her. Take that ham we haven't sliced into. Start cooking for the funeral, if others didn't beat you to it yesterday."

"Yes'm."

"Mind you learn to appreciate your good kitchen when you stand over a wood stove all day."

"I was comin' back. Sister's place a place once you get to it—hard time gettin' out."

Mrs. Stark snapped her fingers. "You and all your sisters!" She rose and walked, with her walk like a girl's, to the front door, looking down over her hill, the burned, patchy grass no better than Katie Rainey's, and the thirsty shrubs; but the Morgan sweet olive, her own grandmother's age, her grandmother's tree, was blooming. She murmured over her shoulder, "I never had cause to set foot in the Rainey house for over five minutes in my life. And I don't suppose they need me now. But I hope I know what any old woman owes another old woman. It doesn't matter if it's too late. Do you hear me? Go back and put on a clean apron."

The Raineys, Miss Katie and her daughter Virgie, still held

on to the house beyond the pavement, on the MacLain Road. There on the ridge the tin roof shed the light under the crape myrtle and privet, gone to trees, that edged the porch. The cannas with their scorched edges, together with the well, made the three familiar islands in the whitened grass of the yard. Across and back again, with effort but bobbinlike, had moved Miss Katie, Mrs. Fate Rainey, in her dress the hard blue of a morning-glory.

In old age Miss Katie showed what a neat, narrow head she had under the hair no longer disheveled and flyaway. When she came outdoors, her carefully dressed and carefully held head was as silver-looking as a new mail box. It was out of the autocracy of her stroke—she had suffered "a light stroke" five years ago, "while separating my cows and calves," she would recount it—that she'd begun ordering things done by set times. When it was time for Virgie to come home from work in the afternoon, Miss Katie fretted herself for fear she wouldn't be in time to milk before dark. She still had her two favorite Jerseys, pastured near. She stood out in the front yard, or moved the best way she could back and forth, waiting for Virgie.

A fiery streak of salvia that ran around the side of the house would turn darker in the leveling light. Though the shade broadened, she still walked her narrow path, not yielding even to the kind sun. She held up poorly there, propped by an old thornstick. Bleaching down by the roadside was a chair, an old chair she sold things from once, under the borrowed shade of the chinaberry across the road; but she didn't seem to want to sit down any more, or to be quite that near the trafficking. Clear up where she was, she felt the world tremble; day and night the loggers went by, to and from Morgan's Woods. That wore her out too. While she lived, she was going to wait—and she did wait, standing up—until Virgie her daughter, past forty now and too dressed up, came home to milk Bossy and Juliette the way she should. Virgie worked for the very people that were out depleting the woods, Mr. Nesbitt's company.

Miss Katie couldn't spare her good hand to put up and shade her eyes; yet after you passed, you saw her in that position, in your vision if not in your sight. She looked ready to ward you off, too, in case of pity, there in her gathered old-lady dress, sometimes in an old bonnety church-hat. There's the old lady that watches the turn of the road, thought the old countrymen, Sissums and Sojourners and Holifields, passing in trucks or wagons on Saturday, going home, lifting their hats. Young courting people, Little Sister Spights' crowd, giggled at her, but small children and Negroes did not; they took her for granted like the lady on the Old Dutch Cleanser can.

The old people in Morgana she reminded of Snowdie MacLain, her neighbor once, who watched and waited for her husband so long. They were reminded vaguely of themselves, too, now that they were old enough to see it, still watching and waiting for something they didn't really know about any longer, wouldn't recognize to see it coming in the road.

As she looked out from her hill in the creeping shade, Miss Katie Rainey might have liked to be argued with and prevailed upon to go back in the house; at the last she might have suffered contradiction, but from whom? Not from Virgie.

"Where's my girl? Have you seen my girl?"

Miss Katie thought she called to the road, but she didn't; shame drew down her head, for she could still feel one thing if she could feel little else coming to her from the outside world: lack of chivalry.

Waiting, she heard circling her ears like the swallows beginning, talk about lovers. Circle by circle it twittered, church talk, talk in the store and postoffice, vulgar man talk possibly in the barbershop. Talk she could never get near now was coming to her.

"So long as the old lady's alive, it's all behind her back."

"Daughter wouldn't run off and leave her, she's old and crippled."

"Left once, will again."

"That fellow Mabry's been taking out his gun and leaving Virgie a bag o' quail every other day. Anybody can see him go by the back door."

"I declare."

"He told her the day she got tired o' quail, let him know and he'd quit and go on off, that's what I heard."

"Do tell."

"Furthermore, I reckon it would be possible for a human being, a woman, to live off them rich birds for the remaining space of time. Her ma can help her eat 'em. Her ma ain't lost her appetite!"

"Hush."

"Guess it wouldn't be polite for her or him neither one to stop on the quails. Even if he heard. Got to keep on now."

"Oh, sure. Fate Rainey's a clean shot, too."

"But ain't he heard?"

Not Fate Rainey at all; but Mr. Mabry. It was just that the talk Miss Katie heard was in voices of her girlhood, and some times they slipped.

Then, in an odd set way, for she lied badly, she would lie to Virgie when she came. "I asked Passing. And not one of 'em said they could tell me where you were, what kept you so long in town."

But it's my last summer, and she ought to get back here and milk on time, the old lady thought, stubbornly and yet pityingly, the two ways she was.

"Look where the sun is," she called, as Virgie did drive up in the yard in the old coupe Miss Katie kept forgetting she had, the battered thing she took in trade for the poor little calf.

"I see it, Mama."

Virgie's long, dark, too heavy hair swung this way and that as she came up in her flowered voile dress, on her high heels through the bearded grass.

"You have to milk before dark, after driving them in, and there's four little quails full of shot for you to dress, lying on my kitchen table."

"Come on back in the house, Mama. Come in with me."

"I been by myself all day."

Virgie bent and gave her mother her evening kiss.

Miss Katie knew then that Virgie would drive the cows home and milk and feed them and deliver the milk on the road, and come back and cook the little quails.

"It's a wonder, though," she thought. "A blessed wonder to see the child mind."

The day Miss Katie died, Virgie was kneeling on the floor

of her bedroom cutting out a dress from some plaid material. She was sewing on Sunday.

"There's nothing Virgie Rainey loves better than struggling against a real hard plaid," Miss Katie thought, with a thrust of pain from somewhere unexpected. Whereas, there was a simple line down through her own body now, dividing it in half; there should be one in every woman's body—it would need to be the long way, not the cross way—that was too easy—making each of them a side to feel and know, and a side to stop it, to be waited on, finally.

But she wanted to drop to her knees there where Virgie's plaid spread out like a pretty rug for her. Her last clear feeling as she stood there, holding herself up, was that she wanted to be down and covered up, in, of all things, Virgie's hard-to-match-up plaid. But she turned herself around by an act of strength which tore her within and walked, striking her cane, the width of the hall and two rooms and lay down on her own bed.

"Stop and fan me a minute," she called aloud. She was thinking rapidly to herself, though, that Virgie had said, "I aim to get married on my bulb money."

Virgie, who worked in her gown, came in with pins in her mouth and her thumb marked green from the scissors, and stood over her. She brought a paper up and down over her mother's face. She fanned her with the *Market Bulletin*.

Dying, Miss Katie went rapidly over the list in it, her list. As though her impatient foot would stamp at each item, she counted it, corrected it, and yet she was about to forget the seasons, and the places things grew. Purple althea cuttings, true box, four colors of cannas for 15¢, moonvine seed by teaspoonful, green and purple jew. Roses: big white rose, little thorn rose, beauty-red sister rose, pink monthly, old-fashioned red summer rose, very fragrant, baby rose. Five colors of verbena, candlestick lilies, milk and wine lilies, blackberry lilies, lemon lilies, angel lilies, apostle lilies. Angel trumpet seed. The red amaryllis.

Faster and faster, Mrs. Rainey thought: Red salvia, four-o'clock, pink Jacob's ladder, sweet geranium cuttings, sword fern and fortune grass, century plants, vase palm, watermelon pink and white crape myrtle, Christmas cactus, golden bell.

White Star Jessamine. Snowball. Hyacinthus. Pink fairy lilies. White. The fairy white.

"Fan me. If you stop fanning, it's worse than if you never started."

And when Mama is gone, almost gone now, she meditated, I can tack on to my ad: the quilts! For sale, Double Muscadine Hulls, Road to Dublin, Starry Sky, Strange Spider Web, Hands All Around, Double Wedding Ring. Mama's rich in quilts, child.

Miss Katie lay there, carelessly on the counterpane, thinking, Crochet tablecloth, Sunburst design, very lacy. She knew Virgie stood over her, fanning her in rhythmic sweeps. Presently Miss Katie's lips shut tight.

She was thinking, Mistake. Never Virgie at all. It was me, the bride—with more than they guessed. Why, Virgie, go away, it was me.

She put her hand up and never knew what happened to it, her protest.

Virgie knelt, crouched there. She held her head, her mouth opened, and one by one the pins fell out on the floor. She was not much afraid of death, either of its delay or its surprise. As yet nothing in the place of fear came into her head; only something about her dress.

The bed, the headboard dark and ungiving as an old mirror on the wall, to her as a child a vast King Arthur shield that might have concealed a motto, cast its afternoon shadow down dark as muscadines, to her mother's waist. The old shadow, familiar as sleep the life long, always ran down over the bolster this time of year, the warm and knotty medallions of the familiar counterpane—the overworked, inherited, and personal pattern—from which her mother's black shoes now pointed up.

Behind the bed the window was full of cloudy, pressing flowers and leaves in heavy light, like a jar of figs in syrup held up. A humming bird darted, fed, darted. Every day he came. He had a ruby throat. The clock jangled faintly as cymbals struck under water, but did not strike; it couldn't. Yet a torrent of riches seemed to flow over the room, submerging it, loading it with what was over-sweet.

Virgie ran to the porch. Waiting on a passing Negro, she called, in a moment, "Go get me Dr. Loomis out of church!" The Negro began to sprint in his Sunday clothes.

By mid-afternoon the house was filling with callers and helpers. Each one who came seemed stopped by the enormous dead boxwood, like a yellow sponge, that stood by the steps; it had to be gone around. Coffee was being kept on the stove and iced tea in the pitcher in the hall. Virgie was dressed, in the dress she had ironed that morning for Monday, and at the front of the house. Moving around her, a lady watered the ferns and evened the shades in the parlor, then watered and evened again, as if some obscure sums were being balanced and checked. Every seat in the parlor and Virgie's room was taken, the porch and the steps creaked under the men who stood outside.

Cassie Morrison, her black-stockinged legs seeming to wade among the impeding legs of the other women, crossed the parlor to where Virgie sat in the chair at the closed sewing machine. Cassie had chosen the one thin, gold-rimmed coffee cup for herself, and balanced it serenely.

"Papa sent his sympathy. Let me sit by you, Virgie." She kissed her. "You know I know what it's like."

"Excuse me," Virgie was saying. All at once she slept, straight in the cane chair. When she opened her eyes, she watched and listened to the even fuller roomful as carefully, and as carelessly, as vacillating as though she were on the point of departure. Through their murmur she heard herself circle the room to speak to them and be kissed. She made the steps of the walk they had to watch, head, breasts, and hips in their helpless agitation, like a rope of bells she started in their ears.

"She can't help it," Cassie Morrison was saying to the person beside her in the gentle tones of a verdict. "She can't take in what's happened quite yet and she doesn't really know us."

The unnaturally closed door led from Miss Katie's room out to the parlor. Behind it, they all knew—waiting as they were for it to open—Miss Snowdie MacLain was laying Miss Katie out. She washed and dressed her herself, tolerating only two old Loomis Negroes to wait on her, and Miss Snowdie was nearly seventy too, and had come seven miles from

MacLain. There was something about it nobody liked, perhaps a break in custom. Miss Lizzie Stark, whose place they felt it to be to supervise the house while old Miss Emmy Holifield laid out the dead, had felt too weak today, and sent word she had had to lie down. And old Emmy herself was gone.

It was true that none of the callers except Miss Snowdie had been inside the Rainey house since Mr. Fate Rainey's funeral. No wonder Virgie looked at them now, staring, at moments.

Always in a house of death, Virgie was thinking, all the stories come evident, show forth from the person, become a part of the public domain. Not the dead's story, but the living's.

She could see Ran MacLain, standing at the door shaking hands with Mr. Nesbitt who was coming in. And didn't it show on Ran, that once he had taken advantage of a country girl who had died a suicide? It showed at election time as it showed now, and he won the election for mayor over Mr. Carmichael, for all was remembered in his middle-age when he stood on the platform. Ran was smiling—holding on to a countryman now. They had voted for him for that—for his glamour and his story, for being a MacLain and the bad twin, for marrying a Stark and then for ruining a girl and the thing she did. Old Man Moody found her on the floor of his store—the place she worked—and walked out into the street with her in his arms. They voted for the revelation; it had made their hearts faint, and they would assert it again. Ran knew that every minute, there in the door he stood it.

"Cheer up, now, cheer up," Mr. Nesbitt was saying to her, seeming to lift her to her feet by running his finger under her chin. His eyes—so willed by him, she thought—ran tears and dried. "Come here," he called over his shoulder.

"Virgie, tell Mr. Thisbee who's your best friend in this town." He had brought the new man in the company.

"You, Mr. Bitts," Virgie said.

"Everybody in Morgana calls me Mr. Bitts, Thisbee; you can too. Now wait. Tell him who hired you when nobody else was in the hiring mood, Virgie. Tell him. And was always kind to you and stood up for you."

She never turned away until it was finished; today this seemed somehow brief and easy, a relief.

"Hurry up, Virgie. Got to cheer my daughter up next."

Nina Carmichael, Mrs. Junior Nesbitt heavy with child, was seated where he could see her, head fine and indifferent, one puffed white arm stretched along the sewing machine. He winked at her across the room.

"You, Mr. Bitts."

"Tell him how long you've been working for old Mr. Bitts."

"A long time."

"No, tell him how long it's been—my my my, tell him. I've been in three different businesses, Thisbee. How long?"

"Since 1920, Mr. Bitts."

"And if you ever made any mistakes in your letters and figgers, who was it stood behind you with the company?"

"I'm very sorry for you in your sorrow," Mr. Thisbee said suddenly, letting go her hand. She almost fell.

"But who? Who stood behind you?"

Mr. Nesbitt extended his arms overly wide, as he did when asking her to dance with him in Vicksburg. Abruptly he wheeled and went off; he was hurt, disappointed in her for the hundredth time. She saw Mr. Nesbitt's fat, hurt back as he wandered as if lost and stood a long time contemplating and cheering up Nina Carmichael.

Food—two banana cakes and a baked ham, a platter of darkly deviled eggs, new rolls—and flowers kept arriving at the back, and the kitchen filled with women as the parlor now filled with men come farther in. Virgie went back once more to the kitchen, but again the women stopped what they were doing and looked at her as though something—not only today—should prevent her from knowing at all how to cook—the thing they knew. She went to the stove, took a fork, and turned over a piece or two of the chicken, to see Missie Spights look at her with eyes wide in a kind of wonder and belligerence.

Then she walked through them and stood on the quiet back porch to feel the South breeze. The packed freezer, wrapped in a croker sack, the old, golden stopper of newspaper hidden and waiting on tomorrow, stood in the dishpan. The cut flowers were plunged stem-down and head-down in shady water buckets. Virgie had a sudden recollection of recital night at Miss Eckhart's—the moment when she was to be called out. She was thirteen, waiting outside, on guard at a vast calming spectacle of turmoil, and saving it. A little drop spilled, she remembered it now: an anxiety which brought her to the point of sickness, that back in there they were laughing at her mother's hat.

She went back into the parlor. Like a forest murmur the waiting talk filled the room.

The door opened. Miss Snowdie stood against it, sideways, looking neither in nor out.

Immediately the ladies rose and filled the doorway; some of them went in. Only the end of the bed and Miss Katie's feet could be seen from within the parlor. There were soft cries. "Snowdie!" "Miss Snowdie! She looks beautiful!" Then the rest of the ladies tiptoed forward and could be seen bending over the bed as they would bend over the crib of a little kicking baby. They came out again.

"Come see your mother."

They pulled pre-emptorily at Virgie's arms, their voices bright.

"Don't touch me."

They pulled harder, still smiling but in silence, and Virgie pulled back. Her hair fell over her eyes. She shook it back. "Don't touch me."

"Honey, you just don't know what you lost, that's all."

They were all people who had never touched her before who tried now to struggle with her, their faces hurt. She was hurting them all, shocking them. They leaned over her, agonized, pleading with the pull of their hands. It was a Mrs. Flewellyn, pulling the hardest, who had caught the last breath of her husband in a toy balloon, by his wish, and had it at home still—most of it, until a Negro stole it.

Miss Perdita Mayo's red face looked over their wall. "Your mama was too fine for you, Virgie, too fine. That was always the trouble between you."

In that truth, Virgie looked up at them lightheadedly and they lifted her to her feet and drew her into the bedroom and showed her her mother.

She lay in the black satin. It had been lifted, heavy as a child, out of her trunk, the dress in which diminished, pea-sized mothballs had shone and rolled like crystals all Virgie's life, in waiting, taken out twice, and now spread out in full triangle. Her head was in the center of the bolster, the widow's place in which she herself laid it. Miss Snowdie had rouged her cheeks.

They watched Virgie, but Virgie gave them no sign now. She felt their hands smooth down her and leave her, draw away from her body and then give it a little shove forward, even their hands showing sorrow for a body that did not fall, giving back to hands what was broken, to pick up, smooth again. For people's very touch anticipated the falling of the body, the own, the single and watchful body.

Later, back in the parlor, she cried. They said, "She used to set out yonder and sell muscadines, see out there? There's where she got rid of all her plums, the early and late, blackberries and dewberries, and the little peanuts you boil. Now the road goes the wrong way." Though that was like a sad song, it was not true: the road still went the same, from Morgana to MacLain, from Morgana to Vicksburg and Jackson, of course. Only now the wrong people went by on it. They were all riding trucks, very fast or heavily loaded, and carrying blades and chains, to chop and haul the big trees to mill. They were not eaters of muscadines, and did not stop to pass words on the season and what grew. And the vines had dried. She wept because they could not tell it right, and they didn't press for her reasons.

"Call Mr. Mabry now. She's let loose."

Mr. Mabry, fresh from the barbershop, took Virgie's hands and swung them, then dropped them. She dried her eyes instantly and withdrew, giving him permission to go into the other room. She wondered when she had seen him leave her on tiptoe before. Old country fellows in the hall began to speak of him now, respectfully, as he looked down at the dead with his face so rubylike, so recently complimented upon, that in the next moment it would fill with concern for itself.

"He aims to get closer to Ives. Where he don't have to use hoot owls for roosters and fox for yard dogs, is the way he put it to me."

"Then why on earth don't he come to Morgana? No nicer place than right here, 's what I think, if I wanted to be close in."

"He prefers Ives."

"I see."

But in the parlor it was generally felt polite now to consider Miss Katie as the center of conversation, since the door was now open.

"Virgie might get a little bit of dairyfood savings now, bet she'll spend it on something 'sides the house, hm?" A lady Virgie couldn't place said it halfway in her direction, leaning toward her now and then as she had been doing, with her full weight. "Her pretty quilts, she can't ship those to the Fair no more. What does Virgie care about housekeeping and china plates without no husband, hm? Wonder what Virgie'll do with the chickens, Katie always enjoyed a mixed yard. Wonder who Virgie'll give the deer to if she don't want it. That picture of the deer Miss Katie's mother hooked in Tishomingo with the mistletoe crown over the horns, and the oak leaves, Miss Katie considered it the prettiest thing in the world. The cloth doll with the china head and hands, that she used to let any and all play with—"

"Guinevere! Oh, I wish I had her now!" Cassie Morrison held out both gloved hands.

"Her fern stand. Virgie won't stay here to keep care of ferns, I bet. Her begonia, thirty-five years old. Not much older than Virgie, is it, Virgie? She left her recipes to the Methodist Church—I hope."

"She was a living saint," answered another lady, as if this would agree with everything.

"Look at my diamond."

Jinny MacLain, Ran's wife, was coming in. With her hand out, she showed a ring about the room on her way to Virgie. "I deserved me a diamond," she went on to say to Cassie Morrison, twisting her hand on its wrist. "That's what I told Ran." Softly, abruptly, she turned and kissed Virgie's cheek, whispering, "I don't have to see her—do I, Virgie?"

Then they all rose as Miss Snowdie came in.

"I don't have to see anybody!" whispered Jinny fiercely.

Virgie, still holding a cup of coffee, walked out and waited on the porch, for she knew Miss Snowdie would come outside. She could hear her in the parlor now, staying to take a certain amount of praise. Then Miss Snowdie came out, now as at all times a gentle lady, her face white and graciously folded, gently concerned but no more. She stood and looked out, at once shading her eyes, to the house across the road where she used to live. She kissed Virgie then, almost idly.

"I think she looks all right, Virgie."

Her albino's hands were cruelly reddened. But she never seemed really to feel their redness any more. Her soft black-and-white dotted dress smelled as freshly as always of verbena.

"I saw to her well as I knew how. If Emmy Holifield were still living, she might have thought of things I didn't."

But her eyes went past Virgie, across the road, where the old house was a ruin now. In between where the women were standing and the sight of the old place, in the Rainey yard, the children waiting for their parents stood still, fell still, at that moment, and not knowing where to look all at once, listened—listened to the locusts, perforce, which sounded like the sound of the world going around to them as they suddenly beat their cupped hands over their ears.

"Virgie? You know Lizzie Stark and I long ago made up. About Ran and Jinny's trouble; that's over, all over. But do you reckon, at such a time, it was old feelings rising up that kept her away?"

Miss Snowdie sighed, as if she had forgotten her question with the asking, as if a reply would interrupt her. Across there was a place where she had lived a long time, the old deserted time, when Virgie played with Ran and Eugene under her trees, on her porch, under her house, along the river bank, and in Morgan's Woods. There were leggy cedars still lining the old property, their trunks white and knobbed like chicken bones. The old summer-house was still back there, lattices leaning inward and not matching at the joinings, in the shadow like a place where long ago something had been kept that could peep out now; in the sun like a little temple raised to it. The big chinaberry tree had been cut down with the other lawn trees when the house burned, but its many suckers sprayed up from the stump like a fountain. Negroes had carried away most of the sides and roof that remained of the house, but had hardly made inroad on the chimney, surprisingly enough; it was its full height still, visible from here, dove-pink through the dust and leafiness. Little locusts and castor plants tall as a man had come up all around, the altheas had come back and made trees, shaggy as old giants holding twilit, flimsy little flowers up high. Vines had taken the yard and the walk, the brick cross of the foundation, and the trees and all.

Virgie removed herself from Miss Snowdie's arm which had gone around her waist. The two women stood quiet in the afternoon light.

"I said I'd want *her* to lay *me* out," the old lady said. She trembled very slightly but did not go back. She looked out still.

From around the big boxwood Mr. King MacLain, treading so lightly they didn't hear him, came up the steps.

"You know Virgie," Miss Snowdie murmured, still motionless.

"And Katie Blazes, that's what we used to call your mother," Mr. King nodded at Virgie. The little patch of hair under his lip—not silky, coarse, a pinkish white—shook in a ruminating way. Viola, their Negro, had driven him over after giving him his dinner; she could be seen going to the back now, to visit the kitchen.

"Sir?"

"I'll take that coffee if it's hot and you ain't drinking it. Katie Blazes. Didn't you ever hear your mother tell how she never took a dare to put a match to her stockings, girl? Whsst! Up went the blazes, up to her knee! Sometimes both legs. Cotton stockings the girls used to wear—fuzzy, God knows they were. Nobody else among the girls would set fire to their legs. She had the neighborhood scared she'd go up in flames at an early age."

"Did you eat your dinner?" Miss Snowdie turned to him.

Virgie watched the black coffee beginning to shake in the little cup. There was something terrifying about that old man—he was too old.

"In flames!"

He left them and went into the hall of men.

"I don't know what to do with him," Miss Snowdie said,

in a murmur as quiet as the world around them now. She did not know she had spoken. When her flyaway husband had come home a few years ago, at the age of sixty-odd, and stayed, they said she had never gotten over it—first his running away, then his coming back to her. "He didn't want to come at all. Now he has her mixed up with Nellie Loomis."

"Virgie, we've got enough ready to feed an army," Missie Spights called up the hall. She was coming, untying Miss Katie's apron from her dress, her arms shining red. "Ham, chickens, potato salad, deviled eggs, and all the cake and folderol people send besides."

"Does there have to be so much?" Virgie asked, going in to meet her.

"Watch. The out-of-town relatives are always hungry!"

Her busyness gave Missie an air of abandon, quite impregnable. Parnell Moody stood behind her, drying every circle of the potato masher with care. The others were clattering the dishes, putting them in stacks, talking.

"My husband's been waiting on me an hour."

"Mr. King MacLain took himself a nap pretty as you please. Viola had to shriek in his ear to get him up."

"We'll all be back early for the funeral, Virgie—wish you'd let us stay." Cassie drew her delicate brows, surveying the kitchen which she had never got to. "Everybody who would, I let stay with me."

"It's a good thing we cut all our flowers," Missie called, fastening her corset behind the door. "Virgie, you haven't a solitary one."

She saw them all, except Miss Snowdie who stayed, get into their cars in the yard, or walk down the path and into the road. As they went, they seemed to drag some mythical gates and barriers away from her view. She looked at the lighted distance, the little last crescent of hills before the country of the river, and the fields. The world shimmered. Cotton fields look busy on Sunday even; while they are not being picked they push out their bloom the same. The frail screens of standing trees still measured, broke, divided—Stark from Loomis from Spights from Holifield, and the summer from the rain. Each tree like a single leaf, half hair-fine skeleton, half gauze and green, let the first suspicious wind through its old, pressed shape, its summertime branches. The air came smelling of what it was, the end of September.

Down the settling dust of the road came an ancient car. It would turn in here. Old Plez, up until his death, had stopped by to milk and feed the chickens for Miss Katie Rainey on his way to and from the Starks'. His grandchildren, still country people, would come today. The car pounded up the hill to her. It was cracked like some put-together puzzle of the globe of the world. Its cracks didn't meet from one side across to the other, and it was all held together with straightened-out baling wire, for today. Next day, next year, it would sit in the front yard for decoration, at rest on its axles, the four wheels gone and the tires divided up between women and children: two for flowerbeds and two for swings.

They had brought the flowers from their dooryard, princess feathers, snow-on-the-mountain. It took them a long time to turn around and get a start back. A little boy ran back with the pan of butterbeans and okra.

"All come to the funeral if you can get away!" she called after them, too late.

Virgie walked down the hill too, crossed the road, and made her way through the old MacLain place and the pasture and down to the river. She stood on the willow bank. It was bright as mid-afternoon in the openness of the water, quiet and peaceful. She took off her clothes and let herself into the river.

She saw her waist disappear into reflectionless water; it was like walking into sky, some impurity of skies. All was one warmth, air, water, and her own body. All seemed one weight, one matter—until as she put down her head and closed her eyes and the light slipped under her lids, she felt this matter a translucent one, the river, herself, the sky all vessels which the sun filled. She began to swim in the river, forcing it gently, as she would wish for gentleness to her body. Her breasts around which she felt the water curving were as sensitive at that moment as the tips of wings must feel to birds, or antennae to insects. She felt the sand, grains intricate as little cogged wheels, minute shells of old seas, and the many dark ribbons of grass and mud touch her and leave her, like suggestions and withdrawals of some bondage that might have been dear, now dismembering and losing itself. She moved but like a cloud in skies, aware but only of the nebulous edges of her feeling and the vanishing opacity of her will, the carelessness for the water of the river through which her body had already passed as well as for what was ahead. The bank was all one, where out of the faded September world the little ripening plums started. Memory dappled her like no more than a paler light, which in slight agitations came through leaves, not darkening her for more than an instant. The iron taste of the old river was sweet to her, though. If she opened her eyes she looked at blue-bottles, the skating waterbugs. If she trembled it was at the smoothness of a fish or snake that crossed her knees.

In the middle of the river, whose downstream or upstream could not be told by a current, she lay on her stretched arm, not breathing, floating. Virgie had reached the point where in the next moment she might turn into something without feeling it shock her. She hung suspended in the Big Black River as she would know to hang suspended in felicity. Far to the west, a cloud running fingerlike over the sun made her splash the water. She stood, walked along the soft mud of the bottom and pulled herself out of the water by a willow branch, which like warm rain brushed her back with its leaves.

At a distance, two little boys lying naked in the red light on the sandbar looked at her as she disappeared into the leaves. They did not move or speak.

The moon, while she looked into the high sky, took its own light between one moment and the next. A wood thrush, which had begun to sing, hushed its long moment and began again. Virgie put her clothes back on. She would have given much for a cigarette, always wishing for a little more of what had just been.

She went back to the pasture, where the enormous ant hills shone, with long shadows, like pyramids on the other side of the world, and drove the cows home.

The crape myrtle had a last crown of bloom on top, once

white, now faintly nutmegged. The ground below was littered with its shed bark, and the limbs shone like human limbs, lithe and warm, pink.

She went out to milk and came back to the house.

From the hall she looked into her mother's room. The window and the room were the one blue of first-dark. Only the black dress, the density of skirt, was stamped on it, like some dark chip now riding mid-air on blue lakes.

Miss Snowdie MacLain had elected to "sit up" the first hours of night. She slept in the bedroom rocker, in the luminous veil of her dress, the cocoon of her head hanging upon it, and the fan let fall from her fingers.

II.

Virgie waked to see the morning star hanging over the fields. What had she meant to do so early? She made and drank her coffee, milked, drove the cows to pasture through mist, chopped wood, and at last she attacked the high grass in the yard. Yesterday cutting the Rainey grass in time for the funeral was considered a project so impossible that even if men could be spared and given scythes, success was never guaranteed. Virgie took her sewing scissors from the little bundle of plaid material in her room, and went outdoors. She crouched in the pink early light, clipping and sawing the heads off the grass—it had all gone to seed—a handful at a time. She could feel dimmed round Venus still, for she must feel some presence, there was always something, someone, and Venus watching her made the imperceptible work almost leisurely, then again fierce. The choked-out roses scratched, surprised her, drew blood drops on her legs. She had to come in when Miss Snowdie, whose presence she had forgotten, stepped out on the porch and called her. As though for a long time she had been extremely angry and had wept many tears, she allowed Miss Snowdie to drive her inside the house and cook her breakfast.

Then Miss Lizzie Stark's Juba arrived, followed by a little stairsteps of Negro children bearing curtain stretchers, and Miss Snowdie and Juba began taking down all the curtains. In half an hour these were out in the backyard, stretched and set forth like the tents in the big Bible's Wilderness of Kadesh. The ladies soon were everywhere, radiating once more from the kitchen.

"First thing," Missie Spights told Virgie, "you called me Missie Spights yesterday. I'm married."

"Oh. Yes, I remember."

"I'm Missie Spights Littlejohn, and I've got three children. I married from off."

"I remember, Missie."

Some of Miss Katie's people arrived by noon, in good time for the funeral—big dark people named Mayhew, men and women alike with square, cleft chins and blue eyes. A little string of tow-headed children made a row behind, finishing some bananas. Virgie couldn't remember all the Mayhews or tell them apart; they all came upon her at once, after knocking on the porch to bring her out, all kissed her in greedy turn and begged before they got through the door for ice water or iced tea or both. They had ridden in in several trucks, now drawn up by the porch, from the Stockstill and Lastingwell communities near the Tennessee line. The first thing the largest Mayhew man did, once inside the house, was to catch up a little child of Missie Spights', who was swatting flies, and tickle her violently, speaking soberly over her screams, "Now wait: you don't know who I am."

Only the same old Rainey came from Louisiana who had come to Fate's funeral years ago and hadn't sent word since. Again he brought his own coffee. Again he offered to fix the front porch and in time, and again was prevented. He was the only Rainey that made the trip. The Raineys were mostly all died out, or couldn't leave the fields, or were too far to buy a ticket. The old man explained it all again, and told what had happened to the French name with all the years.

"Yes, some are missing," Miss Perdita Mayo told Virgie when she arrived and saw the lined-up kin. "But you got in touch, or I did for you. If the funeral's small we can't reproach ourselves."

Screams surrounded the house. The little MacLain children and their nurse had gotten away from old Miss Lizzie, their grandmother, and come to play in the Rainey yard. Gradually other children, Loomis and Maloney, attracted by the magnetic MacLains, played there too, all drunk with the attractions of an untried place, and a place sinister for the day. The little Mayhews, every time they were gathered up and brought away from these into the house, cried. Blue jays were scolding the whole morning over the roof, and the logging trucks thundered by, shaking their chains and threatening the clean curtains.

Miss Perdita Mayo, who had got into the bedroom and formed a circle, was telling a story. "Sister couldn't get her new shoes back on after that funeral, because while she was in the cemetery—" Suddenly Miss Perdita appeared backing out of the room, thinking herself still telling her story, but mistaken. She had heard the coffin come, and ran to meet it. Mr. Holifield at the hardware store sent his grandsons, Hughie and Dewey Holifield, with it on their produce truck. The boys came inside and made it steady, the Mayhews watching.

"Where's all them Mayhews going to bed down?" old Mr. Rainey, with nothing to do, asked Virgie, indicating Mayhews with a thumb purpled like a fig.

"They won't stay. They're striking right out for Stockstill after the funeral, sir," said Virgie. "As soon as they've packed some lunch." And they were taking the bed, Katie's bed; they could set it right up in the truck, they said, looking at it detached from its owner who was lying on it; and the children could ride home on it instead of standing.

Mr. Rainey was shaking his head. "Pity. Never a chance to know those." He put up a little horned finger and touched a string on the old banjo of her father's, which hung on its nail in the hall, the head faintly luminous by morning light. But he didn't play the note. "*He* traveled around a bit," he said at length. "And settled hereabouts for the adventure of it."

The home-grown flowers came early, and the florist flowers late. Mr. Nesbitt sent word by the janitor in the barbershop, who wore gold-rimmed spectacles, that he must be out of town during the funeral, the Negro then bringing out from behind his back a large cross of gladiolas and ferns on a stand, evidently from Vicksburg, with Mr. Nesbitt's card tied on. The Mayhews moved upon it and placed it in front of all the other flowers—now steadily being made into wreaths on the back porch—where they could look at it during the service, to remember. The Sunday School chairs arrived by wagon, and the Mayhews took them at the door and set them in cater-cornered rows. Had Miss Lizzie Stark been able to come, people said, it wouldn't have happened quite the same way.

Old Mr. King MacLain did not appear happy over having to come to the Rainey house again today. He fumed, and went back to visit in the kitchen.

"Little conversation with your mother in '18, or along there," he said to Virgie, who was folding napkins with the Stark "S" on them. "You know in those days I was able to make considerable trips off, and only had my glimpses of the people back here."

Miss Snowdie had come to stand folding napkins too.

"I'd come and I'd go again, only I ended up at the wrong end, wouldn't you say?" He suddenly smiled, rather fiercely, but at neither woman. He wore the stiffest-starched white suit Virgie ever saw on any old gentleman; it looked fierce too—the lapels alert as ears. "Saw your mother in a pink sunbonnet. Rosy-cheeked. 'Hello!'—'I declare, King MacLain, you look to me as you ever did, strolling here in the road. You rascal.'—'Just for that, what would you rather have than anything? I'm asking because I'm going to get it for you.'—'A swivel chair. So I can sit out front and sell crochet and peaches, if my good-for-nothing husband'll let me.' Ah, we all knew sweet old Fate, he was a sweet man among us. 'Shucks, that's too easy. Say something else. I'd have got you anything your living heart desired.'—'Well, I told you. And you mischief, I believe you.'

"Three niggers black as dirtdaubers up to the house in a wagon, bang-up noon next day. Up to the door, pounding.

" 'Oh, King MacLain! You've brought it so quick-like!'

"But I! I was no telling where by that time. Looked to her, I know, like I couldn't wait long enough to hear her pleasure. So bent, so bent I was on all I had to do, on what was ahead of me.

"*She* told me how she flew around the yard. 'Watch out,

now, don't set that down a minute till I tell you where it'll go!' Had niggers carrying here, carrying there. Then she put it spang by the road, close as she could get.

"And her chair always too big for her, little heels wouldn't touch ground. It was big enough for a man, big enough for Drewsie Carmichael, 'cause it was his. I prevailed on the widow. Oh, Katie Rainey was a sight, I saw her swing her chair round many's the time, to hear me coming down the road or starting out, waving her hand to me. And sold more eggs than you'd dream. Oh, then, she could see where Fate Rainey had fallen down, and a lovely man, too; never got her the thing she wanted. I set her on a throne!"

"Mr. King, I never knew the chair came from you," Virgie said, smiling.

He looked all at once inconsolable, but Miss Snowdie shook her head.

"Have a little refreshments, sir. There's ham and potato salad—"

"Oh, is there ham?"

Virgie led him down the hall. The Negroes stood by the table with fly swatters. She laid a little piccalilli with the ham on his plate, which he held for her as long as she'd help it.

When Virgie returned to the parlor, Jinny MacLain came forward to greet her: as if their positions were reversed.

Jinny, who in childhood had seemed more knowing than her years, was in her thirties strangely childlike; was it old perversity or further tactics? She too arrived at close range, looked at the burns and scars on Virgie's hands, as Missie Spights had done, making them stigmata of something at odds in her womanhood.

"Listen. You should marry now, Virgie. Don't put it off any longer," she said, making a face, any face, at her own words. She was grimacing out of the iron mask of the married lady. It appeared urgent with her to drive everybody, even Virgie for whom she cared nothing, into the state of marriage along with her. Only then could she resume as Jinny Love Stark, her true self. She was casting her eye around the room, as if to pick Virgie some husband then and there; and her eyes rested over Virgie's head on—Virgie knew it—Ran MacLain.

Virgie smiled faintly; now she felt, without warning, that two passionate people stood in this roomful, with their indifferent backs to each other.

A great many had gathered now. People sat inside and outside, listening and not listening. Young people held hands, all of them taking seats early to reserve the back row. Then some of the Mayhews carried the coffin into the parlor and placed it over the hearth on the four chairs from around the table. The wreaths were stood on edge to hide the chair legs.

"What are my children up to?" Jinny whispered hurriedly, and swept a curtain aside to expose the front yard. "My daughter has chosen today to catch lizards. She's wearing lizard earrings! How can she stand those little teeth in her!" Jinny laughed delightedly as she settled herself by the window.

"Sit by me, Virgie," said Cassie Morrison, who began to put her handkerchief to her eyes. "This is when it's the worst, or almost."

There was a new arrival just before the service. Brother Dampeer from Goodnight, whose father was the preacher when Mrs. Rainey was a child and baptized her as a girl in Cold Creek, in North Mississippi, couldn't let her go without one more glimpse, he said. Virgie had never seen Brother Dampeer; he sized her up and kissed her. There was a tuning fork in his shirt pocket that showed when he walked sideways back of the coffin and leaned over it full front to scrutinize the body.

"Come up to my crossroads church some pretty Sunday, ever' one of y'all," was all he said, straightening up and addressing the living. Why had he no comment to make on the dead? they felt as a hushed roomful—with him, it seemed marked, as if he found nothing sufficiently remarkable about the body to give him anything flattering to say. "I guarantee nobody'll bite you if you put in at the collection for the piano, either," he added, rocking sidewise off.

"Where were his manners! But of course, he couldn't be turned away," Miss Snowdie, back of Virgie, was whispering. "Coming was his privilege." She drew her fan deeply back and forth, with the pressure of a heavy tail on the air. "A perfect stranger, and he handed out fans from Katie's deer horns out there, because he was a preacher; gave one to everybody."

"It's not time for the Last Look," Parnell Moody said in her natural, school voice. But the little Mayhews had to follow right behind Brother Dampeer. There came the prompting voice of Mrs. Junie Mayhew, "Chirren? Want to see your cousin Kate? Go look in, right quick. She raised your Uncle Berry. Take hands and go now, while there's nobody else; so you'll have her to remember." And they came in dipping their heads and pulling one another. The oldest little boy came hopping; it was remembered that at one point during the day he had run a nail in his foot.

"Brothers and sisters." Dr. Williams was facing the room.

Virgie rose right up. In the pink china jar on the mantel shelf, someone had placed her mother's old stick—like a peach branch, as though it would flower. Brother Dampeer cleared his throat: his work. Before his eyes and everybody's she marched over, took the stick out of the vase, and carried it away to the hall, where she placed it in the ring on the hatrack. When she was back in her chair, Dr. Williams opened the book and held the service.

Every now and then Mr. King, his tender-looking old head cocked sidewise, his heels lifted, his right hand pricking the air, tiptoed down the hall to the table to pick at the ham—all as if nobody could see him. While Mamie C. Loomis, a child in peach, sang "O Love That Will Not Let Me Go," Mr. King sucked a little marrow bone and lifted his wobbly head and looked arrogantly at Virgie through the two open doors of her mother's bedroom. Even Weaver Loomis and Little Sister Spights, holding hands on the back row, were crying by now, listening to music, but Mr. King pushed out his stained lip. Then he made a hideous face at Virgie, like a silent yell. It was a yell at everything—including death, not leaving it out—and he did not mind taking his present animosity out on Virgie Rainey; indeed, he chose her. Then he cracked the little bone in his teeth. She felt refreshed all of a sudden at that tiny but sharp sound.

She sat up straight and touched her hair, which sprang to

her fingers, as always. Turning her head, looking out of the one bright window through which came the cries of the little MacLains playing in the yard, she knew another moment of alliance. Was it Ran or King himself with whom she really felt it? Perhaps that confusion among all of them was the great wound in Ran's heart, she was thinking at the same time. But she knew the kinship for what it was, whomever it settled upon, an indelible thing which may come without friendship or even too early an identity, may come even despisingly, in rudeness, intruding in the middle of sorrow. Except in a form too rarefied for her, it lacked future as well as past; but she knew when even a rarefied thing had become a matter of loyalty and alliance.

"Child, you just don't know yet what you've lost," said Miss Hattie Mayo through the words of the service. It was the only thing Virgie remembered ever hearing Miss Hattie say; and then it was a thing others had been saying before her.

Miss Lizzie Stark—for she had, after all, been able to come to the funeral—waved her own little fan—black chiffon—at Virgie's cheeks from a jet chain. Miss Lizzie looked very rested, and had succeeded in exchanging seats with Cassie Morrison. She let a hand fall plumply on Virgie's thigh, and did not lift it again.

Down the hall, with the blue sky at his back, Mr. King MacLain sent for coffee, tasted it, and put out his tongue in the air to cool, a bright pink tongue wagging like a child's while they sang "Nearer, My God, to Thee."

"Go back," they told Virgie as they all moved out of the parlor. "Be alone with her before you come with us."

"You're the onliest one now," a Mayhew said. The Mayhews had asked to carry Katie home to Lastingwell Church to bury her, but acknowledged that Mr. Fate, whom the Raineys had wanted likewise to take back to their home place, was in Morgana ground, and Victor—"And so will you be," they had concluded to Virgie.

Virgie drew back while they marked time, and then she wasn't alone in the parlor. There was little Jinny MacLain, shoes and socks in hand, quietly bent over the coffin, looking boldly in. She had prized open the screen and climbed in the window. Green lizards hung like tiny springs at her ears, their eyes and jaws busy. At any other house today, Virgie knew, more care would have been exercised by them all; here, a child could slip through.

Jinny looked up at Virgie; the expression on her face was disappointment.

"Hi, Jinny."

"This doesn't look like a coffin. Did you have to use a bureau drawer?"

"They haven't put the lid down, that's all."

"Well, will you put the lid down for me?"

"Run on. Go the back way," said Virgie. "Wait—how is it that you make lizards catch on to your ears?"

"Press their heads," Jinny said languidly, over her shoulder. She walked out beating her shoes softly together with her hands.

Virgie walked over and pressed her forehead against the broken-into screen. She looked far out, over the fields, down to the far, low trees—the old vision belonging to this window. It was the paper serpent with the lantern lights through whose interior was flowing the Big Black.

"So here you are," said Miss Perdita Mayo.

The procession—the coffin passing through their ranks and now going before—marched humped and awkward down the path. They were like people waked by night, in the shimmering afternoon.

This was the children's dispensation: what they'd been waiting for. Little Jinny, her face bright and important, stood by little King, who—he was exactly timing the funeral—sucked a four-o'clock. "Move, Clara," she was saying to the nurse. They adored seeing beyond dodging aprons and black protecting arms (except Clara at the moment was smoking) the sight of grown people streaming tears and having to be held up. They liked coffins carried out because of the chance they could perceive that coffins might be dropped and the dead people spilled right out. But the chance would fade a little more with today. No dead people had ever been spilled while any of them watched, just as no freight train had ever wrecked while they prayed for it to, so they could get the bananas.

"But mainly, Mr. MacLain, you should remember to keep off rich food," Miss Snowdie said, leading her husband down a divergent path. They were not going to the cemetery with the rest; no one expected it of them. Their Negro girl chauffeur waited with their car turned the other way. "At home we've got that nice Moody fish from Moon Lake."

Virgie watched the mysterious, vulnerable back of the old man. Even as Miss Snowdie, unmysterious, led him away, he was eating still. At some moment today she had said, "Virgie, I spent all Mama and Papa had tracing after him. The Jupiter Detective Agency in Jackson. I never told. They never found or went after the right one. But I'll never forgive myself for tracing after him." Virgie had wanted to say, "Forgive yourself, yes," but could not speak the words. And they would not have mattered that much to Miss Snowdie.

"Granddaddy's almost a hundred," said little King clearly. "When you get to be a hundred, you pop."

The old people did not think to say good-bye. Mr. MacLain pressed ahead, a white inch of hair in the nape of his neck curling over in the breeze.

Virgie was again seized by both arms, as if, in the open, she might try to bolt. Her body ached from the firm hand of—in the long run—Miss Lizzie Stark. She was escorted to the Stark automobile parked in the road, where Ran now waited in the driver's seat. The line of cars and trucks had started.

"Poor Mr. Mabry, he didn't show up." Miss Perdita Mayo's flushed face appeared a moment at the window. "He's down with a cold. It came on him yesterday: I saw it coming."

They had to drive the length of Morgana to the cemetery. It was spacious and quiet within, once they rolled over the cattle-guard; yet wherever Virgie looked from the Starks' car window, she seemed to see the same gravestones again, Mr. Comus Stark, old Mr. Tim Carmichael, Mr. Tertius Morgan, like the repeating towers in the Vicksburg park. Twice she thought she saw Mr. Sissum's grave, the same stone pulled down by the same vines—the grave into which Miss Eckhart, her old piano teacher whom she had hated, tried to throw herself on the day of his funeral. And more than once she looked for the squat, dark stone that marked Miss Eckhart's own grave; it would turn itself from them, as she'd seen it do before, when they wound near and passed. And a seated angel, first visible from behind with the stone hair spread on the shoulders, turned up later from the side, further away, showing the steep wings.

"Do you like it?" Cassie was asking from the front seat beside Ran (Jinny had to go home with the children).

So it was Mrs. Morrison's angel. After being so gay and flighty always, Cassie's mother went out of the room one morning and killed herself. "I was proud of it," said Cassie. "It took everything I had."

"Where's Loch these days?" Ran asked.

"Ran, don't you remember he's in New York City? Likes it there. He writes us."

Loch was too young for Virgie ever to have known well in Morgana—always polite, "too good," "too young," people said when he went to war, and she remembered him only as walking up the wooden staircase to his father's printing office. He gave a bent, intent nod of the head, too young and already too distant.—But he's not dead! she thought—it's something else.

"What did you say, Virgie?"

"Nothing, Cassie." Yet she must have hurt Cassie some way, if only by that moment's imagining that what was young was all gone—disappeared wholly.

Virgie leaned out to look for a certain blackened lamb on a small hump of earth that was part of her childhood. It was the grave of some lady's stillborn child (now she knew it must have been that baby sister of Miss Nell Loomis's), the lamb flattened by rains into a little fairy table. There she had entertained a large imaginary company with acorn cups, then ridden away on the table.

"You staying on in Morgana, Virgie?" came Miss Nell's undertone. She talked on—the same in a moving car as she was in a parlor.

"Going away. In the morning," Virgie was saying.

"Auction off everything?"

Virgie said nothing more; she had decided to leave when she heard herself say so—decided by ear.

"Turn to the right and stop, Ran."

That was the first thing Miss Lizzie had said; perhaps she had felt too crowded in her own car to break silence.

Ran stopped, and lifted the ladies out. The group of three fat ones—Ran with Miss Lizzie and Miss Nell in arm—moved in hobbled walk ahead. The Rainey lot was well back under the trees. Cassie put her fingers in Virgie's. All around, the yuccas were full of bells, the angels were reared and horsily dappled. The magnolias' inflamed cones and their brown litter smoldered in the tail of the eye. And also in the tail of the eye was Miss Billy Texas Spights: they had let her come. She wore purple—the costume she had worn on election day.

"Thank goodness Snowdie's not here to see that," Miss Perdita remarked ahead to Miss Hattie. "Ran's here, but nothing bothers Ran."

Virgie, as if nudged, knew they must be near the poor little country girl's grave, with the words "Thy Will Be Done" on the stone. She was buried here with the Sojourners.

I hate her, Virgie thought calmly, not turning her head. Hate her grave.

Mr. Holifield passed by, mowing the grass, and raised his hat significantly. Virgie saw the familiar stone of her father's grave, his name spelled out Lafayette, and the red hole torn out beside it. In spite of the flowers waiting, the place still smelled of the sweat of Negro diggers and of a big cedar root which had been cut through and glimmered wetly in the bed of the grave. Victor was buried on the other side. Perhaps there was nothing there. The box that came back from the other war—who knew what had been sent to the Raineys in that? Somewhere behind her, Virgie could hear the hollow but apologetic coughing of Mr. Mabry. Except that it could not be he, of course; he had not been able to come, after all.

Brother Dampeer was with them still; with his weight thrown to one hip, he stood in front of them all, ahead of the row of Mayhews, and watched the success of the lowering of the coffin and the filling of the grave.

After Dr. Williams' prayer, little crumbs and clods ran down the mound, pellmell; the earth grew immediately vivacious and wild as a creature. Virgie never moved. People taking their turns went up and scattered the wreaths about and slowly stuck the clods with paper cornucopias of flowers with pins to hold them. The cornucopias were none of them perfectly erect but leaned to one side or the other, edging the swollen pink mound, monstrous, wider than it was long until it should "settle."

As the party moved away, one of the cornucopias fell over and spilled its weight of red zinnias. No one returned to right it. A feeling of the tumbling activity and promptitude of the elements had settled over people and stirred up, of all things, their dignity; they could not go back now.

They left the cemetery without looking at anything, and some parted with the company at the gate. Attrition was their wisdom. Already, tomorrow's rain pelted the grave with loudness, and made hasty streams run down its sides, like a mountain red with rivers, already settling the patient work of them all; not one little "made" flower holder, but all, would topple; and so had, or might as well have, done it already; this was the past now.

Brother Dampeer said good-bye and climbed on his mount. He had ridden twenty miles on a mule for this; he did not disclose whether, today, it had been worth it.

The evening fields were still moving, people busy, the sun gone yet busy, where their uneven cotton country tilted and fell riverward into the West. Most of the funeral party had returned to the Raineys' for refreshments. Virgie, with a slip from even Miss Lizzie's arm, which was tired, had not yet gone in.

Four little Mayhews waited for her, perched like birds on the old swivel chair. They hopped off, put their arms around her knees, and pleaded with her too to come in the house now. From the road the lighted-up house had a roof sheared sharp as a fold of paper. The serried leaves of the chinaberry trembled over the road, the branches spread winglike in a breeze that meant change. It was the last of the month of beautiful evening skies, of the lovely East, behind the dark double-twinkling of swallows.

Smells of ham, banana cake, and tuberoses came out and the longing children ran to meet it. Ferns seemed in the early alcoves of twilight to creep, or suddenly to descend like waterfalls in between the deserted porch chairs, and over old man Rainey sitting along the edge of the porch, feet dangling. Juba came running forth, saying Miss Lizzie said for Miss Virgie to come and eat with her company.

Virgie had often felt herself at some moment callous over, go opaque; she had known it to happen to others; not only when her mother changed on the bed while she was fanning her. Virgie had felt a moment in life after which nobody could see through her, into her—felt it young. But Mr. King MacLain, an old man, had butted like a goat against the wall he wouldn't agree to himself or recognize. What fortress indeed would ever come down, except before hard little horns, a rush and a stampede of the pure wish to live?

The feeling had been strong upon her from the moment she came home that she had lived the moment before; it was a moment that found Virgie too tender. She had needed a little time, she needed it now. On the path, with the funeral company at her heels, then surrounding her and passing her and now sitting down to her table without her, she strained against the feeling of the double coming-back.

"Take your time, Virge!" Old Man Rainey said softly. He climbed to his feet and walked into the house without waiting for her.

At seventeen, coming back, she'd jumped the high step from the Y. & M. V. train. She had reached earth dazzled, the first moment, at its unrocked calm. Grass tufted like the back of a dog that had been rolling the moment before shone brown under the naked sprawled-out light of a still-stretching outer world. She heard nothing but the sigh of the vanished train and the single drumbeat of thunder on a bright July day. Across the train yard was Morgana, the remembered oaks like the counted continents against the big blue. Having just jumped from the endless, grinding interior of the slow train from Memphis, she had come back to something—and she began to run toward it, with her suitcase as light as a shoebox, so little had she had to go away with and now to bring back—the lightness made it easier.

"You're back at the right time to milk for me," her mother said when she got there, and untied her bonnet and dashed it to the floor between them, looking up at her daughter. Nobody was allowed weeping over hurts at her house, unless it was Mrs. Rainey herself first, for son and husband, both her men, were gone.

For Virgie, there were practical changes to begin at once with the coming back—no music, no picture show job any more, no piano.

But in that interim between train and home, she walked and ran looking about her in a kind of glory, by the back way.

Virgie never saw it differently, never doubted that all the opposites on earth were close together, love close to hate, living to dying; but of them all, hope and despair were the closest blood—unrecognizable one from the other sometimes, making moments double upon themselves, and in the doubling double again, amending but never taking back.

For that journey, it was ripe afternoon, and all about her was that light in which the earth seems to come into its own, as if there would be no more days, only this day—when fields glow like deep pools and the expanding trees at their edges seem almost to open, like lilies, golden or dark. She had always loved that time of day, but now, alone, untouched now, she felt like dancing; knowing herself not really, in her essence, yet hurt; and thus happy. The chorus of crickets was as unprogressing and out of time as the twinkling of a star.

Her fingers set, after coming back, set half-closed; the strength in her hands she used up to type in the office but most consciously to pull the udders of the succeeding cows, as if she would hunt, hunt, hunt daily for the blindness that lay inside the beast, inside where she could have a real and living wall for beating on, a solid prison to get out of, the most real stupidity of flesh, a mindless and careless and calling body, to respond flesh for flesh, anguish for anguish. And if, as she dreamed one winter night, a new piano she touched had turned, after the one pristine moment, into a calling cow, it was by her own desire.

After she had gone in and served her company and set the Mayhews ("You'd sure better come live with us. If it wasn't for leaving such a nice house," they murmured to her) on the right road (they had come clear around by Greenwood), and after Old Man Rainey had gone to bed in the old bedroom up under the roof, Virgie sat down in the uncleared kitchen and ate herself, while Juba ate nearby—a little chicken, at first, then ham, then bacon and eggs. She drank her milk. Then she sent Juba home and turned out a fantastic number of lights.

After she was in bed and her own light out, there was a pre-emptory pounding on the porch floor.

She walked to the open front door, her nightgown blowing about her in the moist night wind. She was trembling, and put on a light in the hall.

From the gleam falling over the transom behind her she could see an old lady in a Mother Hubbard and clayed boots, holding out something white in a dark wrapping.

"It's you," the old lady said abruptly. "Child, you don't know me, but I know you and brought you somethin'. Mighty late, ain't it? My night-blooming cereus throwed a flower tonight, and I couldn't forbear to bring you it. Take it—unwrop it."

Virgie looked at the naked, luminous, complicated flower, large and pale as a face on the dark porch. For a moment she felt more afraid than she had coming to the door.

"It's for you. Keep it—won't do the dead no good. And tomorrow it'll look like a wrung chicken's neck. Look at it enduring the night."

A horse stamped and whimpered from the dark road. The old woman declined to come in.

"No, oh no. You used to play the pi-anna in the picture show when you's little and I's young and in town, dear love," she called, turning away through the dark. "Sorry about your mama: didn't suppose anybody make as pretty music as you *ever* have no trouble.—I thought you's the prettiest little thing ever was."

Virgie was still trembling. The flower troubled her; she threw it down into the weeds.

She knew that now at the river, where she had been before on moonlit nights in autumn, drunken and sleepless, mist lay on the water and filled the trees, and from the eyes to the moon would be a cone, a long silent horn, of white light. It was a connection visible as the hair is in air, between the self and the moon, to make the self feel the child, a daughter far, far back. Then the water, warmer than the night air or the self that might be suddenly cold, like any other arms, took the body under too, running without visibility into the mouth. As she would drift in the river, too alert, too insolent in her heart in those days, the mist might thin momentarily and brilliant jewel eyes would look out from the water-line and the bank. Sometimes in the weeds a lightning bug would lighten, on and off, on and off, for as long in the night as she was there to see.

Out in the yard, in the coupe, in the frayed velour pocket next to the pistol, was her cache of cigarettes. She climbed inside and shielding the matchlight, from habit, began to smoke cigarettes. All around her the dogs were barking.

III.

"I'll sell the cows to the first white man I meet in the road," Virgie thought, waking up.

After she had milked them and driven them to pasture and come back, she saw Mrs. Stark's Juba back at the kitchen door.

"Leavin'? One thing, I seen your mama's ghost already," Juba said. She picked up a plate. As she began wrapping the china in newspaper, she explained that Virgie's goods must be packed in papers and locked in trunks before Virgie left, or Mrs. Stark would not think it fitting to the dead or to departure either. Virgie was to come up to the house and bid Mrs. Stark good-bye—before noon.

"Still in the house," Juba said. "Ghost be's."

"Well, I don't want to hear about ghosts," Virgie said. They were now crouched together over a shelf in the china closet.

"Don't?"

Juba courteously ignored Virgie's clashing two plates together. Things? Miss Virgie must despise things more than the meanest people, more than any throwing ghosts.

"I don't. I don't like ghosts."

"Now!" Juba said, by way of affirmation. "However, this'n, your mama, her weren't in two pieces, or floatin' upside down, or any those things yet. Her lyin' up big on a stuff davenport like a store window, three four *us* fannin' her."

"I still don't want to hear about it," Virgie said. "Just wrap everything up quick for Mrs. Stark and put it away, then you can go."

"Yes, ma'am. Her ghost restin'. Not stren'us-minded like some. I sees ghosts go walkin' and carryin' on. But your mama." To be the ghost, Juba laid her hand on her chest and put her head to one side, fluttering her eyelids tenderly and not breathing. "Yes'm. Yonder up the wall, is where her was. I says Juba, tell Miss Virgie, her would appreciate word of that."

"Did you come here to make me wrap stuff up and then get in my way?" Virgie said. "You know I'm in a hurry to shut up this house."

"Goin' off and leave all these here clean curtains?"

"Juba, when I was in my worst trouble, I scared everybody off, did you know that? Now I'm not scarey any more. Like Ran MacLain; he's not," Virgie said absently as they wrapped together.

Juba laughed in an obscure glee. "You'll scare 'em when you's a ghost."

"Hurry."

"I seen more ghosts than live peoples, round here. Black and white. I seen plenty both. Miss Virgie, some is given to see, some try but is not given. I seen that Mrs. Morrison from 'cross the road in long white nightgown, no head atall, in her driveway Saddy. Rackanize her freckle arms. You ever see her? I seen her here. She die in pain?"

Juba lowered her lids hypocritically.

"Pain a plenty and I don't ever want to see her." Virgie got to her feet. "Go on, go on back to Mrs. Stark. Tell her I can pack up better without you. Do I have to pack everything?"

"Yes'm. Her idea is," Juba said, "pack 'em up strong for the day the somebody come *un*pack. And I done bent over and stoop best I could. Held all them curlycue plates without spillin' one."

"Do that for Mrs. Stark."

Juba picked herself up. She shook her head at the open cupboard, the dwindled and long-sugared jelly, the rusty cream of tartar box, the Mason jar of bay leaves, the spindly and darkened vanilla bottle, all the old confusion. Her eyes fastened and held to the twenty-year-old box of toothpicks, and Virgie, seeing, got it for her.

"Juba, take it all," she said then. "Plates, knives and forks, the plants on the porch, whatever you want, take. And what's in the trunks. You and Minerva divide." Then she had to burst out and say something to Juba. "And I saw Minerva! I saw her take Mama's hair switch—her young hair that was yellow and I never saw when it matched any more and she could do anything but keep it in that trunk, and I saw it put down in that paper sack. And my brother's baby clothes and my own, yellow and all the lace—I saw all stolen and put with Minerva's umbrella to take home, and I let them go. You tell that Negro. Tell her I know I was robbed, and that I don't care."

Juba nodded and changed the subject. "Thank you, Miss Virgie, for men's clothes. That salt-and-pepper of poor Mr. Rainey."

"Mama kept everything," Virgie said after a moment.

"Glory."

"Now you can go."

"Why, it's a-rainin'. Do hate rain."

Juba left. But she came back.

"That's it," she called softly, appearing once more in her fedora at the kitchen door. "That's right. Cry. Cry. Cry."

"Taking a trip? Think I might come along with you," said Old Man Rainey. "I always aimed to see the world." He looked at her closely.

"Please, sir, don't you come! Yes—I may go far—"

He gave her a hug before he turned to his coffee.

"Do you want to put our cows in your truck to take along?" She gave over to him everything she could think of, hoping he would accept something, something at least.

Virgie went out into the rainy morning and got into her car. She drove it, bumping, down the hill. In the road, the MacLains' old chinaberry tree brushed her window, enjoying the rain like a bird.

She drove through Morgana, hearing a horn blow from

another car; it was Cassie Morrison. Cassie called out, driving abreast.

"I want you to come see Mama's Name in the Spring, Virgie. This morning before it rained I divided all the bulbs again, and it ought to be prettier than ever!"

"Always see it when I pass your yard," Virgie called back.

"Virgie! I know how you feel. You'll never get over it, never!"

They called from car to car, running parallel along the road with the loose gravel from the unpaved part knocking loudly, bounced from one car to the other.

"Well. You come."

"I guess it takes a lot of narcissus to spell Catherine," Virgie called, when Cassie still did not pass her.

"Two hundred and thirty-two bulbs! And then Miss Katie's hyacinthus all around those, and I've got it bordered in violets, you know, to tell me where it is in summer!" Cassie's voice, growing louder, grew at the same time more anxious and more reverent. She was not hurt, not suspecting, only anxious. But it was for Cassie that Virgie had turned her car toward town, to not let her see. "Now you come. We were friends that summer—" (Virgie remembered Cassie and herself in the revival tent, pulling light bugs off each other's shoulders while singing "Throw Out the Life Line.") "You could come play my piano, nobody does but my pupils."

Virgie, and Cassie too, circled the cemetery and drove back the length of Morgana. Then, "Where are you going? Are you going somewhere, Virgie?"

Virgie slowed for a minute as Cassie turned in at her own house. The Morrisons' looked the same as always, except, as the MacLain house had had before it—when Miss Eckhart was there—it now had a fly-like cluster of black mailboxes at its door; it had been cut up for road workers and timber people. In the upstairs corner room, where they tried to keep poor Mr. Morrison, the shade was still down, but she felt him look out through his telescope. Across the front yard stretched the violet frame in which Mama's Name was planted against the coming of spring.

Virgie lifted her hand, and the girls waved.

"You'll go away like Loch," Cassie called from the steps.

"A life of your own, away—I'm so glad for people like you and Loch, I am really."

Virgie drove on, the seven winding miles to MacLain and stopped the car in front of the courthouse.

She had often done this, if only to turn around and go right back after a rest of a few moments and a Coca-Cola standing up in Billy Hudson's drugstore. MacLain pleased her—the uncrowded water tank, catching the first and last light; the old iron bell in the churchyard looking as heavy as a fallen meteor. The courthouse pleased her—space itself, with the columns standing away from its four faces, and the pea-green blinds flat to the wall, and the stile rising in pepper grass over the iron fence to it—and a quail just now running across the yard; and the live oaks—trunks flaky black and white now, as if soot, not rain, had once fallen from heaven on them, and the wet eyes of cut-off limbs on them; and the whole rain-lighted spread roof of green leaves that moved like children's lips in speech, high up.

Virgie left the car and running through the light drops reached the stile and sat down on it in the open shelter of trees. She touched the treads, worn not by feet so much as by their history of warm, spreading seats. At this distance the Confederate soldier on the shaft looked like a chewed-on candle, as if old gnashing teeth had made him. On past him, pale as a rainbow, the ancient circus posters clung to their sheds, they no longer the defacing but the defaced.

There was nobody out in the rain. The land across from the courthouse used to be Mr. Virgil MacLain's park. He was old Mr. King's father; he used to keep deer. Now like a callosity, a cataract of the eye over what was once transparent and bright—for the park racing with deer was an idea strangely transparent to Virgie—was the line of store fronts and the MacLain Bijou, and the cemetery that was visible on the cedar hill.

Here the MacLains buried, and Miss Snowdie's people, the Hudsons. Here lay Eugene, the only MacLain man gone since her memory, after old Virgil himself. Eugene, for a long interval, had lived in another part of the world, learning while he was away that people don't have to be answered just because they want to know. His very wife was never known here, and he did not make it plain whether he had children somewhere now or had been childless. His wife did not even come to the funeral, although a telegram had been sent. A foreigner? "Why, she could even be a Dago and we wouldn't know it." His light, tubercular body seemed to hesitate on the street of Morgana, hold averted, anticipating questions. Sometimes he looked up in the town where he was young and said something strangely spiteful or ambiguous (he was never reconciled to his father, they said, was sarcastic to the old man—all he loved was Miss Snowdie and flowers) but he bothered no one. "He never did bother a soul," they said at his graveside that day, forgetting his childhood. And all Mr. King's family lay over there, Cedar Hill was bigger than the Courthouse; his father Virgil in the Confederate section, and his mother, his grandfather—who remembered his name and what he did? The name was on the stone.

Didn't he kill a man, or have to, and what would be the long story behind it, the vaunting and the wandering from it?

And Miss Eckhart was over there. When Miss Eckhart died, up in Jackson, Miss Snowdie had her brought here and buried in her lot. Her grave was there near to Eugene's. There was the dark, squat stone Virgie had looked for yesterday, confusing her dead.

Before her ran rain-colored tin and red brick, doors weathered down to the whorl and color of river water. The vine over the jail was deep as a bed with brown leaves. At the MacLain Bijou, directly across from Virgie on the stile, there was a wrinkled blue sheen of rain on the two posters and deeper in, the square of yellow card ("Deposit Required for Going In to Talk") hung always like a lighted window in a traveler's gloom. She had sometimes come alone to the MacLain Bijou after Mr. Nesbitt let her go in the afternoon.

Footsteps sounded on the walk, a white man's. It was Mr. Nesbitt, she thought at first, but then saw it was another man almost like him—hurrying, bent on something, furious at being in the rain, speechless. He was all alone out here. His round face, not pushed out now, away from other faces, looked curiously deep, womanly, dedicated. Mr. Nesbitt's twin passed close to her, and down the street he turned flamboyantly and entered what must have been his own door, splashing frantically through a puddle.

Virgie, picking the irresistible pepper grass, saw Mr. Mabry too. It was really himself, looking out under his umbrella for somebody. How wretchedly dignified and not quite yet alarmed he looked, and how his cold would last! Mr. Mabry imagined he was coming to her eventually, but was it to him that she had come, backward to protection? She'd have had to come backward, not simply stand still, to get from the wild spirit of Bucky Moffitt (and where was he? Never under the ground! She smiled, biting the seed in the pepper grass), back past the drunk Simon Sojourner that didn't want her, and on to embarrassed Mr. Mabry, behind whom waited loud, harmless, terrifying Mr. Nesbitt who wanted to stand up for her. She had reached Mr. Mabry but she had passed him and it had not mattered about her direction, since here she was. She sat up tall on the stile, feeling that he would look right through her—Virgie Rainey on a stile, bereaved, hatless, unhidden now, in the rain—and he did. She watched him march by. Then she was all to herself.

Was she that? Could she ever be, would she be, where she was going? Miss Eckhart had had among the pictures from Europe on her walls a certain threatening one. It hung over the dictionary, dark as that book. It showed Perseus with the head of the Medusa. "The same thing as Siegfried and the Dragon," Miss Eckhart had occasionally said, as if explaining second-best. Around the picture—which sometimes blindly reflected the window by its darkness—was a frame enameled with flowers, which was always self-evident—Miss Eckhart's pride. In that moment Virgie had shorn it of its frame.

The vaunting was what she remembered, that lifted arm.

Cutting off the Medusa's head was the heroic act, perhaps, that made visible a horror in life, that was at once the horror in love, Virgie thought—the separateness. She might have seen heroism prophetically when she was young and afraid of Miss Eckhart. She might be able to see it now prophetically, but she was never a prophet. Because Virgie saw things in their time, like hearing them—and perhaps because she must believe in the Medusa equally with Perseus—she saw the stroke of the sword in three moments, not one. In the three was the damnation—no, only the secret, unhurting because not caring in itself—beyond the beauty and the sword's stroke and the terror lay their existence in time—far out and endless, a constellation which the heart could read over many a night.

Miss Eckhart, whom Virgie had not, after all, hated—had come near to loving, for she had taken Miss Eckhart's hate, and then her love, extracted them, the thorn and then the overflow—had hung the picture on the wall for herself. She had absorbed the hero and the victim and then, stoutly, could sit down to the piano with all Beethoven ahead of her. With her hate, with her love, and with the small gnawing feelings that ate them, she offered Virgie her Beethoven. She offered, offered, offered—and when Virgie was young, in the strange wisdom of youth that is accepting of more than is given, she had accepted *the* Beethoven, as with the dragon's blood. That was the gift she had touched with her fingers that had drifted and left her.

In Virgie's reach of memory a melody softly lifted, lifted of itself. Every time Perseus struck off the Medusa's head, there was the beat of time, and the melody. Endless the Medusa, and Perseus endless.

An old wrapped-up Negro woman with a red hen under her arm came and sat down on the step below Virgie.

"Mornin'."

Occasional drops of rain fell on Virgie's hair and her cheek, or rolled down her arm, like a cool finger; only it was not, as if it had never been, a finger, being the rain out of the sky. October rain on Mississippi fields. The rain of fall, maybe on the whole South, for all she knew on the everywhere. She stared into its magnitude. It was not only what expelled some shadow of Mr. Bitts, and pressed poor Mr. Mabry to search the street—it was the air's and the earth's fuming breath, it could come and go. As if her own modesty could also fall upon her now, freely and coolly, outside herself and on the everywhere, she sat a little longer on the stile.

She smiled once, seeing before her, screenlike, the hideous and delectable face Mr. King MacLain had made at the funeral, and when they all knew he was next—even he. Then she and the old beggar woman, the old black thief, were there alone and together in the shelter of the big public tree, listening to the magical percussion, the world beating in their ears. They heard through falling rain the running of the horse and bear, the stroke of the leopard, the dragon's crusty slither, and the glimmer and the trumpet of the swan.

THE BRIDE OF THE INNISFALLEN

and Other Stories

TO ELIZABETH BOWEN

Contents

No Place for You, My Love

THEY WERE strangers to each other, both fairly well strangers to the place, now seated side by side at luncheon—a party combined in a free-and-easy way when the friends he and she were with recognized each other across Galatoire's. The time was a Sunday in summer—those hours of afternoon that seem Time Out in New Orleans.

The moment he saw her little blunt, fair face, he thought that here was a woman who was having an affair. It was one of those odd meetings when such an impact is felt that it has to be translated at once into some sort of speculation.

With a married man, most likely, he supposed, slipping quickly into a groove—he was long married—and feeling more conventional, then, in his curiosity as she sat there, leaning her cheek on her hand, looking no further before her than the flowers on the table, and wearing that hat.

He did not like her hat, any more than he liked tropical flowers. It was the wrong hat for her, thought this Eastern businessman who had no interest whatever in women's clothes and no eye for them; he thought the unaccustomed thing crossly.

It must stick out all over me, she thought, so people think they can love me or hate me just by looking at me. How did it leave us—the old, safe, slow way people used to know of learning how one another feels, and the privilege that went with it of shying away if it seemed best? People in love like me, I suppose, give away the short cuts to everybody's secrets.

Something, though, he decided, had been settled about her predicament—for the time being, anyway; the parties to it were all still alive, no doubt. Nevertheless, her predicament was the only one he felt so sure of here, like the only recognizable shadow in that restaurant, where mirrors and fans were busy agitating the light, as the very local talk drawled across and agitated the peace. The shadow lay between her fingers, between her little square hand and her cheek, like something always best carried about the person. Then suddenly, as she took her hand down, the secret fact was still there—it lighted her. It was a bold and full light, shot up under the brim of that hat, as close to them all as the flowers in the center of the table.

Did he dream of making her disloyal to that hopelessness that he saw very well she'd been cultivating down here? He knew very well that he did not. What they amounted to was two Northerners keeping each other company. She glanced up at the big gold clock on the wall and smiled. He didn't smile back. She had that naive face that he associated, for no good reason, with the Middle West—because it said "Show me," perhaps. It was a serious, now-watch-out-everybody face, which orphaned her entirely in the company of these Southerners. He guessed her age, as he could not guess theirs: thirty-two. He himself was further along.

Of all human moods, deliberate imperviousness may be the most quickly communicated—it may be the most successful, most fatal signal of all. And two people can indulge in imperviousness as well as in anything else. "You're not very hungry either," he said.

The blades of fan shadows came down over their two heads, as he saw inadvertently in the mirror, with himself smiling at her now like a villain. His remark sounded dominant and rude enough for everybody present to listen back a moment; it even sounded like an answer to a question she might have just asked him. The other women glanced at him. The Southern look—Southern mask—of life-is-a-dream irony, which could turn to pure challenge at the drop of a hat, he could wish well away. He liked naïveté better.

"I find the heat down here depressing," she said, with the heart of Ohio in her voice.

"Well—I'm in somewhat of a temper about it, too," he said.

They looked with grateful dignity at each other.

"I have a car here, just down the street," he said to her as the luncheon party was rising to leave, all the others wanting to get back to their houses and sleep. "If it's all right with—Have you ever driven down south of here?"

Out on Bourbon Street, in the bath of July, she asked at his shoulder, "South of New Orleans? I didn't know there was any south to *here*. Does it just go on and on?" She laughed, and adjusted the exasperating hat to her head in a different way. It was more than frivolous, it was conspicuous, with some sort of glitter or flitter tied in a band around the straw and hanging down.

"That's what I'm going to show you."

"Oh—you've been there?"

"No!"

His voice rang out over the uneven, narrow sidewalk and dropped back from the walls. The flaked-off, colored houses were spotted like the hides of beasts faded and shy, and were hot as a wall of growth that seemed to breathe flower-like down onto them as they walked to the car parked there.

"It's just that it couldn't be any worse—we'll see."

"All right, then," she said. "We will."

So, their actions reduced to amiability, they settled into the car—a faded-red Ford convertible with a rather threadbare canvas top, which had been standing in the sun for all those lunch hours.

"It's rented," he explained. "I asked to have the top put down, and was told I'd lost my mind."

"It's out of this world. *Degrading* heat," she said and added, "Doesn't matter."

The stranger in New Orleans always sets out to leave it as though following the clue in a maze. They were threading through the narrow and one-way streets, past the pale-violet bloom of tired squares, the brown steeples and statues, the balcony with the live and probably famous black monkey dipping along the railing as over a ballroom floor, past the grill-work and the lattice-work to all the iron swans painted flesh color on the front steps of bungalows outlying.

Driving, he spread his new map and put his finger down on it. At the intersection marked Arabi, where their road led out of the tangle and he took it, a small Negro seated beneath a black umbrella astride a box chalked "Shou Shine" lifted his pink-and-black hand and waved them languidly good-by. She didn't miss it, and waved back.

Below New Orleans there was a raging of insects from both sides of the concrete highway, not quite together, like the playing of separated marching bands. The river and the levee were still on her side, waste and jungle and some occasional settlements on his—poor houses. Families bigger than housefuls thronged the yards. His nodding, driving head would veer from side to side, looking and almost lowering. As time passed and the distance from New Orleans grew, girls ever darker and younger were disposing themselves over the porches and the porch steps, with jet-black hair pulled high, and ragged palm-leaf fans rising and falling like rafts of butterflies. The children running forth were nearly always naked ones.

She watched the road. Crayfish constantly crossed in front of the wheels, looking grim and bonneted, in a great hurry.

"How the Old Woman Got Home," she murmured to herself.

He pointed, as it flew by, at a saucepan full of cut zinnias which stood waiting on the open lid of a mailbox at the roadside, with a little note tied onto the handle.

They rode mostly in silence. The sun bore down. They met fishermen and other men bent on some local pursuits, some in sulphur-colored pants, walking and riding; met wagons, trucks, boats in trucks, autos, boats on top of autos—all coming to meet them, as though something of high moment were doing back where the car came from, and he and she were determined to miss it. There was nearly always a man lying with his shoes off in the bed of any truck otherwise empty—with the raw, red look of a man sleeping in the daytime, being jolted about as he slept. Then there was a sort of dead man's land, where nobody came. He loosened his collar and tie. By rushing through the heat at high speed, they brought themselves the effect of fans turned onto their cheeks. Clearing alternated with jungle and canebrake like something tried, tried again. Little shell roads led off on both sides; now and then a road of planks led into the yellow-green.

"Like a dance floor in there." She pointed.

He informed her, "In there's your oil, I think."

There were thousands, millions of mosquitoes and gnats—a universe of them, and on the increase.

A family of eight or nine people on foot strung along the road in the same direction the car was going, beating themselves with the wild palmettos. Heels, shoulders, knees, breasts, back of the heads, elbows, hands, were touched in turn—like some game, each playing it with himself.

He struck himself on the forehead, and increased their speed. (His wife would not be at her most charitable if he came bringing malaria home to the family.)

More and more crayfish and other shell creatures littered their path, scuttling or dragging. These little samples, little jokes of creation, persisted and sometimes perished, the more of them the deeper down the road went. Terrapins and turtles came up steadily over the horizons of the ditches.

Back there in the margins were worse—crawling hides you could not penetrate with bullets or quite believe, grins that had come down from the primeval mud.

"Wake up." Her Northern nudge was very timely on his arm. They had veered toward the side of the road. Still driving fast, he spread his map.

Like a misplaced sunrise, the light of the river flowed up; they were mounting the levee on a little shell road.

"Shall we cross here?" he asked politely.

He might have been keeping track over years and miles of how long they could keep that tiny ferry waiting. Now skidding down the levee's flank, they were the last-minute car, the last possible car that could squeeze on. Under the sparse shade of one willow tree, the small, amateurish-looking boat slapped the water, as, expertly, he wedged on board.

"Tell him we put him on hub cap!" shouted one of the numerous olive-skinned, dark-eyed young boys standing dressed up in bright shirts at the railing, hugging each other with delight that that last straw was on board. Another boy drew his affectionate initials in the dust of the door on her side.

She opened the door and stepped out, and, after only a moment's standing at bay, started up a little iron stairway. She appeared above the car, on the tiny bridge beneath the captain's window and the whistle.

From there, while the boat still delayed in what seemed a trance—as if it were too full to attempt the start—she could see the panlike deck below, separated by its rusty rim from the tilting, polished water.

The passengers walking and jostling about there appeared oddly amateurish, too—amateur travelers. They were having such a good time. They all knew each other. Beer was being passed around in cans, bets were being loudly settled and new bets made, about local and special subjects on which they all doted. One red-haired man in a burst of wildness even tried to give away his truckload of shrimp to a man on the other side of the boat—nearly all the trucks were full of shrimp—causing taunts and then protests of "They good! They good!" from the giver. The young boys leaned on each other thinking of what next, rolling their eyes absently.

A radio pricked the air behind her. Looking like a great tomcat just above her head, the captain was digesting the news of a fine stolen automobile.

At last a tremendous explosion burst—the whistle. Everything shuddered in outline from the sound, everybody said something—everybody else.

They started with no perceptible motion, but her hat blew off. It went spiraling to the deck below, where he, thank heaven, sprang out of the car and picked it up. Everybody looked frankly up at her now, holding her hands to her head.

The little willow tree receded as its shade was taken away. The heat was like something falling on her head. She held the hot rail before her. It was like riding a stove. Her shoulders dropping, her hair flying, her skirt buffeted by the sudden strong wind, she stood there, thinking they all must see that with her entire self all she did was wait. Her set hands, with the bag that hung from her wrist and rocked back and forth—all three seemed objects bleaching there, belonging to no one; she could not feel a thing in the skin of her face; perhaps she was crying, and not knowing it. She could look down and see him just below her, his black shadow, her hat, and his black hair. His hair in the wind looked unreasonably long and rippling. Little did he know that from here it had a red undergleam like an animal's. When she looked up and outward, a vortex of light drove through and over the brown waves like a star in the water.

He did after all bring the retrieved hat up the stairs to her. She took it back—useless—and held it to her skirt. What they were saying below was more polite than their searchlight faces.

"Where you think he come from, that man?"

"I bet he come from Lafitte."

"Lafitte? What you bet, eh?"—all crouched in the shade of trucks, squatting and laughing.

Now his shadow fell partly across her; the boat had jolted into some other strand of current. Her shaded arm and shaded hand felt pulled out from the blaze of light and water, and she hoped humbly for more shade for her head. It had seemed so natural to climb up and stand in the sun.

The boys had a surprise—an alligator on board. One of them pulled it by a chain around the deck, between the cars and trucks, like a toy—a hide that could walk. He thought, Well they had to catch one sometime. It's Sunday afternoon. So they have him on board now, riding him across the Mississippi River. . . . The playfulness of it beset everybody on the ferry. The hoarseness of the boat whistle, commenting briefly, seemed part of the general appreciation.

"Who want to rassle him? Who want to, eh?" two boys cried, looking up. A boy with shrimp-colored arms capered from side to side, pretending to have been bitten.

What was there so hilarious about jaws that could bite? And what danger was there once in this repulsiveness—so that the last worldly evidence of some old heroic horror of the dragon had to be paraded in capture before the eyes of country clowns?

He noticed that she looked at the alligator without flinching at all. Her distance was set—the number of feet and inches between herself and it mattered to her.

Perhaps her measuring coolness was to him what his bodily shade was to her, while they stood pat up there riding the river, which felt like the sea and looked like the earth under them—full of the red-brown earth, charged with it. Ahead of the boat it was like an exposed vein of ore. The river seemed to swell in the vast middle with the curve of the earth. The sun rolled under them. As if in memory of the size of things, uprooted trees were drawn across their path, sawing at the air and tumbling one over the other.

When they reached the other side, they felt that they had been racing around an arena in their chariot, among lions. The whistle took and shook the stairs as they went down. The young boys, looking taller, had taken out colored combs and were combing their wet hair back in solemn pompadour above their radiant foreheads. They had been bathing in the river themselves not long before.

The cars and trucks, then the foot passengers and the alligator, waddling like a child to school, all disembarked and wound up the weed-sprung levee.

Both respectable and merciful, their hides, she thought, forcing herself to dwell on the alligator as she looked back. Deliver us all from the naked in heart. (As she had been told.)

When they regained their paved road, he heard her give a little sigh and saw her turn her straw-colored head to look back once more. Now that she rode with her hat in her lap, her earrings were conspicuous too. A little metal ball set with small pale stones danced beside each square, faintly downy cheek.

Had she felt a wish for someone else to be riding with them? He thought it was more likely that she would wish for her husband if she had one (his wife's voice) than for the lover in whom he believed. Whatever people liked to think, situations (if not scenes) were usually three-way—there was somebody else always. The one who didn't—couldn't—understand the two made the formidable third.

He glanced down at the map flapping on the seat between them, up at his wristwatch, out at the road. Out there was the incredible brightness of four o'clock.

On this side of the river, the road ran beneath the brow of the levee and followed it. Here was a heat that ran deeper and brighter and more intense than all the rest—its nerve. The road grew one with the heat as it was one with the unseen river. Dead snakes stretched across the concrete like markers—inlaid mosaic bands, dry as feathers, which their tires licked at intervals that began to seem clocklike.

No, the heat faced them—it was ahead. They could see it waving at them, shaken in the air above the white of the road, always at a certain distance ahead, shimmering finely as a cloth, with running edges of green and gold, fire and azure.

"It's never anything like this in Syracuse," he said.

"Or in Toledo, either," she replied with dry lips.

They were driving through greater waste down here, through fewer and even more insignificant towns. There was water under everything. Even where a screen of jungle had been left to stand, splashes could be heard from under the trees. In the vast open, sometimes boats moved inch by inch through what appeared endless meadows of rubbery flowers.

Her eyes overcome with brightness and size, she felt a panic rise, as sudden as nausea. Just how far below questions and answers, concealment and revelation, they were running now—that was still a new question, with a power of its own, waiting. How dear—how costly—could this ride be?

"It looks to me like your road can't go much further," she remarked cheerfully. "Just over there, it's all water."

"Time out," he said, and with that he turned the car into a sudden road of white shells that rushed at them narrowly out of the left.

They bolted over a cattle guard, where some rayed and crested purple flowers burst out of the vines in the ditch, and rolled onto a long, narrow, green, mowed clearing: a churchyard. A paved track ran between two short rows of raised tombs, all neatly white-washed and now brilliant as faces against the vast flushed sky.

The track was the width of the car with a few inches to spare. He passed between the tombs slowly but in the manner of a feat. Names took their places on the walls slowly at a level with the eye, names as near as the eyes of a person stopping in conversation, and as far away in origin, and in all their music and dead longing, as Spain. At intervals were set packed bouquets of zinnias, oleanders, and some kind of purple flowers, all quite fresh, in fruit jars, like nice welcomes on bureaus.

They moved on into an open plot beyond, of violent-green grass, spread before the green-and-white frame church with worked flower beds around it, flowerless poinsettias growing up to the windowsills. Beyond was a house, and left on the doorstep of the house a fresh-caught catfish the size of a baby—a fish wearing whiskers and bleeding. On a clothesline in the yard, a priest's black gown on a hanger hung airing, swaying at man's height, in a vague, trainlike, lady-like sweep along an evening breath that might otherwise have seemed imaginary from the unseen, felt river.

With the motor cut off, with the raging of the insects about them, they sat looking out at the green and white and black and red and pink as they leaned against the sides of the car.

"What is your wife like?" she asked. His right hand came up and spread—iron, wooden, manicured. She lifted her eyes to his face. He looked at her like that hand.

Then he lit a cigarette, and the portrait, and the right-hand testimonial it made, were blown away. She smiled, herself as unaffected as by some stage performance; and he was annoyed in the cemetery. They did not risk going on to her husband—if she had one.

Under the supporting posts of the priest's house, where a boat was, solid ground ended and palmettos and water hyacinths could not wait to begin; suddenly the rays of the sun, from behind the car, reached that lowness and struck the flowers. The priest came out onto the porch in his underwear, stared at the car a moment as if he wondered what time it was, then collected his robe off the line and his fish off the doorstep and returned inside. Vespers was next, for him.

After backing out between the tombs he drove on still south, in the sunset. They caught up with an old man walking in a sprightly way in their direction, all by himself, wearing a clean bright shirt printed with a pair of palm trees fanning green over his chest. It might better be a big colored woman's shirt, but she didn't have it. He flagged the car with gestures like hoops.

"You're coming to the end of the road," the old man told them. He pointed ahead, tipped his hat to the lady, and pointed again. "End of the road." They didn't understand that he meant, "Take me."

They drove on. "If we do go any further, it'll have to be by water—is that it?" he asked her, hesitating at this odd point.

"You know better than I do," she replied politely.

The road had for some time ceased to be paved; it was made of shells. It was leading into a small, sparse settlement like the others a few miles back, but with even more of the camp about it. On the lip of the clearing, directly before a green willow blaze with the sunset gone behind it, the row of houses and shacks faced out on broad, colored, moving water that stretched to reach the horizon and looked like an arm of the sea. The houses on their shaggy posts, patchily built, some with plank runways instead of steps, were flimsy and alike, and not much bigger than the boats tied up at the landing.

"Venice," she heard him announce, and he dropped the crackling map in her lap.

They coasted down the brief remainder. The end of the road—she could not remember ever seeing a road simply end—was a spoon shape, with a tree stump in the bowl to turn around by.

Around it, he stopped the car, and they stepped out, feeling put down in the midst of a sudden vast pause or subduement that was like a yawn. They made their way on foot toward the water, where at an idle-looking landing men in twos and threes stood with their backs to them.

The nearness of darkness, the still uncut trees, bright water partly under a sheet of flowers, shacks, silence, dark shapes of boats tied up, then the first sounds of people just on the other side of thin walls—all this reached them. Mounds of shells like day-old snow, pink-tinted, lay around a central shack with a beer sign on it. An old man up on the porch there sat holding an open newspaper, with a fat white goose sitting opposite him on the floor. Below, in the now shadowless and sunless open, another old man, with a colored pencil bright under his hat brim, was late mending a sail.

When she looked clear around, thinking they had a fire burning somewhere now, out of the heat had risen the full moon. Just beyond the trees, enormous, tangerine-colored, it was going solidly up. Other lights just striking into view, looking farther distant, showed moss shapes hanging, or slipped and broke matchlike on the water that so encroached upon the rim of ground they were standing on.

There was a touch at her arm—his, accidental.

"We're at the jumping-off place," he said.

She laughed, having thought his hand was a bat, while her eyes rushed downward toward a great pale drift of water hyacinths—still partly open, flushed and yet moonlit, level with her feet—through which paths of water for the boats had been hacked. She drew her hands up to her face under the brim of her hat; her own cheeks felt like the hyacinths to her, all her skin still full of too much light and sky, exposed. The harsh vesper bell was ringing.

"I believe there must be something wrong with me, that I came on this excursion to begin with," she said, as if he had already said this and she were merely in hopeful, willing, maddening agreement with him.

He took hold of her arm, and said, "Oh, come on—I see we can get something to drink here, at least."

But there was a beating, muffled sound from over the darkening water. One more boat was coming in, making its way through the tenacious, tough, dark flower traps, by the shaken light of what first appeared to be torches. He and she waited for the boat, as if on each other's patience. As if borne in on a mist of twilight or a breath, a horde of mosquitoes and gnats came singing and striking at them first. The boat bumped, men laughed. Somebody was offering somebody else some shrimp.

Then he might have cocked his dark city head down at her; she did not look up at him, only turned when he did. Now the shell mounds, like the shacks and trees, were solid purple. Lights had appeared in the not-quite-true window squares. A narrow neon sign, the lone sign, had come out in bright blush on the beer shack's roof: "Baba's Place." A light was on on the porch.

The barnlike interior was brightly lit and unpainted, looking not quite finished, with a partition dividing this room from what lay behind. One of the four cardplayers at a table in the middle of the floor was the newspaper reader; the paper was in his pants pocket. Midway along the partition was a bar, in the form of a pass-through to the other room, with a varnished, second-hand fretwork overhang. They crossed the floor and sat, alone there, on wooden stools. An eruption of humorous signs, newspaper cutouts and cartoons, razor-blade cards, and personal messages of significance to the owner or his friends decorated the overhang, framing where Baba should have been but wasn't.

Through there came a smell of garlic and cloves and red pepper, a blast of hot cloud escaped from a cauldron they could see now on a stove at the back of the other room. A massive back, presumably female, with a twist of gray hair on top, stood with a ladle akimbo. A young man joined her and with his fingers stole something out of the pot and ate it. At Baba's they were boiling shrimp.

When he got ready to wait on them, Baba strolled out to the counter, young, black-headed, and in very good humor.

"Coldest beer you've got. And food— What will you have?"

"Nothing for me, thank you," she said. "I'm not sure I could eat, after all."

"Well, I could," he said, shoving his jaw out. Baba smiled. "I want a good solid ham sandwich."

"I could have asked him for some water," she said, after he had gone.

While they sat waiting, it seemed very quiet. The bubbling of the shrimp, the distant laughing of Baba, and the slap of cards, like the beating of moths on the screens, seemed to come in fits and starts. The steady breathing they heard came from a big rough dog asleep in the corner. But it was bright. Electric lights were strung riotously over the room from a kind of spider web of old wires in the rafters. One of the written messages tacked before them read, "Joe! At the boyy!!" It looked very yellow, older than Baba's Place. Outside, the world was pure dark.

Two little boys, almost alike, almost the same size, and just cleaned up, dived into the room with a double bang of the screen door, and circled around the card game. They ran their hands into the men's pockets.

"Nickel for some pop!"

"Nickel for some pop!"

"Go 'way and let me play, you!"

They circled around and shrieked at the dog, ran under the lid of the counter and raced through the kitchen and back, and hung over the stools at the bar. One child had a live lizard on his shirt, clinging like a breast pin—like lapis lazuli.

Bringing in a strong odor of geranium talcum, some men had come in now—all in bright shirts. They drew near the counter, or stood and watched the game.

When Baba came out bringing the beer and sandwich, "Could I have some water?" she greeted him.

Baba laughed at everybody. She decided the woman back there must be Baba's mother.

Beside her, he was drinking his beer and eating his sandwich—ham, cheese, tomato, pickle, and mustard. Before he finished, one of the men who had come in beckoned from across the room. It was the old man in the palm-tree shirt.

She lifted her head to watch him leave her, and was looked at, from all over the room. As a minute passed, no cards were laid down. In a far-off way, like accepting the light from Arcturus, she accepted it that she was more beautiful or perhaps more fragile than the women they saw every day of their lives. It was just this thought coming into a woman's face, and at this hour, that seemed familiar to them.

Baba was smiling. He had set an opened, frosted brown bottle before her on the counter, and a thick sandwich, and stood looking at her. Baba made her eat some supper, for what she was.

"What the old fellow wanted," said he when he came back at last, "was to have a friend of his apologize. Seems church is just out. Seems the friend made a remark coming in just now. His pals told him there was a lady present."

"I see you bought him a beer," she said.

"Well, the old man looked like he wanted *something*."

All at once the juke box interrupted from back in the corner, with the same old song as anywhere. The half-dozen slot machines along the wall were suddenly all run to like Maypoles, and thrown into action—taken over by further battalions of little boys.

There were three little boys to each slot machine. The local custom appeared to be that one pulled the lever for the friend he was holding up to put the nickel in, while the third covered the pictures with the flat of his hand as they fell into place, so as to surprise them all if anything happened.

The dog lay sleeping on in front of the raging juke box, his ribs working fast as a concertina's. At the side of the room a man with a cap on his white thatch was trying his best to open a side screen door, but it was stuck fast. It was he who had come in with the remark considered ribald; now he was trying to get out the other way. Moths as thick as ingots were trying to get in. The card players broke into shouts of derision, then joy, then tired derision among themselves; they might have been here all afternoon—they were the only ones not cleaned up and shaved. The original pair of little boys ran in once more, with the hyphenated bang. They got nickels this time, then were brushed away from the table like mosquitoes, and they rushed under the counter and on to the cauldron behind, clinging to Baba's mother there. The evening was at the threshold.

They were quite unnoticed now. He was eating another sandwich, and she, having finished part of hers, was fanning her face with her hat. Baba had lifted the flap of the counter and come out into the room. Behind his head there was a sign lettered in orange crayon: "Shrimp Dance Sun. PM." That was tonight, still to be.

And suddenly she made a move to slide down from her stool, maybe wishing to walk out into that nowhere down the front steps to be cool a moment. But he had hold of her hand. He got down from his stool, and, patiently, reversing her hand in his own—just as she had had the look of being about to give up, faint—began moving her, leading her. They were dancing.

"I get to thinking this is what we get—what you and I deserve," she whispered, looking past his shoulder into the room. "And all the time, it's real. It's a real place—away off down here . . ."

They danced gratefully, formally, to some song carried on in what must be the local patois, while no one paid any attention as long as they were together, and the children poured the family nickels steadily into the slot machines, walloping the handles down with regular crashes and troubling nobody with winning.

She said rapidly, as they began moving together too well, "One of those clippings was an account of a shooting right here. I guess they're proud of it. And that awful knife Baba was carrying . . . I wonder what he called me," she whispered in his ear.

"Who?"

"The one who apologized to you."

If they had ever been going to overstep themselves, it would be now as he held her closer and turned her, when she became aware that he could not help but see the bruise at her temple. It would not be six inches from his eyes. She felt it come out like an evil star. (Let it pay him back, then, for the hand he had stuck in her face when she'd tried once to be sympathetic, when she'd asked about his wife.) They danced on still as the record changed, after standing wordless and motionless, linked together in the middle of the room, for the moment between.

Then, they were like a matched team—like professional, Spanish dancers wearing masks—while the slow piece was playing.

Surely even those immune from the world, for the time being, need the touch of one another, or all is lost. Their arms encircling each other, their bodies circling the odorous, just-nailed-down floor, they were, at last, imperviousness in motion. They had found it, and had almost missed it: they had had to dance. They were what their separate hearts desired that day, for themselves and each other.

They were so good together that once she looked up and half smiled. "For whose benefit did we have to show off?"

Like people in love, they had a superstition about themselves almost as soon as they came out on the floor, and dared not think the words "happy" or "unhappy," which might strike them, one or the other, like lightning.

In the thickening heat they danced on while Baba himself sang with the mosquito-voiced singer in the chorus of *"Moi pas l'aimez ça,"* enumerating the *ça*'s with a hot shrimp between his fingers. He was counting over the platters the old woman now set out on the counter, each heaped with shrimp in their shells boiled to iridescence, like mounds of honeysuckle flowers.

The goose wandered in from the back room under the lid of the counter and hitched itself around the floor among the table legs and people's legs, never seeing that it was neatly avoided by two dancers—who nevertheless vaguely thought of this goose as learned, having earlier heard an old man read to it. The children called it Mimi, and lured it away. The old thatched man was again drunkenly trying to get out by the stuck side door; now he gave it a kick, but was prevailed on to remain. The sleeping dog shuddered and snored.

It was left up to the dancers to provide nickels for the juke box; Baba kept a drawerful for every use. They had grown fond of all the selections by now. This was the music you heard out of the distance at night—out of the roadside taverns you fled past, around the late corners in cities half asleep, drifting up from the carnival over the hill, with one odd little strain always managing to repeat itself. This seemed a homey place.

Bathed in sweat, and feeling the false coolness that brings, they stood finally on the porch in the lapping night air for a moment before leaving. The first arrivals of the girls were coming up the steps under the porch light—all flowered fronts, their black pompadours giving out breathlike feelers from sheer abundance. Where they'd resprinkled it since church, the talcum shone like mica on their downy arms. Smelling solidly of geranium, they filed across the porch with short steps and fingers joined, just timed to turn their smiles loose inside the room. He held the door open for them.

"Ready to go?" he asked her.

Going back, the ride was wordless, quiet except for the motor and the insects driving themselves against the car. The windshield was soon blinded. The headlights pulled in two other spinning storms, cones of flying things that, it seemed, might ignite at the last minute. He stopped the car and got out to clean the windshield thoroughly with his brisk, angry motions of driving. Dust lay thick and cratered on the roadside scrub. Under the now ash-white moon, the world traveled through very faint stars—very many slow stars, very high, very low.

It was a strange land, amphibious—and whether water-covered or grown with jungle or robbed entirely of water and trees, as now, it had the same loneliness. He regarded the great sweep—like steppes, like moors, like deserts (all of which were imaginary to him); but more than it was like any likeness, it was South. The vast, thin, wide-thrown, pale, unfocused star-sky, with its veils of lightning adrift, hung over this land as it hung over the open sea. Standing out in the night alone, he was struck as powerfully with recognition of the extremity of this place as if all other bearings had vanished—as if snow had suddenly started to fall.

He climbed back inside and drove. When he moved to slap furiously at his shirtsleeves, she shivered in the hot, licking night wind that their speed was making. Once the car lights picked out two people—a Negro couple, sitting on two facing chairs in the yard outside their lonely cabin—half undressed, each battling for self against the hot night, with long white rags in endless, scarflike motions.

In peopleless open places there were lakes of dust, smudge fires burning at their hearts. Cows stood in untended rings around them, motionless in the heat, in the night—their horns standing up sharp against that glow.

At length, he stopped the car again, and this time he put his arm under her shoulder and kissed her—not knowing ever whether gently or harshly. It was the loss of that distinction that told him this was now. Then their faces touched unkissing, unmoving, dark, for a length of time. The heat came inside the car and wrapped them still, and the mosquitoes had begun to coat their arms and even their eyelids.

Later, crossing a large open distance, he saw at the same time two fires. He had the feeling that they had been riding for a long time across a face—great, wide, and upturned. In its eyes and open mouth were those fires they had had glimpses of, where the cattle had drawn together: a face, a head, far down here in the South—south of South, below it. A whole giant body sprawled downward then, on and on, always, constant as a constellation or an angel. Flaming and perhaps falling, he thought.

She appeared to be sound asleep, lying back flat as a child, with her hat in her lap. He drove on with her profile beside his, behind his, for he bent forward to drive faster. The earrings she wore twinkled with their rushing motion in an almost regular beat. They might have spoken like tongues. He looked straight before him and drove on, at a speed that, for the rented, overheated, not at all new Ford car, was demoniac.

It seemed often now that a barnlike shape flashed by, roof and all outlined in lonely neon—a movie house at a cross roads. The long white flat road itself, since they had followed it to the end and turned around to come back, seemed able, this far up, to pull them home.

A thing is incredible, if ever, only after it is told—returned to the world it came out of. For their different reasons, he thought, neither of them would tell this (unless something was dragged out of them): that, strangers, they had ridden down into a strange land together and were getting safely back—by a slight margin, perhaps, but margin enough. Over the levee wall now, like an aurora borealis, the sky of New Orleans, across the river, was flickering gently. This time they crossed by bridge, high above everything, merging into a long light-stream of cars turned cityward.

For a time afterward he was lost in the streets, turning almost at random with the noisy traffic until he found his bearings. When he stopped the car at the next sign and leaned forward frowning to make it out, she sat up straight on her side. It was Arabi. He turned the car right around.

"We're all right now," he muttered, allowing himself a cigarette.

Something that must have been with them all along suddenly, then, was not. In a moment, tall as panic, it rose, cried like a human, and dropped back.

"I never got my water," she said.

She gave him the name of her hotel, he drove her there, and he said good night on the sidewalk. They shook hands.

"Forgive . . ." For, just in time, he saw she expected it of him.

And that was just what she did, forgive him. Indeed, had she waked in time from a deep sleep, she would have told him her story. She disappeared through the revolving door, with a gesture of smoothing her hair, and he thought a figure in the lobby strolled to meet her. He got back in the car and sat there.

He was not leaving for Syracuse until early in the morning. At length, he recalled the reason; his wife had recommended that he stay where he was this extra day so that she could entertain some old, unmarried college friends without him underfoot.

As he started up the car, he recognized in the smell of exhausted, body-warm air in the streets, in which the flow of drink was an inextricable part, the signal that the New Orleans evening was just beginning. In Dickie Grogan's, as he passed, the well-known Josefina at her organ was charging up and down with *"Clair de Lune."* As he drove the little Ford safely to its garage, he remembered for the first time in years when he was young and brash, a student in New York, and the shriek and horror and unholy smother of the subway had its original meaning for him as the lilt and expectation of love.

The Burning

DELILAH was dancing up to the front with a message; that was how she happened to be the one to see. A horse was coming in the house, by the front door. The door had been shoved wide open. And all behind the horse, a crowd with a long tail of dust was coming after, all the way up their road from the gate between the cedar trees.

She ran on into the parlor, where they were. They were standing up before the fireplace, their white sewing dropped over their feet, their backs turned, both ladies. Miss Theo had eyes in the back of her head.

"Back you go, Delilah," she said.

"It ain't me, it's them," cried Delilah, and now there were running feet to answer all over the downstairs; Ophelia and all had heard. Outside the dogs were thundering. Miss Theo and Miss Myra, keeping their backs turned to whatever shape or ghost Commotion would take when it came—as long as it was still in the yard, mounting the steps, crossing the porch, or even, with a smell of animal sudden as the smell of snake, planting itself in the front hall—they still had to see it if it came in the parlor, the white horse. It drew up just over the ledge of the double doors Delilah had pushed open, and the ladies lifted their heads together and looked in the mirror over the fireplace, the one called the Venetian mirror, and there it was.

It was a white silhouette, like something cut out of the room's dark. July was so bright outside, and the parlor so dark for coolness, that at first nobody but Delilah could see. Then Miss Myra's racing speech interrupted everything.

"Will you take me on the horse? Please take me first."

It was a towering, sweating, grimacing, uneasy white horse. It had brought in two soldiers with red eyes and clawed, mosquito-racked faces—one a rider, hang-jawed and head-hanging, and the other walking by its side, all breathing in here now as loud as trumpets.

Miss Theo with shut eyes spoke just behind Miss Myra. "Delilah, what is it you came in your dirty apron to tell me?"

The sisters turned with linked hands and faced the room.

"Come to tell you we got the eggs away from black broody hen and sure enough, they's addled," said Delilah.

She saw the blue rider drop his jaw still lower. That was his laugh. But the other soldier set his boot on the carpet and heard the creak in the floor. As if reminded by tell-tale, he took another step, and with his red eyes sticking out he went as far as Miss Myra and took her around that little bending waist. Before he knew it, he had her lifted as high as a child, she was so light. The other soldier with a grunt came down from the horse's back and went toward Miss Theo.

"Step back, Delilah, out of harm's way," said Miss Theo, in such a company-voice that Delilah thought harm was one of two men.

"Hold my horse, nigger," said the man it was.

Delilah took the bridle as if she'd always done that, and held the horse that loomed there in the mirror—she could see it there now, herself—while more blurred and blindlike in the room between it and the door the first soldier shoved the tables and chairs out of the way behind Miss Myra, who flitted when she ran, and pushed her down where she stood and dropped on top of her. There in the mirror the parlor remained, filled up with dusted pictures, and shuttered since six o'clock against the heat and that smell of smoke they were all so tired of, still glimmering with precious, breakable things white ladies were never tired of and never broke, unless they were mad at each other. Behind *her*, the bare yawn of the hall was at her back, and the front stair's shadow, big as a tree and empty. Nobody went up there without being seen, and nobody was supposed to come down. Only if a cup or a silver spoon or a little string of spools on a blue ribbon came hopping down the steps like a frog, sometimes Delilah was the one to pick it up and run back up with it. Outside the mirror's frame, the flat of Miss Theo's hand came down on mankind with a boisterous sound.

Then Miss Theo lifted Miss Myra without speaking to her; Miss Myra closed her eyes but was not asleep. Her bands of black hair awry, her clothes rustling stiffly as clothes through winter quiet, Miss Theo strode half-carrying Miss Myra to the chair in the mirror, and put her down. It was the red, rubbed velvet, pretty chair like Miss Myra's ringbox. Miss Myra threw her head back, face up to the little plaster flowers going around the ceiling. She was asleep somewhere, if not in her eyes.

One of the men's voices spoke out, all gone with righteousness. "We just come in to inspect."

"You presume, you dare," said Miss Theo. Her hand came down to stroke Miss Myra's back-flung head in a strong, forbidding rhythm. From upstairs, Phinny threw down his breakfast plate, but Delilah did not move. Miss Myra's hair streamed loose behind her, bright gold, with the combs caught like leaves in it. Maybe it was to keep her like this, asleep in the heart, that Miss Theo stroked her on and on, too hard.

"It's orders to inspect beforehand," said the soldier.

"Then inspect," said Miss Theo. "No man in the house to prevent it. Brother—no word. Father—dead. Mercifully so—" She spoke in an almost rough-and-tumble kind of way used by ladies who didn't like company—never did like company, for anybody.

Phinny threw down his cup. The horse, shivering, nudged Delilah who was holding him there, a good obedient slave in her fresh-ironed candy-stripe dress beneath her black apron. She would have had her turban tied on, had she known all this ahead, like Miss Theo. "Never is Phinny away. Phinny here. He a he," she said.

Miss Myra's face was turned up as if she were dead, or as if she were a fierce and hungry little bird. Miss Theo rested her hand for a moment in the air above her head.

"Is it shame that's stopping your inspection?" Miss Theo asked. "I'm afraid you found the ladies of this house a trifle out of your element. My sister's the more delicate one, as you see. May I offer you this young kitchen Negro, as I've always understood—"

That Northerner gave Miss Theo a serious, recording look as though she had given away what day the mail came in.

"My poor little sister," Miss Theo went on to Miss Myra, "don't mind what you hear. Don't mind this old world." But

Miss Myra knocked back the stroking hand. Kitty came picking her way into the room and sat between the horse's front feet; Friendly was her name.

One soldier rolled his head toward the other. "What was you saying to me when we come in, Virge?"

"I was saying I opined they wasn't gone yet."

"*Wasn't* they?"

Suddenly both of them laughed, jolting each other so hard that for a second it looked like a fight. Then one said with straight face, "We come with orders to set the house afire, ma'am," and the other one said, "General Sherman."

"I hear you."

"Don't you think we're going to do it? We done just burnt up Jackson twice," said the first soldier with his eye on Miss Myra. His voice made a man's big echo in the hall, like a long time ago. The horse whinnied and moved his head and feet.

"Like I was telling you, you ladies ought to been out. You didn't get no word here we was coming?" The other soldier pointed one finger at Miss Theo. She shut her eyes.

"Lady, they told you." Miss Myra's soldier looked hard at Miss Myra there. "And when your own people tell you something's coming to burn your house down, the business-like thing to do is get out of the way. And the right thing. I ain't beholden to tell you no more times now."

"Then go."

"Burning up *people's* further'n I go yet."

Miss Theo stared him down. "I see no degree."

So it was Miss Myra's soldier that jerked Delilah's hand from the bridle and turned her around, and cursed the Bedlam-like horse which began to beat the hall floor behind. Delilah listened, but Phinny did not throw anything more down; maybe he had crept to the landing, and now looked over. He was scared, if not of horses, then of men. He didn't know anything about them. The horse did get loose; he took a clattering trip through the hall and dining room and library, until at last his rider caught him. Then Delilah was set on his back.

She looked back over her shoulder through the doorway, and saw Miss Theo shake Miss Myra and catch the peaked face with its purple eyes and slap it.

"Myra," she said, "collect your senses. We have to go out in front of them."

Miss Myra slowly lifted her white arm, like a lady who has been asked to dance, and called, "Delilah!" Because that was the one she saw being lifted onto the horse's hilly back and ridden off through the front door. Skittering among the iron shoes, Kitty came after, trotting fast as a little horse herself, and ran ahead to the woods, where she was never seen again; but Delilah, from where she was set up on the horse and then dragged down on the grass, never called after her.

She might have been saving her breath for the screams that soon took over the outdoors and circled that house they were going to finish for sure now. She screamed, young and strong, for them all—for everybody that wanted her to scream for them, for everybody that didn't; and sometimes it seemed to her that she was screaming her loudest for Delilah, who was lost now—carried out of the house, not knowing how to get back.

Still inside, the ladies kept them waiting.

Miss Theo finally brought Miss Myra out through that wide-open front door and across the porch with the still perfect and motionless vine shadows. There were some catcalls and owl hoots from under the trees.

"Now hold back, boys. They's too lady-like for you."

"Ladies must needs take their time."

"And then they're no damn good at it!" came a clear, youthful voice, and under the branches somewhere a banjo was stroked to call up the campfires further on, later in the evening, when all this would be over and done.

The sisters showed no surprise to see soldiers and Negroes alike (old Ophelia in the way, talking, talking) strike into and out of the doors of the house, the front now the same as the back, to carry off beds, tables, candlesticks, washstands, cedar buckets, china pitchers, with their backs bent double; or the horses ready to go; or the food of the kitchen bolted down—and so much of it thrown away, this must be a second dinner; or the unsilenceable dogs, the old pack mixed with the strangers and fighting with all their hearts over bones. The last skinny sacks were thrown on the wagons—the last flour, the last scraping and clearing from Ophelia's shelves, even her pepper-grinder. The silver Delilah could count was counted on strange blankets and then, knocking against the teapot, rolled together, tied up like a bag of bones. A drummer boy with his drum around his neck caught both Miss Theo's peacocks, Marco and Polo, and wrung their necks in the yard. Nobody could look at those bird-corpses; nobody did.

The sisters left the porch like one, and in step, hands linked, came through the high grass in their crushed and only dresses, and walked under the trees. They came to a stop as if it was moonlight under the leafy frame of the big tree with the swing, without any despising left in their faces which were the same as one, as one face that didn't belong to anybody. This one clarified face, looking both left and right, could make out every one of those men through the bushes and tree trunks, and mark every looting slave also, as all stood momently fixed like serenaders by the light of a moon. Only old Ophelia was talking all the time, all the time, telling everybody in her own way about the trouble here, but of course nobody could understand a thing that day anywhere in the world.

"What are they fixing to do now, Theo?" asked Miss Myra, with a frown about to burn into her too-white forehead.

"What they want to," Miss Theo said, folding her arms.

To Delilah that house they were carrying the torches to was like one just now coming into being—like the showboat that slowly came through the trees just once in her time, at the peak of high water—bursting with the unknown, sparking in ruddy light, with a minute to go before that ear-aching cry of the calliope.

When it came—but it was a bellowing like a bull, that came from inside—Delilah drew close, with Miss Theo's skirt to peep around, and Miss Theo's face looked down like death itself and said, "Remember this. You black monkeys," as the blaze outdid them all.

A while after the burning, when everybody had gone away, Miss Theo and Miss Myra, finding and taking hold of Delilah who was face-down in a ditch with her eyes scorched open, did at last go beyond the tramped-down gate and away through the grand worthless fields they themselves had had burned long before.

It was a hot afternoon, hot out here in the open, and it played a trick on them with a smell and prophecy of fall—it was the burning. The brown wet standing among the stumps in the cracked cup of the pond tasted as hot as coffee and as bitter. There was still and always smoke between them and the sun.

After all the July miles, there Jackson stood, burned twice, or who knew if it was a hundred times, facing them in the road. Delilah could see through Jackson like a haunt, it was all chimneys, all scooped out. There were soldiers with guns among the ashes, but these ashes were cold. Soon even these two ladies, who had been everywhere and once knew their way, told each other they were lost. While some soldiers looked them over, they pointed at what they couldn't see, traced gone-away spires, while a horse without his rider passed brushing his side against them and ran down a black alley softly, and did not return.

They walked here and there, sometimes over the same track, holding hands all three, like the timeless time it snowed, and white and black went to play together in hushed woods. They turned loose only to point and name.

"The State House."—"The school."

"The Blind School."—"The penintentiary!"

"The big stable."—"The Deaf-and-Dumb."

"Oh! Remember when we passed three of *them*, sitting on a hill?" They went on matching each other, naming and claiming ruin for ruin.

"The lunatic asylum!"—"The State House."

"No, I said that. Now where are we? That's surely Captain Jack Calloway's hitching post."

"But why would the hitching post be standing and the rest not?"

"And ours not."

"I think I should have told you, Myra—"

"Tell me now."

"Word *was* sent to us to get out when it was sent to the rest on Vicksburg Road. Two days' warning. I believe it was a message from General Pemberton."

"Don't worry about it now. Oh no, of course we couldn't leave," said Miss Myra. A soldier watched her in the distance, and she recited:

"There was a man in our town
And he was wondrous wise.
He jumped into a bramble bush
And scratched out both his eyes."

She stopped, looking at the soldier.

"He sent word," Miss Theo went on, "General Pemberton sent word, for us all to get out ahead of what was coming. You were in the summerhouse when it came. It was two days' warning—but I couldn't bring myself to call and tell you, Myra. I suppose I couldn't convince myself—couldn't quite *believe* that they meant to come and visit that destruction on us."

"Poor Theo. I could have."

"No you couldn't. I couldn't *understand* that message, any more than Delilah here could have. I can reproach myself now, of course, with everything." And they began to walk boldly through and boldly out of the burnt town, single file.

"Not everything, Theo. Who had Phinny? Remember?" cried Miss Myra ardently.

"Hush."

"If I hadn't had Phinny, that would've made it all right. Then Phinny wouldn't have—"

"Hush, dearest, that wasn't *your* baby, you know. It was Brother Benton's baby. I won't have your nonsense now." Miss Theo led the way through the ashes, marching in front. Delilah was in danger of getting left behind.

"—perished. Dear Benton. So good. Nobody else would have felt so *bound*," Miss Myra said.

"Not after I told him what he owed a little life! Each little life is a *man's* fault, I said that. Oh, who'll ever forget that awful day?"

"Benton's forgotten, if he's dead. He was so good after that too, never married."

"Stayed home, took care of his sisters. Only wanted to be forgiven."

"There has to be somebody to take care of everybody."

"I told him, he must never dream he was *inflicting* his sisters. That's what we're for."

"And it never would have inflicted us. We could have lived and died. Until *they* came."

"In at the front door on the back of a horse," said Miss Theo. "If Benton had been there!"

"I'll never know what possessed them, riding in like that," said Miss Myra almost mischievously; and Miss Theo turned.

"And *you said*—"

"I said something wrong," said Miss Myra quickly. "I apologize, Theo."

"No, I blame only myself. That I let you remain one hour in that house after it was doomed. I thought I was equal to it, and I proved I was, but not you."

"Oh, to my shame you saw me, dear! Why do you say it wasn't my baby?"

"Now don't start that nonsense over again," said Miss Theo, going around a hole.

"I had Phinny. When we were all at home and happy together. Are you going to take Phinny away from me now?"

Miss Theo pressed her cheeks with her palms and showed her pressed, pensive smile as she looked back over her shoulder.

Miss Myra said, "Oh, don't *I* know who it really belonged to, who it loved the best, that baby?"

"I won't have you misrepresenting yourself."

"It's never what I intended."

"Then reason dictates you hush."

Both ladies sighed, and so did Delilah; they were so tired of going on. Miss Theo still walked in front but she was looking behind her through the eyes in the back of her head.

"You hide him if you want to," said Miss Myra. "Let Papa shut up all upstairs. I had him, dear. It was an officer, no, one of our beaux that used to come out and hunt with Benton. It's because I was always the impetuous one, highstrung and so easily carried away . . . And if Phinny *was* mine—"

"Don't you know he's black?" Miss Theo blocked the path.

"He *was* white." Then, "He's black *now*," whispered Miss Myra, darting forward and taking her sister's hands. Their shoulders were pressed together, as if they were laughing or waiting for something more to fall.

"If I only had something to eat!" sobbed Miss Myra, and once more let herself be embraced. One eye showed over the tall shoulder. "Oh, Delilah!"

"Could be he got out," called Delilah in a high voice. "He strong, he."

"Who?"

"Could be Phinny's out loose. Don't cry."

"Look yonder. What do I see? I see the Dicksons' perfectly good hammock still under the old pecan trees," Miss Theo said to Miss Myra, and spread her hand.

There was some little round silver cup, familiar to the ladies, in the hammock when they came to it down in the grove. Lying on its side with a few drops in it, it made them smile.

The yard was charged with butterflies. Miss Myra, as if she could wait no longer, climbed into the hammock and lay down with ankles crossed. She took up the cup like a story book she'd begun and left there yesterday, holding it before her eyes in those freckling fingers, slowly picking out the ants.

"So still out here and all," Miss Myra said. "Such a big sky. Can you get used to that? And all the figs dried up. I wish it would rain."

"Won't rain till Saturday," said Delilah.

"Delilah, don't go 'way."

"Don't you try, Delilah," said Miss Theo.

"No'm."

Miss Theo sat down, rested a while, though she did not know how to sit on the ground and was afraid of grasshoppers, and then she stood up, shook out her skirt, and cried out to Delilah, who had backed off far to one side, where some chickens were running around loose with nobody to catch them.

"Come back here, Delilah! Too late for that!" She said to Miss Myra, "The Lord will provide. We've still got Delilah, and as long as we've got her we'll use her, my dearie."

Miss Myra "let the cat die" in the hammock. Then she gave her hand to climb out, Miss Theo helped her, and without needing any help for herself Miss Theo untied the hammock from the pecan trees. She was long bent over it, and Miss Myra studied the butterflies. She had left the cup sitting on the ground in the shade of the tree. At last Miss Theo held up two lengths of cotton rope, the red and the white strands untwisted from each other, bent like the hair of ladies taken out of plaits in the morning.

Delilah, given the signal, darted up the tree and hooking her toes made the ropes fast to the two branches a sociable distance apart, where Miss Theo pointed. When she slid down, she stood waiting while they settled it, until Miss Myra repeated enough times, in a spoiled sweet way, "I bid to be first." It was what Miss Theo wanted all the time. Then Delilah had to squat and make a basket with her fingers, and Miss Myra tucked up her skirts and stepped her ashy shoe in the black hands.

"Tuck under, Delilah."

Miss Myra, who had ordered that, stepped over Delilah's head and stood on her back, and Delilah felt her presence tugging there as intimately as a fish's on a line, each longing Miss Myra had to draw away from Miss Theo, draw away from Delilah, away from that tree.

Delilah rolled her eyes around. The noose was being tied by Miss Theo's puckered hands like a bonnet on a windy day, and Miss Myra's young, lifted face was looking out.

"I learned as a child how to tie, from a picture book in Papa's library—not that I ever was called on," Miss Theo said. "I guess I was always something of a tomboy." She kissed Miss Myra's hand and at almost the same instant Delilah was seized by the ribs and dragged giggling backwards, out from under—not soon enough, for Miss Myra kicked her in the head—a bad kick, almost as if that were Miss Theo or a man up in the tree, who meant what he was doing.

Miss Theo stood holding Delilah and looking up—helping herself to grief. No wonder Miss Myra used to hide in the summerhouse with her reading, screaming sometimes when there was nothing but Delilah throwing the dishwater out on the ground.

"I've proved," said Miss Theo to Delilah, dragging her by more than main force back to the tree, "what I've always suspicioned: that I'm brave as a lion. That's right: look at me. If I ordered you back up that tree to help my sister down to the grass and shade, you'd turn and run: I know your minds. You'd desert me with your work half done. So I haven't said a word about it. About mercy. As soon as you're through, you can go, and leave us where you've put us, unspared, just alike. And that's the way they'll find us. The sight will be good for them for what they've done," and she pushed Delilah down and walked up on her shoulders, weighting her down like a rock.

Miss Theo looped her own knot up there; there was no mirror or sister to guide her. Yet she was quicker this time than last time, but Delilah was quicker too. She rolled over in a ball, and then she was up running, looking backward, crying. Behind her Miss Theo came sailing down from the tree. She was always too powerful for a lady. Even those hens went flying up with a shriek, as if they felt her shadow on their backs. Now she reached in the grass.

There was nothing for Delilah to do but hide, down in the jungly grass choked with bitterweed and black-eyed susans, wild to the pricking skin, with many heads nodding, cauldrons of ants, with butterflies riding them, grasshoppers hopping them, mosquitoes making the air alive, down in the loud and lonesome grass that was rank enough almost to matt the sky over. Once, stung all over and wild to her hair's ends, she ran back and asked Miss Theo, "What must I do now? Where must I go?" But Miss Theo, whose eyes from the ground were looking straight up at her, wouldn't tell. Delilah danced away from her, back to her distance and crouched down. She believed Miss Theo twisted in the grass like a dead snake until the sun went down. She herself held still like a mantis until the grass had folded and spread apart at the falling of dew. This was after the chickens had gone to roost in a strange uneasy tree against the cloud where the guns still boomed and the way from Vicksburg was red. Then Delilah could find her feet.

She knew where Miss Theo was. She could see the last white of Miss Myra, the stockings. Later, down by the swamp, in a wading bird tucked in its wing for sleep, she saw Miss Myra's ghost.

•

After being lost a day and a night or more, crouching awhile, stealing awhile through the solitudes of briar bushes, she came again to Rose Hill. She knew it by the chimneys and by the crape myrtle off to the side, where the bottom of the summerhouse stood empty as an egg basket. Some of the flowers looked tasty, like chicken legs fried a little black.

Going around the house, climbing over the barrier of the stepless back doorsill, and wading into ashes, she was lost still, inside that house. She found an iron pot and a man's long boot, a doorknob and a little book fluttering, its leaves spotted and fluffed like guinea feathers. She took up the book and read out from it, "Ba-ba-ba-ba-ba—trash." She was being Miss Theo taking away Miss Myra's reading. Then she saw the Venetian mirror down in the chimney's craw, flat and face-up in the cinders.

Behind her the one standing wall of the house held notched and listening like the big ear of King Solomon into which poured the repeated asking of birds. The tree stood and flowered. What must she do? Crouching suddenly to the ground, she heard the solid cannon, the galloping, the low fast drum of burning. Crawling on her knees she went to the glass and rubbed it with spit and leaned over it and saw a face all neck and ears, then gone. Before it she opened and spread her arms; she had seen Miss Myra do that, try that. But its gleam was addled.

Though the mirror did not know Delilah, Delilah would have known that mirror anywhere, because it was set between black men. Their arms were raised to hold up the mirror's roof, which now the swollen mirror brimmed, among gold leaves and gold heads—black men dressed in gold, looking almost into the glass themselves, as if to look back through a door, men now half-split away, flattened with fire, bearded, noseless as the moss that hung from swamp trees.

Where the mirror did not cloud like the horse-trampled spring, gold gathered itself from the winding water, and honey under water started to flow, and then the gold fields were there, hardening gold. Through the water, gold and honey twisted up into houses, trembling. She saw people walking the bridges in early light with hives of houses on their heads, men in dresses, some with red birds; and monkeys in velvet; and ladies with masks laid over their faces looking from pointed windows. Delilah supposed that was Jackson before Sherman came. Then it was gone. In this noon quiet, here where all had passed by, unless indeed it had gone in, she waited on her knees.

The mirror's cloudy bottom sent up minnows of light to the brim where now a face pure as a water-lily shadow was floating. Almost too small and deep down to see, they were quivering, leaping to life, fighting, aping old things Delilah had seen done in this world already, sometimes what men had done to Miss Theo and Miss Myra and the peacocks and to slaves, and sometimes what a slave had done and what anybody now could do to anybody. Under the flicker of the sun's licks, then under its whole blow and blare, like an unheard scream, like an act of mercy gone, as the wall-less light and July blaze struck through from the opened sky, the mirror felled her flat.

She put her arms over her head and waited, for they would all be coming again, gathering under her and above her, bees saddled like horses out of the air, butterflies harnessed to one another, bats with masks on, birds together, all with their weapons bared. She listened for the blows, and dreaded that whole army of wings—of flies, birds, serpents, their glowing enemy faces and bright kings' dresses, that banner of colors forked out, all this world that was flying, striking, stricken, falling, gilded or blackened, mortally splitting and falling apart, proud turbans unwinding, turning like the spotted dying leaves of fall, spiraling down to bottomless ash; she dreaded the fury of all the butterflies and dragonflies in the world riding, blades unconcealed and at point—descending, and rising again from the waters below, down under, one whale made of his own grave, opening his mouth to swallow Jonah one more time.

Jonah!—a homely face to her, that could still look back from the red lane he'd gone down, even if it was too late to speak. He was her Jonah, her Phinny, her black monkey; she worshiped him still, though it was long ago he was taken from her the first time.

Stiffly, Delilah got to her feet. She cocked her head, looked sharp into the mirror, and caught the motherly image—head wagging in the flayed forehead of a horse with ears and crest up stiff, the shield and the drum of big swamp birdskins, the horns of deer sharpened to cut and kill with. She showed her teeth. Then she looked in the feathery ashes and found Phinny's bones. She ripped a square from her manifold fullness of skirts and tied up the bones in it.

She set foot in the road then, walking stilted in Miss Myra's shoes and carrying Miss Theo's shoes tied together around her neck, her train in the road behind her. She wore Miss Myra's willing rings—had filled up two fingers—but she had had at last to give up the puzzle of Miss Theo's bracelet with the chain. They were two stones now, scalding-white. When the combs were being lifted from her hair, Miss Myra had come down too, beside her sister.

Light on Delilah's head the Jubilee cup was set. She paused now and then to lick the rim and taste again the ghost of sweet that could still make her tongue start clinging—some sweet lapped up greedily long ago, only a mystery now when or who by. She carried her own black locust stick to drive the snakes.

Following the smell of horses and fire, to men, she kept in the wheel tracks till they broke down at the river. In the shade underneath the burned and fallen bridge she sat on a stump and chewed for a while, without dreams, the comb of a dirt-dauber. Then once more kneeling, she took a drink from the Big Black, and pulled the shoes off her feet and waded in.

Submerged to the waist, to the breast, stretching her throat like a sunflower stalk above the river's opaque skin, she kept on, her treasure stacked on the roof of her head, hands laced upon it. She had forgotten how or when she knew, and she did not know what day this was, but she knew—it would not rain, the river would not rise, until Saturday.

The Bride of the Innisfallen

THERE WAS something of the pavilion about one raincoat, the way—for some little time out there in the crowd—it stood flowing in its salmony-pink and yellow stripes down toward the wet floor of the platform, expanding as it went. In the Paddington gloom it was a little dim, but it was parading through now, and once inside the compartment it looked rainbow-bright.

In it a middle-aged lady climbed on like a sheltered girl—a boost up from behind she pretended not to need or notice. She was big-boned and taller than the man who followed her inside bringing the suitcase—he came up round and with a doll's smile, his black suit wet; she turned a look on him; this was farewell. The train to Fishguard to catch the Cork boat was leaving in fifteen minutes—at a black four o'clock in the afternoon of that spring that refused to flower. She, so clearly, was the one going.

There was nobody to share the compartment yet but one girl, and she not Irish.

Over a stronghold of a face, the blue hat of the lady in the raincoat was settled on like an Indian bonnet, or, rather, like an old hat, which it was. The hair that had been pulled out of its confines was flirtatious and went into two auburn-and-gray pomegranates along her cheeks. Her gaze was almost forgiving, if unsettled; it held its shine so long. Even yet, somewhere, sometime, the owner of those eyes might expect to rise to a tragic occasion. When the round man put the suitcase up in the rack, she sank down under it as if something were now done that could not be undone, and with tender glances brushed the soot and raindrops off herself, somewhat onto him. He perched beside her—it was his legs that were short—and then, as her hands dropped into her bright-stained lap, they both stared straight ahead, as if waiting for a metamorphosis.

The American girl sitting opposite could not have taken in anything they said as long as she kept feeling it necessary, herself, to subside. As long as the train stood in the station, her whole predicament seemed betrayed by her earliness. She was leaving London without her husband's knowledge. She was wearing rather worn American clothes and thin shoes, and, sitting up very straight, kept pulling her coat collar about her ears and throat. In the strange, diminished light of the station people seemed to stand and move on some dark stage; by now platform and train must be almost entirely Irish in their gathered population.

A fourth person suddenly came inside the compartment, a small, passionate-looking man. He was with them as suddenly as a gift—as if an arm had thrust in a bunch of roses or a telegram. There seemed something in him about to explode, but—he pushed off his wet coat, threw it down, threw it up overhead, flung himself into the seat—he was going to be a good boy.

"What's the time?" The round man spoke softly, as if perhaps the new man had brought it.

The lady bowed her head and looked up at him: *she* had it: "Six minutes to four." She wore an accurate-looking wristwatch.

The round man's black eyes flared, he looked out at the rain, and asked the American if she, too, were going to Cork—a question she did not at first understand; his voice was very musical.

"Yes—that is—"

"Four minutes to four," the lady in the raincoat said, those fours sounding fated.

"You don't need to get out of the carriage till you get to Fishguard," the round man told her, murmuring it softly, as if he'd told her before and would tell her again. "Straight through to Fishguard, then you book a berth. You're in Cork in the morning."

She looked fondly as though she had never heard of Cork, wouldn't believe it, and opened and shut her great white heavy eyelids. When he crossed his knees she stole her arm through his and seesawed him on the seat. Holding his rows of little black-rimmed fingers together like a modest accordion, he said, "Two ladies going to Cork."

"Two minutes to four," she said, rolling her eyes.

"You'll go through the customs when you get to Fishguard," he told her. "They'll open your case and see what there is to detect. They'll be wanting to discover if you are bringing anything wrongly and improperly into the country." He eyed the lady, above their linked arms, as if she had been a stranger inquiring into the uses and purposes of customs inspection in the world. By ceasing to smile he appeared to anchor himself; he said solidly, "Following that, you go on board."

"Where you won't be able to buy drink for three miles out!" cried the new passenger. Up to now he had been simply drawing quick breaths. He had a neat, short, tender, slightly alarmed profile—dark, straight hair cut not ten minutes ago, a slight cut over the ear. But this still-bleeding customer, a Connemara man as he was now announcing himself, always did everything last-minute, because that was the way he was made.

There was a feel of the train's being about to leave. Then the guard was shouting.

The round man and the lady in the raincoat rose and moved in step to the door together, all four hands enjoined. She bent her head. Hers was a hat of drapes and shapes. There in the rainy light it showed a chaos of blue veil falling behind, and when it sadly turned, shining directly over the eyes was a gold pin in the shape of a pair of links, like those you are supposed to separate in amateur-magician sets. Her raincoat gave off a peppermint smell that might have been stored up for this moment.

"You won't need to get out of the carriage at all," he said. She put her head on one side. Their cheeks glittered as did their eyes. They embraced, parted; the man from Connemara watched him out the door. Then the pair clasped hands through the window. She might have been standing in a tower and he elevated to her level as far as possible by ladder or rope, in the rain.

There was a great rush of people. At the very last minute four of them stormed this compartment. A little boy flung in over his own bags, whistling wildly, paying no attention to being seen off, no attention to feet inside, consenting to let a young woman who had followed him in put a small bag of his in the rack and save him a seat. She was being pelted with thanks for this by young men and girls crowding at the door; she smiled calmly back at them; even in this she was showing pregnancy, as she showed it under her calm blue coat. A pair of lovers slid in last of all, like a shadow, and filled two seats by the corridor door, trapping into the middle the man from Connemara and somewhat crowding the American girl into her corner. They were just not twining, touching, just not angry, just not too late. Without the ghost of impatience or struggle, without shifting about once, they were settled in speechlessness—two profiles, his dark and cleared of temper, hers young, with straight cut hair.

"Four o'clock."

The lady in the raincoat made the announcement in a hollow tone; everybody in the compartment hushed as though almost taken by surprise. She and the wistful round man still clasped hands through the window and continued to shine in the face like lighthouses smiling. The outside doors were banged shut in a long retreat in both directions, and the train moved. Those outside appeared running beside the train, then waving handkerchiefs, the young men shouting questions and envious things, the girls—they were certainly all Irish, wildly pretty—wildly retreating, their hair whipped forward in long bright and dark pennants by the sucking of the train. The round little man was there one moment and, panting, vanished the next.

The lady, still standing, was all at once very noticeable. Her body might have solidified to the floor under that buttoned cover. (What she had on under her raincoat was her own business and remained so.) The next moment she put out her tongue, at everything just left behind.

"*Oh* my God!" The man from Connemara did explode; it sounded like relief.

Then they were underway fast; the lady, having seated herself, smoothed down the raincoat with rattles like the reckless slamming of bureau drawers, and took from her purse a box of Players. She extracted a cigarette already partly burned down, and requested a light. The lover was so quick he almost anticipated her. When the butt glowed, her hand dropped like a shot bird from the flame he rather blindly stuck out.

Between draws she held her cigarette below her knees and turned inward to her palm—her hand making a cauldron into which the little boy stared.

The American girl opened a book, but closed it. Every time the lady in the raincoat walked out over their feet—she immediately, after her cigarette, made several excursions—she would fling them a look. It was like "Don't say a word, start anything, fall into each other's arms, read, or fight, until I get back to you." She might both inspire and tantalize them with her glare. And she was so unpretty she ought to be funny, like somebody on the stage; perhaps she would be funny later.

The little boy whistled *"Funiculi, Funicula"* in notes almost too high for the ear to hear. On the windows it poured, poured rain. The black of London swam like a cinder in the eye and did not go away. The young wife, leaning back and letting her eyes fall a little while on the child, gave him dim, languorous looks, not quite shaking her head at him. He stopped whistling, but at the same time it could be felt how she was not his mother; her face showed degrees of maternity as other faces show degrees of love or anger; she was only acting his mother for the journey.

It was nice of her then to begin to sing *"Funiculi, Funicula,"* and the others joined, the little boy very seriously, as if he now hated the song. Then they sang something more Irish, about the sea and coming back. But the throb of the rails made the song oddly Spanish and hopelessly desirous; they were near the end of the car, where the beat was single and strong.

After the lady in the raincoat undid her top button and suggested "Wild Colonial Boy," her hatted head kept time, started to lead them—perhaps she kept a pub. The little boy, giving the ladies a meeting look, brought out a fiercely shining harmonica, as he would a pistol, and almost drowned them out. The American girl looked as if she did not know the words, but the lovers now sang, with faces strangely brave.

At some small, forgotten station a schoolgirl got on, took the vacant seat in this compartment, and opened a novel to page 1. They quieted. By the look of her it seemed they must be in Wales. They had scarcely got a word at the child before she began reading. She sat by the young wife; especially from her, the school hat hid the bent head like a candle snuffer; of her features only the little mouth, slightly open and working, stayed visible. Even her upper lip was darkly freckled, even the finger that lifted and turned the page.

The little boy sped his breath up the harmonica scale; the young wife said "Victor!" and they all felt sorry for him and had his name.

"Air," she suddenly said, as if she felt their look. The man from Connemara hurled himself at the window and slid the pane, then at the corridor door, and opened it wide onto a woman passing with an eight- or nine-months-old baby. It was a red-haired boy with queenly jowls, squinting in at the world as if to say, "Will what has just been said be very kindly repeated?"

"Oh, isn't he *beautiful*!" the young wife cried reproachfully through the door. She would have put out her hands.

There was no response. On they went.

"An English nurse traveling with an Irish child, look at that, he's so grand, and such style, that dress, that petticoat, do you think she's kidnaped the lad?" suggested the lady in the raincoat, puffing.

"*Oh* my God," said the man from Connemara.

For a moment the schoolgirl made the only sounds—catching her breath and sobbing over her book.

"Kidnaping's farfetched," said the man from Connemara. "Maybe the woman's deaf and dumb."

"I couldn't sleep this night thinking such wickedness was traveling on the train and on the boat with me." The young wife's skin flooded to her temples.

"It's not *your* fault."

The schoolgirl bent lower still and, still reading, opened a canvas satchel at her feet, in which—all looked—were a thermos, a lunchbox under lock and key, a banana, and a Bible. She selected the banana by feel, and brought it up and ate it as she read.

"If it's kidnaping, it'll be in the Cork paper Sunday morning," said the lady in the raincoat with confidence. "Railway trains are great systems for goings on of all kinds. You'll never take me by surprise."

"But this is *our* train," said the young wife. "Women alone, sometimes exceptions, but often on the long journey alone or with children."

"There's evil where you'd least expect it," the man from Connemara said, somehow as if he didn't care for children. "There's one thing and another, so forth and so on, run your finger down the alphabet and see where it stops."

"I'll never see the Cork paper," replied the young wife. "But oh, I tell you I would rather do without air to breathe than see that poor baby pass again and put out his little arms to me."

"Ah, then. Shut the door," the man from Connemara said, and pointed it out to the lover, who after all sat nearer.

"Excuse me," the young man whispered to the girl, and shut the door at her knee and near where her small open hand rested.

"But why would she be kidnaping the baby *into* Ireland?" cried the young wife suddenly.

"Yes—you've been riding backwards: if we were going the other way, 'twould be a different story." And the lady in the raincoat looked at her wisely.

The train was grinding to a stop at a large station in Wales. The schoolgirl, after one paralyzed moment, rose and got off through the corridor in a dream; the book she closed was seen to be *Black Stallion of the Downs.* A big tall man climbed on and took her place. It was this station, it was felt, where they actually ceased leaving a place and from now on were arriving at one.

The tall Welshman drove into the compartment through any remarks that were going on and with great strength like a curse heaved his bag on top of several of theirs in the rack, where it had been thought there was no more room, and took the one seat without question. With serious sets of his shoulders he settled down in the middle of them, between Victor and the lady in the raincoat, facing the man from Connemara. His hair was in two corner bushes, and he had a full eye—like that of the horse in the storm in old chromos in the West of America—the kind of eye supposed to attract lightning. In the silence of the dreary stop, he slapped all his pockets—not having forgotten anything, only making sure. His hands were powdered over with something fairly black.

"Well! How far do *you* go?" he put to the man from Connemara and then to them in turn, and each time the answer came, "Ireland." He seemed unduly astonished.

He lighted a pipe, and pointed it toward the little boy. "What have you been doing in England, eh?"

Victor writhed forward and set his teeth into the strap of the outer door.

"He's been to a wedding," said the young wife, as though she and Victor were saying the same thing in two different ways, and smiled on him fully for the first time.

"Who got married?"

"Me brother," Victor said in a strangled voice, still holding on recklessly while the train, starting with a jerk, rocked him to the side.

"Big wedding?"

Two greyhounds in plaid blankets, like dangerously ecstatic old ladies hoping no one would see them, rushed into, out of, then past the corridor door which the incoming Welshman had failed to shut behind him. The glare in the eye of the man who followed, with his belt flying about him as he pulled back on the dogs, was wild, too.

"Big wedding?"

"Me family was all over the place if that's what you mean." Victor wildly chewed; there was a smell of leather.

"Ah, it has driven his poor mother to her bed, it was that grand a wedding," said the young wife. "That's why she's in England, and Victor here on his own."

"You must have missed school. What school do you go to—you *go* to school?" By the power of his eye, the Welshman got Victor to let go the strap and answer yes or no.

"School, yes."

"You study French and so on?"

"Ah, them languages is no good. What good is Irish?" said Victor passionately, and somebody said, "Now what does your mother tell you?"

"What ails your mother?" said the Welshman.

"Ah, it's her old trouble. Ask *her*. But there's two of me brothers at one end and five at the other."

"You're divided."

The young wife let Victor stand on the seat and haul her paper parcel off the rack so she could give him an orange. She drew out as well a piece of needlepoint, square and tarnished, which she spread over her pretty arm and hung before their eyes.

"Beautiful!"

" 'A Wee Cottage' is the name it has."

"I see the cottage. 'Tis very wee, and so's every bit about it."

" 'Twould blind you: 'tis a work of art."

"The little rabbit peeping out!"

"Makes you wish you had your gun," said the Welshman to Victor.

The young wife said, "Me grandmother. At eighty she died, very sudden, on a visit to England. God rest her soul. Now I'm bringing this masterpiece home to Ireland."

"Who could blame you."

"Well you should bring it away, all those little stitches she put in."

She wrapped it away, just as anyone could see her—as she might for the moment see herself—folding a blanket down into the crib and tucking the ends. Victor, now stained and fragrant with orange, leapt like a tiger to pop the parcel back overhead.

"No, I shouldn't think learning Irish would do you much good," said the Welshman. "No real language."

"Why not?" said the lady in the raincoat instantly. "I've a brother who is a very fluent Irish speaker and a popular man. You cannot doubt yourself that when the English hear you speaking a tongue they cannot follow, in the course of time they are due to start holding respect for you."

"From London you are." The Welshman bit down on his pipe and smoked.

"*Oh* my God." The man from Connemara struck his head. "I have an English wife. How would she like that, I wouldn't like to know? If all at once I begun on her in Irish! How would you like it if your husband would only speak to you in Irish? Or Welsh, my God?" He searched the eyes of all the women, and last of the young Irish sweetheart—who did not seem to grasp the question. "Aha ha ha!" he cried urgently and despairingly at her, asking her only to laugh with him.

But the young man's arm was thrust along the seat and she was sitting under its arch as if it were the entrance to a cave, which surely they all must see.

"Will you eat a biscuit now?" the young wife gently asked the man from Connemara. He took one wordlessly; for the moment he had no English or Irish. So she broke open another paper parcel beside her. "I have oceans," she said.

"Oh, *you wait*," said the lady in the raincoat, rising. And *she* opened a parcel as big as a barrel and it was full of everything to eat that anybody could come out of England with alive.

She offered candy, jam roll, biscuits, bananas, nuts, sections of bursting orange, and bread and butter, and they all in the flush of the hospitality and heat sat eating. Everybody partook but the Welshman, who had presumably had a dinner in Wales. It was more than ever like a little party, all the finer somehow, sadly enough, for the nose against the windowpane. They poured out tea from a couple of steaming thermoses; the black windows—for the sun was down now, never having been out of the fogs and rains all day—coated warmly over between them and what flew by out there.

"Could you tell me the name of a place to stay in Cork?" The American girl spoke up to the man from Connemara as he gave her a biscuit.

"In Cork? Ah, but you don't want to be stopping in Cork. Killarney is where you would do well to go, if you're wanting to see the wonders of Ireland. The lakes and the hills! Blue as blue skies, the lakes. That's where you want to go, Killarney."

"She wants to climb the Hill of Tara, you mean," said the guard, who with a burst of cold wind had entered to punch their tickets again. "All the way up, and into the raths, too, to lay her eyes by the light of candles on something she's never seen before; if that's what she's after. Have you never climbed the Hill and never crept into those, lady? Maybe 'twould take a little boost from behind, I don't know your size; but I think 'twould not be difficult getting you through." He gave her ticket its punch, with a keen blue glance at her, and banged out.

"Well, *I'm* going to the sitting in the dining car now." The lady in the raincoat stood up under the dim little lights in the ceiling that shone on her shoulders. Then down her long nose she suggested to them each to come, too. Did she really mean to eat still, and after all that largess? They laughed, as if to urge her by their shock to go on, and the American girl witlessly murmured, "No, I have a letter to write."

Off she went, that long coat shimmering and rattling. The little boy looked after her, the first sea wind blew in at the opened door, and his cowlick nodded like a dark flower.

"Very grand," said the Connemara man. "Very high and mighty she is, indeed."

Out there, nuns, swept by untoward blasts of wind, shrieked soundlessly as in nightmares in the corridors. It must be like the Tunnel of Love for them—the thought drifted into the young sweetheart's head.

She was so stiff! She struggled up, staggered a little as she left the compartment. All alone she stood in the corridor. A young man went past, soft fair mustache, soft fair hair, combing the hair—oh, delicious. Here came a hat like old Cromwell's on a lady, who had also a fur cape, a stick, flat turning-out shoes, and a heavy book with a pencil in it. The old lady beat her stick on the floor and made a sweet old man in gaiters and ribbon-tied hat back up into a doorway to let her by. All these people were going into the dining cars. She hung her head out the open corridor window into the Welsh night, which, seen from inside itself—her head in its mouth—could look not black but pale. Wales was formidable, barrier-like. What contours which she could not see were raised out there, dense and heraldic? Once there was a gleam from their lights on the walls of a tunnel, from the everlasting springs that the tunnelers had cut. Should they ever have started, those tunnelers? Sometimes there were sparks. She hung out into the wounded night a minute: let him wish her back.

"What do you do with yourself in England, keep busy?" said the man from Wales, pointing the stem of his pipe at the man from Connemara.

"I do, I raise birds in Sussex, if you're asking my hobby."

"A terrific din, I daresay. Birds keep you awake all night?"

"On the contrary. Never notice it for a minute. Of course there are the birds that engage in conversation rather than sing. I might be listening to the conversation."

"Parrots, you mean. You have parrots? You teach them to talk?"

"Budgies, man. Oh, I did have one that was a lovely talker, but curious, very strange and curious, in his habits of feeding."

"What was it he ate? How much would you ask for a bird like that?"

"Like what?"

"Parrot that could talk but didn't eat well, that you were just mentioning you had."

"That bird was an exception. Not for sale."

"Are you responsible for your birds?"

They all sat waiting while a tunnel banged.

"What do you mean responsible?"

"Responsible: you sell me a bird. Presently he doesn't talk or sing. Can I bring it back?"

"You cannot. That's God-given, lads."

"How old is the bird now? Good health?"

"Owing to conditions in England I could not get him the specialties he liked, and came in one morning to find the bird stiff. Still it's a nice hobby. Very interesting."

"Would you have got five pounds for this bird if you had found a customer for her? What was it the bird craved so?"

"'Twas a male, not on the market, and if there had been another man, that would sell him to you, 'twould have cost you eight pounds."

"Ah. He ate inappropriate food?"

"You might say he *could not get* inappropriate food. He was destroyed by a mortal appetite for food you'd call it unlikely for a bird to desire at all. Myself, I never raised a bird that thrived so, learned faster, and had more to say."

"You never tried to sell him."

"For one thing I could not afford to turn him loose in Sussex. I told my wife not to be dusting his cage without due caution, not to be talking to him so much herself, the way she did."

The Welshman looked at him. He said, "Well, he died."

"Pass by my house!" cried the man from Connemara. "And look in the window, as you'll likely do, and you'll see the bird—stuffed. You'll think he's alive at first. Open beak! Talking up to the last, like you or I that have souls to be saved."

"Souls: Is the leading church in Ireland Catholic, would you call Ireland a Catholic country?" The Welshman settled himself anew.

"I would, yes."

"Is there a Catholic church where you live, in your town?"

"There is."

"And you go?"

"I do."

"Suppose you miss. If you miss going to church, does the priest fine you for it?"

"Of course he does not! Father Lavery! What do you mean?"

"Suppose it's Sunday—tomorrow's Sunday—and you don't go to church. Would you have to pay a fine to the priest?"

The man from Connemara lowered his dark head; he glared at the lovers—for she had returned to her place. "Of course I would not!" Still he looked at the girl.

"Ah, in the windows black as they are, we do look almost like ghosts riding by," she breathed, looking past him.

He said at once, "A castle I know, you see them on the wall."

"What castle?" said the sweetheart.

"You mean what ghosts. First she comes, then he comes."

"In Connemara?"

"Ah, you've never been there. Late tomorrow night I'll be there. She comes first because she's mad, and he slow—got the dagger stuck in him, you see? Destroyed by her. She walks along, carries herself grand, not shy. Then he comes, unwilling, not touching with his feet—pulled through the air. By the dagger, you might say, like a hooked fish. Because they're a pair, himself and herself, sure as they was joined together —and while you look go leaping in the bright air, moonlight as may be, and sailing off together cozy as a couple of kites to start it again."

That girl's straight hair, cut like a little train to a point at the nape of her neck, her little pointed nose that came down in the one unindented line which began at her hair, her swimming, imagining eyes, held them all, like her lover, perfectly still. Love was amazement now. The lovers did not touch, for a thousand reasons, but that was one.

"Start what again?" said the Welshman. "Have you personally seen them?"

"I have, I'm no exception."

"Can you say who they might be?"

"Visit the neighborhood for yourself and there'll be those who can acquaint you with the gory details. Myself I'm acquainted with only the general idea of their character and disposition, formed after putting two and two together. Have you never seen a ghost, then?"

The Welshman gave a look as if he'd been unfairly struck, as if a question coming at him now in here was carrying things too far. But he only said, "Heard them."

"Ah, do keep it to yourself then, for the duration of the journey, and not go bragging, will you?" the young wife cried at him. "Irish ghosts are enough for some of us for the one night without mixing them up with the Welsh and them shrieking things, and just before all of us are going on the water except yourself."

"You don't mind the Lord and Lady Beagle now, do you? They shouldn't frighten you, they're lovely and married. Married still. Why, their names just come to me, did you hear that? Lord and Lady Beagle—like they sent in a card. Ha! Ha!" Again the man from Connemara tried to bring that singing laugh out of the frightened sweetheart, from whom he had not yet taken his glances away.

"Don't," the young wife begged him, forcing her eyes to his salver-like palm. "Those are wild, crazy names for ghosts."

"Well, what kind of ghosts do you think they ever are!" Their glances met through their laughter and remorse. She tossed her head.

"There ain't no ghosts," said Victor.

"Now suck this good orange," she whispered to him, as if he were being jealous.

"Here comes the bride," announced the Welshman.

"*Oh* my God." But what business was she of the Welshman's?

In came the lady in the raincoat beaming from her dinner, but he talked right around her hip. "Do you have to confess?" he said. "Regularly? Suppose you make a confession—swear words, lewd thoughts, or the like: *then* does the priest make you pay a fine?"

"Confession's free, why not?" remarked the lady, stepping over all their feet.

"You're a Catholic, too?" he said, as she hung above his knee.

And as they all closed their eyes she fell into his lap, right down on top of him. Even the dogs, now rushing along in the other direction, hung on the air a moment, their tongues out. Then one dog was inside with them. This greyhound flung herself forward, back, down to the floor, her tail slapped out like a dragon's. Her eyes gazed toward the confusion, and little bubbles of boredom and suspicion played under the skin of her jowls, puff, puff, puff, while wrinkles of various memories and agitations came and went on her forehead like little forks of lightning.

"Well, look what's with us," said the lover. "Here, lad, here, lad."

"That's Telephone Girl," said the lady in the raincoat, now on her feet and straightening herself with distant sweepings of both hands. "I was just in conversation with the keeper of those. Don't be getting her stirred up. She's a winner, he has it." She let herself down into the seat and spread a look on all of them as if she had always been too womanly for the place. Her mooning face turned slowly and met the Welshman's stern, strong glance: *he* appeared to be expecting some apology from some source.

" 'Tisn't everybody runs so fast and gets nothing for it in the end herself, either," said the lady. Telephone Girl shuddered, ate some crumbs, coughed.

"I'm ashamed to hear you saying that, she gets the glory,"

said the man from Connemara. "How many human beings of your acquaintance get half a dog's chance at glory?"

"You don't like dogs." The lady looked at him, bowing her head.

"They're not my element. That's not the way I'm made, no."

The man in charge rushed in, and out he and the dog shot together. Somebody closed the door; it was the Welshman.

"Now: what time of the night do you get to Cork?" he asked.

The lover spoke, unexpectedly. "Tomorrow morning." The girl let out a long breath after him.

"What time of the morning?"

"Nine!" shouted everybody but the American.

"Travel all night," he said.

"Book a berth in Fishguard!"

The mincing woman with the red-haired baby boy passed—the baby with his same fat, enchanted squint looked through the glass at them.

"Oh, I always get seasick!" cried the young wife in fatalistic enthusiastic tones, only distantly watching the baby, who, although he stretched his little hand against the glass, was not being kidnaped now. She leaned over to tell the young girl, "Let me only step off the train at Fishguard and I'm dying already."

"What do you usually do for an attack of seasickness when you're on the Cork boat?"

"*I* just stay in one place and never move, that's what *I* do!" she cried, the smile that had never left her sad, sweet lips turned upon them all. "I don't try to move at all and I die all the way." Victor edged a little away from her.

"The boat rocks," suggested the Welshman. Victor edged away from him.

"The *Innisfallen*? Of course she rocks, there's a far, wide sea, very deep and treacherous, and very historic." The man from Connemara folded his arms.

"It takes six weeks, don't you think?" The young wife appealed to them all. "To get over the journey. I tell me husband, a fortnight is never enough. Me husband is English, though. I've never liked England. I have six aunts all living there, too. Me mother's sisters." She smiled. "They all are hating it. Me grandmother died while she was in England."

His cheeks sunk on his fists, Victor leaned forward over his knees. His hair, blue-black, whorled around the cowlick like a spinning gramophone record; he seemed to dream of being down on the ground, and fighting somebody on it.

"God rest her soul," said the lady in the raincoat, as if she might have passed through the goods car and seen where Grandmother was riding with them, to her grave in Ireland; but in that case the young wife would have been with the dead, and not playing at mother with Victor.

"Then how much does the passage cost you? Fishguard to Cork, Cork back to Fishguard? I may decide to try it on holiday sometime."

"Where are you leaving us this night?" asked the young wife, still in the voice in which she had spoken of her grandmother and her mother's sisters.

He gave out a name to make her look more commiserating, and repeated, "What is the fare from Fishguard to Cork?"

They stopped just then at a dark station and a paper boy's voice called his papers into the train.

"*Oh* my God. Where are we!"

The Welshman put up his finger and called for a paper, and one was brought inside to him by a strange, dark child.

At the sight of the man opening his newspaper, the lady in the raincoat spoke promptly and with her lips wooden, like an actress. "How did the race come out?"

"What's that? Race? What race would that be?" He gave her that look he gave her the time she sat down on him. He stretched and rattled his paper without exposing it too widely to anybody.

She tilted her head. "Little Boy Blue, yes," she murmured over his shoulder.

A discussion of Little Boy Blue arose while he kept on reading.

"How much money at a time do you bet on the races?" the Welshman asked suddenly, coming out from behind the paper. Then as suddenly he retreated, taking back the question entirely.

"Now the second race," murmured the lady in the raincoat.

Everybody wreathed in the Welshman. He was in the middle of the Welsh news, silent as the dead.

The man from Connemara put up a hand as the page might have been turned, "Long Gone the favorite! You were long gone yourself," he added politely to the lady in the raincoat. Possibly she had been punished enough for going out to eat and coming in to fall down all over a man.

"Yes I was," she said, lifting her chin; she brought out a Player and lighted it herself. She puffed. "'Twas a long way, twelve cars. 'Twas a lovely dinner—chicken. One man rose up in the aisle when it was put before him and gave a cry, 'It's rabbit!' "

They were pleased. The man from Connemara gave his high, free laugh. The lovers were strung like bows in silent laughter, but the lady blew a ring of smoke, at which Victor aimed an imaginary weapon.

"A lovely, long dinner. A man left us but returned to the car to say that while we were eating they shifted the carriages about and he had gone up the train, down the train, and could not find himself at all." Her voice was so moody and remote now it might be some wandering of long ago she spoke to them about.

The Welshman said, over his paper, "Shifted the carriages?" All laughed the harder.

"He said his carriage was gone, yes. From where he had left it: he hoped to find it yet, but I don't think he has. He came back the second time to the dining car and spoke about it. He laid his hand on the guard's arm. 'While I was sitting at the table and eating my dinner, the carriages have been shifted about,' he said. 'I wandered through the cars with the dogs running and cars with boxes in them, and through cars with human beings sitting in them I never laid eyes on in the journey—one party going on among some young people that would altogether block the traffic in the corridor.' "

"All Irish," said the young wife, and smoothed Victor's head; he looked big-eyed into space.

"The guard was busy and spoke to a third party, a gentleman eating. Yes, they were, all Irish. 'Will you mercifully take and show this gentleman where he is traveling, when you can, since he's lost?' 'Not lost,' he said, 'distracted,' and went through his system of argument. The gentleman said he could jolly well find his own carriage. The man opposite him rose up and that was when he declared the chicken was rabbit. The gentleman put down his knife and said man lost or not, carriage shifted or not, the stew rabbit or not, the man could just the same fight back to where he had come from, as he himself jolly well intended to do when he could finish the dinner on his plate in peace." She opened her purse, and passed licorice drops around.

"He sounds vulgar," said the man from Connemara.

"'Twas a lovely dinner."

"*You* weren't lost, I take it?" said the Welshman, accepting a licorice drop. "Traveled much?"

"Oh dear Heaven, traveled? Well, I have. Yes, no end to it."

"*Oh* my God."

"No, *I'm* never lost."

"Let's drop the subject," said the Welshman.

The lovers settled back into the cushions. They were the one subject nobody was going to discuss.

"Look," the young girl said in a low voice, from within the square of the young man's arm, but not to him. "I see a face that keeps going past, looking through the window. A man, plying up and down, could he be the one so unfortunate?"

"Not him, he's leading greyhounds, didn't we see him come in?" The young man spoke eagerly, to them all. "Leading, or they leading him."

"'Tis a long train," the lady murmured to the Welshman. "The longest, most populated train leaving England, I would suppose, the one going over to catch the *Innisfallen*."

"Is that the name of the boat? You were glad to leave England?"

"It is and I was—pleased to be starting my journey, pleased to have it over." She gave a look at him—then at the others, the compartment, the tumbled baggage, everything. Outside, dim Wales clapped strongly at the window, like some accompanying bird. "I'll just lower the shade, will I?" she said.

She pulled at the window shade and fastened it down, and pulled down the door shade after it. The minute she did that, the window shade flew up, with a noise like a turkey.

They shouted for joy—they knew it! She *was* funny.

The train stopped and waited a long time in the dark, out from nowhere. They sat awhile, swung their feet; the man from Connemara whistled for a minute marvelously, Victor had his third orange.

"Suppose we're late!" shouted the man from Connemara. The mountains could hear him; they had opened the window to look out hoping to see the trouble, but could not. "And the *Innisfallen* sails without us! And we don't reach the other side in this night!"

"Then you'll all have to spend the night in Fishguard," said the Welshman.

"Oh, what a scene there'll be in Cork, when we don't arrive!" cried the young wife merrily. "When the boat sails in without us, oh poor souls."

Victor laughed harshly. He had made a pattern with his orange peel on the window ledge, which he now swept away.

"There's none too much room for the traveler in the town of Fishguard," said the Welshman over his pipe. "You'll do best to keep dry in the station."

"Won't they *die* of it in Cork?" The young wife cocked her head.

"Me five brothers will stand ready to give me a beating!" Victor said, then looked proud.

"I daresay it won't be the first occasion you've put in the night homeless in Fishguard."

"In Fishguard?" warningly cried the man from Connemara. A scowl lit up his face and his eyes opened wide with innocence. "Didn't you know this was the boat train you're riding, man?"

"Oh, is that what you call it?" said the Welshman in equal innocence.

"They *hold* the boat for us. I feel it's safe to say that every soul on board this train saving yourself is riding to catch the boat."

"Hold the *Innisfallen* at Fishguard Harbor? For how long?"

"If need be till doomsday, but we are generally sailing at midnight."

"No sir, we'll never be left helpless in Fishguard, this or any other night," said the lady in the raincoat.

"Or!" cried the man from Connemara. "Or! We could take the other boat if we're as late as that, to Rosslare, oh my God! And spend the Sunday bringing ourselves back to Cork!"

"You're going to Connemara to see your mother," the young wife said psychically.

"I'm sure as God's truth staying the one night in Cork first!" he shouted across at her, and banged himself on the knees, as if they were trying to take Cork away from him.

The Welshman asked, "What is the longest on record they have ever held the boat?"

"Who knows?" said the lady in the raincoat. "Maybe 'twill be tonight."

"Only can I get out now and see where we've stopped?" asked Victor.

"*Oh* my God—we've started! *Oh* that Cork City!"

"When you travel to Cork, do the lot of you generally get seasick?" inquired the Welshman, swaying among them as they got under way.

The lady in the raincoat made him a grand gesture with one hand, and rose and pulled down her suitcase. She opened it and fetched out from beneath the hot water bottle in pink flannel a little pasteboard box.

"What's that going to be—pills for seasickness?" he said.

She lifted the lid and passed the box under his eyes and then under their eyes, although too fast to be quite offering anything. " 'Tis a present," she said. "A present of seasick pills, given me for the journey."

The lovers smiled simultaneously, as they would at the thought of any present.

The train stopped again, started; stopped, started. Here on the outer edge of Wales it advanced and hesitated as rhythmically and as interminably as a needle in a hem. The wheels had taken on that defenseless sound peculiar to running near the open sea. Oil lamps burned in their little boxes at the halts; there was a pull at the heart from the feeling of the trees all being bent the same way.

"*Now* where?" They had stopped again.

A sigh escaped the lovers, who had drawn a breath of the

sea. A single lamp stared in at their window, like the eye of a dragon lifted out of the lid of sleep.

"It's my station!" The Welshman suddenly addressed himself. He reared up, banged down the bushes on his head under a black hat, collected his suitcase and overcoat, and almost swept away with it the parcel with the "Wee Cottage" in it, belonging to the young wife. He got past them, dragging his suitcase with a great heave of the shoulder—God knew what was inside. He wrenched open the door, turned and looked at the lot of them, and then gently backed down into the outdoors.

Only to reappear. He had mistaken the station after all. But he simply held his ground there in the doorway, brazening it out as the train darted on.

"I may decide on raising my own birds some day," he said in a somewhat louder voice. "What did you begin with, a cock and a hen?"

On the index finger which the man from Connemara raised before he answered was a black fingernail, like the mark of a hammer blow; it might have been a reminder not to do something or other before he got home to Ireland.

"I would advise you to begin with a cock and two hens. Don't go into it without getting advice."

"What did you start with?"

"Six cocks—"

Another dark station, and down the Welshman dropped.

"And six hens!"

It was almost too much that his face rose there *again*. He wasn't embarrassed at himself, any more than he was by how black and all impenetrable it was outside in Wales, and asked, "Do you have to produce a passport to go into Ireland?"

"Certainly, a passport or a travel card. *Oh* my God."

"What do you mean by a travel card? Let me see yours. Every one of you carry one with you?"

Travel cards and passports were produced and handed up to him.

"Oh, how beautiful your mother is!" cried the young wife to Victor, over his shoulder. "Is that a wee strawberry mark she has there on her cheek?"

" 'Tis!" he cried in agony.

The Welshman was holding the American's different-looking passport open in his hand; she looked startled, herself, that she had given it up and at once, as if this were required and he had waked her up in the night. He read out her name, nationality, age, her husband's name, nationality. It was not that he read it officially—worse: as if it were a poem in the paper, only with the last verse missing.

"My husband is a photographer. We've made a little dark-room in our flat," she told him.

But he all at once turned back and asked the man from Connemara, "And you give it as your opinion your prize bird died of longings for food from far away."

"There've been times when I've dreamed a certain *person* may have had more to do with it!" the man from Connemara cried in crescendo. "That I've never mentioned till now. But women are jealous and uncertain creatures, I've been thinking as we came this long way along tonight."

"Of *birds*!" cried the young wife, her fingers going to her shoulders.

"Name your poison."

"Why birds?"

"Why not?"

"Because it talked?"

"Name your poison."

Another lantern, another halt of the train.

"It'll be raining over the water," the Welshman called as he swung open his door. From the step he looked back and said, "What do you take the seasick pills in, have you drink to take them in?"

"I have."

He said out of the windy night, "Can you buy drink on board the ship? Or is it not too late for that?"

"Three miles out 'tis only the sea and glory," shouted the man from Connemara.

"Be good," the Welshman tossed back at him, and quite lightly he dropped away. He disappeared for the third time into the Welsh black, this time for keeps. It was as though a big thumb had snuffed him out.

They smoothed and straightened themselves behind him,

all but the young lovers spreading out in the seats; she rubbed her arm, up and down. Not a soul had inquired of that poor vanquished man what he did, if he had wife and children living—he might have only had an auntie. They never let him tell what he was doing with himself in either end of Wales, or why he had to come on this very night, or even what in the world he was carrying in that heavy case.

As they talked, the American girl laid her head back, a faint smile on her face.

"Just one word of advice," said the man from Connemara in her ear, putting her passport, warm from his hand, into hers. "Be careful in future who you ask questions of. You were safe when you spoke to me, I'm a married man. I was pleased to tell you what I could—go to Killarney and so forth and so on, see the marvelous beauty of the lakes. But next time ask a guard."

Victor's head tumbled against the watchful side of the young wife, his right hand was flung in her lap, a fist floating away. In Fishguard, they had to shake him awake and pull him out into the rain.

No traveler out of that compartment was, actually, booked for a berth on the *Innisfallen* except the lady in the raincoat, who marched straight off. Most third-class train passengers spent the night third-class in the *Innisfallen* lounge. The man from Connemara was the first one stretched, a starfish of exhaustion, on a cretonne-covered couch. The American girl stared at a page of her book, then closed it until they were under way. The lovers disappeared. In the deeps of night that bright room reached some vortex of quiet, like a room where all brains are at work and great decisions are on the brink. Occasionally there was a tapping, as of drumming fingernails—that meant to closed or hypnotized eyes that dogs were being sped through. The random, gentle old men who were walking the corridors in their tweeds and seemed lost as Jesus's lambs, were waiting perhaps for the bar to open. The young wife, as desperate as she'd feared, saw nothing, forgot everything, and even abandoned Victor, as if there could never be any time or place in the world but this of her suffering. She spoke to the child as if she had never seen him before and would never see him again. Victor took the last little paper of biscuits she had given him away to a corner and slowly emptied it, making a mountain of the crumbs; then he bent his head over his travel card with its new stamp, on which presently he rolled his cheek and floated unconscious.

Once the man from Connemara sat up out of his sleep and stared at the American girl pinned to her chair across the room, as if he saw somebody desperate who had left her husband once, endangered herself among strangers, been turned back, and was here for the second go-round, asking again for a place to stay in Cork. She stared back motionless, until he was a starfish again.

Then it was morning—a world of sky coursing above, streaming light. The *Innisfallen* had entered the Lee. Almost at arm's reach were the buff, pink, gray, salmon fronts of houses, trees shining like bird wings, and bells that jumped toward sound as the ship, all silent, flowed past. The Sunday, the hour, too, were encroaching-real. Each lawn had a flag-like purity that braved and invited all the morning senses, even smell, as snow can—as if snow had fallen in the night, and this sun and this ship had come to trace it and melt it.

It was that passing, short, yet inviolate distance between ship and land on both sides that made an arrow-like question in the heart. Someone cried at random, "What town is this?" Any of them should have known, but the senses waked back home can fill too full, until black lines and framework vanish like names, leaving only shapes of light and color without knowledge or memory to inform them.

To wake up to the river, no longer the sea! There was more than one little town, that in their silent going they saluted while not touching or deviating to it at all. After the length of the ship had passed a ringing steeple, and the hands had glinted gold at them from the clockface, an older, harsher, more distant bell rang from an inland time: *now*.

Now sea gulls paced city lawns. *They* moved through the hedges, the ship in the garden. A thrush could be heard singing, and there he sang—so clear and so early it all was. On deck a little girl clapped her hands. "Why do you do that!" her brother lovingly encouraged her.

On shore a city street appeared, and now cars were following the ship along; passengers inside blew auto horns and waved handkerchiefs up and down. There was a sidewise sound of a harmonica, frantic, tiny and bold. Victor was up where he ought not to be on deck, handing out black frowns and tunes to the docks sliding into sight. Now he had to look out for his brothers. Perhaps deep in the lounge his guardian was now sleeping at last, white and exhausted, inhumanly smiling in her sleep.

The lovers stood on the lower, more shaded deck—two backs. A line of sun was between them like a thread that could be picked off. One ought not yet to look into their faces, watching water. How far, how deep was this day to cut into their hearts? From now on everything would cut deeper than yesterday. Her wintry boots stiff from their London wet looked big on the ship, pricked with ears, at that brink of light they hung over. And suddenly she changed position—one shoe tapped, pointing, back of the other. She poised there. The boat whistle thundered like a hundred organ notes, but she did not quake—now as used to boat whistles as one of the sea gulls; or as far away.

"There's a bride on board!" called somebody. "Look at her, look!"

Sure enough, a girl who had not yet showed herself in public now appeared by the rail in a white spring hat and, over her hands, a little old-fashioned white bunny muff. She stood there all ready to be met, now come out in her own sweet time. Delight gathered all around, singing began on board, bells could by now be heard ringing urgently in the town. Surely that color beating in their eyes came from flags hung out up the looming shore. The bride smiled but did not look up; she was looking down at her dazzling little fur muff.

They were in, the water held still about them. The gulls converged; just under the surface a newspaper slowly went down with its drowned news.

In the crowd of the dock, the lady in the raincoat was being confronted with a flock of beautiful children—red flags in their cheeks, caps on their heads, little black boots like pipes—and by a man bigger than she was. He stood smoking while the children hurled themselves up against her. As people hurried around her carrying their bundles and bags in the windy bright of the Cork dock, she stood camouflaged like a sportsman in his own polychrome fields, a hand on her striped hip. Vague, luminous, smiling, her big white face held a moment and bent down for its kiss. The man from Connemara strode by, looking down on her as if now her head were in the basket. His cap set at a fairly desperate angle, he went leaping into the streets of Cork City.

Victor was shouting at the top of his lungs, "Here I am!" The young wife, coming forth old but still alive, was met by old women in cloaks, three young men to embrace her, and a donkey and cart to ride her home, once she had put Victor with his brothers.

Perhaps regardless of the joy or release of an arrival, or because of it, there is always for someone a last-minute, fingerlike touch, a reminder, a promise of confusion. Behind shut lids the American girl saw the customs' chalk mark just now scrawled on the wall of her suitcase. Like a gypsy's sign found on her own front door, it stared at her from the sensitized optic dark, and she felt exposed—as if, in spite of herself, when she didn't know it, something had been told on her. "A rabbit ran over my grave," she thought. She left her suitcase in the parcel room and walked out into Cork.

When it rained late in that afternoon, the American girl was still in Cork, and stood sheltering in the doorway of a pub. She was listening to the pub sounds and the alley sounds as she might to a garden's and a fountain's.

She had had her day, her walk, that began at the red, ferny, echo-hung rock against which the lowest houses were set, where the ocean-river sent up signals of mirrored light. She had walked the hill and crossed the swan-bright bridges, her way wound in among people busy at encounters, meetings, it seemed to her reunions. After church in the streets of Cork dozens of little girls in confirmation dresses, squared off by their veils into animated paper snowflakes, raced and danced out of control and into charmed traffic—like miniature and more conscious brides. The trees had almost rushed with light and blossom; they nearly had sound, as the bells did. Boughs that rocked on the hill were tipped and weighted as if with birds, which were really their own bursting and almost-bursting leaves. In all Cork today every willow stood with gold-red hair springing and falling about it, like Venus alive. Rhododendrons swam in light, leaves and flowers alike; only a shadow could separate them into colors. She had felt no lonelier than that little bride herself, who had come off the boat. Yes, somewhere in the crowd at the dock there must have been a young man holding flowers: he had been taken for granted.

In the future would the light, that had jumped like the man from Connemara into the world, be a memory, like that of a meeting, or must there be mere faith that it had been like that?

Shielding the telegraph-form from her fellow writers at the post-office table, she printed out to her husband in England, "England was a mistake." At once she scratched that out, and took back the blame but without words.

Love with the joy being drawn out of it like anything else that aches—that was loneliness; not this. *I* was nearly destroyed, she thought, and again was threatened with a light head, a rush of laughter, as when the Welshman had come so far with them and then let them off.

If she could never tell her husband her secret, perhaps she would never tell it at all. You must never betray pure joy—the kind you were born and began with—either by hiding it or by parading it in front of people's eyes; they didn't want to be shown it. And still you must tell it. Is there no way? she thought—for here I am, this far. I see Cork's streets take off from the waterside and rise lifting their houses and towers like note above note on a page of music, with arpeggios running over it of green and galleries and belvederes, and the bright sun raining at the top. Out of the joy I hide for fear it is promiscuous, I may walk for ever at the fall of evening by the river, and find this river street by the red rock, this first, last house, that's perhaps a boarding house now, standing full-face to the tide, and look up to that window—that upper window, from which the mystery will never go. The curtains dyed so many times over are still pulled back and the window looks out open to the evening, the river, the hills, and the sea.

For a moment someone—she thought it was a woman—came and stood at the window, then hurled a cigarette with its live coal down into the extinguishing garden. But it was not the impatient tenant, it was the window itself that could tell her all she had come here to know—or all she could bear this evening to know, and that was light and rain, light and rain, dark, light, and rain.

"Don't expect me back yet" was all she need say tonight in the telegram. What was always her trouble? "You hope for too much," he said.

When early this morning the bride smiled, it might almost have been for her photograph; but she still did not look up—as though if even her picture were taken, she would vanish. And now she had vanished.

Walking on through the rainy dusk, the girl again took shelter in the warm doorway of the pub, holding her message, unfinished and unsent.

"Ah, it's a heresy, I told him," a man inside was shouting, out of the middle of his story. A barmaid glimmered through the passage in her frill, a glad cry went up at her entrance, as if she were the heresy herself, and when they all called out something fresh it was like the signal for a song.

The girl let her message go into the stream of the street, and opening the door walked into the lovely room full of strangers.

Ladies in Spring

THE PAIR moved through that gray landscape as though no one would see them—dressed alike in overalls and faded coats, one big, one little, one black-headed, one tow-headed, father and son. Each carried a cane fishing pole over his shoulder, and Dewey carried the bucket in his other hand. It was a soft, gray, changeable day overhead—the first like that, here in the month of March.

Just a quarter of an hour before, Dewey riding to school in the school bus had spotted his father walking right down the road, the poles on his shoulder—two poles. Dewey skimmed around the schoolhouse door, and when his father came walking through Royals, he was waiting at the tree by the post office.

"Scoot. Get on back in the schoolhouse. You been told," said his father.

In a way, Dewey would have liked to obey that: Miss Pruitt had promised to read them about *Excalibur*. What had made her go and pick today?

"But I can see you're bound to come," said his father. "Only we ain't going to catch us no fish, because there ain't no water left to catch 'em in."

"The river!"

"All but dry."

"You been many times already?"

"Son, this is my first time this year. Might as well keep still about it at home."

The sky moved, soft and wet and gray, but the ground underfoot was powder dry. Where an old sycamore had blown over the spring before, there was turned up a tough round wall of roots and clay all white, like the moon on the ground. The river had not backed up into the old backing places. Vines, leafless and yet abundant and soft, covered the trees and thickets as if rainclouds had been dropped down from the sky over them. The swamp looked gray and endless as pictures in the Bible; wherever Dewey turned, the world held perfectly still for moments at a time—then a heron would pump through.

"Papa, what's that lady doing?"

"Why, I believe that's Miss Hattie Purcell on foot ahead."

"Is she supposed to be way out here?"

"Miss Hattie calls herself a rainmaker, son. She could be at it. We sure can use the rain. She's most generally on hand at the post office."

"I know now." He opened his mouth.

"Don't be so apt to holler," said his father. "We may can keep to the rear of her, if we try good."

The back of Miss Hattie rose up a little steep place, her black hat sharp above the trees. She was ahead of them by a distance no longer than the street of Royals. Her black coat was a roomy winter one and hung down in the back to her ankles, when it didn't catch on things. She was carrying, like a rolling pin, a long furled umbrella, and moved straight forward in some kind of personal zigzag of a walk—it would be hard to pass *her*.

Now Miss Hattie dipped out of sight into a gully.

"Miss Hattie's making a beeline, ain't she," said Dewey's father. "Look at her go. Let's you and me take us a plain *path*."

But as they came near the river in a little while, Dewey pointed his finger. Fairly close, through the trees, they saw a big strong purse with a handle on it like a suitcase, set down on the winter leaves. Another quiet step and they could see Miss Hattie. There on the ground, with her knees drawn up the least bit, skirt to her ankles, coat spread around her like a rug, hat over her brow, steel glasses in her hand, sat Miss Hattie Purcell, bringing rain. She did not even see them.

Miss Hattie brought rain by sitting a vigil of the necessary duration beside the nearest body of water, as everybody knew. She made no more sound at it than a man fishing. But something about the way Miss Hattie's comfort shoes showed their tips below her skirt and carried a dust of the dry woods on them made her look as though she'd be there forever: longer than they would.

His father made a sign to Dewey, and they got around Miss Hattie there and went on.

"This is where I had in mind the whole time," he said.

It was where there was an old, unrailed, concrete bridge across the Little Muscadine. A good jump—an impossible jump—separated the bridge from land, for the Old Road—overgrown, but still coming through the trees this far—fell away into a sandy ravine when it got to the river. The bridge stood out there high on its single foot, like a table in the water.

There was a sign, "Cross at Own Risk," and a plank limber as a hammock laid across to the bridge floor. Dewey ran the plank, ran the bridge's length, and gave a cry—it was an island.

The bearded trees hung in a ring around it all, the Little Muscadine without a sound threaded through the sand among fallen trees, and the two fishermen sat on the bridge, halfway across, baited their hooks from the can of worms taken out of a pocket, and hung their poles over the side.

They didn't catch anything, sure enough.

About noon, Dewey and his father stopped fishing and went into a lunch of biscuits and jelly the father took out of another pocket.

"This bridge don't belong to nobody," his father said, then. "It's just going begging. It's a wonder somebody don't stretch a tent over this good floor and live here, high and dry. You could have it clean to yourself. Know you could?"

"Me?" asked Dewey.

His father faintly smiled and ate a biscuit before he said, "You'd have to ask your ma about it first."

"There's another one!" said Dewey.

Another lady had dared to invade this place. Over the water and through the trees, on the same side of the river they'd come from, her face shone clear as a lantern light in nighttime. She'd found them.

"Blackie?" she called, and a white arm was lifted too. The sound was like the dove-call of April or May, and it carried as unsurely as something she had tried to throw them across that airy distance.

Blackie was his father's name, but he didn't answer. He sat just as he was, out in the open of the bridge, both knees pointed up blue, a biscuit with a bite gone out of it in his hand.

Then the lady turned around and disappeared into the trees.

Dewey could easily think she had gone off to die. Or if she hadn't, she would have had to die there. It was such a complaint she sent over, it was so sorrowful. And about what but death would ladies, anywhere, ever speak with such soft voices—then turn and run? Before she'd gone, the lady's face had been white and still as magic behind the trembling willow boughs that were the only bright-touched thing.

"I think she's gone," said Dewey, getting to his feet.

Turtles now lay on logs sticking up out of the low water, with their small heads raised. An old log was papped with baby turtles. Dewey counted fourteen, seven up one side and seven down the other. Just waiting for rain, said his father. On a giant log was a giant turtle, gray-tailed, the size of a dishpan, set at a laughable angle there, safe from everybody and everything.

With lunch over, they still didn't catch anything. And then the lady looked through the willow boughs again, in nearly the same place. She was giving them another chance.

She cupped her hands to her silent lips. She meant "Blackie!"

"Blackie!" There it was.

"You hold still," said his father. "She ain't calling you."

Nobody could hold so still as a man named Blackie.

That mysterious lady never breathed anything but the one word, and so softly then that it was all the word could do to travel over the water; still his father never said anything back, until she disappeared. Then he said, "Blackie yourself."

He didn't even bait his hook or say any longer what he would do to the fish if they didn't hurry up and change their minds. Yet when nothing came up on the hook, he looked down at his own son like a stranger cast away on this bridge from the long ago, before it got cut off from land.

Dewey baited his hook, and the first thing he knew he'd caught a fish.

"What is it, what is it?" he shouted.

"You got you a little goggle-eye there, son."

Dewey, dancing with it—it was six inches long and jumping

on the hook—hugged his father's neck and said, "Well—ready to go?"

"No . . . Best not to stay either too long or too little-bit. I favor tarrying awhile," said his father.

Dewey sat back down, and gazed up at his father's solemn side-face—then followed the look his father shot across the river like a fishing line of great length, one that took hold.

Across the river the lady looked out for the third time. She was almost out of the willows now, on the sand. She put the little shells of her hands up to her throat. What did that mean? It was the way she'd pull her collar together if she'd been given a coat around her. It was about to rain. She knew as well as they did that people were looking at her hard; but she must not feel it, Dewey felt, or surely people would have to draw their looks away, and not fasten her there. She didn't have even one word to say, this time.

The bay tree that began moving and sighing over her head was the tall slender one Dewey had picked as his marker. With its head in a stroke of sun, it nodded like a silver flower. There was a little gentle thunder, and Dewey knew that her eyes shut, as well as he would know even in his sleep when his mother put down the windows in their house if a rain was coming. That way, she stood there and waited. And Dewey's father—whose sweat Dewey took a deep breath of as he stood up beside him—believed that the one *that* lady waited for was never coming over the bridge to her side, any more than she would come to his.

Then, with a little sound like a mouse somewhere in the world, a scratch, then a patter like many mice racing—and then at last the splash on Dewey's cheek—it simply began raining. Dewey looked all around—the river was dancing.

"Run now, son! Run for cover! It's fixing to pour down! I'll be right behind you!" shouted his father, running right past him and then jumping over the side of the bridge. Arms and legs spread wide as surprise itself he did a grand leap to the sand. But instead of sheltering under the bridge, he kept going, and was running up the bank now, toward Royals. Dewey resigned himself to go the same way. As for the lady, if she was still where they left her, about to disappear perhaps, she was getting wet.

They ran under the sounding trees and vines. It came down in earnest, feeling warm and cool together, a real spring shower.

"Trot under here!" called a pre-emptory voice.

"Miss Hattie! Forgot she was anywhere near," said Dewey's father, falling back. "Now we got to be nice to *her*."

"Good evening, Lavelle."

At that name, Dewey fell back, but his father went on. Maybe he was getting used to being called, today, and it didn't make any difference what name he got, by now.

Something as big as a sail came out through the brambles.

"Did you hear me?" said Miss Hattie—there she stood. "Get you both under this umbrella. I'm going straight back to town, and I'll take you with me. Can't take your fishing poles, unless you drag 'em."

"Yes'm," they said, and got under.

Starting forward, Miss Hattie held her own umbrella, a man with her or not, branches of trees coming or not, and the harder the rain fell the more energetically she held to the handle. There were little cowlicks of damp standing up all around the black fur of her collar. Her spectacles were on her nose, and both windows had drops all over them like pearls. Miss Hattie's coat tapered up like one tent, and the umbrella spread down like another one. They marched abreast or single file, as the lay of the land allowed, but always politely close together under the umbrella, either despising paths or taking a path so fragrant and newly slick it didn't seem familiar. But there was an almost forgotten landmark of early morning, boarded twin towers of a colored church, set back closet-like in the hanging moss. Dewey thought he knew where he was. Suddenly frogs from everywhere let loose on the world, as if they'd been wound up.

In no time, Miss Hattie brought them to the edge of the woods. Next they were at the gravel road and walking down the middle of it. The turn was coming where Royals could be seen spread out from Baptist church to schoolhouse.

Dewey, keeping watch around Miss Hattie's skirt, saw the lady appear in the distance behind them, running like a ghost across the road in the shining rain—shining, for the sun had looked through.

"The Devil is beating his wife," said Miss Hattie in a professional voice.

There ran the figure that the rain sheathed in a spinning cocoon of light—as if it ran in peril. It was cutting across Mr. Jep Royal's yard, where the Royals were all sitting inside the house and some cows as black as blackbirds came close and watched her go.

"Look at that, to the side," said Miss Hattie suddenly. "Who's that, young eyes?"

Dewey looked shyly under her forward sleeve and asked his father, "Reckon it's the lady?"

"Well, *call* her," said Miss Hattie. "Whoever she is, she can trot under this umbrella just as easy as we can. It's good size."

"La-dy!"

That was Dewey, hollering.

They stood and waited for the lady to come across the pasture, though his father looked very black, trapped under the umbrella. Had Miss Hattie looked at him, that showed what his name was and how he got it.

But the lady, now opposite, in a whole field of falling light, was all but standing still. Starting here, starting there, wavering, retreating, she made no headway at all. Then abruptly she disappeared into the Royals' pear orchard—this time for good.

"Maybe somebody new has escaped from the lunatic asylum," said Miss Hattie. "March."

On they went in the rain.

Opal Purcell slipped sideways through the elderberry bushes at the creek bank, with both hands laid, like a hat, on top of her head, and waited for them.

"Why, it's only my own niece," said Miss Hattie. "Trot under here, Opal. How do you like this rain?"

"Hey, Aunt Hat. Hey," said Opal to Dewey.

She was grown. Sometimes she waited on people in the Seed & Feed. She was plump as ever. She didn't look far enough around her aunt to speak to his father.

Miss Hattie touched Opal on the head. "Has it rained that much?" she said in a gratified way.

"I thought I saw you in the post office, Aunt Hat," objected Opal.

"I expect you did. I had the mail to tie up. I'm a fast worker when the case demands."

They were all compelled, of course, to keep up with Miss Hattie and stay with her and be company all the way back to town. Her black cotton umbrella lacked very little of being big enough for four, but it lacked some. Dewey gave Opal his place.

He marched ahead of them, still in step with his father, but out in the open rain, with his fish now let up high on its pole behind him. He felt the welcome plastering down of his hair on his forehead, and the relentless way the raindrops hit and bounced on him.

Opal Purcell had a look, to Dewey, as if she didn't know whether she was getting wet or not. It was his father's fishing look. And Miss Hattie's rainmaking look. He was the only one—out here in the rain itself—that didn't have it.

Like a pretty lady's hand, to tilt his face up a little and make him smile, deep satisfaction, almost love came down and touched him.

"Miss Hattie," he turned walking and said over his shoulder, "I caught me a goggle-eye perch back yonder, see him? I wish I could give him to you—for your supper!"

"You good and wet, honey?" she said back, marching there in the middle.

The brightest thing in Royals—rain was the loudest, on all the tin roofs—was the empty school bus drawn up under the shed of the filling station. The movie house, high up on its posts, was magnesia-bottle blue. Three red hens waited on the porch. Dewey's and Opal's eyes together looked out of their corners at the "Coming Saturday" poster of the charging white horse. But Miss Hattie didn't dismiss them at the movie house.

They passed the Baptist church getting red as a rose, and the Methodist church getting streaky. In the middle of the first crossing, the water tank stood and they walked under; water from its bottom, black and cold as ice, fell a drop for each head as always. And they passed along the gin, which alone would sleep the spring out. All around were the well-known ditches and little gullies; there were the chinaberry trees, and some Negroes and some dogs underneath them; but it all looked like some different place to Dewey—not Royals. There was a line of faces under the roof of the long store porch, but they looked, white and black, like the faces of new people. Nevertheless, all spoke to Miss Hattie, Blackie, Opal, and Dewey by name; and from their umbrella—out in the middle of the road, where it was coming down hardest—Miss Hattie did the speaking back.

"It's the beginning!" she called. "I'd a heap rather see it come this way than in torrents!"

"We're real proud of you, Miss Hattie!"

"You're still a credit to Royals, Miss Hattie!"

"Don't you drown yourself out there!"

"Oh, I won't," said Miss Hattie.

At the bank corner, small spotty pigs belonging to nobody, with snouts as long as corncobs, raced out in a company like clowns with the Circus, and ran with Dewey and Miss Hattie and all, for the rest of the way. There was one more block, and that was where the post office was. Also the Seed & Feed, and the schoolhouse beyond, and the Stave Mill Road; and also home was that way.

"Well, good-by, everybody," said Miss Hattie, arrived at the post office tree.

Dewey's father—the darkest Coker of the family, much darker than Uncle Lavelle, who had run off a long time ago, by Dewey's reckoning—bowed himself out backwards from under the umbrella and straightened up in the rain.

"Much obliged for the favor, Miss Hattie," he said. With a quiet hand he turned over his fishing pole to Dewey, and was gone.

"Thank you, ma'am, I enjoyed myself," said Dewey.

"You're wet as a drowned rat," said Miss Hattie admiringly.

Up beyond, the schoolhouse grew dim behind its silver yard. The bell mounted at the gate was making the sound of a bucket filling.

"I'll leave you with the umbrella, Opal. Opal, run home," said Miss Hattie, pointing her finger at Opal's chest, "and put down the south windows, and bring in the quilts and dry them out again before the fire. I can't tell you why I forgot clean about my own windows. You might stand on a chair and find a real pretty quart of snapbeans and put them on with that little piece of meat out of the safe. Run now. Where've you been?"

"Nowheres.—Hunting poke salad," said Opal, making a little face twice. She had wet cheeks, and there was a blue violet in her dress, hanging down from a buttonhole, and no coat on her back of any kind.

"Then dry yourself," said Miss Hattie. *"What's that?"*

"It's the train whistle," said Dewey.

Far down, the mail train crossed the three long trestles over Little Muscadine swamp like knocking three knocks at the door, and blew its whistle again through the rain.

Miss Hattie never let her powers interfere with mail time, or mail time interfere with her powers. She had everything worked out. She pulled open the door of her automobile, right there. There on the back seat was her mail sack, ready to go.

Miss Hattie lived next door—where Opal had now gone inside—and only used her car between here and the station; it stayed under the post office tree. Some day old Opal was going to take that car, and ride away. Miss Hattie climbed up inside.

The car roared and took a leap out into the rain. At the corner it turned, looking two stories high, swinging wide as Miss Hattie banked her curve, with a lean of her whole self deep to the right. She made it. Then she sped on the diagonal to the bottom of the hill and pulled up at the station just in time for Mr. Frierson to run out in his suspenders and hand the mail as the train rushed through. It hooked the old sack and flung off the new to Royals.

The rain slacked just a little on Miss Hattie while she hauled the mail uphill. Dewey stamped up the post office runway by her side to help her carry it in—the post office used to be a stable. He held the door open, they went inside, and the rain slammed down behind them.

"Dewey Coker?"

"Ma'am?"

"Why aren't you in school?"

In a sudden moment she dropped the sack and rubbed his head—just any old way—with something out of her purse; it might have been a dinner napkin. He rubbed cornbread crumbs as sharp as rocks out of his eye. Across the road, while this drying was happening, a wonderful white mule that had gotten into the cemetery and rolled himself around till he was green and white like a marble monument, got up to his feet and shivered and shook the raindrops everywhere.

"I may can still go," he said dreamily. *"Excalibur—"*

"Nonsense! Don't you see that rain?" cried Miss Hattie. "You'll stay here in this post office till I tell you."

The post office inside was a long bare room that looked and smelled like a covered bridge, with only a little light at the other end where Miss Hattie's window was. Dewey had never stayed inside here more than a minute at a time, in his life.

"You make yourself at home," said Miss Hattie, and disappeared into the back.

Dewey stood the poles by the front door and kept his fish in his hand on the bit of line, while Miss Hattie put up the mail. After she had put it all up as she saw fit, then she gave it out: pretty soon here came everybody. There was a lot of conversation through the window.

"Sure is a treat, Miss Hattie! Only wish it didn't have to stop."

"It looks like a gully washer to me, Miss Hat!"

And someone leaned down and said to Dewey, "Hi, Dewey! I saw you! And what was *you* up to this evening?"

"It's a beginning," was all Miss Hattie would say. "I'll go back out there tomorrow, if I have the time, and if I live and don't nothing happen, and do some more on it. But depends on the size of the mail."

After everybody had shed their old letters and papers on the floor and tracked out, there would have been silence everywhere but for the bombardment on the roof. Miss Hattie still didn't come out of her little room back there, of which Dewey could see nothing but the reared-back honeycomb of her desk with nine letters in the holes.

Out here, motes danced lazily as summer flies in the running green light of the cracks in the walls. The hole of a missing stovepipe high up was blocked with a bouquet of old newspapers, yellow as roses. It was a little chilly. It smelled of rain, of fish, of pocket money and pockets. Whether the lonely dangling light was turned on or off it was hard to see. Its bulb hung down fierce in a little mask like a biting dog.

On the high table against the wall there was an ink well and a pen, as in a school desk, and an old yellow blotter limp as biscuit dough. Reaching tall, he rounded up the pen and with a great deal of the ink drew a picture on the blotter. He drew his fish. He gave it an eye and then mailed it through the slot to Miss Hattie.

Presently he hung his chin on the little ledge to her window, to see if she got it.

Miss Hattie was asleep in her rocking chair. She was sitting up with her head inclined, beside her little gas stove. She had laid away her hat, and there was a good weight to her hair, which was shaped and colored like the school bell. She looked noble, as if waiting to have the headsman chop off her head. All was quietness itself. For the rain had stopped. The only sound was the peeping of baby chicks from the parcel post at her feet.

"Can I go now?" he hollered.

"Mercy!" she exclaimed at once. "Did it bite? Nothing for you today! Who's that? I wasn't asleep! Whose face is that smiling at me? For pity's sakes!" She jumped up and shook her dress—some leaves fell out. Then she came to the window and said through it, "You want to go leave me? Run then! Because if you dream it's stopped, child, I won't be surprised a bit if it don't turn around and come back."

At that moment the post office shook with thunder, as if horses ran right through it.

Miss Hattie came to the door behind him. He slid down the runway with all he had. She remained there looking out, nodding a bit and speaking a few words to herself. All she had to say to him was "Trot!"

It was already coming down again, with the sound of making up for the lapse that had just happened. As Dewey began to run, he caught a glimpse of a patchwork quilt going like a camel through the yard next door toward Miss Hattie's house. He supposed Opal was under it. Fifteen years later it occurred to him it had very likely been Opal in the woods.

Just in time, he caught and climbed inside the rolling school bus with the children in it, and rode home after all with the others, a sort of hero.

After the bus put him down, he ran cutting across under the charred pines. The big sky-blue violets his mother loved were blooming, wet as cheeks. Pear trees were all but in bloom under the purple sky. Branches were being jogged with the rush and commotion of birds. The Cokers' patch of mustard that had gone to seed shone like gold from here. Dewey ran under the last drops, through the hooraying mud of the pasture, and saw the corrugations of their roof shining across it like a fresh pan of cornbread sticks. His father was off at a distance, on his knees—back at mending the fences. Minnie Lee, Sue, and Annie Bess were ready for Dewey and came flocking from the door, with the baby behind on all fours. None of them could hope to waylay him.

His mother stood in the back lot. Behind her, blue and white, her morning wash hung to the ground, as wet as clouds. She stood with a switch extended most strictly over the head of the silky calf that drank from the old brown cow—as though this evening she knighted it.

"Whose calf will that be? Mine?" he cried out to her. It was to make her turn, but this time, he thought, her answer would be yes.

"You have to ask your pa, son."

"Why do you always tell me the same thing? *Mama!*"

Arm straight before him, he extended toward her dear face his fish—still shining a little, held up by its tail, its eye and its mouth as agape as any big fish's. She turned.

"Get away from me!" she shrieked. "You and your pa! Both of you get the sight of you clear away!" She struck with her little green switch, fanning drops of milk and light. "Get in the house. Oh! If I haven't had enough out of you!"

Days passed—it rained some more, sometimes in the night—before Dewey had time to go back and visit the bridge. He didn't take his fishing pole, he just went to see about it. The sky had cleared in the evening, after school and the work at home were done with.

The river was up. It covered the sandbars and from the

bridge he could no longer remember exactly how the driftwood had lain—only its upper horns stuck out of the water, where parades of brown bubbles were passing down. The gasping turtles had all dived under. The water must now be swimming with fish of all sizes and kinds.

Dewey walked the old plank back, there being no sand to drop down to. Then he visited above the bridge and wandered around in new places. They were drenched and sweet. The big fragrant bay was his marker.

He stood in the light of birdleg-pink leaves, yellow flower vines, and scattered white blooms each crushed under its drop of water as under a stone, the maples red as cinnamon drops and the falling, thready nets of willows, and heard the lonesomest sound in creation, an unknown bird singing through the very moment when he was the one that listened to it. Across the Little Muscadine the golden soldier-tassels of distant oaks filled with light, and there the clear sun dropped.

Before he got out of the river woods, it was nearly first-dark. The sky was pink and blue. The great moon had slid up in it, but not yet taken light, like the little plum tree that had sprung out in flower below. At that mysterious colored church, the one with the two towers and the two privies to the rear, that stood all in darkness, a new friend sat straight up on the top church step. Head to one side, little red tongue hanging out, it was a little black dog, his whole self shaking and alive from tip to tip. He might be part of the church, that was the way he acted. On the other hand, there was no telling where he might have come from.

Yet he had something familiar about him too. He had a look on his little pointed face—for all he was black; and was it he, or she?—that reminded Dewey of Miss Hattie Purcell, when she stood in the door of the post office looking out at the rain she'd brought and remarking to the world at large: "Well, I'd say that's right persnickety."

Circe

NEEDLE in air, I stopped what I was making. From the upper casement, my lookout on the sea, I saw them disembark and find the path; I heard that whole drove of mine break loose on the beautiful strangers. I slipped down the ladder. When I heard men breathing and sandals kicking the stones, I threw open the door. A shaft of light from the zenith struck my brow, and the wind let out my hair. Something else swayed my body outward.

"Welcome!" I said—the most dangerous word in the world.

Heads lifted to the smell of my bread, they trooped inside—and with such a grunting and frisking at their heels to the very threshold. Star-gazers! They stumbled on my polished floor, strewing sand, crowding on each other, sizing up the household for gifts (thinking already of sailing away), and sighted upwards where the ladder went, to the sighs of the island girls who peeped from the kitchen door. In the hope of a bath, they looked in awe at their hands.

I left them thus, and withdrew to make the broth.

With their tear-bright eyes they watched me come in with the great winking tray, and circle the room in a winding wreath of steam. Each in turn with a pair of black-nailed hands swept up his bowl. The first were trotting at my heels while the last still reached with their hands. Then the last drank too, and dredging their snouts from the bowls, let go and shuttled into the company.

That moment of transformation—only the gods really like it! Men and beasts almost never take in enough of the wonder to justify the trouble. The floor was swaying like a bridge in battle. "Outside!" I commanded. "No dirt is allowed in this house!" In the end, it takes phenomenal neatness of housekeeping to put it through the heads of men that they are swine. With my wand seething in the air like a broom, I drove them all through the door—twice as many hooves as there had been feet before—to join their brothers, who rushed forward to meet them now, filthily rivaling, but welcoming. What tusks I had given them!

As I shut the door on the sight, and drew back into my privacy—deathless privacy that heals everything, even the effort of magic—I felt something from behind press like the air of heaven before a storm, and reach like another wand over my head.

I spun round, thinking, O gods, it has failed me, it's drying up. Before everything, I think of my power. One man was left.

"What makes you think you're different from anyone else?" I screamed; and he laughed.

Before I'd believe it, I ran back to my broth. I had thought it perfect—I'd allowed no other woman to come near it. I tasted, and it was perfect—swimming with oysters from my reef and flecks of golden pork, redolent with leaves of bay and basil and rosemary, with the glass of island wine tossed in at the last: it has been my infallible recipe. Circe's broth: all the gods have heard of it and envied it. No, the fault had to be in the drinker. If a man remained, unable to leave that magnificent body of his, then enchantment had met with a hero. Oh, I know those prophecies as well as the back of my hand—only nothing is here to warn me when it is *now*.

The island girls, those servants I support, stood there in the kitchen and smiled at me. I threw kettle and all at their withering heels. Let them learn that unmagical people are put into the world to justify and serve the magical—not to smile at them!

I whirled back again. The hero stood as before. But his laugh had gone too, after his friends. His gaze was empty, as though I were not in it—I was invisible. His hand groped across the rushes of a chair. I moved beyond him and bolted the door against the murmurous outside. Still invisibly, I took away his sword. I sent his tunic away to the spring for washing, and I, with my own hands, gave him his bath. Then he sat and dried himself before the fire—carefully, the only mortal man on an island in the sea. I rubbed oil on his shadowy shoulders, and on the rope of curls in which his jaw was set. His rapt ears still listened to the human silence there.

"I know your name," I said in the voice of a woman, "and you know mine by now."

I took the chain from my waist, it slipped shining to the floor between us, where it lay as if it slept, as I came forth. Under my palms he stood warm and dense as a myrtle grove at noon. His limbs were heavy, braced like a sleep-walker's who has wandered, alas, to cliffs above the sea. When I passed before him, his arm lifted and barred my way. When I held up the glass he opened his mouth. He fell among the pillows, his still-open eyes two clouds stopped over the sun, and I lifted and kissed his hand.

It was he who in a burst of speech announced the end of day. As though the hour brought a signal to the wanderer, he told me a story, while the owl made comment outside. He told me of the monster with one eye—he had put out the eye, he said. Yes, said the owl, the monster is growing another, and a new man will sail along to blind it again. I had heard it all before, from man and owl. I didn't want his story, I wanted his secret.

When Venus leaned at the window, I called him by name, but he had talked himself into a dream, and his dream had him fast. I now saw through the cautious herb that had protected him from my broth. From the first, he had found some way to resist my power. He must laugh, sleep, ravish, he must talk and sleep. Next it would be he must die. I looked an age into that face above the beard's black crescent, the eyes turned loose from mine like the statues' that sleep on the hill. I took him by the locks of his beard and hair, but he rolled away with his snore to the very floor of sleep—as far beneath my reach as the drowned sailor dropped out of his, in the tale he told of the sea.

I thought of my father the Sun, who went on his divine way untroubled, ambitionless—unconsumed; suffering no loss, no heroic fear of corruption through his constant shedding of light, needing no story, no retinue to vouch for where he has been—even heroes could learn of the gods!

Yet I know they keep something from me, asleep and

awake. There exists a mortal mystery, that, if I knew where it was, I could crush like an island grape. Only frailty, it seems, can divine it—and I was not endowed with that property. They live by frailty! By the moment! I tell myself that it is only a mystery, and mystery is only uncertainty. (There is no mystery in magic! Men are swine: let it be said, and no sooner said than done.) Yet mortals alone can divine where it lies in each other, can find it and prick it in all its peril, with an instrument made of air. I swear that only to possess that one, trifling secret, I would willingly turn myself into a harmless dove for the rest of eternity!

When presently he leapt up, I had nearly forgotten he would move again—as a golden hibiscus startles you, all flowers, when you are walking in some weedy place apart.

Yes, but he would not dine. Dinner was carried in, but he would not dine with me until I would undo that day's havoc in the pigsty. I pointed out that his portion was served in a golden bowl—the very copy of that bowl my own father the Sun crosses back in each night after his journey of the day. But he cared nothing for beauty that was not of the world, he did not want the first taste of anything new. He wanted his men back. In the end, it was necessary for me to cloak myself and go down in the dark, under the willows where the bones are hung to the wind, into the sty; and to sort out and bring up his friends again from their muddy labyrinth. I had to pass them back through the doorway as themselves. I could not skip or brush lightly over one—he named and counted. Then he could look at them all he liked, staggering up on their hind legs before him. Their jaws sank asthmatically, and he cried, "Do you know me?"

"It's Odysseus!" I called, to spoil the moment. But with a shout he had already sprung to their damp embrace.

Reunions, it seems, are to be celebrated. (I have never had such a thing.) All of us feasted together on meat and bread, honey and wine, and the fire roared. We heard out the flute player, we heard out the story, and the fair-haired sailor, whose name is now forgotten, danced on the table and pleased them. When the fire was black, my servants came languishing from the kitchen, and all the way up the ladder to the beds above they had to pull the drowsy-kneed star-gazers, spilling laughter and songs all the way. I could hear them calling away to the girls as they would call them home. But the pigsty was where they belonged.

Hand in hand, we climbed to my tower room. His cheeks were grave and his eyes black, put out with puzzles and solutions. We conversed of signs, omens, premonitions, riddles and dreams, and ended in fierce, cold sleep. Strange man, as unflinching and as wound up as I am. His short life and my long one have their ground in common. Passion is our ground, our island—do others exist?

His sailors came jumping down in the morning, full of themselves and stories. Preparing the breakfast, I watched them tag one another, run rough-and-tumble around the table, regaling the house. "What did *I* do? How far did *I* go with it?" and in a reckless reassurance imitating the sounds of pigs at each other's backs. They were certainly more winsome now than they could ever have been before; I'd made them younger, too, while I was about it. But tell me of one that appreciated it! Tell me one now who looked my way until I had brought him his milk and figs.

When he made his appearance, we devoured a god's breakfast—all, the very sausages, taken for granted. The kitchen girls simpered and cried that if this went on, we'd be eaten out of house and home. But I didn't care if I put the house under greater stress for this one mortal than I ever dreamed of for myself—even on those lonely dull mornings when mist wraps the island and hides every path of the sea, and when my heart is black.

But a stir was upon them all from the moment they rose from the table. Treading on their napkins, tracking the clean floor with honey, they deserted me in the house and collected, arms wound on each other's shoulders, to talk beneath the sky. There they were in a knot, with him in the center of it. He folded his arms and sank his golden weight on one leg, while every ear on the island listened. I stood in the door and waited.

He walked up and said, "Thank you, Circe, for the hospitality we have enjoyed beneath your roof."

"What is the occasion for a speech?" I asked.

"We are setting sail," he said. "A year's visit is visit enough. It's time we were on our way."

Ever since the morning Time came and sat on the world, men have been on the run as fast as they can go, with beauty flung over their shoulders. I ground my teeth. I raised my wand in his face.

"You've put yourself to great trouble for us. You may have done too much," he said.

"I undid as much as I did!" I cried. "That was hard."

He gave me a pecking, recapitulating kiss, his black beard thrust at me like a shoe. I kissed it, his mouth, his wrist, his shoulder, I put my eyes to his eyes, through which I saw seas toss, and to the cabinet of his chest.

He turned and raised an arm to the others. "Tomorrow."

The knot broke and they wandered apart to the shore. They were not so forlorn when they could eat acorns and trot quickly where they would go.

It was as though I had no memory, to discover how early and late the cicadas drew long sighs like the playing out of all my silver shuttles. Wasn't it always the time of greatest heat, the Dog Star running with the Sun? The sea the color of honey looked sweet even to the tongue, the salt and vengeful sea. My grapes had ripened all over again while we stretched and drank our wine, and I ordered the harvest gathered and pressed—but this wine, I made clear to the servants, was to store. Hospitality is one thing, but I must consider how my time is endless, how I shall need wine endlessly. They smiled; but magic is the tree, and intoxication is just the little bird that flies in it to sing and flies out again. But the wanderers were watching the sun and waiting for the stars.

Now the night wind was rising. I went my way over the house as I do by night to see if all is well and holding together. From the rooftop I looked out. I saw the vineyards spread out like wings on the hill, the servants' huts and the swarthy groves, the sea awake, and the eye of the black ship. I saw in the moonlight the dance of the bones in the willows. "Old, displeasing ones!" I sang to them on the wind. "There's another now more displeasing than you! Your bite would be sweeter to my mouth than the soft kiss of a wanderer." I looked up at Cassiopeia, who sits there and needs nothing, pale in her chair in the stream of heaven. The old Moon was still at work. "Why keep it up, old woman?" I whispered to her, while the lions roared among the rocks; but I could hear plainly the crying of birds nearby and along the mournful shore.

I swayed, and was flung backward by my torment. I believed that I lay in disgrace and my blood ran green, like the wand that breaks in two. My sight returned to me when I awoke in the pigsty, in the red and black aurora of flesh, and it was day.

They sailed from me, all but one.

The youngest—Elpenor was his name—fell from my roof. He had forgotten where he had gone to sleep. Drunk on the last night, the drunkest of them all—so as not to be known any longer as only the youngest—he'd gone to sleep on the rooftop, and when they called him, his step went off into air. I saw him beating down through the light with rosy fists, as though he'd never left his mother's side till then.

They all ran from the table as though a star had fallen. They stood or they crouched above Elpenor fallen in my yard, low-voiced now like conspirators—as indeed they were. They wept for Elpenor lying on his face, and for themselves, as *he* wept for them the day they came, when I had made them swine.

He knelt and touched Elpenor, and like a lover lifted him; then each in turn held the transformed boy in his arms. They brushed the leaves from his face, and smoothed his red locks, which were still in their tangle from his brief attempts at lovemaking and from his too-sound sleep.

I spoke from the door. "When you dig the grave for that one, and bury him in the lonely sand by the shadow of your fleeing ship, write on the stone: 'I died of love.' "

I thought I spoke in epitaph—in the idiom of man. But when they heard me, they left Elpenor where he lay, and ran. Red-limbed, with linens sparkling, they sped over the windy path from house to ship like a rainbow in the sun, like new butterflies turned erratically to sea. While he stood in the prow and shouted to them, they loaded the greedy ship.

They carried off their gifts from me—all unappreciated, unappraised.

I slid out of their path. I had no need to see them set sail, knowing as well as if I'd been ahead of them all the way, the far and wide, misty and islanded, bright and indelible and menacing world under which they all must go. But foreknowledge is not the same as the last word.

My cheek against the stony ground, I could hear the swine like summer thunder. These were with me still, pets now, once again—grumbling without meaning. I rose to my feet. I was sickened, with child. The ground fell away before me, blotted with sweet myrtle, with high oak that would have given me a ship too, if I were not tied to my island, as Cassiopeia must be to the sticks and stars of her chair. We were a rim of fire, a ring on the sea. His ship was a moment's gleam on a wave. The little son, I knew, was to follow—follow and slay him. That was the story. For whom is a story enough? For the wanderers who will tell it—it's where they must find their strange felicity.

I stood on my rock and wished for grief. It would not come. Though I could shriek at the rising Moon, and she, so near, would wax or wane, there was still grief, that couldn't hear me—grief that cannot be round or plain or solid-bright or running on its track, where a curse could get at it. It has no heavenly course; it is like mystery, and knows where to hide itself. At last it does not even breathe. I cannot find the dusty mouth of grief. I am sure now grief is a ghost—only a ghost in Hades, where ungrateful Odysseus is going—waiting on him.

Kin

"Mingo?" I repeated, and for the first moment I didn't know what my aunt meant. The name sounded in my ears like *something* instead of *somewhere.* I'd been making a start, just a little start, on my own news when Rachel came in in her stately way with the letter.

My aunt was bridling daintily at the unopened envelope in her hand. "Of course you'll be riding out there Sunday, girls, and without me."

"Open it—what does she say now?" said Kate to her mother. "Ma'am? If Uncle Felix—"

"Uncle Felix! Is *he* still living?"

Kate went "Shh!"

But I had only arrived the day before yesterday; and we had of course had so much to catch up with, besides, necessarily, parties. They expected me to keep up in spite of being gone almost my whole life, except for visits—I was taken away from Mississippi when I was eight. I was the only one in Aunt Ethel's downstairs bedroom neither partially undressed nor, to use my aunt's word, "reclining."

"Of course he is," said Aunt Ethel, tearing open the envelope at once, and bringing out an old-fashioned "correspondence card" filled up on both sides with a sharp, jet-black hand, and reading the end. Uncle Felix was her uncle, only my great-uncle. "He is," she said to Kate.

"*Still* this, *still* that," murmured Kate, looking at me sidelong. She was up on the bed too. She leaned lightly across her mother, who was in pink negligée, read ahead of her for an instant, and plucked the last piece of the city candy I had brought from the big shell dish Rachel had seen fit to put it in.

Uncontrite, I rocked. However, I did see I must stop showing what might be too much exuberance in Aunt Ethel's room, since she was old and not strong, and take things more as they came. Kate and I were double first cousins, I was the younger, and neither married yet, but *I* was not going to be an old maid! I was already engaged up North; though I had not yet come to setting a date for my wedding. Kate, though, as far as I could tell, didn't have anybody.

My little aunt, for her heart's sake, had to lie propped up. There inside her tester bed she sometimes looked out as if, I thought, she were riding in some old-fashioned carriage or litter. Now she had drawn that card and its envelope both to her pillowed face. She was smelling them. Mingo, of course, was the home place. It was miles from anywhere, and I saw that she was not to go there any more.

"Look at the gilt edge," she said, shining it. "Isn't it *remarkable* about Sister Anne? I wonder what drawer she went into to find *that* to favor us with? . . . 'Had to drop—' watch?—no, 'water on his tongue—yesterday so he could talk . . . Must *watch* him—day and night,' underlined. *Poor* old man. She insists, you know, Dicey, that's what she does."

"Buzzard," said Kate.

"Who," I sighed, for I thought she had said "sister," and there was no sister at all left of my Aunt Ethel's. But my mind had wandered for a moment. It was two-thirty in the afternoon, after an enormous dinner at which we had had company—six girls, chattering almost like ready-made bridesmaids—ending with wonderful black, bitter, moist chocolate pie under mountains of meringue, and black, bitter coffee. We could hear Rachel now, off in the distance, peacefully dropping the iced-tea spoons into the silver drawer in the pantry.

In this little courthouse town, several hours by inconvenient train ride from Jackson, even the cut grass in the yards smelled different from Northern grass. (Even by evidence of smell, I knew that really I was a stranger in a way, still, just at first.) And the spring was so much farther advanced—the birds so busy you turned as you would at people as they plunged by. Bloom was everywhere in the streets, wistaria just ending, Confederate jasmine beginning. And down in the gardens!—they were deep colored as old rugs in the morning and evening shade. Everybody grew some of the best of everybody else's flowers; by the way, if you thank a friend for a flower, it will not grow for you. Everywhere we went calling, Kate brought me out saying, "Here she is! Got off the train talking, and hasn't stopped yet." And everywhere, the yawning, inconvenient, and suddenly familiar rooms were as deep and inviting and compelling as the yawning big roses opening and shattering in one day in the heating gardens. At night, the moths were already pounding against the screens.

Aunt Ethel and Kate, and everybody I knew here, lived as if they had never heard of anywhere else, even Jackson—in houses built, I could judge now as a grown woman and a stranger, in the local version of the 1880's—tall and spread out at the bottom, with porches, and winged all over with awnings and blinds. As children, Kate and I were brought up across the street from each other—they were her grandfather's and my grandmother's houses. From Aunt Ethel's front window I could see our chinaberry tree, which Mother had always wanted to cut down, standing in slowly realized bloom. Our old house was lived in now by a family named Brown, who were not very much, I gathered—the porch had shifted, and the screens looked black as a set of dominoes.

Aunt Ethel had gone back to the beginning of her note now. "Oh-oh. Word has penetrated even Mingo, Miss Dicey Hastings, that you're in this part of the world! The minute you reached Mississippi our little paper had that notice you laughed at, that was all about your mother and me and your grandmother, so of course there's repercussions from Sister Anne. 'Why didn't we tell her!' But honestly, she might be the remotest kin in the world, for all you know when you're well, but let yourself get to ailing, and she'd show up in Guinea, if that's where you were, and *stay.* Look at Cousin Susan, 'A year if need be' is the way she put it about precious Uncle Felix."

"She'll be coming to you next if you don't hush about her," said Kate, sitting bolt upright on the bed. She adored her mother, her family. What she had was company-excitement. And I guess I had trip-excitement—I giggled. My aunt eyed us and tucked the letter away.

"But who is she, pure and simple?" I said.

"You'd just better not let her *in*," said Aunt Ethel to Kate. "That's what. Sister Anne Fry, dear heart. Declares she's wild to lay eyes on you. I *should* have shown you the letter. Recalls your sweet manners toward your elders. Sunday's our usual day to drive out there, you remember, Dicey, but I'm inclined to think—I feel now—it couldn't be just your coming brought on this mid-week letter. Uncle Felix was taken sick on Valentine's Day and she got there by Saturday. Kate, since you're not working this week—if you're going, you'd better go on today."

"Oh, curses!" cried Kate to me. Kate had told them at the bank she was not working while I was here. We had planned something.

"Mama, what is she?" asked Kate, standing down in her cotton petticoat with the ribbon run in. She was not as tall as I. "I may be as bad as Dicey but I don't intend to go out there today without you and not have her straight."

Aunt Ethel looked patiently upwards as if she read now from the roof of the tester, and said, "Well, she's a remote cousin of Uncle Felix's, to begin with. Your third cousin twice removed, and your Great-aunt Beck's half-sister, my third cousin once removed and my aunt's half-sister, Dicey's—"

"Don't tell me!" I cried. "I'm not that anxious to claim kin!"

"She'll claim you! She'll come visit you!" cried Kate.

"I won't be here long enough." I could not help my smiles.

"When your mother was alive and used to come bringing you, visits were different," said my Aunt Ethel. "She stayed long enough to make us believe she'd fully got here. There'd be time enough to have alterations, from Miss Mattie, too, and transplant things in the yard if it was the season, even start a hook-rug—do a morning glory, at least—even if she'd never really see the grand finale. . . . Our generation knew more how to visit, whatever else escaped us, not that I mean to criticize one jot."

"Mama, what do you *want*?" said Kate in the middle of the floor. "Let me get you something."

"I don't want a thing," said her mother. "Only for my girls to please themselves."

"Well then, tell me who it was that Sister Anne one time, long time ago, was going to marry and stood up in the church? And she was about forty years old!" Kate said, and lightly, excitedly, lifted my hat from where I'd dropped it down on the little chair some time, to her own head—bare feet, petticoat, and all. She made a face at me.

Her mother was saying, "Now *that* is beyond me at the moment, perhaps because it didn't come off. Though he was some kind of off-cousin, too, I seem to recall . . . I'll have it worked out by the time you girls get back from where you're going.—Very becoming, dear."

"Kate," I said, "I thought Uncle Felix was old beyond years when I was a child. And now *I'll* be old in ten years, and so will you. And he's still alive."

"He *was* old!" cried Kate. "He *was*!"

"Light somewhere, why don't you," said her mother.

Kate perched above me on the arm of my chair, and we gently rocked.

I said, "He had red roses on his suspenders."

"When did he ever take his coat off for you to see that?" objected my aunt. "The whole connection always went out there for *Sundays*, and he was a very strict gentleman all his life, you know, and made us be ladies out there, more even than Mama and Papa did in town."

"But I can't remember a thing about Sister Anne," I said. "Maybe she was too much of a lady."

"Foot," said my aunt.

Kate said in a prompting, modest voice, "She fell in the well."

I cried joyously, "And she came out! Oh, I remember her fine! Mournful! Those old black drapey dresses, and plastered hair."

"That was just the way she looked when she came out of the well," objected Kate.

"Mournful isn't exactly the phrase," said my aunt.

"Plastered black hair, and her mouth drawn down, exactly like that aunt in the front illustration of your *Eight Cousins*," I told Kate. "I used to think that was who it was."

"You're so bookish," said my aunt flatly.

"This is where all the books *were*!"—and there were the same ones now, no more, no less.

"On purpose, I think she fell," continued Kate. "Knowing there were plenty to pull her out. That was her contribution to Cousin Eva's wedding celebrations, and snitching a little of *her* glory. You're joggling me the way you're rocking."

"There's such a thing as being unfair, Kate," said her mother. "I always say, *poor* Sister Anne."

"*Poor* Sister Anne, then."

"And I think Dicey just *thinks* she remembers it because she's heard it."

"Well, at least she had something to be poor about!" I said irrepressibly. "Falling in the well, and being an old maid, that's two things!"

Kate cried, "Don't rock so headlong!"

"Maybe she even knew what she was about. Eva's Archie Fielder got drunk every whipstitch for the rest of his life," said Aunt Ethel.

"Only tell me this, somebody, and I'll be quiet," I said. "What poor somebody's Sister Anne was she to begin with?"

Then I held the rocker and leaned against my cousin. I was terrified that I had brought up Uncle Harlan. Kate had warned me again how, ever since his death seventeen years ago, Aunt Ethel could not bear to hear the name of her husband spoken, or to speak it herself.

"Poor Beck's, of course," said Aunt Ethel. "She's a little bit kin on both sides. Since you ask, Beck's *half*-sister—that's why we were always so careful to call her Sister."

"Oh. I thought that was just for teasing," said Kate.

"Well, of course the teasing element is not to be denied," said Aunt Ethel.

"Who began—" My hat was set, not at all rightly, on my own head by Kate—like a dunce cap.

The town was so quiet the doves from the river woods could be heard plainly. In town, the birds were quiet at this hour. Kate and I went on bobbing slowly up and down together as we rocked very gently by Aunt Ethel's bed. I saw us in the pier glass across the room. Looking at myself as the visitor, I considered myself as having a great deal still waiting to confide. My lips opened.

"He was ever so courtly," said my aunt. "Nobody in the family more so."

Kate with a tiny sting pulled a little hair from my neck, where it has always grown too low. I slapped at her wrist.

"But this last spell when I couldn't get out, and he's begun failing, what I remember about him is what I used to be told as a child, isn't that strange? When I knew him all my life and loved him. For instance, that he was a great one for serenading as a young man."

"Serenading!" said Kate and I together, adoring her and her memory. "I didn't know he could sing," said Kate.

"He couldn't. But he *was* a remarkable speller," said my aunt. "A born speller. I remember how straight he stood when they called the word. You know the church out there, like everything else in the world, raised its money by spelling matches. He knew every word in the deck. One time—one time, though!—I turned Uncle Felix down. I was not so bad myself, child though I was. And it isn't . . ."

"Ma'am?"

"It just isn't fair to have water dropped on your tongue, is it!"

"She ought not to have told you, the old buzzard!"

"The word," said Aunt Ethel, "the word was knick-knack. K-n-i-c-k, knick, hyphen, k-n-a-c-k, knack, knick-knack."

"She only writes because she has nothing else to do, away out yonder in the country!"

"She used to get *dizzy* very easily," Aunt Ethel spoke out in a firm voice, as if she were just waking up from a nap. "Maybe she did well—maybe a girl might do well sometimes *not* to marry, if she's not cut out for it."

"Aunt Ethel!" I exclaimed. Kate, sliding gently off the arm of my chair, was silent. But as if I had said something more, she turned around, her bare foot singing on the matting, her arm turned above her head, in a saluting, mocking way.

"Find me her letter again, Kate, where is it?" said Aunt Ethel, feeling under her solitaire board and her pillow. She held that little gilt-edged card, shook it, weighed it, and said, "All that really troubles me is that I can't bear for her to be on Uncle Felix's hands for so long! He was always so courtly, and his family's all, all in the churchyard now (but us!)—or New York!"

"Mama, let me bring you a drink of water."

"Dicey, I'm going to *make* you go to Mingo."

"But I want to go!"

She looked at me uncomprehending. Kate gave her a glass of water, with ice tinkling in it. "That reminds me, whatever you do, Kate, if you do go today, take that fresh Lady Baltimore cake out to the house—Little Di can sit and hold it while you drive. Poor Sister Anne can't cook and loves to eat. She can *eat* awhile. And make Rachel hunt through the shelves for some more green tomato pickle. Who'll put that up next year!"

"If you talk like that," said Kate, "we're going to go right this minute, right out into the heat. I thought this was going to be a good day."

"Oh, it is! Grand— Run upstairs both, and get your baths, you hot little children. You're supposed to go to Suzanne's, I know it." Kate, slow-motion, leaned over and kissed her mother, and took the glass. "Kate!—If only I could see him one more time. As he was. And Mingo. Old Uncle Theodore. The peace. Listen: you give him my love. He's *my* Uncle Felix. Don't tell him why I didn't come. That might distress him more than not seeing me there."

"What's Uncle Felix's trouble?" I asked, shyly at last: but things, even fatal things, did have names. I wanted to know.

Aunt Ethel smiled, looked for a minute as if she would not be allowed to tell me, and then said, "Old age.—I think Sister Anne's lazy, *idle*!" she cried. "You're drawing it out of me. She never cooked nor sewed nor even cultivated her mind! She was a lily of the field." Aunt Ethel suddenly showed us both highly polished little palms, with the brave gesture a girl uses toward a fortune teller—then looked into them a moment absently and hid them at her sides. "She just hasn't got anybody of her own, that's her trouble. And she needs somebody."

"Hush! She *will* be coming here next!" Kate cried, and our smiles began to brim once more.

"She has no inner resources," confided my aunt, and watched to see if I were too young to guess what that meant. "How you girls do set each other off! Not that you're bothering me, I love you in here, and wouldn't deprive myself *of* it. Yes, you all just better wait and go Sunday. Make things as usual." She shut her eyes.

"Look—look!" chanted Kate.

Rachel, who believed in cutting roses in the heat of the day—and nobody could prevent her now, since we forgot to cut them ourselves or slept through the mornings—came in Aunt Ethel's room bearing a vaseful. Aunt Ethel's roses were at their height. A look of satisfaction on Rachel's face was like something nobody could interrupt. To our sighs, for our swooning attitudes, she paraded the vase through the room and around the bed, where she set it on the little table there and marched back to her kitchen.

"*Rachel* wants you to go. All right, you tell Uncle Felix," said Aunt Ethel, turning toward the roses, spreading her little hand out chordlike over them, "—of course he must have these—that *that's* Souvenir de Claudius Pernet—and *that's* Mermaid—Mary Wallace—Silver Moon—those three of course Étoiles—and oh, Duquesa de Penaranda—Gruss an Aachen's of course his cutting he grew for me a thousand years ago—but there's my Climbing Thor! Gracious!" she sighed, looking at it. Still looking at the roses she waited a moment. Pressing out of the vase, those roses of hers looked heavy, drunken with their own light and scent, their stems, just two minutes ago severed with Rachel's knife, vivid with pale thorns through cut-glass. "You know, Sundays always *are* hotter than any other days, and I tell you what: I do think you'd better go on to Mingo today, regardless of what you find."

Circling around in her mind like old people—which Aunt Ethel never used to do, she never used to get back!—she got back to where she started.

"Yes'm," said Kate.

"Aunt Ethel, wouldn't it be better for everybody if he'd come in town to the hospital?" I asked, with all my city seriousness.

"He wouldn't consider it. So give Sister Anne my love, and give Uncle Felix my dear love. Will you remember? Go on, naked," said my aunt to her daughter. "Take your cousin upstairs in her city bonnet. You both look right feverish to me. Start in a little while, so you can get your visit over and come back in the cool of the evening."

"These nights now are so bright," said my cousin Kate, with a strange stillness in her small face, transfixed, as if she didn't hear the end of the messages and did not think who was listening to her either, standing with bare arms pinned behind her head, with the black slick hair pinned up, "these nights are so bright I don't mind, I don't care, how long any ride takes, or how late I ever get home!"

I jumped up beside her and said, pleadingly somehow, to them both, "Do you know—I'd *forgotten* the Milky Way!"

My aunt didn't see any use answering that either. But Kate and I were suddenly laughing and running out together as if we were going to the party after all.

Before we set out, we tiptoed back into Aunt Ethel's room and made off with the roses. Rachel had darkened it. Again I saw us in the mirror, Kate pink and me blue, both our dresses stiff as boards (I had gone straight into Kate's clothes) and creaking from the way Rachel starched them, our teeth set into our lips, half-smiling. I had tried my hat, but Kate said, "Leave that, it's entirely too grand for out there, didn't you hear Mama?" Aunt Ethel stayed motionless, and I thought she was bound to look pretty, even asleep. I wasn't quite sure she was asleep.

"Seems mean," said Kate, looking between the horns of the reddest rose, but I said, "She meant us to."

"Negroes always like them full blown," said Kate.

Out in the bright, "Look! Those crazy starlings have come. They always pick the greenest day!" said Kate.

"Well, maybe because they look so pretty in it," I said.

There they were, feeding all over the yard and every yard, iridescently black and multiplied at our feet, bound for the North. Around the house, as we climbed with our loads into the car, I saw Rachel looking out from the back hall window, with her cheek in her hand. She watched us go, carrying off her cake and her flowers too.

I was thinking, if I always say "still," Kate still says "always," and laughed, but would not tell her.

Mingo, I learned, was only nine miles and a little more away. But it was an old road, in a part the highway had deserted long ago, lonely and winding. It dipped up and down, and the hills felt high, because they were bare of trees, but they probably weren't very high—this was Mississippi. There was hardly ever a house in sight.

"So green," I sighed.

"Oh, but poor," said Kate, with her look of making me careful of what I said. "Gone to pasture now."

"Beautiful to me!"

"It's clear to Jericho. Looks like that cake would set heavy on your knees, in that old tin Christmas box."

"I'm not ever tired in a strange place. Banks and towers of honeysuckle hanging over that creek!" We crossed an iron bridge.

"That's the Hushomingo River."

We turned off on a still narrower, bumpier road. I began to see gates.

Near Mingo, we saw an old Negro man riding side saddle, except there was no saddle at all, on a slow black horse. He was coming to meet us—that is, making his way down through the field. As we passed, he saluted by holding out a dark cloth cap stained golden.

"Good evening, Uncle Theodore," nodded Kate. She murmured, "Rachel's his daughter, did you know it? But she never comes back to see him."

I sighed into the sweet air.

"Oh, Lordy, we're too late!" Kate exclaimed.

On the last turn, we saw cars and wagons and one yellow wooden school bus standing empty and tilted to the sides up and down the road. Kate stared back for a moment toward where Uncle Theodore had been riding so innocently away. Primroses were blowing along the ditches and between the wheelspokes of wagons, above which empty cane chairs sat in rows, and some of the horses were eating the primroses. That was the only sound as we stood there. No, a chorus of dogs was barking in a settled kind of way.

From the gate we could look up and see the house at the head of the slope. It looked right in size and shape, but not in something else—it had a queer intensity for afternoon. Was every light in the house burning? I wondered. Of course: very quietly out front, on the high and sloping porch, standing and sitting on the railing between the four remembered, pale, square cypress posts, was stationed a crowd of people, dressed darkly, but vaguely powdered over with the golden dust of their thick arrival here in mid-afternoon.

Two blackly spherical Cape Jessamine bushes, old presences, hid both gateposts entirely. Such old bushes bloomed fantastically early and late so far out in the country, the way they did in old country cemeteries.

"The whole countryside's turned out," said Kate, and gritted her teeth, the way she did last night in her sleep.

What I could not help thinking, as we let ourselves through the gate, was that I'd either forgotten or never known how *primitive* the old place was.

Immediately my mind remembered the music box up there in the parlor. It played large, gilt-like metal discs, pierced with holes—eyes, eyelids, slits, mysterious as the symbols in a lady's dress pattern, but a whole world of them. When the disc was turned in the machine, the pattern of holes unwound a curious, metallic, depthless, cross music, with silences clocked between the notes. Though I did not like especially to hear it, I used to feel when I was here I must beg for it, as you should ask an old lady how she is feeling.

"I hate to get there," said Kate. She cried, "What a welcome for you!" But I said, "Don't say that." She fastened that creaky gate. We trudged up the straight but uneven dirt path, then the little paved walk toward the house. We shifted burdens, Kate took the cake and I took the flowers—the roses going like headlights in front of us. The solemnity on the porch was overpowering, even at this distance. It was serene, imperturbable, gratuitous: it was of course the look of "good country people" at such times.

On either side of us were Uncle Felix's roses—hillocks of bushes set in hillocks of rank grass and ragged-robins, hung with roses the size of little biscuits; indeed they already had begun to have a baked look, with little carmine edges curled. Kate dipped on one knee and came up with a four-leaf clover. She could always do that, even now, even carrying a three-layer cake.

By the house, wistaria had taken the scaffolding where a bell hung dark, and gone up into a treetop. The wistaria trunk, sinews raised and twined, like some old thigh, rose above the porch corner, above roof and all, where its sheet of bloom, just starting to go, was faded as an old sail. In spite of myself, I looked around the corner for that well: there it was, squat as a tub beneath the overpiece, a tiger-cat asleep on its cover.

The crowd on the porch were men and women, mostly old, some young, and some few children. As we approached they made no motion; even the young men sitting on the steps did not stand up. Then an old man came out of the house and a lady behind him, the old man on canes and the lady tiptoeing. Voices were murmuring softly all around.

Viewing the body, I thought, my breath gone—but nobody here's kin to me.

The lady had advanced to the head of the steps. It had to be Sister Anne. I saw her legs first—they were old—and her feet were set one behind the other, like an "expression teacher's," while the dress she had on was rather girlish, black taffeta with a flounce around it. But to my rising eyes she didn't look half so old as she did when she was pulled back out of the well. Her hair was not black at all. It was rusty brown, soft and unsafe in its pins. She didn't favor Aunt Ethel and Mama and them, or Kate and me, or any of us in the least, I thought—with that short face.

She was beckoning—a gesture that went with her particular kind of uncertain smile.

"What do I see? Cake!"

She ran down the steps. I bore down on Kate's shoulder behind her. Ducking her head, Kate hissed at me. What had I said? "Who pulled her out?"?

"You *surprised* me!" Sister Anne cried at Kate. She took the cake box out of her hands and kissed her. Two spots of red stabbed her cheeks. I was sorry to observe that the color of her hair was the very same I'd been noticing that spring in robins' breasts, a sort of stained color.

"Long-lost cousin, ain't you!" she cried at me, and gave me the same kiss she had given Kate—a sort of reprisal-kiss. Those head-heavy lights of Aunt Ethel's roses smothered between our unequal chests.

"Monkeys!" she said, leading us up, looking back and forth between Kate and me, as if she had to decide which one she liked best, before anything else in the world could be attended to. She had a long neck and that short face, and round, brown, jumpy eyes with little circles of wrinkles at each blink, like water wrinkles after something's popped in; that looked somehow like a twinkle, at her age. "Step aside for the family, please?" she said next, in tones I thought rather melting.

Kate and I did not dare look at each other. We did not dare look anywhere. As soon as we had moved through the porch crowd and were arrived inside the breezeway—where, however, there were a few people too, standing around—I looked and saw the corner clock was wrong. I was deeply aware that all clocks worked in this house, as if they had been keeping time just for me all this while, and I remembered that the bell in the yard was rung every day at straight-up noon, to bring them in out of the fields at picking time. And I had once supposed they rang it at midnight too.

Around us, voices sounded as they always did everywhere, in a house of death, soft and inconsequential, and tidily assertive.

"I believe Old Hodge's mules done had an attack of the wanderlust. Passed through my place Tuesday headed East, and now you seen 'em in Goshen."

Sister Anne was saying bodingly to us, "You just come *right* on *through*."

This was where Kate burst into tears. I held her to me, to protect her from more kisses. "When, when?" she gasped. "When did it happen, Sister Anne?"

"Now when did what happen?"

That was the kind of answer one kind of old maid loves to give. It goes with "Ask me sometime, and I'll tell you." Sister Anne lifted her brow and fixed her eye on the parlor doorway. The door was opened into that room, but the old red curtain was drawn across it, with bright light, looking red too, streaming out around it.

Just then there was a creaking sound inside there, like an old winter suit bending at the waist, and a young throat was cleared.

"Little bit of commotion here today, but I *would* rather you didn't tell Uncle Felix anything about it," said Sister Anne.

"Tell him! Is he alive?" Kate cried wildly, breaking away from me, and then even more wildly, "I might have known it! What sort of frolic are you up to out here, Sister Anne?"

Sister Anne suddenly marched to the other side of us and

brought the front bedroom door to with a good country slam. That room—Uncle Felix's—had been full of people too.

"I beg your pardon," said Kate in a low voice in the next moment. We were still just inside the house—in the breezeway that was almost as wide as the rooms it ran between from front porch to back. It was a hall, really, but still when I was a child called the breezeway. Open at the beginning, it had long been enclosed, and papered like the parlor, in red.

"Why, Kate. You all would be the first to *know*. Do you think I'd have let everybody come, regardless of promises, if Uncle Felix had chosen *not* to be with us still, on the day?"

While we winced, a sudden flash filled the hall with light, changing white to black, black to white—I saw the roses shudder and charge in my hands, Kate with white eyes rolled, and Sister Anne with the livid brow of a hostess and a pencil behind one ear.

"That's what you mean," said Sister Anne. "That's a photographer. He's here in our house today, taking pictures. He's *itinerant*," she said, underlining in her talk. "And he *asked* to use our parlor—we didn't ask *him*. Well—it *is* complete."

"What is?"

"Our parlor. And all in shape—curtains washed—*you know*."

Out around the curtain came the very young man, dressed in part in a soldier's uniform not his, looking slightly dazed. He tiptoed out onto the porch. The bedroom door opened on a soft murmuring again.

"Listen," said Sister Anne, leaning toward it. "Hear them in yonder?"

A voice was saying, "My little girl says she'd rather have come on this trip than gone to the zoo."

There was a look on Sister Anne's face as fond and startling as a lover's. Then out the door came an old lady with sidecombs, in an enormous black cotton dress. An old man came out behind her, with a mustache discolored like an old seine. Sister Anne pointed a short strict finger at them.

"We're together," said the old man.

"I've got everything under control," Sister Anne called over her shoulder to us, leaving us at once. "Luckily, I was always able to be in two places at the same time, so I'll be able to visit with you back yonder and keep things moving up front, too. Now, what was your name, sir?"

At the round table in the center of the breezeway, she leaned with the old man over a ledger opened there, by the tray of glasses and the water pitcher.

"But where could Uncle Felix be?" Kate whispered to me. As for me, I was still carrying the roses.

Sister Anne was guiding the old couple toward the curtain, and then she let them into the parlor.

"Sister Anne, where have you got him put?" asked Kate, following a step.

"You just come right on through," Sister Anne called to us. She said, behind her hand, "They've left the fields, dressed up like Sunday and Election Day put together, but I can't say they all stopped long enough to bathe, ha-ha! April's a pretty important time, but having your picture taken beats that! Don't have a chance of that out this way more than once or twice in a lifetime. Got him put back out of all the commotion," she said, leading the way. "The photographer's name is—let me see. He's of the Yankee persuasion, but that don't matter any longer, eh, Cousin Dicey? But I shouldn't be funny. Anyway, traveled all the way from some town somewhere since *February*, he tells me. Mercy, but it's hot as churchtime up there, with 'em so packed in! Did it ever occur to you how vain the human race can be if you just give 'em a chance?"

There was that blinding flash again—curtain or not, it came right around it and through it, and down the hall.

"Smells like gunpowder," said Kate stonily.

"Does," agreed Sister Anne. She looked flattered, and said, "May *be*."

"I feel like a being from another world," I said all at once, just to the breezeway.

"Come on, then," said Sister Anne. "Kate, leave her alone. Oh, Uncle Felix'll eat you two little boogers up."

Not such small haunches moved under that bell-like skirt; the skirt's hem needed mending where a point hung down. Just as I concentrated and made up my mind that Sister Anne weighed a hundred and forty-five pounds and was sixty-nine years old, she mounted on tiptoe like a little girl, and I had to bite my lip to keep from laughing. Kate was steering me by the elbow.

"Now how could she have *moved* him away back here," Kate marveled. Her voice might even have been admiring, with Sister Anne not there.

"Hold your horses while I look at this cake," said Sister Anne, turning off at the kitchen. "What I want to see is *what kind*."

She squealed as if she had seen a mouse. She took a lick of the icing on her finger before she covered the cake again and set it on the table. "My favorite. And how is Cousin Ethel?" Then she reached for my roses.

"Your ring!" she cried—a cry only at the last second subdued. "Your ring!"

She took my face between her fingers and thumb and shook my cheeks, as though I could not hear what she said at all. She could do this because we were kin to each other.

With unscratchable hands she began sticking the roses into a smoky glass vase too small for them, into which she'd run too little water. Of course there was plumbing. The well was abandoned.

"Well," she said, poking in the flowers, as though suddenly we had all the time in the world, "the other morning, I was looking out at the road, and along came a dusty old-time Ford with a trunk on the back, real slow, then stopped. Was a man. I wondered. And in a minute, knock knock knock. I changed my shoes and went to the door with my finger to my lips." She showed us.

"He was still there, on the blazing porch—eleven-fifteen. He was a middle-age man all in hot black, short, but reared back, like a stove handle. He gave me a calling card with a price down in the corner, and leaned in and whispered he'd like to use the parlor. He was an itinerant! That's almost but not quite the same thing as a Gypsy. I hadn't seen a living person in fourteen days, except here, and he was an itinerant photographer with a bookful of orders to take pictures. I made him open and show me his book. It was chock-full. All kinds of names of all kinds of people from all over everywhere.

New pages clean, and old pages scratched out. In purple, indelible pencil. I flatter myself I *don't get* lonesome, but I felt sorry for *him*.

"I first told him he had taken me by surprise, and then thanked him for the compliment, and then said, after persuasion like that, he *could* use the parlor, *providing* he would make it quiet, because my cousin here wasn't up to himself. And he assured me it was the quietest profession on earth. That he had chosen it because it *was* such quiet, refined work, and also so he could see the world and so many members of the human race. I said I was a philosopher too, only I thought the sooner the better, and we made it today. And he borrowed a bucket of water and poured it steaming down the radiator, and returned the bucket, and was gone. I almost couldn't believe he'd been here.

"Then here today, right after dinner, in they start pouring. There's more people living in and around Mingo community than you can shake a stick at, more than you would ever dream. Here they come, out of every little high road and by road and cover and dell, four and five and six at the time—draw up or hitch up down at the foot of the hill and come up and shake hands like Sunday visitors. Everybody that can walk, and two that can't. I've got one preacher out there brought by a delegation. Oh, it's like Saturday and Sunday put together. The rounds the fella must have made! It's not as quiet as all he said, either. There's those mean little children, he never said a word about them, the spook.

"So I said all right, mister, I'm ready for you. I'll show them where they can sit and where they can wait, and I'll call them. I says to them, 'When it's not your turn, please don't get up. If you want anything, ask me.' And I told them that any that had to, could smoke, but I wasn't ready to have a fire today, so mind out.

"And he took the parlor right over and unpacked his suitcase, and put up his lights, and unfolded a camp stool, until he saw the organ bench with the fringe around it. And shook out a big piece of scenery like I'd shake out a bedspread and hooked it to the wall, and commenced pouring that little powder along something like a music stand. "First!" he says, and commenced calling them in. I took over that. He and I go by his book and take them in order one at a time, all fair, honest, and above-board."

"And so what about Uncle Felix!" cried Kate, as if now she had her.

"The niggers helped, to get him back there, but it was mostly my fat little self," said Sister Anne. "Oh, you mean how come he consented? I expect I told him a story." She led us back to the hall, where a banjo hung like a stopped clock, and some small, white-haired children were marching to meet each other, singing "Here Comes the Duke A-Riding, Riding," in flat, lost voices. I too used to think that breezeway was as long as a tunnel through some mountain.

"Get!" said Sister Anne, and clapped her hands at them. They flung to the back, off the back porch into the sun and scattered toward the barn. With reluctance I observed that Sister Anne's fingers were bleeding from the roses. Off in the distance, a herd of black cows moved in a light of green, the feathery April pastures deep with the first juicy weeds of summer.

There was a small ell tacked onto the back of the house, down a turn of the back porch, leading, as I knew, to the bathroom and the other little room behind that. A young woman and little boy were coming out of the bathroom.

"Look at that," shuddered Sister Anne. "Didn't take them long to find out what *we've* got."

I never used to think that back room was to be taken seriously as part of the house, because apples were kept in it in winter, and because it had an untrimmed, flat board door like a shed door, where you stuck your finger through a rough hole to lift up the latch.

Sister Anne stuck in her finger, opened the door, and we all three crowded inside the little room, which was crowded already.

Uncle Felix's side and back loomed from a featherbed, on an old black iron frame of a bedstead, which tilted downwards toward the foot with the sinking of the whole house from the brow of the hill toward the back. He sat white-headed as one of those escaping children, but not childlike—a heavy bulk, motionless, in a night-shirt, facing the window. A woven cotton spread was about his knees. His hands, turned under, were lying one on each side of him, faded from outdoor burn, mottled amber and silver.

"That's a nigger bed," said Kate, in one tone, one word. I turned and looked straight into her eyes.

"It—is—not," said Sister Anne. Her whole face shook, as if Kate could have made it collapse. Then she bowed her head toward us—that we could go on, now, if that was the spirit we had come in.

"Good evening, sir," said Kate, in a changed voice.

I said it after her.

Uncle Felix's long, mute, grizzly head poked around his great shoulder and, motionless again, looked out at us. He visited this gaze a long time on a general point among the three different feminine faces—if you could call Sister Anne's wholly feminine—but never exactly on any of them. Gradually something left his eyes. Conviction was what I missed. Then even that general focus altered as though by a blow, a rap or a tap from behind, and his old head swung back. Again he faced the window, the only window in the house looking shadeless and shameless to the west, the glaring west.

Sister Anne bore the roses to the window and set them down on the window sill in his line of sight. The sill looked like the only place left where a vase could safely be set. Furniture, odds and ends, useless objects were everywhere, pushed by the bed even closer together. There were trunks, barrels, chairs with the cane seats hanging in a fringe. I remembered how sometimes in winter, dashing in here where the window then blew icily upon us, we would snatch an apple from the washed heap on the floor and run slamming out before we would freeze to death; that window always stayed open, then as now propped with a piece of stovewood. The walls were still rough boards with cracks between. Dust had come in everywhere, rolls of dust or lint or cottonwood fuzz hung even from the ceiling, glinting like everything else in the unfair light. I was afraid there might be dirt-daubers' nests if I looked. Our roses glared back at us as garish as anything living could be, almost like paper flowers, a magician's bouquet that had exploded out of a rifle to shock and amaze us.

"We'll enjoy our sunset from over the pasture this evening, won't we, Uncle Felix!" called Sister Anne, in a loud voice. It was the urgent opposite of her conspiratorial voice. "I bet we're fixing to have a gorgeous one—it's so dusty! You were saying last week, Cousin Felix, we already need a rain!"

Then to my amazement she came and rested her foot on a stack of mossy books by the bed—I was across from her there—and leaned her elbow on her lifted knee, and looked around the room with the face of a brand-new visitor. I thought of a prospector. I could look if she could. What must have been a Civil War musket stood like a forgotten broom in the corner. On the coal bucket sat an old bread tray, split like a melon. There was even a dress form in here, rising among the trunks, its inappropriate bosom averted a little, as though the thing might still be able to revolve. If it were spanked, how the dust would fly up!

"Well, he's not going to even know *me* today," said Sister Anne, teasing me. "Well! I mustn't stay away too long at a time. Excuse me, Uncle Felix! I'll be right back," she said, taking down her tomboy foot. At the door she turned, to look as us sadly.

Kate and I looked at each other across the bed.

"Isn't this just—like—her!" said Kate with a long sigh.

As if on second thought she pulled open the door suddenly and looked off after her. From the other part of the house came the creakings of that human tiptoeing and passing going on in the breezeway. A flash of light traveled around the bend. Very close by, a child cried. Kate shut the door.

Back came Sister Anne—she really was back in a minute. She looked across at me. "Haven't you spoken? Speak! Tell him who you are, child! What did you come for?"

Instead—without knowing I was going to do it—I stepped forward and my hand moved out of my pocket with my handkerchief where the magnolia-fuscata flowers were knotted in the corner, and I put it under Uncle Felix's heavy brown nose.

He opened his mouth. I drew the sweet handkerchief back. The old man said something, with dreadful difficulty.

"Hide," said Uncle Felix, and left his mouth open with his tongue out for anybody to see.

Sister Anne backed away from us all and kept backing, to

the front of the paper-stuffed fireplace, as if she didn't even know the seasons. I almost expected to see her lift her skirt a little behind her. She gave me a playful look instead.

"Hide," said Uncle Felix.

We kept looking at her. Sister Anne gave a golden, listening smile, as golden as a Cape Jessamine five days old.

"Hide," gasped the old man—and I made my first movement. "And I'll go in. Kill 'em all. I'm old enough I swear you Bob. Told you. Will for sure if you don't hold me, hold me."

Sister Anne winked at me.

"Surrounded . . . They're inside." On this word he again showed us his tongue, and rolled his eyes from one of us to the other, whoever we were.

Sister Anne produced a thermometer. With professional motions, which looked so much like showing off, and yet were so derogatory, she was shaking it down. "All right, Cousin Felix, that's enough for now! You pay attention to that sunset, and see what it's going to do!—Listen, that picture made twenty-six," she murmured. She was keeping some kind of tally in her head, as you do most exactly out of disbelief.

Uncle Felix held open his mouth and she popped the thermometer straight in, and he had to close it. It looked somehow wrong, dangerous—it was like daring to take the temperature of a bear.

"I don't know where he thinks he is," she said, nodding her head gently at him, Yes—yes.

Before I knew it, his hand raked my bare arm down. I felt as if I had been clawed, but when I bent toward him, the hand had fallen inert again on the bed, where it looked burnished with hundreds of country suns and today's on top of them all.

"Please, ma'am," said a treble voice at the door. A towheaded child looked in solemnly; his little red tie shone as his hair did, as with dewdrops. "Miss Sister Anne, the man says it's one more and then you."

"Listen at that. My free picture," said Sister Anne, drawing breath like a little girl going to recite, about to be martyrized.

For whom! I thought.

"Don't you think I need to freshen up a little bit?" she said with a comical expression. "My hair hasn't been combed since four o'clock this morning."

"You go right ahead," said Kate. "Right ahead."

Sister Anne bent to sight straight into Uncle Felix's face, and then took the thermometer out of his lips and sighted along it. She read off his temperature to herself and almost sweetly firmed her lips. That was *hers*, what he gave *her*.

Uncle Felix made a hoarse sound as she ran out again. Kate moved to the trunk, where on a stack of old books and plates was a water pitcher that did not look cold, and a spoon. She poured water into the spoon, and gave the old man some water on his tongue, which he offered her. But already his arm had begun to stir, to swing, and he put the same work-heavy, beast-heavy hand, all of a lump, against my side again and found my arm, which this time went loose in its socket, waiting. He groped and pulled at it, down to my hand. He pulled me all the way down. On my knees I found the pencil lying in the dust at my feet. He wanted it.

My Great-Uncle Felix, without his right hand ever letting me go, received the pencil in his left. For a moment our arms crossed, but it was not awkward or strange, more as though we two were going to skate off, or dance off, out of here. Still holding me, but without stopping a moment, as if all the thinking had already been done, he knocked open the old hymnbook on top of the mossy stack at the bedside and began riding the pencil along over the flyleaf; though none of the Jerrolds that I ever heard of were left-handed, and certainly not he. I turned away my eyes.

There, lying on the barrel in front of me, looking vaguely like a piece of worn harness, was an object which I slowly recognized as once beloved to me. It was a stereopticon. It belonged in the parlor, on the lower shelf of the round table in the middle of the room, with the Bible on the top. It belonged to Sunday and to summertime.

My held hand pained me through the wish to use it and lift that old, beloved, once mysterious contraption to my eyes, and dissolve my sight, all our sights, in that. In that delaying, binding pain, I remembered Uncle Felix. That is, I remembered the real Uncle Felix, and could hear his voice, respectful again, asking the blessing at the table. Then I heard the cataract of talk, which I knew he engendered; that was what Sunday at Mingo began with.

I remembered the house, the real house, always silvery, as now, but then cypressy and sweet, cool, reflecting, dustless. Sunday dinner was eaten from the table pulled to the very head of the breezeway, almost in the open door. The Sunday air poured in through it, and through the frail-ribbed fanlight and side lights, down on the island we made, our cloth and our food and our flowers and jelly and our selves, so lightly enclosed there—as though we ate in pure running water. So many people were gathered at Mingo that the Sunday table was pulled out to the limit, from a circle to the shape of our race track. It held my mother, my father and brother; Aunt Ethel; Uncle Harlan, who could be persuaded, if he did not eat too much, to take down the banjo later; my Jerrold grandmother, who always spoke of herself as "nothing but a country bride, darling," slicing the chicken while Uncle Felix cut the ham; Cousin Eva and Cousin Archie; and Kate, Kate everywhere, like me. And plenty more besides; it was eating against talking, all as if nobody would ever be persuaded to get up and leave the table: everybody, we thought, that we needed. And some were so pretty!

And when they were, the next thing, taking their naps all over the house, it was then I got my chance, and there would be, in lieu of any nap, pictures of the world to see.

I ran right through, with the stereoptican, straight for the front porch steps, and sitting there, stacked the slides between my bare knees in the spread of my starched skirt. The slide belonging on top was "The Ladies' View, Lakes of Killarney."

And at my side sat Uncle Felix.

That expectation—even alarm—that the awareness of happiness can bring! Of any happiness. It need not even be yours. It is like being able to prophesy, all of a sudden. Perhaps Uncle Felix loved the stereopticon most; he had it first. With his coat laid folded on the porch floor on the other side of him, sitting erect in his shirtsleeves for this, he would reach grandly for the instrument as I ran bringing it out. He saddled his full-size nose with the stereopticon and said, "All right, Skeeta." And then as he signaled ready for each slide, I handed it up to him.

Some places took him a long time. As he perspired there in his hard collar, looking, he gave off a smell like a cut watermelon. He handed each slide back without a word, and I was ready with the next. I would no more have spoken than I would have interrupted his blessing at the table.

Eventually they—all the rest of the Sunday children—were awake and wanting to be tossed about, and they hung over him, pulling on him, seeking his lap, his shoulders, pinning him down, riding on him. And he with his giant size and absorption went on looking his fill. It was as though, while he held the stereopticon to his eye, *we* did not see *him*. Gradually his ear went red. I thought all the blood had run up to his brain then, as it had run to mine.

It's strange to think that since then I've gone to live in one of those picture cities. If I asked him something about what was in there, he never told me more than a name, never saw fit. (I couldn't read then.) We passed each other those sand-pink cities and passionate fountains, the waterfall that rocks snuffed out like a light, islands in the sea, red Pyramids, sleeping towers, checkered pavements on which strollers had come out, with shadows that seemed to steal further each time, as if the strollers had moved, and where the statues had rainbow edges; volcanoes; the Sphinx, and Constantinople; and again the Lakes, like starry fields—brought forward each time so close that it seemed to me the tracings from the beautiful face of a strange coin were being laid against my brain. Yet there were things too that I couldn't see, which could make Uncle Felix pucker his lips as for a kiss.

"Now! Dicey! I want *you* to tell me how I look!"

Sister Anne had opened the door, to a flash from the front. A low growl filled the room.

"You look mighty dressed up," said Kate for me.

Sister Anne had put on a hat—a hat from no telling where, what visit, what year, but it had been swashbuckling. It was a sort of pirate hat—black, of course.

"Thank you. Oh! Everything comes at once if it comes at all!" she said, looking piratically from one to the other of us. "So you can't turn around fast enough! You come on Mr. Dolollie's day! Now what will I do for Sunday!"

Under that, I heard an inching, delicate sound. Uncle Felix

had pulled loose the leaf of the book he had labored over. Now he let me go, and took both swollen fists and over the lump of his body properly folded his page. He nudged it into my tingling hand.

"*He'll* keep you busy!" said Sister Anne nodding. "*That* table looks ready to go to market!" Her eyes were so bright, she was in such a state of excitement and pride and suspense that she seemed to lose for the moment all ties with us or the house or any remembrance where anything was and what it was for. The next minute, with one blunder of her hatbrim against the door, she was gone.

I had slipped the torn page from the book, still folded, into my pocket, working it down through the starch-stuck dimity. Now I leaned down and kissed Uncle Felix's long unshaven, unbathed cheek. He didn't look at me—Kate stared, I felt it—but in a moment his eyes pinched shut.

Kate turned her back and looked out the window. The scent was burrowing into the roses, their heads hung. Out there was the pasture. The small, velvety cows had come up to the far fence and were standing there looking toward the house. They were little, low, black cows, soot-black, with their calves among them, in a green that seemed something to drink from more than something to eat.

Kate groaned under her breath, "I don't care, I've got to see her do it."

"She's doing it now," I said.

We stood on either side of the bed. Again Uncle Felix's head poked forward and held still, the western light full and late on him now.

"Never mind, Uncle Felix. Listen to me, I'll be back," Kate said. "It's nothing—it's all nothing—"

I felt that I had just showed off a good deal in some way. She bent down, hands on knees, but his face did not consult either of us again, although his eyes had opened. Tiptoeing modestly, we left him by himself. In his bleached gown he looked like the story book picture of the Big Bear, the old white one with star children on his back and more star children following, in triangle dresses, starting down the Milky Way.

•

We saw Sister Anne at the table signing the book. We hid in the front bedroom before she saw us.

The overflow from outside was sitting in here. Thick around the room, on the rocking chair, on parlor chairs and the murmurous cane chairs from the dining room, our visitors were visiting. A few were standing or sitting at the windows to talk, and leaning against the mantle. The four-poster held, like a paddock, a collection of cleaned-up little children, mostly girls, some of them mutinous and tearful, one little girl patiently holding a fruit jar with something alive inside.

"Writing herself in, signing herself out all in one," Kate whispered, watching. "No! She mustn't forget that."

She gripped my wrist wickedly and we tiptoed out across the breezeway, and stood by the parlor curtain until Kate lifted it, and I saw her smile into the parlor to make watching all right; and perhaps I did the same.

Sister Anne was shaking out her skirt, and white crumbs scattered on the rug. She had managed a slice of that cake. The parlor in its plush was radiant in the spectacular glare of multiplied lights brought close around. The wallpaper of course was red, but now it had a cinnamon cast. Its design had gone into another one—it, too, faded and precise, ringed by rain and of a queerly intoxicating closeness, like an old trunk that has been opened still again for the children to find costumes. White flags and amaryllis in too big a vase, where they parted themselves in the middle and tried to fall out, were Sister Anne's idea of what completed the mantle shelf. The fireplace was banked with privet hedge, as for a country wedding. I could almost hear a wavery baritone voice singing, "O Promise Me."

One with his camera and flash apparatus, the photographer stood with his back to us. He was baldheaded. We could see over him; he was short, and he leaned from side to side. He had long since discarded his coat, and his suspenders crossed tiredly on that bent back.

Sister Anne sat one way, then the other. A variety of expressions traveled over her face—pensive, eager, wounded, sad, and businesslike.

"I don't know why she can't make up her mind," I said all at once. "She's done nothing but practice all afternoon."

"Wait, wait, wait," said Kate. "Let her get to it."

What would show in the picture was none of Mingo at all, but the itinerant backdrop—the same old thing, a scene that never was, a black and white and gray blur of unrolled, yanked-down moonlight, weighted at the bottom with the cast-iron parlor rabbit doorstop, just behind Sister Anne's restless heel. The photographer raised up with arms extended, as if to hold and balance Sister Anne just exactly as she was now, with some special kind of semaphore. But Sister Anne was not letting him off that easily.

"Just a minute—I feel like I've lost something!" she cried, in a voice of excitement. "My handkerchief?"

I could feel Kate whispering to me, sideways along my cheek.

"Did poor Uncle Felix have to kill somebody when he was young?"

"I don't know." I shrugged, to my own surprise.

"Do you suppose she told him today there was a Yankee in the house? He might be thinking of Yankees." Kate slanted her whisper into my hair. It was more feeling, than hearing, what she said. "But he was almost too young for killing them . . . Of course he wasn't too young to be a drummer boy . . ." Her words sighed away.

I shrugged again.

"Mama can tell us! I'll make her tell us. What did the note say, did it go on just warning us to hide?"

I shook my head. But she knew I must have looked at it.

"Tell you when we get out," I whispered back, stepping forward a little from her and moving the curtain better.

"Oh, wait!" Sister Anne exclaimed again.

I could never have cared, or minded, less how Sister Anne looked. I had thought of what was behind the photographer's backdrop. It was the portrait in the house, the one picture on the walls of Mingo, where pictures ordinarily would be considered frivolous. It hung just there on the wall that was before me, crowded between the windows, high up—the romantic figure of a young lady seated on a fallen tree under brooding skies: my Great-Grandmother Jerrold, who had been Evelina Mackaill.

And I remembered—rather, more warmly, *knew*, like a

secret of the family—that the head of this black-haired, black-eyed lady who always looked the right, mysterious age to be my sister, had been fitted to the ready-made portrait by the painter who had called at the door—he had taken the family off guard, I was sure of it, and spoken to their pride. The yellow skirt spread fanlike, straw hat held ribbon-in-hand, orange beads big as peach pits (to conceal the joining at the neck)—none of that, any more than the forest scene so unlike the Mississippi wilderness (that enormity she had been carried to as a bride, when the logs of this house were cut, her bounded world by drop by drop of sweat exposed, where she'd died in the end of yellow fever) or the melancholy clouds obscuring the sky behind the passive figure with the small, crossed feet—none of it, world or body, was really hers. *She* had eaten bear meat, seen Indians, she had married into the wilderness at Mingo, to what unknown feelings. Slaves had died in her arms. She had grown a rose for Aunt Ethel to send back by me. And still those eyes, opaque, all pupil, belonged to Evelina—I knew, because they saw out, as mine did; weren't warned, as mine weren't, and never shut before the end, as mine would not. I, her divided sister, knew who had felt the wildness of the world behind the ladies' view. We were homesick for somewhere that was the same place.

I returned the touch of Kate's hand. This time, I whispered, "What he wrote was, 'River—Daisy—Midnight—Please.' "

" 'Midnight'!" Kate cried first. Then, "River daisy? His mind has wandered, the poor old man."

"Daisy's a lady's name," I whispered impatiently, so impatiently that the idea of the meeting swelled right out of the moment, and I even saw Daisy.

Then Kate whispered, "You must mean Beck, Dicey, that was his wife, and he meant her to meet him in Heaven. Look again.—*Look* at Sister Anne!"

Sister Anne had popped up from the organ bench. Whirling around, she flung up the lid—hymnbooks used to be stuffed inside—and pulled something out. To our amazement and delight, she rattled open a little fan, somebody's old one—it even sounded rusty. As she sat down again she drew that fan, black and covered over with a shower of forget-me-nots, languidly across her bosom. The photographer wasted not another moment. The flash ran wild through the house, singeing our very hair at the door, filling our lungs with gunpowder smoke as though there had been a massacre. I had a little fit of coughing.

"Now let her try forgiving herself for this," said Kate, and almost lazily folded her arms there.

"Did you see me?" cried Sister Anne, running out crookedly and catching onto both of us to stop herself. "Oh, I hope it's good! Just as the thing went off—I blinked!" She laughed, but I believed I saw tears start out of her eyes. "Look! Come meet Mr. Puryear. Come have your pictures taken! It's only a dollar down and you get them in the *mail*!"

And for a moment, I wanted to—wanted to have my picture taken, to be sent in the mail to someone—even against that absurd backdrop, having a vain, delicious wish to torment someone, then have something to laugh about together afterwards.

Kate drew on ladylike white cotton gloves, that I had not noticed her bringing. Whatever she had been going to say turned into, "Sister Anne? What have you been telling Uncle Felix?"

"What I *didn't* tell him," replied Sister Anne, "was that people were getting their pictures taken: I didn't want him to feel left out. It was just for one day. Mr. Alf J. Puryear is the photographer's name—there's some Puryears in Mississippi. I'll always remember his sad face."

"Thank you for letting us see Uncle Felix, in spite of the trouble we were," said Kate in her clear voice.

"You're welcome. And come back. But if I know the signs," said Sister Anne, and looked to me, the long-lost, for confirmation of herself the specialist, "we're losing him fast, ah me. Well! I'm used to it, I can stand it, that's what I'm for. But oh, I can't stand for you all to go! Stay—stay!" And she turned into our faces that outrageous, yearning smile she had produced for the photographer.

I knew I hadn't helped Kate out yet about Sister Anne. And so I said, "Aunt Ethel didn't come today! Do you know why? Because she just can't abide you!"

The bright lights inside were just then turned off. Kate and I turned and ran down the steps, just as a voice out of the porch shadow said, "It seems to me that things are moving in too great a rush." It sounded sexless and ageless both to me; it sounded deaf.

Somehow, Kate and I must have expected everybody to rush out after us. Sister Anne's picture, the free one, had been the last. But nobody seemed to be leaving. Children were the only ones flying loose. Maddened by the hour and the scene, they were running barefoot and almost silent, skimming around and around the house. The others sat and visited on, in those clouds of dust, all holding those little tickets or receipts I remembered wilting in their hands; some of the old men had them stuck in their winter hats. At last, maybe the Lady Baltimore cake would have to be passed.

"Sister Anne, greedy and all as she is, will cut that cake yet, if she can keep them there a little longer!" said Kate in answer to my thoughts.

"Yes," I said.

"She'll forget what you said. Oh the sweet evening air!"

I took so for granted once, and when had I left for ever, I wondered at that moment, the old soft airs of Mingo as I knew them—the interior airs that were always kitchen-like, of oil lamps, wood ashes, and that golden scrapement off cake-papers—and outside, beyond the just-watered ferns lining the broad strong railing, the fragrances winding up through the luster of the fields and the dim, gold screen of trees and the river beyond, fragrances so rich I once could almost see them, untransparent and Oriental? In those days, fresh as I was from Sunday School in town, I could imagine the Magi riding through, laden.

At other times—perhaps later, during visits back from the North—that whole big congregated outside smell, like the ripple of an animal's shining skin, used suddenly to travel across and over to my figure standing on the porch, like a marvel of lightning, and by it I could see myself, by myself, a child on a visit to Mingo, hardly under any auspices that I knew of, but wild myself, at the mercy of that touch.

"It's a wonder she didn't let the niggers file in at the back and have theirs taken too. If you didn't know it was Sister Anne, it would be past understanding," Kate said. "It would kill Mama—we must spare her this."

"Of course!" Sparing was our family trait.

We were going down the walk, measuredly, like lady callers who had left their cards; in single file. That was the one little strip of cement in miles and miles—narrow as a ladder.

"But listen, who was Daisy, have you thought? *Daisy*," said Kate in front. She looked over her shoulder. "I don't believe it."

I smoothed out that brown page of the hymn book with the torn edge, that purple indelible writing across it where the print read "Round & Shaped Notes." Coming around, walking in the dampening uncut grass, I showed it to Kate. You could still make out the big bold D with the cap on.

" *'Midnight!'* But they always go to bed at dark, out here."

I put the letter back inside my pocket. Kate said, "Daisy must have been smart. I don't understand that message at all."

"Oh, I do," I lied. I felt it was up to me. I told Kate, "It's a kind of shorthand." Yet it had seemed a very long letter—didn't it take Uncle Felix a long time to write it!

"Oh, I can't think even out here, but mustn't Daisy be dead? . . . Not Beck?" Kate ventured, then was wordless.

"Daisy was Daisy," I said. It was the "please" that had hurt me. It was I who put the old iron ring over the gate and fastened it. I saw the Cape Jessamines were all in bud, and for a moment, just at the thought, I seemed to reel from a world too fragrant, just as I suspected Aunt Ethel had reeled from one too loud.

"I expect by now Uncle Felix has got his names mixed up, and Daisy was a mistake," Kate said.

She could always make the kind of literal remark, like this, that could alienate me, even when we were children—much as I love her. I don't know why, yet, but some things are too important for a mistake even to be considered. I was sorry I had showed Kate the message, and said, "Look, how we've left him by himself."

We stood looking back, in our wonder, until out of the house came the photographer himself, all packed up—a small, hurrying man, black-coated as his subjects were. He wore a pale straw summer hat, which was more than they had. It was to see him off, tell him good-by, reassure him, that they had waited.

"Open it again! Look out, Dicey," said Kate, "get back."

He did not tarry. With paraphernalia to spare, he ran out between the big bushes ahead of us with a strange, rushing, fuse-like, Yankee sound—out through the evening and into his Ford, and was gone like that.

I felt the secret pang behind him—I know I did feel the cheat he had found and left in the house, the helpless, asking cheat. I felt it more and more, too strongly.

And then we were both excruciated by our terrible desire, and catching each other at the same moment with almost fierce hands, we did it, we laughed. We leaned against each other and on the weak, open gate, and gasped and choked into our handkerchiefs, and finally we cried. "Maybe she kissed him!" cried Kate at random. Each time we tried to stop ourselves, we sought each other's faces and started again. We laughed as though we were inspired.

"She forgot to take the pencil out of her hair!" gasped Kate.

"Oh no! What do you think Uncle Felix wrote with! He managed—it was the pencil out of Sister Anne's head!" That was almost too much for me. I held onto the gate.

I was aware somehow that birds kept singing passionately all around us just the same, and hurling themselves like bolts in front of our streaming eyes.

Kate tried to say something new—to stop us disgracing ourselves and each other, our visit, our impending tragedy, Aunt Ethel, everything. Not that anybody, anything in the world could hear us, reeled back in those bushes now, except ourselves.

"You know Aunt Beck—she never let us leave Mingo without picking us our nosegay on the way down this walk, every little thing she grew that smelled nice, pinks, four-o'clocks, verbena, heliotrope, bits of nicotiana—she grew all such little things, just for that, Di. And she wound their stems, round and round and round, with a black or white thread she would take from a needle in her collar, and set it all inside a rose-geranium leaf, and presented it to you at the gate—right here. That was Aunt Beck," said Kate's positive voice. "She wouldn't *let* you leave without it."

But it was no good. We had not laughed together that way since we were too little to know any better.

With tears streaming down my cheeks, I said, "I don't remember her."

"But she wouldn't *let* you forget. She *made* you remember her!"

Then we stopped.

I stood there and folded the note back up. There was the house, floating on the swimming dust of evening, its gathered, safe-shaped mass darkening. A dove in the woods called its five notes—two and three—at first unanswered. The last gleam of sunset, except for the threadbare curtain of wistaria, could be seen going on behind. The cows were lowing. The dust was in windings, the roads in their own shapes in the air, the exhalations of where the people all had come from.

"They'll all be leaving now," said Kate. "It's first-dark, almost."

But the grouping on the porch still held, that last we looked back, posed there along the rail, quiet and obscure and never-known as passengers on a ship already embarked to sea. Their country faces were drawing in even more alike in the dusk, I thought. Their faces were like dark boxes of secrets and desires to me, but locked safely, like old-fashioned caskets for the safe conduct of jewels on a voyage.

Something moved. The little girl came out to the front, holding her glass jar, like a dark lantern, outwards. Kate and I turned, wound our arms around each other, and got down to the car. We heard the horses.

It was all one substance now, one breath and density of blue. Along the back where the pasture was, the little, low black cows came in, in a line toward the house, with their sober sides one following the other. Where each went looked like simply where nothing was. But across the quiet we heard Theodore talking to them.

Across the road was Uncle Theodore's cabin, where clumps of privet hedge in front were shaped into a set of porch furniture, god-size, table and chairs, and a snake was hung up in a tree.

We drew out of the line of vehicles, and turned back down the dark blue country road. We neither talked, confided, nor sang. Only once, in a practical voice, Kate spoke.

"I hate going out there without Mama. Mama's too nice to say it about Sister Anne, but I will. You know what it is: it's in there somewhere."

Our lips moved together. "She's common . . ."

All around, something went on and on. It was hard without thinking to tell whether it was a throbbing, a dance, a rattle, or a ringing—all louder as we neared the bridge. It was everything in the grass and trees. Presently Mingo church, where Uncle Felix had been turned down on "knick-knack," revolved slowly by, with its faint churchyard. Then all was April night. I thought of my sweetheart, riding, and wondered if he were writing to me.

Going to Naples

THE *Pomona* sailing out of New York was bound for Palermo and Naples. It was the warm September of a Holy Year. Along with the pilgrims and the old people going home, there rode in *turistica* half a dozen pairs of mothers and daughters—these seemed to take up the most room. If Mrs. C. Serto, going to Naples, might miss by a hair's breadth being the largest mother, there was no question about which was the largest daughter—that was hers. And how the daughter did love to scream! From the time the *Pomona* began to throb and move down the river, Gabriella Serto regaled the deck with clear, soprano cries. As she romped up and down after the other girls—she was the youngest, too: eighteen—screaming and waving good-by to the Statue of Liberty, a hole broke through her stocking and her flesh came through like a pear.

Before land was out of sight, everybody knew that whatever happened during the next two weeks at sea, Gabriella had a scream in store for it. It was almost as though their ship—not a large ship at all, the rumor began to go round—had been appointed for this. "Why do I have to be taken to Naples! Why? I was happy in Buffalo, with you and Papa and Aunt Rosalia and Uncle Enrico!" she wailed to her mother along the passages—where of course everybody else, as well as the Sertos, was lost.

"Enough for you it is *l'Anno Santo*," said Mama. "Hold straight those shoulders. Look the others."

The others were going to pair off any minute—as far as pairing would go. There were six young girls, but though there were six young men too, they were only Joe Monteoliveto, Aldo Scampo, Poldy somebody, and three for the priesthood. As for Poldy, he was a Polish-American who was on his way now to marry a girl in Italy that he had never seen.

Every morning, to reach their deck, Mrs. Serto and Gabriella had to find their way along the whole length of the ship, right along its humming and pounding bottom, where the passage was wet (Did the ship leak? people asked) and narrow as a schoolroom aisle; past the quarters of the crew—who looked wild in their half-undress, even their faces covered with black—and the *Pomona* engines; and at last up a steep staircase toward the light. Gabriella complained all the way. Mrs. Serto, feeling this was the uphill journey, only puffed. On the long way back to the dining room—downhill—Mrs. Serto had her say.

"You saw! Every girl on ship is fat"—exactly what she said about school and church at home. "In *Napoli*, when I was a girl, your *Nonna* told me a hundred times, 'Little daughter: girls do well to be strong. Also, be *delicata*.' You wait! She'll tell you the same. What's the matter? You got pretty little feet like me." Mama framed herself in the engine-room door, and showed her shoe.

But not every girl coming into the dining room had to pass seven tables to reach her own, as Gabriella did—bouncing along sideways, with each table to measure her hips again as briskly as a mother's tape measure; while Joe Monteoliveto, for example, might be looking her way.

"You are youngest of six daughters, all beautiful and strong, five married to smart boys, Maria's Arrigo smart enough to be pharmacist. Five with babies to show. And what would you call every one those babies?"

The word rushed out. "Adorable!"

"*Bellissimo!* But you hang back."

"So O.K.! If you wouldn't follow me all the time!"

"I know the time to drop behind," said Mama sharply.

On deck all day, where she could see all that water, the smoother the ocean looked behind, the more apprehensive Gabriella felt; tourist deck faced backwards. She yelled that she wished the ship would turn around right where it was and take her back to the good old Statue of Liberty again. At that, Mama cast her eyes heavenward and a little to the left, like St. Cecilia on the cake plate at home, won on stunt night at the Sodality.

"Walk!" said the mothers to their daughters.

"You hear, Gabriella? Get up and walk!"

There was nowhere to go but in a circle—six of them walking arm-in-arm, dissolved in laughter; Maria-Pia Arpista almost had to be held up—especially when they wheeled at the turns and Gabriella gave her scream. For every time, there were the same black shawls, the same old caps, backed up against the blue—faces coming out of them that grew to be the only faces in the world, more solid a group than a family's, more persistent one by one than faces held fast in the memory or floating to nearness in dreams. On the best benches sat the old people, old enough to be going home to die—not noticing of the water, of the bad smells here and there, of where the warnings read *"Pittura Fresca,"* or when the loudspeaker cried *"Attenzione!"* and the others flew to the rail to learn the worst. They cared only for which side of the boat the sun was shining on. If they heard Gabriella screaming, it would be hard to tell. They could not even speak English.

On the last bench on one side two black men sat together by themselves. They never said a word, they did not smile. Their feet were long as loaves of bread, and black as beetles, and each pair pointed outward east and west; together their four feet formed a big black M, for getting married, set out for young girls to fall over.

"Why you put your tongue out those black people? Is that nice?" said Mama. "Signora Arpista, your Maria-Pia needs to sit down, look her expression."

But by the third day out, Maria-Pia walked with Joe Monteoliveto, and her expression had changed. So did Mama's—she stepped up and joined Maria-Pia's mama, a few paces behind the new couple's heels, where she would get in on everything.

Gabriella took a long running jump to the other side of the deck. And there, only a little distance away, stood Aldo Scampo, all by himself, as though the breezes had just set him down. He stood at the rail looking out, his rich pompadour blowing. The shadow of the upper deck hung over him like a big jaw, or the lid of a trunk, with priests on it.

As Gabriella drew near, slowly, as though she brought bad news, he leaned low on his elbows, watching the birds drop into the water where the crew, below, were shooting guns through the portholes. Except for white frown marks, Aldo's forehead was all bright copper, and so were his nose and chin, his chest, his folded arms—as if he were dressed up in somebody's kitchen dowry over his well-known costume of yellow T-shirt and old army pants. The story Mama had of Aldo Scampo was that he was unmarried, was *Californese*, had mother, father, sisters, and brothers in America, and his mother's people lived in Nettuno, where they partly owned a boat; but as he rattled around in a cabin to himself, the complete story was not yet known.

Pop—pop—pop.

These were the small, tireless, black-and-gold island birds that had kept up with their ship so far today that Gabriella felt like telling them, "Go home, dopes"—only of course, having followed for such a long way, by now they could never fly all the way back. (*"Attenzione!"* the loudspeaker had warned—all for some land you couldn't see, the Azores.) Another small body plummeted down before Aldo, so close he might have caught it in his hand. Did Aldo Scampo, mopping his radiant brow, know how many poor little birds that made?

Like a mind-reader, he turned brilliantly toward her; she thought he was going to answer with the number of birds, but when he spoke it was even more electrifying than an answer; it was a question.

"Ping pong?"

She screamed and raced him to the table.

This must have been the very moment that Aldo Scampo himself gave something up. Until now he had not had more than a passing glance for the girls who went walking by in a row with their chocolate cigarettes in the air. Like Joe Monteoliveto before him, he had brooded over La Zìngara the popular passenger said to be an actress; there she was now, further down the rail, talking to an almost *old* man. As Aldo and Gabriella pounded past her, La Zìngara—thin, but no one could say how young—leaned back into a life preserver as though it were a swing. Her lips, moving like a scissors, could be read: she was talking about the Jersey Highway.

While Aldo went begging the balls from the children, Gabriella seized her paddle and beat the table like an Indian drum. In a moment, many drew near.

Up to now, Gabriella's only partner had been a choice between a boy of nine, who had since broken his arm and would have to wear a sling to see the Pope, and the Polish-American fellow, who was engaged. Both, of course, had beaten her—but not as she would be beaten today! And her extra-long skirt, made by Mama in a nice strong red for the trip, rocked on her like a panoply as she readied herself for the opening ball, and missed it.

Everybody cheered. Even if she did not miss the ball, Gabriella was almost certain to fall down; finally, rushing in an ill-advised arc, she did collide with a priest, a large one, who was down from above to see how things in *turistica* were going. He rolled away in his skirts like a ball of yarn and had to be picked up by two of the three for the priesthood, while Gabriella clapped her hands to her ears and yelped like a puppy.

Everybody had begun to wonder if Gabriella could help screaming—especially now, after three days. It was true her screams were sometimes justified, out on a ship at sea, and always opportune—but there were also screams that seemed offered through the day for their own sake, endeavors of pure anguish or joy that youth and strength seemed able to put out faster than the steady, pounding quiet of the voyage could ever overtake and heal.

Only her long brows were calm in her face with its widened mouth, stretched eyes, and flying dark hair, in her whole contending body, as though some captive, that had never had news of the world, land or sea, would sometimes stand there and look out from that pure arch—but never to speak; that could not even be thought to hear.

The evening after her overthrow at ping pong, the dining room saw Gabriella come to the door and for a breath pause there. There was an ineffable quality about Mrs. Serto's daughter now. An evening after a storm comes with such bright drops—so does a child whose tantrum is over, even the reason for it almost, if not quite, forgotten. Through large, oval eyes whose shine made them look over-forgiving, she regarded the dining room now. And as she came through the door, they saw appearing from behind her Aldo Scampo, almost luminous himself in a clean white shirt.

As she and Aldo started hand in hand across the room,

there was a sudden *"Tweeeeet!"* Papa, an old man from the table farthest back in the corner, blew a tin whistle whenever he felt like it—his joke and his privilege. Immediately everybody laughed.

Was it on every boat that tried to cross the ocean that some old fellow and his ten-cent whistle alerted the whole assembly at life's most precious moments? Papa was an outrageous, halfway dirty, twice-married old man in an olive-green sweater who at each meal fought for the whole carafe of wine for himself and then sent the waiter for another. On top of his long head rose a crest of grizzly hair. A fatherly mustache, well-stained, draped itself over the whistle when he blew it. Except for one old crippled lady in this room, he was surely the only Italian in the world who could cross the ocean without suffering for it at all. His black eyes were forever traveling carelessly beyond his own table. And just when it was least expected, when it was least desired, when your thoughts were all gentle and reassured and forgiving and triumphant—then it would be your turn: *"Tweeeeet!"*

Gabriella and Aldo, after stopping dead in their tracks—for there was something official about the sound—marched to their separate tables like punished children. But by the time Gabriella had reached hers safely, she was able to lift her face like a dish of something fresh and delicious she had brought straight to them; and Mrs. Serto smiled her circle round: Mr. Fossetta, for Bari; Poldy, who was engaged, and Mr. Ambrogio, for Rome.

"Dressed up!" said Mama, a gesture of blessing for all falling from her plump little hand. Mama was even more dressed up. They had on silk blouses.

"We've been strolling, with Maria-Pia and Joe!" And Gabriella took her seat on Mama's right hand.

Tonight, the dining room felt, the missing sixth should have been at that table. Between Poldy and Mr. Ambrogio waited the vacant chair and spotless napkin of one assigned who had never come. Even if appetite had gone, he should have shown his face to complete the happiness of a mother.

Later that very night, Gabriella was fallen against Mrs. Serto on the rearmost bench on deck, trying not to watch the flagpole ride, while at gentle intervals her mother gave her a little more of the account of the bride's dress reported to be traveling on this ship in the Polish-American's cabin. Without those screams, the *Pomona* sailed in a strange, almost sad tranquillity under the stars, as in a trance that might never be broken again. So there had come a night, almost earlier than they had expected, when they all had their chance to feel sorry for Gabriella.

Between tea and dinner time next day, everybody who was able was sitting about on the benches enjoying the warm sea. All afternoon, with the sun going down on their backs, they had been drawing nearer and nearer the tinted coast of Spain. It grew long, pink, and caverned as the side of a melon. Chances were it would never come close enough for them to see much: they would see no face. But to Gabriella, the faces here on deck appeared bemused enough. Beside her, sitting up on their bench, Mama seemed to be asleep, with Mrs. Arpista, beyond her, also asleep; the two maternal heads under their little black buns nodded together like twin buoys in the waves.

Only the two black men looked the same as always. Not yet had they laughed, or asked a single question. Not yet had they expressed consternation at mealtime, or a moment's doubt about the course of the ship. Their very faith was enough to put other passengers off.

Aldo Scampo, like a man pining to be teased, was reading. He lay sprawled in the solitary deck chair—the one that the steward had opened out and set up in the center of the deck to face everybody, and labeled "Crosby"—very likely the name of the unattached lady who could not speak a word of Italian. All afternoon Aldo had held at various angles in front of his eyes a paper-back book bought on board, *The Bandit Giuliano, Dopo Bellolampo*. Or else he got up and disappeared into the public room to drink cherry soda and play cards with three little gray fellows going to Foggia.

When Aldo was about to open that book again, Gabriella rose from Mama's bench, took a hop, skip and jump to the chair, and pulled Aldo out of it. He came down to the deck floor on hands and knees, with a laughable crash.

She dropped beside him to make a violent face into his. Aldo, as though he drew a gun from a holster, put up a toothpick between his lips. On the softly vibrating floor, ringed around with the well-filled benches, they knelt confronting each other, eyes open wide. Just out of range, the ship's cat picked his way in and out the circle of feet, then, cradled in a pair of horny hands, disappeared upward.

It did not matter that the passengers on the warm *Pomona* deck had heads that were nodding or dreaming of home. It took only their legs from the knees down to listen like ears and watch like eyes—to wait dense and still as a ring of trees come near. The sailors softly beating the air with their paintbrushes, up in Second Class, could look down and see them too, over the signs *"Pittura Fresca"* hung on ropes festooning the stairs.

Aldo's and Gabriella's hands suddenly interlocked, and their arms were as immobilized as wings that failed. Gabriella drove her face into Aldo's warm shirt. She set her teeth into his sleeve. But when she pierced that sleeve she found his arm—rigid and wary, with a muscle that throbbed like a heart. She would have bitten a piece out of him then and there for the scare his arm gave her, but he moved like a spring and struck at her with his playful weapon, the toothpick between his teeth. In return she butted his chest, driving her head against the hard, hot rayon, while, still in the character of an airy bird, he pecked with his little beak that place on the back of the neck where women no longer feel. (Weren't all women made alike? she wondered: *she* could no longer feel there.) She screamed as if she could feel everything. But if she hadn't screamed so hard at Aldo yesterday, she wouldn't have had to bite him today. Now she knew *that* about Aldo.

The circle was still. Mama's own little feet might speak to them—there they rested, so well known. For a space Mama opened her eyes and contemplated her screaming daughter as she would the sunset behind her.

"Help! He's killing me!" howled Gabriella, but Mama dropped her eyes and was nodding Mrs. Arpista's way again.

Aldo buried his face in Gabriella's blouse, and she looked

out over his head and presently smiled—not into any face in particular. Her smile was as rare as her silence, and as vulnerable—it was meant for everybody. A gap where a tooth was gone showed childishly.

And it lifted the soul—for a thing like crossing the ocean could depress it—to sit in the sun and contemplate among companions the weakness and the mystery of the flesh. Looking, dreaming, down at Gabriella, they felt something of an old, pure loneliness come back to them—like a bird sent out over the waters long ago, when they were young, perhaps from their same company. Only the long of memory, the brave and experienced of heart, could bear such a stirring, an awakening—first to have listened to that screaming, and in a flash to remember what it was.

Aldo climbed to his feet and set himself back in his chair, and Gabriella went back to her mother, but the *Pomona*, turning, sailed on to the south, down the coast of Europe—so near now that Father's vesper bell might almost be taken for a little goat bell on shore. The air colored, and a lighthouse put up its arm.

Even the morning sky told them they were in the Mediterranean now. They could see it glowing through the windows of church, while waiting for Father to come and start Mass. In the middle of the night before, they had slipped through the Gates of Gibraltar—even touched there, so it was said. While everybody was asleep, the two black passengers had been put off the boat.

"They're going to the Cape Verde Islands," Mrs. Arpista cried to Mrs. Serto two rows ahead. "They don't know nothing but French."

"Poveretti!" Mrs. Serto cried back, with the sympathy that comes too late. "And where were their wives, *i Mori*?"

"My sweetheart and I are going to have a happy, happy Christmas," Poldy announced, rubbing his hands together. His straw-blond hair was thin enough to show a baby-like scalp beneath.

"So you never seen your girl, eh?" remarked Mr. Fossetta, a small dark father of five, who sat just in front of him. All the Serto table sat together in church—Mama thought it was nice. Today they made a little square around her. At her right, Poldy locked his teeth and gave a dazzling grin.

"We've never seen each other. But do we love each other? Oh boy!"

Mr. Fossetta made the abrupt gesture with which he turned away the fresh sardines at the table, and faced front again.

Poldy reached in his breast pocket and produced his papers. He prodded under the elastic band that held them all together to take out a snapshot, and passed this up to Mr. Fossetta. The first time he'd tried to pass that was in the middle of the movie while the lights blinked on for them to change the reel.

"Yes, a happy, happy Christmas," said Poldy. "Pass that. Why *wouldn't* we be happy, we'll be married then. I'm taking the bridesmaids' dresses, besides the bride's I told you about, and her mother's dress too, in store boxes. Her aunt in Chicago, that's who gave me the address in the first place—she knows everything! The names and the sizes. Everything is going to fit. Wait! I'll show you something else—the ticket I bought for my wife to come back to the U.S.A. on. Guess who we're going to live with? Her aunt."

Everybody took a chance to yawn or look out the window, but Mama inclined her head at Poldy going through his papers and said, "Sweetest thing in the world, Christmas, second to love." She suddenly looked to the other side of her. "You paying attention, Gabriella?"

Gabriella had been examining her bruises, old and new. She shook her head; under the kerchief it was burgeoning with curlers. Here came the snapshot on its way from the row ahead.

"Take that bride," said Mama.

"Hey, she's little!" said Gabriella. "You can't hardly see her."

Old Papa put his head in the door, gave Gabriella his red eye, and vanished. He was only passing by, the ship's cat in his arms, with no intention in the world of coming in, but he looked in.

Poldy reached across Mama as though she were nothing but a man. That golden-haired wrist with its yellow-gold watch was under Gabriella's nose, and those golden-haired fingers snatched the picture from her and Mama's hands and stuck it at Mr. Ambrogio, behind.

"Wait, wait! There went who I love best in world," said Mama. "Little bride. Was that nice?"

"We haven't got all day," said Poldy. "Gee, I can't find her ticket anywhere. Don't worry, folks, I'll show it to you at breakfast."

"She knows how to pose," said Mr. Ambrogio politely. He was a widower of long standing.

"All right, pass it."

At that moment, who but Aldo Scampo elected to come to church! Just in time, as he dropped to his knee by the last chair in the row, to be greeted with Poldy's bride stuck under his nose.

"Curlers!" hissed Mama in Gabriella's ear. She gave Gabriella's cheek one of her incredibly quick little slaps—it looked for all the world like only a pat, belonging to no time and place but pure motherhood.

There Aldo studied the bride from his knees, sighting down his blue chin before breakfast.

"O.K., O.K., partner!" said Poldy, his hand on the reach again, as Father came bustling in with fresh paint on his skirts; and there was quiet except for two noisy, almost simultaneous smacks: Poldy kissing his bride and snapping her back under the elastic band.

"You stay after Mass and confess sloth, you hear?" whispered Mama.

Gabriella and Aldo were looking along the rows of rolled-down eyelids at each other. They put out exactly simultaneous tongues.

By nine o'clock, Gabriella and Aldo were strolling up on deck; so was everybody. Aldo pushed out his lips and offered Gabriella a kiss.

"Oh, look what I found," said Mrs. Serto from behind them, causing them to jump apart as if she'd exploded something. She had opened a little gold locket. Now she held out, cupped in her pink palm, a ragged little photograph, oval and pearl-colored, snatched from its frame. "Who but my Gabriella as a baby?"

Gabriella seized it, where Mama bent over it smiling as at a little foundling, and tucked it inside her blouse.

"No longer a child now, Gabriella," announced Mama to the sky.

"Somebody told me," Aldo said, "it's nifty up front."

"Cielo azzurro!" said Mama. "Go 'head. *Pellegrini, pellegrini* everywhere, beautiful day like this!"

Three priests strolled by, their skirts gaily blowing, and as Joe Monteoliveto ran their gamut, juggling ping pong balls, Mama held Gabriella fast for a moment and whispered, "Not the prize Arpistas may think—he leaves the boat at Palermo."

"Keep my purse," was all Gabriella said.

The long passage through the depths of the ship, that was too narrow for Mrs. Serto and Gabriella to walk without colliding, seemed made for Gabriella and Aldo. True, it was close with the smell of the sour wine the crew drank. In the deepest part, the engines pounding just within that open door made a human being seem to go in momentary danger of being shaken asunder. It sounded here a little like the Niagara Falls at home, but she had never paid much attention to *them.* Yet with all the deafening, Gabriella felt as if she and Aldo were walking side by side in some still, lonely, even high place never seen before now, with mountains above, valleys below, and sky. The old man in the red knit cap who slept all day on top of that box was asleep where he always was, but now as if he floated, with no box underneath him at all, in some spell. Even the grandfather clock, even the map, when these came into sight, looked faceless, part of a landscape. And the remembered sign, so beautifully penned, on the bulletin board—"Lost, a golden brooch for the tie, with initials F. A."—it shone at them like a star.

By steep stairs at the end, they came out on an altogether new deck, where the air was bright and stiff as an open eye. It was white and narrowing, set about with mysterious shapes of iron wound with chains. No passenger was in sight. Leaning into the very beak ahead, with her back to them, a *cameriera* was drying her hair; when she let it loose from the towel it blew behind her straight as an arm. A sailor, seated cross-legged on an eminence like a drum, with one foot bare, the blackened toes fanned out like a circus clown's, sewed with all his might on a sock with a full shape to it. All was still. No—as close as a voice that was speaking to them now, the *Pomona* was parting the water.

"Wait—a—minute," said Aldo still looking, with his hands on his hips.

So this was where Miss Crosby came with her book. Still as a mouse, she was sitting on the floor close to the rail, drawn up with the book on her knees.

"Don't bother her, and maybe she won't bother us," said Gabriella. "That's how *I* treat people."

Aldo came back, reached in his hand, and took the picture away from Gabriella, then sat down cross-legged on this barely slanting floor to see what he'd got.

At last he hit his leg a slap. He said, "They took one of me the same age! They had me dressed up like a little St. John the Baptist. Can you beat 'em?"

Gabriella had been standing behind him, where she could see anew. Suddenly she grasped a length of the hem of her skirt and blindfolded him with it. Aldo threw up both hands, the hand with the snapshot releasing it to the milky sea. The uncovered part of his face expressed solemnity. Like all blindfolded persons, he was holding his breath. Gabriella couldn't see his face; hers above it waited with eyes tight-shut.

A moment went by, and she jumped away; that was all that had come to her to do. Aldo promptly wheeled himself around, one leg flailing the deck, and caught her by the ankle and threw her.

She came down headlong; her fall, like a single clap of thunder, was followed by that burst of expectancy in the air that can almost be heard too. The *cameriera* bound down her hair, and the sailor put on his sock; as if they'd been together a long time, they disappeared together through the door, down the stairs.

Neither Gabriella nor Aldo stirred. They lay, a little apart, like the victims of a passing wind. Presently Aldo, moving one finger at a time, began to thump on the calf of Gabriella's leg—1, 2, 3, 4—while she lay as before, with her back to him. Intermittently the 1, 2, 3, 4 kept up, then it slowed and fell away. Gradually the sounds of the dividing sea came back to Gabriella's ear, as though a seashell were once more held lifted.

She turned her head and opened her eyes onto Aldo's clay-colored shoe, hung loose on his sockless foot. Far away now was his hand, gaping cavelike in sleep beside her forgotten leg. Past the pink buttress of his jaw rose the little fountain, not playing now, where his mouth stood open to the sky. He lay there sound asleep over the Mediterranean Sea.

Gabriella stayed as she was, caught in an element as languorous as it was strange, like a mermaid who has been netted into a fisherman's boat, only to find that the fisherman is dreaming. Where no eye oversaw them, the sea lifted and dropped them both, mindless as a cradle, up and down.

Even when La Zìngara clattered out on deck, with a spectacled youth at her heels, and, seeing Aldo, gave the sharp laugh of experience, Aldo only shut his lips, like a reader who has just licked his finger to turn a page. But Gabriella sat up and caught her hair and her skirt, seeing those horn-rims: that young man was marked for the priesthood.

With the pop of corks being drawn from wine bottles, La Zìngara kicked off her shoes. Then she began dancing in her polished, bare feet over the deck. ("Practicing," she had replied with her knifelike smile when the mothers wondered where she went all day—furiously watching an actress rob the church.) She made the horn-rimmed young man be her partner; to dance like La Zìngara meant having someone to catch you. In a few turns they had bounded to the other side of the deck.

"Excuse me," said a new voice. Miss Crosby had unfolded herself and come over on her long legs. Speaking across the sleeping Aldo as though she only called through a window, she asked, "What do you call those birds in Italian?"

"What birds?"

"There! Making all that racket!" Miss Crosby pointed out to sea with her book, *First Lessons in Italian Conversation.* "Ever since we've been passing Sardinia."

"Didn't you ever see seagulls before?"

"I just want to know the Italian."

"I gabbiani," said Gabriella.

In a moment, Miss Crosby made a face, as if she were about to grit her teeth, and said *"Grazie."* She went away then. Gabriella crossed her legs beneath her and sat there, guarding Aldo.

Three members of the crew presently materialized, one raising his gun toward the birds that were flying and calling there, shifting up and down in the light.

"No!" cried Aldo in his sleep.

In two minutes he was up shooting with the sailors, and she was merely waiting on him.

"Terrible responsibility to be coming into property—who knows how soon!" said Mama.

"It's nothing to be sneezed at," said Gabriella. A white triangle of salve—Maria's Harry had tucked that into her suitcase—was laid over her nose; the rest of her face still carried a carnation glow.

Just those three sat propped on the back of the rear-most bench—Gabriella, Aldo Scampo, and Mama. They could see the long blue wake flowing back from them, smooth as a lady's train.

"Look at the dolphins!" cried Aldo.

"Where, where? Wanting their dinner. A terrible responsibility," said Mama. She ran her loving little finger over the brooches settled here and there on her bosom, like St. Sebastian over his arrows. If she had had to slap Gabriella at the lunch table for getting lost on her morning walk, all was *delicato* now. Nice naps had been taken, tea was over with, and real estate in the vicinity of Naples had come up in conversation.

"And tomorrow, Gala Night," said Mama. "Am I right, Mr. Scampo?"

"Yeah, Mrs. Serto, I guess you are," said Aldo.

Mama slipped down from between them to her feet, her fingers threw them a little wave that looked like a pinch of salt, and she began a last march around deck. Her opposite turn was the public room, where her friends would by now be collecting, the *indisposti* propped deadweight among them but able to listen, and the well ones speculating peacefully out of the wind.

When Mama passed the bench again—really her farewell time, and then she would leave the sunset to young sweethearts—all seemed well. With the obsessiveness that characterizes a family man, Aldo was drumming a soft fist into Gabriella's plump young back, which held there unflinchingly, while her words came out in snatches with the breath cut off between.

"Nothing to be sneezed at— We'll have to wear paper caps—and dance—"

The wake of the ship turned to purple and gold. The dolphins, in silhouette, performed a rainbow of leaps. Gabriella screamed and her laugh ran down the scale.

Mama bowed herself into the public room, where the mothers were expecting her, the full congregation; and taking the seat by Mrs. Arpista, she continued with the subject she loved the best—under its own name, now: love.

But the day of Gala Night broke forth with a trick from the Mediterranean. Its blue had darkened and changed, and here and there at the edge of things could be seen a little whitecap. Father did not look too cheerful at Mass, and among other sad messages coming in from either side to Mama was the one that Aldo Scampo himself had not been able to rise. When a wave was seen at the glass of the porthole, looking in the dining room at lunch, Mama retreated upward to the public room, with Gabriella to sit by her side; and through the afternoon she declared herself unanswerable for the night.

But when the dinner gong was sounded, Mrs. Serto found she could raise her head. She believed, if she were helped to dress up a little . . . After she had pinned and patted Mama together, Gabriella got out of her skirt, into her blue, and up on her high heels; then she guided Mama down that final flight of stairs.

And when they had crossed the dining room to the Serto table, one of the old, old ladies was sitting in Mama's place. Was it simply a mistake? Was it a visit? She was far too old to be questioned. Every little pin trembling, Mama sat down in Gabriella's place, which left Gabriella the vacant one, with Mr. Ambrogio between them. The first thing the waiter brought was the paper hats.

The old lady put on hers, and so did they all after her. Gabriella's was an open yellow crown, cut in points that tended to fall outward like the petals of a daisy. But poor Mama could not take her eyes away from the old lady who sat in her place.

She was a Sicilian. With her pierced ears and mosaic eardrops, the skin of her face around eyes and mouth like water where stones have dropped in, her body wrapped around in shawls and her head in a black silk rag—and now the paper hat of Gala Night atop that, looking no more foolish there than a little cloud hanging to a mountain—their guest was so old that her chin perpetually sank nearly to the level of the table. She treated their waiter like dirt.

He was bringing every course tonight to the old lady first, instead of to Mama, and with a croak and a flick of the hand the old lady was sending it back—not only the *antipasto*, but now the soup. She wanted to see something better. Their waiter treated her dismissals with respect—with more than respect; some deeper, more everlasting relationship was implied.

And suddenly, as the *pasta* was coming in, their long-missing table mate chose to make his appearance. Another chair had to be wedged between the old lady's and Mr. Fossetta's, where he sat down, with pale cheeks, snow-white hair, and mustaches that were black as night. He looked at them all in their paper caps. His first words were to demand, "Is it true? There is no one for Genoa but me?"

Mama looked back at him, in a little soldier hat with a tassel on top, and said, "This boat is *Pomona*, going to *Napoli*."

"And after *Napoli*," said he, "Genoa." A paper cap was put in his hand by the waiter, and he put it on—it was a chef's cap—and lowered his head at Mama. "Genoa I leave only on holiday. Only for pleasure I travel. Now I return to Genoa."

"Please," said Mr. Ambrogio politely, "what is there beautiful in Genoa?"

He was handed a calling card. Mama's little hand asked for it, and she read to them in English: "C. C. Ugone. The man to see is Ugone. Genoa."

"For one thing, is in Genoa most beautiful cemetery in world," said Mr. Ugone—and did well to speak in English; otherwise who could have understood this voice from the north tonight? "You have never seen? No one? Ah, the statues—you could find nowhere in *Italia* more beautiful, more sad, more real. Envision with me now, I will take you there gladly. Ah! See here—a mama, how she hold high the little daughter to kiss picture of Papa—all lifesize. See here! You see angel flying out the tomb—lifesize! See here! You see family of ten, eleven, twelve, all kneeling lifesize at deathbed. You would marvel how splendid is Genoa with the physical. Oh, I tell you here tonight, you making a mistake to leave this boat at Naples."

Mama returned Mr. Ugone's card.

"I go to Rome," Mr. Ambrogio said.

"Say, mister," said Poldy. "What you say sounds worth coming all the way to Italy to see."

"Signore," said Mr. Ugone, turning toward Poldy—he had to lean across Mr. Fossetta and his *pasta*—"you will see this and more. Oh, I guarantee, you will find it sad! You want to see tear on little child's cheek? Solid tear?" Mr. Ugone made a gesture of silence at the waiter coming with the fish. "*Ecco!* Bringing the news! Is turned over, the little boat. Look how hand holds tight the hat. Mmm!"

"No sardine!" said Mama, ahead of the old lady, but there was no need of warning. The waiter had dropped his tray on the floor.

But Mr. Ugone, with his untoward respect for Poldy, went on above all confusion. "*Signore*, we have in Genoa a sculptor who is a special for angels. See this tomb! Don't you see that soul look glad to be reaching Heaven? Oh! Here a sister die young. See her dress—the fold is caught in the tomb-door—*delicato*, you accord? How she enjoin the other sister she die too, before her wedding day. Sad, mmm?"

"Say!" said Poldy.

"Gabriella, you please listen to me, hold tight that hat!" said Mama. "You shake your head and it goes round and round."

"I show you," said Mr. Ugone to all, "the tomb my blessed mother."

Back in the corner, old Papa had been fixing his eye on Mr. Ugone for some time. Now he blew his whistle.

"Go ahead," said Poldy. Mr. Ugone had stopped with his

napkin over his heart. "He does that all the time—we're used to it."

"Of course," said Mr. Ugone, "other beautiful things I show to you in Genoa. I enjoin you direct your attention to back of old wall where Paganini born."

"Say, what are you?" Gabriella asked him, holding her crown on straight.

"Who's Paganini?" said Poldy.

But Mr. Ugone, who had never really taken his eyes off Papa, waiting there still in that red engineer's cap with his whistle raised, now rose to his feet. With the words, "Also well-known skyscraper!" flung to them all, he suddenly left them—almost as though he hadn't ever come.

Mr. Fossetta brushed off his hands, and poured more wine around. Under cover of Mr. Ugone's departure, the old lady stole a roll from Mama's plate, and Mama watched it disappearing into that old, old mouth. But Mama remained throughout the evening just as nice to the old lady as Gabriella was nice to Mama. Even when the old lady described the Cathedral of Monreale from front to back, and more than one time said, "First church in the world for beauty, Saint Peter second," Mama only closed her eyes and gave a brief click of the tongue.

"Mama," said Gabriella, "are we coming back home on this boat too?"

"No more *Pomona*!" said Mama. "We come home *Colomba*. By grace of Holy Mother it will not rock—beautiful white boat, *Colomba*."

"You are full of thoughts too." Mr. Ambrogio turned to Gabriella. "I am still missing my tiepin. Do you feel I will ever find it?"

"Who knows?" said Mama. "You never know when you find something. That's what I tell my poor daughter every morning she wants to sleep late the nice bed."

"Ah, it could have been lost into the sea—before we start, who knows? Standing to wave at friends, from the rail—'Good-by! Good-by!'" and Mr. Ambrogio half rose from his chair to wave at them now.

"But you're *wearing* a tiepin!" said Poldy, and laughed loudly at poor Mr. Ambrogio, who sat down; and it was true that he was doing so, and true too that he had been showing them from the first night out the way he had said good-by to all those friends he had in America.

"It is my second pin, not my first. Only a cameo." Mr. Ambrogio's feelings were hurt now. He was going eventually home to Sicily but certainly he wanted his first pin for his audience with the Pope. He asked not to be given any of the fish, which the waiter now brought in for the second time.

The boat lurched. A black wave could be felt looking in at the nearest porthole, out of the night.

"Ah, the Captain this boat—has he anywhere a wife?" cried Mama, and rolled her head toward the old lady, who gave no answer.

Poldy at once took out his papers. Hadn't Mr. Ugone's card at the table been enough?—even supposing it had not been Gala Night, with *gelati* somewhere on the way. Now Poldy was finding an envelope he had never brought out before, with an address written on it in purple ink—a long one.

"What town in Italy is that?" he demanded, and passed the envelope back and forth in front of Mr. Fossetta's eyes. Mr. Fossetta, with one sharp gesture of the hand and a shake of the head, went on taking fishbones out of his mouth.

"Can't read? That's the town they're taking me to to get married." Poldy beamed. "My sweetheart and her brother, or cousin, or whoever comes with her to meet the boat in Naples, they'll take me there. How about you, can you read?" he asked Mr. Ambrogio, but on the way to him the envelope had reached the old lady, who deposited it in her lap.

Poldy only shouted to the waiter, "Gee, I'll take another plate of that!", pulling him back by the coat. It was not only Gala Night that Poldy asked for second plates—it was every night. He enjoyed the food.

"If," Mr. Fossetta remarked ostensibly to Mama, with something a little ominous in his voice, "if she has a brother, then it will be her brother come to meet him."

"Only daughters have I ever been sent!" cried Mama—then gave an even sharper cry.

Through the dining-room door, arriving at the same time as the veal course, Aldo Scampo had entered like a ghost. Tentatively, not seeming to see with his eyes at all, he made his way through the dining room with all its caps, past the Serto table without a sign. Even after he had sat down safely in his own chair, who could speak to him? He was so white.

Papa, however, blew his whistle. This time he stood up to do it.

And instantly, another old man—the old man in the red knit cap who slept in the day by the ship's engines and had not exchanged for a paper cap tonight—rose up from the other side of the room and answered Papa, with mumbled words and the vague waving of an arm. He thought somebody had been insulted. Papa blew the whistle back at him, and then, carried away at meeting opposition at last, blew without stopping—*"Tweet! Tweet! Tweet! Tweet!"* The argument filled the dining room to its now gently creaking walls.

The head steward himself came to Papa's table—his first visit to the back of the room. Everybody but the other old man, and the old lady who was crushing a crust, like a bone, between her teeth, grew hushed.

"What is the meaning of this whistle?" asked the steward.

Old Papa, with his head cocked and in the voice of a liar, told the steward that once a little boy, long ago, was going away to America from Italy. Papa's left hand dived low and gave the air a pat. On such a big ship—and his right hand poked the whistle into the girth of the steward—the little boy might have been lost. But his papa said to him, "Never mind. Whenever you hear *this*"—and before the steward knew it, the old man had blown it again, *"Tweeeeeet!"*—"Papa." All this had the old sleepy-head raising both fists in the air and shaking them together as if he denied every word of that tale. The whistle was blowing and everybody else was shouting.

Aldo Scampo moved out of his chair and started silently out of the room the way he had come; only his yellow, pointed crown was crumpled like the antlers of a deer where, as he rose up, he had had to clutch his head.

"No *gelati*?" many called sorrowfully after him through their laughter.

"Why did he think he had to come, anyway?" Gabriella shrieked as he staggered past her. "Who's Aldo Scampo?"

"You imagine the sea is high tonight? Not at all!" The voice of a visiting Father, who was down from above for Gala Night in *turistica*, was heard over the room as the dining-room door fell to. Laughter stopped. This sea was no match at all for what might have been sent them, bearing the season of the year in mind. Up to now there was no word for it but calm. Had due thanks been sent up? Father, an Irishman, appeared to be looking around him for an immediate errand boy. Still, it was a fact, he said: by the essence of their nature, which was frail, all human beings were probably doomed to be seasick. The middle of the deep was never the spot God's children would show wisdom to go wandering over for long. Upstairs, Father said, with another look around, it was taking an equivalent toll.

Mr. Ambrogio leaned over his fork, which waited with a bite of veal the shape of a little ship itself, and spoke as quietly as Father to the Serto table at large. "I think on this ship there are people lower than us. This morning, alone on my way, I have seen other steps going down." And staring down over his shoulder, between himself and Mama, he suddenly sent his hand, fork and all, in a plumb line toward the floor. Consternation rose around the table, led by Mama's cry.

"Am I in wrong place?" A little old man got up from the nearest table and tottering with the roll of the ship began to turn himself around in the aisle. "Why nobody tell me?" That little man always thought he was in the wrong place, on the wrong ship, going the wrong way for Foggia; it always took many to reassure him. But tonight his cone-shaped hat came down nearly over his eyes.

Mr. Fossetta pushed back his chair.

"Looka my hand," he said. He held it up squarely, a small dark hand still burnished with the grease of America, as the little lost man drew near and bent his face over it, standing in Mama's way. Everybody who was near enough to the Serto table watched the hand; a few stood up. Mr. Fossetta rolled his wrist like a magician; then, with the knife from his plate, began to count off the fingers.

"*Firsta* class . . . *Seconda* class . . . *Us.*"

But a finger was left, dangling below the knife. That was seen. Mr. Fossetta got to his feet, drew silence again, and started over, this time counting from the middle finger and in Italian. When he finished, he flicked both hands apart on the empty air.

"Now you believe?" he said, but his own face had gone desperately white. "Nobody below us but the fishes." And poor Mr. Fossetta departed the way Aldo had gone, only it was to unfeeling choruses of "Champagne! *Gelati!*" For here came out the trays, sparkling all over, radiating to every table. Jumping up, Poldy raised his glass. "To my wedding!" he cried to the room, then swallowed the champagne without a stop.

Mama first pulled him down, then rose herself with her own arms stretched empty, like a prophetess.

"Mama! It's Gala Night," said Gabriella, joining her hands and looking into her mother's face.

Mrs. Serto, with a tragic look for all, toppled upon her daughter. Gabriella, struggling up just in time, caught her beneath the arms and then bore her, leaning, from the dining room. As they passed table after table, people who were eating *gelati* rose spoon in hand, paper hats a-bob on their heads, to make way.

It was thought an anticlimax, showing lack of appreciation of the night's feelings, that Gabriella came straight back. The *frutti* was just appearing. Crowned a little nearer to the ears, as though by one last sweep of a failing hand, she took back her real place at the table, where she ate her own *gelati* and then her mother's, and drank both glasses of champagne.

The old lady—as though she were the waiter's own mother, or the V.M., thought Gabriella—finally accepted his bowl of fruit, and Gabriella was allotted, from her fork, a little brown-skinned pear.

It was this old lady who remained last at the Serto table. When the others excused themselves, she was still dropping grapes into her mouth, like a goddess sacrificing a few extra tribes. Scarcely an eyelid flickered from above.

Upstairs in the public room, when the three-piece band began playing "Deep in the Heart of Texas" to start the dancing, an unexpected trio of newcomers turned themselves loose on the girls. Two looked like, and were, the radio operator and the man who brought the bouillon around the deck in the mornings; another, who had the mothers guessing at first, was placed as the *turistica* hairdresser, seen daily, after all, smoking in his doorway. Then Mr. Ambrogio, who had softly perfumed himself again since dinner, with the thin little widow from Rome, went arrowing bravely down the floor; she was the usually distracted mother of those divine, but sometimes bad, little children.

Gabriella stood in the door, in her blue dress mounted with ruffles from which the little pleats had still not quite shaken out—and suddenly she was asked to dance by Joe Monteoliveto. Maria-Pia was out of it too, then; there was no one who could not fall by the wayside tonight, and have a stranger appear in his place. Joe wore on his head a pink stack like a name-day cake, with a cherry on top. Gabriella gave him her hand. Out on the floor, under the stroke of the riding ship, they began circling together as easily as if they had sailed many a time across the sea, and were used to the waves and the way to dance over them.

Tonight was Gala Night, that was the reason—and partners were not real partners, the sea not the sea Mama had had in mind, and paper lanterns masked the lights that climbed and fell over their heads; and there was no colliding with the world. The band went into "Japanese Sandman," and as Gabriella went swinging in the arms of Joe Monteoliveto the whole round of the room, a gentle breath of wonder started after her, too soft to be accusation, too perishable to be hope. Dancing, poor Mrs. Serto's daughter was filled with grace.

The whole company—mothers banked around the walls, card players trapped at the tables, and the shadowy old—all looked her way. *Indisposti* or not, of course they knew what was in front of their eyes. Once more, slipping the way it liked to do through one of life's weak moments, illusion had got in, and they were glad to see it. How many days had they been on the water!

The mothers gently cocked their heads from side to side in time, the old men re-lit their tobacco and poured out a little *vino.* That great, unrewarding, indestructible daughter of Mrs. Serto, round as an onion, and tonight deserted, unadvised, unprompted, and unrestrained in her blue, went dancing around this unlikely floor as lightly as an angel.

Whenever she turned, she whirled, and her ruffles followed—and the music too had to catch up. It began to seem to the general eye that she might be turning around faster inside than out. For an unmarried girl, it was danger. Some radiant pin through the body had set her spinning like that tonight, and given her the power—not the same thing as permission, but what was like a memory of how to do it—to be happy all by herself. Their own poor daughters, trudging uphill and down as the ship tilted them, would have to bide their time until Gabriella learned her lesson.

When La Zìngara arrived, and took Joe Monteoliveto away in the middle of a waltz, Gabriella spread both arms and went on dancing by herself. Lighter than ever on her toes, as the band swung faster and louder into a new chorus of "Let Me Call You Sweetheart," and the very sides of the room began tapping and humming, she began whirling around in place in the middle of the floor.

Arms wide, toes in, four, six, ten, a dozen turns she went, and kept whirling, and at the end, as the cymbal crashed, she stopped. The ruffles ran the other way once, and fell into their pleats. The *Pomona* rose and fell, like a sigh on the breast, but Gabriella held her place—not falling: smiling, intact, a Leaning Tower. A shout of joy went up—even from those that the spectacle of an ungrasped, spinning girl was bound to have made feel worse. "Bravo!" shouted Father Madden, standing dangerously on a chair.

It was the stunt Gabriella was famous for in the St. Cecilia Sodality.

Whistles with toy balloons attached arrived on a dining-room tray, and were blown in every direction. For a moment Papa was missed. He would have enjoyed this!

"May I have the pleasure of the next?" Mr. Ambrogio asked Gabriella, moving a saffron handkerchief over his brow above dilated eyes.

Poldy, in the end, broke up the evening—he did not dance—by rushing in pretending to be Gene Autry on horseback and shooting an imaginary pistol at all the girls and all the boys and at all the lights in this room afloat in the night at sea.

•

It was as though they'd *forgotten* Palermo!

Everybody, at sun-up, crowded to the rail to turn one concerted gaze, full and ardent, on the first big black island rocks. They pointed fingers that trembled up at crags, into caves. They smiled on a man they had surprised in his frail little craft with the pomegranate-colored sail, far out in the early morning under the drop of some cliff. How fast now they were slipping through the silver light! Shafts of the clearing sun forked down from battlements higher than the ship was. The mist lifted and revealed something dim and green sliding near, something adored.

Smiling, they turned and admired one another. Everybody was dressed up for Palermo—not only the Sicilians, who would be reaching home. Gone were the shawls except on the oldest ladies—those were eternal. All about were the coats and hats of city streets; new stockings flashed in the light. Gone were the caps—there had been a felt hat on the grayest old grandfather since six o'clock in the morning.

Gabriella, though not specially in honor of Palermo, had got back into her blue. Only Aldo must still be untouched by where they were. Back in the canary sweatshirt, he was spread out in Miss Crosby's chair, not even looking when a passing cave was hailed as Giuliano's, and Joe Monteoliveto, with Maria-Pia pulling on his coattails, nearly fell overboard trying to see who was in it.

As they were being tugged into the harbor, it looked as though Palermo itself could wait no longer on the *Pomona*. One by one, bobbing out on the water's altered green, appeared tiny rowboats, and out of them presently came small, urgent cries. The boats worked their way nearer and nearer the ship, shirtsleeved arms shot up from them like flags, cries turned into names, and suddenly everywhere at once there was welcome. One boat was bringing thirteen, all fat, still unrecognized, one man in shirtsleeves rowing, the rest in a frenzy of waving.

"Enrico!"

"Achille!"

"Rosalia!"

"Massimiliano!"

The little old lady who had invited herself to the Serto table on Gala Night was all ready to disembark. She was the one with the limp. She made her way around deck like a wounded bird on the ground, opening her mouth now and then to scream "Fortunato!"

And suddenly she was answered from the water: "Pepi-i-ina!"

Mama, rushing to look out by first one side, then the other, was wildly excited. Her crisis last night had done her good. She was dressed as though for Sunday. She easily found *Signora* Pepina's relative for her—that was his boat. No, it was that one!

"Fortunato!"

"Fortunato! I see him!" Mrs. Serto could be heard above all the rest. "Fortunato and seven. Have no doubt. It is he."

"Why couldn't he wait? We'll get there soon enough," said Gabriella.

"He is the rower!" Mrs. Serto swung her purse in a wild arc; now her crucifix, having come unpinned once but discovered thus by Mr. Ambrogio, was pinned back all crooked.

"Francesco!"

"Pepi-i-ina!"

"Massimiliano!"

"But where is Achille?"

"He has had heart attack!" screamed Mama fearfully.

In the dock—now in plain view from shipboard—a fight was going on among those who had been patient enough to wait on shore; a big man in a straw hat who had got past the rope was struggling in the hands of the police. Here, crowded to the *Pomona*'s landward side, the passengers could hear the warm, worldly sound of fisticuffs traveling across the last reach of water, the insults rolling and falling on solid ground.

"Francesco!"

"Assunta!"

"Achille, Achille, Achille!"

"Pepi-i-ina!"

"*Ecco, ecco* Pepina!" screamed Mama. "Must we tell you which one is she?"

In the background, by the flagpole, Maria-Pia Arpista and Joe Monteoliveto were trying to say good-by. Maria-Pia was weeping into a silk handkerchief, and Joe was so swallowed up in a winter suit—the one from whose sleeves he had nearly fallen out—as to look entirely different from last night.

"Moto perpetuo." The little man who had never been sure where the boat was taking them smiled at Gabriella, stirring the air with his black-nailed finger. He remembered her.

Gabriella nodded to him. She set her shoulders and posed beside her mother, frowning out from under her Buffalo hat, facing the dock.

"Fortunato, he is your brother?" Mama was asking the old woman at her other side. "Your nephew? Cousin? He was not your husband?"

"He is all I have," the old woman replied.

La Zìngara managed to be the first from *turistica* to disembark. She went swaying down the gangway, arms outstretched—secretly for balance, Gabriella felt, but outwardly to extend a tender greeting. Below, with his arms also outflung, waited, alas, a country clown, with red face and yellow shoes. La Zìngara had saved for this moment those two thin but brilliant red foxes that bit each other around her neck, both with blue eyes.

"Well, there *she* goes," said the voice of Aldo, a yawn all through it. He had wandered to the rail where the three for the priesthood stood.

Gabriella did not even look at him. From Maria-Pia she had heard what all the boys called La Zìngara among themselves—*Il Cadavere.*

"You will see tomorrow," her mother told her with a nod. "It will be much more than this. These are only Sicilians. Why don't we go 'head to Naples?"

Gabriella screamed, "Where's the fire? What's going to happen when we do get there?"

"L'Anno Santo, l'Anno Santo," said Mama. "But listen." She pulled Gabriella to her. "If you don't pay attention, you be like Zìngara some day—old maid! You see her neck? Then you cry for somebody to take you even to *Sicilia*! But who? I'll be dead then, in cemetery!" Mama gave a cross little laugh and pushed her away.

At last the Sicilians were all off the boat, and all their trunks and boxes and bundles had been flung down behind them, with the electric toasters and irons tied on like Christmas tags. The struggling and shouting and claiming ceased on shore, kissing and embracing fell off, and the final semaphores from the shirtsleeved arms were diminishing away. Once more the *Pomona* throbbed and moved in blue water.

"When did that Joe Monteoliveto sneak off the ship?" wondered Mama aloud, not yet going inside. "He never said good-by to me."

This sunset was the last. Gabriella stood at the flagpole and looked off the back of the ship; it moved smoothly now as if by magic.

Once—she couldn't remember how long ago—there had been some country they sailed near—Africa—with mountains like coals, and above, the scimitar and star of evening. The country had vanished like the two black men who got off in the night for Cape Verde. The moon and star tonight looked as though they had never been close together in their lives, to hang one from the tip of the other to go down over the edge of the world.

Was now the time to look forward to the doom of parting, and stop looking back at the doom of meeting? The thought of either made sorrow go leaping and diving, like those dolphins in the water. Gabriella would only have to say "Good-by, Aldo," and while she was saying the words, the time would be flying by; parting would be over with almost before it began, no matter what Aldo had in store for an answer. "Hello, Aldo!" had been just the other way.

"What d'you think you see out there?" came Aldo's voice. "A whale?"

Reflecting the rosy light, a half-denuded stalk of bananas at his feet—for Aldo Scampo had slipped off the boat in Palermo and back on again, without a word to anybody—he was where you could find him still, in the old place, eating away and turning over pages he could hardly see any longer.

She made her way slowly to his chair and sat down on the arm of it, and like a modest confession let out the weight of her side against his shoulder. He offered her a bite of his banana. Tiredly and quietly, in alternation, they ate it. His book dropped to the floor; the toe of her shoe found it and drew it under the chair. Her heel went down, almost without her knowing, on the idealized, dreaming, and predatory face of that Sicilian bandit.

"Almost over now," said Aldo into the evening.

Their thoughts had met. Curtained into her bed that night, and after Mama had fallen silent, Gabriella could go to sleep thinking of those three words. Just now she dropped her head and put a kiss on Aldo somewhere, the way she would upon a little baby.

Near them, there was a patter of applause. Without their noticing, the nightly circle of sitters had gathered outside tonight, on the warm apron of deck—their ranks thinned now, since Palermo, by a number of the solidest. The clapping was for old Papa, who had come forward to sing.

His verses were like little rags that fluttered on the wind from his frail and prancing person. He carried a willowy cane. He had saved his paper hat, which showed against the first stars, jutting like a rooster's crown. So he must have known all along he would sing on the last night.

He stepped back and came forward again, tapped his cane, and sang a verse; retired, and came back with a new one. His voice was old and light, a little cracked. Each time, they gave him back the chorus, sitting in close array, moved in nearer together than ever on the benches and on the floor, a row reclining against billowy knees and another leaning on billowy shoulders behind, as if for some strange, starlit group-photograph, to be found years later in a trunk. A girl went to the well for water, Papa sang, and a traveler jumped out and surprised her, and she dropped her pitcher.

Mama's benchful moved in closer to make room for Gabriella and Aldo. After they sat down, they joined in the chorus with everybody. Whatever the verse, it was the same chorus—in Buffalo, in New York, in California, in Naples, perhaps even in Genoa. As the song went on, Aldo turned his head and on Gabriella's moving lips returned her kiss.

If only that had been good-by! But here they still were. Mama in the next instant rapped Aldo's skull with her knuckle—the crack of her wedding ring went out all over the Mediterranean night. Mama was still not speaking to Aldo for his ruining Gala Night for her. He obediently caught up with the song. Everything was in darkness now—there were only the *Pomona*'s lights and the stars.

Presently Mama called out to ask Poldy the hour by his wristwatch, but Poldy did not reply. He was stretched on a bench nearby, face-down on his sleeve, asleep; his hair had turned to silver.

"Time for my Gabriella to say good night," announced Mama anyway.

"I'm not sleepy!" said Gabriella. "There's lots more songs!"

Old Papa tapped. This is for me, thought Gabriella, and stood up. Mama flew up beside her, boxed her ears, and pulled her out of Papa's way, calling to them all, "My youngest! Look once more my baby Gabriella! Tomorrow she will be in Naples!"

"Good night!" they said, the women all embracing Gabriella and one another. "The last night—the last!" Mama kissed Mrs. Arpista back, and cried, "In Naples, who knows how soon something will happen?" Gabriella waved her hand at Mr. Ambrogio, who rose speechless from among the men, and then Mama led her away.

"Don't fall down the stairs!" called Aldo after her in a strangely discordant voice, almost as if it came from out over the water.

But old Papa, tapping his cane, brought in his circle closer. He could sing the night to sleep.

When the *Pomona* came in sight of land, it was sunrise. Sailors were lifting away tarpaulins, and hauling ropes and chains over the feet of a crowd, while joking indecipherably among themselves; for this once-secret, foremost deck had by now been discovered by everyone.

The body of the sea had been cut off. The *Pomona* sailed among dark, near islands, like shaggy beings asleep on one arm or kneeling now forever. Far ahead, Vesuvius, frail as a tent, almost transparent, lifted up under the morning. Gabriella watched it coming nearer and nearer to her. At last it was exactly like the picture over the dining-room mantel at home, which hung above the row of baby photographs and the yellow one of Nonna with the startled eyes under a mound of black hair.

Tightening her hand to a fist, Gabriella banged herself on the chest three times under Aldo's eyes. Holding his eyes wide open to keep himself awake gave him an expression of black indignation.

"Man Mountain Dean!" she wailed at him. "I'm a big girl now and I want my nourishment!" This had never failed to bring a laugh from the girls in Sacred Heart typewriting class.

But that breakfast was the one *Pomona* meal Gabriella could never remember afterwards; though she could see the table-cloth stained like a map with old wine. Surely she and Aldo had sat there, where neither had ever sat before, and eaten one meal together, in the hue and cry of what was about to happen.

Arrival in Naples was not so simple as being welcomed to Palermo. Only officials came out on the water to meet them, speeding direct by motor and climbing up on board. *"Attenzione!"* was broadcast every moment; everybody was being herded somewhere, only where? Mama, who could find the heart of confusion wherever it moved, constantly darted into it, striking her brow. And then, up in First Class as they stood in line to wait, the man who had charge of the S's couldn't find something he needed, his seal. Then Poldy's passport was lost—by the *Pomona*, not Poldy—and there was much running about, until all at once the spelling of his name, hailed through the room, seemed to clear things up everywhere. The feeling ran strong that landing would be soon. Mr. Ambrogio steered two of the ancient shawled ladies, like old black poodles, one on each arm, outside on deck and started a line at the rail. But Aldo Scampo still reclined in one of the overstuffed chairs, hideously yawning.

Half an hour later, with everybody watching from high on board, the docks of Naples in a bloom of yellow sun slid directly under their side. They could hear the first street sounds—*they* had awakened them!—the whipping of horses, the creaking of wooden wheels over stones, the cry of a child from somewhere deep in the golden labyrinth.

The gangway was an apparatus of steps and ropes. As it dropped like an elephant's trunk from the height of the ship, streams of Neapolitans came running toward it across a sweep of walled-in yard floored over with sun, with yellow trees stirring their leaves and buildings whose sides danced with light.

"Hey! Naples smells like a kitchen!" cried Gabriella; for all that couldn't be helped in life had stolen over her, sweet as a scent, just then.

"Not the kitchen on *this* boat!" said Aldo beside her.

"Where's Nonna?" screamed Gabriella. "Where's my Nonna?"

The first passengers, the priests, were already descending, fast as firemen down a pole. Then a shower of nuns went down.

And down rushed Mrs. Serto headlong. She flew from Mr. Ambrogio, who wished to offer her his arm, as if she'd never seen him before. She clopped down the slatted steps like a little black pony, her spangled veil flying. Then all were let loose!

And where was Mama now? Gabriella frowned down over the rail, and could recognize nobody in the spinning crowd but Mr. Fossetta. Looking flattened, taking long steps, he seemed already making for Bari, dressed in a Chicago overcoat, long, thick and green, with a felt hat over his eyes and his lips pushing out a cigar. He did not seem ever to have had a delicate stomach; he looked bent on demonstrating that the most intimate crowd, when the moment came, could tear itself apart, hurry to vanish.

Where was Aldo? He was still behind her, breathing on first one side of her, then the other—breathing as he took the coats both out of her arms, hers and Mama's. She was left at the head of the ladder with only her purse and the pasteboard box for the hat she had fastened on her head.

"Now?" she asked him.

"See Naples and die!" he said loudly in her face, as if he had been preparing the best thing to say.

She took a step down, and the gangway all but swung free. Everything moved below, travelers and relatives running in and out of each other's arms, as if rendered by the Devil unrecognizable; a band of ragged boys with a ball; a family of dogs, another of blind and crippled people; and what looked like generations of guides and porters, in hereditary caps; and now moving in through the big arched gate (an outer rim of carriages, horn-blowing taxis, streetcars and cars reached around the Piazza beyond) a school of nuns with outstretched plates, all but late for the boat. Loudest of all, a crowd of little girls all dressed in black were jumping up and down shaking noisy boxes and singing like a flock of birds, *"Orfanelli, orfanelli, orfanelli—"* Then she felt Aldo's step behind her shake the whole scene again, as if they were treading the spokes of a wheel, and now it began to turn steadily beneath them.

"Poldy!" Aldo hailed him from the air. "See Naples and die, Poldy! Where's your girl?"

Poldy was running up and down the dock pitching a ball with some little boys of Naples. He wore the feathered hat, the bright yellowish coat with the big buttons that had galvanized them all so on the first day at sea, before they knew all about him. He shouted back, "Oh, she'll find me! I sent her a whole dozen poses!"

Poldy's and Aldo's laughs met like clapped hands over Gabriella's head, and she could hardly take another step down for anger at that girl, and outrage for her, as if she were her dearest friend, her little sister. Even now, the girl probably languished in tears because the little country train she was coming on, from her unknown town, was late. Perhaps, even more foolishly, she had come early, and was languishing just beyond that gate, not knowing if she were allowed inside the wall or not—how would she know? No matter—they would meet. The *Pomona* had landed, and that was enough. Poor girl, whose name Poldy had not even bothered to tell them, her future was about to begin.

"Watch me!" Poldy, just below, was shouting to the little boys. "I'll teach you how to throw a ball!"

But he turned his shining face upward and threw the ball at Gabriella. It only struck the *Pomona*'s side and bounced back; all the same, she dodged and swayed, and Poldy covered his head with his sleeve in imitation shame, while the little urchins stamped up and down beside him, laughing in a contagious-sounding joy like the *orfanelli's.*

"Rock-a-bye baby!" she yelled down over their heads. "On the tree top! When the wind blows—"

Aldo, coming out of the family coats, put a grip around her neck for the last time. But even while he did it, instinct, too, told her she could not scream that way any longer. She was here.

"Ecco! Ecco!" came Mama's own voice, wildly excited. *"Mamma mia!"* There she was, halfway across the yard.

And where she pointed, almost in the center of everything, was a little, low, black figure waiting. It was the quietest and most substantial figure there, unagitated as a little settee, a black horsehair settee, in a room where people are dancing.

"But she doesn't look like her picture!" cried Gabriella. And her foot came down and touched something hard, the hard ground of Naples. Out of it came a strange, rocking response—as if the earth were shocked on its part, to be meeting their feet. Then the coats were bundled in her arms.

"O.K.," said Aldo. "Got to line up my stuff and try for a train. Good-by, Mr. Ambrogio!" he shouted. "Don't let 'em try to keep you over here!" And off he went, at an odd trot.

"We shall never meet again!" Mr. Ambrogio, standing at the foot of the gangway now with his arm raised like a gladiator, had found words. Then, raising the other arm too, he half ran through the moving game of ball, to be gathered in by some old ladies—just like the ones he'd been escorting across the ocean. But in his consideration he did not even knock down Poldy's stack of suitcases and cardboard boxes, neat as a little house in the thick of the disembarkation.

"Gabriella Serto! You want to stay on ship?" Mama had seized her and was taking her through the crowd. "Think who you keep waiting! You want to go to Genoa?" Mama was first pushing her ahead, then pulling her back and shoving herself in front.

"Mamma mia!"

"Crocefissa!"

Mama threw herself forward and arms came up and embraced her.

Then Mama herself was set to one side by a small brown hand with a thin gold ring on it. And there was Nonna, her big, upturned, diamond-shaped face shimmering with wrinkles under its cap of white hair and its second little cap of black silk. So low and so full of weight in all her shawls, she not only looked to be seated there—she was. Amply, her skirts covered whatever she was resting on.

Nonna drew Gabriella down toward all her blackness, which the sun must have drenched through and through until light and color yielded to it together, and to which the very essence of that smell in the air—of cinnamon and cloves, bananas and coffee—clung. Raising Gabriella's chin, Nonna set a kiss on one of her cheeks, then the other. Nonna's own cheek, held waiting, was brown as a nut and dainty as a rose. She gave Gabriella an ancient, inviting smile.

"Si," she said. *"Si."*

As Nonna began to address Gabriella, the very first words were so beautiful and without reproach, that they seemed to leave her out. Nothing had prepared Gabriella for the *sound* of Nonna. She couldn't understand a word. Her gaze wavered and fell. A little way off in the crowd she saw the feet of Miss Crosby, raised on tiptoe beside a suitcase. *She* had learned only one thing the whole way over, *i gabbiani*. And there, poor Maria-Pia Arpista, rigid as though bound and gagged, was being carried off by a large and shouting family, who were proudest of all of the baby's coming to meet her. But Nonna had not finished, already? Here was Mama rushing her off to the Customs.

Afterwards, there was Nonna watching for them in her same place, as they came out of the shed with their baggage behind them. The porter in a kind of madness—he was an old man—had thrown their trunk over his back, taken their suitcases, and then had seized the coats as well, and even the little hatbox that had been swinging since early morning on its string from Gabriella's finger, like a reminder. Now she had nothing but her purse.

And there apart stood Papa. Nobody had come to meet Papa. Even as Gabriella saw him, he was deciding not to wait. Bearing on his cane, still in the same old olive-colored sweater—why should she have expected that hole to be sewed up by this morning?—he walked, with nothing to carry, away into the widening sunlight as if he had blinders on. He's only come home to die, thought Gabriella. All the way over, *he* might have been the oldest and the poorest one. Mama pretended not to see him go. Her curiosity about Papa had long ago been satisfied: he had nobody: she knew it. It was the punishment for marrying twice.

Nonna, when they reached her, said calmly, "We will wait one little moment longer. A dizziness—it will pass."

Mama crossed herself, and laid her instant, tender hand to Nonna's cheek. The porter just as instantly shed every bit of the baggage to the ground.

"Are you seventy-six too, Signora?" he asked. But he had meant it not disrespectfully, but respectfully, for he stood inclined, with a musing finger against his cheek, against a pillar he had made of the trunk dressed with the coats. She raised her eyes to the empty *Pomona* standing over them still—not empty, for Mr. Ugone still rode aboard, with Genoa yet to come. She could actually see him at that minute, standing at the rail with his cigar in his hand; but he did not see her. His gaze was bent and seemed lost on Poldy—still playing there with some of the little urchins, so that the dock took on the echoing sound of a playground just before dark. Maybe the surest people, thought Gabriella, are also the most forgetful of what comes next. All around was the smell of yellow leaves.

"Look what I see!" cried Mama, without ceasing to pat Nonna's cheek. "Mr. Scampo! Ah, I thought we had seen the last of him. On board ship—poor *mamma mia!*—he was passionately running after our Gabriella. It was necessary to keep an eye on her every minute."

"Her fatefulness is inherited from you, Crocefissa, my child," said Nonna.

"All my girls have been so afflicted, but five, like me, married by eighteen," Mama said—pat, pat, pat.

Aldo was coming toward them slowly, with his strange new walk of today, almost hidden by a large number of hopeful porters attacking him like flies from all sides. He did not wave; but how could he? He was loaded down. Gabriella did not wave herself, but suddenly missing the old, known world of the *Pomona*, she gave one brief scream. Nonna bent a considering head her way, as though to place the pitch.

"*That* she gets from her father," said Mama. "The *Siracusano*!"

"Ah," replied Nonna. "Daughter, where is my little fan? Somewhere in my skirts, thank you. With the years he has calmed himself, Achille? You no longer tremble to cross him?"

Gabriella said absently, "She should've seen him hit the ceiling when I flunked old typewriting."

"Per favore!" cried Mama to her. "Quiet about things you know nothing about, yet! Say good-by to Mr. Scampo."

Aldo had pulled a disreputable raincoat over his thick, new brown suit; even now he wore no hat, and his hair was down in his eyes. In addition to two suitcases he was carrying something as tall, bulky, and toppling as a man. It towered above his head.

Mama said, "If you think this fellow looks strong, *mamma mia*, I tell you now it is an illusion. He is delicate!"

"Only on Gala Night," protested Gabriella. "That's the one and only time he faded out of the picture. And so did you, Mama."

"We stop first thing at Santa Maria, to thank Holy Mother for one fate she saved you from!" Mama said. She shook her head one way, Nonna nodded hers in another.

"Hey! What you got in that thing, a dead body?" cried Gabriella to Aldo in good old English. She went bounding out to meet him.

"Watch out!" said Aldo, who seemed to have to walk in a straight line, by now, or fall. "You got nothing but just one trunk and those suitcases? You're luckier than you know."

"*You* watch out who you bump with that funeral coffin."

"*You* watch out how you talk about what I got. This is a musical instrument." With Gabriella there in his path, Aldo had to come to a full stop. The porters closed in in fresh circles of hope. "A cello," Aldo said, embracing it. Even one ear was being used to help hold it. "And after I rode it all the way in the bed over mine on the boat, the Naples Customs grabbed it right out the cover and banged the strings and took a stick and knocked all around inside it! I bet you heard it out here."

"What did you have in it?" called Mama.

"My socks!" Aldo shouted to Gabriella. "All my socks that my aunt knitted! It's going to be *cold* in Italy this winter!"

"Aldo, don't yell," said Gabriella. "That's my grandmother."

"Oh, yeah. She looks pretty well to me," said Aldo. "She ought not to've tried to meet a boat in Naples, though."

"Mother—excuse me—Mr. Scampo, a shipboard acquaintance," said Mama.

"*Il Romeo? Il pellegrino, Signore* Scampo?" murmured Nonna serenely. She moved a glistening black silk fan back and forth in front of her now, in a way that seemed to invite any confidence.

"I'm just saying good-by to Mrs. Serto and Gabriella, ma'am," said Aldo.

Gabriella had clapped her hand over her mouth. She cried, "Aldo! Did you hear her? *Romeo!* First Mama thought you were Dick Tracy or somebody, the time you spent studying crime the whole way over—now Nonna is asking if you're not a pilgrim!"

"And what did *you* ever think I was?" Aldo stared at her rudely, clasping his burden round in that clumsy and painful way that made him look as though *he* were the one to wonder how people ever parted.

"Yes, *Signore*?" said Nonna. "Perhaps you will tell us?"

"Well, ma'am, what I came to Italy for, since somebody really *asks* me, is study cello in Rome under the G.I. Bill," said Aldo. *"Musicista, Signora."*

"Sfortunato!" exclaimed Nonna, and gave a familiar-sounding click of the tongue.

"I already have a son-in-law in Buffalo the same!" cried Mama.

There Aldo stood before the three of them.

"Hey, Aldo. Want to see our trunk real quick?" asked Gabriella gently. She moved over to it, and the porter swept off the coats, unveiling it. The Serto trunk stood there—its size, shape, and weight all apparent, also the rope that went around it and the original lock that nobody trusted, and the name "Serto" painted on the lid in the confident lettering of a pharmacist. It did not matter that the hand of Customs had gone romping through it—it was restored now to the miracle of ownership.

"It's full of presents, I can tell you," said Gabriella.

Advice arrived almost like gratitude upon Aldo's face, as pride had come upon hers. "Then keep your eye on it till you get it home," he told her. "A fellow in New York told me they'll steal them even from over your head, in Naples. With a kind of tongs, very nifty. Running around over the rafters of the Customs shed, or even hanging over the gate as you go out. Everybody here knows about it, and don't even try to stop it."

"Shame," said Mama. "That's not talking nice about Naples."

And again, as Nonna spoke to him too, he was pulled around in a daze.

"My mother is telling you, Mr. Scampo, the human voice alone is divine," said Mama with her little chin up. "Not the screeching of cats. She is telling you there still may be time to set right your mistake—she sees you so young. Of course, in *Napoli*, she once sang with Caruso."

Nonna was looking up at Aldo. No two smiles were the same in her face. Aldo had now turned dark red, and his head hung.

"Well, good-by, Aldo," said Gabriella in English, and he looked up already startled, as if to see someone he had never expected to see again.

"Be good," he replied formally, and momentarily setting the suitcases down, he shook hands with them all, even their porter, who joined the circle.

"Good-by, Mr. Scampo! Maybe we all meet at St. Peter's *Ognissanti*—who knows?" said Mama. That was what she'd said to everybody.

As Aldo staggered away, Gabriella reached out her hand and with her fingertips touched his cello—or rather its wrinkled outer covering, at once soft and imperious. It was like touching the forehead of an animal, from which horns might even start; but indeed, the old lady's withered and feminine cheek had felt just as mysterious to Gabriella's kiss. Aldo's back grew less and less familiar with every step, while the porters like a family of acrobats were leaping and crying in chorus, *"Stazione! Stazione!"* all around him. They all saw him pass, unrobbed and unaided, through the archway into the big Piazza, and away into the sliding life of the streets, and then Mama brought her handkerchief up to her face like a little nosegay of tears. *She* was being the daughter—the better daughter.

But Nonna was still the mother. Her brown face might be creased like a fig-skin, but her eyes were brighter now than tears had left Mama's, or than the lightning of bewilderment that struck so often into the eyes of Gabriella. Surely they knew everything. They had taken Gabriella for granted.

"Come now," Nonna said.

She stood up. She was smaller than Mama, she came only to Gabriella's shoulder. But as she turned around, a motion of her hand, folding shut the little fan and pointing away with it, told them they were none of them any too soon. She stood perfectly straight, and could have walked by herself, though Mama, with a cry of remembrance, seized hold of her. Gabriella took her place a step behind. The porter once more—he, one man, all alone, and possibly for nothing—shouldered the backbreaking luggage of women, to which now something extra was added—the little rush-bottomed fireside stool on which the old lady had been sitting. They all set off toward the gate.

Only for the space of a breath did Gabriella feel she would rather lie down on that melon cart pulled by a donkey, that she could see just disappearing around the corner ahead. Then the melons and the arch of the gate, the grandmother's folding of the fan and Mama's tears, the volcano of early morning, and even the long, dangerous voyage behind her—all seemed caught up and held in something: the golden moment of touch, just given, just taken, in saying good-by. The moment—bright and effortless of making, in the end, as a bubble—seemed to go ahead of them as they walked, to tap without sound across the dust of the emptying courtyard, and alight in the grandmother's homely buggy, filling it. The yellow leaves of the plane trees came down before their feet; and just beyond the gate the black country horse that would draw the buggy shivered and tossed his mane, which fell like one long silver wave as the first of the bells in the still-hidden heart of Naples began to strike the hour.

"And the nightingale," Mama's voice just ahead was beseeching, "is the nightingale with us yet?"

OTHER STORIES

Contents

Where Is the Voice Coming From?

I SAYS to my wife, "You can reach and turn it off. You don't have to set and look at a black nigger face no longer than you want to, or listen to what you don't want to hear. It's still a free country."

I reckon that's how I give myself the idea.

I says, I could find right exactly where in Thermopylae that nigger's living that's asking for equal time. And without a bit of trouble to me.

And I ain't saying it might not be because that's pretty close to where *I* live. The other hand, there could be reasons you might have yourself for knowing how to get there in the dark. It's where you all go for the thing you want when you want it the most. Ain't that right?

The Branch Bank sign tells you in lights, all night long even, what time it is and how hot. When it was quarter to four, and 92, that was me going by in my brother-in-law's truck. He don't deliver nothing at that hour of the morning.

So you leave Four Corners and head west on Nathan B. Forrest Road, past the Surplus & Salvage, not much beyond the Kum Back Drive-In and Trailer Camp, not as far as where the signs starts saying "Live Bait," "Used Parts," "Fireworks," "Peaches," and "Sister Peebles Reader and Adviser." Turn before you hit the city limits and duck back towards the I.C. tracks. And his street's been paved.

And there was his light on, waiting for me. In his garage, if you please. His car's gone. He's out planning still some other ways to do what we tell 'em they can't. I *thought* I'd beat him home. All I had to do was pick my tree and walk in close behind it.

I didn't come expecting not to wait. But it was so hot, all I did was hope and pray one or the other of us wouldn't melt before it was over.

Now, it wasn't no bargain I'd struck.

I've heard what you've heard about Goat Dykeman, in Mississippi. Sure, everybody knows about Goat Dykeman. Goat he got word to the Governor's Mansion he'd go up yonder and shoot that nigger Meredith clean out of school, if he's let out of the pen to do it. Old Ross turned *that* over in his mind before saying him nay, it stands to reason.

I ain't no Goat Dykeman, I ain't in no pen, and I ain't ask no Governor Barnett to give me one thing. Unless he wants to give me a pat on the back for the trouble I took this morning. But he don't have to if he don't want to. I done what I done for my own pure-D satisfaction.

As soon as I heard wheels, I knowed who was coming. That was him and bound to be him. It was the right nigger heading in a new white car up his driveway towards his garage with the light shining, but stopping before he got there, maybe not to wake 'em. That was him. I knowed it when he cut off the car lights and put his foot out and I knowed him standing dark against the light. I knowed him then like I know me now. I knowed him even by his still, listening back.

Never seen him before, never seen him since, never seen anything of his black face but his picture, never seen his face alive, any time at all, or anywheres, and didn't want to, need to, never hope to see that face and never will. As long as there was no question in my mind.

He had to be the one. He stood right still and waited against the light, his back was fixed, fixed on me like a preacher's eyeballs when he's yelling "Are you saved?" He's the one.

I'd already brought up my rifle, I'd already taken my sights. And I'd already got him, because it was too late then for him or me to turn by one hair.

Something darker than him, like the wings of a bird, spread on his back and pulled him down. He climbed up once, like a man under bad claws, and like just blood could weigh a ton he walked with it on his back to better light. Didn't get no further than his door. And fell to stay.

He was down. He was down, and a ton load of bricks on his back wouldn't have laid any heavier. There on his paved driveway, yes sir.

And it wasn't till the minute before, that the mockingbird had quit singing. He'd been singing up my sassafras tree. Either he was up early, or he hadn't never gone to bed, he was like me. And the mocker he'd stayed right with me, filling the air till come the crack, till I turned loose of my load. I was like him. I was on top of the world myself. For once.

I stepped to the edge of his light there, where he's laying flat. I says, "Roland? There was one way left, for me to be ahead of you and stay ahead of you, by Dad, and I just taken it. Now I'm alive and you ain't. We ain't never now, never going to be equals and you know why? One of us is dead. What about that, Roland?" I said. "Well, you seen to it, didn't you?"

I stood a minute—just to see would somebody inside come out long enough to pick him up. And there she comes, the woman. I doubt she'd been to sleep. Because it seemed to me she'd been in there keeping awake all along.

It was mighty green where I skint over the yard getting back. That nigger wife of his, she wanted nice grass! I bet my wife would hate to pay her water bill. And for burning her electricity. And there's my brother-in-law's truck, still waiting with the door open. "No Riders"—that didn't mean me.

There wasn't a thing I been able to think of since would have made it to go any nicer. Except a chair to my back while I was putting in my waiting. But going home, I seen what little time it takes after all to get a thing done like you really want it. It was 4:34, and while I was looking it moved to 35. And the temperature stuck where it was. All that night I guarantee you it had stood without dropping, a good 92.

My wife says, "What? Didn't the skeeters bite you?" She said, "Well, they been asking that—why somebody didn't trouble to load a rifle and get some of these agitators out of Thermopylae. Didn't the fella keep drumming it in, what a good idea? The one that writes a column ever' day?"

I says to my wife, "Find *some* way I don't get the credit."

"He says do it for Thermopylae," she says. "Don't you ever skim the paper?"

I says, "Thermopylae never done nothing for me. And I don't owe nothing to Thermopylae. Didn't do it for you. Hell, any more'n I'd do something or other for them Kennedys! I done it for my own pure-D satisfaction."

"It's going to get him right back on TV," says my wife. "You watch for the funeral."

I says, "You didn't even leave a light burning when you

went to bed. So how was I supposed to even get me home or pull Buddy's truck up safe in our front yard?"

"Well, hear another good joke on you," my wife says next. "Didn't you hear the news? The N. double A. C. P. is fixing to send somebody to Thermopylae. Why couldn't you waited? You might could have got you somebody better. Listen and hear 'em say so."

I ain't but one. I reckon you have to tell *somebody.*

"Where's the gun, then?" my wife says. "What did you do with our protection?"

I says, "It was scorching! It was scorching!" I told her, "It's laying out on the ground in rank weeds, trying to cool off, that's what it's doing now."

"You dropped it," she says. "Back there."

And I told her, "Because I'm so tired of ever'thing in the world being just that hot to the touch! The keys to the truck, the doorknob, the bedsheet, ever'thing, it's all like a stove lid. There just ain't much going that's worth holding onto it no more," I says, "when it's a hundred and two in the shade by day and by night not too much difference. I wish *you'd* laid *your* finger to that gun."

"Trust you to come off and leave it," my wife says.

"Is that how no-'count I am?" she makes me ask. "*You* want to go back and get it?"

"You're the one they'll catch. I say it's so hot that even if you get to sleep you wake up feeling like you cried all night!" says my wife. "Cheer up, here's one more joke before time to get up. Heard what *Caroline* said? Caroline said, 'Daddy, I just can't wait to grow up big, so I can marry *James Meredith.*' I heard that where I work. One rich-bitch to another one, to make her cackle."

"At least I kept some dern teen-ager from North Thermopylae getting there and doing it first," I says. "Driving his own car."

On TV and in the paper, they don't know but half of it. They know who Roland Summers was without knowing who I am. His face was in front of the public before I got rid of him, and after I got rid of him there it is again—the same picture. And none of me. I ain't ever had one made. Not ever!

The best that newspaper could do for me was offer a five-hundred-dollar reward for finding out who I am. For as long as they don't know who that is, whoever shot Roland is worth a good deal more right now than Roland is.

But by the time I was moving around uptown, it was hotter still. That pavement in the middle of Main Street was so hot to my feet I might've been walking the barrel of my gun. If the whole world could've just felt Main Street this morning through the soles of my shoes, maybe it would've helped some.

Then the first thing I heard 'em say was the N. double A. C. P. done it themselves, killed Roland Summers, and proved it by saying the shooting was done by a expert (I hope to tell you it was!) and at just the right hour and minute to get the whites in trouble.

You can't win.

"They'll never find him," the old man trying to sell roasted peanuts tells me to my face.

And it's so hot.

It looks like the town's on fire already, whichever ways you turn, ever' street you strike, because there's those trees hanging them pones of bloom like split watermelon. And a thousand cops crowding ever'where you go, half of 'em too young to start shaving, but all streaming sweat alike. I'm getting tired of 'em.

I was already tired of seeing a hundred cops getting us white people nowheres. Back at the beginning, I stood on the corner and I watched them new babyface cops loading nothing but nigger children into the paddy wagon and they come marching out of a little parade and into the paddy wagon singing. And they got in and sat down without providing a speck of trouble, and their hands held little new American flags, and all the cops could do was knock them flagsticks aloose from their hands, and not let 'em pick 'em up, that was all, and give 'em a free ride. And children can just get 'em more flags.

Everybody: It don't get you nowhere to take nothing from nobody unless you make sure it's for keeps, for good and all, for ever and amen.

I won't be sorry to see them brickbats hail down on us for

a change. Pop bottles too, they can come flying whenever they want to. Hundreds, all to smash, like Birmingham. I'm waiting on 'em to bring out them switchblade knives, like Harlem and Chicago. Watch TV long enough and you'll see it all to happen on Deacon Street in Thermopylae. What's holding it back, that's all?—Because it's *in* 'em.

I'm ready myself for that funeral.

Oh, they may find me. May catch me one day in spite of 'emselves. (But I grew up in the country.) May try to railroad me into the electric chair, and what that amounts to is something hotter than yesterday and today put together.

But I advise 'em to go careful. Ain't it about time us taxpayers starts to calling the moves? Starts to telling the teachers *and* the preachers *and* the judges of our so-called courts how far they can go?

Even the President so far, he can't walk in my house without being invited, like he's my daddy, just to say whoa. Not yet!

Once, I run away from my home. And there was a ad for me, come to be printed in our county weekly. My mother paid for it. It was from her. It says: "SON: You are not being hunted for anything but to find you." That time, I come on back home.

But people are dead now.

And it's so hot. Without it even being August yet.

Anyways, I seen him fall. I was evermore the one.

So I reach me down my old guitar off the nail in the wall. 'Cause I've got my guitar, what I've held onto from way back when, and I never dropped that, never lost or forgot it, never hocked it but to get it again, never give it away, and I set in my chair, with nobody home but me, and I start to play, and sing a-Down. And sing a-down, down, down, down. Sing a-down, down, down, down. Down.

The Demonstrators

NEAR eleven o'clock that Saturday night, the doctor stopped again by his office. He had recently got into playing a weekly bridge game at the club, but tonight it had been interrupted for the third time, and he'd just come from attending to Miss Marcia Pope. Now bedridden, scorning all medication and in particular tranquillizers, she had a seizure every morning before breakfast and often on Saturday night for some reason, but had retained her memory; she could amuse herself by giving out great wads of Shakespeare and *"Arma virumque cano,"* or the like. The more forcefully Miss Marcia Pope declaimed, the more innocent grew her old face—the lines went right out.

"She'll sleep naturally now, I think," he'd told the companion, still in her rocker.

Mrs. Warrum did well, perhaps hadn't hit yet on an excuse to quit that suited her. She failed to be alarmed by Miss Marcia Pope, either in convulsions or in recitation. From where she lived, she'd never gone to school to this lady, who had taught three generations of Holden, Mississippi, its Latin, civics, and English, and who had carried, for forty years, a leather satchel bigger than the doctor's bag.

As he'd snapped his bag shut tonight, Miss Marcia had opened her eyes and spoken distinctly: "Richard Strickland? I have it on my report that Irene Roberts is not where she belongs. Now which of you wants the whipping?"

"It's all right, Miss Marcia. She's still my wife," he'd said, but could not be sure the answer got by her.

In the office, he picked up the city newspaper he subscribed to—seeing as he did so the picture on the front of a young man burning his draft card before a camera—and locked up, ready to face home. As he came down the stairway onto the street, his sleeve was plucked.

It was a Negro child. "We got to hurry," she said.

His bag was still in the car. She climbed into the back and stood there behind his ear as he drove down the hill. He met the marshal's car as both bounced over the railroad track—no passenger rode with the marshal that he could see—and the doctor asked the child, "Who got hurt? Whose house?" But she could only tell him how to get there, an alley at a time, till they got around the cottonseed mill.

Down here, the street lights were out tonight. The last electric light of any kind appeared to be the one burning in the vast shrouded cavern of the gin. His car lights threw into relief the dead goldenrod that stood along the road and made it look heavier than the bridge across the creek.

As soon as the child leaned on his shoulder and he had stopped the car, he heard men's voices; but at first his eyes could make out little but an assembly of white forms spaced in the air near a low roof—chickens roosting in a tree. Then he saw the reds of cigarettes. A dooryard was as packed with a standing crowd as if it were funeral time. They were all men. Still more people seemed to be moving from the nearby churchyard and joining onto the crowd in front of the house.

The men parted before them as he went following the child up broken steps and across a porch. A kerosene lamp was being held for him in the doorway. He stepped into a roomful of women. The child kept going, went to the foot of an iron bed and stopped. The lamp came up closer behind him and he followed a path of newspapers laid down on the floor from the doorway to the bed.

A dark quilt was pulled up to the throat of a girl alive on the bed. A pillow raised her at the shoulders. The dome of her forehead looked thick as a battering ram, because of the rolling of her eyes.

Dr. Strickland turned back the quilt. The young, very black-skinned woman lay in a white dress with her shoes on. A maid? Then he saw that of course the white was not the starched material of a uniform but shiny, clinging stuff, and there was a banner of some kind crossing it in a crumpled red line from the shoulder. He unfastened the knot at the waist and got the banner out of the way. The skintight satin had been undone at the neck already; as he parted it farther, the girl kicked at the foot of the bed. He exposed the breast and then, before her hand had pounced on his, the wound below the breast. There was a small puncture with little evidence of external bleeding. He had seen splashes of blood on the dress, now almost dry.

"Go boil me some water. Too much excitement to send for the doctor a little earlier?"

The girl clawed at his hand with her sticky nails.

"Have you touched her?" he asked.

"See there? And she don't want you trying it, either," said a voice in the room.

A necklace like sharp and pearly teeth was fastened around her throat. It was when he took that off that the little girl who had been sent for him cried out. "I bid that!" she said, but without coming nearer. He found no other wounds.

"Does it hurt you to breathe?" He spoke almost absently as he addressed the girl.

The nipples of her breasts cast shadows that looked like figs; she would not take a deep breath when he used the stethoscope. Sweat in the airless room, in the bed, rose and seemed to weaken and unstick the newspapered walls like steam from a kettle already boiling; it glazed his own white hand, his tapping fingers. It was the stench of sensation. The women's faces coming nearer were streaked in the hot lamplight. Somewhere close to the side of his head something glittered; hung over the knob of the bedpost, where a boy would have tossed his cap, was a tambourine. He let the stethoscope fall, and heard women's sighs travel around the room, domestic sounds like a broom being flirted about, women getting ready for company.

"Stand back," he said. "You got a fire on in here?" Warm as it was, crowded as it was in here, he looked behind him and saw the gas heater burning, half the radiants burning blue. The girl, with lips turned down, lay pulling away while he took her pulse.

The child who had been sent for him and then had been sent to heat the water brought the kettle in from the kitchen too soon and had to be sent back to make it boil. When it was ready and in the pan, the lamp was held closer; it was beside his elbow as if to singe his arm.

"Stand back," he said. Again and again the girl's hand had to be forced away from her breast. The wound quickened spasmodically as if it responded to light.

"Icepick?"

"You right this time," said voices in the room.

"Who did this to her?"

The room went quiet; he only heard the men in the yard laughing together. "How long ago?" He looked at the path of newspapers spread on the floor. "Where? Where did it happen? How did she get here?"

He had an odd feeling that somewhere in the room somebody was sending out beckoning smiles in his direction. He lifted, half turned his head. The elevated coal that glowed at regular intervals was the pipe of an old woman in a boiled white apron standing near the door.

He persisted. "Has she coughed up anything yet?"

"Don't you know her?" they cried, as if he never was going to hit on the right question.

He let go the girl's arm, and her hand started its way back again to her wound. Sending one glowing look at him, she covered it again. As if she had spoken, he recognized her.

"Why, it's Ruby," he said.

Ruby Gaddy *was* the maid. Five days a week she cleaned up on the second floor of the bank building where he kept his office and consulting rooms.

He said to her, "Ruby, this is Dr. Strickland. What have you been up to?"

"Nothin'!" everybody cried for her.

The girl's eyes stopped rolling and rested themselves on the expressionless face of the little girl, who again stood at the foot of the bed watching from this restful distance. Look equalled look: sisters.

"Am I supposed to just know?" The doctor looked all around him. An infant was sitting up on the splintery floor near his feet, he now saw, on a clean newspaper, a spoon stuck pipelike in its mouth. From out in the yard at that moment came a regular guffaw, not much different from the one that followed the telling of a dirty story or a race story by one of the clowns in the Elks' Club. He frowned at the baby; and the baby, a boy, looked back over his upside-down spoon and gave it a long audible suck.

"She married? Where's her husband? That where the trouble was?"

Now, while the women in the room, too, broke out in sounds of amusement, the doctor stumbled where he stood. "What the devil's running in here? Rats?"

"You wrong there."

Guinea pigs were running underfoot, not only in this room but on the other side of the wall, in the kitchen where the water had finally got boiled. Somebody's head turned toward the leaf end of a stalk of celery wilting on top of the Bible on the table.

"Catch those things!" he exclaimed.

The baby laughed; the rest copied the baby.

"They lightning. Get away from you so fast!" said a voice.

"Them guinea pigs ain't been caught since they was born. Let you try."

"Know why? 'Cause they's Dove's. Dove left 'em here when he move out, just to be in the way."

The doctor felt the weight recede from Ruby's fingers, and saw it flatten her arm where it lay on the bed. Her eyes had closed. A little boy with a sanctimonious face had taken the bit of celery and knelt down on the floor; there was scrambling about and increasing laughter until Dr. Strickland made himself heard in the room.

"All right. I heard you. Is Dove who did it? Go on. Say."

He heard somebody spit on the stove. Then:

"It's Dove."

"Dove."

"Dove."

"Dove."

"You got it right that time."

While the name went around, passed from one mouth to the other, the doctor drew a deep breath. But the sigh that filled the room was the girl's own, luxuriously uncontained.

"Dove Collins? I believe you. I've had to sew him up enough times on Sunday morning, you all know that," said the doctor. "I know Ruby, I know Dove, and if the lights would come back on I can tell you the names of the rest of you and you know it." While he was speaking, his eyes fell on Oree, a figure of the Holden square for twenty years, whom he had inherited—sitting here in the room in her express wagon, the flowered skirt spread down from her lap and tucked in over the stumps of her knees.

While he was preparing the hypodermic, he was aware that more watchers, a row of them dressed in white with red banners like Ruby's, were coming in to fill up the corners. The lamp was lifted—higher than the dipping shadows of their heads, a valentine tacked on the wall radiated color—and then, as he leaned over the bed, the lamp was brought down closer and closer to the girl, like something that would devour her.

"Now I can't see what I'm doing," the doctor said sharply, and as the light jumped and swung behind him he thought he recognized the anger as a mother's.

"Look to me like the fight's starting to go out of Ruby mighty early," said a voice.

Still her eyes stayed closed. He gave the shot.

"Where'd he get to—Dove? Is the marshal out looking for him?" he asked.

The sister moved along the bed and put the baby down on it close to Ruby's face.

"Remove him," said the doctor.

"She don't even study him," said the sister. "Poke her," she told the baby.

"Take him out of here," ordered Dr. Strickland.

The baby opened one of his mother's eyes with his fingers. When she shut it on him he cried, as if he knew it to be deliberate of her.

"Get that baby out of here and all the kids, I tell you," Dr. Strickland said into the room. "This ain't going to be pretty."

"Carry him next door, Twosie," said a voice.

"I ain't. You all promised me if I leave long enough to get the doctor I could stand right here until." The child's voice was loud.

"O.K. Then you got to hold Roger."

The baby made a final reach for his mother's face, putting out a hand with its untrimmed nails, gray as the claw of a squirrel. The woman who had held the lamp set that down and grabbed the baby out of the bed herself. His legs began churning even before she struck him a blow on the side of the head.

"You trying to raise him an idiot?" the doctor flung out.

"*I* ain't going to raise him," the mother said toward the girl on the bed.

The deliberation had gone out of her face. She was drifting into unconsciousness. Setting her hand to one side, the doctor inspected the puncture once more. It was clean as the eye of a needle. While he stood there watching her, he lifted her hand and washed it—the wrist, horny palm, blood-caked fingers one by one.

But as he again found her pulse, he saw her eyes opening. As long as he counted he was aware of those eyes as if they loomed larger than the watch face. They were filled with the unresponding gaze of ownership. She knew what she had. Memory did not make the further effort to close the lids when he replaced her hand, or when he took her shoes off and set them on the floor, or when he stepped away from the bed and again the full lamplight struck her face.

The twelve-year-old stared on, over the buttress of the baby she held to her chest.

"Can you ever hush that baby?"

A satisfied voice said, "He going to keep-a-noise till he learn better."

"Well, I'd like a little peace and consideration to be shown!" the doctor said. "Try to remember there's somebody in here with you that's going to be pumping mighty hard to breathe." He raised a finger and pointed it at the old woman in the boiled apron whose pipe had continued to glow with regularity by the door. "You stay. You sit here and watch Ruby," he called. "The rest of you clear out of here."

He closed his bag and straightened up. The woman stuck the lamp hot into his own face.

"Remember Lucille? I'm Lucille. I was washing for your mother when you was born. Let me see you do something," she said with fury. "You ain't even tied her up! You sure ain't your daddy!"

"Why, she's bleeding inside," he retorted. "What do you think *she's* doing?"

They hushed. For a minute all he heard was the guinea pigs racing. He looked back at the girl; her eyes were fixed with possession. "I gave her a shot. She'll just go to sleep. If she doesn't, call me and I'll come back and give her another one. One of you kindly bring me a drink of water," the doctor continued in the same tone.

With a crash, hushed off like cymbals struck by mistake, something was moved on the kitchen side of the wall. The little boy who had held the celery to catch the guinea pigs came in carrying a teacup. He passed through the room and out onto the porch, where he could be heard splashing fresh water from a pump. He came back inside and at arm's length held the cup out to the doctor.

Dr. Strickland drank with a thirst they all could and did follow. The cup, though it held the whole smell of this house in it, was of thin china, was an old one.

Then he stepped across the gaze of the girl on the bed as he would have had to step over a crack yawning in the floor.

"Fixing to leave?" asked the old woman in the boiled white apron, who still stood up by the door, the pipe gone from her lips. He then remembered her. In the days when he travelled East to medical school, she used to be the sole factotum at the Holden depot when the passenger train came through sometime between two and three in the morning. It was always late. Circling the pewlike benches of the waiting rooms, she carried around coffee which she poured boiling hot into paper cups out of a white-enamelled pot that looked as long as her arm. She wore then, in addition to the apron, a white and flaring head covering—something between a chef's cap and a sunbonnet. As the train at last steamed in, she called the stations. She didn't use a loudspeaker but just the power of her lungs. In all the natural volume of her baritone voice she thundered them out to the scattered and few who had waited under lights too poor to read by—first in the colored waiting room, then in the white waiting room, to echo both times from the vault of the roof: ". . . Meridian. Birmingham. Chattanooga. Bristol. Lynchburg. Washington. Baltimore. Philadelphia. And New York." Seizing all the bags, two by two, in her own hands, walking slowly in front of the passengers, she saw to it that they left.

He said to her, "I'm going, but you're not. You're keeping a watch on Ruby. Don't let her slide down in the bed. Call me if you need me." As a boy, had he never even wondered what her name was—this tyrant? He didn't know it now. He put the cup into her reaching hand. "Aren't you ready to leave?" he asked Oree, the legless woman. She still lived by the tracks where the train had cut off her legs.

"I ain't in no hurry," she replied and as he passed her she called her usual "Take it easy, Doc."

When he stepped outside onto the porch, he saw that there was moonlight everywhere. Uninterrupted by any lights from Holden, it filled the whole country lying out there in the haze of the long rainless fall. He himself stood on the edge of Holden. Just one house and one church farther, the Delta began, and the cotton fields ran into the scattered paleness of a dimmed-out Milky Way.

Nobody called him back, yet he turned his head and got a sideways glimpse all at once of a row of dresses hung up across the front of the house, starched until they could have stood alone (as his mother complained), and in an instant had recognized his mother's gardening dress, his sister Annie's golf dress, his wife's favorite duster that she liked to wear to the breakfast table, and more dresses, less substantial. Elevated across the front of the porch, they were hung again between him and the road. With sleeves spread wide, trying to scratch his forehead with the tails of their skirts, they were flying around this house in the moonlight.

The moment of vertigo passed, as a small black man came up the steps and across the porch wearing heeltaps on his shoes.

"Sister Gaddy entered yet into the gates of joy?"

"No, Preacher, you're in time," said the doctor.

As soon as he left the house, he heard it become as noisy as the yard had been, and the men in the yard went quiet to let him through. From the road, he saw the moon itself. It was above the tree with the chickens in it; it might have been one of the chickens flown loose. He scraped children off the hood of his car, pulled another from position at the wheel, and climbed inside. He turned the car around in the churchyard. There was a flickering light inside the church. Flat-roofed as a warehouse, it had its shades pulled down like a bedroom. This was the church where the sounds of music and dancing came from habitually on many another night besides Sunday, clearly to be heard on top of the hill.

He drove back along the road, across the creek, its banks glittering now with the narrow bottles, the size of harmonicas, in which paregoric was persistently sold under the name of Mother's Helper. The telephone wires along the road were hung with shreds of cotton, the sides of the road were strewn with them too, as if the doctor were out on a paper chase.

He passed the throbbing mill, working on its own generator. No lights ever shone through the windowless and now moonlit sheet iron, but the smell came out freely and spread over the town at large—a cooking smell, like a dish ordered by a man with an endless appetite. Pipes hung with streamers of lint fed into the moonlit gin, and wagons and trucks heaped up round as the gypsy caravans or circus wagons of his father's, or even his grandfather's, stories, stood this way and that, waiting in the yard outside.

Far down the railroad track, beyond the unlighted town, rose the pillow-shaped glow of a grass fire. It was gaseous, unveined, unblotted by smoke, a cloud with the November flush of the sedge grass by day, sparkless and nerveless, not to be confused with a burning church, but like anesthetic made visible.

Then a long beam of electric light came solid as a board from behind him to move forward along the long loading platform, to some bales of cotton standing on it, some of them tumbled one against the others as if pushed by the light; then it ran up the wall of the dark station so you could read the name, "Holden." The hooter sounded. This was a grade crossing with a bad record, and it seemed to the doctor that he had never started over it in his life that something was not bearing down. He stopped the car, and as the train in its heat began to pass in front of him he saw it to be a doubleheader, a loaded freight this time. It was going right on through Holden.

He cut off his motor. One of the sleepers rocked and complained with every set of wheels that rolled over it. Presently the regular, slow creaking reminded the doctor of an old-fashioned porch swing holding lovers in the dark.

He had been carried a cup tonight that might have been his own mother's china or his wife's mother's—the rim not a perfect round, a thin, porcelain cup his lips and his fingers had recognized. In that house of murder, comfort had been brought to him at his request. After drinking from it he had all but reeled into a flock of dresses stretched wide-sleeved across the porch of that house like a child's drawing of angels.

Faintly rocked by the passing train, he sat bent at the wheel of the car, and the feeling of well-being persisted. It increased, until he had come to the point of tears.

The doctor was the son of a doctor, practicing in his father's office; all the older patients, like Miss Marcia Pope—and like Lucille and Oree—spoke of his father, and some confused the young doctor with the old; but not they. The watch he carried was the gold one that had belonged to his father. Richard had grown up in Holden, married "the prettiest girl in the Delta." Except for his years at the university and then at medical school and during his interneship, he had lived here at home and had carried on the practice—the only practice in town. Now his father and his mother both were dead, his sister had married and moved away, a year ago his child had died. Then, back in the summer, he and his wife had separated, by her wish.

Sylvia had been their only child. Until her death from pneumonia last Christmas, at the age of thirteen, she had never sat up or spoken. He had loved her and mourned her all her life; she had been injured at birth. But Irene had done more; she had dedicated her life to Sylvia, sparing herself nothing, tending her, lifting her, feeding her, everything. What do you do after giving all your devotion to something that cannot be helped, and that has been taken away? You give all your devotion to something else that cannot be helped. But you shun all the terrible reminders, and turn not to a human being but to an idea.

Last June, there had come along a student, one of the civil-rights workers, calling at his office with a letter of introduction. For the sake of an old friend, the doctor had taken him home to dinner. (He had been reminded of him once tonight, already, by a photograph in the city paper.) He remembered that the young man had already finished talking about his work. They had just laughed around the table after Irene had quoted the classic question the governor-before-this-one had asked, after a prison break: "If you can't trust a trusty, who can you trust?" Then the doctor had remarked, "Speaking of who can you trust, what's this I read in your own paper, Philip? It said some of your outfit over in the next county were forced at gunpoint to go into the fields at hundred-degree temperature and pick cotton. Well, that didn't happen—there isn't any cotton in June."

"I asked myself the same question you do. But I told myself, 'Well, they won't know the difference where the paper is read,' " said the young man.

"It's lying, though."

"We are dramatizing your hostility," the young bearded man had corrected him. "It's a way of reaching people. Don't forget—what they *might* have done to us is even worse."

"Still—you're not justified in putting a false front on things, in my opinion," Dr. Strickland had said. "Even for a good cause."

"*You* won't tell Herman Fairbrothers what's the matter with him," said his wife, and she jumped up from the table.

Later, as a result of this entertainment, he supposed, broken glass had been spread the length and breadth of his driveway. He hadn't seen in time what it wouldn't have occurred to him to look for, and Irene, standing in the door, had suddenly broken into laughter. . . .

He had eventually agreed that she have her wish and withdraw herself for as long as she liked. She was back now where she came from, where, he'd heard, they were all giving parties for her. He had offered to be the one to leave. "Leave Holden without its Dr. Strickland? You wouldn't to save your soul, would you?" she had replied. But as yet it was not divorce.

He thought he had been patient, but patience had made him tired. He was so increasingly tired, so sick and even bored with the bitterness, intractability that divided everybody and everything.

And suddenly, tonight, things had seemed just the way they used to seem. He had felt as though someone had stopped him on the street and offered to carry his load for a while—had insisted on it—some old, trusted, half-forgotten family friend that he had lost sight of since youth. Was it the sensation, now returning, that there was still allowed to everybody on earth a *self*—savage, death-defying, private? The pounding of his heart was like the assault of hope, throwing itself against him without a stop, merciless.

It seemed a long time that he had sat there, but the cars were still going by. Here came the caboose. He had counted them without knowing it—seventy-two cars. The grass fire at the edge of town came back in sight.

The doctor's feeling gradually ebbed away, like nausea put down. He started up the car and drove across the track and on up the hill.

Candles, some of them in dining-room candelabra, burned clear across the upstairs windows in the Fairbrothers' house. His own house, next door, was of course dark, and while he was wondering where Irene kept candles for emergencies he had driven on past his driveway for the second time that night. But the last place he wanted to go now was back to the club. He'd only tried it anyway to please his sister Annie. Now that he'd got by Miss Marcia Pope's dark window, he smelled her sweet-olive tree, solid as the bank building.

Here stood the bank, with its doorway onto the stairs to Drs. Strickland & Strickland, their names in black and gilt on three windows. He passed it. The haze and the moonlight were one over the square, over the row of storefronts opposite with the line of poles thin as matchsticks rising to prop the one long strip of tin over the sidewalk, the drygoods store with its ornamental top that looked like opened paper fans held up by acrobats. He slowly started around the square. Behind its iron railings, the courthouse-and-jail stood barely emerging from its black cave of trees and only the slicked iron steps of the stile caught the moon. He drove on, past the shut-down movie house with all the light bulbs unscrewed from the sign that spelled out in empty sockets "BROADWAY." In front of the new post office the flagpole looked feathery, like the track of a jet that is already gone from the sky. From in front of the fire station, the fire chief's old Buick had gone home.

What was there, who was there, to keep him from going home? The doctor drove on slowly around. From the center of the deserted pavement, where cars and wagons stood parked helter-skelter by day, rose the water tank, pale as a balloon that might be only tethered here. A clanking came out of it, for the water supply too had been a source of trouble this summer—a hollow, irregular knocking now and then from inside, but the doctor no longer heard it. In turning his car, he saw a man lying prone and colorless in the arena of moonlight.

The lights of the car fastened on him and his clothes turned golden yellow. The man looked as if he had been sleeping all day in a bed of flowers and rolled in their pollen and were sleeping there still, with his face buried. He was covered his length in cottonseed meal.

Dr. Strickland stopped the car short and got out. His footsteps made the only sound in town. The man raised up on his hands and looked at him like a seal. Blood laced his head like a net through which he had broken. His wide tongue hung down out of his mouth. But the doctor knew the face.

"So you're alive, Dove, you're still alive?"

Slowly, hardly moving his tongue, Dove said: "Hide me." Then he hemorrhaged through the mouth.

Through the other half of the night, the doctor's calls came to him over the telephone—all chronic cases. Eva Duckett Fairbrothers telephoned at daylight.

"Feels low in his mind? Of course he feels low in his mind," he had finally shouted at her. "If I had what Herman has, I'd go down in the back yard and shoot myself!"

The *Sentinel*, owned and edited by Horatio Duckett, came out on Tuesdays. The next week's back-page headline read, "TWO DEAD, ONE ICE PICK, FREAK EPISODE AT NEGRO CHURCH." The subhead read, "No Racial Content Espied."

The doctor sat at the table in his dining room, finishing breakfast as he looked it over.

> An employee of the Fairbrothers Cotton Seed Oil Mill and a Holden maid, both Negroes, were stabbed with a sharp instrument judged to be an ice pick in a crowded churchyard here Saturday night. Both later expired. The

incident was not believed by Mayor Herman Fairbrothers to carry racial significance.

"It warrants no stir," the Mayor declared.

The mishap boosted Holden's weekend death toll to 3. Billy Lee Warrum Jr. died Sunday before reaching a hospital in Jackson where he was rushed after being thrown from his new motorcycle while on his way there. He was the oldest son of Mrs. Billy Lee Warrum, Rt. 1. Reputedly en route to see his fiance he was pronounced dead on arrival. Multiple injuries was listed as the cause, the motorcycle having speeded into an interstate truck loaded to capacity with holiday turkeys. (See eye-witness account, page 1.)

As Holden marshal Curtis "Cowboy" Stubblefield reconstructed the earlier mishap, Ruby Gaddy, 21, was stabbed in full view of the departing congregation of the Holy Gospel Tabernacle as she attempted to leave the church when services were concluded at approximately 9:30 P.M. Saturday.

Witnesses said Dave Collins, 25, appeared outside the church as early as 9:15 P.M. having come directly from his shift at the mill where he had been employed since 1959. On being invited to come in and be seated he joked and said he preferred to wait outdoors as he was only wearing work clothes until the Gaddy woman, said to be his common-law wife, came outside the frame structure.

In the ensuing struggle at the conclusion of the services, the woman, who was a member of the choir, is believed to have received fatal ice-pick injuries to a vital organ, then to have wrested the weapon from her assailant and paid him back in kind. The Gaddy woman then walked to her mother's house but later collapsed.

Members of the congregation said they chased Collins 13 or 14 yds. in the direction of Snake Creek on the South side of the church then he fell to the ground and rolled approximately ten feet down the bank, rolling over six or seven times. Those present believed him to have succumbed since it was said the pick while in the woman's hand had been seen to drive in and pierce either his ear or his eye, either of which is in close approximation to the brain. However, Collins later managed to crawl unseen from the creek and to make his way undetected up Railroad Avenue and to the Main St. door of an office occupied by Richard Strickland, M.D., above the Citizens Bank & Trust.

Witnesses were divided on which of the Negroes struck the first blow. Percy McAtee, pastor of the church, would not take sides but declared on being questioned by Marshal Stubblefield he was satisfied no outside agitators were involved and no arrests were made.

Collins was discovered on his own doorstep by Dr. Strickland who had been spending the evening at the Country Club. Collins is reported by Dr. Strickland to have expired shortly following his discovery, alleging his death to chest wounds.

"He offered no statement," Dr. Strickland said in response to a query.

Interviewed at home where he is recuperating from an ailment, Mayor Fairbrothers stated that he had not heard of there being trouble of any description at the Mill. "We are not trying to ruin our good reputation by inviting any, either," he said. "If the weatherman stays on our side we expect to attain capacity production in the latter part of next month," he stated. Saturday had been pay day as usual.

When Collins' body was searched by officers the pockets were empty however.

An ice pick, reportedly the property of the Holy Gospel Tabernacle, was later found by Deacon Gaddy, 8, brother of Ruby Gaddy, covered with blood and carried it to Marshal Stubblefield. Stubblefield said it had been found in the grounds of the new $100,000.000 Negro school. It is believed to have served as the instrument in the twin slayings, the victims thus virtually succeeding in killing each other.

"Well, I'm surprised didn't more of them get hurt," said Rev. Alonzo Duckett, pastor of the Holden First Baptist Church. "And yet they expect to be seated in our churches." County Sheriff Vince Lasseter, reached fishing at Lake Bourne, said: "That's one they can't pin the blame on us for. That's how they treat their own kind. Please take note our conscience is clear."

Members of the Negro congregation said they could not account for Collins having left Snake Creek at the unspecified time. "We stood there a while and flipped some bottle caps down at him and threw his cap down after him right over his face and didn't get a stir out of him," stated an official of the congregation. "The way he acted, we figured he was dead. We would not have gone off and left him if we had known he was able to subsequently crawl up the hill." They stated Collins was not in the habit of worshipping at Holy Gospel Tabernacle.

The Gaddy woman died later this morning, also from chest wounds.

No cause was cited for the fracas.

The cook had refilled his cup without his noticing. The doctor dropped the paper and carried his coffee out onto the little porch; it was still his morning habit.

The porch was at the back of the house, screened on three sides. Sylvia's daybed used to stand here; it put her in the garden. No other houses were in sight; the gin could not be heard or even the traffic whining on the highway up off the bypass.

The roses were done for, the perennials too. But the surrounding crape-myrtle tree, the redbud, the dogwood, the Chinese tallow tree, and the pomegranate bush were bright as toys. The ailing pear tree had shed its leaves ahead of the rest. Past a falling wall of Michaelmas daisies that had not been tied up, a pair of flickers were rifling the grass, the cock in one part of the garden, the hen in another, picking at the devastation right through the bright leaves that appeared to have been left lying there just for them, probing and feeding. They stayed year round, he supposed, but it was only in the fall of the year that he ever noticed them. He was pretty sure that Sylvia had known the birds were there. Her eyes would follow birds when they flew across the garden. As he watched, the cock spread one wing, showy as a zebra's hide, and with a turn of his head showed his red seal.

Dr. Strickland swallowed the coffee and picked up his bag. It was all going to be just about as hard as seeing Herman and Eva Fairbrothers through. He thought that in all Holden, as of now, only Miss Marcia Pope was still quite able to take care of herself—or such was her own opinion.

SELECTED ESSAYS

Contents

A Pageant of Birds

ONE SUMMER EVENING on a street in my town I saw two Negro women walking along carrying big colored paper wings in their hands and talking and laughing. They proceeded unquestioned, the way angels did in their day, possibly, although anywhere else but on such a street the angels might have been looked back at if they had taken their wings off and carried them along over their arms. I followed them to see where they were going, and, sure enough, it was to church.

They walked in at the Farish Street Baptist Church. It stands on a corner in the Negro business section, across the street from the Methodist Church, in a block with the clothing stores, the pool hall, the Booker-T movie house, the doctor's office, the pawnshop with gold in the windows, the café with the fish-sign that says "If They Don't Bite We Catch 'em Anyhow," and the barbershop with the Cuban hair styles hand-drawn on the window. It is a solid, brick-veneered church, and has no hollering or chanting in the unknown tongue. I looked in at the door to see what might be going on.

The big frame room was empty of people but ready for something. The lights were shining. The ceiling was painted the color of heaven, bright blue, and with this to start on, decorators had gone ahead to make the place into a scene that could only be prepared to receive birds. Pinned all around the walls were drawings of birds—bluebirds, redbirds, quail, flamingos, wrens, lovebirds—some copied from pictures, and the redbird a familiar cover taken from a school tablet. There was greenery everywhere. Sprigs of snow-on-the-mountain—a bush which grows to the point of complete domination in gardens of the neighborhood this time of year—were tied in neat bunches, with single zinnias stuck in, at regular intervals around the room, on the pews and along the altar rail. Over in the corner the piano appeared to be a large mound of vines, with the keyboard bared rather startlingly, like a row of teeth from ambush. On the platform where the pulpit had been was a big easy chair, draped with a red and blue robe embroidered in fleur-de-lys. Above it, two American flags were crossed over a drawing of an eagle copied straight off the back of a dollar bill.

As soon as people began coming into the church, out walked Maude Thompson from the rear, bustling and starched in the obvious role of church leader. She came straight to welcome me. Yes indeed, she said, there was to be a Pageant of Birds at seven o'clock sharp. I was welcome and all my friends. As she talked on, I was pleased to learn that she had written the Pageant herself and had not got it from some Northern YWCA or missionary society, as might be feared. "I said to myself, 'There have been pageants about everything else—why not about birds?' " she said. She told me proudly that each costume had been made by the bird who would wear it.

I brought a friend, and presently we were seated—unavoidably, because we were white—in the front row, with our feet turned sidewise by a large can of zinnias, but in the first of the excitement we were forgotten, and all proceeded as if we weren't there.

Maude Thompson made an announcement to the audience that everybody had better be patient. "Friends, the reason we are late starting is that several of the birds have to work late and haven't arrived yet. If there are any birds in the audience now, will they *kindly get on back here*?" Necks craned and eyes popped in delight when one girl in a dark-blue tissue-paper dress jumped up from a back pew and skittered out. Maude Thompson clapped her hands for order and told how a collection to be taken up would be used to pay for a piano—"not a new one, but a better one." Her hand was raised solemnly: we were promised, if we were quiet and nice, the sight of even more birds than we saw represented on the walls. The audience fanned, patted feet dreamily, and waited.

The Pageant, decidedly worth waiting for, began with a sudden complete silence in the audience, as if by mass intuition. Every head turned at the same time and all eyes fastened upon the front door of the church.

Then came the entrance of the Eagle Bird. Her wings and tail were of gold and silver tin foil, and her dress was a black and purple kimono. She began a slow pace down the aisle with that truly majestic dignity which only a vast, firmly matured physique, wholly unselfconscious, can achieve. Her hypnotic majesty was almost prostrating to the audience as she moved, as slowly as possible, down the aisle and finally turned and stood beneath the eagle's picture on the wall, in the exact center of the platform. A little Eaglet boy, with propriety her son, about two and a half feet tall, very black, entered from the Sunday School room and trotted around her with a sprightly tail over his knickers, flipping his hands dutifully from the wrist out. He wore bows on each shoulder. No smiles were exchanged—there was not a smile in the house. The Eagle then seated herself with a stifled groan in her chair, there was a strangled chord from the piano, where a Bird now sat, and with the little Eaglet to keep time by waving a flag jutting out from each wing, the congregation rose and sang "The Star-Spangled Banner."

Then the procession of lesser Birds began, and the music —as the pianist watched in a broken piece of mirror hidden in the vines—went gradually into syncopation.

The Birds would enter from the front door of the church, portentously, like members of a bridal party, proceed in absolute and easily distinguishable character down the aisle, cross over, and take their places in a growing circle around the audience. All came in with an assurance that sprang from complete absorption in their roles—erect in their bright wings and tails and crests, flapping their elbows, dipping their knees, hopping and turning and preening to the music. It was like a dance only inasmuch as birds might dance under the circumstances. They would, on reaching the platform, bow low, first to the Eagle Bird, who gave them back a stern look, and then to the audience, and take their positions—never ceasing to fly in place and twitter now and then, never showing recognition or saying one human word to anyone, even each other. There were many more Birds of some varieties than of others; I understood that "you could be what you want to." Maude Thompson, standing in a white uniform beside the piano, made a little evocation of each variety, checking down a list.

"The next group of Birds to fly will be the Bluebirds," she said, and in they flew, three big ones and one little one, in clashing shades of blue crepe paper. They were all very pleased and serious with their movements. The oldest wore shell-rimmed glasses. There were Redbirds, four of them; two Robin Redbreasts with diamond-shaped gold speckles on their breasts; five "Pink-birds"; two Peacocks who simultaneously spread their tails at a point halfway down the aisle; Goldfinches with black tips on their tails, who waltzed slowly and somehow appropriately; Canary birds, announced as "the beautiful Canaries, for pleasure as well as profit," who whistled vivaciously as they twirled, and a small Canary who had a yellow ostrich plume for a crest. There was only one "beautiful Blackbird, alone but not lonesome," with red caps on her wings; there was a head-wagging Purple Finch, who wore gold earrings. There was the Parrot-bird, who was a man and caused shouts—everyone's instant favorite; he had a yellow breast, one green trouser-leg, one red; he was in his shirt sleeves because it was hot, and he had red, green, blue and yellow wings. The lady Parrot (his wife) followed after in immutable seriousness—she had noticed parrots well, and she never got out of character: she ruffled her shoulder feathers, she was cross, she pecked at her wings, she moved her head rapidly from side to side and made obscure sounds, not quite words; she was so good she almost called up a parrot. There was loud appreciation of the Parrots—I thought they would have to go back and come in again. The "Red-headed Peckerwood" was a little boy alone. The "poor little Mourning Dove" was called but proved absent. "And last but not least, the white Dove of Peace!" cried Maude Thompson. There came two Doves, very sanctimonious indeed, with long sleeves, nurse's shoes and white cotton gloves. They flew with restraint, almost sadly.

When they had all come inside out of the night, the Birds filled a complete circle around the congregation. They performed a finale. They sang, lifting up their wings and swaying from side to side to the mounting music, bending and rolling their hips, all singing. And yet in their own and in everybody's eyes they were still birds. They were certainly birds to me.

> "And I want TWO wings
> To veil my face
> And I want TWO wings

To fly away,
And I want TWO wings
To veil my face,
And the world can't do me no harm."

That was their song, and they circled the church with it, singing and clapping with their wings, and flew away by the back door, where the ragamuffins of the alley cried "Oooh!" and jumped aside to let them pass.

I wanted them to have a picture of the group to keep and offered to take it. Maude Thompson said, "Several of the Birds could meet you in front of the church door tomorrow afternoon at four."

There turned out to be a number of rendezvous; but not all the Birds showed up, and I almost failed to get the Eagle, who has some very confining job. The Birds who could make it were finally photographed, however, Maude Thompson supervising the poses. I did not dare interfere. She instructed them to hold up their necks, and reproached the Dove of Peace for smiling. "You ever see a bird smile?"

Since our first meeting I have chanced on Maude Thompson several times. Every time I would be getting on a train, I would see her in the station; she would be putting on a coffin, usually, or receiving one, in a church capacity. She would always tell me how the Pageant was doing. They were on the point of taking it to Forrest or Mount Olive or some other town. Also, the Birds have now made themselves faces and beaks.

"This is going to be one of those things going to grow," said Maude Thompson.

Some Notes on River Country

A PLACE that ever was lived in is like a fire that never goes out. It flares up, it smolders for a time, it is fanned or smothered by circumstance, but its being is intact, forever fluttering within it, the result of some original ignition. Sometimes it gives out glory, sometimes its little light must be sought out to be seen, small and tender as a candle flame, but as certain.

I have never seen, in this small section of old Mississippi River country and its little chain of lost towns between Vicksburg and Natchez, anything so mundane as ghosts, but I have felt many times there a sense of place as powerful as if it were visible and walking and could touch me.

The clatter of hoofs and the bellow of boats have gone, all old communications. The Old Natchez Trace has sunk out of use; it is deep in leaves. The river has gone away and left the landings. Boats from Liverpool do not dock at these empty crags. The old deeds are done, old evil and old good have been made into stories, as plows turn up the river bottom, and the wild birds fly now at the level where people on boat deck once were strolling and talking of great expanding things, and of chance and money. Much beauty has gone, many little things of life. To light up the nights there are no mansions, no celebrations. Just as, when there were mansions and celebrations, there were no more festivals of an Indian tribe there; before the music, there were drums.

But life does not forsake any place. People live still in Rodney's Landing; flood drives them out and they return to it. Children are born there and find the day as inexhaustible and as abundant as they run and wander in their little hills as they, in innocence and rightness, would find it anywhere on earth. The seasons come as truly, and give gratefulness, though they bring little fruit. There is a sense of place there, to keep life from being extinguished, like a cup of the hands to hold a flame.

To go there, you start west from Port Gibson. This was the frontier of the Natchez country. Postmen would arrive here blowing their tin horns like Gabriel where the Old Natchez Trace crosses the Bayou Pierre, after riding three hundred wilderness miles from Tennessee, and would run in where the tavern used to be to deliver their mail, change their ponies, and warm their souls with grog. And up this now sand-barred bayou trading vessels would ply from the river. Port Gibson is on a highway and a railroad today, and lives on without its river life, though it is half diminished. It is still rather smug because General Grant said it was "too pretty to burn." Perhaps it was too pretty for any harsh fate, with its great mossy trees and old camellias, its exquisite little churches, and galleried houses back in the hills overlooking the cotton fields. It has escaped what happened to Grand Gulf and Bruinsburg and Rodney's Landing.

A narrow gravel road goes into the West. You have entered the loess country, and a gate might have been shut behind you for the difference in the world. All about are hills and chasms of cane, forests of cedar trees, and magnolia. Falling away from your road, at times merging with it, an old trail crosses and recrosses, like a tunnel through the dense brakes, under arches of branches, a narrow, cedar-smelling trace the width of a horseman. This road joined the Natchez Trace to the river. It, too, was made by buffaloes, then used by man, trodden lower and lower, a few inches every hundred years.

Loess has the beautiful definition of aeolian—wind-borne. The loess soil is like a mantle; the ridge was laid down here by the wind, the bottom land by the water. Deep under them both is solid blue clay, embalming the fossil horse and the fossil ox and the great mastodon, the same preserving blue clay that was dug up to wrap the head of the Big Harp in bandit days, no less a monstrous thing when it was carried in for reward.

Loess exists also in China, that land whose plants are so congenial to the South; there the bluffs rise vertically for five hundred feet in some places and contain cave dwellings without number. The Mississippi bluffs once served the same purpose; when Vicksburg was being shelled from the river during the year's siege there in the War Between the States, it was the daily habit of the three thousand women, children and old men who made up the wartime population to go on their all-fours into shelters they had tunneled into the loess bluffs. Mark Twain reports how the Federal soldiers would shout from the river in grim humor, "Rats, to your holes!"

Winding through this land unwarned, rounding to a valley, you will come on a startling thing. Set back in an old gray field, with horses grazing like small fairy animals beside it, is a vast ruin—twenty-two Corinthian columns in an empty oblong and an L. Almost seeming to float like lace, bits of wrought-iron balcony connect them here and there. Live cedar trees are growing from the iron black acanthus leaves, high in the empty air. This is the ruin of Windsor, long since burned. It used to have five stories and an observation tower—Mark Twain used the tower as a sight when he was pilot on the river.

Immediately the cane and the cedars become more impenetrable, the road ascends and descends, and rather slowly, because of the trees and shadows, you realize a little village is before you. Grand Gulf today looks like a scene in Haiti. Under enormous dense trees where the moss hangs long as ladders, there are hutlike buildings and pale whitewashed sheds; most of the faces under the straw hats are black, and only narrow jungly paths lead toward the river. Of course this is not Grand Gulf in the original, for the river undermined that and pulled it whole into the river—the opposite of what it did to Rodney's Landing. A little corner was left, which the Federals burned, all but a wall, on their way to Vicksburg. After the war the population built it back—and the river moved away. Grand Gulf was a British settlement before the Revolution and had close connection with England, whose ships traded here. It handled more cotton than any other port in Mississippi for about twenty years. The old cemetery is there still, like a roof of marble and moss overhanging the town and about to tip into it. Many names of British gentry stare out from the stones, and the biggest snakes in the world must have their kingdom in that dark-green tangle.

Two miles beyond, at the end of a dim jungle track where you can walk, is the river, immensely wide and vacant, its bluff occupied sometimes by a casual camp of fishermen under the willow trees, where dirty children playing about and nets drying have a look of timeless roaming and poverty and sameness . . . By boat you can reach a permanent fishing camp, inaccessible now by land. Go till you find the hazy shore where the Bayou Pierre, dividing in two, reaches around the swamp to meet the river. It is a gray-green land, softly flowered, hung with stillness. Houseboats will be tied there among the cypresses under falls of the long moss, all of a color. Aaron Burr's "flotilla" tied up there, too, for this is Bruinsburg Landing, where the boats were seized one wild day of apprehension. Bruinsburg grew to be a rich, gay place in cotton days. It is almost as if a wand had turned a noisy cotton port into a handful of shanty boats. Yet Bruinsburg Landing has not vanished: it is this.

Wonderful things have come down the current of this river, and more spectacular things were on the water than could ever have sprung up on shores then. Every kind of treasure, every kind of bearer of treasure has come down, and armadas and flotillas, and the most frivolous of things, too, and the most pleasure-giving of people.

Natchez, downstream, had a regular season of drama from 1806 on, attended by the countryside—the only one in English in this part of the world. The plays would be given outdoors, on a strip of grass on the edge of the high bluff overlooking the landing. With the backdrop of the river and the endless low marsh of Louisiana beyond, some version of Elizabethan or Restoration comedy or tragedy would be given, followed by a short farcical afterpiece, and the traveling company would run through a little bird mimicry, ventriloquism and magical tricks in-between. Natchez, until lately a bear-baiting crowd, watched eagerly "A Laughable Comedy in 3 Acts written by Shakespeare and Altered by Garrick called Catherine & Petrucio," followed by "A Pantomime Ballet Called a Trip through the Vauxhall Gardens into which is introduced the humorous song of Four and Twenty Fiddlers concluding with a dance by the characters." Or sometimes the troupe would arrive with a program of "divertissements"—recitations of Lochinvar, Alexander's Feast, Cato's Soliloquy of the Soul, and Clarence's Dream, interspersed with Irish songs by the boys sung to popular requests and concluding with "A Laughable Combat between Two Blind Fiddlers."

The Natchez country took all this omnivorously to its heart. There were rousing, splendid seasons, with a critic writing pieces in the newspaper to say that last night's Juliet spoke just a *bit* too loudly for a girl, though Tybalt kept in perfect character to delight all, even after he was dead—signed "X.Y.Z."

But when the natural vigor of the day gave clamorous birth to the minstrel show, the bastard Shakespeare went; and when the showboat really rounded the bend, the theatre of that day, a child of the plantation and the river, came to its own. The next generation heard calliopes filling river and field with their sound, and saw the dazzling showboats come like enormous dreams up the bayous and the little streams at floodtime, with whole French Zouave troops aboard, whole circuses with horses jumping through paper hoops, and all the literal rites of the minstrel show, as ever true to expectations as a miracle play.

Now if you pick up the Rodney Road again, through twenty miles of wooded hills, you wind sharply round, the old sunken road ahead of you and following you. Then from a great height you descend suddenly through a rush of vines, down, down, deep into complete levelness, and there in a strip at the bluff's foot, at the road's end, is Rodney's Landing.

Though you walk through Rodney's Landing, it long remains a landscape, rather than a center of activity, and seems to exist altogether in the sight, like a vision. At first you think there is not even sound. The thick soft morning shadow of the bluff on the valley floor, and the rose-red color of the brick church which rises from this shadow, are its dominant notes—all else seems green. The red of the bricks defies their element; they were made of earth, but they glow as if to remind you that there is fire in earth. No one is in sight.

Eventually you see people, of course. Women have little errands, and the old men play checkers at a table in front of the one open store. And the people's faces are good. Theirs seem *actually* the faces your eyes look for in city streets and never see. There is a middle-aged man who always meets you when you come. He is like an embodiment of the simplicity and friendliness not of the mind—for his could not teach him—but of the open spirit. He never remembers you, but he speaks courteously. "I am Mr. John David's boy—where have you come from, and when will you have to go back?" He has what I have always imagined as a true Saxon face, like a shepherd boy's, light and shy and set in solitude. He carries a staff, too, and stands with it on the hill, where he will lead you—looking with care everywhere and far away, warning you of the steep stile . . . The river is not even in sight here. It is three miles beyond, past the cotton fields of the bottom, through a dense miasma of swamp.

The houses merge into a shaggy fringe at the foot of the bluff. It is like a town some avenging angel has flown over, taking up every second or third house and leaving only this. There are more churches than houses now; the edge of town is marked by a little wooden Catholic church tiny as a matchbox, with twin steeples carved like icing, over a stile in a flowery pasture. The Negro Baptist church, weathered black with a snow-white door, has red hens in the yard. The old galleried stores are boarded up. The missing houses were burned—they were empty, and the little row of Negro inhabitants have carried them off for firewood.

You know instinctively as you stand here that this shelf of forest is the old town site, and you find that here, as in Grand Gulf, the cemetery has remained as the roof of the town. In a mossy wood the graves, gently tended here, send up mossy shafts, with lilies flowering in the gloom. Many of the tombstones are marked "A Native of Ireland," though there are German names and graves neatly bordered with sea shells and planted in spring-flowering bulbs. People in Rodney's Landing won silver prizes in the fairs for their horses; they planted all this land; some of them were killed in battle, some in duels fought on a Grand Gulf sand bar. The girls who died young of the fevers were some of them the famous "Rodney heiresses." All Mississippians know descendants of all the names. I looked for the grave of Dr. Nutt, the man who privately invented and used his cotton gin here, previous to the rest of the world. The Petit Gulf cotton was known in England better than any other as superior to all cotton, and was named for the little gulf in the river at this landing, and Rodney, too, was once called Petit Gulf.

Down below, Mr. John David's boy opens the wrought-iron gate to the churchyard of the rose-red church, and you go up the worn, concave steps. The door is never locked, the old silver knob is always the heat of the hand. It is a church, upon whose calm interior nothing seems to press from the outer world, which, though calm itself here, is still "outer." (Even cannonballs were stopped by its strong walls, and are in them yet.) It is the kind of little church in which you might instinctively say prayers for your friends; how is it that both danger and succor, both need and response, seem intimately near in little country churches?

Something always hangs imminent above all life—usually claims of daily need, daily action, a prescribed course of movement, a schedule of time. In Rodney, the imminent thing is a natural danger—the town may be flooded by the river, and every inhabitant must take to the hills. Every house wears a belt of ineradicable silt around its upper walls. I asked the storekeeper what his store would be like after the river had been over it, and he said, "You know the way a fish is?" Life threatened by nature is simplified, most peaceful in present peace, quiet in seasons of waiting and readiness. There are rowboats under all the houses.

Even the women in sunbonnets disappear and nothing moves at noon but butterflies, little white ones, large black ones, and they are like some flutter of heat, some dervishes of the mid-day hour, as in pairs they rotate about one another, ascending and descending, appearing to follow each other up and down some swaying spiral staircase invisible in the dense light. The heat moves. Its ripples can be seen, like the ripples in some vertical river running between earth and sky. It is so still at noon. I was never there before the river left, to hear the thousand swirling sounds it made for Rodney's Landing, but could it be that its absence is so much missed in the life of sound here that a stranger would feel it? The stillness seems absolute, as the brightness of noon seems to touch the point of saturation. Here the noon sun does make a trance; here indeed at its same zenith it looked down on life sacrificed to it and was worshipped.

It is not strange to think that a unique nation among Indians lived in this beautiful country. The origin of the Natchez is still in mystery. But their people, five villages in the seventeenth century, were unique in this country and they were envied by the other younger nations—the Choctaws helped the French in their final dissolution. In Mississippi they were remnants surely of medievalism. They were proud and cruel, gentle-mannered and ironic, handsome, extremely tall, intellectual, elegant, pacific and ruthless. Fire, death, sacrifice formed the spirit of the Natchez' worship. They did not now, however, make war.

The women—although all the power was in their blood, and a Sun woman by rigid system married a low-caste Stinkard and bore a Sun child by him—were the nation's laborers still. They planted and they spun, they baked their red jugs for the bear oil, and when the men came from the forests, they would throw at the feet of their wives the tongues of the beasts they had shot from their acacia bows—both as a tribute to womanhood and as a command to the wives to go out and hunt on the ground for what they had killed, and to drag it home.

The town of Natchez was named after this nation, although the French one day, in a massacre for a massacre, slew or sent into slavery at Santo Domingo every one of its namesakes, and the history of the nation was done in 1773. The French amusedly regarded the Natchez as either *"sauvages"* or *"naturels, innocents."* They made many notes of their dress and quaint habits, made engravings of them looking like Cupids and Psyches, and handed down to us their rites and customs with horrified withholdings or fascinated repetitions. The women fastened their knee-length hair in a net of mulberry threads, men singed theirs short into a crown except for a lock over the left ear. They loved vermilion and used it delicately, men and women, the women's breasts decorated in tattooed designs by whose geometrics they strangely match ancient Aztec bowls. *"En été"* male and female wore a draped garment from waist to knee. *"En hyver"* they threw about them swan-feather mantles, made as carefully as wigs. For the monthly festivals the men added bracelets of skin polished like ivory, and thin disks of feathers went in each hand. They were painted fire-color, white puffs of down decorated their shorn heads, the one lock left to support the whitest feathers. As children, the Natchez wore pearls handed down by their ancestors—pearls which they had ruined by piercing them with fire.

The Natchez also laughed gently at the French. (Also they massacred them when they were betrayed by them.) Once a Frenchman asked a Natchez noble why these Indians would laugh at them, and the noble replied that it was only because the French were like geese when they talked—all clamoring at once. The Natchez never spoke except one at a time; no one was ever interrupted or contradicted; a visitor was always allowed the opening speech, and that after a rest in silence of fifteen or twenty minutes, to allow him to get his breath and collect his thoughts. (Women murmured or whispered; their game after labor was a silent little guessing game played with three sticks that could not disturb anyone.) But this same nation, when any Sun died, strangled his wife and a great company of loyal friends and ambitious Stinkards to attend him in death, and walked bearing his body over the bodies of strangled infants laid before him by their parents. A Sun once expressed great though polite astonishment that a certain Frenchman declined the favor of dying with him.

Their own sacrifices were great among them. When Iberville came, the Natchez had diminished to twelve hundred. They laid it to the fact that the fire had once been allowed to go out and that a profane fire burned now in its place. Perhaps they had prescience of their end—the only bit of their history that we really know.

Today Rodney's Landing wears the cloak of vegetation which has caught up this whole land for the third time, or the fourth, or the hundredth. There is something Gothic about the vines, in their structure in the trees—there are arches, flying buttresses, towers of vines, with trumpet flowers swinging in them for bells and staining their walls. And there is something of a warmer grandeur in their very abundance—stairways and terraces and whole hanging gardens of green and flowering vines, with a Babylonian babel of hundreds of creature voices that make up the silence of Rodney's Landing. Here are nests for birds and thrones for owls and trapezes for snakes, every kind of bower in the world. From earliest spring there is something, when garlands of yellow jasmine swing from tree to tree, in the woods aglow with dogwood and redbud, when the green is only a floating veil in the hills.

And the vines make an endless flourish in summer and fall. There are wild vines of the grape family, with their lilac and turquoise fruits and their green, pink and white leaves. Muscadine vines along the stream banks grow a hundred feet high, mixing their dull, musky, delicious grapes among the bronze grapes of the scuppernong. All creepers with trumpets and panicles of scarlet and yellow cling to the treetops. On shady stream banks hang lady's eardrops, fruits and flowers dangling pale jade. The passionflower puts its tendrils where it can, its strange flowers of lilac rays with their little white towers shining out, or its fruit, the maypop, hanging. Wild wistaria hangs its flowers like flower-grapes above reach, and the sweetness of clematis, the virgin's-bower which grows in Rodney, and of honeysuckle, must fill even the highest air. There is a vine that grows to great heights, with heart-shaped leaves as big and soft as summer hats, overlapping and shading everything to deepest jungle blue-green.

Ferns are the hidden floor of the forest, and they grow, too, in the trees, their roots in the deep of mossy branches.

All over the hills the beautiful white Cherokee rose trails its glossy dark-green leaves and its delicate luminous-white flowers. Foliage and flowers alike have a quality of light and dark as well as color in Southern sun, and sometimes a seeming motion like dancing due to the flicker of heat, and are luminous or opaque according to the time of day or the density of summer air. In early morning or in the light of evening they become translucent and ethereal, but at noon they blaze or darken opaquely, and the same flower may seem sultry or delicate in its being all according to when you see it.

It is not hard to follow one of the leapings of old John Law's mind, then, and remember how he displayed diamonds in the shop windows in France—during the organization of his Compagnie d'Occident—saying that they were produced in the cups of the wildflowers along the lower Mississippi. And the closer they grew to the river, the more nearly that might be true.

Deep in the swamps the water hyacinths make solid floors

you could walk on over still black water, the Southern blue flag stands thick and sweet in the marsh. Lady's-tresses, greenish-white little orchids with spiral flowers and stems twisted like curls and braids, grow there, and so do nodding lady's-tresses. Water lilies float, and spider lilies rise up like little coral monsters.

The woods on the bluffs are the hardwood trees—dark and berried and flowered. The magnolia is the spectacular one with its heavy cups—they look as heavy as silver—weighing upon its aromatic, elliptical, black-green leaves, or when it bears its dense pink cones. I remember an old botany book, written long ago in England, reporting the magnolia by hearsay, as having blossoms "so large as to be distinctly visible a mile or more—seen in the mass, we presume." But I tested the visibility power of the magnolia, and the single flower can be seen for several miles on a clear day. One magnolia cousin, the cucumber tree, has long sleevelike leaves and pale-green flowers which smell strange and cooler than the grandiflora flower. Set here and there in this country will be a mimosa tree, with its smell in the rain like a cool melon cut, its puffs of pale flowers settled in its sensitive leaves.

Perhaps the live oaks are the most wonderful trees in this land. Their great girth and their great spread give far more feeling of history than any house or ruin left by man. Vast, very dark, proportioned as beautifully as a church, they stand majestically in the wild or line old sites, old academy grounds. The live oaks under which Aaron Burr was tried at Washington, Mississippi, in this section, must have been old and impressive then, to have been chosen for such a drama. Spanish moss invariably hangs from the live oak branches, moving with the wind and swaying its long beards, darkening the forests; it is an aerial plant and strangely enough is really a pineapple, and consists of very, very tiny leaves and flowers, springy and dustily fragrant to the touch; no child who has ever "dressed up" in it can forget the sweet dust of its smell. It would be hard to think of things that happened here without the presence of these live oaks, so old, so expansive, so wonderful, that they might be sentient beings. W. H. Hudson, in his autobiography, *Far Away and Long Ago*, tells of an old man who felt reverentially toward the ancient trees of his great country house, so that each night he walked around his park to visit them one by one, and rest his hand on its bark to bid it goodnight, for he believed in their knowing spirits.

Now and then comes a report that an ivory-billed woodpecker is seen here. Audubon in his diary says the Indians began the slaughter of this bird long before Columbus discovered America, for the Southern Indians would trade them to the Canadian Indians—four buckskins for an ivory bill. Audubon studied the woodpecker here when he was in the Natchez country, where it lived in the deepest mossy swamps along the windings of the river, and he called it "the greatest of all our American woodpeckers and probably the finest in the world." The advance of agriculture rather than slaughter has really driven it to death, for it will not live except in a wild country.

This woodpecker used to cross the river "in deep undulations." Its notes were "clear, loud, and rather plaintive . . . heard at a considerable distance . . . and resemble the false high note of a clarinet." "Pait, pait, pait," Audubon translates it into his Frenchlike sound. It made its nest in a hole dug with the ivory bill in a tree inclined in just a certain way—usually a black cherry. The holes went sometimes three feet deep, and some people thought they went spirally. The bird ate the grapes of the swampland. Audubon says it would hang by its claws like a titmouse on a grapevine and devour grapes by the bunch—which sounds curiously as though it knew it would be extinct before very long. This woodpecker also would destroy any dead tree it saw standing—chipping it away "to an extent of twenty or thirty feet in a few hours, leaping downward with its body . . . tossing its head to the right and left, or leaning it against the bark to ascertain the precise spot where the grubs were concealed, and immediately renewing its blows with fresh vigor, all the while sounding its loud notes, as if highly delighted." The males had beautiful crimson crests, the females were "always the most clamorous and the least shy." When caught, the birds would fight bitterly, and "utter a mournful and very piteous cry." All vanished now from the earth—the piteous cry and all; unless where

Rodney's swamps are wild enough still, perhaps it is true, the last of the ivory-billed woodpeckers still exist in the world, in this safe spot, inaccessible to man.

Indians, Mike Fink the flatboatman, Burr, and Blennerhassett, John James Audubon, the bandits of the Trace, planters, and preachers—the horse fairs, the great fires—the battles of war, the arrivals of foreign ships, and the coming of floods: could not all these things still move with their true stature into the mind here, and their beauty still work upon the heart? Perhaps it is the sense of place that gives us the belief that passionate things, in some essence, endure. Whatever is significant and whatever is tragic in its story live as long as the place does, though they are unseen, and the new life will be built upon these things—regardless of commerce and the way of rivers and roads, and other vagrancies.

Writing and Analyzing a Story

WRITERS are often asked to give their own analysis of some story they have published. I never saw, as reader or writer, that a finished story stood in need of any more from the author: for better or worse, there the story is. There is also the question of whether or not the author could provide the sort of analysis asked for. Story writing and critical analysis are indeed separate gifts, like spelling and playing the flute, and the same writer proficient in both has been doubly endowed. But even he can't rise and do both at the same time.

To me as a story writer, generalizations about writing come tardily and uneasily, and I would limit them, if I were wise, by saying that any conclusions I feel confidence in are stuck to the particular story, part of the animal. The most trustworthy lesson I've learned from work so far is the simple one that the writing of each story is sure to open up a different prospect and pose a new problem; and that no past story bears recognizably on a new one or gives any promise of help, even if the writing mind had room for help and the wish that it would come. Help offered from outside the frame of the story would be itself an intrusion.

It's hard for me to believe that a writer's stories, taken in their whole, are written in any typical, predictable, systematically developing, or even chronological way—for all that a serious writer's stories are ultimately, to any reader, so clearly identifiable as his. Each story, it seems to me, thrives in the course of being written only as long as it seems to have a life of its own.

Yet it may become clear to a writer in retrospect (or so it did to me, although I may have been simply tardy to see it) that his stories have repeated themselves in shadowy ways, that they have returned and may return in future too—in variations—to certain themes. They may be following, in their own development, some pattern that's been very early laid down. Of course, such a pattern is subjective in nature; it may lie too deep to be consciously recognized until a cycle of stories and the actions of time have raised it to view. All the same, it is a pattern of which a new story is not another copy but a fresh attempt made in its own full-bodied right and out of its own impulse, with its own pressure, and its own needs of fulfillment.

It seems likely that all of one writer's stories do tend to spring from the same source within him. However they differ in theme or approach, however they vary in mood or fluctuate in their strength, their power to reach the mind or heart, all of one writer's stories carry their signature because of the one impulse most characteristic of his own gift—to praise, to love, to call up into view. But then, what countless stories by what countless authors share a common source! For the source of the short story is usually lyrical. And all writers speak from, and speak to, emotions eternally the same in all of us: love, pity, terror do not show favorites or leave any of us out.

The tracking down of a story might do well to start not in the subjective country but in the world itself. What in this world leads back most directly, makes the clearest connection to these emotions? What is the pull on the line? For some outside signal has startled or moved the story-writing mind to complicity: some certain irresistible, alarming (pleasurable or disturbing), magnetic person, place or thing. The outside world and the writer's response to it, the story's quotients, are always different, always differing in the combining; they are always—or so it seems to me—most intimately connected with each other.

This living connection is one that by its nature is not very open to generalization or discoverable by the ordinary scrutinies of analysis. Never mind; for its existence is, for any purpose but that of the working writer, of little importance to the story itself. It is of merely personal importance. But it is of extraordinary, if temporary, use to the writer for the particular story. Keeping this connection close is a writer's testing device along the way, flexible, delicate, precise, a means of guidance. I would rather submit a story to the test of its outside world, to show what it was doing and how it went about it, than to the method of critical analysis which would pick the story up by its heels (as if it had swallowed a button) to examine the writing process as analysis in reverse, as though a story—or any system of feeling—could be more accessible to understanding for being hung upside down.

It is not from criticism but from this world that stories come in the beginning; their origins are living reference plain to the writer's eye, even though to his eye alone. The writer's mind and heart, where all this exterior is continually *becoming* something—the moral, the passionate, the poetic, hence the *shaping* idea—can't be mapped and plotted. (Would this help—any more than a map hung on the wall changes the world?) It's the form it takes when it comes out the other side, of course, that gives a story something unique—its life. The story, in the way it has arrived at what it is on the page, has been something learned, by dint of the story's challenge and the work that rises to meet it—a process as uncharted for the writer as if it had never been attempted before.

Since analysis has to travel backward, the path it goes is an ever-narrowing one, whose goal is the vanishing point, beyond which only "influences" lie. But the writer of the story, bound in the opposite direction, works into the open. The choices multiply, become more complicated and with more hanging on them, as with everything else that has a life and moves. "This story promises me fear and joy and so I write it" has been the writer's beginning. The critic, coming to the end of his trail, may call out the starting point he's found, but the writer knew his starting point first and for what it was—the jumping-off place. And all along, the character of the choices—the critic's decisions and the writer's—is wholly different. I think that the writer's out-bound choices were to him the *believable* ones, not necessarily defensible on other grounds; impelled, not subject to scheme but to feeling; that they came with an arrow inside them. They have been *fiction's* choices: one-way and fateful; strict as art, obliged as feeling, powerful in their authenticity.

The story and its analysis are not mirror-opposites of each other. They are not reflections, either one. Criticism indeed is an art, as a story is, but only the story is to some degree a vision; there is no explanation outside fiction for what its writer is learning to do. The simplest-appearing work may have been brought off (when it does not fail) on the sharp edge of experiment, and it was for this its writer was happy to leave behind him all he knew before, and the safety of that, when he began the new story.

I feel that our ever-changing outside world and some learnable lessons about writing fiction are always waiting side by side for us to put into connection, if we can. A writer should say this only of himself and offer an example. In a story I wrote recently called "No Place for You, My Love," the outside world—a definite place in it, of course—not only suggested how to write it but repudiated a way I had already tried. What follows has no claim to be critical analysis; it can be called a piece of hindsight from a working point of view.

What changed my story was a trip. I was invited to drive with an acquaintance, one summer day, down south of New Orleans to see that country for the first (and so far, only) time; and when I got back home, full of the landscape I'd seen, I realized that without being aware of it at the time, I had treated the story to my ride, and it had come into my head in an altogether new form. I set to work and wrote the new version from scratch.

As first written, the story told, in subjective terms, of a girl in a claustrophobic predicament: she was caught fast in the over-familiar, monotonous life of her small town, and immobilized further by a prolonged and hopeless love affair; she could see no way out. As a result of my ride, I extricated—not the girl, but the story.

This character had been well sealed inside her world, by nature and circumstance, just where I'd put her. But she was sealed in to the detriment of the story, because I'd made hers the point of view. The primary step now was getting outside her mind; on that instant I made her a girl from the Middle West. (She'd been before what I knew best, a Southerner.) I kept outside her by taking glimpses of her through the eyes of a total stranger: casting off the half-dozen familiars the first girl had around her, I invented a single new character, a man whom I brought into the story *to be* a stranger, and I was to keep out of his mind, too. I had double-locked the doors behind me.

It would have been for nothing had the original impulse

behind the story not proved itself alive; it now took on new energy. That country—that once-submerged, strange land of "south from South"—which had so stamped itself upon my imagination put in an unmistakable claim now as the very image of the story's predicament. It pointed out to me at the same time where the real point of view belonged. Once I'd escaped those characters' minds, I saw it was outside them—suspended, hung in the air between two people, fished alive from the surrounding scene. As I wrote further into the story, something more real, more essential, than the characters were on their own was revealing itself. In effect, though the characters numbered only two, there had come to be a sort of third character along on the ride—the presence of a relationship between the two. It was what grew up between them meeting as strangers, went on the excursion with them, nodded back and forth from one to the other—listening, watching, persuading or denying them, enlarging or diminishing them, forgetful sometimes of who they were or what they were doing here—in its domain—and helping or betraying them along.

(Here I think it perhaps should be remembered that characters in a short story have not the size and importance and capacity for development they have in a novel, but are subservient altogether to the story as a whole.)

This third character's role was that of hypnosis—it was what a relationship *can do*, be it however brief, tentative, potential, happy or sinister, ordinary or extraordinary. I wanted to suggest that its being took shape as the strange, compulsive journey itself, was palpable as its climate and mood, the heat of the day—but was its spirit too, a spirit that held territory, that which is seen fleeting past by two vulnerable people who might seize hands on the run. There are moments in the story when I say neither "she felt" nor "he felt" but "they felt."

This is to grant that I rode out of the old story on the back of the girl and then threw away the girl; but I saved my story, for, entirely different as the second version was, it was what I wanted to tell. Now my subject was out in the open, provided at the same time with a place to happen and a way to say it was happening. All I had to do was recognize it, which I did a little late.

Anyone who has visited the actual scene of this story will possibly recognize it when he meets it here, for the story is visual and the place is out of the ordinary. The connection between a story and its setting may not always be so plain. For no matter whether the "likeness" is there for all to see or not, the place, once entered into the writer's mind in a story, is, in the course of writing the story, *functional.*

Thus I wanted to make seen and believed what was to me, in my story's grip, literally apparent—that secret and shadow are taken away in this country by the merciless light that prevails there, by the river that is like an exposed vein of ore, the road that descends as one with the heat—its nerve (these are all terms in the story), and that the heat is also a visual illusion, shimmering and dancing over the waste that stretches ahead. I was writing of a real place, but doing so in order to write about my subject. I was writing of exposure, and the shock of the world; in the end I tried to make the story's inside outside and then leave the shell behind.

The vain courting of imperviousness in the face of exposure is this little story's plot. Deliver us all from the naked in heart, the girl thinks (this is what I kept of her). "So strangeness gently steels us," I read today in a poem of Richard Wilbur's. Riding down together into strange country is danger, a play at danger, secretly poetic, and the characters, in attempting it as a mutual feat, admit nothing to each other except the wicked heat and its comical inconvenience. The only time they will yield or touch is while they are dancing in the crowd that to them is comically unlikely (hence insulating, non-conducting) or taking a kiss outside time. Nevertheless it happens that they go along aware, from moment to moment, as one: as my third character, the straining, hallucinatory eyes and ears, the roused-up sentient being of that place. Exposure begins in intuition; and the intuition comes to its end in showing the heart that has expected, while it dreads, that exposure. Writing it as I'd done before, as a story of concealment, in terms of the hermetic and the familiar, had somehow resulted in my own effective concealment of what I meant to show.

Now, the place had suggested to me that something demonaic was called for—the speed of the ride pitted against the danger of an easy or conventionally tempting sympathy, the heat that in itself drives on the driver in the face of an inimical world. Something wilder than ordinary communication between well-disposed strangers, and more ruthless and more tender, more pressing and acute, than their automatic, saving ironies and graces, I felt, and do so often feel, has to come up against a world like that.

I did my best to merge, or even to identify, the abstract with the concrete as it became possible in this story—where setting, characters, mood, and method of writing all worked as parts of the same thing and subject to related laws and conditionings. The story *had* to be self-evident, and to hold its speed to the end—a speed I think of as racing, though it may not seem so to the reader.

Above all, I had no wish to sound mystical, but I admit that I did expect to sound mysterious now and then, if I could: this was a circumstantial, realistic story in which the reality *was* mystery. The cry that rose up at the story's end was, I hope unmistakably, the cry of that doomed relationship—personal, mortal, psychic—admitted in order to be denied, a cry that the characters were first able (and prone) to listen to, and then able in part to ignore. The cry was authentic to my story: the end of a journey *can* set up a cry, the shallowest provocation to sympathy and love does hate to give up the ghost. A relationship of the most fleeting kind has the power inherent to loom like a genie—to become vocative at the last, as it has already become present and taken up room; as it has spread out as a destination however unlikely; as it has glimmered and rushed by in the dark and dust outside, showing occasional points of fire. Relationship *is* a pervading and changing mystery; it is not words that make it so in life, but words have to make it so in a story. Brutal or lovely, the mystery waits for people wherever they go, whatever extreme they run to.

I had got back at the end of the new story to suggesting what I had taken as the point of departure in the old, but there was no question in my mind which story was nearer the mark of my intention. This may not reflect very well on the brightness of the author at work; it may cause a reader to wonder how often a story has to rescue itself. I think it goes to show, all the same, that subject, method, form, style, all wait upon—indeed hang upon—a sort of double thunderclap at the author's ears: the break of the living world upon what is already stirring inside the mind, and the answering impulse that in a moment of high consciousness fuses impact and image and fires them off together. There never really was a sound, but the impact is always recognizable, granting the author's sensitivity and sense; and if the impulse so projected is to some degree fulfilled, it may give some pleasure in its course to the writer and reader. The living world itself remains just the same as it always was, and luckily enough for the story, among other things, for it can test and talk back to the story any day in the week. Between the writer and the story he writes, *there* is the undying third character.

Place in Fiction

PLACE is one of the lesser angels that watch over the racing hand of fiction, perhaps the one that gazes benignly enough from off to one side, while others, like character, plot, symbolic meaning, and so on, are doing a good deal of wing-beating about her chair, and feeling, who in my eyes carries the crown, soars highest of them all and rightly relegates place into the shade. Nevertheless, it is this lowlier angel that concerns us here. There have been signs that she has been rather neglected of late; maybe she could do with a little petitioning.

What place has place in fiction? It might be thought so modest a one that it can be taken for granted: the location of a novel; to use a term of the day, it may make the novel "regional." The term, like most terms used to pin down a novel, means little; and Henry James said there isn't any difference between "the English novel" and "the American novel," since there are only two kinds of novels at all, the good and the bad. Of course Henry James didn't stop there, and we all hate generalities, and so does place. Yet as soon as we step down from the general view to the close and particular, as writers must and readers may and teachers well know how to, and consider what good writing may be, place can be seen, in her own way, to have a great deal to do with that goodness, if not to be responsible for it. How so?

First, with the goodness—validity—in the raw material of writing. Second, with the goodness in the writing itself—the achieved world of appearance, through which the novelist has his whole say and puts his whole case. There will still be the lady, always, who dismissed *The Ancient Mariner* on grounds of implausibility. Third, with the goodness—the worth—in the writer himself: place is where he has his roots, place is where he stands; in his experience out of which he writes, it provides the base of reference; in his work, the point of view. Let us consider place in fiction in these three wide aspects.

Wide, but of course connected—vitally so. And if in some present-day novels the connection has apparently slipped, that makes a fresh reason for us to ponder the subject of place.

For novels, besides being the pleasantest things imaginable, are powerful forces on the side. Mutual understanding in the world being nearly always, as now, at low ebb, it is comforting to remember that it is through art that one country can nearly always speak reliably to another, if the other can hear at all. Art, though, is never the voice of a country; it is an even more precious thing, the voice of the individual, doing its best to speak, not comfort of any sort, indeed, but truth. And the art that speaks it most unmistakably, most directly, most variously, most fully, is fiction; in particular, the novel.

Why? Because the novel from the start has been bound up in the local, the "real," the present, the ordinary day-to-day of human experience. Where the imagination comes in is in directing the use of all this. That use is endless, and there are only four words, of all the millions we've hatched, that a novel rules out: "Once upon a time." They make a story a fairy tale by the simple sweep of the remove—by abolishing the present and the place where we are instead of conveying them to us. Of course we shall have some sort of fairy tale with us always—just now it is the historical novel. Fiction is properly at work on the here and now, or the past made here and now; for in novels *we* have to be there. Fiction provides the ideal texture through which the feeling and meaning that permeate our own personal, present lives will best show through. For in his theme —the most vital and important part of the work at hand—the novelist has the blessing of the inexhaustible subject: you and me. You and me, here. Inside that generous scope and circumference—who could ask for anything more?—the novel can accommodate practically anything on earth; and has abundantly done so. The novel so long as it be *alive* gives pleasure, and must always give pleasure, enough to stave off the departure of the Wedding Guest forever, except for that one lady.

It is by the nature of itself that fiction is all bound up in the local. The internal reason for that is surely that *feelings* are bound up in place. The human mind is a mass of associations—associations more poetic even than actual. I say, "The Yorkshire Moors," and you will say, *"Wuthering Heights,"* and I have only to murmur, "If Father were only alive—" for you to come back with "We could go to Moscow," which certainly is not even so. The truth is, fiction depends for its life on place. Location is the crossroads of circumstance, the proving ground of "What happened? Who's here? Who's coming?" —and that is the heart's field.

Unpredictable as the future of any art must be, one condition we may hazard about writing: of all the arts, it is the one least likely to cut the cord that binds it to its source. Music and dancing, while originating out of place—groves!—and perhaps invoking it still to minds pure or childlike, are no longer bound to dwell there. Sculpture exists out in empty space: that is what it commands and replies to. Toward painting, place, to be so highly visible, has had a curious and changing relationship. Indeed, wasn't it when landscape invaded painting, and painting was given, with the profane content, a narrative content, that this worked to bring on a revolution to the art? Impressionism brought not the likeness-to-life but the mystery of place onto canvas; it was the method, not the subject, that told this. Painting and writing, always the closest two of the sister arts (and in ancient Chinese days only the blink of an eye seems to have separated them), have each a still closer connection with place than they have with each other; but a difference lies in their respective requirements of it, and even further in the way they use it—the written word being ultimately as different from the pigment as the note of the scale is from the chisel.

One element, which has just been mentioned, is surely the underlying bond that connects all the arts with place. All of them celebrate its mystery. Where does this mystery lie? Is it in the fact that place has a more lasting identity than we have, and we unswervingly tend to attach ourselves to identity? Might the magic lie partly, too, in the *name* of the place—since that is what *we* gave it? Surely, once we have it named, we have put a kind of poetic claim on its existence; the claim works even out of sight—may work forever sight unseen. The Seven Wonders of the World still give us this poetic kind of gratification. And notice we do not say simply "The Hanging Gardens"—that would leave them dangling out of reach and dubious in nature; we say "The Hanging Gardens of Babylon," and there they are, before our eyes, shimmering and garlanded and exactly elevated to the Babylonian measurement.

Edward Lear tapped his unerring finger on the magic of place in the limerick. There's something unutterably convincing about that Old Person of Sparta who had twenty-five sons and one darta, and it is surely beyond question that he fed them on snails and weighed them in scales, because we know where that Old Person is *from*—Sparta! We certainly do not need further to be told his *name*. "Consider the source." Experience has ever advised us to base validity on point of origin.

Being shown how to locate, to place, any account is what does most toward *making* us believe it, not merely allowing us to, may the account be the facts or a lie; and that is where place in fiction comes in. Fiction is a lie. Never in its inside thoughts, always in its outside dress.

Some of us grew up with the china night-light, the little lamp whose lighting showed its secret and with that spread enchantment. The outside is painted with a scene, which is one thing; then, when the lamp is lighted, through the porcelain sides a new picture comes out through the old, and they are seen as one. A lamp I knew of was a view of London till it was lit; but then it was the Great Fire of London, and you could go beautifully to sleep by it. The lamp alight is the combination of internal and external, glowing at the imagination as one; and so is the good novel. Seeing that these inner and outer surfaces do lie so close together and so implicit in each other, the wonder is that human life so often separates them, or appears to, and it takes a good novel to put them back together.

The good novel should be steadily alight, revealing. Before it can hope to be that, it must of course be steadily visible from its outside, presenting a continuous, shapely, pleasing and finished surface to the eye.

The sense of a story when the visibility is only partial or intermittent is as endangered as Eliza crossing the ice. Forty hounds of confusion are after it, the black waters of disbelief open up between its steps, and no matter which way it jumps it is bound to slip. Even if it has a little baby moral in its arms, it is more than likely a goner.

The novel must get Eliza across the ice; what it means—the way it proceeds—is always in jeopardy. It must be given a surface that is continuous and unbroken, never too thin to trust, always in touch with the senses. Its world of experience must be at every step, through every moment, within reach as the world of appearance.

This makes it the business of writing, and the responsibility of the writer, to disentangle the significant—in character, incident, setting, mood, everything—from the random and meaningless and irrelevant that in real life surround and beset it. It is a matter of his selecting and, by all that implies, of changing "real" life as he goes. With each word he writes, he acts—as literally and methodically as if he hacked his way through a forest and blazed it for the word that follows. He makes choices at the explicit demand of this one present story; each choice implies, explains, limits the next, and illuminates the one before. No two stories ever go the same way, although in different hands one story might possibly go any one of a thousand ways; and though the woods may look the same from outside, it is a new and different labyrinth every time. What tells the author his way? Nothing at all but what he knows inside himself: the same thing that hints to him afterward how far he has missed it, how near he may have come to the heart of it. In a working sense, the novel and its place have become one: work has made them, for the time being, the same thing, like the explorer's tentative map of the known world.

The reason why every word you write in a good novel is a lie, then, is that it is written expressly to serve the purpose; if it does not apply, it is fancy and frivolous, however specially dear to the writer's heart. Actuality, it is true, is an even bigger risk to the novel than fancy writing is, being frequently even more confusing, irrelevant, diluted and generally far-fetched than ill-chosen words can make it. Yet somehow, the world of appearance in the novel has got to *seem* actuality. Is there a reliable solution to the problem? Place being brought to life in the round before the reader's eye is the readiest and gentlest and most honest and natural way this can be brought about, I think; every instinct advises it. The moment the place in which the novel happens is accepted as true, through it will begin to glow, in a kind of recognizable glory, the feeling and thought that inhabited the novel in the author's head and animated the whole of his work.

Besides furnishing a plausible abode for the novel's world of feeling, place has a good deal to do with making the characters real, that is, themselves, and keeping them so. The reason is simply that, as Tristram Shandy observed, "We are not made of glass, as characters on Mercury might be." Place *can* be transparent, or translucent: not people. In real life we have to express the things plainest and closest to our minds by the clumsy word and the half-finished gesture; the chances are our most usual behavior makes sense only in a kind of daily way, because it has become familiar to our nearest and dearest, and still demands their constant indulgence and understanding. It is our describable outside that defines us, willy-nilly, to others, that may save us, or destroy us, in the world; it may be our shield against chaos, our mask against exposure; but whatever it is, the move we make in the place we live has to signify our intent and meaning.

Then think how unprotected the poor character in a novel is, into whose mind the author is inviting us to look—unprotected and hence surely unbelievable! But no, the author has expressly seen to believability. Though he must know all, again he works with illusion. Just as the world of a novel is more highly selective than that of real life, so character in a novel is much more definite, less shadowy than our own, in order that we may believe in it. This is not to say that the character's scope must be limited; it is our vision of it that is guided. It is a kind of phenomenon of writing that the likeliest character has first to be enclosed inside the bounds of even greater likelihood, or he will fly to pieces. Paradoxically, the more narrowly we can examine a fictional character, the greater he is likely to loom up. We must see him set to scale in his proper world to know his size. Place, then, has the most delicate control over character too: by confining character, it defines it.

Place in fiction is the named, identified, concrete, exact and exacting, and therefore credible, gathering spot of all that has been felt, is about to be experienced, in the novel's progress. Location pertains to feeling; feeling profoundly pertains to place; place in history partakes of feeling, as feeling about history partakes of place. Every story would be another story, and unrecognizable as art, if it took up its characters and plot and happened somewhere else. Imagine *Swann's Way* laid in London, or *The Magic Mountain* in Spain, or *Green Mansions* in the Black Forest. The very notion of moving a novel brings ruder havoc to the mind and affections than would a century's alteration in its time. It is only too easy to conceive that a bomb that could destroy all trace of places as we know them, in life and through books, could also destroy all feelings as we know them, so irretrievably and so happily are recognition, memory, history, valor, love, all the instincts of poetry and praise, worship and endeavor, bound up in place. From the dawn of man's imagination, place has enshrined the spirit; as soon as man stopped wandering and stood still and looked about him, he found a god in that place; and from then on, that was where the god abided and spoke from if ever he spoke.

Feelings are bound up in place, and in art, from time to time, place undoubtedly works upon genius. Can anyone well explain otherwise what makes a given dot on the map come passionately alive, for good and all, in a novel—like one of those novae that suddenly blaze with inexplicable fire in the heavens? What brought a *Wuthering Heights* out of Yorkshire, or a *Sound and the Fury* out of Mississippi?

If place does work upon genius, how does it? It may be that place can focus the gigantic, voracious eye of genius and bring its gaze to point. Focus then means awareness, discernment, order, clarity, insight—they are like the attributes of love. The act of focusing itself has beauty and meaning; it is the act that, continued in, turns into meditation, into poetry. Indeed, as soon as the least of us stands still, that is the moment something extraordinary is seen to be going on in the world. The drama, old beyond count as it is, is no older than the first stage. Without the amphitheatre around it to persuade the ear and bend the eye upon a point, how could poetry ever have been spoken, how have been heard? Man is articulate and intelligible only when he begins to communicate inside the strict terms of poetry and reason. Symbols in the end, both are permanent forms of the act of focusing.

Surely place induces poetry, and when the poet is extremely attentive to what is there, a meaning may even attach to his poem out of the spot on earth where it is spoken, and the poem signify the more because it does spring so wholly out of its place, and the sap has run up into it as into a tree.

But we had better confine ourselves here to prose. And then, to take the most absolutely unfanciful novelist of them all, it is to hear him saying, *"Madame Bovary—c'est moi."* And we see focusing become so intent and aware and conscious in this most "realistic" novel of them all as to amount to fusion. Flaubert's work is indeed of the kind that is embedded immovably as rock in the country of its birth. If, with the slicers of any old (or new) criticism at all, you were to cut down through *Madame Bovary*, its cross section would still be the same as the cross section of that living earth, in texture, color, composition, all; which would be no surprise to Flaubert. For such fusion always means accomplishment no less conscious than it is gigantic—effort that must exist entirely as its own reward. We all know the letter Flaubert wrote when he had just found, in the morning paper, in an account of a minister's visit to Rouen, a phrase in the Mayor's speech of welcome

> which I had written the day before, textually, in my *Bovary* . . . Not only were the idea and the words the same, but even the rhythm of the style. It's things like this that give me pleasure . . . Everything one invents is true, you may be perfectly sure of that! Poetry is as precise as geometry . . . And besides, after reaching a certain point, one no longer makes any mistakes about the things of the soul. My poor Bovary, without a doubt, is suffering and weeping this very instant in twenty villages of France.

And now that we have come to the writer himself, the question of place resolves itself into the point of view. In this changeover from the objective to the subjective, wonderful and unexpected variations may occur.

Place, to the writer at work, is seen in a frame. Not an

empty frame, a brimming one. Point of view is a sort of burning-glass, a product of personal experience and time; it is burnished with feelings and sensibilities, charged from moment to moment with the sun-points of imagination. It is an instrument—one of intensification; it acts, it behaves, it is temperamental. We have seen that the writer must accurately choose, combine, superimpose upon, blot out, shake up, alter the outside world for one absolute purpose, the good of his story. To do this, he is always seeing double, two pictures at once in his frame, his and the world's, a fact that he constantly comprehends; and he works best in a state of constant and subtle and unfooled reference between the two. It is his clear intention—his passion, I should say—to make the reader see only one of the pictures—the author's—under the pleasing illusion that it is the world's; this enormity is the accomplishment of a good story. I think it likely that at the moment of the writer's highest awareness of, and responsiveness to, the "real" world, his imagination's choice (and miles away it may be from actuality) comes closest to being infallible for his purpose. For the spirit of things is what is sought. No blur of inexactness, no cloud of vagueness, is allowable in good writing; from the first seeing to the last putting down, there must be steady lucidity and uncompromise of purpose. I speak, of course, of the ideal.

One of the most important things the young writer comes to see for himself is that point of view *is* an instrument, not an end in itself, that is useful as a glass, and not as a mirror to reflect a dear and pensive face. Conscientiously used, point of view will discover, explore, see through—it may sometimes divine and prophesy. Misused, it turns opaque almost at once and gets in the way of the book. And when the good novel is finished, its cooled outside shape, what Sean O'Faoláin has called "the veil of reality," has all the burden of communicating that initial, spontaneous, overwhelming, driving charge of personal inner feeling that was the novel's reason for being. The measure of this representation of life corresponds most tellingly with the novel's life expectancy: whenever its world of outside appearance grows dim or false to the eye, the novel has expired.

Establishing a chink-proof world of appearance is not only

the first responsibility of the writer; it is the primary step in the technique of every sort of fiction: lyric and romantic, of course; the "realistic," it goes without saying; and other sorts as well. Fantasy itself must touch ground with at least one toe, and ghost stories must have one foot, so to speak, in the grave. The black, squat, hairy ghosts of M. R. James come right out of Cambridge. Only fantasy's stepchild, poor science-fiction, does not touch earth anywhere; and it is doubtful already if happenings entirely confined to outer space are ever going to move us, or even divert us for long. Satire, engaged in its most intellectual of exercises, must first of all establish an impeccable *locus operandi*; its premise is the kingdom where certain rules apply. The countries Gulliver visits are the systems of thought and learning Swift satirizes made visible one after the other and set in operation. But while place in satire is a purely artificial construction, set up to be knocked down, in humor place becomes its most revealing and at the same time is itself the most revealed. This is because humor, it seems to me, of all forms of fiction, entirely accepts place for what it is.

"Spotted Horses," by William Faulkner, is a good case in point. At the same time that this is just about Mr. Faulkner's funniest story, it is the most thorough and faithful picture of a Mississippi crossroads hamlet that you could ever hope to see. True in spirit, it is also true to everyday fact. Faulkner's art, which often lets him shoot the moon, tells him when to be literal too. In all its specification of detail, both mundane and poetic, in its complete adherence to social fact (which nobody knows better than Faulkner, surely, in writing today), by its unerring aim of observation as true as the sights of a gun would give, but Faulkner has no malice, only compassion; and even and also in the joy of those elements of harlequinade-fantasy that the spotted horses of the title bring in—in all that shining fidelity to place lies the heart and secret of this tale's comic glory.

Faulkner is, of course, the triumphant example in America today of the mastery of place in fiction. Yoknapatawpha County, so supremely and exclusively and majestically and totally itself, is an everywhere, but only because Faulkner's first concern is for what comes first—Yoknapatawpha, his own created world. I am not sure, as a Mississippian myself, how widely it is realized and appreciated that these works of such marvelous imaginative power can also stand as works of the carefulest and purest representation. Heightened, of course: their specialty is they are twice as true as life, and that is why it takes a genius to write them. "Spotted Horses" may not have happened yet; if it had, some others might have tried to make a story of it; but "Spotted Horses" could happen to-morrow—that is one of its glories. It could happen today or tomorrow at any little crossroads hamlet in Mississippi; the whole combination of irresistibility is there. We have the Snopses ready, the Mrs. Littlejohns ready, nice Ratliff and the Judge ready and sighing, the clowns, sober and merry, settled for the evening retrospection of it in the cool dusk of the porch; and the Henry Armstids armed with their obsessions, the little periwinkle-eyed boys armed with their indestructi-bility; the beautiful, overweening spring, too, the moonlight on the pear trees from which the mockingbird's song keeps returning; and the little store and the fat boy to steal and steal away at its candy. There are undoubtedly spotted horses too, in the offing—somewhere in Texas this minute, straining to-ward the day. After Faulkner has told it, it is easy for one and all to look back and see it.

Faulkner, simply, knew it already; it is a different kind of knowledge from Flaubert's, and proof could not add much to it. He was born knowing, or rather learning, or rather proph-esying, all that and more; and having it all together at one time available while he writes is one of the marks of his mind. If there *is* any more in Mississippi than is engaged and dilated upon, and made twice as real as it used to be and applies now to the world, in the one story "Spotted Horses," then we would almost rather not know it—but I don't bet a piece of store candy that there is. In Faulkner's humor, even more measurably than in his tragedy, it is all there.

It may be going too far to say that the exactness and con-creteness and solidity of the real world achieved in a story correspond to the intensity of feeling in the author's mind and to the very turn of his heart; but there lies the secret of our confidence in him.

Making reality real is art's responsibility. It is a practical assignment, then, a self-assignment: to achieve, by a cultivated sensitivity for observing life, a capacity for receiving its impressions, a lonely, unremitting, unaided, unaidable vision, and transferring this vision without distortion to it onto the pages of a novel, where, if the reader is so persuaded, it will turn into the reader's illusion. How bent on this peculiar joy we are, reader and writer, willingly to practice, willingly to undergo, this alchemy for it!

What is there, then, about place that is transferable to the pages of a novel? The best things—the explicit things: physical texture. And as place has functioned between the writer and his material, so it functions between the writer and reader. Location is the ground conductor of all the currents of emotion and belief and moral conviction that charge out from the story in its course. These charges need the warm hard earth underfoot, the light and lift of air, the stir and play of mood, the softening bath of atmosphere that give the likeness-to-life that life needs. Through the story's translation and ordering of life, the unconvincing raw material becomes the very heart's familiar. Life *is* strange. Stories hardly make it more so; with all they are able to tell and surmise, they make it more believably, more inevitably so.

I think the sense of place is as essential to good and honest writing as a logical mind; surely they are somewhere related. It is by knowing where you stand that you grow able to judge where you are. Place absorbs our earliest notice and attention, it bestows on us our original awareness; and our critical powers spring up from the study of it and the growth of experience inside it. It perseveres in bringing us back to earth when we fly too high. It never really stops informing us, for it is forever astir, alive, changing, reflecting, like the mind of man itself. One place comprehended can make us understand other places better. Sense of place gives equilibrium; extended, it is sense of direction too. Carried off we might be in spirit, and should be, when we are reading or writing something good; but it is the sense of place going with us still that is the ball of golden thread to carry us there and back and in every sense of the word to bring us home.

What can place *not* give? Theme. It can present theme, show it to the last detail—but place is forever illustrative: it is a picture of what man has done and imagined, it is his visible past, result. Human life is fiction's only theme.

Should the writer, then, write about home? It is both natural and sensible that the place where we have our roots should become the setting, the first and primary proving ground, of our fiction. Location, however, is not simply to be used by the writer—it is to be discovered, as each novel itself, in the act of writing, is discovery. Discovery does not imply that the place is new, only that we are. Place is as old as the hills. Kilroy at least has been there, and left his name. Discovery, not being a matter of writing our name on a wall, but of seeing what that wall is, and what is over it, is a matter of vision.

One can no more say, "To write stay home," than one can say, "To write leave home." It is the writing that makes its own rules and conditions for each person. And though place is home, it is for the writer writing simply *locus.* It is where the particular story he writes can be pinned down, the circle it can spin through and keep the state of grace, so that for the story's duration the rest of the world suspends its claim upon it and lies low as the story in peaceful extension, the *locus* fading off into the blue.

Naturally, it is the very breath of life, whether one writes a word of fiction or not, to go out and see what is to be seen of the world. For the artist to be unwilling to move, mentally or spiritually or physically, out of the familiar is a sign that spiritual timidity or poverty or decay has come upon him; for what is familiar will then have turned into all that is tyrannical.

One can only say: writers must always write best of what they know, and sometimes they do it by staying where they know it. But not for safety's sake. Although it is in the words of a witch—or all the more because of that—a comment of Hecate's in *Macbeth* is worth our heed: "Security/Is mortal's chiefest enemy." In fact, when we think in terms of the spirit, which are the terms of writing, is there a conception more stupefying than that of security? Yet writing of what you know has nothing to do with security: what is more dangerous? How can you go out on a limb if you do not know your own tree? No art ever came out of not risking your neck. And risk—experiment—is a considerable part of the joy of doing, which is the lone, simple reason all writers of serious fiction are willing to work as hard as they do.

The open mind and the receptive heart—which are at last and with fortune's smile the informed mind and the experienced heart—are to be gained anywhere, any time, without necessarily moving an inch from any present address. There must surely be as many ways of seeing a place as there are pairs of eyes to see it. The impact happens in so many different ways.

It may be the stranger within the gates whose eye is smitten by the crucial thing, the essence of life, the moment or act in our long-familiar midst that will forever define it. The inhabitant who has taken his fill of a place and gone away may look back and see it for good, from afar, still there in his mind's eye like a city over the hill. It was in the New Zealand stories, written eleven thousand miles from home and out of homesickness, that Katherine Mansfield came into her own. Joyce transplanted not his subject but himself while writing about it, and it was as though he had never left it at all: there it was, still in his eye, exactly the way he had last seen it. From the Continent he wrote the life of Dublin as it was then into a book of the future, for he went translating his own language of it on and on into a country of its own, where it set up a kingdom as renowned as Prester John's. Sometimes two places, two countries, are brought to bear on each other, as in E. M. Forster's work, and the heart of the novel is heard beating most plainly, most passionately, most personally when two places are at meeting point.

There may come to be new places in our lives that are second spiritual homes—closer to us in some ways, perhaps, than our original homes. But the home tie is the blood tie. And had it meant nothing to us, any other place thereafter would have meant less, and we would carry no compass inside ourselves to find home ever, anywhere at all. We would not even guess what we had missed.

It is noticeable that those writers who for their own good reasons push out against their backgrounds nearly always passionately adopt the new one in their work. Revolt itself is a reference and tribute to the potency of what is left behind. The substitute place, the adopted country, is sometimes a very much stricter, bolder, or harsher one than the original, seldom more lax or undemanding—showing that what was wanted was structure, definition, rigidity—perhaps these were wanted, and understanding was not.

Hemingway in our time has sought out the formal and ruthless territories of the world, archaic ones often, where there are bullfight arenas, theatres of hunting and war, places with a primitive, or formidable, stripped-down character, with implacable codes, with inscrutable justices and inevitable retributions. But whatever the scene of his work, it is the *places* that never are hostile. People give pain, are callous and insensitive, empty and cruel, carrying with them no pasts as they promise no futures. But place heals the hurt, soothes the outrage, fills the terrible vacuum that these human beings make. It heals actively, and the response is given consciously, with the ardent care and explicitness, respect and delight of a lover, when fishing streams or naming over streets becomes almost something of the lover's secret language—as the careful conversations between characters in Hemingway bear hints of the secret language of hate. The response to place has the added intensity that comes with the place's not being native or taken for granted, but found, chosen; thereby is the rest more heavily repudiated. It is the response of the aficionado; the response, too, is adopted. The title "A Clean Well Lighted Place" is just what the human being is not, for Hemingway, and perhaps it is the epitome of what man would like to find in his fellow-man but never has yet, says the author, and never is going to.

We see that point of view is hardly a single, unalterable vision, but a profound and developing one of great complexity. The vision itself may move in and out of its material, shuttle-fashion, instead of being simply turned on it, like a telescope on the moon. Writing is an expression of the writer's own peculiar personality, could not help being so. Yet in reading great works one feels that the finished piece transcends the personal. All writers great and small must sometimes have felt that they have become part of what they wrote even more than it still remains a part of them.

When I speak of writing from where you have put down roots, it may be said that what I urge is "regional" writing. "Regional," I think, is a careless term, as well as a condescending one, because what it does is fail to differentiate between the localized raw material of life and its outcome as art. "Regional" is an outsider's term; it has no meaning for the insider who is doing the writing, because as far as he knows he is simply writing about life. Jane Austen, Emily Brontë, Thomas Hardy, Cervantes, Turgenev, the authors of the books of the Old Testament, all confined themselves to regions, great or small—but are they regional? Then who from the start of time has not been so?

It may well be said that all work springing out of such vital impulse from its native soil has certain things in common. But what signifies is that these are not the little things that it takes a fine-tooth critic to search out, but the great things, that could not be missed or mistaken, for they are the beacon lights of literature.

It seems plain that the art that speaks most clearly, explicitly, directly and passionately from its place of origin will remain the longest understood. It is through place that we put out roots, wherever birth, chance, fate or our traveling selves set us down; but where those roots reach toward—whether in America, England or Timbuktu—is the deep and running vein, eternal and consistent and everywhere purely itself, that feeds and is fed by the human understanding. The challenge to writers today, I think, is not to disown any part of our heritage. Whatever our theme in writing, it is old and tried. Whatever our place, it has been visited by the stranger, it will never be new again. It is only the vision that can be new; but that is enough.

A Sweet Devouring

WHEN I used to ask my mother which we were, rich or poor, she refused to tell me. I was then nine years old and of course what I was dying to hear was that we were poor. I was reading a book called *Five Little Peppers* and my heart was set on baking a cake for my mother in a stove with a hole in it. Some version of rich, crusty old Mr. King—up till that time not living on our street—was sure to come down the hill in his wheelchair and rescue me if anything went wrong. But before I could start a cake at all I had to find out if we were poor, and poor *enough*; and my mother wouldn't tell me, she said she was too busy. I couldn't wait too long; I had to go on reading and soon Polly Pepper got into more trouble, some that was a little harder on her and easier on me.

Trouble, the backbone of literature, was still to me the original property of the fairy tale, and as long as there was plenty of trouble for everybody and the rewards for it were falling in the right spots, reading was all smooth sailing. At that age a child reads with higher appetite and gratification, and with those two stars sailing closer together, than ever again in his growing up. The home shelves had been providing me all along with the usual books, and I read them with love—but snap, I finished them. I read everything just alike—snap. I even came to the *Tales from Maria Edgeworth* and went right ahead, without feeling the bump—then. It *was* noticeable that when her characters suffered she punished them for it, instead of rewarding them as a reader had rather been led to hope. In her stories, the children had to make their choice between being unhappy and good about it and being unhappy and bad about it, and then she helped them to choose wrong. In *The Purple Jar*, it will be remembered, there was the little girl being taken through the shops by her mother and her downfall coming when she chooses to buy something beautiful instead of something necessary. The purple jar, when the shop sends it out, proves to have been purple only so long as it was filled with purple water, and her mother knew it all the time. They don't deliver the water. That's only the cue for stones to start coming through the hole in the victim's worn-out shoe. She bravely agrees she must keep walking on stones until such time as she is offered another choice between the beautiful and the useful. Her father tells her as far as he is concerned she can stay in the house. If I had been at all easy to disappoint, that story would have disappointed me. Of course, I did feel, what is the good of walking on rocks if they are going to let the water out of the jar too? And it seemed to me that even the illustrator fell down on the characters in that book, not alone Maria Edgeworth, for when a rich, crusty old gentleman gave Simple Susan a guinea for some kind deed she'd done him, there was a picture of the transaction and where was the guinea? I couldn't make out a feather. But I liked *reading* the book all right—except that I finished it.

My mother took me to the Public Library and introduced me: "Let her have any book she wants, except *Elsie Dinsmore.*" I looked for the book I couldn't have and it was a row. That was how I learned about the Series Books. The *Five Little Peppers* belonged, so did *The Wizard of Oz*, so did *The Little Colonel*, so did *The Green Fairy Book*. There were many of everything, generations of everybody, instead of one. I wasn't coming to the end of reading, after all—I was saved.

Our library in those days was a big rotunda lined with shelves. A copy of *V. V.'s Eyes* seemed to follow you wherever you went, even after you'd read it. I didn't know what I liked, I just knew what there was a lot of. After *Randy's Spring* there came *Randy's Summer*, *Randy's Fall* and *Randy's Winter*. True, I didn't care very much myself for her spring, but it didn't occur to me that I might not care for her summer, and then her summer didn't prejudice me against her fall, and I still had hopes as I moved on to her winter. I was disappointed in her whole year, as it turned out, but a thing like that didn't keep me from wanting to read every word of it. The pleasures of reading itself—who doesn't remember?—were like those of a Christmas cake, a sweet devouring. The "Randy Books" failed chiefly in being so soon over. Four seasons doesn't make a series.

All that summer I used to put on a second petticoat (our librarian wouldn't let you past the front door if she could see through you), ride my bicycle up the hill and "through the

Capitol" (shortcut) to the library with my two read books in the basket (two was the limit you could take out at one time when you were a child and also as long as you lived), and tiptoe in ("Silence") and exchange them for two more in two minutes. Selection was no object. I coasted the two new books home, jumped out of my petticoat, read (I suppose I ate and bathed and answered questions put to me), then in all hope put my petticoat back on and rode those two books back to the library to get my next two.

The librarian was the lady in town who wanted to be it. She called me by my full name and said, "Does your mother know where you are? You know good and well the fixed rule of this library: *Nobody is going to come running back here with any book on the same day they took it out*. Get both those things out of here and don't come back till tomorrow. And I can practically see through you."

My great-aunt in Virginia, who understood better about needing more to read than you *could* read, sent me a book so big it had to be read on the floor—a bound volume of six or eight issues of *St. Nicholas* from a previous year. In the very first pages a serial began: *The Lucky Stone* by Abbie Farwell Brown. The illustrations were right down my alley: a heroine so poor she was ragged, a witch with an extremely pointed hat, a rich, crusty old gentleman in—better than a wheelchair—a runaway carriage; and I set to. I gobbled up installment after installment through the whole luxurious book, through the last one, and then came the words, turning me to *un*lucky stone: "To be concluded." The book had come to an end and *The Lucky Stone* wasn't finished! The witch had it! I couldn't believe this infidelity from my aunt. I still had my secret childhood feeling that if you hunted long enough in a book's pages, you could find what you were looking for, and long after I knew books better than that, I used to hunt again for the end of *The Lucky Stone*. It never occurred to me that the story had an existence anywhere else outside the pages of that single green-bound book. The last chapter was just something I would have to do without. Polly Pepper could do it. And then suddenly I tried something—I read it again, as much as I had of it. I was in love with books at least partly for what they looked like; I loved the printed page.

In my little circle books were almost never given for Christmas, they cost too much. But the year before, I'd been given a book and got a shock. It was from the same classmate who had told me there was no Santa Claus. She gave me a book, all right—*Poems by Another Little Girl.* It looked like a real book, was printed like a real book—but it was *by her. Homemade* poems? Illusion-dispelling was her favorite game. She was in such a hurry, she had such a pile to get rid of—her mother's electric runabout was stacked to the bud vases with copies—that she hadn't even time to say, "Merry Christmas!" With only the same raucous laugh with which she had told me, "Been filling my own stocking for years!" she shot me her book, received my Japanese pencil box with a moonlight scene on the lid and a sharpened pencil inside, jumped back into the car and was sped away by her mother. I stood right where they had left me, on the curb in my Little Nurse's uniform, and read that book, and I had no better way to prove when I got through than I had when I started that this was not a real book. But of course it wasn't. The printed page is not absolutely everything.

Then this Christmas was coming, and my grandfather in Ohio sent along in his box of presents an envelope with money in it for me to buy myself the book I wanted.

I went to Kress's. Not everybody knew Kress's sold books, but children just before Christmas know everything Kress's ever sold or will sell. My father had showed us the mirror he was giving my mother to hang above her desk, and Kress's is where my brother and I went to reproduce that by buying a mirror together to give her ourselves, and where our little brother then made us take him and he bought her one his size for fifteen cents. Kress's had also its version of the Series Books, called, exactly like another series, "The Camp Fire Girls," beginning with *The Camp Fire Girls in the Woods.*

I believe they were ten cents each and I had a dollar. But they weren't all that easy to buy, because the series stuck, and to buy some of it was like breaking into a loaf of French bread. Then after you got home, each single book was as hard to open as a box stuck in its varnish, and when it gave way it popped like a firecracker. The covers once prized apart would never close; those books once open stayed open and lay on their backs helplessly fluttering their leaves like a turned-over June bug. They were as light as a matchbox. They were printed on yellowed paper with corners that crumbled, if you pinched on them too hard, like old graham crackers, and they smelled like attic trunks, caramelized glue, their own confinement with one another and, over all, the Kress's smell—bandannas, peanuts and sandalwood from the incense counter. Even without reading them I loved them. It was hard, that year, that Christmas is a day you can't read.

What could have happened to those books?—but I can tell you about the leading character. His name was Mr. Holmes. He was not a Camp Fire Girl: he wanted to catch one. Through every book of the series he gave chase. He pursued Bessie and Zara—those were the Camp Fire Girls—and kept scooping them up in his touring car, while they just as regularly got away from him. Once Bessie escaped from the second floor of a strange inn by climbing down a gutter pipe. Once she escaped by driving away from Mr. Holmes in his own automobile, which she had learned to drive by watching him. What Mr. Holmes wanted with them—either Bessie or Zara would do—didn't give me pause; I was too young to be a Camp Fire Girl; I was just keeping up. I wasn't alarmed by Mr. Holmes—when I cared for a chill, I knew to go to Dr. Fu Manchu, who had his own series in the library. I wasn't fascinated either. There was one thing I wanted from those books, and that was for me to have ten to read at one blow.

Who in the world wrote those books? I knew all the time they were the false "Camp Fire Girls" and the ones in the library were the authorized. But book reviewers sometimes say of a book that if anyone else had written it, it might not have been this good, and I found it out as a child—their warning is justified. This was a proven case, although a case of the true not being as good as the false. In the true series the characters were either totally different or missing (Mr. Holmes was missing), and there was too much time given to teamwork. The Kress's Campers, besides getting into a more reliable kind of trouble than the Carnegie Campers, had adventures that even they themselves weren't aware of: the pages were in wrong. There were transposed pages, repeated pages, and whole sections in upside down. There was no way of telling if there was anything missing. But if you knew your way in the woods at all, you could enjoy yourself tracking it down. I read the library "Camp Fire Girls," since that's what they were there for, but though they could be read by poorer light they were not as good.

And yet, in a way, the false Campers were no better either. I wonder whether I felt some flaw at the heart of things or whether I was just tired of not having any taste; but it seemed to me when I had finished that the last nine of those books weren't as good as the first one. And the same went for all Series Books. As long as they are keeping a series going, I was afraid, nothing can really happen. The whole thing is one grand prevention. For my greed, I might have unwittingly dealt with myself in the same way Maria Edgeworth dealt with the one who put her all into the purple jar—I had received word it was just colored water.

And then I went again to the home shelves and my lucky hand reached and found Mark Twain—twenty-four volumes, not a series, and good all the way through.

Must the Novelist Crusade?

NOT TOO LONG AGO I read in some respectable press that Faulkner would have to be reassessed because he was "after all, only a white Mississippian." For this reason, it was felt, readers could no longer rely on him for knowing what he was writing about in his life's work of novels and stories, laid in what he called "my country."

Remembering how Faulkner for most of his life wrote in all but isolation from critical understanding, ignored impartially by North and South, with only a handful of critics in forty years who were able to "assess" him, we might smile at this journalist as at a boy let out of school. Or there may have been an instinct to smash the superior, the good, that is endurable enough to go on offering itself. But I feel in these words and others like them the agonizing of our times. I think they come of an honest and understandable zeal to allot every writer his chance to better the world or go to his grave reproached for the mess it is in. And here, it seems to me, the heart of fiction's real reliability has been struck at—and not for the first time by the noble hand of the crusader.

It would not be surprising if the critic I quote had gained his knowledge of the South from the books of the author he repudiates. At any rate, a reply to him exists there. Full evidence as to whether any writer, alive or dead, can be believed is always at hand in one place: any page of his work. The color of his skin would modify it just about as much as would the binding of his book. Integrity can be neither lost nor concealed nor faked nor quenched nor artificially come by nor outlived, nor, I believe, in the long run denied. Integrity is no greater and no less today than it was yesterday and will be tomorrow. It stands outside time.

The novelist and the crusader who writes both have their own place—in the novel and the editorial respectively, equally valid whether or not the two happen to be in agreement. In my own view, writing fiction places the novelist and the crusader on opposite sides. But they are not the sides of right and wrong. Honesty is not at stake here and is not questioned;

the only thing at stake is the proper use of words for the proper ends. And a mighty thing it is.

Because the printed page is where the writer's work is to be seen, it may be natural for people who do not normally read fiction to confuse novels with journalism or speeches. The very using of words has these well-intentioned people confused about the novelist's purpose.

The writing of a novel is taking life as it already exists, not to report it but to make an object, toward the end that the finished work might contain this life inside it, and offer it to the reader. The essence will not be, of course, the same thing as the raw material; it is not even of the same family of things. The novel is something that never was before and will not be again. For the mind of one person, its writer, is in it too. What distinguishes it above all from the raw material, and what distinguishes it from journalism, is that inherent in the novel is the possibility of a shared act of the imagination between its writer and its reader.

"All right, Eudora Welty, what are you going to do about it? Sit down there with your mouth shut?" asked a stranger over long distance in one of the midnight calls that I suppose have waked most writers in the South from time to time. It is part of the same question: Are fiction writers on call to be crusaders? For us in the South who are fiction writers, is writing a novel *something we can do about it*?

It can be said at once, I should think, that we are all agreed upon the most important point: that morality as shown through human relationships is the whole heart of fiction, and the serious writer has never lived who dealt with anything else.

And yet, the zeal to reform, which quite properly inspires the editorial, has never done fiction much good. The exception occurs when it can rise to the intensity of satire, where it finds a better home in the poem or the drama. Large helpings of naïveté and self-esteem, which serve to refresh the crusader, only encumber the novelist. How unfair it is that when a novel is to be written, it is never enough to have our hearts in the right place! But good will all by itself can no more get a good novel written than it can paint in watercolor or sing Mozart.

Nevertheless, let us suppose that we feel we might help if we were to write a crusading novel. What will our problems be?

Before anything else, speed. The crusader's message is prompted by crisis; it has to be delivered on time. Suppose John Steinbeck had only now finished *The Grapes of Wrath*? The ordinary novelist has only one message: "I submit that this is one way we are." This can wait. When we think of Ibsen, we see that causes themselves may in time be forgotten, their championship no longer needed; it is Ibsen's passion that keeps the plays alive.

Next, we as the crusader-novelist shall find awkward to use the very weapon we count on most: the generality. On fiction's pages, generalities clank when wielded, and hit with equal force at the little and the big, at the merely suspect and the really dangerous. They make too much noise for us to hear what people might be trying to say. They are fatal to tenderness and are in themselves non-conductors of any real, however modest, discovery of the writer's own heart. This discovery is the best hope of the ordinary novelist, and to make it he begins not with the generality but with the particular in front of his eyes, which he is able to examine.

Taking a particular situation existing in his world, and what he feels about it in his own breast and what he can make of it in his own head, he constructs on paper, little by little, an equivalent of it. Literally it may correspond to a high degree or to none at all; emotionally it corresponds as closely as he can make it. Observation and the inner truth of that observation as he perceives it, the two being tested one against the other: to him this is what the writing of a novel is.

We, the crusader-novelist, having started with our generality, must end with a generality; they had better be the same. In the place of climax, we can deliver a judgment. How can the plot seem disappointing when it is a lovely argument spread out? It is because fiction is stone-deaf to argument.

The ordinary novelist does not argue; he hopes to show, to disclose. His persuasions are all toward allowing his reader to see and hear something for himself. He knows another bad thing about arguments: they carry the menace of neatness into fiction. Indeed, what we as the crusader-novelist are scared of most is confusion.

Great fiction, we very much fear, abounds in what makes for confusion; it generates it, being on a scale which copies life, which it confronts. It is very seldom neat, is given to sprawling and escaping from bounds, is capable of contradicting itself, and is not impervious to humor. There is absolutely everything in great fiction but a clear answer. Humanity itself seems to matter more to the novelist than what humanity thinks it can prove.

When a novelist writes of man's experience, what else is he to draw on but the life around him? And yet the life around him, on the surface, can be used to show anything, absolutely anything, as readers know. The novelist's real task and real responsibility lie in the way he uses it.

Situation itself always exists; it is whatever life is up to here and now, it is the living and present moment. It is transient, and it fluctuates. Using the situation, the writer populates his novel with characters invented to express it in their terms.

It is important that it be in their terms. We cannot in fiction set people to acting mechanically or carrying placards to make their sentiments plain. People are not Right and Wrong, Good and Bad, Black and White personified; flesh and blood and the sense of comedy object. Fiction writers cannot be tempted to make the mistake of looking at people in the generality—that is to say, of seeing people as not at all *like us.* If human beings are to be comprehended as real, then they have to be treated as real, with minds, hearts, memories, habits, hopes, with passions and capacities like ours. This is why novelists begin the study of people from within.

The first act of insight is throw away the labels. In fiction, while we do not necessarily write about ourselves, we write out of ourselves, using ourselves; what we learn from, what we are sensitive to, what we feel strongly about—these become our characters and go to make our plots. Characters in fiction are conceived from within, and they have, accordingly, their own interior life; they are individuals every time. The character we care about in a novel we may not approve of or agree with—that's beside the point. But he has got to seem alive. Then and only then, when we read, we experience or surmise things about life itself that are deeper and more lasting and less destructive to understanding than approval or disapproval.

The novelist's work is highly organized, but I should say it is organized around anything but logic. Just as characters are not labels but are made from the inside out and grow into their own life, so does a plot have a living principle on which it hangs together and gradually earns its shape. A plot is a thousand times more unsettling than an argument, which may be answered. It is not a pattern imposed; it is inward emotion acted out. It is arbitrary, indeed, but not artificial. It is possibly so odd that it might be called a vision, but it is organic to its material: it is a working vision, then.

A writer works *through* what is around him if he wishes to get to what he is after—no kind of proof, but simply an essence. In practice he will do anything at all with his material: shape it, strain it to the breaking point, double it up, or use it backward; he will balk at nothing—see *The Sound and the Fury*—to reach that heart and core. But even in a good cause he does not falsify it. The material itself receives deep ultimate respect: it has given rise to the vision of it, which in turn has determined what the novel shall be.

The ordinary novelist, who can never make a perfect thing, can with every novel try again. But if we write a novel to prove something, one novel will settle it, for why prove a thing more than once? And what, then, is to keep all novels by all right-thinking persons from being pretty much alike? Or exactly alike? There would be little reason for present writers to keep on, no reason for the new writers to start. There's no way to know, but we might guess that the reason the young write no fiction behind the Iron Curtain is the obvious fact that to be acceptable there, all novels must conform, and so must be alike, hence valueless. If the personal vision can be made to order, then we should lose, writer and reader alike, our own gift for perceiving, seeing through the fabric of everyday to what to each pair of eyes on earth is a unique thing. We'd accept life exactly like everybody else, and so, of course, be content with it. We should not even miss our vanished novelists. And if life ever became not worth writing fiction about, that, I believe, would be the first sign that it wasn't worth living.

With a blueprint to work with instead of a vision, there is a good deal that we as the crusader-novelist must be at pains to leave out. Unavoidably, I think, we shall leave out one of the greatest things. This is the mystery in life. Our blueprint for sanity and of solution for trouble leaves out the dark. (This is odd, because surely it was the dark that first troubled us.) We leave out the wonder because with wonder it is impossible to argue, much less to settle. The ordinary novelist thinks it had better be recognized. Reckless as this may make him, he believes the insoluble is part of his material too.

The novelist works neither to correct nor to condone, not at all to comfort, but to make what's told alive. He assumes at the start an enlightenment in his reader equal to his own, for they are hopefully on the point of taking off together from that base into the rather different world of the imagination.

It's not only the fact that this world is bigger and that fewer constrictions apply that may daunt us as crusaders. But the imagination itself is the problem. It is capable of saying everything but no. In our literature, what has traveled the longest way through time is the great affirmative soul of Chaucer. The novel itself always affirms, it seems to me, by the nature of itself. It says what people are like. It doesn't, and doesn't know how to, describe what they are *not* like, and it would waste its time if it told us what we ought to be like, since we already know that, don't we? But we may not know nearly so well what we are as when a novel of power reveals this to us. For the first time we may, as we read, see ourselves in our own situation, in some curious way reflected. By whatever way the novelist accomplishes it—there are many ways—truth is borne in on us in all its great weight and angelic lightness, and accepted as home truth.

Passing judgment on his fellows, which is trying enough for anybody, is frustrating for an author. It is hardly the way to make the discoveries about living that he must have hoped for when he began to write. If he does not pass judgment, does this mean he has no conscience? Of course he has a conscience; it is, like his temperament, his own, and he is one hundred percent answerable to it, whether it is convenient or not. What matters is that a writer is committed to his own moral principles. If he is, when we read him we cannot help but be aware of what these are. Certainly the characters of his novel and the plot they move in are their ultimate reflections. But these convictions are implicit; they are deep down; they are the rock on which the whole structure of more than that novel rests.

Indeed, we are more aware of his moral convictions through a novel than any flat statement of belief from him could make us. We are aware in that part of our mind that tells us truths about ourselves. Yet it is only by way of the imagination—the novelist's to ours—that such private neighborhoods are reached.

There is still to mention what I think will give us, as the crusader-novelist, the hardest time: our voice will not be our own. The crusader's voice is the voice of the crowd and must rise louder all the time, for there is, of course, the other side to be drowned out. Worse, the voices of most crowds sound alike. Worse still, the voice that seeks to do other than communicate when it makes a noise has something brutal about it; it is no longer using words as words but as something to brandish, with which to threaten, brag or condemn. The noise is the simple assertion of self, the great, mindless, general self. And for all its volume it is ephemeral. Only meaning lasts. Nothing was ever learned in a crowd, from a crowd, or by addressing or trying to please a crowd. Even to deplore, yelling is out of place. To deplore a thing as hideous as the murder of the three civil rights workers demands the quiet in which to absorb it. Enormities can be lessened, cheapened, just as good and delicate things can be. We can and will cheapen all feeling by letting it go savage or parading in it.

Writing fiction is an interior affair. Novels and stories always will be put down little by little out of personal feeling and personal beliefs arrived at alone and at firsthand over a period of time as time is needed. To go outside and beat the drum is only to interrupt, interrupt, and so finally to forget and to lose. Fiction has, and must keep, a private address. For life is *lived* in a private place; where it means anything is inside the mind and heart. Fiction has always shown life where it is lived, and good fiction, or so I have faith, will continue to do this.

A Passage to India is an old novel now. It is an intensely moral novel. It deals with race prejudice. Mr. Forster, not by preaching at us, while being passionately concerned, makes us know his points unforgettably as often as we read it. And does he not bring in the dark! The points are good forty years after their day *because of the splendor of the novel.* What a lesser novelist's harangues would have buried by now, his imagination still reveals. Revelation of even the strongest forces is delicate work.

Indeed, great fiction shows us not how to conduct our behavior but how to feel. Eventually, it may show us how to face our feelings and face our actions and to have new inklings about what they mean. A good novel of any year can initiate us into our own new experience.

From the working point of view of the serious writer of fiction, nothing has changed today but the externals. They are important externals; we may have developed an increased awareness of them, which is certainly to the good; we have at least the same capacity as ever for understanding, the same eyes and ears, same hearts to feel, same minds to agonize or remember or to try to put things together, see things in proportion with. While the raw material of our fiction is changing dramatically—as indeed it is changing everywhere—we are the same instruments of perceiving that we ever were. I should not trust us if we were not. And we do not know what is to be made out of experience at any time until the personal quotient has been added. To convey what we see around us, whatever it is, so as to let it speak for itself according to our lights is the same challenge it ever was, not a different one, not a greater one, only perhaps made harder by the times. Now as ever we must keep writing from what we know; and we must really know it.

No matter how fast society around us changes, what remains is that there is a relationship in progress between ourselves and other people; this was the case when the world seemed stable, too. There are relationships of the blood, of the passions and the affections, of thought and spirit and deed. There is the relationship between the races. How can one kind of relationship be set apart from the others? Like the great root system of an old and long-established growing plant, they are all tangled up together; to separate them you would have to cleave the plant itself from top to bottom.

What must the Southern writer of fiction do today? Shall he do anything different from what he has always done?

There have already been giant events, some of them wrenchingly painful and humiliating. And now there is added the atmosphere of hate. We in the South are a hated people these days; we were hated first for actual and particular reasons, and now we may be hated still more in some vast unparticularized way. I believe there must be such a thing as sentimental hate. Our people hate back.

I think the worst of it is we are getting stuck in it. We are like trapped flies with our feet not in honey but in venom. It's not love that is the gluey emotion; it's hate. As far as writing goes, which is as far as living goes, this is a devastating emotion. It could kill us. This hate seems in part shame for self, in part self-justification, in part panic that life is really changing.

Fury at ourselves and hurt pride, anger aroused too often, outrage at being hated need not obscure forever the sore spots we Southerners know better than our detractors. For some of us have shown bad hearts. As in the case of our better qualities, we are locally blessed with an understanding and intimate knowledge of our faults that our worst detractors cannot match, and have been in a less relentless day far more relentless, more eloquent, too, than they have yet learned to be.

I do not presume to speak for my fellow Southern writers, a group of individuals if there ever was one. Yet I would like to point something out: in the rest of the country people seem suddenly aware now of what Southern fiction writers have been writing about in various ways for a great long time. We do not need reminding of what our subject is. It is humankind, and we are all part of it. When we write about people, black or white, in the South or anywhere, if our stories are worth the reading, we are writing about everybody.

In the South, we who are now at work may not learn to write it before we learn, or learn again, to live it—our full life in the South within its context, in its relation to the rest of the world. "Only connect," Forster's ever wise and gentle and daring words, could be said to us in our homeland quite literally at this moment. And while the Southern writer goes on portraying his South, which I think nobody else can do and which I believe he must do, then if his work is done well enough, it will reflect a larger mankind as it has done before.

And so finally I think we need to write with love. Not in self-defense, not in hate, not in the mood of instruction, not in rebuttal, in any kind of militance, or in apology, but with love. Not in exorcisement, either, for this is to make the reader bear a thing for you.

Neither do I speak of writing forgivingly; out of love you can write with straight fury. It is the *source* of the understanding that I speak of; it's this that determines its nature and its reach.

We are told that Turgenev's nostalgic, profoundly reflective, sensuously alive stories that grew out of his memories of early years reached the Czar and were given some credit by him when he felt moved to free the serfs in Russia. Had Turgenev set out to write inflammatory tracts instead of the sum of all he knew, could express, of life learned at firsthand, how much less of his mind and heart with their commitments, all implicit, would have filled his stories! But he might be one of us now, so directly are we touched with a hundred and thirteen years gone by since they were first published.

Indifference would indeed be corrupting to the fiction writer, indifference to any part of man's plight. Passion is the chief ingredient of good fiction. It flames right out of sympathy for the human condition and goes into all great writing. (And of course passion and the temper are different things; writing in the heat of passion can be done with extremely good temper.) But to distort a work of passion for the sake of a cause is to cheat, and the end, far from justifying the means, is fairly sure to be lost with it. Then the novel will have been not the work of imagination, at once passionate and objective, made by a man struggling in solitude with something of his own to say, but a piece of catering.

To cater to is not to love and not to serve well either. We do need to bring to our writing, over and over again, all the abundance we possess. To be able, to be ready, to enter into the minds and hearts of our own people, all of them, to comprehend them (us) and then to make characters and plots in stories that in honesty and with honesty reveal them (ourselves) to us, in whatever situation we live through in our own times: this is the continuing job, and it's no harder now than it ever was, I suppose. Every writer, like everybody else, thinks he's living through the crisis of the ages. To write honestly and with all our powers is the least we can do, and the most.

Time, though it can make happenings and trappings out of date, cannot do much to change the realities apprehended by the imagination. History will change in Mississippi, and the hope is that it will change in a beneficial direction and with a merciful speed, and above all bring insight, understanding. But when William Faulkner's novels come to be pictures of a society that is no more, they will still be good and still be authentic because of what went into them from the man himself. Mankind still tries the same things and suffers the same falls, climbs up to try again, and novels are as true at one time as at another. Love and hate, hope and despair, justice and injustice, compassion and prejudice, truth-telling and lying work in all men; their story can be told in whatever skin they are wearing and in whatever year the writer can put them down.

Faulkner is not receding from us. Indeed, his work, though it can't increase in itself, increases us. His work throws light on the past and on today as it becomes the past—the day in its journey. This being so, it informs the future too.

What is written in the South from now on is going to be taken into account by Faulkner's work; I mean the remark literally. Once Faulkner had written, we could never unknow what he told us and showed us. And his work will do the same thing tomorrow. We inherit from him, while we can get fresh and firsthand news of ourselves from his work at any time.

A source of illumination is not dated by what passes along under its ray, is not qualified or disqualified by the nature of the traffic. When the light of Faulkner's work will be discovering things to us no more, it will be discovering *us*. Even we shall lie enfolded in perspective one day: what we hoped along with what we did, what we didn't do, and not only what we were but what we missed being, what others yet to come might dare to be. For we *are* our own crusade. Before ever we write, we are. Instead of our judging Faulkner, he will be revealing us in books to later minds.

"Is Phoenix Jackson's Grandson Really Dead?"

A STORY WRITER is more than happy to be read by students; the fact that these serious readers think and feel something in response to his work he finds life-giving. At the same time he may not always be able to reply to their specific questions in kind. I wondered if it might clarify something, for both the questioners and myself, if I set down a general reply to the question that comes to me most often in the mail, from both students and their teachers, after some classroom discussion. The unrivaled favorite is this: "Is Phoenix Jackson's grandson really *dead*?"

It refers to a short story I wrote years ago called "A Worn Path," which tells of a day's journey an old woman makes on foot from deep in the country into town and into a doctor's office on behalf of her little grandson; he is at home, periodically ill, and periodically she comes for his medicine; they give it to her as usual, she receives it and starts the journey back.

I had not meant to mystify readers by withholding any fact; it is not a writer's business to tease. The story is told through Phoenix's mind as she undertakes her errand. As the author at one with the character as I tell it, I must assume that the boy is alive. As the reader, you are free to think as you like, of course: the story invites you to believe that no matter what happens, Phoenix for as long as she is able to walk and can hold to her purpose will make her journey. The *possibility* that she would keep on even if he were dead is there in her devotion and its single-minded, single-track errand. Certainly the *artistic* truth, which should be good enough for the fact, lies in Phoenix's own answer to that question. When the nurse asks, "He isn't dead, is he?" she speaks for herself: "He still the same. He going to last."

The grandchild is the incentive. But it is the journey, the going of the errand, that is the story, and the question is not whether the grandchild is in reality alive or dead. It doesn't affect the outcome of the story or its meaning from start to finish. But it is not the question itself that has struck me as much as the idea, almost without exception implied in the asking, that for Phoenix's grandson to be dead would somehow make the story "better."

It's *all right*, I want to say to the students who write to me, for things to be what they appear to be, and for words to mean what they say. It's all right, too, for words and appearances to mean more than one thing—ambiguity is a fact of life. A fiction writer's responsibility covers not only what he presents as the facts of a given story but what he chooses to stir up as their implications; in the end, these implications, too, become facts, in the larger, fictional sense. But it is not all right, not in good faith, for things *not* to mean what they say.

The grandson's plight was real and it made the truth of the story, which is the story of an errand of love carried out. If the child no longer lived, the truth would persist in the "wornness" of the path. But his being dead can't increase the truth of the story, can't affect it one way or the other. I think I signal this, because the end of the story has been reached before old Phoenix gets home again: she simply starts back. To the question "Is the grandson really dead?" I could reply that it doesn't make any difference. I could also say that I did not make him up in order to let him play a trick on Phoenix. But my best answer would be: "*Phoenix* is alive."

The origin of a story is sometimes a trustworthy clue to the author—or can provide him with the clue—to its key image; maybe in this case it will do the same for the reader. One day I saw a solitary old woman like Phoenix. She was walking; I saw her, at middle distance, in a winter country landscape, and watched her slowly make her way across my line of vision. That sight of her made me write the story. I invented an errand for her, but that only seemed a living part of the figure she was herself: what errand other than for someone else could be making her go? And her going was the first thing, her persisting in her landscape was the real thing, and the first and the real were what I wanted and worked to keep. I brought her up close enough, by imagination, to describe her face, make her present to the eyes, but the full-length figure moving across the winter fields was the indelible one and the image to keep, and the perspective extending into the vanishing distance the true one to hold in mind.

I invented for my character, as I wrote, some passing adventures—some dreams and harassments and a small triumph or two, some jolts to her pride, some flights of fancy to console her, one or two encounters to scare her, a moment that gave her cause to feel ashamed, a moment to dance and preen—for it had to be a *journey*, and all these things belonged to that, parts of life's uncertainty.

A narrative line is in its deeper sense, of course, the tracing out of a meaning, and the real continuity of a story lies in this probing forward. The real dramatic force of a story depends on the strength of the emotion that has set it going. The emotional value is the measure of the reach of the story. What gives any such content to "A Worn Path" is not its circumstances but its *subject*: the deep-grained habit of love.

What I hoped would come clear was that in the whole surround of this story, the world it threads through, the only certain thing at all is the worn path. The habit of love cuts through confusion and stumbles or contrives its way out of difficulty, it remembers the way even when it forgets, for a dumbfounded moment, its reason for being. The path is the thing that matters.

Her victory—old Phoenix's—is when she sees the diploma in the doctor's office, when she finds "nailed up on the wall the document that had been stamped with the gold seal and framed in the gold frame, which matched the dream that was hung up in her head." The return with the medicine is just a matter of retracing her own footsteps. It is the part of the journey, and of the story, that can now go without saying.

In the matter of function, old Phoenix's way might even do as a sort of parallel to your way of work if you are a writer of stories. The way to get there is the all-important, all-absorbing problem, and this problem is your reason for undertaking the story. Your only guide, too, is your sureness about your subject, about what this subject is. Like Phoenix, you work all your life to find your way, through all the obstructions and the false appearances and the upsets you may have brought on yourself, to reach a meaning—using inventions of your imagination, perhaps helped out by your dreams and bits of good luck. And finally too, like Phoenix, you have to assume that what you are working in aid of is life, not death.

But you would make the trip anyway—wouldn't you?—just on hope.

The Little Store

TWO BLOCKS away from the Mississippi State Capitol, and on the same street with it, where our house was when I was a child growing up in Jackson, it was possible to have a little pasture behind your backyard where you could keep a Jersey cow, which we did. My mother herself milked her. A thrifty homemaker, wife, mother of three, she also did all her own cooking. And as far as I can recall, she never set foot inside a grocery store. It wasn't necessary.

For her regular needs, she stood at the telephone in our front hall and consulted with Mr. Lemly, of Lemly's Market and Grocery downtown, who took her order and sent it out on his next delivery. And since Jackson at the heart of it was still within very near reach of the open country, the blackberry lady clanged on her bucket with a quart measure at your front door in June without fail, the watermelon man rolled up to your house exactly on time for the Fourth of July, and down through the summer, the quiet of the early-morning streets was pierced by the calls of farmers driving in with their plenty. One brought his with a song, so plaintive we would sing it with him:

"Milk, milk,
Buttermilk,
Snap beans—butterbeans—
Tender okra—fresh greens . . .
And buttermilk."

My mother considered herself pretty well prepared in her kitchen and pantry for any emergency that, in her words, might choose to present itself. But if she should, all of a sudden, need another lemon or find she was out of bread, all she had to do was call out, "Quick! Who'd like to run to the Little Store for me?"

I would.

She'd count out the change into my hand, and I was away. I'll bet the nickel that would be left over that all over the country, for those of my day, the neighborhood grocery played a similar part in our growing up.

Our store had its name—it was that of the grocer who owned it, whom I'll call Mr. Sessions—but "the Little Store" is what we called it at home. It was a block down our street toward the capitol and half a block further, around the corner, toward the cemetery. I knew even the sidewalk to it as well as I knew my own skin. I'd skipped my jumping-rope up and down it, hopped its length through mazes of hopscotch, played jacks in its islands of shade, serpentined along it on my Princess bicycle, skated it backward and forward. In the twilight I had dragged my steamboat by its string (this was homemade out of every new shoebox, with candle in the bottom lighted and shining through colored tissue paper pasted over windows scissored out in the shapes of the sun, moon and stars) across every crack of the walk without letting it bump or catch fire. I'd "played out" on that street after supper with my brothers and friends as long as "first-dark" lasted; I'd caught its lightning bugs. On the first Armistice Day (and this will set the time I'm speaking of) we made our own parade down that walk on a single velocipede—my brother pedaling, our little brother riding the handlebars, and myself standing on the back, all with arms wide, flying flags in each hand. (My father snapped that picture as we raced by. It came out blurred.)

As I set forth for the Little Store, a tune would float toward me from the house where there lived three sisters, girls in their teens, who ratted their hair over their ears, wore headbands like gladiators, and were considered to be very popular. They practiced for this in the daytime; they'd wind up the Victrola, leave the same record on they'd played before, and you'd see them bobbing past their dining-room windows while they danced with each other. Being three, they could go all day, cutting in:

"Everybody ought to know-oh
How to do the Tickle-Toe
(how to do the Tickle-Toe)"—

they sang it and danced to it, and as I went by to the same song, I believed it.

A little further on, across the street, was the house where the principal of our grade school lived—lived on, even while we were having vacation. What if she would come out? She would halt me in my tracks—she had a very carrying and well-known voice in Jackson, where she'd taught almost everybody—saying, "Eudora Alice Welty, spell OBLIGE." OBLIGE was the word that she of course knew had kept me from making 100 on my spelling exam. She'd make me miss it again now, by boring her eyes through me from across the street. This was my vacation fantasy, one good way to scare myself on the way to the store.

Down near the corner waited the house of a little boy named Lindsey. The sidewalk here was old brick, which the roots of a giant chinaberry tree had humped up and tilted this way and that. On skates, you took it fast, in a series of skittering hops, trying not to touch ground anywhere. If the chinaberries had fallen and rolled in the cracks, it was like skating through a whole shooting match of marbles. I crossed my fingers that Lindsey wouldn't be looking.

During the big flu epidemic he and I, as it happened, were being nursed through our sieges at the same time. I'd hear my father and mother murmuring to each other, at the end of a long day, "And I wonder how poor little *Lindsey* got along today?" Just as, down the street, he no doubt would have to hear his family saying, "And I wonder how is poor *Eudora* by now?" I got the idea that a choice was going to be made soon between poor little Lindsey and poor Eudora, and I came up with a funny poem. I wasn't prepared for it when my father told me it wasn't funny and my mother cried that if I couldn't be ashamed for myself, she'd have to be ashamed for me:

> There was a little boy and his name was Lindsey.
> He went to heaven with the influinzy.

He didn't, he survived it, poem and all, the same as I did. But his chinaberries could have brought me down in my skates in a flying act of contrition before his eyes, looking pretty funny myself, right in front of his house.

Setting out in this world, a child feels so indelible. He only comes to find out later that it's all the others along his way who are making themselves indelible to him.

•

Our Little Store rose right up from the sidewalk; standing in a street of family houses, it alone hadn't any yard in front, any tree or flowerbed. It was a plain frame building covered over with brick. Above the door, a little railed porch ran across on an upstairs level and four windows with shades were looking out. But I didn't catch on to those.

Running in out of the sun, you met what seemed total obscurity inside. There were almost tangible smells—licorice recently sucked in a child's cheek, dill-pickle brine that had leaked through a paper sack in a fresh trail across the wooden floor, ammonia-loaded ice that had been hoisted from wet croker sacks and slammed into the icebox with its sweet butter at the door, and perhaps the smell of still-untrapped mice.

Then through the motes of cracker dust, cornmeal dust, the Gold Dust of the Gold Dust Twins that the floor had been swept out with, the realities emerged. Shelves climbed to high reach all the way around, set out with not too much of any one thing but a lot of things—lard, molasses, vinegar, starch, matches, kerosene, Octagon soap (about a year's worth of octagon-shaped coupons cut out and saved brought a signet ring addressed to you in the mail. Furthermore, when the postman arrived at your door, he blew a whistle). It was up to you to remember what you came for, while your eye traveled from cans of sardines to ice cream salt to harmonicas to flypaper (over your head, batting around on a thread beneath the blades of the ceiling fan, stuck with its testimonial catch).

Its confusion may have been in the eye of its beholder. Enchantment is cast upon you by all those things you weren't supposed to have need for, it lures you close to wooden tops you'd outgrown, boy's marbles and agates in little net pouches, small rubber balls that wouldn't bounce straight, frazzly kite-string, clay bubble-pipes that would snap off in your teeth, the stiffest scissors. You could contemplate those long narrow boxes of sparklers gathering dust while you waited for it to be the Fourth of July or Christmas, and noisemakers in the shape of tin frogs for somebody's birthday party you hadn't been invited to yet, and see that they were all marvelous.

You might not have even looked for Mr. Sessions when he came around his store cheese (as big as a doll's house) and in front of the counter looking for you. When you'd finally asked him for, and received from him in its paper bag, whatever single thing it was that you had been sent for, the nickel that was left over was yours to spend.

Down at a child's eye level, inside those glass jars with mouths in their sides through which the grocer could run his scoop or a child's hand might be invited to reach for a choice, were wineballs, all-day suckers, gumdrops, peppermints. Making a row under the glass of a counter were the Tootsie Rolls, Hershey Bars, Goo-Goo Clusters, Baby Ruths. And whatever was the name of those pastilles that came stacked in a cardboard cylinder with a cardboard lid? They were thin and dry, about the size of tiddlywinks, and in the shape of twisted rosettes. A kind of chocolate dust came out with them when you shook them out in your hand. Were they chocolate? I'd say rather they were brown. They didn't taste of anything at all, unless it was wood. Their attraction was the number you got for a nickel.

Making up your mind, you circled the store around and around, around the pickle barrel, around the tower of Cracker Jack boxes; Mr. Sessions had built it for us himself on top of a packing case, like a house of cards.

If it seemed too hot for Cracker Jacks, I might get a cold drink. Mr. Sessions might have already stationed himself by the cold-drinks barrel, like a mind reader. Deep in ice water that looked black as ink, murky shapes that would come up as Coca-Colas, Orange Crushes, and various flavors of pop, were all swimming around together. When you gave the word, Mr. Sessions plunged his bare arm in to the elbow and fished out your choice, first try. I favored a locally bottled concoction called Lake's Celery. (What else could it be called? It was made by a Mr. Lake out of celery. It was a popular drink here for years but was not known universally, as I found out when I arrived in New York and ordered one in the Astor bar.) You drank on the premises, with feet set wide apart to miss the drip, and gave him back his bottle.

But he didn't hurry you off. A standing scales was by the door, with a stack of iron weights and a brass slide on the balance arm, that would weigh you up to three hundred pounds. Mr. Sessions, whose hands were gentle and smelled of carbolic, would lift you up and set your feet on the platform, hold your loaf of bread for you, and taking his time while you stood still for him, he would make certain of what you weighed today. He could even remember what you weighed the last time, so you could subtract and announce how much you'd gained. That was goodbye.

Is there always a hard way to go home? From the Little Store, you could go partway through the sewer. If your brothers had called you a scarecat, then across the next street beyond the Little Store, it was possible to enter this sewer by passing through a privet hedge, climbing down into the bed of a creek, and going into its mouth on your knees. The sewer—it might have been no more than a "storm sewer"—came out and emptied here, where Town Creek, a sandy, most often shallow little stream that ambled through Jackson on its way to the Pearl River, ran along the edge of the cemetery. You could go in darkness through this tunnel to where you next saw light (if you ever did) and climb out through the culvert at your own street corner.

I was a scarecat, all right, but I was a reader with my own refuge in storybooks. Making my way under the sidewalk, under the street and the streetcar track, under the Little Store, down there in the wet dark by myself, I could be Persephone entering into my six-month sojourn underground—though I didn't suppose Persephone had to crawl, hanging onto a loaf of bread, and come out through the teeth of an iron grating. Mother Ceres would indeed be wondering where she could find me, and mad when she knew. "Now am I going to have to start marching to the Little Store for *myself*?"

I couldn't picture it. Indeed, I'm unable today to picture the Little Store with a grown person in it, except for Mr. Sessions and the lady who helped him, who belonged there. We children thought it was ours. The happiness of errands was in part that of running for the moment away from home, a free spirit. I believed the Little Store to be a center of the outside world, and hence of happiness—as I believed what I found in the Cracker Jack box to be a genuine prize, which was as simply as I believed in the Golden Fleece.

But a day came when I ran to the store to discover, sitting on the front step, a grown person, after all—more than a grown person. It was the Monkey Man, together with his monkey. His grinding-organ was lowered to the step beside him. In my whole life so far, I must have laid eyes on the Monkey Man no more than five or six times. An itinerant of rare and wayward appearances, he was not punctual like the Gipsies, who every year with the first cool days of fall showed up in the aisles of Woolworth's. You never knew when the Monkey Man might decide to favor Jackson, or which way he'd go. Sometimes you heard him as close as the next street, and then he didn't come up yours.

But now I saw the Monkey Man at the Little Store, where I'd never seen him before. I'd never seen him sitting down. Low on that familiar doorstep, he was not the same any longer, and neither was his monkey. They looked just like an old man and an old friend of his that wore a fez, meeting quietly together, tired, and resting with their eyes fixed on some place far away, and not the same place. Yet their romance for me didn't have it in its power to waver. I wavered. I simply didn't know how to step around them, to proceed on into the Little Store for my mother's emergency as if nothing had happened. If I could have gone in there after it, whatever it was, I would have given it to them—putting it into the monkey's cool little fingers. I would have given them the Little Store itself.

In my memory they are still attached to the store—so are all the others. Everyone I saw on my way seemed to me then part of my errand, and in a way they were. As I myself, the free spirit, was part of it too.

All the years we lived in that house where we children were born, the same people lived in the other houses on our street too. People changed through the arithmetic of birth, marriage and death, but not by going away. So families just accrued stories, which through the fullness of time, in those times, their own lives made. And I grew up in those.

But I didn't know there'd ever been a story at the Little Store, one that was going on while I was there. Of course, all the time the Sessions family had been living right overhead there, in the upstairs rooms behind the little railed porch and the shaded windows; but I think we children never thought of that. Did I fail to see them as a family because they weren't living in an ordinary house? Because I so seldom saw them close together, or having anything to say to each other? She sat in the back of the store, her pencil over a ledger, while he stood and waited on children to make up their minds. They worked in twin black eyeshades, held on their gray heads by elastic bands. It may be harder to recognize kindness—or unkindness, either—in a face whose eyes are in shadow. His face underneath his shade was as round as the little wooden wheels in the Tinker Toy box. So was her face. I didn't know, perhaps didn't even wonder: were they husband and wife or brother and sister? Were they father and mother? There were a few other persons, of various ages, wandering singly in by the back door and out. But none of their relationships could I imagine, when I'd never seen them sitting down together around their own table.

The possibility that they had any other life at all, anything beyond what we could see within the four walls of the Little Store, occurred to me only when tragedy struck their family. There was some act of violence. The shock to the neighborhood traveled to the children, of course; but I couldn't find out from my parents what had happened. They held it back from me, as they'd already held back many things, "until the time comes for you to know."

You could find out some of these things by looking in the unabridged dictionary and the encyclopedia—kept to hand in our dining room—but you couldn't find out there what had happened to the family who for all the years of your life had lived upstairs over the Little Store, who had never been anything but patient and kind to you, who never once had sent you away. All I ever knew was its aftermath: they were the only people ever known to me who simply vanished. At the point where their life overlapped into ours, the story broke off.

We weren't being sent to the neighborhood grocery for facts of life, or death. But of course those are what we were on the track of, anyway. With the loaf of bread and the Cracker Jack prize, I was bringing home the intimations of pride and disgrace, and rumors and early news of people coming to hurt one another, while others practiced for joy—storing up a portion for myself of the human mystery.

Preface to "Collected Stories"

WITHOUT the love and belief my family gave me, I could not have become a writer to begin with. But all my stories brought together here speak with their own voice to me of a source of strength on which I leaned as well, and do lean. In the presence of the stories, taking in forty years of time, I feel the presences also of those whose support of my work made all the difference in its fate and in my life as a writer. For beyond their being written—I do know they would have been *written*—there is what happens to the writer's stories when they are submitted to the world of strangers.

It happened for me that the strangers—the first readers of my first stories—included Robert Penn Warren and Cleanth Brooks, the editors of *The Southern Review*. This distinguished quarterly, between 1937 and 1939, gave space to six stories of mine. Katherine Anne Porter, when she read some of them there, sat down and wrote me a letter of encouragement. The generosity of these writers' openness to me, their critical regard when it mattered most, not to mention the long friendships that began by letter in those days, have nourished my life.

Submitting stories to *The Southern Review* had needed its own encouragement. That had come about when John Rood published "Death of a Traveling Salesman," my first, in *Manuscript*, the "little" magazine he issued from Athens, Ohio. Following my good fortune with *The Southern Review*, other good things happened. John Woodburn, an editor with Doubleday, Doran (as it was then), who was driving through the South on a scouting trip, stopped on *The Southern Review*'s suggestion to see me, and left carrying some of my manuscripts with him. As was to be expected, a book publisher was not interested in a collection of short stories by an obscure young writer. But when Diarmuid Russell was opening his literary agency of Russell and Volkening, John Woodburn offered him the names of some new young writers he'd come across who might need an agent, among them mine. I became his client (I believe, his first), a decisive event in my writing life.

Diarmuid Russell's integrity was a clear stream proceeding undeflected and without a ripple on its own way through the fields of publishing. On his quick perception, his acute and steady judgment in regard to my work, as well as on his friendship, I relied without reservation. (When, presently, he sent back to me a story I'd written called "The Delta Cousins," saying that to him it looked like Chapter Two of a novel, I saw then where the story had come from and where it was going, and wrote my first novel, *Delta Wedding*.)

It was Diarmuid Russell's own belief in my work, and his hardheaded persistence in sending it out again and again when it was rejected, that resulted after a year's time in the acceptance of a story of mine in a magazine of general circulation. Edward Weeks took "A Worn Path" for *The Atlantic Monthly* in 1941. He had opened the door. Mary Louise Aswell, the fiction editor of *Harper's Bazaar*, who was a passionate advocate of new young writers, was able to clear the way for "The Key," the first of many of my stories she later introduced.

Diarmuid Russell was thus eventually able to interest a publisher in a first book of stories by a writer hardly known, true, but now in print. The publisher was Doubleday, Doran, and the book went straight into the shepherding of the same John Woodburn who a few years earlier had carried the manuscripts there. It was through his editorship that Katherine Anne Porter, once more to encourage me, out of her shining bounty introduced the book, *A Curtain of Green*.

John Woodburn, one of the great editors in a time of great ones, was a true champion of young writers; others writing today have him to thank as I do. When he moved to Harcourt, Brace (as it was then), I moved along with him.

The present collection holds all my published stories: those in *A Curtain of Green* and the three volumes that followed; and two that appear here for the first time in book form. In general, my stories as they've come along have reflected their own present time, beginning with the Depression in which *I* began; they came out of my response to it. These two written in the changing sixties reflect the unease, the ambiguities, the sickness and desperation of those days in Mississippi. If they have any special virtue in this respect, it would lie in the fact that they, like the others, are stories written from within. They come from living here—they were *part* of living here, of my long familiarity with the thoughts and feelings of those around me, in their many shadings and variations and contradictions.

"Where Is the Voice Coming From?" is unique, however, in the way it came about.

That hot August night when Medgar Evers, the local civil rights leader, was shot down from behind in Jackson, I thought, with overwhelming directness: Whoever the murderer is, I know him: not his identity, but his coming about, in this time and place. That is, I ought to have learned by now, from here, what such a man, intent on such a deed, had going on in his mind. I wrote his story—my fiction—in the first person: about that character's point of view, I felt, through my shock and revolt, I could make no mistake. The story pushed its way up through a long novel I was in the middle of writing, and was finished on the same night the shooting had taken place. (It's only two pages long.) At *The New Yorker*, where it was sent and where it was taken for the immediately forthcoming issue, William Maxwell, who had already known on sight all I could have told him about this story and its reason for being, edited it over the telephone with me. By then, an arrest had been made in Jackson, and the fiction's outward details had to be changed where by chance they had resembled too closely those of actuality, for the story must not be found prejudicial to the case of a person who might be on trial for his life.

I have been told, both in approval and in accusation, that I seem to love all my characters. What I do in writing of any character is to try to enter into the mind, heart, and skin of a human being who is not myself. Whether this happens to be a man or a woman, old or young, with skin black or white, the primary challenge lies in making the jump itself. It is the act of a writer's imagination that I set most high.

Jackson, Mississippi EUDORA WELTY.
May 1980

ONE WRITER'S BEGINNINGS

To the memory of my parents

CHRISTIAN WEBB WELTY
1879–1931

CHESTINA ANDREWS WELTY
1883–1966

ACKNOWLEDGMENTS

The origin of this book is the set of three lectures delivered at Harvard University in April, 1983, to inaugurate the William E. Massey lecture series. I am deeply grateful to Harvard University and to the graduate program in the History of American Civilization at whose invitation I wrote and gave the lectures. Mr. David Herbert Donald, of this program, gave me the best of his firm guidance and understanding. I am grateful to Mrs. Aida D. Donald, executive editor of Harvard University Press, for her kindness and patient care during their preparation in present form. To Mr. Daniel Aaron, whose suggestion as to the direction and course the lectures might take strongly encouraged me in their writing, I wish to express particular gratitude.

Jackson, Mississippi, 1983

Eudora, 1929, University of Wisconsin

When I was young enough to still spend a long time buttoning my shoes in the morning, I'd listen toward the hall: Daddy upstairs was shaving in the bathroom and Mother downstairs was frying the bacon. They would begin whistling back and forth to each other up and down the stairwell. My father would whistle his phrase, my mother would try to whistle, then hum hers back. It was their duet. I drew my buttonhook in and out and listened to it—I knew it was "The Merry Widow." The difference was, their song almost floated with laughter: how different from the record, which growled from the beginning, as if the Victrola were only slowly being wound up. They kept it running between them, up and down the stairs where I was now just about ready to run clattering down and show them my shoes.

I

Listening

IN OUR HOUSE on North Congress Street in Jackson, Mississippi, where I was born, the oldest of three children, in 1909, we grew up to the striking of clocks. There was a mission-style oak grandfather clock standing in the hall, which sent its gong-like strokes through the livingroom, diningroom, kitchen, and pantry, and up the sounding board of the stairwell. Through the night, it could find its way into our ears; sometimes, even on the sleeping porch, midnight could wake us up. My parents' bedroom had a smaller striking clock that answered it. Though the kitchen clock did nothing but show the time, the diningroom clock was a cuckoo clock with weights on long chains, on one of which my baby brother, after climbing on a chair to the top of the china closet, once succeeded in suspending the cat for a moment. I don't know whether or not my father's Ohio family, in having been Swiss back in the 1700s before the first three Welty brothers came to America, had anything to do with this; but we all of us have been time-minded all our lives. This was good at least for a future fiction writer, being able to learn so penetratingly, and almost first of all, about chronology. It was one of a good many things I learned almost without knowing it; it would be there when I needed it.

My father loved all instruments that would instruct and fascinate. His place to keep things was the drawer in the "library table" where lying on top of his folded maps was a telescope with brass extensions, to find the moon and the Big Dipper after supper in our front yard, and to keep appointments with eclipses. There was a folding Kodak that was brought out for Christmas, birthdays, and trips. In the back of the drawer you could find a magnifying glass, a kaleidoscope, and a gyroscope kept in a black buckram box, which he would set dancing for us on a string pulled tight. He had also supplied himself with an assortment of puzzles composed of metal rings and intersecting links and keys chained together, impossible for the rest of us, however patiently shown, to take apart; he had an almost childlike love of the ingenious.

In time, a barometer was added to our diningroom wall; but we didn't really need it. My father had the country boy's accurate knowledge of the weather and its skies. He went out and stood on our front steps first thing in the morning and took a look at it and a sniff. He was a pretty good weather prophet.

"Well, I'm *not*," my mother would say with enormous self-satisfaction.

He told us children what to do if we were lost in a strange country. "Look for where the sky is brightest along the horizon," he said. "That reflects the nearest river. Strike out for a river and you will find habitation." Eventualities were much on his mind. In his care for us children he cautioned us to take measures against such things as being struck by lightning. He drew us all away from the windows during the severe electrical storms that are common where we live. My mother stood apart, scoffing at caution as a character failing. "Why, I always loved a storm! High winds never bothered me in West Virginia! Just listen at that! I wasn't a bit afraid of a little lightning and thunder! I'd go out on the mountain and spread my arms wide and *run* in a good big storm!"

So I developed a strong meteorological sensibility. In years ahead when I wrote stories, atmosphere took its influential role from the start. Commotion in the weather and the inner feelings aroused by such a hovering disturbance emerged connected in dramatic form. (I tried a tornado first, in a story called "The Winds.")

From our earliest Christmas times, Santa Claus brought us toys that instruct boys and girls (separately) how to build things—stone blocks cut to the castle-building style, Tinker Toys, and Erector sets. Daddy made for us himself elaborate kites that needed to be taken miles out of town to a pasture long enough (and my father was not afraid of horses and cows watching) for him to run with and get up on a long cord to which my mother held the spindle, and then we children were given it to hold, tugging like something alive at our hands. They were beautiful, sound, shapely box kites, smelling delicately of office glue for their entire short lives. And of course, as soon as the boys attained anywhere near the right age, there was an electric train, the engine with its pea-sized working headlight, its line of cars, tracks equipped with switches, semaphores, its station, its bridges, and its tunnel, which blocked off all other traffic in the upstairs hall. Even from downstairs, and through the cries of excited children, the elegant rush and click of the train could be heard through the ceiling, running around and around its figure eight.

All of this, but especially the train, represents my father's fondest beliefs—in progress, in the future. With these gifts, he was preparing his children.

And so was my mother with her different gifts.

I learned from the age of two or three that any room in our house, at any time of day, was there to read in, or to be read to. My mother read to me. She'd read to me in the big bedroom in the mornings, when we were in her rocker together, which ticked in rhythm as we rocked, as though we had a cricket accompanying the story. She'd read to me in the diningroom on winter afternoons in front of the coal fire, with our cuckoo clock ending the story with "Cuckoo," and at night when I'd got in my own bed. I must have given her no peace. Sometimes she read to me in the kitchen while she sat churning, and the churning sobbed along with *any* story. It was my ambition to have her read to me while *I* churned; once she granted my wish, but she read off my story before I brought her butter. She was an expressive reader. When she was reading "Puss in Boots," for instance, it was impossible not to know that she distrusted *all* cats.

It had been startling and disappointing to me to find out that story books had been written by *people*, that books were not natural wonders, coming up of themselves like grass. Yet regardless of where they came from, I cannot remember a time when I was not in love with them—with the books themselves, cover and binding and the paper they were printed on, with their smell and their weight and with their possession in my arms, captured and carried off to myself. Still illiterate, I was ready for them, committed to all the reading I could give them.

Neither of my parents had come from homes that could afford to buy many books, but though it must have been something of a strain on his salary, as the youngest officer in a young insurance company, my father was all the while carefully selecting and ordering away for what he and Mother thought we children should grow up with. They bought first for the future.

Besides the bookcase in the livingroom, which was always called "the library," there were the encyclopedia tables and dictionary stand under windows in our diningroom. Here to help us grow up arguing around the diningroom table were the Unabridged Webster, the Columbia Encyclopedia, Compton's Pictured Encyclopedia, the Lincoln Library of Information, and later the Book of Knowledge. And the year we moved into our new house, there was room to celebrate it with the new 1925 edition of the Britannica, which my father, his face always deliberately turned toward the future, was of course disposed to think better than any previous edition.

In "the library," inside the mission-style bookcase with its three diamond-latticed glass doors, with my father's Morris chair and the glass-shaded lamp on its table beside it, were books I could soon begin on—and I did, reading them all alike and as they came, straight down their rows, top shelf to bottom. There was the set of Stoddard's Lectures, in all its late nineteenth-century vocabulary and vignettes of peasant life and quaint beliefs and customs, with matching halftone illustrations: Vesuvius erupting, Venice by moonlight, gypsies glimpsed by their campfires. I didn't know then the clue they were to my father's longing to see the rest of the world. I read straight through his other love-from-afar: the Victrola Book of the Opera, with opera after opera in synopsis, with portraits in costume of Melba, Caruso, Galli-Curci, and Geraldine Farrar, some of whose voices we could listen to on our Red Seal records.

My mother read secondarily for information; she sank as a hedonist into novels. She read Dickens in the spirit in which she would have eloped with him. The novels of her girlhood that had stayed on in her imagination, besides those of Dickens and Scott and Robert Louis Stevenson, were *Jane Eyre*, *Trilby*, *The Woman in White*, *Green Mansions*, *King Solomon's Mines.* Marie Corelli's name would crop up but I understood she had gone out of favor with my mother, who had only kept

Eudora with father's watch, c. 1910.

Playing on Congress Street, Davis School in background

Ardath out of loyalty. In time she absorbed herself in Galsworthy, Edith Wharton, above all in Thomas Mann of the *Joseph* volumes.

St. Elmo was not in our house; I saw it often in other houses. This wildly popular Southern novel is where all the Edna Earles in our population started coming from. They're all named for the heroine, who succeeded in bringing a dissolute, sinning roué and atheist of a lover (St. Elmo) to his knees. My mother was able to forgo it. But she remembered the classic advice given to rose growers on how to water their bushes long enough: "Take a chair and *St. Elmo*."

To both my parents I owe my early acquaintance with a beloved Mark Twain. There was a full set of Mark Twain and a short set of Ring Lardner in our bookcase, and those were the volumes that in time united us all, parents and children.

Reading everything that stood before me was how I came upon a worn old book without a back that had belonged to my father as a child. It was called *Sanford and Merton.* Is there anyone left who recognizes it, I wonder? It is the famous moral tale written by Thomas Day in the 1780s, but of him no mention is made on the title page of *this* book; here it is *Sanford and Merton in Words of One Syllable* by Mary Godolphin. Here are the rich boy and the poor boy and Mr. Barlow, their teacher and interlocutor, in long discourses alternating with dramatic scenes—danger and rescue allotted to the rich and the poor respectively. It may have only words of one syllable, but one of them is "quoth." It ends with not one but two morals, both engraved on rings: "Do what you ought, come what may," and "If we would be great, we must first learn to be good."

This book was lacking its front cover, the back held on by strips of pasted paper, now turned golden, in several layers, and the pages stained, flecked, and tattered around the edges; its garish illustrations had come unattached but were preserved, laid in. I had the feeling even in my heedless childhood that this was the only book my father as a little boy had had of his own. He had held onto it, and might have gone to sleep on its coverless face: he had lost his mother when he was seven. My father had never made any mention to his own children of the book, but he had brought it along with him from Ohio to our house and shelved it in our bookcase.

My mother had brought from West Virginia that set of Dickens; those books looked sad, too—they had been through fire and water before I was born, she told me, and there they were, lined up—as I later realized, waiting for *me*.

I was presented, from as early as I can remember, with books of my own, which appeared on my birthday and Christmas morning. Indeed, my parents could not give me books enough. They must have sacrificed to give me on my sixth or seventh birthday—it was after I became a reader for myself—the ten-volume set of Our Wonder World. These were beautifully made, heavy books I would lie down with on the floor in front of the diningroom hearth, and more often than the rest volume 5, *Every Child's Story Book*, was under my eyes. There were the fairy tales—Grimm, Andersen, the English, the French, "Ali Baba and the Forty Thieves"; and there was Aesop and Reynard the Fox; there were the myths and legends, Robin Hood, King Arthur, and St. George and the Dragon, even the history of Joan of Arc; a whack of *Pilgrim's Progress* and a long piece of *Gulliver*. They all carried their classic illustrations. I located myself in these pages and could go straight to the stories and pictures I loved; very often "The Yellow Dwarf" was first choice, with Walter Crane's Yellow Dwarf in full color making his terrifying appearance flanked by turkeys. Now that volume is as worn and backless and hanging apart as my father's poor *Sanford and Merton*. The precious page with Edward Lear's "Jumblies" on it has been in danger of slipping out for all these years. One measure of my love for Our Wonder World was that for a long time I wondered if I would go through fire and water for it as my mother had done for Charles Dickens; and the only comfort was to think I could ask my mother to do it for me.

I believe I'm the only child I know of who grew up with this treasure in the house. I used to ask others, "Did you have Our Wonder World?" I'd have to tell them The Book of Knowledge could not hold a candle to it.

I live in gratitude to my parents for initiating me—and as early as I begged for it, without keeping me waiting—into knowledge of the word, into reading and spelling, by way of the alphabet. They taught it to me at home in time for me to begin to read before starting to school. I believe the alphabet is no longer considered an essential piece of equipment for traveling through life. In my day it was the keystone to knowledge. You learned the alphabet as you learned to count to ten, as you learned "Now I lay me" and the Lord's Prayer and your father's and mother's name and address and telephone number, all in case you were lost.

My love for the alphabet, which endures, grew out of reciting it but, before that, out of seeing the letters on the page. In my own story books, before I could read them for myself, I fell in love with various winding, enchanted-looking initials drawn by Walter Crane at the heads of fairy tales. In "Once upon a time," an "O" had a rabbit running it as a treadmill, his feet upon flowers. When the day came, years later, for me to see the Book of Kells, all the wizardry of letter, initial, and word swept over me a thousand times over, and the illumination, the gold, seemed a part of the word's beauty and holiness that had been there from the start.

Learning stamps you with its moments. Childhood's learning is made up of moments. It isn't steady. It's a pulse.

In a children's art class, we sat in a ring on kindergarten chairs and drew three daffodils that had just been picked out of the yard; and while I was drawing, my sharpened yellow pencil and the cup of the yellow daffodil gave off whiffs just alike. That the pencil doing the drawing should give off the same smell as the flower it drew seemed part of the art lesson—as shouldn't it be? Children, like animals, use all their senses to discover the world. Then artists come along and discover it the same way, all over again. Here and there, it's the same world. Or now and then we'll hear from an artist who's never lost it.

In my sensory education I include my physical awareness of the *word*. Of a certain word, that is; the connection it has with what it stands for. At around age six, perhaps, I was standing by myself in our front yard waiting for supper, just at that hour in a late summer day when the sun is already below the horizon and the risen full moon in the visible sky stops being chalky and begins to take on light. There comes the moment, and I saw it then, when the moon goes from flat to round. For the first time it met my eyes as a globe. The word "moon" came into my mouth as though fed to me out of a silver spoon. Held in my mouth the moon became a word. It had the roundness of a Concord grape Grandpa took off his vine and gave me to suck out of its skin and swallow whole, in Ohio.

This love did not prevent me from living for years in foolish error about the moon. The new moon just appearing in the west was the rising moon to me. The new should be rising. And in early childhood the sun and moon, those opposite reigning powers, I just as easily assumed rose in east and west respectively in their opposite sides of the sky, and like partners in a reel they advanced, sun from the east, moon from the west, crossed over (when I wasn't looking) and went down on the other side. My father couldn't have known I believed that when, bending behind me and guiding my shoulder, he positioned me at our telescope in the front yard and, with careful adjustment of the focus, brought the moon close to me.

The night sky over my childhood Jackson was velvety black. I could see the full constellations in it and call their names; when I could read, I knew their myths. Though I was always waked for eclipses, and indeed carried to the window as an infant in arms and shown Halley's Comet in my sleep, and though I'd been taught at our diningroom table about the solar system and knew the earth revolved around the sun, and our moon around us, I never found out the moon didn't come up in the west until I was a writer and Herschel Brickell, the literary critic, told me after I misplaced it in a story. He said valuable words to me about my new profession: "Always be sure you get your moon in the right part of the sky."

My mother always sang to her children. Her voice came out just a little bit in the minor key. "Wee Willie Winkie's" song was wonderfully sad when she sang the lullabies.

"Oh, but now there's a record. She could have her own record to listen to," my father would have said. For there came a Victrola record of "Bobby Shafftoe" and "Rock-a-Bye Baby", all of Mother's lullabies, which could be played to take

Eudora and Edward, c. 1913

Eudora, Edward, Mother, Walter, c. 1917

her place. Soon I was able to play her my own lullabies all day long.

Our Victrola stood in the diningroom. I was allowed to climb onto the seat of a diningroom chair to wind it, start the record turning, and set the needle playing. In a second I'd jumped to the floor, to spin or march around the table as the music called for—now there were all the other records I could play too. I skinned back onto the chair just in time to lift the needle at the end, stop the record and turn it over, then change the needle. That brass receptacle with a hole in the lid gave off a metallic smell like human sweat, from all the hot needles that were fed it. Winding up, dancing, being cocked to start and stop the record, was of course all in one the act of *listening*—to "Overture to *Daughter of the Regiment*," "Selections from *The Fortune Teller*," "Kiss Me Again," "Gypsy Dance from *Carmen*," "Stars and Stripes Forever," "When the Midnight Choo-Choo Leaves for Alabam," or whatever came next. Movement must be at the very heart of listening.

Ever since I was first read to, then started reading to myself, there has never been a line read that I didn't *hear*. As my eyes followed the sentence, a voice was saying it silently to me. It isn't my mother's voice, or the voice of any person I can identify, certainly not my own. It is human, but inward, and it is inwardly that I listen to it. It is to me the voice of the story or the poem itself. The cadence, whatever it is that asks you to believe, the feeling that resides in the printed word, reaches me through the reader-voice. I have supposed, but never found out, that this is the case with all readers—to read as listeners—and with all writers, to write as listeners. It may be part of the desire to write. The sound of what falls on the page begins the process of testing it for truth, for me. Whether I am right to trust so far I don't know. By now I don't know whether I could do either one, reading or writing, without the other.

My own words, when I am at work on a story, I hear too as they go, in the same voice that I hear when I read in books. When I write and the sound of it comes back to my ears, then I act to make my changes. I have always trusted this voice.

•

In that vanished time in small-town Jackson, most of the ladies I was familiar with, the mothers of my friends in the neighborhood, were busiest when they were sociable. In the afternoons there was regular visiting up and down the little grid of residential streets. Everybody had calling cards, even certain children; and newborn babies themselves were properly announced by sending out their tiny engraved calling cards attached with a pink or blue bow to those of their parents. Graduation presents to high-school pupils were often "card cases." On the hall table in every house the first thing you saw was a silver tray waiting to receive more calling cards on top of the stack already piled up like jackstraws; they were never thrown away.

My mother let none of this idling, as she saw it, pertain to her; she went her own way with or without her calling cards, and though she was fond of her friends and they were fond of her, she had little time for small talk. At first, I hadn't known what I'd missed.

When we at length bought our first automobile, one of our neighbors was often invited to go with us on the family Sunday afternoon ride. In Jackson it was counted an affront to the neighbors to start out for anywhere with an empty seat in the car. My mother sat in the back with her friend, and I'm told that as a small child I would ask to sit in the middle, and say as we started off, "Now *talk*."

There was dialogue throughout the lady's accounts to my mother. "I said" . . . "He said" . . . "And I'm told she very plainly said" . . . "It was midnight before they finally heard, and what do you think it *was*?"

What I loved about her stories was that everything happened in *scenes*. I might not catch on to what the root of the trouble was in all that happened, but my ear told me it was dramatic. Often she said, "The crisis had come!"

This same lady was one of Mother's callers on the telephone who always talked a long time. I knew who it was when my mother would only reply, now and then, "Well, I declare," or "You don't say so," or "Surely not." She'd be standing at the wall telephone, listening against her will, and I'd sit on the stairs close by her. Our telephone had a little bar set into the handle which had to be pressed and held down to keep the connection open, and when her friend had said goodbye, my mother needed me to prize her fingers loose from the little bar; her grip had become paralyzed. "What did she say?" I asked.

"She wasn't *saying* a thing in this world," sighed my mother. "She was just ready to talk, that's all."

My mother was right. Years later, beginning with my story "Why I Live at the P.O.," I wrote reasonably often in the form of a monologue that takes possession of the speaker. How much more gets told besides!

This lady told everything in her sweet, marveling voice, and meant every word of it kindly. She enjoyed my company perhaps even more than my mother's. She invited me to catch her doodlebugs; under the trees in her backyard were dozens of their holes. When you stuck a broom straw down one and called, "Doodlebug, doodlebug, your house is on fire and all your children are burning up," she believed this is why the doodlebug came running out of the hole. This was why I loved to call up her doodlebugs instead of ours.

My mother could never have told me her stories, and I think I knew why even then; my mother didn't believe them. But I could listen to this murmuring lady all day. She believed everything she heard, like the doodlebug. And so did I.

This was a day when ladies' and children's clothes were very often made at home. My mother cut out all the dresses and her little boys' rompers, and a sewing woman would come and spend the day upstairs in the sewing room fitting and stitching them all. This was Fannie. This old black sewing woman, along with her speed and dexterity, brought along a great provision of up-to-the-minute news. She spent her life going from family to family in town and worked right in its bosom, and nothing could stop her. My mother would try, while I stood being pinned up. "Fannie, I'd rather Eudora didn't hear that." "That" would be just what I was longing to hear, whatever it was. "I don't want her exposed to gossip"—as if gossip were measles and I could catch it. I did catch some of it but not enough. "Mrs. O'Neil's oldest daughter she had her wedding dress *tried on*, and all her fine underclothes featherstitched and ribbon run in and then—" "I think that will do, Fannie," said my mother. It was tantalizing never to be exposed long enough to hear the end.

Fannie was the worldliest old woman to be imagined. She could do whatever her hands were doing without having to stop talking; and she could speak in a wonderfully derogatory way with any number of pins stuck in her mouth. Her hands steadied me like claws as she stumped on her knees around me, tacking me together. The gist of her tale would be lost on me, but Fannie didn't bother about the ear she was telling it to; she just liked telling. She was like an author. In fact, for a good deal of what she said, I daresay she *was* the author.

Long before I wrote stories, I listened for stories. Listening *for* them is something more acute than listening *to* them. I suppose it's an early form of participation in what goes on. Listening children know stories are *there.* When their elders sit and begin, children are just waiting and hoping for one to come out, like a mouse from its hole.

It was taken entirely for granted that there wasn't any lying in our family, and I was advanced in adolescence before I realized that in plenty of homes where I played with schoolmates and went to their parties, children lied to their parents and parents lied to their children and to each other. It took me a long time to realize that these very same everyday lies, and the stratagems and jokes and tricks and dares that went with them, were in fact the basis of the *scenes* I so well loved to hear about and hoped for and treasured in the conversation of adults.

My instinct—the dramatic instinct—was to lead me, eventually, on the right track for a storyteller: the *scene* was full of hints, pointers, suggestions, and promises of things to find out and know about human beings. I had to grow up and learn to listen for the unspoken as well as the spoken—and to know a truth, I also had to recognize a lie.

It was when my mother came out onto the sleeping porch to tell me goodnight that her trial came. The sudden silence in the double bed meant my younger brothers had both keeled over in sleep, and I in the single bed at my end of the porch would be lying electrified, waiting for this to be the night when she'd tell me what she'd promised for so long.

Just as she bent to kiss me I grabbed her and asked: "Where do babies come from?"

My poor mother! But something saved her every time. Almost any night I put the baby question to her, suddenly, as if the whole outdoors exploded, Professor Holt would start to sing. The Holts lived next door; he taught penmanship (the Palmer Method), typing, bookkeeping and shorthand at the high school. His excitable voice traveled out of their dining-room windows across the two driveways between our houses, and up to our upstairs sleeping porch. His wife, usually so quiet and gentle, was his uncannily spirited accompanist at the piano. "High-ho! Come to the Fair!" he'd sing, unless he sang "Oho ye oho ye, who's bound for the ferry, the briar's in bud and the sun's going down!"

"Dear, this isn't a very good time for you to hear Mother, is it?"

She couldn't get started. As soon as she'd whisper something, Professor Holt galloped into the chorus, "And 'tis but a penny to Twickenham town!" "Isn't that enough?" she'd ask me. She'd told me that the mother and the father had to both *want* the baby. This couldn't be enough. I knew she was not trying to fib to me, for she never did fib, but also I could not help but know she was not really *telling* me. And more than that, I was afraid of what I was going to hear next. This was partly because she wanted to tell me in the dark. I thought *she* might be afraid. In something like childish hopelessness I thought she probably *couldn't* tell, just as she *couldn't* lie.

On the night we came the closest to having it over with, she started to tell me without being asked, and I ruined it by yelling, "Mother, look at the lightning bugs!"

In those days, the dark was dark. And all the dark out there was filled with the soft, near lights of lightning bugs. They were everywhere, flashing on the slow, horizontal move, on the upswings, rising and subsiding in the soundless dark. Lightning bugs signaled and answered back without a stop, from down below all the way to the top of our sycamore tree. My mother just gave me a businesslike kiss and went on back to Daddy in their room at the front of the house. Distracted by lightning bugs, I had missed my chance. The fact is she never did tell me.

I doubt that any child I knew ever was told by her mother any more than I was about babies. In fact, I doubt that her own mother ever told her any more than she told me, though there were five brothers who were born after Mother, one after the other, and she was taking care of babies all her childhood.

Not being able to bring herself to open that door to reveal its secret, one of those days, she opened another door.

In my mother's bottom bureau drawer in her bedroom she kept treasures of hers in boxes, and had given me permission to play with one of them—a switch of her own chestnut-colored hair, kept in a heavy bright braid that coiled around like a snake inside a cardboard box. I hung it from her doorknob and unplaited it; it fell in ripples nearly to the floor, and it satisfied the Rapunzel in me to comb it out. But one day I noticed in the same drawer a small white cardboard box such as her engraved calling cards came in from the printing house. It was tightly closed, but I opened it, to find to my puzzlement and covetousness two polished buffalo nickels, embedded in white cotton. I rushed with this opened box to my mother and asked if I could run out and spend the nickels.

"No!" she exclaimed in a most passionate way. She seized the box into her own hands. I begged her; somehow I had started to cry. Then she sat down, drew me to her, and told me that I had had a little brother who had come before I did, and who had died as a baby before I was born. And these two nickels that I'd wanted to claim as my find were his. They had lain on his eyelids, for a purpose untold and unimaginable. "He was a fine little baby, my first baby, and he shouldn't have died. But he did. It was because your mother almost died at the same time," she told me. "In looking after me, they too nearly forgot about the little baby."

She'd told me the wrong secret—not how babies could come but how they could die, how they could be forgotten about.

I wondered in after years: how could my mother have kept those two coins? Yet how could someone like herself have disposed of them in any way at all? She suffered from a morbid streak which in all the life of the family reached out on occasions—the worst occasions—and touched us, clung around us, making it worse for her; her unbearable moments could find nowhere to go.

The future story writer in the child I was must have taken unconscious note and stored it away then: one secret is liable to be revealed in the place of another that is harder to tell, and the substitute secret when nakedly exposed is often the more appalling.

Perhaps telling me what she did was made easier for my mother by the two secrets, told and still not told, being connected in her deepest feeling, more intimately than anyone ever knew, perhaps even herself. So far as I remember now, this is the only time this baby was ever mentioned in my presence. So far as I can remember, and I've tried, he was never mentioned in the presence of my father, for whom he had been named. I am only certain that my father, who could never bear pain very well, would not have been able to bear it.

It was my father (my mother told me at some later date) who saved her own life, after that baby was born. She had in fact been given up by the doctor, as she had long been unable to take any nourishment. (That was the illness when they'd cut her hair, which formed the switch in the same bureau drawer.) What had struck her was septicemia, in those days nearly always fatal. What my father did was to try champagne.

I once wondered where he, who'd come not very long before from an Ohio farm, had ever heard of such a remedy, such a measure. Or perhaps as far as he was concerned he invented it, out of the strength of desperation. It would have been desperation augmented because champagne couldn't be bought in Jackson. But somehow he knew what to do about that too. He telephoned to Canton, forty miles north, to an Italian orchard grower, Mr. Trolio, told him the necessity, and asked, begged, that he put a bottle of his wine on Number 3, which was due in a few minutes to stop in Canton to "take on water" (my father knew everything about train schedules). My father would be waiting to meet the train in Jackson. Mr. Trolio did—he sent the bottle in a bucket of ice and my father snatched it off the baggage car. He offered my mother a glass of chilled champagne and she drank it and kept it down. She was to live, after all.

Now, her hair was long again, it would reach in a braid down her back, and now I was her child. She hadn't died. And when I came, I hadn't died either. Would she ever? Would I ever? I couldn't face *ever*. I must have rushed into her lap, demanding her like a baby. And she had to put her first-born aside again, for me.

Of course it's easy to see why they both overprotected me, why my father, before I could wear a new pair of shoes for the first time, made me wait while he took out his thin silver pocket knife and with the point of the blade scored the polished soles all over, carefully, in a diamond pattern, to prevent me from sliding on the polished floor when I ran.

As I was to learn over and over again, my mother's mind was a mass of associations. Whatever happened would be forever paired for her with something that had happened before it, to one of us or to her. It became a private anniversary. Every time any possible harm came near me, she thought of how she lost her first child. When a Roman candle at Christmas backfired up my sleeve, she rushed to smother the blaze with the first thing she could grab, which was a dish towel hanging in the kitchen, and the burn on my arm became infected. I was nothing but proud of my sling, for I could wear it to school, and her repeated blaming of herself—for even my sling—puzzled and troubled me.

When my mother would tell me that she wanted me to have something because she as a child had never had it, I wanted, or I partly wanted, to give it back. All my life I continued to feel that bliss for me would have to imply my mother's deprivation or sacrifice. I don't think it would have occurred to her what a double emotion I felt, and indeed I know that it was being unfair to her, for what she said was simply the truth.

"I'm going to let you go to the Century Theatre with your father tonight on my ticket. I'd rather you saw *Blossom Time* than go myself."

In the Century first-row balcony, where their seats always were, I'd be sitting beside my father at this hour beyond my bedtime carried totally away by the performance, and then suddenly the thought of my mother staying home with my sleeping younger brothers, missing the spectacle at this

With my father, Christian Welty

moment before my eyes, and doing without all the excitement and wonder that filled my being, would arrest me and I could hardly bear my pleasure for my guilt.

There is no wonder that a passion for independence sprang up in me at the earliest age. It took me a long time to manage the independence, for I loved those who protected me—and I wanted inevitably to protect them back. I have never managed to handle the guilt. In the act and the course of writing stories, these are two of the springs, one bright, one dark, that feed the stream.

When I was six or seven, I was taken out of school and put to bed for several months for an ailment the doctor described as "fast-beating heart." I felt all right—perhaps I felt too good. It was the feeling of suspense. At any rate, I was allowed to occupy all day my parents' double bed in the front upstairs bedroom.

I was supposed to rest, and the little children didn't get to run in and excite me often. Davis School was as close as across the street. I could keep up with it from the window beside me, hear the principal ring her bell, see which children were tardy, watch my classmates eat together at recess: I knew their sandwiches. I was homesick for school; my mother made time for teaching me arithmetic and hearing my spelling.

An opulence of story books covered my bed; it was the "Land of Counterpane." As I read away, I was Rapunzel, or the Goose Girl, or the Princess Labam in one of the *Thousand and One Nights* who mounted the roof of her palace every night and of her own radiance faithfully lighted the whole city just by reposing there, and I daydreamed I could light Davis School from across the street.

But I never dreamed I could learn as long as I was away from the schoolroom, and that bits of enlightenment far-reaching in my life went on as ever in their own good time. After they'd told me goodnight and tucked me in—although I knew that after I'd finally fallen asleep they'd pick me up and carry me away—my parents draped the lampshade with a sheet of the daily paper, which was tilted, like a hatbrim, so that they could sit in their rockers in a lighted part of the room and I could supposedly go to sleep in the protected dark of the bed. They sat talking. What was thus dramatically made a present of to me was the secure sense of the hidden observer. As long as I could make myself keep awake, I was free to listen to every word my parents said between them.

I don't remember that any secrets were revealed to me, nor do I remember any avid curiosity on my part to learn something I wasn't supposed to—perhaps I was too young to know what to listen for. But I was present in the room with the chief secret there was—the two of them, father and mother, sitting there as one. I was conscious of this secret and of my fast-beating heart in step together, as I lay in the slant-shaded light of the room, with a brown, pear-shaped scorch in the newspaper shade where it had become overheated once.

What they talked about I have no idea, and the subject was not what mattered to me. It was no doubt whatever a young married couple spending their first time privately in each other's company in the long, probably harried day would talk about. It was the murmur of their voices, the back-and-forth, the unnoticed stretching away of time between my bedtime and theirs, that made me bask there at my distance. What I felt was not that I was excluded from them but that I was included, in—and because of—what I could hear of their voices and what I could see of their faces in the cone of yellow light under the brown-scorched shade.

I suppose I was exercising as early as then the turn of mind, the nature of temperament, of a privileged observer; and owing to the way I became so, it turned out that I became the loving kind.

A conscious act grew out of this by the time I began to write stories: getting my distance, a prerequisite of my understanding of human events, is the way I begin work. Just as, of course, it was an initial step when, in my first journalism job, I stumbled into making pictures with a camera. Frame, proportion, perspective, the values of light and shade, all are determined by the distance of the observing eye.

I have always been shy physically. This in part tended to keep me from rushing into things, including relationships, headlong. Not rushing headlong, though I may have wanted to, but beginning to write stories about people, I drew near slowly; noting and guessing, apprehending, hoping, drawing my eventual conclusions out of my own heart, I *did* venture closer to where I wanted to go. As time and my imagination led me on, I did plunge.

From the first I was clamorous to learn—I wanted to know and begged to be told not so much what, or how, or why, or where, as when. How soon?

> Pear tree by the garden gate,
> How much longer must I wait?

This rhyme from one of my nursery books was the one that spoke for me. But I lived not at all unhappily in this craving, for my wild curiosity was in large part suspense, which carries its own secret pleasure. And so one of the godmothers of fiction was already bending over me.

When I was five years old, I knew the alphabet, I'd been vaccinated (for smallpox), and I could read. So my mother walked across the street to Jefferson Davis Grammar School and asked the principal if she would allow me to enter the first grade after Christmas.

"Oh, all right," said Miss Duling. "Probably the best thing you could do with her."

Miss Duling, a lifelong subscriber to perfection, was a figure of authority, the most whole-souled I have ever come to know. She was a dedicated schoolteacher who denied herself all she might have done or whatever other way she might have lived (this possibility was the last that could have occurred to us, her subjects in school). I believe she came of well-off people, well-educated, in Kentucky, and certainly old photographs show she was a beautiful, high-spirited-looking young lady—and came down to Jackson to its new grammar school that was going begging for a principal. She must have earned next to nothing; Mississippi then as now was the nation's lowest-ranking state economically, and our legislature has always shown a painfully loud reluctance to give money to public education. That challenge *brought* her.

In the long run she came into touch, as teacher or principal, with three generations of Jacksonians. My parents had not, but everybody else's parents had gone to school to her. She'd taught most of our leaders somewhere along the line. When she wanted something done—some civic oversight corrected, some injustice made right overnight, or even a tree spared that the fool telephone people were about to cut down—she telephoned the mayor, or the chief of police, or the president of the power company, or the head doctor at the hospital, or the judge in charge of a case, or whoever, and calling them by their first names, *told* them. It is impossible to imagine her meeting with anything less than compliance. The ringing of her brass bell from their days at Davis School would still be in their ears. She also proposed a spelling match between the fourth grade at Davis School and the Mississippi Legislature, who went through with it; and that told the Legislature.

Her standards were very high and of course inflexible, her authority was total; why *wouldn't* this carry with it a brass bell that could be heard ringing for a block in all directions? That bell belonged to the figure of Miss Duling as though it grew directly out of her right arm, as wings grew out of an angel or a tail out of the devil. When we entered, marching, into her school, by strictest teaching, surveillance, and order we learned grammar, arithmetic, spelling, reading, writing, and geography; and she, not the teachers, I believe, wrote out the examinations: need I tell you, they were "hard."

She's not the only teacher who has influenced me, but Miss Duling, in some fictional shape or form, has stridden into a larger part of my work than I'd realized until now. She emerges in my perhaps inordinate number of schoolteacher characters. I loved those characters in the writing. But I did not, in life, love Miss Duling. I was afraid of her high-arched bony nose, her eyebrows lifted in half-circles above her hooded, brilliant eyes, and of the Kentucky R's in her speech, and the long steps she took in her hightop shoes. I did nothing but fear her bearing-down authority, and did not connect this (as of course we were meant to) with our own need or desire to learn, perhaps because I already had this wish, and did not need to be driven.

She was impervious to lies or foolish excuses or the insufferable plea of not knowing any better. She wasn't going to have any frills, either, at Davis School. When a new governor moved into the mansion, he sent his daughter to Davis

School; her name was Lady Rachel Conner. Miss Duling at once called the governor to the telephone and told him, "She'll be plain Rachel here."

Miss Duling dressed as plainly as a Pilgrim on a Thanksgiving poster we made in the schoolroom, in a longish black-and-white checked gingham dress, a bright thick wool sweater the red of a railroad lantern—she'd knitted it herself—black stockings and her narrow elegant feet in black hightop shoes with heels you could hear coming, rhythmical as a parade drum down the hall. Her silky black curly hair was drawn back out of curl, fastened by high combs, and knotted behind. She carried her spectacles on a gold chain hung around her neck. Her gaze was in general sweeping, then suddenly at the point of concentration upon you. With a swing of her bell that took her whole right arm and shoulder, she rang it, militant and impartial, from the head of the front steps of Davis School when it was time for us all to line up, girls on one side, boys on the other. We were to march past her into the school building, while the fourth-grader she nabbed played time on the piano, mostly to a tune we could have skipped to, but we didn't skip into Davis School.

Little recess (open-air exercises) and big recess (lunchboxes from home opened and eaten on the grass, on the girls' side and the boys' side of the yard) and dismissal were also regulated by Miss Duling's bell. The bell was also used to catch us off guard with fire drill.

It was examinations that drove my wits away, as all emergencies do. Being expected to measure up was paralysing. I failed to make 100 on my spelling exam because I missed one word and that word was "uncle." Mother, as I knew she would, took it personally. "You couldn't spell *uncle*? When you've got those five perfectly splendid uncles in West Virginia? What would *they* say to that?"

It was never that Mother wanted me to beat my classmates in grades; what she wanted was for me to have my answers right. It was unclouded perfection I was up against.

My father was much more tolerant of possible error. He only said, as he steeply and impeccably sharpened my pencils on examination morning, "Now just keep remembering: the examinations were made out for the *average* student to pass. That's the majority. And if the majority can pass, think how much better *you* can do."

I looked to my mother, who had her own opinions about the majority. My father wished to treat it with respect, she didn't. I'd been born left-handed, but the habit was broken when I entered the first grade in Davis School. My father had insisted. He pointed out that everything in life had been made for the convenience of right-handed people, because they were the majority, and he often used "what the majority wants" as a criterion for what was for the best. My mother said she could not promise him, could not promise him at all, that I wouldn't stutter as a consequence. Mother had been born left-handed too; her family consisted of five left-handed brothers, a left-handed mother, and a father who could write with both hands at the same time, also backwards and forwards and upside down, different words with each hand. She had been broken of it when she was young, and she said she used to stutter.

"But you still stutter," I'd remind her, only to hear her say loftily, "You should have heard me when I was your age."

In my childhood days, a great deal of stock was put, in general, in the value of doing well in school. Both daily newspapers in Jackson saw the honor roll as news and published the lists, and the grades, of all the honor students. The city fathers gave the children who made the honor roll free season tickets to the baseball games down at the grandstand. We all attended and all worshiped some player on the Jackson Senators: I offered up my 100's in arithmetic and spelling, reading and writing, attendance and, yes, deportment—I must have been a prig!—to Red McDermott, the third baseman. And our happiness matched that of knowing Miss Duling was on her summer vacation, far, far away in Kentucky.

Every school week, visiting teachers came on their days for special lessons. On Mondays, the singing teacher blew into the room fresh from the early outdoors, singing in her high soprano "How do you do?" to do-mi-sol-do, and we responded in chorus from our desks, "I'm ve-ry well" to do-sol-mi-do. Miss Johnson taught us rounds—"Row row row

My mother coming down the stairs at 741 North Congress Street, Jackson. (My father took all these photos.)

your boat gently down the stream"—and "Little Sir Echo," with half the room singing the words and the other half being the echo, a competition. She was from the North, and she was the one who wanted us all to stop the Christmas carols and see snow. The snow falling that morning outside the window was the first most of us had ever seen, and Miss Johnson threw up the window and held out wide her own black cape and caught flakes on it and ran, as fast as she could go, up and down the aisles to show us the real thing before it melted.

Thursday was Miss Eyrich and Miss Eyrich was Thursday. She came to give us physical training. She wasted no time on nonsense. Without greeting, we were marched straight outside and summarily divided into teams (no choosing sides), put on the mark, and ordered to get set for a relay race. Miss Eyrich cracked out "Go!" Dread rose in my throat. My head swam. Here was my turn, nearly upon me. (Wait, have I been touched—was that slap the touch? Go on! Do I go on without our passing a word? What word? Now am I racing too fast to turn around? Now I'm nearly home, but where is the hand waiting for mine to touch? Am I too late? Have I lost the whole race for our side?) I lost the relay race for our side before I started, through living ahead of myself, dreading to make my start, feeling too late prematurely, and standing transfixed by emergency, trying to think of a password. Thursdays still can make me hear Miss Eyrich's voice. "On your mark—get set—GO!"

Very composedly and very slowly, the art teacher, who visited each room on Fridays, paced the aisle and looked down over your shoulder at what you were drawing for her. This was Miss Ascher. Coming from behind you, her deep, resonant voice reached you without being a word at all, but a sort of purr. It was much the sound given out by our family doctor when he read the thermometer and found you were running a slight fever: "Um-hm. Um-hm." Both alike, they let you go right ahead with it.

The school toilets were in the boys' and girls' respective basements. After Miss Duling had rung to dismiss school, a friend and I were making our plans for Saturday from adjoining cubicles. "Can you come spend the day with me?" I called out, and she called back, "I might could."

"Who—said—MIGHT—COULD?" It sounded like "Fe Fi Fo Fum!"

We both were petrified, for we knew whose deep measured words those were that came from just outside our doors. That was the voice of Mrs. McWillie, who taught the other fourth grade across the hall from ours. She was not even our teacher, but a very heavy, stern lady who dressed entirely in widow's weeds with a pleated black shirtwaist with a high net collar and velvet ribbon, and a black skirt to her ankles, with black circles under her eyes and a mournful, Presbyterian expression. We children took her to be a hundred years old. We held still.

"You might as well tell me," continued Mrs. McWillie. "I'm going to plant myself right here and wait till you come out. Then I'll see who it was I heard saying 'MIGHT-COULD.' "

If Elizabeth wouldn't go out, of course I wouldn't either. We knew her to be a teacher who would not flinch from standing there in the basement all afternoon, perhaps even all day Saturday. So we surrendered and came out. I priggishly hoped Elizabeth would clear it up which child it was—it wasn't me.

"So it's you." She regarded us as a brace, made no distinction: whoever didn't say it was guilty by association. "If I ever catch you down here one more time saying 'MIGHT-COULD,' I'm going to carry it to Miss Duling. You'll be kept in every day for a week! I hope you're both sufficiently ashamed of yourselves?" Saying "might-could" was bad, but saying it in the basement made bad grammar a sin. I knew Presbyterians believed that you could go to Hell.

Mrs. McWillie never scared us into grammar, of course. It was my first-year Latin teacher in high school who made me discover I'd fallen in love with it. It took Latin to thrust me into bona fide alliance with words in their true meaning. Learning Latin (once I was free of Caesar) fed my love for words upon words, words in continuation and modification, and the beautiful, sober, accretion of a sentence. I could see the achieved sentence finally standing there, as real, intact, and built to stay as the Mississippi State Capitol at the top of my street, where I could walk through it on my way to school and hear underfoot the echo of its marble floor, and over me the bell of its rotunda.

On winter's rainy days, the schoolrooms would grow so dark that sometimes you couldn't see the figures on the blackboard. At that point, Mrs. McWillie, that stern fourth-grade teacher, would let her children close their books, and she would move, broad in widow's weeds like darkness itself, to the window and by what light there was she would stand and read aloud "The King of the Golden River." But I was excluded—in the other fourth grade, across the hall. Miss Louella Varnado, my teacher, didn't copy Mrs. McWillie; we had a spelling match: you could spell in the dark. I did not then suspect that there was any other way I could learn the story of "The King of the Golden River" than to have been assigned in the beginning to Mrs. McWillie's cowering fourth grade, then wait for her to treat you to it on the rainy day of her choice. I only now realize how much the treat depended, too, on there not having been money enough to put electric lights in Davis School. John Ruskin had to come in through courtesy of darkness. When in time I found the story in a book and read it to myself, it didn't seem to live up to my longings for a story with that name; as indeed, how could it?

Jackson's Carnegie Library was on the same street where our house was, on the other side of the State Capitol. "Through the Capitol" was the way to go to the Library. You could glide through it on your bicycle or even coast through on roller skates, though without family permission.

I never knew anyone who'd grown up in Jackson without being afraid of Mrs. Calloway, our librarian. She ran the Library absolutely by herself, from the desk where she sat with her back to the books and facing the stairs, her dragon eye on the front door, where who knew what kind of person might come in from the public? SILENCE in big black letters was on signs tacked up everywhere. She herself spoke in her normally commanding voice; every word could be heard all over the Library above a steady seething sound coming from her electric fan; it was the only fan in the Library and stood on her desk, turned directly onto her streaming face.

As you came in from the bright outside, if you were a girl, she sent her strong eyes down the stairway to test you; if she could see through your skirt she sent you straight back home: you could just put on another petticoat if you wanted a book that badly from the public library. I was willing; I would do anything to read.

My mother was not afraid of Mrs. Calloway. She wished me to have my own library card to check out books for myself. She took me in to introduce me and I saw I had met a witch. "Eudora is nine years old and has my permission to read any book she wants from the shelves, children or adult," Mother said. "With the exception of *Elsie Dinsmore*," she added. Later she explained to me that she'd made this rule because Elsie the heroine, being made by her father to practice too long and hard at the piano, fainted and fell off the piano stool. "You're too impressionable, dear," she told me. "You'd read that and the very first thing you'd do, you'd fall off the piano stool." "Impressionable" was a new word. I never hear it yet without the image that comes with it of falling straight off the piano stool.

Mrs. Calloway made her own rules about books. You could not take back a book to the Library on the same day you'd taken it out; it made no difference to her that you'd read every word in it and needed another to start. You could take out two books at a time and two only; this applied as long as you were a child and also for the rest of your life, to my mother as severely as to me. So two by two, I read library books as fast as I could go, rushing them home in the basket of my bicycle. From the minute I reached our house, I started to read. Every book I seized on, from *Bunny Brown and His Sister Sue at Camp Rest-a-While* to *Twenty Thousand Leagues under the Sea*, stood for the devouring wish to read being instantly granted. I knew this was bliss, knew it at the time. Taste isn't nearly so important; it comes in its own time. I wanted to read *immediately*. The only fear was that of books coming to an end.

My mother was very sharing of this feeling of insatiability.

Now, I think of her as reading so much of the time while doing something else. In my mind's eye *The Origin of Species* is lying on the shelf in the pantry under a light dusting of flour—my mother was a bread maker; she'd pick it up, sit by the kitchen window and find her place, with one eye on the oven. I remember her picking up *The Man in Lower Ten* while my hair got dry enough to unroll from a load of kid curlers trying to make me like my idol, Mary Pickford. A generation later, when my brother Walter was away in the Navy and his two little girls often spent the day in our house, I remember Mother reading the new issue of *Time* magazine while taking the part of the Wolf in a game of "Little Red Riding Hood" with the children. She'd just look up at the right time, long enough to answer—in character—"The better to eat you with, my dear," and go back to her place in the war news.

Both our parents had grown up in religious households. In our own family, we children were christened as babies, and were taught our prayers to say at night, and sent as we were growing up to Sunday school, but ours was never a church-going family. At home we did not, like Grandpa Welty, say grace at table. In this way we were variously different from most of the families we knew. On Sundays, Presbyterians were not allowed to eat hot food or read the funnypapers or travel the shortest journey; parents believed in Hell and believed tiny babies could go there. Baptists were not supposed to know, up until their dying day, how to play cards or dance. And so on. We went to the Methodist Episcopal Church South Sunday School, and of course we never saw anything strange about Methodists.

But we grew up in a religious-minded society. Even in high school, pupils were used to answering the history teacher's roll call with a perfectly recited verse from the Bible. (No fair "Jesus wept.")

In the primary department of Sunday school, we little girls rose up in taffeta dresses and hot white gloves, with a nickel for collection embedded inside our palms, and while elastic bands from our Madge Evans hats sawed us under the chin, we sang songs led and exhorted by Miss Hattie. This little lady was a wonder of animation, also dressed up, and she stood next to the piano making wild chopping motions with both arms together, a chairleg off one of our Sunday school chairs in her hand to beat time with, and no matter how loudly we sang, we could always hear her even louder: "Bring them in! Bring them in! Bring them in from the fields of sin! Bring the little ones to Jesus!" Those favorite Methodist hymns all sounded happy and pleased with the world, even though the words ran quite the other way. "Throw out the lifeline! Throw out the lifeline! Someone is sinking today!" went to a cheering tune. "I was sinking deep in sin, Far from the peaceful shore, Very deeply stained within, Sinking to rise no more" made you want to dance, and the chorus—"Love lifted me! Love lifted me! When nothing else would help, Love lifted me!"—would send you leaping. Those hymns set your feet moving like the march played on the piano for us to enter Davis School—"Dorothy, an Old English Dance" was the name of that, and of course so many of the Protestant hymns reached down to us from the same place; they *were* old English rounds and dance tunes, and Charles Wesley and the rest had—no wonder—taken them over.

Evangelists visited Jackson then; along with the Redpath Chautauqua and political speakings, they seemed to be part of August. Gypsy Smith was a great local favorite. He was an evangelist, but the term meant nothing like what it stands for today. He had no "team," no organization, no big business, no public address system; he wasn't a showman. Billy Sunday, a little later on, who preached with the athletics of a baseball player, threw off his coat when he got going, and in his shirt-sleeves and red suspenders, he wound up and pitched his punchlines into the audience.

Gypsy Smith was a real Gypsy; in this may have lain part of his magnetism, though he spoke with sincerity too. He was so persuasive that, as night after night went by, he saved "everybody in Jackson," saved all the well-known businessmen on Capitol Street. They might well have been church-goers already, but they never had been saved by Gypsy Smith. While amalgamated Jackson church choirs sang "Softly and Tenderly Jesus Is Calling" and "Just as I Am," Gypsy Smith called, and being saved—standing up and coming forward—

Chestina Andrews Welty

swept Jackson like an epidemic. Most spectacular of all, the firebrand editor of the evening newspaper rose up and came forward one night. It made him lastingly righteous so that he knew just what to say in the *Jackson Daily News* when one of our fellow Mississippians had the unmitigated gall to publish, and expect other Mississippians to read, a book like *Sanctuary*.

Gypsy Smith may have been a Methodist; I don't know. At any rate, our Sunday school class was expected to attend, but I did not go up to be saved. Though all my life susceptible to anyone on a stage, I never would have been able to hold up my hand in front of the crowd at the City Auditorium and "come forward" while the choir leaned out singing "Come home! Come home! All God's children, come home, come home!" And I never felt anything like the pang of secular longing that I'd felt as a much younger child to go up onto the stage at the Century Theatre when the magician dazzlingly called for the valuable assistance of a child from the audience in the performance of his next feat of magic.

Neither was my father among the businessmen who were saved. As if the whole town were simply going through a temperamental meteorological disturbance, he remained calm and at home on Congress Street.

My mother did too. She liked reading her Bible in her own rocking chair, and while she rocked. She considered herself something of a student. "Run get me my Concordance," she'd say, referring to a little book bound in thin leather, falling apart. She liked to correct herself. Then from time to time her lips would twitch in the stern books of the Bible, such as Romans, providing her as they did with memories of her Grandfather Carden who had been a Baptist preacher in the days when she grew up in West Virginia. She liked to try in retrospect to correct Grandpa too.

I painlessly came to realize that the reverence I felt for the holiness of life is not ever likely to be entirely at home in organized religion. It was later, when I was able to travel farther, that the presence of holiness and mystery seemed, as far as my vision was able to see, to descend into the windows of Chartres, the stone peasant figures in the capitals of Autun, the tall sheets of gold on the walls of Torcello that reflected the light of the sea; in the frescoes of Piero, of Giotto; in the shell of a church wall in Ireland still standing on a floor of sheep-cropped grass with no ceiling other than the changing sky.

I'm grateful that, from my mother's example, I had found the base for this worship—that I had found a love of sitting and reading the Bible for myself and looking up things in it.

How many of us, the South's writers-to-be of my generation, were blessed in one way or another, if not blessed alike, in not having gone deprived of the King James Version of the Bible. Its cadence entered into our ears and our memories for good. The evidence, or the ghost of it, lingers in all our books.

"In the beginning was the Word."

After Sunday school, Daddy might take us children to visit his office. The Lamar Life was in those days housed in a little one-story four-columned Greek temple, next door to the Pythian Castle—a building with crenellations and a high roof that looked as though Douglas Fairbanks might come swinging out of the top window on a rope. On Sunday, nobody else was in Daddy's building, and the water in the cooler was dead quiet too, warm and flat. There was a low mahogany fence around his office with a little gate for people to enter by, and he let us swing on his gate and bounce on the leather davenport while he went over his mail. He put the earphones over my ears to let me discover what I could hear on his dictaphone (I believe he had the first in Jackson). I heard his voice speaking to Miss Montgomery; this was his secretary, who always wore her hair in stylish puffs over her ears, and I had seen her seated at her typewriter while wearing these earphones right on top of her puffs.

He allowed us all our turns to peck at the typewriter. We used the Lamar Life stationery, which carried on its letterhead an oval portrait of Lucius Quintus Cincinnatus Lamar, for whom the Company had been named: a Mississippian who had been a member of Congress, Secretary of the Interior under Cleveland, and a U.S. Supreme Court Justice, a powerful orator who had pressed for the better reconciliation of North and South after the Civil War. Under his bearded portrait we all wrote letters to Mother.

She kept one of Walter's. There wasn't much of it he could

spell, but it said, to help her guess who had written it, "Dear Mrs. C. W. Welty. I think you know me. I think you like me."

I can't think I had much of a sense of humor as long as I remained the only child. When my brother Edward came along after I was three, we both became comics, making each other laugh. We set each other off, as we did for life, from the minute he learned to talk. A sense of the absurd was communicated between us probably before that.

Though he hated to see me reading to myself, he accepted my reading to him as long as it made him laugh. We read the same things over and over, chapters from *Alice*, stretches from *Tom Sawyer*, Edward Lear's "Story of the Four Little Children Who Went Around the World." Whenever we came to the names of the four little children we rang them out in unison—"Violet, Slingsby, Guy, and Lionel!" And fell over. We kept this up at mealtimes, screaming nonsense at each other. My mother would warn us that we were *acting* the fool and would very shortly be asked to leave the table. She wouldn't call one of us a fool, or allow us to do it either. "He who calleth his brother a fool," she'd interrupt us, "is in danger of hell fire." I think she never in her life called anyone a fool, though she never bore one gladly, but she *would* say, "Well, it appears to me that Mrs. So-and-So is the least bit *limited*."

Walter, three years again younger than Edward, was soberer than we. In his long baby dress he looked like a judge. I snatched up his baby bathtub and got behind it and danced for him, to hear him really crow. On the pink bottom of his tub I'd drawn a face with crayons, and all he could see of anybody's being there was my legs prancing under it. Walter wore a little kimono when he was up from acidosis, and, another way of adoring him, Edward tried to teach him to fly off Daddy's chair in his kimono, spreading the sleeves, then cried on the floor with him. Walter grew up to be the most serious in his expression of the three of us, and remained the calmest—the one who most took after our father.

When one of us caught measles or whooping cough and we were isolated in bed upstairs, we wrote notes to each other perhaps on the hour. Our devoted mother would pass them for us, after first running them in a hot oven to kill the germs.

They came into our hands curled up and warm, sometimes scorched, like toast. Edward replied to my funny notes with his funny drawings. He was a born cartoonist.

In the Spanish influenza epidemic, when Edward had high fever in one room and I high fever in another, I shot him off a jingle about the little boy down our street who was in bed with the same thing: "There was a little boy and his name was Lindsey. He went to Heaven with the influenzy." My mother, horrified, told me to be ashamed of myself and refused to deliver it. So I saw we were all pretty sick, though a proper horror, on finding out what heedless written words of mine have really said, had to come later, as it has. But Edward and I and Lindsey all three got well, and so did Mother, who had much the worst case.

All children in those small-town, unhurried days had a vast inner life going on in the movies. Whole families attended together in the evenings, at least once a week, and children were allowed to go without chaperone in the long summer afternoons—schoolmates with their best friends, pairs of little girls trotting on foot the short distance through the park to town under their Japanese parasols.

In devotion to Buster Keaton, Charlie Chaplin, Ben Blue, and the Keystone Kops, my brother Edward and I collapsed in laughter. My sense of making fictional comedy undoubtedly caught its first spark from the antic pantomime of the silent screen, and from having a kindred soul to laugh with.

The silent movies were a source also of words that you might never have learned anywhere else. You read them in the captions. "Jeopardy," for example, I got to know from *Drums of Jeopardy* with Alice Brady, who was wearing a leopard skin, a verbal connection I shall never forget. *The Cabinet of Dr. Caligari* turned up by some strange fluke in place of the Saturday western on the screen of the Istrione Theatre (known as the Eyestrain) where it was seen by an attendance consisting entirely of children. I learned "somnambulist" in terror, a word I still never hear or read without seeing again Conrad Veidt in black tights and bangs, making his way at night alongside a high leaning wall with eyes closed, one arm reaching high, seeing with his fingers. But of course all of us together in the movie had screamed with laughter, laughing at what terrified us, exactly as if it were funny, and exactly as grown-up audiences do today.

Events that weren't quite clear in meaning, things we children were shielded from, seemed to have their own routes, their own streets in town, and you might hear them coming near but then they never came, like the organ grinder with his monkey—surely you'd see him, but then the music went down the other street, and the monkey couldn't find you, though you waited with your penny.

In Davis School days, there lived a little boy two or three streets over from ours who was home sick in bed, and when the circus came to town that year, someone got the parade to march up a different street from the usual way to the Fairgrounds, to go past his house. He was carried to the window to watch it go by. Just for him the ponderous elephants, the plumes, the spangles, the acrobats, the clowns, the caged lion, the band playing, the steam calliope, the whole thing! When not long after that he disappeared forever from our view, having died of what had given him his special privilege, none of this at all was acceptable to the rest of us children. He had been tricked, not celebrated, by the parade's brazen marching up his street with the band playing, and we had somehow been tricked by envying him—betrayed into it.

It is not for nothing that an ominous feeling often attaches itself to a procession. This was when I learned it. "The Pied Piper of Hamelin" had done more than just hint at this. In films and stories we see spectacles forming in the street and parades coming from around the corner, and we know to greet them with distrust and apprehension: their intent is still to be revealed. (Think what it was in "My Kinsman, Major Molineux.")

I never resisted it when, in almost every story I ever wrote, some parade or procession, impromptu or ceremonious, comic or mocking or funereal, has risen up to mark some stage of the story's unfolding. They've started from far back.

We all had something like the same sense of humor. It was in losing our tempers that we were wide apart. Our tempers were all strong and intense. When we children quarreled, my brother Edward, in the terrible position of having to hit either a girl or a baby, yelled the loudest in outrage and was driven to bite. Walter, resourceful and practical in his childish fury as in everything else, was locked into the basement once by Edward who had grown tired of being followed around; but our little brother found the ax and made a good start on chopping himself a hole through the bottom of the door before rescue came.

I didn't hit other people or hit purposefully, I just hit. Some object would be at fault. In one case it was a pin-oak tree in the park which I had climbed all the way up and now couldn't get down. So I screamed and hit it with my head, the only part I could spare, and did my best to have a tantrum, while my family stood below making fun and arguing that nobody could bring me down but me. My anger was at myself, every time, all vanity. As an adolescent I was a slammer of drawers and a packer of suitcases. I was responsible for scenes.

Control came imperfectly to all of us: we reached it at different times of life, frustrated, shot into indignation, by different things—some that are grown out of, and others not.

"I don't understand where you children *get* it," said my mother. "I never lose my temper. I just get hurt." (But that was it.)

One time, and one time only, she told us in a voice that opens a subject to close it, "I believe your father himself had a terrible temper once. But he learned to control his, a long time ago."

We tried to imagine Daddy swinging our ax. We could not, even our precious Walter, who had done it.

Of all my strong emotions, anger is the one least responsible for any of my work. I don't write out of anger. For one thing, simply as a fiction writer, I am minus an adversary—except, of course, that of time—and for another thing, the act of writing in itself brings me happiness.

There was one story that anger certainly lit the fuse of. In the 1960s, in my home town of Jackson, the civil rights leader Medgar Evers was murdered one night in darkness, and I wrote a story that same night about the murderer (his identity then unknown) called "Where Is the Voice Coming From?" But all that absorbed me, though it started as outrage, was the necessity I felt for entering into the mind and inside the skin of a character who could hardly have been more alien or repugnant to me. Trying for my utmost, I wrote it in the first person. I was wholly vaunting the prerogative of the short-story writer. It is always vaunting, of course, to imagine yourself inside another person, but it is what a story writer does in every piece of work; it is his first step, and his last too, I suppose. I'm not sure this story was brought off; and I don't believe that my anger showed me anything about human character that my sympathy and rapport never had.

Even as we grew up, my mother could not help imposing herself between her children and whatever it was they might take it in mind to reach out for in the world. For she would get it for them, if it was good enough for them—she would have to be very sure—and give it to them, at whatever cost to herself: valiance was in her very fibre. She stood always prepared in herself to challenge the world in our place. She did indeed tend to make the world look dangerous, and so it had been to her. A way had to be found around her love sometimes, without challenging *that*, and at the same time cherishing it in its unassailable strength. Each of us children did, sooner or later, in part at least, solve this in a different, respectful, complicated way.

But I think she was relieved when I chose to be a writer of stories, for she thought writing was safe.

II

Learning To See

WHEN WE set out in our five-passenger Oakland touring car on our summer trip to Ohio and West Virginia to visit the two families, my mother was the navigator. She sat at the alert all the way at Daddy's side as he drove, correlating the AAA Blue Book and the speedometer, often with the baby on her lap. She'd call out, "All right, Daddy: '86-point-2, crossroads. Jog right, past white church. Gravel ends.'—And there's the church!" she'd say, as though we had scored. Our road always became her adversary. "This doesn't surprise me at all," she'd say as Daddy backed up a mile or so into our own dust on a road that had petered out. "I could've told you a road that looked like that had little intention of going anywhere."

"It was the first one we'd seen all day going in the right direction," he'd say. His sense of direction was unassailable, and every mile of our distance was familiar to my father by rail. But the way we set out to go was popularly known as "through the country."

My mother's hat rode in the back with the children, suspended over our heads in a pillowcase. It rose and fell with us when we hit the bumps, thumped our heads and batted our ears in an authoritative manner when sometimes we bounced as high as the ceiling. This was 1917 or 1918; a lady couldn't expect to travel without a hat.

Edward and I rode with our legs straight out in front of us over some suitcases. The rest of the suitcases rode just outside the doors, strapped on the running boards. Cars weren't made with trunks. The tools were kept under the back seat and were heard from in syncopation with the bumps; we'd jump out of the car so Daddy could get them out and jack up the car to patch and vulcanize a tire, or haul out the tow rope or the tire chains. If it rained so hard we couldn't see the road in front of us, we waited it out, snapped in behind the rain curtains and playing "Twenty Questions."

My mother was not naturally observant, but she could scrutinize; when she gave the surroundings her attention, it was to verify something—the truth or a mistake, hers or another's. My father kept his eyes on the road, with glances toward the horizon and overhead. My brother Edward periodically stood up in the back seat with his eyelids fluttering while he played the harmonica, "Old Macdonald had a farm" and "Abdul the Bulbul Amir," and the baby slept in Mother's lap and only woke up when we crossed some rattling old bridge. "*There's* a river!" he'd crow to us all. "Why, it certainly *is*," my mother would reassure him, patting him back to sleep. I rode as a hypnotic, with my set gaze on the landscape that vibrated past at twenty-five miles an hour. We were all wrapped by the long ride into some cocoon of our own.

The journey took about a week each way, and each day had my parents both in its grip. Riding behind my father I could see that the road had him by the shoulders, by the hair under his driving cap. It took my mother to make him stop. I inherited his nervous energy in the way I can't stop writing on a story. It makes me understand how Ohio had him around the heart, as West Virginia had my mother. Writers and travelers are mesmerized alike by knowing of their destinations.

And all the time that we think we're getting there so fast, how slowly we do move. In the days of our first car trip, Mother proudly entered in her log, "Mileage today: 161!" with an exclamation mark.

"A Detroit car passed us yesterday." She always kept those logs, with times, miles, routes of the day's progress, and expenses totaled up.

That kind of travel made you conscious of borders; you rode ready for them. Crossing a river, crossing a county line, crossing a state line—especially crossing the line you couldn't see but knew was there, between the South and the North—you could draw a breath and feel the difference.

The Blue Book warned you of the times for the ferries to run; sometimes there were waits of an hour between. With rivers and roads alike winding, you had to cross some rivers three times to be done with them. Lying on the water at the foot of a river bank would be a ferry no bigger than somebody's back porch. When our car had been driven on board

—often it was down a roadless bank, through sliding stones and runaway gravel, with Daddy simply aiming at the two-plank gangway—father and older children got out of the car to enjoy the trip. My brother and I got barefooted to stand on wet, sun-warm boards that, weighted with your car, seemed exactly on the level with the water; our feet were the same as in the river. Some of these ferries were operated by a single man pulling hand over hand on a rope bleached and frazzled as if made from cornshucks.

I watched the frayed rope running through his hands. I thought it would break before we could reach the other side.

"No, it's not going to break," said my father. "It's never broken before, has it?" he asked the ferry man.

"No sirree."

"You see? If it never broke before, it's not going to break this time."

His general belief in life's well-being worked either way. If you had a pain, it was "Have you ever had it before? You have? It's not going to kill you, then. If you've had the same thing before, you'll be all right in the morning."

My mother couldn't have more profoundly disagreed with that.

"You're such an optimist, dear," she often said with a sigh, as she did now on the ferry.

"You're a good deal of a pessimist, sweetheart."

"I certainly *am*."

And yet I was well aware as I stood between them with the water running over my toes, he the optimist was the one who was prepared for the worst, and she the pessimist was the daredevil: he the one who on our trip carried chains and a coil of rope and an ax all upstairs to our hotel bedroom every night in case of fire, and she the one—before I was born—when there *was* a fire, had broken loose from all hands and run back—on crutches, too—into the burning house to rescue her set of Dickens which she flung, all twenty-four volumes, from the window before she jumped out after them, all for Daddy to catch.

"I make no secret of my lifelong fear of the water," said my mother, who on ferry boats remained inside the car, clasping the baby to her—my brother Walter, who was destined to prowl the waters of the Pacific Ocean in a minesweeper.

As soon as the sun was beginning to go down, we went more slowly. My father would drive sizing up the towns, inspecting the hotel in each, deciding where we could safely spend the night. Towns little or big had beginnings and ends, they reached to an edge and stopped, where the country began again as though they hadn't happened. They were intact and to themselves. You could see a town lying ahead in its whole, as definitely formed as a plate on a table. And your road entered and ran straight through the heart of it; you could see it all, laid out for your passage through. Towns, like people, had clear identities and your imagination could go out to meet them. You saw houses, yards, fields, and people busy in them, the people that had a life where they were. You could hear their bank clocks striking, you could smell their bakeries. You would know those towns again, recognize the salient detail, seen so close up. Nothing was blurred, and in passing along Main Street, slowed down from twenty-five to twenty miles an hour, you didn't miss anything on either side. Going somewhere "through the country" acquainted you with the whole way there and back.

My mother never fully gave in to her pleasure in our trip—for pleasure every bit of it was to us all—because she knew we were traveling with a loaded pistol in the pocket on the door of the car on Daddy's side. I doubt if my father fired off any kind of gun in his life, but he could not have carried his family from Jackson, Mississippi to West Virginia and Ohio through the country, unprotected.

This was not the first time I'd been brought here to visit Grandma in West Virginia, but the first visit I barely remembered. Where I stood now was inside the house where my mother had been born and where she grew up. It was a low, gray-weathered wooden house with a broad hall through the middle of it with the light of day at each end, the house that Ned Andrews, her father, had built to stand on the very top of the highest mountain he could find.

"And here's where I first began to read my Dickens,"

Mother said, pointing. "Under that very bed. Hiding my candle. To keep them from knowing what I was up to all night."

"But where did it all *come* from?" I asked her at last. "All that Dickens?"

"Why, Papa gave me that set of Dickens for agreeing to let them cut off my hair," she said, as if surprised that a reason like that wouldn't have occurred to me. "In those days, they thought very long thick hair like mine would sap a child's strength. I said *No!* I wanted my hair left the very way it was. They offered me gold earrings first—in those days little girls often developed a wish to have their ears pierced and fitted with little gold rings. I said *No!* I'd rather keep my hair. Then Papa said, 'What about books? I'll have them send a whole set of Charles Dickens to you, right up the river from Baltimore, in a barrel.' I agreed."

Ned Andrews had been the county's youngest member of the bar. He quickly made a name for himself on the side as an orator. When he gave the dedicatory address for the opening of a new courthouse in Nicholas County, West Virginia, my mother put away a copy. He is praising the architecture of the building: "The student turns with a sigh of relief from the crumbling pillars and columns of Athens and Alexandria to the symmetrical and colossal temples of the New World. As time eats from the tombstones of the past the epitaphs of primeval greatness, and covers the pyramids with the moss of forgetfulness, she directs the eye to the new temples of art and progress that make America the monumental beacon-light of the world."

People may have expected the highfalutin in oratory in those days, but they might not have expected Ned's courtroom flair. There was a murder trial of a woman given to fortunetelling. She had been overheard reading in an old man's cards that his days were numbered. When, the very next day, this old man had been found in his bed dead from a gunshot wound, it appeared to the public that that fortuneteller might have known too much about it. She was put on trial for murder. Ned Andrews' defense centered on the well-known fact that the old man kept his loaded gun mounted at all times over the head of his bed. This was the gun that had shot him. The old man could have discharged it perfectly easily himself, Ned argued, by carelessly bouncing on the bed a little bit. He proposed to prove it, and invited the jury of dubious mountaineers to watch him do it. Leading them all the way up the mountain to the old man's cabin, he mounted the gun in place on its rests, having first loaded it with blank shells, and while they watched he mimicked the old man and made a running jump onto the bed. The gun jarred loose, tumbled down, and fired at him. He rested his case. The fortuneteller was without any more ado declared not guilty.

He was brim full of talents. He'd attended Trinity College (later, Duke University) where he organized a literary society; he'd been a journalist and a photographer in Norfolk, Virginia, and in West Virginia where he'd run away to, to seek adventure, he'd turned into a lawyer. He seems to have been a legendary fisherman in those mountain streams, is still now and then referred to in local sportsmen's tales. Ned was impervious to the sting of bees and could always be summoned to capture a wild swarm. Ned was the one they sent for when someone fell down an empty well, because he was not afraid to harness himself and be lowered into the deathly gasses at the bottom and bring the unconscious victim up again.

Yet the human failings Mother could least forgive in other people, she regarded with only tenderness in him. I gathered—slowly and over the years I gathered—that sometimes he drank. He told tall tales to his wife, Eudora Carden. He told one to begin with, in order to marry her, saying he was of age to do so, when he was nineteen and four years younger than she. She was superstitious; he loved to tease her with tricks, to stage elaborate charades with the connivance of one of his little boys, that preyed on her fear of ghosts. He shocked her with a tale—Mother said there was nothing to prove it wasn't a fact—that one of the Andrews ancestors had been hanged in Ireland. Eudora Carden came from the home of a strongly dedicated Baptist preacher, and about all preachers he was irreverent and irrepressible. I have seen photographs he took of her—tintypes; it's clear that he took them with great care to show how beautiful he found her. In one she is standing up behind a chair, with her long hands crossed at the wrist over the back of it; she is dressed in her best, with her dark hair drawn high above her oval face and tucked with a flower that looks like a wild rose. She is very young. She has long gray eyes over high cheekbones; she is gazing to the front, looking straight at him. Her mouth is sensitive, her lips youthfully full. She told her daughter Chessie years later that she was objecting to his taking this picture because she was pregnant at the time, and the pose—the crossed hands on the back of a chair—had been to hide that. (With my mother herself, I wondered, her first child?) When she came back from the well on cold mornings, her hands would be bleeding from breaking the ice on it: this is what my mother would remember when she looked at those soft hands in the tintypes.

I don't know from whom it came or to whom it was passed, but at one time an old, home-made drawing of the Andrews family tree came into my mother's hands. It was rolled up; if unrolled it was capable of rattling shut the next instant. The tree was drawn as a living tree, spreading from a rooted trunk, every branch, twig, and leaf in clear outline, all with names and dates on them in a copperplate handwriting. The most riveting feature was the thick branch stemming from near the base of the main trunk: it was broken off short to a jagged end, branchless and leafless, and labeled "Joseph, Killed by lightning."

It had been executed with the finest possible pen in ink grown very pale, as if it had been drawn in watered maple syrup. The leaves weren't stiffly drawn or conventional ellipses, all alike, but each one daintily fashioned with a pointed tip and turned on its stem this way or that, as if this family tree were tossed by a slight breeze. The massed whole had the look, at that time to me, of a children's puzzle in which you were supposed to find your mother. I found mine—only a tiny leaf on a twig of a branch near the top, hardly big enough to hold her tiny name.

The Andrews branch my mother came from represents the mix most usual in the Southeast—English, Scottish, Irish, with a dash of French Huguenot. The first American one, Isham, who fought in the Revolutionary War, was born in Virginia and moved to Georgia, where succeeding generations lived. The Andrewses were not a rural clan, like the Weltys; they lived in towns, were educators and preachers, with some

My mother's mother, Eudora Carden Andrews. Photograph of a tintype made by Edward Raboteau Andrews, in West Virginia, c. 1882

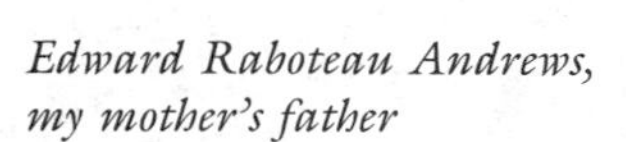

Edward Raboteau Andrews, my mother's father

Methodist circuit riders; one cousin of Ned's (Walter Hines Page) was an ambassador to England. Trinity College educated some of them, including, for an impatient time, young Ned. By the time my mother's father, Edward Raboteau Andrews (Ned) was born in 1862, the family had returned to Virginia. He broke from the mold and at eighteen ran away from a home of parents, grandparents, sisters, brothers, and aunts in Norfolk to become the first West Virginian.

Here in the center of the Andrews kitchen, at the same long table where the family always ate, not too far from where Grandma seemed to be always busy at the warm stove, Ned had sat and worked up his cases for the defense in Clay Courthouse, far below and out of sight straight down the mountain. Mother remembered him transposing band music there, too; he had sent off for the instruments, got together a band, and proceeded to teach them to play in concert, lined up on the courthouse lawn: he had a strong need of music. His children had an instrument to learn to play too: he assigned my mother the cornet. (When I think back to how she sang "Blessed Assurance" while washing the dishes, I realize she flatted her high notes just where a child's cornet might.)

It was in the quilted bed in the front room of this house where he lay in so much pain (probably from the affliction that brought on his death, an infected appendix) that he once told Mother, a little girl, to bring the kitchen knife and plunge it into his side; she, hypnotized, almost believed she must obey. It was from that door that later she went with him on the frozen winter night when it was clear he had to get, somehow, to a hospital. The mountain roads were impassable, there was ice in the Elk River: but a neighbor vowed he could make way by raft. She was fifteen. Leaving her mother and the five little brothers at home, Chessie went with him. Her father lay on the raft, on which a fire had been lit to warm him, Chessie beside him. The neighbor managed to pole the raft through the icy river and eventually across it to a railroad. They flagged the train. (It seems likely that the place they flagged it was the same as where my mother and I were let off that train when I was three, arriving on that nearly forgotten visit. It was an early summer dawn; everything was a cloud of mist—we were standing on the bank of a river and I didn't know it. When my mother pulled the rope of an iron bell, we watched a boat come out of the mist to meet us, with her five brothers all inside.)

Mother had to return by herself from Baltimore, her father's body in a coffin on the same train. He had died on the operating table in Johns Hopkins, of a ruptured appendix, at thirty-seven years of age. The last lucid remark he'd made to my mother was "If you let them tie me down, I'll die." (The surgeon had come out where she stood waiting in the hall. "Little girl," he'd said, "you'd better get in touch now with somebody in Baltimore." "Sir, I don't know anybody in Baltimore," she said, and what she never forgot was his astounded reply: "You don't know anybody in *Baltimore*?")

It was from this house that my mother very soon after that piled up her hair and went out to teach in a one-room school, mountain children little and big alike. The first day, some fathers came along to see if she could whip their children, some who were older than she. She told the children that she did intend to whip them if they became unruly and refused to learn, and invited the fathers to stay if they liked and she'd be able to whip them too. Having been thus tried out, she was a great success with them after that. She left home every day on her horse; since she had the river to cross, a little brother rode on her horse behind her, to ride him home, while she rowed across the river in a boat. And he would be there to meet her with her horse again at evening. All this way, to pass the time, she told me, she recited the poems in McGuffey's Readers out loud.

She could still recite them in full when she was lying helpless and nearly blind, in her bed, an old lady. Reciting, her voice took on resonance and firmness, it rang with the old fervor, with ferocity even. She was teaching me one more, almost her last, lesson: emotions do not grow old. I knew that I would feel as she did, and I do.

Teaching, my mother earned, little by little, money enough to go to nearby Marshall College in the summers and in time was graduated. Her mind was filled with *Paradise Lost*, she told me later, showing me the notebook she still kept with its diagrams. It was as a schoolteacher she'd met my father, Christian Welty, a young man from Ohio, who had come to work that summer in the office of a lumber company in the vicinity. While they courted, they used to take long walks up and down the railroad tracks, which I imagine my father found in themselves romantic—they took snapshots of each other, my father with one foot on a milepost, my mother sitting on a stile with an open book and wearing a "fascinator" over her hair. My father had her snap his picture standing on a moving sidecar, his hand at the lever. It was in leaving this house that she married him and set off for a new life and a new part of the world for both of them, in Jackson, Mississippi.

Mother's brothers were called "the boys." Their long-necked banjos hung on pegs along the wide hall, as casually as hats and coats. Coming in from outdoors, Carl and Mose lifted their banjos off the wall and sat down side by side and struck in. This was what I remembered from my early visit; I had till now forgotten. They played together like soulmates. At age three, I'd cried "Two Carls!" They sang in the same perfect beat, perfect unison, "Frog Went A-Courting and He Did Ride."

That effortless, drumlike rhythm, heard in double, too, would have put a claim on any child. They had a repertoire of ballads and country songs and rousing hymns. My mother would tell her brothers, plead with them, to stop—I didn't want to go to bed. "Aw, Sister, let Girlie have her one more song," and one song could keep going without loss of a beat into still one more.

The boys liked to sing together too, all five, without accompaniment. Gus, the heaviest, with his broad chest, dominated the others with a bass down to his toes. Those old hymns they'd grown up with, coming out chorus after chorus, sounded more and more uproarious, especially sung outdoors. "Roll, Jordan, Roll" would fill the air around them and roll back on them from the next mountain in echoes, as if the mountain were full of singers like blackbirds in a pie, just waiting for the song to let them out.

I don't suppose now that my mother ever thought of her father in any other light than the one she saw him in when she was a little girl—for he didn't live much beyond then. All I was given to know of him myself is her same childlike vision, uncorrectable—half of it adoring dream, half brutal memory of his death, the part of his story that she, all by herself, was the one able to tell. Her brothers were all too little to have kept a clear memory of him at all; they remembered his songs best, remembered him when *they* sang, and told how he made up more and more verses to "Where Have You Been, Billy Boy?" putting his own rambunctious words to the tune. What they remember is what the stories tell about him, and what they could see lay in their mother.

What did my father, Christian Welty, think of all these stories of her father my mother told? I never knew. My father was his very opposite, all that was stable, reticent, self-contained, willing to be patient if need be, and, in all *he* said, factual. Before the birth of my brothers, when my mother and I went up on the train alone, my father would come at the end of our visit to shepherd us home. Perhaps I remembered this without too much understanding, but I was not too much of a baby to notice and remember how different it was when my father arrived on the scene. A difference came over whatever we were doing, like a change in the wind.

The fact was my mother and I were the only ones really dying to see him come. Of course he was older than they, the brothers—six years older than Chessie, their older sister—and he was a Yankee, but I came to realize later what must have been the real reason for the polite distance they put into their welcome: ever since he'd first come courting, they'd known he was only here to take their sister away from them.

It was in this house they saw their sister married. Mother's brothers never in my memory called my father other than "Mr. Welty," and certainly they didn't then, on their wedding day; Moses, the youngest, went out and "cried on the ground." The newlyweds left on the train for the World's Fair and Louisiana Purchase Centennial Exposition that had opened (a year late) in St. Louis. It was October 1904. They would then go on to Jackson, Mississippi, and the future. My mother thought it was ill-becoming to brag about your courage; the nearest she came was to say, "Yes, I expect I was pretty venturesome."

It must have seemed to her family behind her that she had been cut off from them forever. They never really got over her absence from home.

I don't think she ever really got over it either. I think she could listen sometimes and hear the mountain's voice—the delayed echo of the unseen and distant old man—"just an old hermit," said Grandma—chopping wood with his ax and calling on God in alternation, in answering blows; the prattling of the Queen's Shoals in Elk river somewhere below, equally out of sight, which I believed I could hear from Grandma's front-yard rocking chair, though I was told that I must be listening to something else; the loss and recovery of traveling sound, the *carrying* of the voice that called as if on long threads the hand could hold to, so I would keep asking who that was, who was still out of sight but calling in the mountains as he neared us, as we brought him near.

I think when my mother came to Jackson she brought West Virginia with her. Of course, I brought some of it with me too.

For as long as she lived, letters went back and forth every day between my grandmother and my mother. Grandma always had to concern herself with her letters getting carried down the mountain to the Court House to make the train.

> Dear Chessie, I wrote to you last night but did not give it to Gus this morning as I thought Carl would be sure to go to the C.H. and as he had letters of his own to mail would not be likely to forget. He had his overcoat on to go before dinner but I told him that dinner was ready and after we had started to eat Moses came in and said the dog was after a fox and all of the boys left as soon as they were through dinner and here is my letter and I hear the train now so it will not go. It stopped raining last night and today it has been snowing part of the time and blowing nearly all of the time and so dark and gloomy looking that I only sit by the fire. I wish you had a half dozen of my chickens. I killed three last week for the boys to take to school. I do wish I could step in a while and see you and as I cannot I think I will take a nap. With lots of love from Mother.

and

> . . . Carl is writing letters to different ones that he thinks might come to school, Gus and Moses are playing on their banjoes as Eudora would say, I do not know what John is doing, he is in the other room . . . Say, do you believe that two pigeons could be sent from here to Eudora say in April or do you think they could not go without some one being along to take care of them. She would like them for they would fly all around her and eat out of her hand if she would let them. We are all well and do hope you are all well, with lots of love from Mother, and kiss Baby.

and one on a November 4:

> My dear child, I received no letter yesterday but had expected to start one to you this morning but failed. I had thought I would walk to the C.H. and started to get ready. It is a beautiful day overhead, you cannot see a cloud and yet the wind is fearful. I have nearly finished my looming [?], scrubbed the dining room and kitchen, picked up three or four bushels of walnuts, I washed yesterday and found two hen's nests with sixteen eggs in them. I told Gus I had saved 75¢ or a dollar and made a quarter, as eggs are 25¢ a dozen . . . The boys have started to school and I believe they will learn, they both seem pleased with their Teacher. Maggie Keeney's fourth sister is teaching the lower room. Maggie Cora and Mattie as you may know are married, that leaves Hester and this one to teach. Gus said last night that one of Clay's teachers died yesterday, a bright young man. I wish I was able to do with my hands as fast as I find jobs to do, and maybe I could set things straight but I cannot do that. I am lonely enough but if you and baby could walk in sometime to see Grandma I would do all right but I hope both and all three of you keep well, with a heart full of love from Mother.

This is a letter she wrote to me:

> My dear Eudora Alice, I do wish I could go on the choo choo train and see you and be at your little party, I

> would bring you two pretty little pigeons, for I know both you and your little friends would enjoy having them, but as I cannot go nor send the little pigeons, I am going to the Court House this morning and see if I can send you a little cup of sugar you can eat and think of Grandma. I hope you will have a nice time and be well. With lots of love from Grandma. P.S. Tell your Ma I will write to her next time.

Such were my mother's component parts.

Grandma had thought my agitation and apprehension of her over-familiar pigeons was love. I can see now that perhaps she was right.

That summer, lying in the long grass with my head propped against the back of a saddle, with the zenith above me and the drop of distance below, I listened to the mountain silence until I could hear as far into it as the faintest clink of a cowbell. In the mountains, what might be out of sight had never really gone away. Like the mountain, that distant bell would always be there. It would keep reminding.

It took the mountain top, it seems to me now, to give me the sensation of independence. It was as if I'd discovered something I'd never tasted before in my short life. Or rediscovered it—for I associated it with the taste of the water that came out of the well, accompanied with the ring of that long metal sleeve against the sides of the living mountain, as from deep down it was wound up to view brimming and streaming long drops behind it like bright stars on a ribbon. It thrilled me to drink from the common dipper. The coldness, the far, unseen, unheard springs of what was in my mouth now, the iron strength of its flavor that drew my cheeks in, its fern-laced smell, all said mountain mountain mountain as I swallowed. Every swallow was making me a part of being here, sealing me in place, with my bare feet planted on the mountain and sprinkled with my rapturous spills. What I felt I'd come here to do was something on my own.

My mother adored her brothers, "the boys," and she was their heart. One day she and the boys, taking me along, were dawdling down the mountain path and talking family together. I thought I'd take off on a superior track I saw for myself, and the next moment I was flying down it, straight down, then falling, rolling and tumbling, gathering dust and leaves in my clothes and hair, and I could hear a long rip coming in my skirt without being able to stop until some bush caught hold of me. I got to my feet and looked back up. It wasn't far, but my mother and the boys might have been standing over the rim of the moon: they were laughing at me, my mother along with the boys, helplessly laughing. One of my uncles dropped down to me and carried me up again. I went back with them, riding on his shoulders. The boys, though not my mother now, were still teasing, and I was aloft up there, hanging my head or holding it up—I can't be sure now.

"Well, now Girlie's learned what a log chute is," said Uncle Carl, putting me down in front of Grandma as if to let her in on the family joke. Her gesture then was the last other thing I remembered from being here before: with her forefinger she pushed my hair behind my ears and bared my face to hers. She looked seriously right into my eyes. Hadn't we come right to the point of our both being named Eudora?

"Run take that little dress of yours off, and Grandma'll sew up the hole in it right quick," she said. Then she looked from me to my mother and back. I learned on our trip what that look meant: it was matching family faces.

The Cardens had been in West Virginia for a while—I believe were there before West Virginia was a state. Eudora Carden's own mother had been Eudora Ayres, of an Orange County, Virginia, family, the daughter of a Huguenot mother and an English father. He was a planter, fairly well-to-do. Eudora Ayres married another young Virginian, William Carden, who was poor and called a "dreamer"; and when these two innocents went to start life in the wild mountainous country, in the unknown part that had separated itself from Virginia, among his possessions he brought his leather-covered Latin dictionary and grammar, and she brought her father's wedding present of five slaves. The dictionary was forever kept in the tiny farmhouse and the slaves were let go. One of the stark facts of their lives in Enon is that during the Civil War Great-

My grandmother, Eudora Carden Andrews, seated in the chair, with five of her six children: my mother and, left to right, John, Moses, Carl, and Edward Columbus (Bus). At their mountain-top home near Clay, West Virginia

On our summer trip.
A road through the Mississippi Delta, c. 1917

Grandfather Carden was taken prisoner and incarcerated in Ohio on suspicion of being, as a Virginian, a Confederate sympathizer, and lost his eyesight in confinement.

Their son, Mother's Grandpa Carden, was a Baptist preacher. Enon-near-Gilboa was the name of his church—taken from the Bible, of course; Gilboa, on the mountain as in the Bible, was the older church it was near to. This was where Eudora Carden and four brothers were born, and where later the Andrews children spent a great deal of their time. He was an enormously strict and vigorous-minded old man.

When his first wife died, leaving him a young man with little children, Grandpa did what so many did then: he sent back to Virginia for her sister. Then, after an interval, he married her. My mother, at a young and knowing age, once praised her to her face for her unselfishness in coming from Virginia and marrying Grandpa for the sake of his motherless children, and the old lady replied tartly, "Who says that's why I married him?"

My mother and the boys spent a lot of time visiting Grandpa and Grandma Carden. This good old man liked to retire to the barn to say his bedtime prayers, where he could thunder them up as he pleased, to the rafters. Mother's little brothers used to delight in hiding in the hay where they could listen to Grandpa pray, and he on his side would be sure to get all their names in when he was asking for forgiveness and beg the Lord to be patient with them, whatever had been their sinful ways, and lead them into righteousness *before it was too late.*

Sometimes at our house, when my mother read the Bible in her rocking chair by the fire, she'd hail a passage to read out oratorically. "I'm just so strongly reminded of Grandpa Carden when I come to Romans," she'd say.

She'd been pretty lively toward Grandpa in her own youth. "I don't agree with Saint Paul," she'd told him once: it was in connection with the rule of wearing a hat to church.

In our picture of Grandpa Carden, his long beard and side whiskers are pure white, and seem to be stirred by some mountain wind. His large black hat is resting upside-down on his knee as he sits on a straight-back bench. His right hand is holding, straight up and down and thin as a rod, his staff; it looks four or five feet tall. The photograph is inscribed across the back in a strict hand, "To Chessie, if she will have it."

Those had been early days. I tend to think that it had been Ned Andrews who saw himself in West Virginia as some original pioneer; he was the lone romantic in this story. He might have delighted in imagining the figure he'd cut to them back in Tidewater Virginia. (They *did* wonder at him: I grew to know the Virginia kin, his remarkable mother and his sisters who, when they knew, rallied around young Chessie and all Ned's family.)

His fine-grained wife lived on as a woman of unceasing courage and of considerable grace, with a great deal to make the best of. In the eyes of all their devoted children, and in every word I ever heard them say, it appeared that neither of their parents could ever have done conscious wrong or made an irretrievable mistake in their lives. When their mother died, the boys came down from the mountain. They married and made their own lives—except for John, who died of pneumonia after enlisting in the Army in 1918—in teaching, banking, civic or business affairs below. Carl became mayor of Charleston. They never let go of the home place. It was kept up as a family retreat, a camp for hunting and fishing. My mother and her brothers were able to visit each other, not only in times of trouble or crisis. It became comparatively easy, one day, after all.

It seems likely to me now that the very element in my character that took possession of me there on top of the mountain, the fierce independence that was suddenly mine, to remain inside me no matter how it scared me when I tumbled, was an inheritance. Indeed it was my chief inheritance from my mother, who was braver. Yet, while she knew that independent spirit so well, it was what she so agonizingly tried to protect me from, in effect to warn me against. It was what we shared, it made the strongest bond between us and the strongest tension. To grow up is to fight for it, to grow old is to lose it after having possessed it. For her, too, it was most deeply connected to the mountains.

When she was old, widowed, ill, and losing her sight, my

mother one day announced to me she would be very glad to have the piano back in our house. It was the Steinway upright she had bought for me when I was nine, so far beyond her means, and had paid for herself out of the housekeeping money, which she added to by buying a Jersey cow, milking her, and selling part of the milk to the neighbors on our street, in quart bottles which I delivered on my bicycle. While I sat on the piano stool practicing my scales, I imagined my mother sitting on her stool in the cowshed, her fingers just as rhythmically pulling the teats of Daisy.

Two of her children had played this piano, I practicing my lessons and my brother Edward all along playing better by ear. When her grand-daughters came along, the piano was sent to their house to practice their lessons on. Now, all those years later, Mother wanted it under her roof again. Right now! It was brought and, the same day, tuned. She asked me to go directly to it and play for her "The West Virginia Hills."

I sat down and remembered how it went, and as I played I heard her singing it—singing it to herself, just as she used to while washing the dishes after supper:

> O the West Virginia hills!
> How my heart with rapture thrills . . .
> O the hills! Beautiful hills! . . .

This one moment seemed to satisfy her. Once from her wheelchair, afterwards, she tried to pick it out herself, laying her finger slowly down on keys she couldn't really see. "A mountaineer," she announced to me proudly, as though she had never told me this before and now I had better remember it, "always will be *free*."

"Oh yes, we're in the North now," said my mother after we'd crossed the state line from West Virginia into Ohio. "The barns are all bigger than the houses. They care more about the horses and cows than they do about—" She forbore to say.

The farm my father grew up on, where Grandpa Welty and Grandma lived, was in southern Ohio in the rolling hills of Hocking County, near the small town of Logan. It was one of the neat, narrow-porched, two-story farmhouses, painted white, of the Pennsylvania-German country. Across its front grew feathery cosmos and barrel-sized peony bushes with stripy heavy-scented blooms pushing out of the leaves. There was a springhouse to one side, down a little walk only one brick in width, and an old apple orchard in front, the barn and the pasture and fields of corn and wheat behind. Periodically there came sounds from the barn, and you could hear the crows, but everything else was still.

In the house it was solid stillness, it seemed to me, at almost any hour, all day, except for dinnertime. Whoever was in the house seemed to remain invisible, but this was because they were all busy. I think in retrospect that my father had set our visit in time to help with the harvest, and certainly he was very busy outside all day. He let my brother Edward go with him.

My mother, in the way she had, never put aside her *first* impression of Grandpa Welty. She was hurt when he had met the train in the spring wagon, not the buggy. All the way home to the farm, he never started a conversation with her. "But that was his *custom*," years later she explained to me. "He never brought out much to say till I was ready to go. Then on my last day, on the long ride to the station, he never stopped talking at all. He talked up one blue streak." They took to each other enormously.

Throughout our visit, as long as the daylight held, he was out stirring about the barn or moving through the fields. He was a quiet, gentle man, with a flourishing mustache, with not much to say to the women and children in his house; when he did sit down, it would be in his wooden platform swing outside, usually with his pipe and holding one of the farm kittens on his knee. Now and then he held me there, and then I could hold the kitten.

My grandmother Welty was my father's stepmother. My mother would remark, "There's one thing I will have to say about Mother Welty: she makes the best *bread* I ever put in my mouth." It really is the only thing I can remember she ever said about Grandma Welty, though she did feel often compelled to repeat it, and never said anything different after the old lady died.

Grandma Welty, with each work day in the week set firmly

aside for a single task, was not very expectant of conversation either. Of course I remember Friday best—baking day. Her pies, enough for a week, were set to cool when done on the kitchen windowsills, side by side like so many cheeky faces telling us "One at a time!"

Like the hub that would make the dinner table go round, if it ever could start, was a tulip-shaped glass in the center in which the bright-polished teaspoons, all the largest family could ever need, stood facing in with their backs turned. I don't believe this spoonholder ever left the table. Even in the dark diningroom at midnight in the sleeping house, it would stand ready there. The smell of all those loaves of bread and the row of pies didn't easily go away either. And in the parlor where the blinds were drawn, the smell of being unvisited would pervade, pervade, pervade.

Compared to the Andrews clan, the Welty family at the time of the first visit I remember was very scarce in the way of uncles and cousins and kin of an older generation. Grandpa, Jefferson Welty, had been the youngest of thirteen children, but he is the only one I ever saw; his parents were Christian and Salome Welty, early settlers in Marion Township, Hocking County. The Weltys were originally German Swiss; the first ones to come to this country, back before the Revolutionary War here, were three brothers, and the whole family is descended from them, I understand—it seems to hark back to German fairy-tale tradition.

My father is not the one who told me this: he never happened to tell us a single family story; could it have been because he'd heard so many of the Andrews stories? I think it was rather because, as he said, he had no interest in ancient history—only the future, he said, should count. At the same time, he was exceedingly devoted to his father, went to see him whenever he could, and wrote to him regularly from his desk at home; I grew up familiar with seeing the long envelopes being addressed in my father's clear, careful hand: Jefferson Welty, Esquire. It was the only use my father made of the word; he saved it for his father. I took "Esquire" for a term of reverence, and I think it stood for that with him; we were always aware that Daddy loved him.

An English Welti, who spelled his name thus with an *i*,

wrote to me once from Kent, in curiosity, after an early book of mine had appeared over there; he asked me about my name. My father, who had never told us anything, had died, and this was before my mother set herself as she did later to looking into records. Mr. Welti knew about the whole throng of them, from medieval times on, and the three brothers who set forth to the New World from German Switzerland and settled from Virginia westward over Pennsylvania, Ohio, and Indiana before the Revolutionary War. "I expect you know," wrote the British Mr. Welti, "that one unfortunate Welty fell at Saratoga."

The only part of his letter that would have interested my father is that about the St. Gotthard Tunnel and the Welty who pushed it through. The fact that this same Welty had been President of Switzerland seven times running would have caused him to say "Pshaw!", his strongest expletive. (That my mother's strongest exclamation was "Pshaw!" too rather took away some of its force for both of them.)

In Grandpa and Grandma's parlor stood the organ, which, my mother had whispered to me, they preferred not to hear played. I tiptoed around it as if it were asleep. There were steep, uphill pedals; the flowered carpet continued right on up them as if they were part of the floor. When opened, the organ gave off a smell sharp as an exclamation, as if opening it were a mistake in company manners, which I already knew. I chilled my finger by touching a key. The key did not yield. The whole keyboard withstood me as if it had been a kitchen table; I suppose the organ had to be pumped.

But either I had been told, or I got the feeling there and then that this organ had belonged to my father's real mother, who had died when he was a little boy. But when I was named Eudora for my Andrews grandmother, I had been named for this grandmother too. Alice was my middle name. Her name had been Allie. Too late, after I was already christened, it came out that Allie stood for not Alice but Almira. Her name had been remembered wrong. I imagined what that would have done to her. It seemed to me to have made her an orphan. That was worse to me than if I had been able to imagine dying.

Barefooted on the slick brick walk I rushed to where I could breathe in the cool breath from the interior of the spring-house. On a cold bubbling spring, covered dishes and crocks and pitchers of butter and milk and so on floated in a circle in the mild whirlpool, like horses on a merry-go-round, in the water that smelled of the mint that grew close by.

Or I ran to the barn where all you touched was warm. Grandpa's barn *was* bigger than his house. The doors had to be rolled back. It had a plank floor like a bridge that came to an end at the wall and another door. The barn was fuller of furnishings than the house, with barrels and tubs and crates and sacks piled on top of one another, odorous of all the different things they held. There was more to see, more to smell, more to climb on; nothing appeared to be forbidden. At times when the animals were down in the pasture, I could hear the dry seedcorn I let run through my fingers in the waiting stillness. After the animals had been led inside, now and then a horse's head would appear looking over the door of his stall. Then I played nearby, to give the head a chance to speak to me, like Falada the white horse's head nailed above the gate in the fairy tale. Falada says to the Goose Girl driving her geese, "Princess, Princess, passing by, / Alas, alas, if thy mother knew it, / Sadly, sadly her heart would rue it." Up in the loft, jumping wild in the new hay, I skinned through the hole in the floor, the way it went down when it was tossed to the trough below, and the trough caught me neatly. My brother Edward, not missing a jump overhead, didn't even know I'd gone.

There was an old buggy being used for hens to nest in, standing in the shadows of the barn. The shiny black buggy next to it, with a fringe on top, was the one in which Grandpa drove us to church. He allowed me to stand between his knees and hold the reins, even though I could not see over the horse's too-busy tail where we were going. But standing up on the back seat, I could see, squinting through the peephole window at the back, where the narrow wheels on a rainy Sunday sliced the road to chocolate ribbons. I got to hear Grandpa's voice on Sunday more than in all the rest of the week, because he sang in the choir; indeed, Grandpa led the choir.

•

At the end of the day at Grandpa's house, there wasn't much talking and no tales were told, even for the first time. Sometimes we all sat listening to a music box play.

There was a rack pulled out from inside the music box; we could see it holding shining metal discs as large as silver waiters, with teeth around the edges, and pierced with tiny holes in the shape of triangles or stars, like the tissue-paper patterns by which my mother cut out cloth for my dresses. When the discs began to turn, taking hold by their little teeth, a strange, chimelike music came about.

Its sounds had no kinship with those of "His Master's Voice" that we could listen to at home. They were thin and metallic, not exactly keeping to time—rather as if the spoons in the spoonholder had started a quiet fretting among themselves. Whatever song it was was slow and halting and remote, as if the music box were playing something I knew as well as "Believe Me If All Those Endearing Young Charms" but did not intend me to recognize. It seemed to be reaching the parlor from far away. It might even have been the sound going through the rooms and up and down the stairs of our house in Jackson at night while all of us were here in Ohio, too far from home even to hear the clock striking from the downstairs hall. While we listened, there at the open window, the moonflowers opened little by little, and the song continued like a wire spring allowing itself slowly, slowly to uncoil, then just stopped trying. Music and moonflower might have been geared to move together.

Then, in my father's grown-up presence, I could not imagine him as a child in this house, the sober way he looked in the little daguerreotype, motherless in his fair bangs and heavy little shoes, sitting on one foot. Now I look back, or listen back, in the same desire to imagine, and it seems possible that the sound of that sparse music, so faint and unearthly to my childhood ears, was the sound he'd had to speak to him in all that country silence among so many elders where he was the only child. To me it was a sound of unspeakable loneliness that I did not know how to run away from. I was there in its company, watching the moonflower open.

I never saw until after he was dead a small keepsake book

Ferrying the Kentucky (?), family car trip to West Virginia and Ohio, in the Oakland car

Grandpa Jefferson Welty, on the farm near Logan, Ohio, with Edward, Walter, Eudora, c. 1917

given to my father in his early childhood. On one page was a message of one sentence written to him by his mother on April 15, 1886. The date is the day of her death. "My dearest Webbie: I want you to be a good boy and to meet me in heaven. Your loving Mother." Webb was his middle name—her maiden name. She always called him by it. He was seven years old, her only child.

He had other messages in his little book to keep and read over to himself. "May your life, though short, be pleasant / As a warm and melting day" is from "Dr. Armstrong," and as it follows his mother's message may have been entered on the same day. Another entry reads: "Dear Webbie, If God send thee a cross, take it up willingly and follow Him. If it be light, slight it not. If it be heavy, murmur not. After the cross is the crown. Your aunt, Nina Welty." This is dated earlier—he was then three years old. The cover of the little book is red and embossed with baby ducklings falling out of a basket entwined with morning glories. It is very rubbed and worn. It had been given him to keep and he had kept it; he had brought it among his possessions to Mississippi when he married; my mother had put it away.

In the farmhouse, the staircase was not in sight until evening prayers were over—it was time to go to bed then, and a door in the kitchen wall was opened and there were the stairs, as if kept put away in a closet. They went up like a ladder, steep and narrow, that we climbed on the way to bed. Step by step became visible as I reached it, by the climbing yellow light of the oil lamp that Grandpa himself carried behind me.

Back on Congress Street, when my father unlocked the door of our closed-up, waiting house, I rushed ahead into the airless hall and stormed up the stairs, pounding the carpet of each step with both hands ahead of me, and putting my face right down into the cloud of the dear dust of our long absence. I was welcoming ourselves back. Doing likewise, more methodically, my father was going from room to room restarting all the clocks.

I think now, in looking back on these summer trips—this one and a number later, made in the car and on the train—that another element in them must have been influencing my mind. The trips were wholes unto themselves. They were stories. Not only in form, but in their taking on direction, movement, development, change. They changed something in my life: each trip made its particular revelation, though I could not have found words for it. But with the passage of time, I could look back on them and see them bringing me news, discoveries, premonitions, promises—I still can; they still do. When I did begin to write, the short story was a shape that had already formed itself and stood waiting in the back of my mind. Nor is it surprising to me that when I made my first attempt at a novel, I entered its world—that of the mysterious Yazoo-Mississippi Delta—as a child riding there on a train: "From the warm window sill the endless fields glowed like a hearth in firelight, and Laura, looking out, leaning on her elbows with her head between her hands, felt what an arriver in a land feels—that slow hard pounding in the breast."

The events in our lives happen in a sequence in time, but in their significance to ourselves they find their own order, a timetable not necessarily—perhaps not possibly—chronological. The time as we know it subjectively is often the chronology that stories and novels follow: it is the continuous thread of revelation.

III

Finding a Voice

I HAD the window seat. Beside me, my father checked the progress of our train by moving his finger down the timetable and springing open his pocket watch. He explained to me what the position of the arms of the semaphore meant; before we were to pass through a switch we would watch the signal lights change. Along our track, the mileposts could be read; he read them. Right on time by Daddy's watch, the next town sprang into view, and just as quickly was gone.

Side by side and separately, we each lost ourselves in the experience of not missing anything, of seeing everything, of knowing each time what the blows of the whistle meant. But of course it was not the same experience: what was new to me, not older than ten, was a landmark to him. My father knew our way mile by mile; by day or by night, he knew where we were. Everything that changed under our eyes, in the flying countryside, was the known world to him, the imagination to me. Each in our own way, we hungered for all of this: my father and I were in no other respect or situation so congenial.

In Daddy's leather grip was his traveler's drinking cup, collapsible; a lid to fit over it had a ring to carry it by; it traveled in a round leather box. This treasure would be brought out at my request, for me to bear to the water cooler at the end of the Pullman car, fill to the brim, and bear back to my seat, to drink water over its smooth lip. The taste of silver could almost be relied on to shock your teeth.

After dinner in the sparkling dining car, my father and I walked back to the open-air observation platform at the end of the train and sat on the folding chairs placed at the railing. We watched the sparks we made fly behind us into the night. Fast as our speed was, it gave us time enough to see the rose-red cinders turn to ash, each one, and disappear from sight. Sometimes a house far back in the empty hills showed a light no bigger than a star. The sleeping countryside seemed itself to open a way through for our passage, then close again behind us.

The swaying porter would be making ready our berths for the night, pulling the shade down just so, drawing the green fishnet hammock across the window so the clothes you took off could ride along beside you, turning down the tight-made bed, standing up the two snowy pillows as high as they were wide, switching on the eye of the reading lamp, starting the tiny electric fan—you suddenly saw its blades turn into gauze and heard its insect murmur; and drawing across it all the pair of thick green theaterlike curtains—billowing, smelling of cigar smoke—between which you would crawl or dive headfirst to button them together with yourself inside, to be seen no more that night.

When you lay enclosed and enwrapped, your head on a pillow parallel to the track, the rhythm of the rail clicks pressed closer to your body as if it might be your heart beating, but the sound of the engine seemed to come from farther away than when it carried you in daylight. The whistle was almost too far away to be heard, its sound wavering back from the engine over the roofs of the cars. What you listened for was the different sound that ran under you when your own car crossed on a trestle, then another sound on an iron bridge; a low or a high bridge—each had its pitch, or drumbeat, for your car.

Riding in the sleeper rhythmically lulled me and waked me. From time to time, waked suddenly, I raised my window shade and looked out at my own strip of the night. Sometimes there was unexpected moonlight out there. Sometimes the perfect shadow of our train, with our car, with me invisibly included, ran deep below, crossing a river with us by the light of the moon. Sometimes the encroaching walls of mountains woke me by clapping at my ears. The tunnels made the train's passage resound like the "loud" pedal of a piano, a roar that seemed to last as long as a giant's temper tantrum.

But my father put it all into the frame of regularity, predictability, that was his fatherly gift in the course of our journey. I saw it going by, the outside world, in a flash. I dreamed over what I could see as it passed, as well as over what I couldn't. Part of the dream was what lay beyond, where the path wandered off through the pasture, the red clay road climbed and went over the hill or made a turn and was hidden in trees, or toward a river whose bridge I could see but whose name I'd never know. A house back at its distance at night showing a light from an open doorway, the morning faces of the children who stopped still in what they were doing, perhaps picking blackberries or wild plums, and watched us go by—I never saw with the thought of their continuing to be there just the same after we were out of sight. For now, and for a long while to come, I was proceeding in fantasy.

I learned much later—after he was dead, in fact, the time when we so often learn fundamental things about our parents—how well indeed he knew the journey, and how he happened to do so. He fell in love with my mother, and she with him, in West Virginia when she was a teacher in the mountain schools near her home and he was a young man from Ohio who'd gone over to West Virginia to work in the office of a lumber construction company. When they decided to marry, they saw it as part of the adventure of starting a new life to go to a place far away and new to both of them, and that turned out to be Jackson, Mississippi. From rural Ohio and rural West Virginia, that must have seemed, in 1904, as far away as Bangkok might possibly seem to young people today. My father went down and got a job in a new insurance company being formed in Jackson. This was the Lamar Life. He was promoted almost at once, made secretary and one of the directors, and he was to stay with the company for the rest of his life. He set about first thing finding a house in Jackson, then a town of six or eight thousand people, for them to live in until they could build a house of their own. So during the engagement, he went the thousand miles to see her when he could afford it. The rest of the time—every day, sometimes twice a day—the two of them sent letters back and forth by this same train.

Their letters had all been kept by that great keeper, my mother; they were in one of the trunks in the attic—the trunk that used to go on the train with us to West Virginia and Ohio on summer trips. I didn't in the end feel like a trespasser when I came to open the letters: they brought my parents before me for the first time as young, as inexperienced, consumed with the strength of their hopes and desires, as *living* on these letters. I would have known my mother's voice in her letters anywhere. But I wouldn't have so quickly known my father's. Annihilating those miles between them—the miles I came along to travel with him, that first time on the train—those miles he knew nearly altogether by heart, he wrote more often than any once a day, and mailed his letters directly onto the mail car—letters that are so ardent, so direct and tender in expression, so urgent, that they seemed to bare, along with his love, the rest of his whole life to me.

On the train I saw that world passing my window. It was when I came to see it was *I* who was passing that my self-centered childhood was over. But it was not until I began to write, as I seriously did only when I reached my twenties, that I found the world out there revealing, because (as with my father now) *memory* had become attached to seeing, love had added itself to discovery, and because I recognized in my own continuing longing to keep going, the need I carried inside myself to know—the apprehension, first, and then the passion, to connect myself to it. Through travel I first became aware of the outside world; it was through travel that I found my own introspective way into becoming a part of it.

This is, of course, simply saying that the outside world is the vital component of my inner life. My work, in the terms in which I see it, is as dearly matched to the world as its secret sharer. My imagination takes its strength and guides its direction from what I see and hear and learn and feel and remember of my living world. But I was to learn slowly that both these worlds, outer and inner, were different from what they seemed to me in the beginning.

The best college in the state was very possibly the private liberal-arts one right here in Jackson, but I was filled with desire to go somewhere away and enter a school I'd never passed on the street. My parents thought that I was too young at sixteen to live for my first year too far from home. Mississippi State College for Women was well enough accredited and two hundred miles to the north.

There I landed in a world to itself, and indeed it was all

Chestina Andrews and Christian Welty in West Virigina, in courtship days, c. 1903

new to me. It was surging with twelve hundred girls. They came from every nook and corner of the state, from the Delta, the piney woods, the Gulf Coast, the black prairie, the red clay hills, and Jackson—as the capital city and the only sizeable town, a region to itself. All were clearly differentiated sections, at that time, and though we were all put into uniforms of navy blue so as to unify us, it could have been told by the girls' accents, by their bearings, the way they came into the classroom and the way they ate, where they'd grown up. This was my first chance to learn what the body of us were like and what differences in background, persuasion of mind, and resources of character there were among Mississippians—at that, among only half of us, for we were all white. I missed the significance of both what was in, and what was out of, our well-enclosed but vibrantly alive society. What was never there was money enough provided by our Legislature for education, and what was always there was a faculty accomplishing that education as a *feat*. Mississippi State College for Women, the oldest institution of its kind in America, poverty-stricken, enormously overcrowded, keeping within the tradition we were all used to in Mississippi, was conscientiously and, on the average, well taught by a dedicated faculty remaining and growing old there.

It was life in a crowd. We'd fight to get our mail in the basement post office, on rainy mornings, surrounded by other girls doing the Three Graces, where the gym teacher would have had to bring her first-period class indoors to practice. Even a gym piano, in competition with girls screaming over their letters and opening the food packages from home, was almost defeated. When we all had to crowd into compulsory chapel, one or two little frail undernourished students would faint sometimes—we had a fifteen-minute long Alma Mater to sing.

Old Main, the dormitory where I lived, had been built in 1860. It was packed to the roof with freshmen, three, four, or a half-dozen sometimes to the room, rising up four steep flights of wooden stairs. The chapel clock striking the hour very close by would shake our beds under us. It was the practice to use the fire escape to go to class, and at night to slip outside for a few minutes before going to bed.

It was the iron standpipe kind of fire escape, with a tin chute running down through it—all corkscrew turns from top to bottom, with holes along its passage where girls at fire drill could pour out of the different floors, and a hole at the bottom to pitch you out onto the ground, head still whirling.

It seemed impossible to be alone. Only music students had a good way. On a spring night you might hear one of them alone in a practice room of the Music Building, playing her heart out at an open window. It would be something like "Pale Hands I Loved Beside the Shalimar (Where Are You Now?)"—she'd be imagining of course that what she sent floating in the air was from someone else singing this song to *her*. At other times, when some strange song with low guttural notes and dragging movement, dramatically working up to a crescendo, was heard later still through that same open window, we freshmen told one another that was Miss Pohl, the spectacular gym teacher with the flying gray hair, who was, we had heard and believed, a Russian by birth, who'd been crossed, long years ago, in love. She may have indeed been crossed in love, but she was a Mississippian, just like us.

A time could be seized, close to bedtime, when it was possible to slip down the fire escape and, before the doors were all locked against my getting back, walk to an iron fountain on the campus and around it, with poetry running through my head. I'd bought the first book for my shelf from the college bookstore, *In April Once*, by William Alexander Percy, our chief Mississippi poet. Its first poem was one written from New York City, entitled "Home."

> I have a need of silence and of stars.
> Too much is said too loudly. I am dazed.
> The silken sound of whirled infinity
> Is lost in voices shouting to be heard . . .

Where I walked at that moment, within the little town of Columbus, and further within the iron gates of the campus of a girls' college at night, now everywhere going to bed, and while I said the poem to myself, around me was nothing *but* silence and stars. This did not impinge upon my longing. In the beautiful spring night, I was dedicated to *wanting* a beautiful spring night. To be *transported* to it was what I wanted.

Whatever a poem was about—that it could be called "Home" didn't matter—it was about somewhere else, somewhere distant and far.

I was lucky enough to have found for myself, at the very beginning, an outside shell, that of freshman reporter on our college newspaper, *The Spectator*. I became a wit and humorist of the parochial kind, and the amount I was able to show off in print must have been a great comfort to me. (I saw *The Bat* and wrote "The Gnat," laid in MSCW. The Gnat assumes the disguise of our gym uniform—navy blue serge one-piece with pleated bloomers reaching below the knee, and white tennis shoes—and enters through the College Library, after hours; our librarian starts screaming at his opening line, "Beulah Culbertson, I have come for those fines.") I'd been a devoted reader of S. J. Perelman, Corey Ford, and other humorists who appeared in *Judge* magazine, and I'd imagined that with these as a springboard, I could swim.

After great floods struck the state and Columbus had been overflowed by the Tombigbee River, I contributed an editorial to *The Spectator* for its April Fool issue. This lamented that five of our freshman class got drowned when the waters rose, but by this Act of God, it went on, there was that much more room now for the rest of us. Years later, a Columbus newspaperman, on whose press our paper was printed, told me that H. L. Mencken had picked up this chirp out of me for *The American Mercury* as sample thinking from the Bible Belt. But by chance, in the home of a town student, I had just met my first intellectual. Within a few moments he had lent me *Candide*! It was just published, the first Modern Library book (I believe the very first)—that thin little book with leatherlike covers that heated up, while you read, warmer than your hand. Voltaire, too, I could call on.

But I learned my vital lesson in the classroom.

Mr. Lawrence Painter, the only man teacher in the college, spent his life conducting the MSCW girls in their sophomore year through English Survey, from "Summer is y-comen in" to "I have a rendezvous with Death." In my time a handsome, learned, sandy-haired man—wildly popular, of course, on campus—he got instant silence when he would throw open the book and begin to read aloud to us.

In high-school freshman English, we had committed to memory "Whan that Aprille with his shoures soote . . ." which as poetry was not less remote to our ears than "Arma virumque cano . . ." I had come unprepared for the immediacy of poetry.

I felt the shock closest to this a year later at the University of Wisconsin when I walked into my art class and saw, in place of the bowl of fruit and the glass bottle and ginger jar of the still life I used to draw at MSCW, a live human being. As we sat at our easels, a model, a young woman, lightly dropped her robe and stood, before us and a little above us, holding herself perfectly contained, in her full self and naked. Often that year in Survey Course, as Mr. Painter read, poetry came into the room where we could see it and all around it, free-standing poetry. As we listened, Mr. Painter's, too, was a life class.

After I transferred, in my junior year, to the University of Wisconsin, I made in this far, new place a discovery for myself that has fed my life ever since. I express a little of my experience in a story, one fairly recent and not yet completed. It's the story of a middle-aged man who'd come from a farm in the Middle West, who's taciturn and unhappy as a teacher of linguistics and now has reached a critical point in his life. The scene is New Orleans; he and a woman are walking at night (they are really saying goodbye) and he speaks of himself without reserve to her for the first time.

He'd put himself through the University of Wisconsin, he tells her:

> "And I happened to discover Yeats, reading through some of the stacks in the library. I read the early and then the later poems all in the same one afternoon, standing up, by the window . . . I read 'Sailing to Byzantium,' standing up in the stacks, read it by the light of falling snow. It seemed to me that if I could stir, if I could move to take the next step, I could go out into the poem the way I could go out into that snow. That it would be falling on my shoulders. That it would pelt me on its way down—that I could move in it, live in it—that I could die in it, maybe. So after that I had to

learn it," he said. "And I told myself that I would. That I accepted the invitation."

The experience I describe in the story had indeed been my own, snow and all; the poem that smote me first was "The Song of Wandering Aengus"; it was the poem that turned up, fifteen years or so later, in my stories of *The Golden Apples* and runs all through that book.

At length too, at Wisconsin, I learned the word for the nature of what I had come upon in reading Yeats. Mr. Riccardo Quintana lecturing to his class on Swift and Donne used it in its true meaning and import. The word is *passion.*

It was my mother who emotionally and imaginatively supported me in my wish to become a writer. It was my father who gave me the first dictionary of my own, a Webster's Collegiate, inscribed on the flyleaf with my full name (he always included Alice, my middle name, after his mother) and the date, 1925. I still consult it. It was also he who expressed his reservations that I wouldn't achieve financial success by becoming a writer, a sensible fear; nevertheless he fitted me out with my first typewriter, my little red Royal Portable, which I carried off to the University of Wisconsin. It was also he who advised me, after I'd told him I still meant to try writing, even though I didn't expect to sell my stories to *The Saturday Evening Post* which paid well, to go ahead and try myself—but to prepare to earn my living some other way. My supportive parents had already very willingly agreed that I go farther from home for my last two years of college and sent me to Wisconsin—my father's choice for its high liberal-arts reputation. Now that I'd been graduated from there, they sent me to my first choice of a place to prepare for a job: New York City, at Columbia University Graduate School of Business. (As certain as I was of wanting to be a writer, I was certain of *not* wanting to be a teacher. I lacked the instructing turn of mind, the selflessness, the patience for teaching, and I had the unreasoning feeling that I'd be trapped. The odd thing is that when I did come to write my stories, the longest list of my characters turns out to be schoolteachers. They are to a great extent my heroines.)

My father did not bring it up, but of course I knew that he had another reason to worry about my decision to write. Though he was a reader, he was not a lover of fiction, because fiction is not true, and for that flaw it was forever inferior to fact. If reading fiction was a waste of time, so was the writing of it. (Why is it, I wonder, that humor didn't count? Wodehouse, for one, whom both of us loved, was a flawless fiction writer.)

But I was not to be in time to show him what I could do, to hear what he thought, on the evidence, of where I was headed.

My father had given immense study to the erection of the new Lamar Life home office building on Capitol Street, which was completed in 1925—"Jackson's first skyscraper." It is a delicately imposing Gothic building of white marble, thirteen stories high with a clock tower at the top. It had been designed, as my father had asked of the Fort Worth architect, to be congenial with the Episcopal parish church that stood next door to it and with the fine Governor's Mansion that faced it from across the street. The architect pleased him with his gargoyles: the stone decorations of the main entrance took the form of alligators, which related it as well to Mississippi.

At every stage of the building, Daddy took his family to see as much as we could climb over, usually on Sunday mornings. At last we could climb by the fire escape to reach the top. We stood on the roof, with the not-yet-working clock towering at our backs, and viewed all Jackson below, spread to its seeable limits, its green rim, where the still river-like Pearl River and the still-unpaved-over Town Creek meandered and joined together in their unmolested swamp, with "the country" beyond. We were located where we stood there—part of our own map.

At the grand opening, the whole of the new building was lighted from a top to bottom and the Company—its business now expanded into other Southern states—had a public reception. My father made a statement at the time: "Not a dollar was borrowed nor a security sold for the erection of this new building, and it is all paid for. The building will stand, now and always, free from all debt, as a most valuable asset to policy-holders."

It was a crowning year of his life. At the same time that the new building was going up, so was our new house, designed by the same architect. The house was on a slight hill (my mother never could see the hill) covered with its original forest pines, on a gravel road then a little out from town, and was built in a style very much of its day, of stucco and brick and beams in the Tudor style. We had moved in, and Mother was laying out the garden.

Six years later, my father was dead.

The Lamar Life tower is overshadowed now, and you can no longer read the time on its clocktower from all over town, as he'd wanted to be possible always, but the building's grace and good proportion contrast tellingly with the overpowering, sometimes brutal, character of some of the structures that rise above it. Renovators have sandblasted away the alligators that graced the entrance. But the Company still has its home there, and my father is remembered.

My father's enthusiasm for business was not the part of him that he passed on to his children. But his imaginative conception of the building, and his pride in seeing it go up and his love of working in his tenth-floor office with the windows open to the view on three sides, may well have entered into his son Edward. He went on to become an architect, especially gifted in design, who had a hand in a number of public buildings and private houses to be seen today in Jackson. Walter was a more literal kind of inheritor; after taking his master's degree in mathematics he went into the office of an insurance company—not the Lamar Life, but another.

Plans for the Company had included the launching of a radio station, and its office was a cubbyhole installed in the base of the tower. After my father was dead and the Great Depression remained with us, I got a part-time job there. My first paid work was in communications: Mississippi's first radio station, operating there under the big clock, to which he would have given his nod of approval.

My first full-time job was rewarding to me in a way I could never have foreseen in those early days of my writing. I went to work for the state office of the Works Progress Administration as junior publicity agent. (This was of course one of President Roosevelt's national measures to combat the Great Depression.) Traveling over the whole of Mississippi, writing news stories for county papers, taking pictures, I saw my home state at close hand, really for the first time.

With the accretion of years, the hundreds of photographs —life as I found it, all unposed—constitute a record of that desolate period; but most of what I learned for myself came right at the time and directly out of the *taking* of the pictures. The camera was a hand-held auxiliary of wanting-to-know.

It had more than information and accuracy to teach me. I learned in the doing how *ready* I had to be. Life doesn't hold still. A good snapshot stopped a moment from running away. Photography taught me that to be able to capture transience, by being ready to click the shutter at the crucial moment, was the greatest need I had. Making pictures of people in all sorts of situations, I learned that every feeling waits upon its gesture; and I had to be prepared to recognize this moment when I saw it. These were things a story writer needed to know. And I felt the need to hold transient life in *words*—there's so much more of life that only words can convey—strongly enough to last me as long as I lived. The direction my mind took was a writer's direction from the start, not a photographer's, or a recorder's.

Along Mississippi roads you'd now and then see bottle trees; you'd see them alone or in crowds in the front yard of remote farmhouses. I photographed one—a bare crape myrtle tree with every branch of it ending in the mouth of a colored glass bottle—a blue Milk of Magnesia or an orange or green pop bottle; reflecting the light, flashing its colors in the sun, it stood as the centerpiece in a little thicket of peach trees in bloom. Later, I wrote a story called "Livvie" about youth and old age: the death of an old, proud, possessive man and the coming into flower, after dormant years, of his young wife—a spring story. Numbered among old Solomon's proud possessions is this bottle tree.

I know that the actual bottle tree, from the time of my actual sight of it, was the origin of my story. I know equally well that the bottle tree appearing in the story is a projection from my imagination; it isn't the real one except in that it is corrected by reality. The fictional eye sees in, through, and around what is really there. In "Livvie," old Solomon's bottle tree stands bright with dramatic significance, it stands vulnerable, ready for invading youth to sail a stone into the bottles and shatter them, as Livvie is claimed by love in the bursting light of spring. This I saw could be brought into being in the form of a story.

I was always my own teacher. The earliest story I kept a copy of was, I had thought, sophisticated, for I'd had the inspiration to lay it in Paris. I wrote it on my new typewriter, and its opening sentence was, "Monsieur Boule inserted a delicate dagger into Mademoiselle's left side and departed with a poised immediacy." I'm afraid it was a perfect example of what my father thought "fiction" mostly was. I was ten years older before I redeemed that in my first published story, "Death of a Traveling Salesman." I back-slid, for I found it hard to save myself from starting stories to show off what I could write.

In "Acrobats in a Park," though I laid the story in my home town, I was writing about Europeans, acrobats, adultery, and the Roman Catholic Church (seen from across the street), in all of which I was equally ignorant. In real life I fell easily under the spell of all traveling artists. En route to New Orleans, entertainments of many kinds would stop over in those days for a single performance in Jackson's Century Theatre. Galli-Curci came, so did Blackstone the Magician, so did Paderewski, so did *The Cat and the Canary* and the extravaganza *Chu Chin Chow*. Our family attended them all. My stories from the first drew visiting performers in, beginning modestly with a ladies' trio of the Redpath Chautauqua in "The Winds" and going so far as Segovia in "Music from Spain." Then, as now, my imagination was magnetized toward transient artists—toward the transience as much as the artists.

I must have seen "Acrobats in a Park" at the time I wrote the story as exotic, free of any experience as I knew it. And yet in the simplest way it isn't unrelated. The acrobats I led in procession into Smith Park in Jackson, Mississippi, were a *family*. They sat down in our family park, eating their lunch under a pin-oak tree I knew intimately. A father, a mother, and their children made up the troupe. At the center of the little story is the Zorros' act: the feat of erecting a structure of their bodies that holds together, interlocked, and stands like a wall, the Zorro Wall. Writing about the family act, I was writing about the family itself, its strength as a unit, testing its frailty under stress. I treated it in an artificial and oddly formal way; the stronghold of the family is put on public view as a structure built each night; on the night before the story opens, the Wall has come down when the most vulnerable member slips, and the act is done for. But from various points within it and from outside it, I've been writing about the structure of the family in stories and novels ever since. In spite of my unpromising approach to it, my fundamental story form might have been trying to announce itself to me.

My first good story began spontaneously, in a remark repeated to me by a traveling man—our neighbor—to whom it had been spoken while he was on a trip into North Mississippi: "He's gone to borry some fire." The words, which carried such lyrical and mythological and dramatic overtones, were real and actual—their hearer repeated them to me.

As usual, I began writing from a distance, but "Death of a Traveling Salesman" led me closer. It drew me toward what was at the center of it, to a cabin back in the red clay hills—perhaps just such a house as I used to see from far off on a train at night, with the firelight or lamplight showing yellow from its open doorway. In writing the story I approached and went inside with my traveling salesman, and had him, pressed by imminent death, figure out what was there:

> Bowman could not speak. He was shocked with knowing what was really in this house. A marriage, a fruitful marriage. That simple thing. Anyone could have had that.

Writing "Death of a Traveling Salesman" opened my eyes. And I had received the shock of having touched, for the first time, on my real subject: human relationships. Daydreaming had started me on the way; but story writing, once I was truly in its grip, took me and shook me awake.

•

My temperament and my instinct had told me alike that the author, who writes at his own emergency, remains and needs to remain at his private remove. I wished to be, not effaced, but invisible—actually a powerful position. Perspective, the line of vision, the frame of vision—these set a distance.

An early story called "A Memory" is a discovery in the making. This is how it begins:

> One summer morning when I was a child I lay on the sand after swimming in the small lake in the park. The sun beat down—it was almost noon. The water shone like steel, motionless except for the feathery curl behind a distant swimmer. From my position I was looking at a rectangle brightly lit, actually glaring at me, with sun, sand, water, a little pavilion, a few solitary people in fixed attitudes, and around it all a border of dark rounded oak trees, like the engraved thunderclouds surrounding illustrations in the Bible. Ever since I had begun taking painting lessons, I had made small frames with my fingers, to look out at everything.
>
> Since this was a weekday morning, the only persons who were at liberty to be in the park were either children, who had nothing to occupy them, or those older people whose lives are obscure, irregular, and consciously of no worth to anything: this I put down as my observation at that time. I was at an age when I formed a judgment upon every person and every event which came under my eye, although I was easily frightened. When a person, or a happening, seemed to me not in keeping with my opinion, or even my hope or expectation, I was terrified by a vision of abandonment and wildness which tore my heart with a kind of sorrow. My father and mother, who believed that I saw nothing in the world which was not strictly coaxed into place like a vine on our garden trellis to be presented to my eyes, would have been badly concerned if they had guessed how often the weak and inferior and strangely turned examples of what was to come showed themselves to me.
>
> I do not know even now what it was that I was waiting to see; but in those days I was convinced that I almost

> saw it at every turn. To watch everything about me I regarded grimly and possessively as a *need*. All through this summer I had lain on the sand beside the small lake, with my hands squared over my eyes, finger tips touching, looking out by this device to see everything: which appeared as a kind of projection. It did not matter to me what I looked at; from any observation I would conclude that a secret of life had been revealed to me—for I was obsessed with notions about concealment, and from the smallest gesture of a stranger I would wrest what was to me a communication or a presentiment.

This is not, on reaching its end, an observer's story. The tableau discovered through the young girl's framing hands is unwelcome realism. How can she accommodate the existence of this view to the dream of love, which she carried already inside her? Amorphous and tender, from now on it will have to remain hidden, her own secret imagining. The frame only raises the question of the vision. It has something of my own dreaming at the train window. But now the dreamer has stopped to look. After that, dreaming or awake, she will be drawn in.

"A Still Moment"—another early story—was a fantasy, in which the separate interior visions guiding three highly individual and widely differing men marvelously meet and converge upon the same single exterior object. All my characters were actual persons who had lived at the same time, who would have been strangers to one another, but whose lives had actually taken them at some point to the same neighborhood. The scene was in the Mississippi wilderness in the historic year 1811—"*anno mirabilis*," the year the stars fell on Alabama and lemmings, or squirrels perhaps, rushed straight down the continent and plunged into the Gulf of Mexico, and an earthquake made the Mississippi River run backwards and New Madrid, Missouri, tumbled in and disappeared. My real characters were Lorenzo Dow the New England evangelist, Murrell the outlaw bandit and murderer on the Natchez Trace, and Audubon the painter; and the exterior object on which they all at the same moment set their eyes is a small heron, feeding.

I never wrote another such story as that, but other sorts of vision, dream, illusion, hallucination, obsession, and that most wonderful interior vision which is memory, have all gone to make up my stories, to form and to project them, to impel them.

The frame through which I viewed the world changed too, with time. Greater than scene, I came to see, is situation. Greater than situation is implication. Greater than all of these is a single, entire human being, who will never be confined in any frame.

Writing a story or a novel is one way of discovering *sequence* in experience, of stumbling upon cause and effect in the happenings of a writer's own life. This has been the case with me. Connections slowly emerge. Like distant landmarks you are approaching, cause and effect begin to align themselves, draw closer together. Experiences too indefinite of outline in themselves to be recognized for themselves connect and are identified as a larger shape. And suddenly a light is thrown back, as when your train makes a curve, showing that there has been a mountain of meaning rising behind you on the way you've come, is rising there still, proven now through retrospect.

It seems to me, writing of my parents now in my seventies, that I see continuities in their lives that weren't visible to me when they were living. Even at the times that have left me my most vivid memories of them, there were connections between them that escaped me. Could it be because I can better see their lives—or any lives I know—today because I'm a fiction writer? See them not as fiction, certainly—see them, perhaps, as even greater mysteries than I knew. Writing fiction has developed in me an abiding respect for the unknown in a human lifetime and a sense of where to look for the threads, how to follow, how to connect, find in the thick of the tangle what clear line persists. The strands are all there: to the memory nothing is ever really lost.

The little keepsake book given to my father so long ago, of which I never heard a word spoken by anybody, has grown in eloquence to me. The messages that were meant to "go with him"—and which did—the farewell from his mother on the day of her death; and the doctor's following words that the child's own life would be short; the admonition from his Aunt Penina to bear his cross and murmur not—made a sum that he had been left to ponder over from the time he had learned to read. It seems to me that my father's choosing life insurance as his work, and indeed he exhausted his life for it, must have always had a deeper reason behind it than his conviction, strong as it was, in which he joined the majority in the twenties, that success in business was the solution to most of the problems of living—security of the family, their ongoing comfort and welfare, and especially the certainty of education for the children. This was partly why the past had no interest for him. He saw life in terms of the future, and he worked to provide that future for his children.

Right along with the energetic practice of optimism, and deeper than this, was an abiding awareness of mortality itself—most of all the mortality of a parent. This care, this caution, that ruled his life in the family, and in the business he chose and succeeded in expanding so far, began very possibly when he was seven years old, when his mother, asking him with perhaps literally her last words to be a good boy and meet her in heaven, died and left him alone.

Strangely enough, what Ned Andrews had extolled too, in all his rhetoric, was the future works of man and the leaving of the past behind. No two characters could have been wider apart than those of Ned Andrews and Christian Welty, or more different in their self-expression. They never knew each other, and the only thing they had in common was my mother's love. Who knows but that this ambition for the betterment of mankind in the attainable future was the quality in them both that she loved first? She would have responded to the ardency of their beliefs. I'm not sure she succeeded in having faith in their predictions. Neither got to live their lives out; the hurt she felt in this was part of her love for both.

My father of course liberally insured his own life for the future provision of his family, and had cause to believe that all was safe ahead. Then the Great Depression arrived. And in 1931 a disease that up to then even he had never heard of, leukemia, caused his death in a matter of weeks, at the age of fifty-two.

I believe the guiding emotion in my mother's life was pity. It encompassed the world. During the war (World War II), she heard on a radio broadcast that the Chinese, fearing their great library would be destroyed, took the books up in their hands and put them onto their backs and carried all of them, on foot, over long mountain paths, away to safety. Mother cried for them, and for their books. Almost more than eventual disaster, brave hope that it could be averted undid her. She had had so many of those brave hopes herself. Crying for the old Chinese scholars carrying their precious books over the mountain gave her a way too of crying for herself, with her youngest child, who was serving with the Navy at the battle of Okinawa.

She suffered perhaps more than an ordinary number of blows in her long life. We her children, like our father before us, had to learn the lesson that we never would be able to console her for any of them; especially could we not console her for what happened to ourselves.

Her strongest habit of thought was association. There is no way to help that.

When my father was dying in the hospital, there was a desperate last decision to try a blood transfusion. How much was known about compatibility of blood types then, or about the procedure itself, I'm unable to say. All I know is that there was no question in my mother's mind as to who the donor was to be.

I was present when it was done; my two brothers were in school. Both my parents were lying on cots, my father had been brought in on one and my mother lay on the other. Then a tube was simply run from her arm to his.

My father, I believe, was unconscious. My mother was looking at him. I could see her fervent face: there was no doubt as to what she was thinking. This time, *she* would save *his* life, as he'd saved hers so long ago, when she was dying of septicemia. What he'd done for her in giving her the champagne, she would be able to do for him now in giving him her own blood.

All at once his face turned dusky red all over. The doctor made a disparaging sound with his lips, the kind a woman knitting makes when she drops a stitch. What the doctor meant by it was that my father had died.

My mother never recovered emotionally. Though she lived for over thirty years more, and suffered other bitter losses, she never stopped blaming herself. She saw this as her failure to save his life.

As the New York train pulled, close to midnight, out of the station at home, your friends stood waving as though they'd never see you again. Your last view of Jackson from your window was an old dark wooden building by the tracks topped by a hand-painted sign under an arc light: "Where Will YOU Spend Eternity?" This sign was also the first thing you saw in the dawn when the train brought you back home again.

As the train picked up speed, rolled faster out of town, I would lie back with an iron cage around my chest of guilt.

In the later times of the Depression, I saved all I could from my part-time or temporary jobs in Jackson to go to New York. I hoped to show my stories and the photographs I'd taken over Mississippi in the Depression to an editor who would like them—either or both—enough to publish them. A two-week stay in the City, which I'd proved could be managed for $100 then—and that included the theatre—seemed long enough to me for a decision; but I would have to come away without knowing. It didn't at all occur to me how many times over my own manuscripts were multiplied on an editor's desk. It was the *encouraging* responses that took so long to come—a year sometimes; the editors who gave me an extraordinary amount of understanding and hope, and praise too, had so far found they still had to say no in the end. All this would go on the train with me, up there and back. It was part of my flying landscape.

I knew that even as I was moving farther away from Jackson, my mother was already writing to me at her desk, telling me she missed me but only wanted what was best for me. She would not leave the house till she had my wire, sent from Penn Station the third day from now, that I had arrived safely. I was not to worry about her or things at home, about how she was getting along. She anxiously awaited my letter after I had tried my stories on the publishers.

I knew this was how she must have waited when my father had left on one of his business trips, and I thought I could guess how he, the train lover, the trip lover, must have felt too while he remained away. I thought of the big box of Fanny May Chocolates he brought back from Chicago, the sheet music to "I Want to Be Happy" from *No, No, Nanette* that would tell us all about the show he'd so much enjoyed and wished we had seen with him. Taking trips tore all of us up inside, for they seemed, each journey away from home, something that might have been less selfishly undertaken, or something that would test us, or something that had better be momentous, to justify such a leap into the dark. The torment and guilt—the torment of having the loved one go, the guilt of being the loved one gone—comes into my fiction as it did and does into my life. And most of all the guilt then was because it was true: I had left to arrive at some future and secret joy, at what was unknown, and what was now in New York, waiting to be discovered. My joy was connected with writing; that was as much as I knew.

In Meridian (I had only gone ninety miles from Jackson) there was a wait of hours for the train that went from New Orleans to New York. The ceiling lights in the station were so lofty that you couldn't see to read. Long after midnight, the first signal came from the blackness outside—the whistle blowing for the curve south of town. The ancient and familiar figure of the black lady who for the last two hours had carried around coffee in a black iron pot as large as a churn would be at your side as you woke up. She was the sole attendant. Now she proceeded to call the stations. Her white frilled bonnet and starched white apron only made her look official at 2 A.M. in Meridian. She shouted out the whole list of destinations exactly as she must have done for fifty years under the echoing vault of the grand railroad station of its day. Above the thunder of the approaching engine, and then a bell heard ringing, rising in pitch as it rang nearer, and its alarm right at our ears now, and over the clanging and banging of arrival at the platform and the shriek of vented steam, one human voice recited the roster of our destination. Slowly and from deep-down inside her each name came measured out to us like words in a church: "Birmingham . . . Chattanooga . . . Bristol . . . Lynchburg . . . Washington . . . Baltimore . . . Philadelphia . . . and New York." And changing herself one more time—now into the porter—she would start loading her arms and shoulders with all our suitcases, as many as she could carry at one time, and herd us down the platform to our day-coach, getting rid of us herself to make sure we were gone. She appears as herself in one story I wrote, "The Demonstrators," but she's there in spirit in many more. She was to me the very Angel of Departure, and I thought how often, parked over there insensible in the sleeping car waiting for the same connection, in those earlier times, I'd slept through her.

The trip to New York meant two nights and parts of three days sitting up and changing trains several times. This cost only $17.50 each way, cheaper if I could run into an excursion rate out of Washington. We spent all one day crossing the width of Tennessee, then peacefully rural. I came to know the layout of any given town we went through, the name of the hardware store, where to look for a bank clock that kept good time. I knew where the shade patches came at mid-afternoon in upland pastures, and remembered to look for the pony among the horses gathered there. The same little dogs from summer to summer would always chase our train past the gates of certain farms. We went through the mountains by night; you could only hear your passage, not see. If I were asleep and a stop awakened me at dawn, I'd look out the window instinctively knowing I'd see the station where the fat, simple-minded boy would be skipping down the sidewalk at the drugstore corner, just in time to greet the train. I could have prophesied I'd see the same man and woman standing on ladders every time we went around a certain long curve, endlessly re-painting their greenhouse.

Yet those were the last years when there seemed to be time-tables, schedules, in operation. With the approach of the War, on crowded and ill-maintained trains, the kind never running on time and often breaking down, the route itself retraced the same country as in those earlier days; landmarks were slower then to fade away. But the train often stopped for no discernible reason in the open country and stood without sound or

Eudora, 1936, at the time of publication of first story, "Death of a Traveling Salesman"

Eudora, 1941, at the time of first book, A Curtain of Green, in the backyard on Pinehurst Street

motion, like a becalmed ship. My father would have been right out there, finding out the trouble from the brakeman or the engineer, taking out his watch, as concerned as they were. You had to expect to stop dead where the track reached a three-way meeting of branchlines in perfectly empty country; a tiny shed-like station carried the name "Ooltewah." Was this "Waterloo" said backwards? But nothing, it seemed to me, ever did happen at this prolonged stop. We met no other train; no train came to pass us. Destination, when the train isn't moving, seems only a forgotten dream.

Once, when my train came to one of those inexplicable stops in open country, this happened: Out there was spread around us a long, high valley, a green peaceful stretch of Tennessee with distant farmhouses and, threading off toward planted fields, a little foot path. It was sunset. Presently, without a word, a soldier sitting opposite me rose and stepped off the halted train. He hadn't spoken to anybody for the whole day and now, taking nothing with him and not stopping to put on his cap, he just left us. We saw him walking right away from the track, into the green valley, making a long shadow and never looking back. The train in time proceeded, and as we left him back there in the landscape, I felt *us* going out of sight for *him*, diminishing and soon to be forgotten.

Eventually, without stirring a mile from home, I fell into the safest possible hands. After I had written enough stories that were the best I could make them, my future literary agent Diarmuid Russell and my future editors, who became my friends for life, found *me*. (John Woodburn, an editor who came through Jackson scouting for his publisher, wrote when he'd persuaded the house to take my first book, "I knew when I tasted your mother's waffles everything would turn out all right.")

Travel itself is part of some longer continuity.

Just this past summer, in some effects of my father's, I came across photographic negatives I'd never seen—even their size was different from all those he made of our family. I had them printed and found before me scenes of unfamiliar places—city streets and buildings and tram cars and docksides, public parks with running children who seemed in costume; young ladies sitting in boats or strolling in long skirts and straw hats; ships, flags, stretches of sea or some wide river—and all at once Niagara Falls, no mistake about that, by day and by night, lit up. On the other hand, there was a frozen waterfall with a man in overcoat and hat posing beside it, holding to one long icicle as to a lady's hand in an opera-length white glove. I was mystified until at a later time this same summer I ran across by chance a railway timetable with ferry-boat schedules and hours for band concerts, and excursion prices from Halifax, for a given week in August, 1903. That was my father's, all right—he would have taken every one of those offers. And the date I recognized now as the summer before the year he married my mother. In those snapshots I was looking at the festival scenes of his last fling.

No, I was looking at more than that. It came back to me that my mother had said he'd offered her a choice between the Thousand Islands and Jackson, Mississippi, as their future home, and she'd chosen Jackson, Mississippi; we had her to thank. But I could see now that of course he would have gone up there to look over the Thousand Islands and ridden the train or sailed the St. Lawrence from Ontario to Halifax, stopping off for Niagara Falls, and taken those pictures to bring her, before he'd say a rash thing like that to Chessie Andrews. And here they were, the choice she didn't take. She'd chosen the other place, and here was I now, one of the results, in it, with pictures of the other choice now turning up in my hand.

Along with the ferry timetable and the schedule of excursions and the souvenir book of the Thousand Islands, I came across a sizeable commercial photograph taken of my father. A slim figure in a light business suit, he is standing, with one foot up on a rock, apparently right in the rapids of Niagara Falls. His usual expression of kind regard is on his face. He'd probably had this trick photograph made just to present to my mother. It made me remember what countless times he tried by joking means to make her laugh. When he did, it took *him* with delighted surprise, too—a triumph for both of them. I could imagine her being handed this picture of her fiancé standing in the rapids above Niagara Falls with his hat in his hand, and saying to him, "I don't see the humor in that." He *knew* how terrified she was of the water!

•

What discoveries I've made in the course of writing stories all begin with the particular, never the general. They are mostly hindsight: arrows that I now find I myself have left behind me, which have shown me some right, or wrong, way I have come. What one story may have pointed out to me is of no avail in the writing of another. But "avail" is not what I want; freedom ahead is what each story promises—beginning anew. And all the while, as further hindsight has told me, certain patterns in my work repeat themselves without my realizing. There would be no way to know this, for during the writing of any single story, there is no other existing. Each writer must find out for himself, I imagine, on what strange basis he lives with his own stories.

I had been writing a number of stories, more or less one after the other, before it belatedly dawned on me that some of the characters in one story were, and had been all the time, the same characters who had appeared already in another story. Only I'd written about them originally under different names, at different periods in their lives, in situations not yet interlocking but ready for it. They touched on every side. These stories were all related (and the fact was buried in their inceptions) by the strongest ties—identities, kinships, relationships, or affinities already known or remembered or foreshadowed. From story to story, connections between the characters' lives, through their motives or actions, sometimes their dreams, already existed: there to be found. Now the whole assembly—some of it still in the future—fell, by stages, into place in one location already evoked, which I saw now was a focusing point for all the stories. What had drawn the characters together there was one strong strand in them all: they lived in one way or another in a dream or in romantic aspiration, or under an illusion of what their lives were coming to, about the meaning of their (now) related lives.

The stories were connected most provocatively of all to me, perhaps, through the entry into my story-telling mind of another sort of tie—a shadowing of Greek mythological figures, gods and heroes that wander in various guises, at various times, in and out, emblems of the characters' heady dreams.

Writing these stories, which eventually appeared joined together in the book called *The Golden Apples*, was an experience in a writer's own discovery of affinities. In writing, as in life, the connections of all sorts of relationships and kinds lie in wait of discovery, and give out their signals to the Geiger counter of the charged imagination, once it is drawn into the right field.

The characters who go to make up my stories and novels are not portraits. Characters I invent along with the story that carries them. Attached to them are what I've borrowed, perhaps unconsciously, bit by bit, of persons I have seen or noticed or remembered in the flesh—a cast of countenance here, a manner of walking there, that jump to the visualizing mind when a story is underway. (Elizabeth Bowen said, "Physical detail cannot be invented." It can only be chosen.) I don't write by invasion into the life of a real person: my own sense of privacy is too strong for that; and I also know instinctively that living people to whom you are close—those known to you in ways too deep, too overflowing, ever to be plumbed outside love—do not yield to, could never fit into, the demands of a story. On the other hand, what I do make my stories out of is the *whole* fund of my feelings, my responses to the real experiences of my own life, to the relationships that formed and changed it, that I have given most of myself to, and so learned my way toward a dramatic counterpart. Characters take on life sometimes by luck, but I suspect it is when you can write most entirely out of yourself, inside the skin, heart, mind, and soul of a person who is not yourself, that a character becomes in his own right another human being on the page.

It was not my intention—it never was—to invent a character who should speak for me, the author, in person. A character is in a story to fill a role there, and the character's life along with its expression of life is defined by that surrounding—indeed is created by his own story. Yet, it seems to me now, years after I wrote *The Golden Apples*, that I did bring forth a character with whom I came to feel oddly in touch. This is Miss Eckhart, a woman who has come from away to give piano lessons to the young of Morgana. She is formidable and eccentric in the eyes of everyone, is scarcely accepted in the town. But she persisted with me, as she persisted in spite of herself with the other characters in the stories.

Where did the character of Miss Eckhart come from? There was my own real-life piano teacher, "eligible" to the extent that she swatted my hands at the keyboard with a fly-swatter if I made a mistake; and when she wrote "Practice" on my page of sheet music she made her "P" as Miss Eckhart did—a cat's face with a long tail. She did indeed hold a recital of her pupils every June that was a fair model for Miss Eckhart's, and of many another as well, I suppose. But the character of Miss Eckhart was miles away from that of the teacher I knew as a child, or from that of anybody I did know. Nor was she like other teacher-characters I was responsible for: my stories and novels suddenly appear to me to be full of teachers, with Miss Eckhart different from them all.

What the story "June Recital" most acutely shows the reader lies in her inner life. I haven't the slightest idea what my real teacher's life was like inside. But I knew what Miss Eckhart's was, for it protruded itself well enough into the story.

As I looked longer and longer for the origins of this passionate and strange character, at last I realized that Miss Eckhart came from me. There wasn't any resemblance in her outward identity: I am not musical, not a teacher, nor foreign in birth; not humorless or ridiculed or missing out in love; nor have I yet let the world around me slip from my recognition. But none of that counts. What counts is only what lies at the solitary core. She derived from what I already knew for myself, even felt I had always known. What I have put into her is my passion for my own life work, my own art. Exposing yourself to risk is a truth Miss Eckhart and I had in common. What animates and possesses me is what drives Miss Eckhart, the love of her art and the love of giving it, the desire to give it until there is no more left. Even in the small and literal way, what I had done in assembling and connecting all the stories in *The Golden Apples*, and bringing them off as one, was not too unlike the June recital itself.

Not in Miss Eckhart as she stands solidly and almost opaquely in the surround of her story, but in the making of her character out of my most inward and most deeply feeling self, I would say I have found my voice in my fiction.

Of course any writer is in part all of his characters. How otherwise would they be known to him, occur to him, become what they are? I was also part Cassie in that same story, the girl who hung back, and indeed part of most of the main characters in the connected stories into whose minds I go. Except for Virgie, the heroine. She is right outside me. She is powerfully like Miss Eckhart, her co-equal in stubborn and passionate feeling, while more expressive of it—but fully apart from me. And as Miss Eckhart's powers shrink and fade away, the young Virgie grows up more rampant, and struggles into some sort of life independent from all the rest.

If somewhere in its course your work seems to you to have come into a life of its own, and you can stand back from it and leave it be, you are looking then at your subject—so I feel. This is how I came to regard the character of Virgie in *The Golden Apples.* She comes into her own in the last of the stories, "The Wanderers." Passionate, recalcitrant, stubbornly undefeated by failure or hurt or disgrace or bereavement, all the while heedlessly wasting of her gifts, she knows to the last that there is a world that remains out there, a world living and mysterious, and that she is of it.

Inasmuch as Miss Eckhart might have been said to come from me, the author, Virgie, at her moments, might have always been my subject.

Through learning at my later date things I hadn't known, or had escaped or possibly feared realizing, about my parents—and myself—I glimpse our whole family life as if it were freed of that clock time which spaces us apart so inhibitingly, divides young and old, keeps our living through the same experiences at separate distances.

It is our inward journey that leads us through time—forward or back, seldom in a straight line, most often spiraling. Each of us is moving, changing, with respect to others. As we discover, we remember; remembering, we discover; and most intensely do we experience this when our separate journeys converge. Our living experience at those meeting points is one of the charged dramatic fields of fiction.

I'm prepared now to use the wonderful word *confluence*, which of itself exists as a reality and a symbol in one. It is the only kind of symbol that for me as a writer has any weight, testifying to the pattern, one of the chief patterns, of human experience.

Here I am leading to the last scenes in my novel, *The Optimist's Daughter*:

> She had slept in the chair, like a passenger who had come on an emergency journey in a train. But she had rested deeply.
>
> She had dreamed that she *was* a passenger, and riding with Phil. They had ridden together over a long bridge.
>
> Awake, she recognized it: it was a dream of something that had really happened. When she and Phil were coming down from Chicago to Mount Salus to be married in the Presbyterian Church, they came on the train. Laurel, when she travelled back and forth between Mount Salus and Chicago, had always taken the sleeper. She and Phil followed the route on the day train, and she saw it for the first time.
>
> When they were climbing the long approach to a bridge after leaving Cairo, rising slowly higher until they rode above the tops of bare trees, she looked down and saw the pale light widening and the river bottoms opening out, and then the water appearing, reflecting the low, early sun. There were two rivers. Here was where they came together. This was the confluence of the waters, the Ohio and the Mississippi.
>
> They were looking down from a great elevation and all they saw was at the point of coming together, the bare trees marching in from the horizon, the rivers moving into one, and as he touched her arm she looked up with him and saw the long, ragged, pencil-faint line of birds within the crystal of the zenith, flying in a V of their own, following the same course down. All they could see was sky, water, birds, light, and confluence. It was the whole morning world.
>
> And they themselves were a part of the confluence. Their own joint act of faith had brought them here at

the very moment and matched its occurrence, and proceeded as it proceeded. Direction itself was made beautiful, momentous. They were riding as one with it, right up front. It's our turn! she'd thought exultantly. And we're going to live forever.

Left bodiless and graveless of a death made of water and fire in a year long gone, Phil could still tell her of her life. For her life, any life, she had to believe, was nothing but the continuity of its love.

She believed it just as she believed that the confluence of the waters was still happening at Cairo. It would be there the same as it ever was when she went flying over it today on her way back—out of sight, for her, this time, thousands of feet below, but with nothing in between except thin air.

Of course the greatest confluence of all is that which makes up the human memory—the individual human memory. My own is the treasure most dearly regarded by me, in my life and in my work as a writer. Here time, also, is subject to confluence. The memory is a living thing—it too is in transit. But during its moment, all that is remembered joins, and lives—the old and the young, the past and the present, the living and the dead.

As you have seen, I am a writer who came of a sheltered life. A sheltered life can be a daring life as well. For all serious daring starts from within.

CHRONOLOGY

NOTE ON THE TEXTS

NOTES

Chronology

1909 Born Eudora Alice Welty on April 13 in Jackson, Mississippi, to Chestina Andrews Welty, b. 1883, and Christian Webb Welty, b. 1879. Father is secretary and a director of Lamar Life Insurance Company in Jackson; mother is a homemaker and avid gardener. (Grandfather Jefferson Welty, a descendant of German-Swiss immigrants who came to America before the Revolutionary War, is the son of Salome and Christian Welty, early settlers in Marion Township, Hocking County, Ohio. Grandfather married Allie Webb and with her established a farm near Logan, Ohio; she died in 1886. Grandfather Edward "Ned" Raboteau Andrews, b. 1862, studied at Trinity College in North Carolina and worked as a journalist and photographer in Norfolk, Virginia, then practiced law in West Virginia; he married Eudora Carden, the daughter of Eudora Ayres and William Carden, a Baptist preacher, and they lived near Clay, West Virginia. After grandfather's death at age 37, mother taught school and earned a degree from Marshall College. Parents met during father's employment at a West Virginia lumber company; they married in 1904 and moved into rented house on North Congress Street in Jackson, where father had joined Lamar. Their first child, Christian, died in infancy.)

1912 Brother Edward Jefferson Welty born.

1915–20 Having learned to read at home, Welty enters first grade at Jefferson Davis Elementary School in January 1915. Also attends Sunday school at Methodist Episcopal Church South, although family are not regular churchgoers. Brother Walter Andrews Welty born in 1915. Around the age of seven, Welty is diagnosed with a fast-beating heart and confined to bed for several months. Enjoys family life, including Sunday drives, summer visits to grandparents in Ohio and West Virginia, and going to theater and concerts with parents, both music lovers; mother is also an avid reader and father is an opera aficionado. Welty reads books from home and public library including myths and nursery rhymes, the Brothers Grimm, Edward Lear, Dickens,

Scott, Robert Louis Stevenson, Mark Twain, Ring Lardner, encyclopedias, and popular sentimental and didactic fiction. Enjoys drawing and playing upright Steinway piano bought by mother with earnings from selling the milk of her Jersey cow. Learns about photography from father, who develops his own pictures, and from mother to study Bible with use of a concordance. Goes to movies weekly. A drawing by Welty is published in children's magazine *St. Nicholas* in August 1920.

1921–24 Wins $25 prize in summer in Jackie Mackie Jingles contest sponsored by Mackie Pine Oil Specialty Co., which sends letter encouraging Welty to "improve in poetry to such an extent as to win fame." Begins attending Jackson's Central High School in fall 1921; publishes sketches and poems in school newspaper and *St. Nicholas* and one of her drawings is accepted by the Memphis *Commercial Appeal.*

1925–26 Parents build new home on Pinehurst Street in Jackson. Welty enrolls in fall 1925 at Mississippi State College for Women in Columbus with plans to become a writer; shares room in Old Main dormitory with three other students. For first time, gets to know people from throughout the state and is fascinated by their different accents. Tries writing a novel; publishes sketches, poems, and stories in campus newspaper, *The Spectator*, and two of her drawings appear in campus magazine *O, Lady!* (later describes herself during these years as "a wit and humorist of the parochial kind").

1927–29 Transfers to University of Wisconsin, Madison, for junior and senior years; concentrates on literature and fine arts and considers career as an artist. Studies literary modernists including Virginia Woolf, Faulkner, and Yeats, who becomes her favorite poet. Also reads Irish writer Æ (George Russell) and Russian novelists. Feels lonely in what she later describes as the "icy world" of Madison, whose people "seemed to me like sticks of flint." Poem "Shadows" published in *Wisconsin Literary Magazine* (April 1928). Makes frequent visits to Chicago and spends time at the Art Institute while waiting for train connections between Mississippi and Madison. Graduates with

B.A. degree in 1929. Becomes seriously interested in photography; uses Kodak camera with a bellows and develops her own prints.

1930 Begins one-year advertising course at Columbia University Graduate School of Business in New York City; rooms with friends from Jackson. Regularly visits galleries, museums, and theater, where she enjoys musical comedy and revues, as well as jazz clubs and vaudeville shows in Harlem.

1931–34 With jobs scarce in the Depression, returns home at completion of Columbia course in 1931. Shortly after, father becomes critically ill with leukemia and dies while receiving a blood transfusion from mother, with Welty at bedside. Welty gets work writing scripts, doing odd jobs, and editing *Lamar Life Radio News* at WJIX, first Jackson radio station, which is housed in Lamar Life building. Also works as Jackson social news correspondent for the Memphis *Commercial Appeal.*

1935–36 Works as publicity agent for the Works Progress Administration in Mississippi, traveling throughout the state to photograph and report on WPA projects and people they serve; uses Recomar camera and in 1936 buys a Rolleiflex. Prepares group of her photographs, titled "Black Saturday," in spring 1935 and sends them to New York publisher Harrison Smith, who rejects them. Visits New York City with the photographs; fails to find a publisher, but Lugene Opticians sponsors exhibition of 45 of the prints at Photographic Galleries, March 31–April 15, 1936, and that summer Samuel Robbins proposes mounting a second exhibit at the Camera House (it is held March 6–31, 1937). Welty applies for, but fails to receive, job as a photographer with the Resettlement Administration in New York City. Submits stories to prestigious little magazine *Manuscript*, published in Athens, Ohio, which accepts "Death of a Traveling Salesman" and "Magic." Begins receiving letters from publishers inquiring about her writing a novel; she suggests a collection of stories, but the proposal is not accepted. Meets at her home with friends including young writers Frank Lyell, Hubert Creekmore, Nash Burger, and composer and conductor Lehman Engel; dubs the group Night-Blooming Cereus Club.

1937 Works on short stories; sends several to Robert Penn Warren and Cleanth Brooks, editors of the newly established *Southern Review* at Louisiana State University. Discouraged when they return "Petrified Man," which was previously rejected by other journals, Welty destroys the only copy of it (when Warren expresses second thoughts about the story, she rewrites it from memory). Six of Welty's photographs appear in *Life* (Nov. 8, 1937) in conjunction with story, for which she did research, about series of deaths in Mount Olive, Mississippi, caused by new form of the prescription drug sulfanilamide. Three other photographs are chosen for *Mississippi: A Guide to the Magnolia State* (published by Federal Writers Project in 1938). Continues to circulate photographs, along with a collection of stories, to New York publishers, but they are rejected partly on grounds that the genre of photo-fiction is saturated.

1938 "Lily Daw and the Three Ladies" (*Prairie Schooner*, Winter 1937) appears in *The Best Short Stories 1938*. Warren, Brooks, and Katherine Anne Porter sponsor Welty in Houghton Mifflin Fellowship contest for first novels; her entry receives high rating but does not win. Ford Madox Ford writes Welty in November praising her work; she sends him a collection of her stories and he submits it to publishers in England and America, but without success.

1939 "A Curtain of Green" (*Southern Review*, Autumn 1938) is chosen for *The Best Short Stories 1939* and "Petrified Man" (*Southern Review*, Spring 1939) for *O. Henry Prize Stories of 1939*. Continues publishing in *Southern Review*. Visited in autumn by John Woodburn, an editor and scout for Doubleday, Doran to whom she has been recommended by Brooks and Warren; he takes back a collection of her stories but it is rejected.

1940 Learns that "The Hitch-Hikers" (*Southern Review*, Autumn 1939) has been chosen for *The Best Short Stories 1940*. Takes on Diarmuid Russell, son of George Russell (Æ) and a founder of new Russell & Volkening literary agency in New York, as her agent in June; he begins working to place her fiction in well-paying magazines such as *Atlantic Monthly*, *The New Yorker*, and *Harper's Bazaar*, and seeks publisher for a story collection. Welty spends part of summer on fellowship at Bread Loaf Writers' Conference in Middlebury, Vermont; sees Russell in New York in August and they begin close working relationship and enduring friendship. Concentrates on writing stories set in the Natchez Trace area; reads Robert Coates' *The Outlaw Years.* In early December, *Atlantic Monthly* accepts "Powerhouse" and "A Worn Path."

1941 Doubleday, Doran offers contract for story collection (published in November, with introduction by Katherine Anne Porter, as *A Curtain of Green*). "A Worn Path" wins second prize in the O. Henry Awards competition. Spends June–July on fellowship at Yaddo writers colony, Saratoga Springs, New York; shares housing with Katherine Anne Porter. Night-Blooming Cereus Club entertains Henry Miller during his three-day visit to Jackson; he offers to put Welty in contact with publishers in the pornographic market.

1942 Wins a Guggenheim fellowship for writing fiction in spring. *The Robber Bridegroom* is published by Doubleday, Doran in October. "The Wide Net" wins first prize in the O. Henry Awards competition for 1942. Hearing in November that Woodburn has left Doubleday for Harcourt, Brace, Welty decides to move with him.

1943 *The Wide Net and Other Stories* is published by Harcourt in September. "Livvie is Back" (later titled "Livvie") wins first prize in O. Henry Awards competition for 1943, "Asphodel" is included in *The Best American Short Stories 1943*, and "Old Mr. Marblehall" and "A Piece of News" are included in Brooks and Warren's textbook *Understanding Fiction.*

1944–45 Moves to New York City for summer to work for Robert Van Gelder at *The New York Times Book Review* (for reviews of books on the war, Welty writes under pseudonym "Michael Ravenna"); continues writing reviews after return to Jackson. Works on story "The Delta Cousins" based on stories and documents of friend John Fraiser Robinson's family; by January 1945 it "boils over" into a novel that she calls "Shellmound" (later *Delta Wedding*).

1946 Story "A Sketching Trip" wins mention in O. Henry Awards competition for 1946. *Delta Wedding* is serialized in *Atlantic Monthly* (Jan.–April 1946) and brought out as a book by Harcourt in April. Begins writing stories that are later collected in *The Golden Apples.* Travels in November to San Francisco for a stay that stretches to four months; while there, writes story "Music from Spain," sees a lot of John Fraiser Robinson, and makes new friends including Art and Antonette Fereva Foff, clients of Russell.

1947 Receives letter from E. M. Forster praising her work, particularly *The Wide Net.* Delivers lecture at Northwest Pacific Writers' Conference at University of Washington in August, then uses fee to stay in San Francisco until late November; buys new Royal typewriter. Continues working on short stories and revises lecture to form first extended essay in literary criticism, "The Reading and Writing of Short Stories" (published in *Atlantic Monthly,* Feb. 1949).

1948 Despite urging of Russell that she finish revisions of *The Golden Apples,* goes to New York to collaborate with Hildegarde Dolson on revue "The Waiting Room" (only Welty's skit "Bye-Bye Brevoort" is later produced). Also collaborates by mail with Robinson on screenplay of *The Robber Bridegroom* (completed in 1949, it is never produced).

1949 Hears that her Guggenheim fellowship has been renewed. After *The Golden Apples* is published by Harcourt, sails to Italy, where she sees Robinson, and to France where she travels with *Harper's Bazaar* editor Mary Louise Aswell. Goes on to England and then by ferry to Ireland; sends note to Elizabeth Bowen, who has reviewed Welty's work favorably, and is invited to visit her at home in County Cork.

1951 "The Burning," published in *Harper's Bazaar* (March 1951), wins second prize in O. Henry competition for 1951. Travels to England in spring to deliver lecture at Cambridge University based on "The Reading and Writing of Short Stories"; visits Bowen in Ireland, where she works on "The Bride of the Innisfallen," and spends June to mid-July in London; also sees Elizabeth Spencer and Stephen Spender. In late November accompanies Bowen to New Orleans and Shreveport on part of her American lecture tour.

1952–54 Elected to the National Institute of Arts and Letters in 1952. *The Ponder Heart* appears in *The New Yorker* (Dec. 5, 1953) and is published by Harcourt in January 1954; it is also a Book-of-the-Month Club selection. Writes "Place in Fiction" for Fulbright program held at Cambridge University in July 1954. *Selected Stories of Eudora Welty*, including *A Curtain of Green* and *The Wide Net*, published by Modern Library.

1955 *The Bride of the Innisfallen and Other Stories*, dedicated to Bowen, published by Harcourt in January. Delivers "Place in Fiction" at Duke University in February; meets Reynolds Price, then editor of student paper *The Archive*. Mother suffers a slow and difficult recuperation from eye surgery. While caring for her, Welty works on a "long story about the country" (eventually *Losing Battles*), writing brief vignettes and scenes which she keeps in shoe boxes for assembling later.

1956 With mother and Jackson friends who charter a plane for the event, attends New York opening on February 16 of Joseph Fields and Jerome Chodorov's adaptation of *The Ponder Heart*; starring David Wayne as Uncle Daniel and Una Merkel as Edna Earle, it runs for 149 performances. Returns to the city for May 22 opening at Phoenix Theatre of *The Littlest Revue* which includes Welty's 1948 skit "Bye-Bye Brevoort."

1959 Brother Walter dies in January.

1960 On Ford Foundation grant spends two seasons of study and observation at Phoenix Theatre in New York.

1962 Serves as guest lecturer at Smith College in Massachusetts in winter term; in May is chosen to present the National Institute of Arts and Letters' Gold Medal for Fiction to William Faulkner.

1963 In response to the assassination in Jackson on June 12 of Mississippi NAACP leader Medgar Evers, writes "Where Is the Voice Coming From?" (published in *The New Yorker*, July 6, 1963).

1964 Children's book *Pepe, The Shoe Bird*, with illustrations by Beth Krush, published by Harcourt, Brace & World Inc. in October.

1965 Russell circulates parts of *Losing Battles*, and in April Bennett Cerf at Random House offers a lucrative contract; Welty remains with Harcourt. Writes essay "Must the Novelist Crusade?" during civil rights disturbances in Mississippi.

1966 Mother dies on January 20 after a long and painful series of illnesses. Brother Edward dies on January 24.

1967 Welty completes a draft of "Poor Eyes" in May 1967, which Russell sends to *The New Yorker* (titled "The Optimist's Daughter," it appears March 15, 1969).

1968 "The Demonstrators" (*The New Yorker*, Nov. 26, 1966) wins first prize in O. Henry competition.

1969 Sends completed draft of *Losing Battles* to Russell in May 1969 and he sends it out for bids to several publishers. When Harcourt demands cuts, Welty terminates contract with them and in August signs with Random House for four books, including *Losing Battles.*

1970 *Losing Battles*, dedicated to her brothers, is published on Welty's birthday; it becomes her biggest seller and precipitates re-issues of her earlier works.

1971 *One Time, One Place*, photographs of Mississippi during the Depression (many part of the 1935 "Black Saturday" group), published by Random House in October. Welty receives nomination for 1971 National Book Award for *Losing Battles.*

1972 *The Optimist's Daughter*, a revision of *The New Yorker* text, published by Random House in spring. In May receives Gold Medal of the National Institute of Arts and Letters; it is presented by Katherine Anne Porter.

1973 Wins Pulitzer Prize for *The Optimist's Daughter* in April. Honored by celebration of May 2, 1973, as Eudora Welty Day in Mississippi. Diarmuid Russell, who had retired in the spring because of illness, dies on December 16.

1978 *The Eye of the Story: Selected Essays and Reviews* published by Random House in April.

1979 Wins National Medal for Literature.

1980 *The Collected Stories of Eudora Welty*, published by Harcourt in October, wins the American Library Association Notable Book and the American Book awards. Awarded the Medal of Freedom by President Jimmy Carter at White House ceremony in June.

1983 Delivers William E. Massey Sr. Lectures in the History of American Civilization at Harvard University in April.

1984 *One Writer's Beginnings*, a version of the Massey lectures, is published by Harvard University Press and wins the American Book and National Book Critics Circle awards.

1987 Made Chevalier de l'Ordre des Arts et Lettres (France). Continues over the next decade to write occasional book reviews, introductory essays, and prefaces.

1989 *Eudora Welty Photographs*, including 226 photographs from the Welty collection at the Mississippi Department of Archives and History, published with foreword by Reynolds Price by University Press of Mississippi.

1996 Inducted into France's Légion d'honneur at ceremony held in Old Capitol building in Jackson.

Note on the Texts

This volume presents 41 short stories by Eudora Welty, including the complete contents of her collections *A Curtain of Green and Other Stories* (1941), *The Wide Net and Other Stories* (1943), *The Golden Apples* (1949), and *The Bride of the Innisfallen and Other Stories* (1955), as well as her later stories "Where Is the Voice Coming From?" (1963) and "The Demonstrators" (1966). It also contains a selection of nine essays that were first published between 1943 and 1980 and the memoir *One Writer's Beginnings* (1984).

Welty's practice was to revise her stories for collection soon after they were first published in periodicals, and early in her career she began to consider periodical publication as an interim step in the completion of her stories. She also took care with the arrangement of her story collections, which she thought of as works in their own right, and was closely involved in the first publications of them. All four collections were later included in *The Collected Stories of Eudora Welty*, published by Harcourt Brace Jovanovich in 1980, with revisions made or authorized by Welty up to forty years after the first publications of her stories.

Welty's first collection of stories was accepted by Doubleday, Doran in January 1941 and published as *A Curtain of Green and Other Stories* that November. The book was also published in London in 1943, without Welty's participation, by John Lane: The Bodley Head, which made numerous editorial changes to accord with British conventions and house style, and in 1947 in New York by Welty's new publisher, Harcourt, Brace, which used the British edition as setting copy. Welty did not make any revisions and apparently did not read proofs for the Harcourt edition, which includes numerous corruptions, such as dropped paragraphs and the rendering of some dialect and colloquialisms as standard English. The Harcourt edition was later used for the Modern Library's *Selected Stories of Eudora Welty* (1954) and Harcourt Brace's *The Collected Stories of Eudora Welty* (1980). Although Welty made some revisions for the Harcourt Brace collection, she did not rectify the corruptions in it, most of which were retained. This volume prints the text of the first 1941 Doubleday, Doran printing. Following is a list of the original publications of the 17 stories in it: "Lily Daw and the Three Ladies," *Prairie Schooner*, Winter 1937; "A Piece of News," *Southern Review*, Summer 1937; "Petrified Man," *Southern Review*, Spring 1939; "The Key," *Harper's Bazaar*, August 1941; "Keela, the Outcast Indian Maiden," *New*

Directions in Prose and Poetry, ed. James Laughlin (Norfolk, Connecticut: New Directions Press, 1940); "Why I Live at the P.O.," *Atlantic Monthly*, April 1941; "The Whistle," *Prairie Schooner*, Fall 1938; "The Hitch-Hikers," *Southern Review*, Autumn 1939; "A Memory," *Southern Review*, Autumn 1937; "Clytie," *Southern Review*, Summer 1941; "Old Mr Marblehall," *Southern Review*, Spring 1938, titled "Old Mr. Grenada"; "Flowers for Marjorie," *Prairie Schooner*, Summer 1937; "A Curtain of Green," *Southern Review*, Autumn 1938; "A Visit of Charity," *Decision*, June 1941; "Death of a Traveling Salesman," *Manuscript*, May–June 1936; "Powerhouse," *Atlantic Monthly*, June 1941; "A Worn Path," *Atlantic Monthly*, February 1941.

Welty's second story collection, *The Wide Net and Other Stories*, was published by Harcourt, Brace on September 23, 1943. It was also published in London in 1945 by John Lane: The Bodley Head, with variants made in accordance with British and house-style conventions, and it was included in Modern Library's *Selected Stories of Eudora Welty* (1954) and, with some late revisions by Welty, in Harcourt Brace's *The Collected Stories of Eudora Welty* (1980). This volume prints the text of the first 1943 Harcourt printing. Following is a list of the original publications of the eight stories in it: "First Love," *Harper's Bazaar*, February 1942; "The Wide Net," *Harper's Magazine*, May 1942; "A Still Moment," *American Prefaces*, Spring 1942; "Asphodel," *Yale Review*, September 1942; "The Winds," *Harper's Bazaar*, August 1942; "The Purple Hat," *Harper's Bazaar*, November 1941; "Livvie," *Atlantic Monthly*, November 1942, titled "Livvie Is Back"; "At the Landing," *Tomorrow*, April 1943.

Welty called the seven stories in her third collection, *The Golden Apples*, "inter-related, but not inter-dependent" and, while preparing the stories for collection by Harcourt, Brace, changed some of the original titles and included a list of "Main Families in Morgana, Mississippi." The collection was published by Harcourt on August 18, 1949, and, with no supervision by Welty, in London in 1950 by John Lane: The Bodley Head. It was also collected, with late revisions by Welty, in *The Collected Stories of Eudora Welty* (1980). This volume prints the text of the first 1949 Harcourt printing. Following is a list of the original publications of the stories in it: "Shower of Gold," *Atlantic Monthly*, May 1948; "June Recital," *Harper's Bazaar*, September 1947, titled "Golden Apples"; "Sir Rabbit," *Hudson Review*, Spring 1949; "Moon Lake," *Sewanee Review*, Summer 1949; "The Whole World Knows," *Harper's Bazaar*, March 1947; "Music from Spain" as a separate publication (Greenville, Mississippi: The Levee Press, December 1948); "The Wanderers," *Harper's Bazaar*, March 1949, as "The Hummingbirds."

Although Welty promised Harcourt, Brace the manuscript of her next story collection, *The Bride of the Innisfallen and Other Stories*, in 1951, the composition of *The Ponder Heart* and its staging as a Broadway play intervened, and she was unable to complete the final typescript for the collection until the spring of 1954. Welty made further revisions to some of the stories in proofs in late 1954, and the collection was published by Harcourt on April 6, 1955. Hamish Hamilton also published the book in London in October 1955, with variants resulting from differences in British and American conventions, and the collection was included, with late revisions by Welty, in *The Collected Stories of Eudora Welty* (1980). This volume prints the text of the first 1955 Harcourt printing. Following is a list of the original publications of the seven stories in it: "No Place for You, My Love," *The New Yorker*, September 20, 1952; "The Burning," *Harper's Bazaar*, March 1951; "The Bride of the Innisfallen," *The New Yorker*, December 1, 1951; "Ladies in Spring," *Sewanee Review*, Winter 1954, titled "Spring"; "Circe," *Accent*, Autumn 1949, titled "Put Me in the Sky!"; "Kin," *The New Yorker*, November 15, 1952; and "Going to Naples," *Harper's Bazaar*, July 1954.

The present volume includes, in a section titled "Other Stories," two stories written in the 1960s. Welty wrote "Where Is the Voice Coming From?" following the murder of Mississippi NAACP leader Medgar Evers in Jackson on June 12, 1963, and revised the story over the telephone with *New Yorker* editor William Maxwell after it was accepted by the magazine on June 26. "By then, an arrest had been made in Jackson," Welty later wrote, "and the fiction's outward details had to be changed where by chance they had resembled too closely those of actuality, for the story must not be found prejudicial to the case of a person who must be on trial for his life." The story was published in *The New Yorker* on July 6, 1963, and reprinted in *Write and Rewrite: A Study of the Creative Process*, ed. John Kuehl (New York: Meredith Press, 1967), along with an unrevised draft of the story titled "From the Unknown." Welty wrote "The Demonstrators" in the fall of 1965; it was published in *The New Yorker* on November 26, 1966. The texts of the two stories presented here are of *The New Yorker* printings. (Both stories were included, without change, in *The Collected Stories of Eudora Welty*.)

This volume also includes, under the heading "Selected Essays," eight pieces from *The Eye of the Story*, Welty's first essay collection, published by Random House in 1978, and the "Preface" to *The Collected Stories of Eudora Welty*, which was published by Harcourt Brace in October 1980. Welty made minor revisions to most of the previously published essays while preparing them for collection in *The Eye of the Story* and had more control over the book, for which she read and corrected proofs, than the periodical publications. For only one of the essays, "Writing and Analyzing a Story," did she heavily revise and rewrite an earlier piece. This volume prints the text of the "Preface" to *The Collected Stories of Eudora Welty* from the first 1980 Harcourt Brace printing of that collection; the texts of the other eight essays are taken from the first 1978 Random House printing of *The Eye of the Story.* Versions of those eight essays first appeared as follows: "A Pageant of Birds" was originally published in *New Republic*, October 25, 1943, and "Some Notes on River Country" in *Harper's Bazaar*, February 1944; "Writing and Analyzing a Story" is a heavily revised version of "How I Write," which appeared in *Virginia Quarterly Review*, Spring 1955; "Place in Fiction" was prepared for a 1954 conference on American studies at Cambridge University and was first published in the Duke University paper *The Archive*, April 1955, and then in *South Atlantic Quarterly*, January 1956; "A Sweet Devouring" appeared in *Mademoiselle*, December 1957; "Must the Novelist Crusade?" appeared in *Atlantic Monthly*, October 1965, and was reprinted in *Writer's Digest*, February 1970; " 'Is Phoenix Jackson's Grandson Really Dead?' " was published in *Critical Inquiry*, September 1974, and in *The New York Times Book Review*, as "The Point of the Story," March 5, 1978; "The Little Store" appeared in *Esquire*, December 1975, as "The Corner Store" and was reprinted in *Mom, the Flag, and Apple Pie: Great American Writers on Great American Things* (Doubleday, 1976; compiled by editors of *Esquire*) as "The Neighborhood Grocery Store."

Welty's memoir, *One Writer's Beginnings*, originated in three lectures that she delivered at Harvard University in April 1983 to inaugurate the William E. Massey Sr. Lectures in the History of American Civilization. She revised her lectures for publication by Harvard University Press, which published the memoir on February 20, 1984; that text is reproduced here.

This volume presents the texts of the original printings chosen for inclusion here, but it does not attempt to reproduce features of their typographic design, such as display capitalization at the beginnings of pieces. The texts are printed without change, except for the correction of typographical errors. Spelling, punctuation, and capitalization are often expressive features, and they are not altered, even when inconsistent or irregular. Except for clear typographical errors, the spelling and usage of foreign words and phrases are left as they appear in the original texts. The following is a list of typographical errors corrected, cited by page and line number: 66.27, ukelele; 70.8, Morton's; 86.30, spent; 101.28, since,; 196.8, of weapon; 206.29,

Beula; 218.38, all,; 219.17, base; 259.30, camp; 469.34, part; 490.39, ideness; 505.35, on; 635.7, "*Excalibur*—; 650.3, Katee; 670.34, stereoptican; 670.38, stereoptican; 671.11, stereoptican; 700.24, Gabriella," are; 758.19, caracter; 763.35, "divertisements"; 787.33, mediation; 789.32, O'Faolàin; 861.15, parent's; 903.9, gread; 910.30, daguerrotype; 914.4, relevation; 922.13, gutteral; 929.31, Chatauqua; 936.39, her on.

Notes

In the notes below, the reference numbers denote page and line of this volume (the line count includes headings). No note is made for material included in standard desk-reference books such as Webster's *Collegiate*, *Biographical*, and *Geographical* dictionaries. Biblical references are keyed to the King James Version. For further background and references to other studies, see Michael Kreyling, *Author and Agent: Eudora Welty and Diarmuid Russell* (New York: Farrar Straus Giroux, 1991); Noel Polk, *Eudora Welty: A Bibliography of Her Work* (Jackson: University Press of Mississippi, 1994); Suzanne Marrs, *The Welty Collection: A Guide to the Eudora Welty Manuscripts and Documents at the Mississippi Department of Archives and History* (Jackson: University Press of Mississippi, 1988); *Conversations with Eudora Welty* (Jackson: University Press of Mississippi, 1984), ed. Peggy Whitman Prenshaw.

A CURTAIN OF GREEN, AND OTHER STORIES

1.1–2 A CURTAIN . . . *Stories*] The first and most later editions include an Introduction by Katherine Anne Porter; it reads:

> Friends of us both first brought Eudora Welty to visit me three years ago in Louisiana. It was hot midsummer, they had driven over from Mississippi, her home state, and we spent a pleasant evening together talking in the cool old house with all the windows open. Miss Welty sat listening, as she must have done a great deal of listening on many such occasions. She was and is a quiet, tranquil-looking, modest girl, and unlike the young Englishman of the story, she has something to be modest about, as this collection of short stories proves.
>
> She considers her personal history as hardly worth mentioning, a fact in itself surprising enough, since a vivid personal career of fabulous ups and downs, hardships and strokes of luck, travels in far countries, spiritual and intellectual exile, defensive flight, homesick return with a determined groping for native roots, and a confusion of contradictory jobs have long been the mere conventions of an American author's life. Miss Welty was born and brought up in Jackson, Mississippi, where her father, now dead, was president of a Southern insurance company. Family life was cheerful and thriving; she seems to have got on excellently with both her parents and her two brothers. Education, in the Southern manner with daughters, was continuous, indulgent, and precisely as serious as she chose to make it. She went from school in Mississippi to the University of Wisconsin, thence to Columbia, New York, and so home again where she lives with her mother, among her

lifelong friends and acquaintances, quite simply and amiably. She tried a job or two because that seemed the next thing, and did some publicity and newspaper work; but as she had no real need of a job, she gave up the notion and settled down to writing.

She loves music, listens to a great deal of it, all kinds; grows flowers very successfully, and remarks that she is "underfoot locally," meaning that she has a normal amount of social life. Normal social life in a medium-sized Southern town can become a pretty absorbing occupation, and the only comment her friends make when a new story appears is, "Why, Eudora, when did you write that?" Not how, or even why, just when. They see her about so much, what time has she for writing? Yet she spends an immense amount of time at it. "I haven't a literary life at all," she wrote once, "not much of a confession, maybe. But I do feel that the people and things I love are of a true and human world, and there is no clutter about them. . . . I would not understand a literary life."

We can do no less than dismiss that topic as casually as she does. Being the child of her place and time, profiting perhaps without being aware of it by the cluttered experiences, foreign travels, and disorders of the generation immediately preceding her, she will never have to go away and live among the Eskimos, or Mexican Indians; she need not follow a war and smell death to feel herself alive: she knows about death already. She shall not need even to live in New York in order to feel that she is having the kind of experience, the sense of "life" proper to a serious author. She gets her right nourishment from the source natural to her—her experience so far has been quite enough for her and of precisely the right kind. She began writing spontaneously when she was a child, being a born writer; she continued without any plan for a profession, without any particular encouragement, and, as it proved, not needing any. For a good many years she believed she was going to be a painter, and painted quite earnestly while she wrote without much effort.

Nearly all the Southern writers I know were early, omnivorous, insatiable readers, and Miss Welty runs reassuringly true to this pattern. She had at arm's reach the typical collection of books which existed as a matter of course in a certain kind of Southern family, so that she had read the ancient Greek and Roman poetry, history and fable, Shakespeare, Milton, Dante, the eighteenth-century English and the nineteenth-century French novelists, with a dash of Tolstoy and Dostoievsky, before she realized what she was reading. When she first discovered contemporary literature, she was just the right age to find first W. B. Yeats and Virginia Woolf in the air around her; but always, from the beginning until now, she loved folk tales, fairy tales, old legends, and she likes to listen to the songs and stories of people who live in old communities whose culture is recollected and bequeathed orally.

She has never studied the writing craft in any college. She has never belonged to a literary group, and until after her first collection was ready to be published she had never discussed with any colleague or older artist any problem of her craft. Nothing else that I know about her could be more satisfactory to me than this; it seems to me immensely right, the very way a young artist should grow, with pride and independence and the courage really to face out the individual struggle; to make and correct mistakes and take the consequences of them, to stand firmly on his own feet in the end. I believe in the rightness of Miss Welty's instinctive knowledge that writing cannot be taught, but only learned, and learned by the individual in his own way, at his own pace and in his own time, for the process of mastering the medium is part of a cellular growth in a most complex organism; it is a way of life and a mode of being which cannot be divided from the kind of human creature you were the day you were born, and only in obeying the law of this singular being can the artist know his true directions and the right ends for him.

Miss Welty escaped, by miracle, the whole corrupting and destructive influence of the contemporary, organized tampering with young and promising talents by professional teachers who are rather monotonously divided into two major sorts: those theorists who are incapable of producing one passable specimen of the art they profess to teach; or good, sometimes first-rate, artists who are humanly unable to resist forming disciples and imitators among their students. It is all well enough to say that, of this second class, the able talent will throw off the master's influence and strike out for himself. Such influence has merely added new obstacles to an already difficult road. Miss Welty escaped also a militant social consciousness, in the current radical-intellectual sense, she never professed Communism, and she has not expressed, except implicitly, any attitude at all on the state of politics or the condition of society. But there is an ancient system of ethics, an unanswerable, indispensable moral law, on which she is grounded firmly, and this, it would seem to me, is ample domain enough; these laws have never been the peculiar property of any party or creed or nation, they relate to that true and human world of which the artist is a living part; and when he dissociates himself from it in favor of a set of political, which is to say, inhuman, rules, he cuts himself away from his proper society—living men.

There exist documents of political and social theory which belong, if not to poetry, certainly to the department of humane letters. They are reassuring statements of the great hopes and dearest faiths of mankind and they are acts of high imagination. But all working, practical political systems, even those professing to originate in moral grandeur, are based upon and operate by contempt of human life and the individual fate; in accepting any one of them and shaping his mind and work to that mold, the artist dehumanizes himself, unfits himself for the practise of any art.

Not being in a hurry, Miss Welty was past twenty-six years when she offered her first story, "The Death of a Traveling Salesman," to the editor of a little magazine unable to pay, for she could not believe that anyone would buy a story from her; the magazine was *Manuscript*, the editor John Rood, and he accepted it gladly. Rather surprised, Miss Welty next tried the *Southern Review*, where she met with a great welcome and the enduring partisanship of Albert Erskine, who regarded her as his personal discovery. The story was "A Piece of News" and it was followed by others published in the *Southern Review*, the *Atlantic Monthly*, and *Harper's Bazaar*.

She has, then, never been neglected, never unappreciated, and she feels simply lucky about it. She wrote to a friend: "When I think of Ford Madox Ford! You remember how you gave him my name and how he tried his best to find a publisher for my book of stories all that last year of his life; and he wrote me so many charming notes, all of his time going to his little brood of promising writers, the kind of thing that could have gone on forever. Once I read in the *Saturday Review* an article of his on the species and the way they were neglected by publishers, and he used me as the example chosen at random. He ended his cry with 'What is to become of both branches of Anglo-Saxondom if this state of things continues?' Wasn't that wonderful, really, and typical? I may have been more impressed by that than would other readers who knew him. I did not know him, but I knew it was typical. And here I myself have turned out to be not at all the martyred promising writer, but have had all the good luck and all the good things Ford chided the world for withholding from me and my kind."

But there is a trap just ahead, and all short-story writers know what it is—The Novel. That novel which every publisher hopes to obtain from every short-story writer of any gifts at all, and who finally does obtain it, nine times out of ten. Already publishers have told her, "Give us first a novel, and then we will publish your short stories." It is a special sort of trap for poets, too, though quite often a good poet can and does write a good novel. Miss Welty has tried her hand at novels, laboriously, dutifully, youthfully thinking herself perhaps in the wrong to refuse, since so many authoritarians have told her that this was the next step. She can very well become a master of the short story, there are almost perfect stories in this book. It is quite possible she can never write a novel, and there is no reason why she should. The short story is a special and difficult medium, and contrary to a widely spread popular superstition it has no formula that can be taught by a correspondence school. There is nothing to hinder her from writing novels if she wishes or believes she can. I only say that her good gift, just as it is now, alive and flourishing, should not be retarded by a perfectly artificial demand upon her to do the conventional thing. It is a fact that the public for short stories is smaller than the public for novels; this seems to me no good reason for depriving the minority. I remember a reader writing to an editor, complaining that he did not like collections of short stories because, just as he had got himself worked into one mood or frame of mind, he was called upon to change to another. If that is an important objection, we might also apply it to music. We might compare the novel to a symphony, and a collection of short stories to a good concert recital. In any case, this complainant is not our reader, yet our reader does exist, and there would be more of him if more and better short stories were offered.

These stories offer an extraordinary range of mood, pace, tone, and variety of material. The scene is limited to a town the author knows well; the farthest reaches of that scene never go beyond the boundaries of her own state, and many of the characters are of the sort that caused a Bostonian to remark that he would not care to meet them socially. Lily Daw is a half-witted girl in the grip of social forces represented by a group of earnest young ladies bent on doing the best thing for her, no matter what the consequences. Keela, the Outcast Indian Maid, is a crippled little Negro who represents a type of man considered most unfortunate by W. B. Yeats: one whose experience was more important than he, and completely beyond his powers of absorption. But the really unfortunate man in this story is the ignorant young white boy, who had innocently assisted at a wrong done the little Negro, and for a most complex reason, finds that no reparation is possible, or even desirable to the victim. . . . The heroine of "Why I Live at the P. O." is a terrifying case of dementia praecox. In this first group—for the stories may be loosely classified on three separate levels—the spirit is satire and the key grim comedy. Of these, "The Petrified Man" offers a fine clinical study of vulgarity—vulgarity absolute, chemically pure, exposed mercilessly to its final subhuman depths. Dullness, bitterness, rancor, self-pity, baseness of all kinds, can be most interesting material for a story provided these are not also the main elements in the mind of the author. There is nothing in the least vulgar or frustrated in Miss Welty's mind. She has simply an eye and an ear sharp, shrewd, and true as a tuning fork. She has given to this little story all her wit and observation, her blistering humor and her just cruelty; for she has none of that slack tolerance or sentimental tenderness toward symptomatic evils that amounts to criminal collusion between author and character. Her use of this material raises the quite awfully sordid little tale to a level above its natural habitat, and its realism seems almost to have the quality of caricature, as complete realism so often does. Yet, as painters of the grotesque make only detailed reports of actual living types observed more keenly than the average eye is capable of observing, so Miss Welty's little human monsters are not really caricatures at all, but individuals exactly and clearly presented: which is perhaps a case against realism, if we cared to go into it. She does better on another level—for the important reason that the themes are richer—in such beautiful stories as "Death of a Traveling Salesman," "A Memory," "A Worn Path." Let me admit a deeply personal preference for this particular kind of story, where external act and internal voiceless life of the human imagination almost meet and mingle on the mysterious threshold between dream and waking, one reality refusing to admit or confirm the existence of the other, yet both conspiring toward the same end. This is not easy to accomplish, but it is always worth trying, and Miss Welty is so successful at it, it would seem her most familiar territory. There is no blurring at the edges, but evidences of an active and disciplined imagination working firmly in the line of continuity, the waking faculty of daylight reason recollecting and recording the crazy logic of the dream. There is in none of these stories any trace of autobiography in the prime sense, except as the author is omnipresent, and knows each character she writes about as only the artist knows the thing he has made, by first experiencing it in imagination. But perhaps in "A Memory," one of the best stories, there might be something of early personal history in the story of the child on the beach, alienated from the world of adult knowledge by her state of childhood, who hoped to learn the secrets of life by looking at everything, squaring her hands before her eyes to bring the observed thing into a frame—the gesture of one born to select, to arrange, to bring apparently disparate elements into harmony within deliberately fixed boundaries. But the author is freed already in her youth from self-love, self-pity, self-preoccupation, that triple damnation of too many of the young and gifted, and has reached an admirable objectivity. In such stories as "Old Mr Marblehall," "Powerhouse," "The Hitch-Hikers," she combines an objective reporting with great perception of mental or emotional states, and in "Clytie" the very shape of madness takes place before your eyes in a straight account of actions and speech, the personal appearance and habits of dress of the main character and her family.

In all of these stories, varying as they do in excellence, I find nothing false or labored, no diffusion of interest, no wavering of mood—the approach is direct and simple in method, though the themes and moods are anything but simple, and there is even in the smallest story a sense of power in reserve which makes me believe firmly that, splendid beginning that this is, it is only the beginning.

*"But now that so much is being changed, is it not time that we should change? Could we not try to develop ourselves a little, slowly and gradually take upon ourselves our share in the labor of love? We have been spared all its hardship . . . we have been spoiled by easy enjoyment. . . . But what if we despised our successes, what if we began from the beginning to learn the work of love which has always been done for us? What if we were to go and become neophytes, now that so much is changing?"**

KATHERINE ANNE PORTER

August 19, 1941

* *The Journal of My Other Self*, by Rainer Maria Rilke. Translated by M. D. Herter Norton and John Linton. Published by W. W. Norton & Company, Inc.

7.8 Ne-Hi] Carbonated beverage made and distributed by the Nehi Corporation, Columbus, Georgia.

7.19 Willys-Knight] Luxury automobile manufactured from 1914 to 1932.

78.17–18 "Love, . . . Love"] Repeated opening line of "Careless Love" (1921) by W. C. Handy, Spencer Williams, and Martha Koenig.

78.32 dirt-dauber] Southern usage for mud dauber, a type of wasp.

114.5 Pilgrimage Week] Annual celebration in spring of the elite lifestyle of the Old South; begun in Mississippi in 1932, it features tours of antebellum houses and gardens, costumed guides, and Confederate balls.

169.34 "Somebody Loves Me"] Popular song (1924) by George Gershwin, with lyrics by Ballard MacDonald and Buddy DeSylva; Welty originally had Powerhouse playing Fats Waller's "Hold Tight," but the editors of *Atlantic Monthly*, which first published "Powerhouse," objected to its suggestive lyrics.

177.31 Old Natchez Trace] An Indian trail later used by European explorers and pioneers that runs 600 miles from Nashville on the Cumberland River to Natchez on the Mississippi (for Welty's essay on it, see page 760 in this volume).

THE WIDE NET, AND OTHER STORIES

225.16 Sacred Harp] Tradition of a cappella singing of the southeastern U.S. that began with the "shape note" practice of musical instruction in the late 18th century. Many of the songs are included in the tunebook *The Sacred Harp*, compiled in Georgia and first published in 1844; they include fuguing and hymn tunes and longer pieces such as odes, anthems, and Biblical texts set to music.

228.2 LORENZO DOW] For the characters of Dow, Audubon, and James Murrell in this story, Welty drew on the writings and legends of itinerant Methodist minister and evangelist Lorenzo Dow (1777–1834), ornithologist and naturalist John James Audubon (1785–1851), and outlaw John A. Murrell (1806–44), first convicted as a horse thief and later for kidnapping slaves whom he would resell or, if they were recognized, murder.

235.39 "H.T."] Horse thief.

237.16–17 my Conspiracy] Murrell was reputed to have planned a slave uprising with his band of outlaws.

237.29 Lost Dauphin] Supposed son of King Louis XVI and Marie Antoinette.

240.10 "In that . . . disclosed."] 1 Corinthians 4:5.

241.13 golden ruin] Based on the ruins of Windsor near Port Gibson, Mississippi, a mansion built 1861 and destroyed by fire in 1890.

259.4 "Beautiful Ohio"] Song (1918) by Robert A. King, with lyrics by Ballard MacDonald; an early version of "The Winds" was titled "Beautiful Ohio."

THE GOLDEN APPLES

314.1–2 *Wells . . . Lyell*] Jackson natives who studied along with Welty at Columbia University in 1930.

325.7 Governor Vardaman] James Kemble Vardaman (1861–1930), governor of Mississippi 1904–8, and U.S. senator, 1913–19; he had long white hair and often wore white frock coats and wide-brimmed hats.

330.3 Y. & M. V.] The Yazoo & Mississippi Valley Rail Road; it operated in the Mississippi Delta until it was absorbed by the Illinois Central (I.C.).

333.9 pompadour cap] A tight-fitting wrap intended to prevent re-infection of a malaria patient by mosquitoes that would be drawn to the moist and feverish skin along the hairline.

339.9 Rook party] A card party organized around games played with a Rook deck of four suits identified only by color and numbered 1–14, with a single Rook card as the highest trump. "Rook" was common in Bible Belt communities where gaming was considered a sin and the picture cards themselves graven images.

343.8 shooting-the-moon] Bidding a slam and taking all the tricks.

345.21 *Für Elise*] Bagatelle in A minor by Beethoven.

345.24 *danke schoen*] Thank you.

346.28 "Though . . . wandering] In William Butler Yeats' "Song of the Wandering Aengus" (1899).

353.28 "The Lucky Stone."] See page 799.21–22 and note.

366.34–35 the Gish and the Talmadge sisters.] Lillian (1893–1993) and Dorothy (1898–1968) Gish and Norma (1893?–1957), Constance (1891–1973), and Natalie (1899–1969) Talmadge.

366.36 tent . . . Valentino] In *The Sheik* (1921).

407.5 in Coventry] Banished or ostracized as undesirable.

421.8 *The Re-Creation . . . Kent*] Novel (1919) by Harold Bell Wright.

432.30–31 "How . . . Aix"] Poem by Robert Browning.

463.6 U.D.C.] United Daughters of the Confederacy.

481.9 *"Open . . . Richard!"*] Novelty hit of 1947, music by Jack McVea and Dan Howell, lyrics by "Dusty" Fletcher and John Mason.

482.36 Monteaux . . . *Babar*] Probably Pierre Monteux (1875–1964), French-born conductor of major symphony orchestras in the U.S., who had a bushy mustache and flowing black hair. Jean de Brunhoff's *Babar* series is about an elephant king who has human friends.

492.24 Traveler's Tree] Folkloric version of the Tree of Life.

498.18–19 *Ouvrez . . . Jacques*] Open the window, Paul or Jacques.

500.29 Dr. Caligari] In the German film *The Cabinet of Dr. Caligari*, released in the U.S. in 1921.

THE BRIDE OF THE INNISFALLEN, AND OTHER STORIES

576.24–25 *"Moi pas l'aimez ça,"*] I don't like that.

595.24–25 dirtdauber] See note 78.32.

602.25 *Black . . . Downs*] Novel in Walter Farley's "Black Stallion" series, begun 1941.

605.34–36 Tara . . . raths] Tara, about 20 miles north of Dublin, was the ancient seat of the kings of Ireland. Raths (circular earthenworks) mark the site of the "halls of Tara" where the national assembly met and gatherings for games, music, and literary contests were held.

639.1 *Circe*] Cf. Homer's *Odyssey*, chap. X.

651.31 *Eight Cousins*] Novel (1875) by Louisa May Alcott (1832–88).

682.5 *turistica*] Tourist class.

682.26 *l'Anno Santo*] Holy (or Jubilee) Year in the Roman Catholic Church.

684.10 *Pittura Fresca*] Fresh Paint.

685.28 La Zìngara] The Gypsy.

690.31–32 *Poveretti!" . . . i Mori*] Poor things! . . . the Moors (or, the dark-complexioned ones).

693.6 *"Cielo azzurro!" . . . Pellegrini*] Blue sky! . . . Pilgrims.

693.36–37 *cameriera*] Chambermaid, waitress.

709.3 *"Moto perpetuo".*] Perpetual motion.

709.26 *Il Cadavere*] The Corpse.

715.8 *"Orfanelli*] Orphans.

720.26 *"Sfortunato!"*] Unfortunate!

721.28 *Ognissanti*] All Saints' Day.

OTHER STORIES

727.1 *Where Is the Voice Coming From?*] Welty discusses the background of this story in "Preface to *Collected Stories*," p. 829 in this volume.

727.25 I.C. tracks] See note 330.3.

728.1 Meredith] James Meredith integrated the University of Mississippi, Oxford, on September 30, 1962, under the protection of U.S. marshals after Governor Ross Barnett attempted to block his admission. When he registered for second semester on January 30, 1963, Meredith was accompanied by Mississippi NAACP leader Medgar Evers.

730.28 *Caroline*] The daughter of President John F. Kennedy.

733.11 "*Arma . . . cano*,"] Virgil, *Aeneid*, I.i.: "Arms and the man I sing."

SELECTED ESSAYS

761.9 "too pretty to burn."] Grant is said to have made the remark when he stopped in the town during his march to Vicksburg in 1863.

761.30 Big Harp] Micajah "Big" Harpe (1768–99) who worked with Wiley "Little" Harpe (1770–1804); the brothers were so pathologically violent that they were shunned even by other outlaws. Big Harpe was killed in Tennessee by vigilantes who brought in his head to claim their reward.

762.2–3 Mark Twain . . . holes!"] In *Life on the Mississippi* (1883), chap. XXXV: "Vicksburg during the Trouble."

763.36–37 Lochinvar . . . Dream] References, respectively, to Walter Scott's *Marmion* (1808), canto 5 (concerning Lochinvar); John Dryden's poem *Alexander's Feast* (1697); Joseph Addison's *Cato* (1713), V.i; and Shakespeare's *Richard III*, I.iv (in which George, Duke of Clarence, describes his dream).

767.33–34 *"En été" . . . "En hyver"*] In summer. In winter.

768.17 Stinkards] A term for the lower caste of Natchez.

778.21–22 "So strangeness . . . Wilbur's.] "Castles and Distances," stanza 3, line 1, in *Ceremony and Other Poems* (1950).

781.29 *The Ancient Mariner*] Samuel Taylor Coleridge's *The Rime of the Ancient Mariner* (1798).

782.39–783.1 "If Father . . . Moscow,"] In Chekhov's *Three Sisters* (1901).

784.36 Eliza] In Harriet Beecher Stowe's *Uncle Tom's Cabin* (1852).

787.6–7 *Swann's . . . Mansions*] *Du Côté de chez Swann* (1913), section 1 of Marcel Proust's *A la recherche du temps perdu*; Thomas Mann's *Der Zauberberg* (1924), centered at the International Sanatorium Berghof in Germany; and W. H. Hudson's *Green Mansions* (1904), set in the forests of British Guiana.

787.27 *Sound and the Fury*] By William Faulkner (1929).

788.11 *"Madame . . . moi."*] "I am Madame Bovary," Flaubert's reputed response when asked to name the person on whom he'd based his heroine.

797.5 *Five Little Peppers*] In Harriett Lothrop's "Pepper family" series, beginning with *Five Little Peppers and How They Grew* (1881).

798.16–17 *Elsie Dinsmore*] Novel (1867) in Martha Farquharson Finley's "Elsie" series.

798.19–20 *The Wizard . . . Book*] Frank L. Baum's *The Wonderful Wizard of Oz* (1900), Annie Fellows Johnston's *The Little Colonel* (1895), and *The Green Fairy Book* (1892) in the series of Fairy Book anthologies edited by Andrew Lang.

799.21–22 *The Lucky Stone . . .* Brown] The story ran January-July 1914.

812.2 "Only connect,"] In *Howards End* (1910), chap. 22.

829.7–8 Medgar Evers . . . shot] A lawyer and, from 1954, Mississippi field secretary for the NAACP, Evers (b. 1925), was shot to death in Jackson shortly after midnight, June 12, 1963, as he returned home from a meeting.

829.23 an arrest] Greenwood fertilizer salesman Byron de la Beckwith was arrested on June 22, 1963; his first two trials for the murder of Evers ended in mistrials, but the case was reopened in 1989 and a third trial resulted in Beckwith's conviction on February 5, 1994.

ONE WRITER'S BEGINNINGS

842.22 Stoddard's Lectures] Massachusetts author and hymn writer John Lawson Stoddard (1850–1931) became well known for his travel lectures accompanied by stereopticon slides; they were collected in 15 volumes, 1897–1901.

842.37–39 *Jane . . . Mines*] Novels by, respectively, Charlotte Brontë (1847), George du Maurier (1894), Wilkie Collins (1860), William Henry Hudson (1904), and H. Rider Haggard (1886).

845.4 *St. Elmo*] By Alabama novelist Augusta Evans (1835–1909).

858.33 *Blossom Time*] American version (1921) of Heinrich Berté's *Das Dreimäderlhaus* (1916), operetta based on the music of Franz Schubert.

871.26 Carnegie Library] The main branch of the public library was renamed for Welty when it moved to new quarters in 1986.

872.15 *Elsie Dinsmore*] See note 798.16–17.

873.6 *The Man . . . Ten*] Mary Roberts Rinehart's second mystery novel (1909).

873.37 Madge Evans] Stage and movie actor (1909–81) who became a silent film star at the age of five.

874.21–22 Redpath Chautauqua] Organization continuing the entertainment, uplift, and educational productions of James Redpath (1833–91).

874.23 Gypsy Smith] A British evangelist expelled from the Salvation Army in 1882 for deviations in doctrine, Rodney "Gipsy" Smith (1860-1947) made more than 50 trips to preach in the United States.

877.2–4 editor . . . *Jackson Daily News*] Frederick Sullens, a segregationist, commented (with particular reference to *Sanctuary*) after Faulkner became a Nobel laureate in November 1950: "those who award the Nobel Prize are now laboring under the delusion that a novel, in order to be excellent, must also be nasty . . . he is a propagandist of degradation and properly belongs in the privy school of literature."

880.31–32 *The Cabinet . . . Caligari*] See note 500.29.

882.37 Medgar Evers] See notes 829.7–8 and 829.23.

922.10–11 "Pale . . . Now?)"] "By the Shalimar" (1922), words and music by Ted Koehler and Frank Magine.

923.8–9 *The Bat*] Whodunnit play (1920) and film (1926) based on Mary Roberts Rinehart's 1908 novel *The Circular Staircase*; it was also filmed in 1931, as *The Bat Whispers*, and 1959.

923.15 Corey Ford] Humorist and parodist born in New York; Ford (1902–69) sometimes used the pen name John Riddell.

923.36–37 "Summer . . . Death."] First lines, respectively, of "Cuckoo Song" (c. 1250) and Alan Seeger's "I Have a Rendezvous With Death" (1916).

924.2–4 "Whan . . . cano] "When April with its sweet showers," opening of Chaucer's *The Canterbury Tales*; see also note 733.11.

929.27 Galli-Curci . . . Blackstone] Italian-born opera star Amelita Galli-Curci (1889–1963), known for her coloratura singing, and Harry Blackstone (1883–1965), rival of and then successor to Howard Thurston (1869–1936) as the premier stage magician in American entertainment. His trademark illusion was making a horse disappear.

929.28 *The Cat . . . Canary*] Mystery-comedy play (1922) by John Willard that was filmed in 1927 by Carl Laemmle; it was also filmed in 1930, as *The Cat Creeps*, and in 1939.

929.29 *Chu Chin Chow*] Musical by Frederick Norton, libretto by Oscar Asche; it opened on Broadway in 1917 and was often revived.

932.30 *"anno mirabilis"*] Year of wonders; miraculous year.

932.35–37 Dow . . . Audubon] See note 228.2.

937.8 *No, No, Nanette*] Popular musical (1924) by Vincent Youmans, book by Irving Caesar and Otto Harbach; it was filmed in 1930 and again in 1940.

THE LIBRARY OF AMERICA SERIES

The Library of America fosters appreciation and pride in America's literary heritage by publishing, and keeping permanently in print, authoritative editions of America's best and most significant writing. An independent nonprofit organization, it was founded in 1979 with seed funding from the National Endowment for the Humanities and the Ford Foundation.

1. Herman Melville: *Typee, Omoo, Mardi*
2. Nathaniel Hawthorne: *Tales and Sketches*
3. Walt Whitman: *Poetry and Prose*
4. Harriet Beecher Stowe: *Three Novels*
5. Mark Twain: *Mississippi Writings*
6. Jack London: *Novels and Stories*
7. Jack London: *Novels and Social Writings*
8. William Dean Howells: *Novels 1875–1886*
9. Herman Melville: *Redburn, White-Jacket, Moby-Dick*
10. Nathaniel Hawthorne: *Collected Novels*
11. Francis Parkman: *France and England in North America*, vol. I
12. Francis Parkman: *France and England in North America*, vol. II
13. Henry James: *Novels 1871–1880*
14. Henry Adams: *Novels, Mont Saint Michel, The Education*
15. Ralph Waldo Emerson: *Essays and Lectures*
16. Washington Irving: *History, Tales and Sketches*
17. Thomas Jefferson: *Writings*
18. Stephen Crane: *Prose and Poetry*
19. Edgar Allan Poe: *Poetry and Tales*
20. Edgar Allan Poe: *Essays and Reviews*
21. Mark Twain: *The Innocents Abroad, Roughing It*
22. Henry James: *Literary Criticism: Essays, American & English Writers*
23. Henry James: *Literary Criticism: European Writers & The Prefaces*
24. Herman Melville: *Pierre, Israel Potter, The Confidence-Man, Tales & Billy Budd*
25. William Faulkner: *Novels 1930–1935*
26. James Fenimore Cooper: *The Leatherstocking Tales*, vol. I
27. James Fenimore Cooper: *The Leatherstocking Tales*, vol. II
28. Henry David Thoreau: *A Week, Walden, The Maine Woods, Cape Cod*
29. Henry James: *Novels 1881–1886*
30. Edith Wharton: *Novels*
31. Henry Adams: *History of the U.S. during the Administrations of Jefferson*
32. Henry Adams: *History of the U.S. during the Administrations of Madison*
33. Frank Norris: *Novels and Essays*
34. W.E.B. Du Bois: *Writings*
35. Willa Cather: *Early Novels and Stories*
36. Theodore Dreiser: *Sister Carrie, Jennie Gerhardt, Twelve Men*

37a. Benjamin Franklin: *Silence Dogood, The Busy-Body, & Early Writings*

37b. Benjamin Franklin: *Autobiography, Poor Richard, & Later Writings*

38. William James: *Writings 1902–1910*
39. Flannery O'Connor: *Collected Works*
40. Eugene O'Neill: *Complete Plays 1913–1920*
41. Eugene O'Neill: *Complete Plays 1920–1931*
42. Eugene O'Neill: *Complete Plays 1932–1943*
43. Henry James: *Novels 1886–1890*
44. William Dean Howells: *Novels 1886–1888*
45. Abraham Lincoln: *Speeches and Writings 1832–1858*
46. Abraham Lincoln: *Speeches and Writings 1859–1865*
47. Edith Wharton: *Novellas and Other Writings*
48. William Faulkner: *Novels 1936–1940*
49. Willa Cather: *Later Novels*
50. Ulysses S. Grant: *Memoirs and Selected Letters*
51. William Tecumseh Sherman: *Memoirs*
52. Washington Irving: *Bracebridge Hall, Tales of a Traveller, The Alhambra*
53. Francis Parkman: *The Oregon Trail, The Conspiracy of Pontiac*
54. James Fenimore Cooper: *Sea Tales: The Pilot, The Red Rover*
55. Richard Wright: *Early Works*
56. Richard Wright: *Later Works*
57. Willa Cather: *Stories, Poems, and Other Writings*
58. William James: *Writings 1878–1899*
59. Sinclair Lewis: *Main Street & Babbitt*
60. Mark Twain: *Collected Tales, Sketches, Speeches, & Essays 1852–1890*
61. Mark Twain: *Collected Tales, Sketches, Speeches, & Essays 1891–1910*
62. *The Debate on the Constitution: Part One*
63. *The Debate on the Constitution: Part Two*
64. Henry James: *Collected Travel Writings: Great Britain & America*
65. Henry James: *Collected Travel Writings: The Continent*

66. *American Poetry: The Nineteenth Century*, Vol. 1
67. *American Poetry: The Nineteenth Century*, Vol. 2
68. Frederick Douglass: *Autobiographies*
69. Sarah Orne Jewett: *Novels and Stories*
70. Ralph Waldo Emerson: *Collected Poems and Translations*
71. Mark Twain: *Historical Romances*
72. John Steinbeck: *Novels and Stories 1932–1937*
73. William Faulkner: *Novels 1942–1954*
74. Zora Neale Hurston: *Novels and Stories*
75. Zora Neale Hurston: *Folklore, Memoirs, and Other Writings*
76. Thomas Paine: *Collected Writings*
77. *Reporting World War II: American Journalism 1938–1944*
78. *Reporting World War II: American Journalism 1944–1946*
79. Raymond Chandler: *Stories and Early Novels*
80. Raymond Chandler: *Later Novels and Other Writings*
81. Robert Frost: *Collected Poems, Prose, & Plays*
82. Henry James: *Complete Stories 1892–1898*
83. Henry James: *Complete Stories 1898–1910*
84. William Bartram: *Travels and Other Writings*
85. John Dos Passos: *U.S.A.*
86. John Steinbeck: *The Grapes of Wrath and Other Writings 1936–1941*
87. Vladimir Nabokov: *Novels and Memoirs 1941–1951*
88. Vladimir Nabokov: *Novels 1955–1962*
89. Vladimir Nabokov: *Novels 1969–1974*
90. James Thurber: *Writings and Drawings*
91. George Washington: *Writings*
92. John Muir: *Nature Writings*
93. Nathanael West: *Novels and Other Writings*
94. *Crime Novels: American Noir of the 1930s and 40s*
95. *Crime Novels: American Noir of the 1950s*
96. Wallace Stevens: *Collected Poetry and Prose*
97. James Baldwin: *Early Novels and Stories*
98. James Baldwin: *Collected Essays*
99. Gertrude Stein: *Writings 1903–1932*
100. Gertrude Stein: *Writings 1932–1946*
101. Eudora Welty: *Complete Novels*
102. Eudora Welty: *Stories, Essays, & Memoir*
103. Charles Brockden Brown: *Three Gothic Novels*
104. *Reporting Vietnam: American Journalism 1959–1969*
105. *Reporting Vietnam: American Journalism 1969–1975*
106. Henry James: *Complete Stories 1874–1884*
107. Henry James: *Complete Stories 1884–1891*
108. *American Sermons: The Pilgrims to Martin Luther King Jr.*
109. James Madison: *Writings*
110. Dashiell Hammett: *Complete Novels*
111. Henry James: *Complete Stories 1864–1874*
112. William Faulkner: *Novels 1957–1962*
113. John James Audubon: *Writings & Drawings*
114. *Slave Narratives*
115. *American Poetry: The Twentieth Century*, Vol. 1
116. *American Poetry: The Twentieth Century*, Vol. 2
117. F. Scott Fitzgerald: *Novels and Stories 1920–1922*
118. Henry Wadsworth Longfellow: *Poems and Other Writings*
119. Tennessee Williams: *Plays 1937–1955*
120. Tennessee Williams: *Plays 1957–1980*
121. Edith Wharton: *Collected Stories 1891–1910*
122. Edith Wharton: *Collected Stories 1911–1937*
123. *The American Revolution: Writings from the War of Independence*
124. Henry David Thoreau: *Collected Essays and Poems*
125. Dashiell Hammett: *Crime Stories and Other Writings*
126. Dawn Powell: *Novels 1930–1942*
127. Dawn Powell: *Novels 1944–1962*
128. Carson McCullers: *Complete Novels*
129. Alexander Hamilton: *Writings*
130. Mark Twain: *The Gilded Age and Later Novels*
131. Charles W. Chesnutt: *Stories, Novels, and Essays*
132. John Steinbeck: *Novels 1942–1952*
133. Sinclair Lewis: *Arrowsmith, Elmer Gantry, Dodsworth*
134. Paul Bowles: *The Sheltering Sky, Let It Come Down, The Spider's House*
135. Paul Bowles: *Collected Stories & Later Writings*
136. Kate Chopin: *Complete Novels & Stories*
137. *Reporting Civil Rights: American Journalism 1941–1963*
138. *Reporting Civil Rights: American Journalism 1963–1973*
139. Henry James: *Novels 1896–1899*
140. Theodore Dreiser: *An American Tragedy*
141. Saul Bellow: *Novels 1944–1953*
142. John Dos Passos: *Novels 1920–1925*
143. John Dos Passos: *Travel Books and Other Writings*

144. Ezra Pound: *Poems and Translations*
145. James Weldon Johnson: *Writings*
146. Washington Irving: *Three Western Narratives*
147. Alexis de Tocqueville: *Democracy in America*
148. James T. Farrell: *Studs Lonigan: A Trilogy*
149. Isaac Bashevis Singer: *Collected Stories I*
150. Isaac Bashevis Singer: *Collected Stories II*
151. Isaac Bashevis Singer: *Collected Stories III*
152. Kaufman & Co.: *Broadway Comedies*
153. Theodore Roosevelt: *The Rough Riders, An Autobiography*
154. Theodore Roosevelt: *Letters and Speeches*
155. H. P. Lovecraft: *Tales*
156. Louisa May Alcott: *Little Women, Little Men, Jo's Boys*
157. Philip Roth: *Novels & Stories 1959–1962*
158. Philip Roth: *Novels 1967–1972*
159. James Agee: *Let Us Now Praise Famous Men, A Death in the Family*
160. James Agee: *Film Writing & Selected Journalism*
161. Richard Henry Dana, Jr.: *Two Years Before the Mast & Other Voyages*
162. Henry James: *Novels 1901–1902*
163. Arthur Miller: *Collected Plays 1944–1961*
164. William Faulkner: *Novels 1926–1929*
165. Philip Roth: *Novels 1973–1977*
166. *American Speeches: Part One*
167. *American Speeches: Part Two*
168. Hart Crane: *Complete Poems & Selected Letters*
169. Saul Bellow: *Novels 1956–1964*
170. John Steinbeck: *Travels with Charley and Later Novels*
171. Capt. John Smith: *Writings with Other Narratives*
172. Thornton Wilder: *Collected Plays & Writings on Theater*
173. Philip K. Dick: *Four Novels of the 1960s*
174. Jack Kerouac: *Road Novels 1957–1960*
175. Philip Roth: *Zuckerman Bound*
176. Edmund Wilson: *Literary Essays & Reviews of the 1920s & 30s*
177. Edmund Wilson: *Literary Essays & Reviews of the 1930s & 40s*
178. *American Poetry: The 17th & 18th Centuries*
179. William Maxwell: *Early Novels & Stories*
180. Elizabeth Bishop: *Poems, Prose, & Letters*
181. A. J. Liebling: *World War II Writings*
182s. *American Earth: Environmental Writing Since Thoreau*
183. Philip K. Dick: *Five Novels of the 1960s & 70s*
184. William Maxwell: *Later Novels & Stories*
185. Philip Roth: *Novels & Other Narratives 1986–1991*
186. Katherine Anne Porter: *Collected Stories & Other Writings*
187. John Ashbery: *Collected Poems 1956–1987*
188. John Cheever: *Collected Stories & Other Writings*
189. John Cheever: *Complete Novels*
190. Lafcadio Hearn: *American Writings*
191. A. J. Liebling: *The Sweet Science & Other Writngs*
192s. *The Lincoln Anthology: Great Writers on His Life and Legacy from 1860 to Now*
193. Philip K. Dick: *VALIS & Later Novels*
194. Thornton Wilder: *The Bridge of San Luis Rey and Other Novels 1926–1948*
195. Raymond Carver: *Collected Stories*
196. *American Fantastic Tales: Terror and the Uncanny from Poe to the Pulps*
197. *American Fantastic Tales: Terror and the Uncanny from the 1940s to Now*
198. John Marshall: *Writings*
199s. *The Mark Twain Anthology: Great Writers on His Life and Works*
200. Mark Twain: *A Tramp Abroad, Following the Equator, Other Travels*
201. Ralph Waldo Emerson: *Selected Journals 1820–1842*
202. Ralph Waldo Emerson: *Selected Journals 1841–1877*
203. *The American Stage: Writing on Theater from Washington Irving to Tony Kushner*
204. Shirley Jackson: *Novels & Stories*
205. Philip Roth: *Novels 1993–1995*
206. H. L. Mencken: *Prejudices: First, Second, and Third Series*
207. H. L. Mencken: *Prejudices: Fourth, Fifth, and Sixth Series*
208. John Kenneth Galbraith: *The Affluent Society and Other Writings 1952–1967*
209. Saul Bellow: *Novels 1970–1982*
210. Lynd Ward: *Gods' Man, Madman's Drum, Wild Pilgrimage*
211. Lynd Ward: *Prelude to a Million Years, Song Without Words, Vertigo*
212. *The Civil War: The First Year Told by Those Who Lived It*
213. John Adams: *Revolutionary Writings 1755–1775*
214. John Adams: *Revolutionary Writings 1775–1783*
215. Henry James: *Novels 1903–1911*
216. Kurt Vonnegut: *Novels & Stories 1963–1973*
217. *Harlem Renaissance: Five Novels of the 1920s*

*This book is set in 10 point Linotron Galliard,
a face designed for photocomposition by Matthew Carter
and based on the sixteenth-century face Granjon. The paper
is acid-free lightweight opaque and meets the requirements
for permanence of the American National Standards Institute.
The binding material is Brillianta, a woven rayon cloth made
by Van Heek-Scholco Textielfabrieken, Holland. Composition by The Clarinda Company. Printing by
Malloy Incorporated. Binding by Dekker Book-
binding. Designed by Bruce Campbell.*